# AT THE END OF THE RAINBOW

Novels published by Midnight Fire Media

Your Own Fate
Night on Earth
Dreams Belong to the Night
ShadowWalk
Alarums of Reality

The Janus Clan series:

The Defenseless
The Slaves
Birds Flying in the Dark

Preliminary release date for next book Lewis of Modern York October 31, 2017

**Poems:**

Amos Keppler: Complete Poems 1989 - 2003

(A few of the) novels to be published:

The Afterglow trilogy
Season of the Witch
Thunder Road: Ice and Fire
Falling
Black Dragon

For a «complete» list of current and current future Amos Keppler and Midnight Fire Media projects see the back of the book and the Midnight Fire/Midnight Fire Media web pages.

The Janus Clan, Book Four

**«The first twenty years - Book Four»**
**The years 1976 - 1979**

# At the End of the Rainbow

## By

## Amos Keppler

MIDNIGHT FIRE MEDIA
2012

Midnight Fire Media

http://midnight-fire.net/mfm
For more about At the End of the Rainbow and the Janus Clan:
http://midnight-fire.net/sw

E-Mail:
ak@midnight-fire.net
manofhood@yahoo.com

Cover, text, design, premedia, art and photos Amos Keppler

Thanks to David Huxley



ISBN 978-82-91693-14-9

# PROLOGUE

Memphis, Tennessee, USA, a hot spring day 1976.

The Vietnam War had finally ended. Gerald Ford remained the country's president. Moon-landings had become bland routine, and had basically been given up on, been given the boot. Ford's blatant pardon of Richard Nixon caused his popularity to fall to a new low. Elvis had about one year left to live, if one could call that living. The racial unrest that had ravaged the nation and its southern states since long before the early sixties raged on.

The gray buildings shook. The crowd surrounding the person the nervous cops had encircled caused that with their loud cries and feet stamping at the ground. The Earth itself seemed to be shaking. The girl on the platform waved her hands and directed the crowd in a relaxed and calm manner.

She was clearly excited. He could easily see that, without aid from his other senses. It was evident in her eyes and the very way her body moved. Her dark skin was covered in sweat. But it didn't look like the heat bothered her much.

He spotted her again a few hours later, as dusk settled in the stone desert. The protesters, still numerous enough to be called a crowd gathered outside a derelict building.

*Another temporary rebellious collective,* he thought.

Squatted houses, old, derelict and abandoned buildings occupied by disgruntled citizens had become commonplace lately. Most places the authorities acted swiftly and threw them out, but other places like here people managed to stay, to make a claim to the house.

He slipped out of the shadows and made sure she would easily spot him. Five, ten, perhaps fifteen seconds passed before she froze. Her face lit up in one huge smile and when he took another step towards her, she ran to him. She embraced him, throwing herself at him, into his arms, filled with excitement.

– TED! She cried. – It is you, isn't it, Ted?

– It is me, he nodded.

She let herself slide down his body, until she stood there breathless looking at him. He looked down at Glory Burns across an abyss not much deeper than a year, deeper than an ocean.

– So what brings you to these parts? She asked innocently.

– Coincidence, he replied lightly. – I thought I should use the opportunity to renew old acquaintances.

She looked at him across the table with badly hidden interest. They sat in a deep corner inside a café, a bit off the ruckus that was still dominating the Memphis streets.

– I can't help being amazed by those eyes of yours. She cheerfully shook her head. – How do you *explain* it?

She was pulled into them, as she studied them, into their dark fire. They sparked like sprigs of spruce a wet night.

– There is nothing to explain. He shrugged. – It's a family trait going back generations.
– Countless generations of *witches,* according to Eric Carr, she grinned cautiously. – What do you think of his book?
– I guess he's got a point. According to folklore witches' eyes did change color, and did glow like fire in the night.
They laughed a lot then.
– You're so funny, she marveled, drying her tears. – I can't recall you ever being so funny.
She grabbed his hands, looking at him with stars in her eyes.
– I heard about what happened in Colorado…
– I keep doing that, too.
She giggled, looking waggishly at him.
– You must be careful not to grow famous.
– Infamous is more like it.
There was intensity in his joking this time, but she laughed some more anyway.
They danced. A lousy pianist played on an old, brittle piano. It didn't faze them. It was like they were dancing to a completely different tune, like they weren't in the room at all.
– I can't believe it, she exclaimed, – you've actually learned to dance.
Then she sobered, an expression of deep regret forming her features.
– I guess you remember what… what they… taught you.
– I do remember, he nodded.
Drying a tear from the edge of her eye.
The dance was slow, relaxed, not really wild at all, but she was still out of breath when it ended.
– You didn't stay there, in Colorado?
– I enjoy wandering, he said simply.
– What about Elizabeth, your cousin?
– She enjoys wandering, too.
They sat by the table again. She held on to his hand.
– I heard about what happened in London, too, in a roundabout way. About Tilla. I'm sorry.
Teetering on the edge of his abyss the catching in her throat turned pronounced.
– It's a long time ago already, he said distantly. – Time heals all wounds, as they say. That's another cliché that is the bullshit of this world.
Some wounds would never heal.
– I'm dealing with it, he added.
– So am I, she said solemnly. – Dealing with what I did, what happened to me, my just reward. It was rough for a while, but I got over it, got over myself.
They sat for a while in silence. She reached for him, but pulled her hand back before it reached his cheek. She wanted to comfort him, but didn't.
After a while he rose abruptly and rushed like the wind to the piano. She drew breath in surprise when he spoke to the pianist in a very pleasant manner. The

man jumped to his feet and hurried nervously away. The man with the beastly eyes sat down, and began playing.

The music flowed through the room, filled it like a sponge. It was difficult at first to know what made it so… so disturbing. Glory realized why with a start. It evoked… evoked *memories*. She actually felt an ice-cold trickle down her spine. Something she had never been even close to experiencing. She, who had experienced quite a lot, a lot bringing forth nausea just by the thought of it.

He brought forth the old, what she had believed buried memories.

Memories of shame and fear and a sickness beyond words.

He wanted her to remember. She choked.

From the edge of her eye she noticed three men in another corner, clearly distraught, more then a bit *excited*. The music filled them up, she could tell, cutting them in a thousand pieces. They enjoyed an extensive conversation, something that to her was akin to a war council. She was convinced Ted Warren noticed them as well.

He stopped playing the moment the three jumped from their chairs in something very much resembling full attack mode. He smiled, but his eyes looked like they were made of glass. Glass. The slag of a thousand nightmares revealed itself to them, and to her. They stopped, more then bewildered, more than stunned, sore afraid.

They had gone to school together. He was about her age, about twenty-one. They had a similar traumatic background. Sometimes, like now, he seemed far older.

A few, quick steps, and he was back by the table.

– That was amazing, she breathed. – The music… is it yours… did you make it? It overwhelmed me like a storm. It sounded so calm at first, but then… then I felt it, felt the *wind*.

He grabbed her arm and pulled her up, pulled her out of there. She just about managed to fetch her jacket.

She attempted to resist his pull, but it was useless, like stopping the Storm. It didn't' even slow him down. She suspected he didn't even notice her resistance. His hand clutched hers so hard that she feared it would be crushed. Her twisted mouth released a whine of pain.

– Those men, you handled them like they were nothing…

– They are nothing, he said.

He stopped deep within the darkness. There was nothing but emptiness in the street around them. He let go of her hand, stared at her, before walking on. She didn't hesitate for long, before rushing after him.

After a while she looked up, surprised.

– I live close by.

– I know that, he said.

And she wasn't surprised at all. A rippling heat spread through her. She felt it grow from between her legs and all over her, violently and unquenchable. He had to take the keys from her and unlock and open the door.

He knew what key fit the door, just like he knew the way to her small house.

– Such a nice flower, he said, touching her jaw. – One already plucked and devoured.

– I don't mind, she whispered. – I don't mind at all.

He went right for the bedroom. She wanted to say something, something meaningful, something critical, a declaration of how much she had longed for him to come to her. Throat constricted. She was unable to utter a sound. He stopped by the large bed. She stopped right inside the door, shyly bowing her head, not understanding why she held back. She had always wanted this.

– Undress! He commanded curtly.

His direct approach made her tremble. She didn't want it to be like this, but wanted to stand close to him, breathing his powerful scent, clinging to his strong body, caressing him, and be caressed back.

She removed her jacket, just letting it slip from her hand. Her fingers had some trouble before they succeeded in grasping the fabric of the blouse and pull it over her head. Her sore domes pushed at the t-shirt beneath. She quickly pushed the pants down her thighs, leaving them in a heap by her feet.

– Horny nigger bitch isn't shy, is she?

She removed her panties and t-shirt in two swift moves, and she stood naked before him, before his ruthless scrutiny. The body, hardly belonging to her anymore turned and displayed itself. He waved her to him, and she eagerly obeyed, rushed to him in a whirl of motion. Confident hands grabbed her and turned her around. He studied and appraised her. She made an attempt to meet his eyes. The fire in them grew even stronger. She felt them no matter how much she stared at the floor.

He placed her at the wall by the bed. Two fingers under the jaw pushed up the head, the quivering lips. She waited in excitement and fear, when he bent down and kissed her. The heat and the relief flowed through her.

– You want me, she mumbled. – I want you. I want you so much.

She hungrily returned his kiss. Her fingers groped his clothes in an attempt to tear them off him. He grabbed her hands and held them with one hand. She tried to free herself, without any discernible effect. He waited until she stopped fighting and then he kissed her again, much rougher this time. She stared at him, a hurt look in her misty eyes. He began exploring her body rough and ruthless, totally without the pretense of kindness. She moaned and strived desperately to express her increasing worry by shaking her head. He released her hands. She smiled to him. He grabbed her hair so hard that it hurt deep in the roots. She cried out in protest and pain. He pinched and squeezed her all over the body, harder the longer he kept it going. The next time his hands reached her breasts it hurt so much that tears jumped from her eyes. Each kiss was a humiliation, not a caress.

– Ted, NO!

He slapped her cheeks. With the right hand. With the left hand. With the right hand. With the left hand… She stared incredulous at him the first time, grew angry the second, fearful the third, and then, by the fifth or seventh she just stood there and took it. For every new slap she grew increasingly paralyzed and passive. She had tried to raise her hands to protect herself, strike back and beg him, everything useless. Now her arms hung straight down, and she made no attempt at raising them. He smiled. A smile making her shake and shake hard.

– That's it, now you're receptive, now you're ready to learn.

He took her between her thighs, finally. Rubbed back and forth, back and forth. He pushed his hand up, and her eyes grew soft and wet. She moaned in need. His hand was wet when he raised it to her mouth. She could smell it.

– Taste, he commanded, and pushed the hand at her mouth.

She kept licking it until he pulled it away.

He pushed her down on the bed. Such a cliché and so real. She heaved a few times, until she lay still on her back. Her breasts kept heaving with her heavy breathing. She lay still, quiet and needy. He undressed in pulls and tears. His limb rose until it pointed right at her. She couldn't recall it… being so big. All of him was big, so mighty. She imagined that his head touched the ceiling, and that he was hidden in shadow. The shadow reached for her. She desperately wanted to flee. As far away from him as she could possibly come. She writhed horny and terribly needy, terrified because she feared he would lose interest in her.

– Please, Ted, she sniffed.

He kept this distance.

– That was much better, he commented. – This clearly shows you're twice the slave, both nigger and woman, a bitch wagging her tail for the strongest.

All this still felt unreal to her. To a part of her. To another it was all too real. The part knowing beyond knowing that she couldn't say no to this man even if she had wanted to. One didn't say no to Ted Warren. One just didn't.

It had all happened so fast, so unexpected.

The Monster towered above her. It still did as it lowered itself down on her shaking body.

– You're probably wondering if this is the same man you laughed with half an hour ago. He spat hoarsely into her ear. – I can assure you it is. The explanation to this perceived discrepancy is simple: You just don't deserve any better.

The sobbing began then, sore and painful. He penetrated deep within her, and he pulled and pushed and tore. Her body responded to his, as he knew it would. She imagined she heard a growl from deep in his throat, but didn't imagine there was any savagery behind it. He emanated cold and his calm was death. He enjoyed her tight, smooth body and was very careful to make her enjoy every move he made. She forgot everything. Her longing, her hopes. So unreal, so pleasant. Incredulity stuck in her. She told herself, a quiet little voice drowning in the onslaught from the Monster. *It can't be true, can't be true, can't be…*

He didn't enjoy what he did. He didn't dislike it. He performed it, as if getting rid of something vile.

Everything turned dark. Everything turned bright.

He rested on her, his large, heavy body crushing her, staying inside her. She had always loved that, but now it only added to her horror and confusion.

– The world is an insane dance, he said casually. – You mirror it, like it mirrors you. All you can hope for is to stay one step ahead, one step behind.

She stared at him, and it was all totally incomprehensible to her. It was like she could see it, actually see the dancing shadow out there in the yard.

– One day you'll thank me for this, he nodded.

He began moving on her again, not giving her a moment's peace. She attempted to look away. Two light slaps on the cheek and she was brought around once more. He moved and she was his mirror. His body straightened slightly, and he emptied himself in her again. And again and again. And it didn't look like to her as if he needed any break at all. If there was any she sure as hell didn't notice them. She just drowned in a pleasant horror of red and heat.

Afterwards, while he took a shower and she crouched on the bed, she felt fairly certain he had come «only» five times in her, but she couldn't tell for sure. She would never more be certain of anything. Her eyelids slid down and stayed there. They felt so heavy, like being pulled down by lead. He had sucked all the power out of her and left nothing.

She heard the whistling as he dressed, heard it in her half-asleep stupor. A slap on her butt woke her brutally. He signed for her to rise. She placed herself at the center of the bed, displaying herself. He studied her without the slightest sign of passion, and she shook in fright. She feared she didn't satisfy his standards. He threw some clothes on the bed. She dressed without looking at them. When he pulled her in front of the mirror she realized it was her old clothes. She still seemed different, completely changed from the person she had been the last time she had worn them, such a short while ago. It was his clothes. He had taken them, like he had overtaken her.

– Let's go.

– W-where? She asked weakly.

He stood behind her, stared into the mirror behind her shoulder. He didn't raise his voice. There was no need for that.

– Look at yourself… what do you see?

– I d-don't k-know…

– I'll tell you. You don't see shit! You see, you're nothing except what I tell you to be. From now on you will do exactly as I tell you to do, when I say it.

– Yes, Ted… Please, Ted!

He unbuttoned her blouse so her breasts almost fell out. That's all.

Mrs. Rawlins looked at her with a triumphant look from the other side of the street as they walked down the stairs outside. She had always viewed her as a whore. It didn't matter anymore.

They sat by a table at a strip joint on the eastside. She sat with a perfect view to the stage, to the dancers. Thoughts kept churning in her head. She didn't want them to, but they didn't ask her for permission.

The incredulity still stuck in her. She still felt it as if she was on a stage, participating in an insane play. She didn't understand anything of what was happening. It dawned on her that she never had. She wondered what he had done to her. What had he done, really? She imagined a trial where his defense lawyer interrogated her. There were no marks on her. How had he forced her? She shrunk on the spot. The thought of a trial, the notion that there would be a trial at all never truly struck her.

The girls on the stage danced with half-closed eyes. The heat under the powerful lamps made them sweat hard. Whirling hair stuck to face and nude skin. Glory noticed that those with long hair routinely brushed the tresses off breasts and butt. She imagined she was up there with them, wriggling her butt, rocking her breasts, dancing to the wild rhythm, sweating under the men's stares.

– You're probably wondering what we're doing here? Ted Warren nodded in acknowledgment, while studying everything happening in the dump.

She nodded numbly.

– I'm gonna sell you, he informed her. – You may not believe so, but they're making loads of money here. You'll bring a good price.

She knew he wasn't joking. She was convinced to her roots he meant every word.

– P-please, she stuttered, completely beside herself. – Don't… I'll do anything to please you.

– I know you will, he said indifferently. – I knew you would learn quickly.

He had his hands under the table. Wide eyed she heard him open his zipper.

– On your knees, he commanded harshly. – Show your worth!

She knelt down by the chair and crawled under the table. She was convinced no one here would help her, that no one could have stopped him even if they had been standing right at the center of a busy shopping mall. He was so strong, so sovereign that no one would stand a change against him.

The shaking girl grabbed his half stiff cock. The very sight of it and then touch made it all hot and sticky again between her thighs. She began fondling it, with her hands and lips and tongue. It was second nature, as half-buried, horrible memories were brought forward again. She knew what to do. He knew she knew.

It quickly grew hard and big. She felt so terribly small. Her hips hurt by the awkward kneeling. Time passed as she moved her lips up and down the pulsing head. Then she felt it, felt it as if he was touching her… touching her below. But he couldn't be. There was no way he could reach it. But she was positive she felt his hands on her cunt, the soaking wet cunt, a touch overwhelming her completely. She had never felt anything like it, not even… not even with David Gidman. The thought exploded in her head the moment the volcanic moisture erupted in her mouth, flowing from her hole below and down her thighs. Thighs turned weak and her body slack like a heap of clothes on the floor. Her head fell into his lap. She kissed and licked the cock with a dreamy look on her face. Eyes stared at him, filled with worship, like he knew they would.

He pushed back the chair.

– Pull yourself together, he snapped. – We have an appointment on the second floor.

She sniffed, quelling her disappointment, and put the limb back in place, closing the zipper. He rose and pulled her up by the hair. It *hurt!* She looked at him in utter disbelief and despair.

– I do care about you, he grinned, replying to her silent question. – I show you how much I appreciate you.

And everything twisted inside her, cutting her to pieces.

She heard no true humor in his voice, and saw nothing of it in his face, nothing but a hard cold edge, a voice from the grave.

– No one can resist a creature like you, she whispered. – I certainly can't. I Love you!

She kissed him, desperately, filled with longing, with despair.

– I know where you're going with this, she stuttered, she insisted. Couldn't she even speak properly anymore? – To survive in a harsh and ruthless world one must become even harder, even more ruthless. Let me be your *student,* please, Ted. *Please!*

She sent him an inviting smile. As if she could deny him anything, give him anything he hadn't long since taken.

He didn't dignify her with a vocal reply. Her spirit fell even more when she realized he had long since demonstrated how he looked at her.

She slinked after him up the stairs. He knew she would. She recalled the play he had done. He and his brother Mike. She had seen a recording of it, after Mike's death. None of the brothers had much in the sense of talent. They had obvious trouble with pretence. Even as children they had had more than a tendency to speak their mind. Ted had played the villain, and Mike had gallantly penetrated his rotten heart in the last act. It had never been convincing, never real. But this was real. This was actually happening.

*No way out. No places to hide.*

The large room resembled any office. The man behind the desk could be taken for any young executive. The suit, the tie, the striped pants and his hairdo stressed the impression of a successful businessman.

There was a loud crack when Ted closed the door behind them.

– Glory, this is Flaherty. Say hello!

– Hello, Flaherty, she huskily greeted the man behind the desk.

Cursing herself.

– It's really her. The man rose behind the desk with an astonished expression in his face, one that slowly transformed into a satisfied grin. – That's excellent. This nigger bitch doesn't know her place. She has aggravated a number of people in high places. Quite infamous as she is, we can only display her at smaller, exclusive venues, but that's okay. The revenue for each outing will rise accordingly.

He studied her. Then he turned to the dark man.

– She's housebroken? I mean… properly trained?

– I'm certain you'll find her a bit defiant after I've left, but not more than you can handle.

– You can take that to the bank, Flaherty exclaimed.

Unable to curtail his excitement he rushed to the large safe and opened it without bothering to hide the code. Glory's eyes were pulled towards the bulge on his pants. She desperately attempted to draw Ted's attention, but he kept behaving as if she didn't exist.

– Cash, right?

– I have a great distaste for the upcoming money-free society, the dark man nodded.

He accepted a thick envelope and put it in a pocket inside his jacket without checking its content.

And then he left, without so much as a glance of farewell.

Flaherty gave Glory her complete attention.

– Get rid off the rags, lazy slut. Give me value for my money.

She opened her mouth, attempting in vain to voice her protest. She shook her head with large, frightened eyes.

Flaherty kept grinning. He signed for her to come to him.

– Come here. I've got something to show you, something that will teach you beyond all doubt not to be willful. Feel free to try the door first. I think you have a fair idea of what happens to insolent girls.

She imagined the angel of death standing outside, waiting for her. She hurried to the other man's side.

He opened a locker in the desk. It hid a large video screen. He laughed pleased when more fear was revealed in her face. The screen showed many nude girls inside a cage. There were marks of whiplashes on their bodies, faded but distinct. The fear hadn't totally left their expression, but their faces had a resigned, docile quality that frightened her much more than open fear would have done.

– These are the ones that will be sent away, that will be sold to the highest bidder. You don't want to be one of them.

She begged him with her eyes. The moisture didn't seem to leave them, leave them ever. He signed for her to begin, totally indifferent to her plight.

There was a choking sound. She stepped out on the floor and began swaying. With half closed eyes she removed her clothes piece by piece. She rubbed her breasts, and they swelled in her hands. She rotated, revealing everything to the man watching her in slow, delicate moves. Her butt rotated as she spread her legs and eagerly displayed herself to him.

– Very convincing, he commented. – There is nothing you want more, is there, than to submit to me.

The final piece of clothing fell from her hands. She flowed naked across the floor, rushing to his side. A playful hand touched the bulge on his pants.

– You're definitely showing potential, as I thought you would, he nodded pleased. – After the right training you'll be quite the attraction, grossing as much dough as five other girls, and the prestige to go with it.

She went at him with a murderous intensity. He caught her hand in a grip like a vice, and hit her hard in the belly with the other hand. It happened so quickly. All her experience, her rage was for naught. All air was pushed from her lungs. She hung paralyzed in his strong grip.

– Delicious. He carried her to the desk, and dropped her upper body on it. – Sweet flavor, pure chocolate, waiting to be filled.

He pulled down his zipper, pulled out his cock. His insensitive hands grabbed around her hips and then he began pumping her up. First she felt him against his thighs, and then deep inside her cunt. She cried out in protest, in need, not wanting the heat to spread, but it still did. One of her hands sought her mouth. She bit it and didn't feel a thing.

– You will be sold, eventually, of course, he breathed. – Our clients grow tired of the merchandize rather fast. If we didn't supplant you gals with fresh meat fairly often we would go bankrupt. There's a large market with a lot of demand out there, and no lack of supply. Without the right products we'll quickly fall behind.

His thick, coarse fingers sought inside the already filled hole, expanding it further. She let out a long, horny wail.

– So tight, he mumbled.

He growled and pushed hard in a series of explosive thrusts. The warm stream flowed into the warm and wet hole.

But the ultimate reward didn't come to her. Her hot water had just begun to trickle, but it didn't flow. She began sobbing then, sore and hard.

He pushed a button on his desk without bothering to put his cock back inside its resting place. Glory lay on her back with weak, unmovable arms and legs. A big, assertive woman entered the room, followed by two smaller in uniform, of the clearly submissive type.

– Rise, girl! The voice was just as authoritative as her appearance. Glory obeyed without a thought, without the slightest resistance. – That's good!

The woman circled her like a predator, and Glory stood there frozen. She felt as if every bit of her pride had been pulled out.

– I'm Alysse, the woman told her. – From this moment I'm your Goddess. You'll obey my every command. A hint of an order from me, and you'll obey it eagerly and joyfully. I know you do understand, beauty.

Alysse found a collar and fit it around the brown neck. The lukewarm metal glued itself to the skin. Glory was led out of the room and into a smaller, darker, empty, and from there into a narrow twilight passageway. The two uniformed servants used their small whips every time she according to them slackened the pace. The passageway led to endless stairs. She knew them to be that, endless, fully aware of what awaited her, but she didn't care. It didn't concern her. From this point on others would tell her what to do and not do. She thought of Ted, a passing fancy quickly slipping away.

She had been wrong when she had thought he had left her nothing. He had left ashes.

## 2

The afternoon sun cast long shadows at the walls of the low houses in Vieux Carrè. Francis Caine stared down at the busy street. He stared up and down it several times. It didn't make him feel like less of a target at the open balcony. The old city of New Orleans had always attracted him. Now, the mere sight of the crowd down below made him sweat hard. He dried the sweat from his brow, using his seventh handkerchief in ten minutes and hating it. Heat had never been a problem for him. Now he wanted to leave it, leave it behind.

But the cool shadows in the apartment weren't inviting either.

– Come inside, the imposing voice called to him. – Don't stand there like an idiot.

He did his best to ignore it, once again cursing the day he had heard it for the first time. His thoughts drifted, but not enough by far. They basically stayed within the last two years. So much had happened, and everything else was a haze of gray and pale red. In his most panicked moments he feared a day would come when he no longer would recall anything before July Fourth 1974, when Stewart had *sent* for him.

And he had charged off to Denver like an idiot.

No more handkerchiefs. He pulled back into the apartment's cool shadows.

Mark Stewart sat in a deep chair by the bed. He was oiling and polishing a revolver, a newly acquired Magnum 44". The man didn't sweat. His hands were steady. Nothing contradicted the impression that here was a man in total harmony with himself. Caine knew better. Whatever sat there relaxed in the chair was no man.

– I've looked at you, Caine breathed. – I know you're playing games with me. Why don't you go away, dissolve into open air? Why are you *hounding* me?

– May I suggest that this isn't the right time to indulge your xenophobia, Stewart commented dryly. – May I remind you that somewhere in this town a pack of barking dogs is searching streets and houses for us.

– For you, the other gritted his teeth. – You!

– C'mon, how long do you think you'll survive without me at your side?

– How long will I survive *with* you? Caine complained bitterly.

Something irritating him beyond anything was the calm Stewart projected, in contrast to his own nervous and erratic behavior. It made him even more down and out. He wondered what was wrong with him, how Stewart's very presence could turn him into an insecure and fumbling jerk. Never before in his adult life had he carried this feeling of inferiority confronted with another human being, and he hated it, hated everything about it.

A twenty-year war had been violently upgraded when David Gidman had escaped the English prison a few months earlier. The last few weeks it had exploded, long since passed the point of reason or rationality. Caine suspected that both Stewart and Gidman wanted a clean sweep because they sensed the end was coming. Caine couldn't keep up with that. Not anymore. What he had taken as a given a few years earlier felt like mountain climbing now. Nothing seemed to faze Stewart. He was the same as ever. Caine didn't like to think about that. It meant that Caine himself had been weakened, diminished. Stewart was the same. And different. The fire was no longer concealed. It burned fully in the open.

– It has taken time, Caine said accusingly, – but now your true self is showing itself, is rearing its ugly head.

– You must explain that one better, old eagle.

Stewart's harmony wasn't rocked, not the slightest.

– Don't play dumb, Caine spat with poison in his voice. – You're building an army, pulling in both the willing and unwilling. And it isn't just about Gidman, is it? He's just one stop for you. Don't think I don't know that. I just wonder how many you'll destroy before you're done.

The last sentence didn't come out as strong as he would have wanted. Stewart bent slightly forward. The fire danced in his eyes, uninterrupted.

– Now, now, Francis, let's not get carried away with the hypocrisy here. We both know whom you are truly worried about…

There was a knock on the door, the prearranged signal. Everything turned black for Caine. He hardly even registered the five men entering the apartment, entering of their own, free will. Their names flashed through his mind. The room shifted, *existence* shifted. In his thoughts he turned a corner. The shadows stretched out before him. There were flashes in them, caused by many weapons being fired simultaneously. All the bullets hit him. He fell on his back, and lay there, while life bled out of him. In the background he heard an insane rhythm of countless drums. He opened wide eyes. Sweat drowned his skin. The cold sweat. Suddenly he was freezing badly. Deeply shocked he realized he had experienced a vision, his very first. Nausea rose in his throat.

The five men dealt exclusively with Stewart. The lemming instinct sought the leader, the strong man.

– Activity increases by the hour, Clayton Prescott, the roughest among them said. – I can't really fathom why they're hesitating. They're many enough to attack us ten times.

– And Gidman? Stewart asked sharply, like a whip.

– No one has seen shit of him. If he's close he must have cut himself in pieces, each piece carried by his devoted followers…

– He will come. Stewart turned towards the window. The shadows from the Venetian blinds fragmented his face. – If not now, then later, someplace, somewhere.

Caine once more heard the beat of the insane drums. Their sound rocked in the air and cut in his ears. Disheartened, he followed the six men down below. It wasn't that many years ago, when he had led and others followed. He desperately wanted that time back.

They walked down two long stairs, to the basement, where hectic activity flowed around them. Guns were everywhere. A wide variety of models. Only two groups of people. For the first time the two to this point separate groups Stewart had spent the last year gathering met. Caine had met up with Clayton Prescott and the experienced mercenaries on various occasions, but he had never even seen any of the other group face to face.

Stewart had gathered them and trained them, all the young and impressionable.

– Good afternoon, Stewart greeted them.

– GOOD AFTERNOON, the youths cried, and the mercenaries mumbled.
– We finally meet, all of us, Stewart stated. – You have all been training hard lately. Now we will become a unit. Now we will become a war.
His words stirred them. That was easily discerned.
– How go the preparations? Prescott grumbled.
He had been Stewart's middleman the last month, Caine his errand boy.
– They are almost complete.
A tall, well-built girl stepped forward and reported to him, but she was turned towards Stewart.
– Excellent, Kelly. Stewart nodded to her. – Is everybody ready? Are you ready, Kelly Regehr?
– We're looking forward to complete whatever you require of us, sir.
She straightened a bit more, staring straight ahead.
– Are you *loyal,* Kelly Regehr?
– Yes, SIR!
*What has he done with you, with you all?*
He had thrown all caution to the wind. That much was clear to Caine. The question was what to do with it.
– Ian Nelson, Stewart shouted sharply.
The boy stepped forward, virtually like a soldier, perhaps overdoing it a bit.
– Are you loyal, boy?
– To my toes, Mr. Stewart.
– Kelly, turn your gun at him!
She turned her gun, a 357" Magnum towards the boy's head. She had obeyed without hesitation. Caine saw her send Nelson a warm smile. They were close.
– Are you loyal, boy?
– Until death! The boy cried.
Silenced reigned.
No, *Stewart* reigned.
– Shoot him!
It was said so casually, in such a normal tone of voice.
Regehr pulled the trigger, without even the slightest hesitation. There was a crack. The bullet hit Nelson on the forehead. The back of his head was blown away. The bullet passed several others by a narrow margin. They stood remarkably still, like statues. No others were hit.
The girl screamed short and sharp. Her arm fell down, along her side, and the gun slipped from weak fingers. No one heard it actually hit the floor, but it lay there, at Kelly's feet.
– Pick up your weapon, Stewart commanded.
The hand reaching down for the gun shook hard. But as the hand closed around the cold and hot steel, it turned calm. Eyes opened wide in the strongest possible horror stared blindly at him when he stepped in front of her.
– Excellent, Kelly Regehr, you didn't fail me.
He dried off a single tear before it left the corner of her eye.
Caine couldn't move, couldn't speak.

– An excellent disciplinary measure, Prescott noted. – May I ask if there was a reason?
– I didn't know I needed any, Stewart replied cheerfully.
– You don't, of course. Prescott grinned. – I should point out that you need a lot of new recruits if you make a habit of this, though.
Stewart pulled a tape from his pocket and put it in a player. He pushed a button and the tape began turning. The first voice said only «yes». No more was needed for Caine. He knew he was listening to David Gidman. Everybody recognized instantly Ian Nelson's voice.
*– I've got invaluable information. Can we meet?*
*– You haven't made yourself deserving of that yet. You'll meet with my envoy. The usual place.*
*– After this you'll want to meet me face to face.*
Nelson sounded extremely confident, but he probably stood there and glared at the phone. Gidman had hung up.
– That asshole, Regehr said, strangely relaxed. – Thank you! Thank you, Fireeyes!
– Fireeyes? The Gambler couldn't resist the temptation.
– It's what my faithful call me, Stewart replied teasingly. – Fitting, isn't it?
The suspicion that his friend had thrown all caution to the wind was finally and explicitly confirmed.
– It's time, Mark Stewart said aloud. – Our enemy knows where we are. We know where he will be: where we are.
He had them. There was no doubt about that either. The mercenaries and the others with some battle experience used the opportunity to grin a bit, but they kept their mouth shut. They were used to leaders' bombastic speech, and they were young, too, admiring the way he had dealt with potential disciplinary problems.
Prescott stepped forward for everybody to see.
– Well said, he acknowledged. – We're with you… Fireeyes.
They walked through the haze and smoke and afternoon heat. No space, no time but a blink from one moment to the next. Stewart's eyes glowed and sparkled constantly behind the shades. The last few weeks he had walked around with a horrible dark wig. As they watched he pulled it off and threw it away. As they stared he removed his shades and broke them in one hand. He hid no more. And those who followed him did as he did, grew in his tracks.
– It's all changing, Caine said bitterly.
They walked through Bourbon Street.
– From a street full of bordellos and «casinos», where people were pulled in and duped, you mean? Stewart countered.
Caine sent him another bitter stare.
– Everything changes. Stewart shrugged. – Unless the changes are fundamental and final they matter little.
Regehr and Prescott and several others surrounded their leader like a living shield. He accepted it, even though he needed it the least. Their close proximity

made his skin tingle even more, made the volcano boil even stronger. He surrounded them all with his power, his living energy. Caine as well. The sun seemed to have descended among them, sharing its power. Caine shook constantly, unable to stop. He observed Phoenix in all its glory, and it scared the shit out of him.

– Can't you feel it? Stewart cried to his old friend. – Feel New Orleans, become one with it.

This city was a melting pot of cultures and races, a unique mix of Spanish, French, English, African and Native, local origin. In Unites States as well as the rest of the world.

– I feel it. Caine nodded. – It's choking me.

He couldn't enjoy it. He just couldn't.

– JESUS! One of the younger men exclaimed. – What's HAPPENING?

– Hush. Regehr put a finger on his lips. – Enjoy it. Be on guard. Prepare yourself.

The street they moved through, Bourbon Street, its narrow sidewalks crawled with people. They made their way towards the modern parts of the city. Thirty in number followed Stewart to the slaughterhouse. Caine tied a sweatband around his head. It did him little good. He still had to blink the sweat from his eyes, the little good that did him.

There were images, nightmarish impressions assaulting them all. Caine couldn't shut them out. He realized that Stewart shared his thoughts, his visions with them all, consciously or not. The youths, judging by the visible awe in their faces were used to it. The older men and women weren't. One thing was certain: steam flowed from under the pushed down lid.

Stewart was sweating ever so little. He concentrated slightly and the impressions from the chaotic minds in his close proximity stopped bothering him. He sensed the focused thoughts from those he led, and from those that were convinced they were about to close a trap ahead somewhere.

– Forty in ambush around the corner, he said. – Perhaps as many as fifty. The fools. They've split up. We attack them head on.

Prescott nodded, both eagerness, confidence and doubt visible in his face.

– Well, Fireeyes, he grinned. – I've known you for months and have never had a reason to doubt you, so why start now?

There was silence for a second or two, silence in the howling buzz.

– Head on? One yelped.

– Very few of them will be in hiding. They're gambling on a frontal assault. All the people in the street make it hard to aim properly anyway. Thanks to Ian they know how inexperienced many of you are. They expect you to fold by the first sight of *blood*. Most of you have killed, but you've never experienced anything remotely like this… Neither have *they*. I trust you'll not let yourself be fooled, be killed, and disappoint me. The wind blows through us. This is the first step on the path for which I've prepared you. Only the first step. Some of you will die, but those that survive will have passed a crucial test, a trial by fire… and you'll be able to face the world on your own terms.

They couldn't fathom how they could hear him, far less hear him like thunder in their ears over the buzzing voices around them, their own fever-hot thoughts, the overwhelming sound of boiling blood.

The group moved as a unit, as one. Every movement, every glance and step seemed economical, measured, like an extension of the person in front or behind or by one's side. Before they knew it, without truly registering it, they left Vieux Carrè, and reached the modern part of the city.

A slight turn of the body and the broad Canal Street embraced them. Nothing seemed out of the ordinary. Everything looked perfectly normal.

They saw a street filled with stores, filled up in the afternoon rush. People crossed and crisscrossed each other in an endless flow. Impressions flooded their brains. There was little or nothing to hold onto, except the deadly weapons they hid on their bodies.

– Urban guerilla! Kelly exclaimed.

The cry distracted her, but didn't divert her from the task.

Urban guerilla. Warriors moving from house to house, with open street shootouts, with spectators and random casualties. She walked two steps behind Stewart. She felt him like skin to skin. Her lips formed *Fireeyes*.

Caine saw it. A look of disgust touched his face.

His right hand touched his revolver and the machinegun. His arm felt stiff and dead.

Stewart seemed totally unfazed. Simultaneously, in his tearing half-smile, flared the Moon and the Sun. Blood flowed in veins, and flowed from wounds. There was the thunder of drums.

Time didn't slow down. The world didn't change into slow motion. Instead their perception of time changed so the world moved faster around them. The whirlwind was blowing. The wheel of fate spun so fast that it made them dizzy.

A woman about twenty steps ahead appeared from behind a random pedestrian, the weapon in her hands about to point forward. Stewart had already aimed his. He fired his Ingram machinegun in a wide bow as he let himself fall. Most of the bullets hit the woman, but a few also hit others, both armed combatants and unarmed «civilians». The screams drowned in the thunder. The murderous salvos the two opposing groups fired at each other quickly cleaned the path between them.

Stewart lay on the ground, stretched flat in the air and sat on his heels, as he moved like a shadow in the bright-lit day. His body twisted as he ran and in midair, making him a beyond hard target. The others almost froze in absolute amazement. His machinegun hit an empty chamber, and he threw it away. He kept firing with a Magnum 44" in each hand. Enemies fell in a shower of blood.

People began dying on both sides of Caine. Stewart drew most of the fire as the enemies attempted to hit him in their desperate fear, but not all of it. A line of blood erupted behind Kelly Regehr's right arm. She spun around and fell, but quickly got back up. She picked up an UZI, and kept firing. There were still a few covers between the groups, especially when the battle spread to the road. Tires howled as cars shrieked to a halt. A driver was hit, and in the moment of death he probably pushed the brakes extra hard, and the car tumbled over and hit another and flew through the air. The gas tank exploded as it hit the ground. Thick, black smoke covered the street. A few police officers came to. They managed to shoot down a few from both sides before they were gunned down.

– How long? A boy cried. – HOW LONG?

Caine understood. He wondered himself, how long the skirmish had lasted. Fifteen seconds? Twenty? Four minutes? Five? Probably somewhere between one and two. When one was fighting for one's life the measure of time truly turned meaningless.

Stewart sheathed the revolvers. He picked up new guns as he advanced. Threw them away when they were empty and picked up others. A bullet penetrated his jacket. Caine didn't see any blood. He could more than imagine how Stewart had to look to those he was attacking. A demon, an invincible dust devil hungering for their tender souls. The first threw away their guns and fled. Stewart fired and fired, no matter his position, moving so fast that it seemed impossible to lock on to him. If something eventually should happen to hit him, it would have to be random fired bullets. Caine had never, ever seen anything like it. He remained half in cover behind a burning car, half out of it, paralyzed by the sight. Two rushed at him with blazing guns. Prescott shot them. Caine shot one firing in pure raving delirium from a window, silencing the man. Thc insane expression in the man's face softened as he died.

Prescott was hit and fell on his belly. He kept firing, but was hit in the arm. Caine fired at a woman, but missed. She pulled the trigger with a totally insane expression in her bloated face. She fell in a hail of bullets.

Stewart rushed in among the enemies. It both paralyzed and inspired his followers. They looked at each other, indecisive, afraid of firing in the fear of hitting him. But here was no need to worry. Stewart shot two and two. Those attempting to hit him usually hit open air or their own people. Kelly and the others weren't lacking in targets among those fleeing from the demon in their midst, driven by a fear they couldn't name. Fireeyes' warriors cried triumphantly and moved forward in ruthless abandon. The massacre ended in an orgy of excitement and blood. This beaten part of David Gidman's army was slaughtered to practically the last person. Stewart fired one and one bullet into the back of those fleeing. He suddenly seemed indifferent, almost bored, as if he was doing target practice.

Canal Street slowly fell into an eerie calm. Two seconds, four, six… sixteen… Shadows walked among the dead and dying, blocking the light. The rumble in the ground persisted. People blinked and they couldn't quite see the person standing next to them because of the dozen dark shapes. Dust and ashes, and millions of microscopic droplets of blood remained in the air. Francis Caine tasted it all, as he rose, unharmed. The shapes slowly faded. It was over. And then Mark Stewart didn't in any way look indifferent anymore. He sat on his heels and held on to a dying enemy soldier, soaking up the last of his energy. Caine realized that, and didn't even feel surprised, shocked. The seconds ticked on, filled with impressions, intensity.

– CANNON FODDER! Stewart shouted into the air. – You sent me cannon fodder. I expected that, but not that they would be to this degree PATHETIC.

He signed to his people. They stopped in their task, relenting. The few that had belonged to the enemy and was still fleeing, was free to keep fleeing into their personal darkness.

There was no blood on him, no sign of any wounds.

– Let's scram, he said. – Carry our heavily wounded, those that cannot walk on their own. Let the dead and other living be.

He threw a bloody sack of clothes and holes over his shoulder, and lifted and carried another in his other arm, without visibly straining.

– I can walk.

Prescott fought himself to his feet with clenched teeth.

Canal Street, the otherwise so busy shopping street didn't look like a disaster area. It was one. Screams of desperation, insanity and pain surrounded the group. People still rushed back and forth in a confused, erratic pattern. The heavily reduced warrior tribe left the place as they had arrived; in silence. The Gambler took the rear, numb, shaken. He still heard the drums, heard the drums of the damned.

– So what do you say, Frankie? Stewart turned with a shadow of a smile. – Perhaps you will survive with me?

A policeman blocked their way, clutching a revolver in his shaking hands. They had all sheathed their weapons. They looked at him with interest as they kept walking. His eyes grew larger and larger and he began sweating. His weapon practically lowered itself. He turned abruptly and fled.

– I who used to be afraid of cops.

Kelly's laughter was hard and accentuated and free.

Gray, square buildings rose around them. Fireeyes led them to safety. Not back to the house in Vieux Carrè, but in the opposite direction, down many a haunted street, to an empty, unpopulated garage in the modern business area. The door rolled down the moment everybody had stepped inside.

– Another secret? Caine said to Stewart.

None of the others had known of this either, judging by their wide eyes, their impressed demeanor.

– I've got tons of them, Stewart grinned. – You should know that by now.

A large panel in the wall slid open, large enough for humans to walk through. Behind was revealed a long passage.

– Is anybody there? Kelly wondered. – Anybody pushing buttons?

– No, Stewart replied.

Caine knew he was the one pushing the buttons. Without being physically close. Such an elaborate system would by default be close to impenetrable. The buttons could be hidden deep within the wall, beneath thick layers of concrete or metal. Only one like Stewart, with Stewart's specific abilities could access it and grant access to others.

At the end of the long passageway they reached a living room, a hospital room, a field hospital.

– That was far, Prescott gasped. – That was a very long way to go. I don't know exactly how long.
Stewart put down the two wounded he had carried all the way. All in all there were eight wounded unable to stay on their feet.
– I'm dying, Fireeyes, a pale boy moaned, striving to keep the tears from his eyes.
Stewart said nothing. He put his hands on naked and bloodied skin. Hands began glowing, pulsing in conjunction with the fireeyes. The boy gasped. Everybody turned to look at what was happening, and once they had done so they couldn't turn away.
The blood flowed and flowed, steaming hot blood. Flowed, and then it stopped. Laurie and Andrew entered the room with their hands full of bandages and equipment. Not many would have survived that way, and they all knew it. Now, they stopped. Laurie Isherwood gasped. Francis suddenly knew her last name, knew the names of everybody in the room. Everybody stared speechless at what happened on the operating tables.
Oliver's eyes cleared. He gasped and gasped.
– Yes, Stewart nodded. – You're fully conscious, now. You know fully how it is to live.
Stewart raged on, from table to table. More wounds closed. They didn't vanish completely, but closed. Bullets hit the floor.
– Don't just stand there, he snarled, staring back at them in an even warm and cold flow unlike anything they had previously experienced. This was their life with Stewart, what it would always be. – Start treating these poor souls.
They laughed nervously, wondering if there was a touch of humor in his voice.
An image rose in Francis's mind, crystal clear: Stewart walking among the shapes, there on the battlefield, among his dying enemies, sucking the energy from them from the very air itself. He was still glowing from it, still filled to the brim with life. Francis saw the souls of the condemned rise in the smoke and the mist, howling in pain, whining in pain… whiiiiiiiiiniiiiiiiing iiiiiiin paiiiiiiin
I'm cracking up cracking up uuuuuuuup
Stewart put his hands on Kelly Regehr, one on the injured arm and one on her shoulder. Her eyes burned in pain. She looked apprehensive, but trusting at him. Then she felt it, felt the heat. Francis felt it, too, felt the fire. Her eyes widened, locked onto Stewart, first in incomprehension and then… then in worship. She shook, as if in cramps and shouted:
– Yes, Fireeyes. Oh, YES! It's so pleasant, so wonderful, wonderful, WONDERFUL
He put her down on an empty table. She blinked several times and smiled half asleep in devotion to Fireeyes.
Prescott hadn't been able to stay on his feet. He sat on a chair and clenched his teeth. Fire and water whirled around him and in the entire room when Stewart touched him.
– The sorcerer keeps finding new tricks, Caine commented dryly. – Where will it end?

*endendendendend*

Sound danced in the room with the fire, and nothing was right with the world.

It was no use. Kelly stared at Fireeyes with worship in her eyes. The women he hadn't touched physically found themselves wishing that they had been hit. The men followed him with a dedicated look. Even Prescott, the hardened warrior had a feverish look in there somewhere. They all stared at him as if he was the second coming or something.

They belonged to *him,* now.

– You don't have more need for me today, Francis heard himself say.

– That's for sure, Prescott grinned.

The scornful laughter was like an echo of his words.

– I'm going out, Francis heard himself say, as if being immersed in water.

– Granted, Fireeyes granted mercifully. – I'll open all the doors for you.

Had he really said that? How much of what Francis saw in here really happened? He wondered what was real and what was not, like he had done for so long, now. When the Gambler turned his back to them, to the spinning coin, he heard his own voice inside his head cry out: *Help me, please, help me!*

He walked into the night, condemned and cursed forever.

## 3

The voice spoke, forming sounds and words out of thin air. If there were lips they didn't move, at least not in any way the black man noticed.

*An old joke. Two men sit on a train. They don't know if it is moving or not. They know it doesn't matter, not in any meaningful way. Both know the train's destination. It never moves from the rails they walk on. So they ask themselves the inevitable question: Why don't they leave? That one is easy to answer: They don't want to go off track.*

The train raged on through the gray, gray night. Lights and shadows played in the face of the gigantic man. He strived to look out of the window with his one, healthy eye.

– Ha ha, very funny. He struck his thigh in a controlled manner. – It made me laugh, you know.

At the other side of the table in the luxurious compartment the other man smiled behind the shades.

There were only the two of them in there, in the entire coach. No one disturbed them. Guards in both ends of the adjacent coaches made sure of that.

The two had been silent for quite a while, now, which was strange, since they never had had any problems communicating before.

– Life sure is strange. The man with the shades smiled and shook his head. – You think you've got it all figured out, and then, WHAM, you realize you know nothing.

– An epiphany? The one-eyed man wondered, moderately interested.

– Sort of, the man with the shades nodded. It would seem that he bent forward slightly. The reality of it was that he was leaning back in his seat. White fangs flashed. – I could show you, if I thought it would do any good, what disastrous impact people like you and I have had on human life the last ten thousand years. We were few and marginal in influence in the time before the first cities. We're dominating the current world, and no one dares opposing us. I find it quite pathetic actually. The poor, oppressed sheep work hard to either become devourers themselves or to be further oppressed. The worst part is that they're among the first to eagerly strike down the minuscule attempt at liberation. In short: humanity has a desperate need to be rescued from itself.

– And you're the man that will do this impossible task?

– Why not? I know myself and the world to the bottom of my heart. There are few people better qualified.

– Bravo! The one-eyed man cried caustically and applauded slowly. – What an excellent self-sacrifice!

– I wouldn't say that. A shrug. – The way I see it I've hardly done anything but shift from one form of egoism to another. Everything a person does have the origin in the Self. We all seek to satisfy something deep-felt and fundamental within ourselves.

His eyes burned like the flames of hell when he stared out of the window, at a point distant in time and space.

– It will take time, and a lot of sweat, but I will succeed, I know that.

– No matter… Now One-Eye's voice was even more sarcastic, – I must thank you from the bottom of my heart for the little service you did for me.

– It wasn't any worse than anything else I've done. A deliberate shrug. – It won't matter one way or another, anyway. It was the last I'll ever do for you. We're even, now. I don't owe you shit anymore.

He rose. He stood slightly crouched, but there was no stench of defeat in him.

– My thanks for the train trip. It has been very… educational. But I'll jump off before the next station.

He turned towards the door, turning his back to the one-eyed man, walking away. He turned around a few seconds in the doorway.

– You'll lose, you know. I almost hope you know that much. One or all of the three titans you're taking on will wipe you off the board. *Au revoir,* old friend, we'll never meet again. I feel a certain need to wish you a long and healthy life, but since I believe it's useless I won't bother.

The man with the dark shades snarled behind the glass. The next moment he was gone. The lone giant had hardly been blinking with his one eye. It had been sufficient for the other to vanish like a ghost.

– I think you'll discover I still have some surprises on hand, he shouted.

The unique laughter made ice flow through his veins. That hadn't happened in many years, since he had been a boy. He heard a door open and close. He saw before his closed eye the beast throwing itself into the night and land steady on all fours, a mighty bird flapping its wings in the dark, filling it to the brim.

– I did laugh, he said to the air. – «They don't want to go off track». That *is* very funny, a punch-line of the first order.

Whatever remained of the eye under the patch always hurt when he laughed. He straightened in the seat to his full height, deliberately avoiding looking out the window.

He had never found comedies particularly funny.

## 4

Four men sat in a train compartment, a younger Francis Caine and a young Stewart, with Peter Clarke and Wolf Connors on their way to the hot, dusty city of San Diego the summer of 1966, to a rendezvous with Death, with Destiny.

– Nobody can change the tide of blood. Caine heard his own voice like an echo, a double voice. A demon from hell somebody had sent to taunt him. – Time passes no matter what we do to stop it. No one can stop the wind.

Stewart was approaching thirty, a fairly mature age, but he still seemed insecure, unmade. It was only when he spoke - when he spoke again - that the older Caine recognized him. Words were hammered in. Like nails, nuts and bolts.

– It's difficult to rock a system rotten to its roots. It has grown itself so large that David Gidman is just a modest beginning. But if you push hard enough the building with feet of clay will eventually fall by the slightest added force applied to it.

No, no, he recalled it all wrong. The words hadn't come out like that. They hadn't cared about such peripheral concerns then. They had shunned the hippies like a disease. They had sought experiences, not prolonged uphill struggles. The battles they had participated in had almost always been personal, against an enemy they could touch and feel.

*What makes you think it's any different, now?*

A blinding, rainbow-like light boiled away the heavy fog and he shook, shook hard.

He shook in frosty cramps in the hot room, burned by Stewart's warm hands. Christ, ten years ago he hadn't believed in warm hands. He hadn't even believed in Santa Claus.

The flow of Life pulled him out of his coma-like state, but it brought him no joy. His eyes, when opening, opened only slowly. With sharpened senses came awareness, understanding. He smelled his own vomit. His own, weary body mixed with alcohol filtered through burned pores.

The small, bombed-out room stank of drunkenness and crushed cockroaches. He heard the sound of his week-old beard without touching it with his hand.

Stewart, *Fireeyes* sat straddling on a chair. To say that knowledge burned in Caine was in no way sufficient. The icy fire itched and warmed and devoured. It dawned on him that Stewart wanted it that way. He wanted to share his knowledge, wanted to make sure Caine knew everything worth knowing.

– I can't keep carrying you, Francis. This is the last time.

More dawned on the man with the week old beard.

– Hatred reaching back to childhood's mists, he said slowly, hardly recognizing himself, as if he wasn't quite himself. – It has taken many forms, hasn't it, been focused at more than one man, going far beyond the vanquishing of David Gidman…

Stewart stared at him with his age-old eyes, stared straight through him.

Someone played accordion somewhere on the streets. It cut through Caine's brain like a razor.

– Funny, isn't it, how a few minutes by a frog pond might form an entire life? An unmovable smile. – Except about the forming part, of course. That's the usual silly interpretation, something therapists have fun with at dinner parties. I took control of my life that day, Francis. And I formed, developed myself, consciously, step by step. I waited, waited patiently. Things come to those who wait. A chain isn't necessarily weakened by what is originally the weakest link.

– You're obsessed with your agenda, Caine said weakly. – I knew that, but not to what degree. It gives new meaning to both words. Congratulations.

– My family has a long tradition of obsession, the man that had once called himself Fontaine laughed. – The trick is to be better at it than any of the others.

And he kept talking, kept talking even as he turned away, as he turned back.

– But now, there is something I must know, Frankie. No more silly jokes or evasive tricks…

He didn't bend forward even if that was how it seemed.

– I must know, Francis. *Are you with me?*

Everything Caine had wanted to say, all the objections just faded away on his lips. All the illusions he had carefully crafted about his life evaporated.

– I'm with you, he replied hoarsely.

Stewart rose. He was smiling.

– That pleases me. Perhaps you will, in time realize the truth I've discovered: that it's possible to stop the flow of time, divert the mighty winds, the flow of history and downfall, if one's wanting it hard enough. If one is willing to make the sacrifices. If one is willing to do absolutely anything in order to finish what one has started. The metal in the forge is about to cool. The time has come.

These words, everything about this seemed so familiar to Caine. By the almighty. He remembered.

A while later he wondered if Stewart had truly been here at all. The man with the week-old beard rested, somewhat on his back on the bed, and listened to the sounds of life outside. He sought it, clung to it desperately, like a lifeline to any kind of distant paradise.

He found himself back in Vieux Carrè. People danced around him in the narrow streets, and he wondered for the thousandth time if people always danced in fucking New Orleans. He levitated between them like a ghost. They didn't notice him, and he hardly noticed them. Jackson Square, its green and lush park area appeared before him, blessed and empty. He made an attempt to rest on a bench. A bunch of drummers passed him, jumping and dancing like madmen. He hurried on, hurried past the old cathedral. Seconds passed, minutes… he couldn't say, before he sought another church. Finding one obsessed him. He couldn't recall seeing it on the streets. It was just there. And he was inside, as if swallowed by a huge black hole.

The catholic church calmed him, chilled him to the bone. The weak light anointed his sore eyes. The drums disrupted him, even as he sat in the confessional, ready to spill his guts. He was unable to think.

– Forgive me, Father, for I have sinned. It has been forty years since my last confession.

There was no sound from the other side of the wall. He didn't see anyone, couldn't decide if there was anyone there. He didn't care.

– I've killed many people, Father. I'm responsible for many people's death, and I've killed. I don't know how many. Such things have a tendency to blur in time. It doesn't really weigh heavily on my conscience. What does concern me is whether or not I've met Satan's emissary on Earth, and what I shall do or not do about it.

He left the church in a hurry. The visit hadn't helped any. The unrest and anxiety inside grew another notch. His eyes moved in slits and pulls, and he constantly turned his head to look behind. He looked to his sides. That didn't seem strange to him. He would have looked under the bed if he felt for it. But not checked out the closet. Never ever. His hand touched the gun every second or so. His wet hand slid across the handle. Slid. He sat outside, at a sidewalk cafeteria. For about ten seconds. He eventually settled somewhat in the deepest corner of a moist and hot dump of a bar. Eyes stared at all the scoundrels and gangsters there. He felt strangely safe.

Later at night. The night had fallen, and he hadn't noticed. He hadn't seen Stewart the entire day (or the entire week), but he was always there, present like a wound, a presence in his mind, walking right there by his side.

– I don't need you, he cried. – I don't fucking need you, okay?

The bright light of day had always been sufficient for him. He had never needed any sort of deeper, fundamental truth.

He stumbled through the streets. He didn't know where he was headed. Perhaps the deeper part of his consciousness steered him? He barked a laughter, one sounding more like choking.

– What's wrong? He shouted. – What are you staring at?

He caught glimpses of himself in the windows he passed. At least he thought it was his own face and indistinct body he saw there in the misty shadows.

New Orleans was his town. But he didn't recognize it anymore, not its smallest parts. Everything seemed eerie and overwhelming.

– It's your fault, he belched to the shadow following him. – Everything was fine until you came along. Go back to the hell you came from.

A sound attracted him, a gathering of sounds. He brightened.

He circled a bit before finding it. His experience told him it would only be one entrance and he was right. He heard cries and the unmistakable sound of cock fighting. And suddenly he was there, among the other desperate people. Bets were made. A lot of dirty, greasy bills exchanged hands and owners. He saw it before his inner eyes, recalling his adolescence in places such as these. The stench settled once more on him, doing so like a second skin.

Smoke covered the room from floor to ceiling. Experience and luck made him reach a good spot. It was simple when one knew the ropes, the tricks. And once again he did.

– Next fight? He inquired.

– Won't be long, the skinny man wailed. – This won't take long. The boy with the colorful feathers looked so promising, and he's the worst kind of crap, having all his feathers plucked.

The Gambler left the place at dawn. He hadn't lost anything, but he hadn't won either. He had lost, really, running away from there, from there, too.

Poker. *Poker*. The word echoed through his head like salvation. Poker dumps were everywhere. They wouldn't be difficult to find. He had to go there, had to go there, now. His hand touched his jaw. He just had to shave first, pull himself together, get his life back in order. The Sun's first, thin rays touched his skin. They didn't improve upon his color. Instead they exposed the gusty texture. He stopped in front of a dark display window. By God, they wouldn't admit him in the worst dump the way he looked.

Morning. Another morning. It had to be. By all saints and demons. He fell down on a bench, already exhausted, burned out. In pure desperation he attempted to listen to the sound of nature surrounding him, the birdsong, details he had always disregarded as silly and useless.

He had enough money left. For now. But not months, years ahead. What would happen then, if he had lost his ability to play, to gamble, to play to win? He rose abruptly from the wreck of a bench. He knew what it was all about. It was about leadership, about leading, taking charge. What was wrong needed to be corrected.

He turned a corner. The entire broad street opened up to him, to his senses, the ironware store fifteen steps ahead, the advertising for IBM computers, the drummer beating his old skin with a demonic grin all over his apeshit face. He wanted to blow them all away. The woman brushing the dusty staircase. The man with the gun. There was one single crack of thunder. A sledgehammer struck his head. He fell on his back and after just a few seconds he lay still, lay there on his back without breathing.

Francis Caine was dead.

# First Part:
# Leaving Las Vegas

# Chapter One: The undying Hunger

The branches whipped her naked body. She hardly even acknowledged them as she ran like the wind through the tight forest. The wind whispered in the leaves around her. She heard him giving chase, and the smile around her lips spread to her entire face. Sore legs and thigh muscles increased the speed further. She ran uphill. A hill seemingly steeper the longer the run lasted. She knew, sensed that he heard her, caught glimpses of her butt now and then, making him double his efforts. He would catch up with her soon.

*They warmed themselves in the heat of the burning castle. The ashes reached for them, but didn't catch them. Six fireeyes flashed in the crossroads between the fire and the night. She had a pretty good idea of how she looked like. Blackened face, torn clothes, busty hair. Blood everywhere. She didn't care. Neither did he.*

*– I look terrible.*

*Her own voice, thick with desire.*

*– You look great.*

*His the same.*

*– I need a bath, she declared.*

*Breathing desire kept dominating her voice and body language, but the echo of the despair and desperation so prevalent such a short time ago remained. He sensed it, and it made everything just so much more potent.*

*Then, with a teasing and irresistible snarl of a smile she pulled backwards, towards the forest.*

*– Will you give me a five minutes head start?*

*She just gave herself time to catch his nod, before setting off with her heart quivering in her chest.*

The last few remaining rags of her clothes vanished on the last stretch of the forest. It was as if his hands removed them, touched her hot skin, and she gasped. She cried out enraged, as she tore it all off with a mind boiling by raging Power.

– You gave me only one, you rascal… I rather thought you would.

The dark laughter from behind enveloped her in its cocoon of fire and shadow, and she returned it, an echo just as loud, if not louder than its origin, and in the end, of course, it was hard to know what had come first.

It rolled through the forest stronger than a storm, shaking the trees. She ran to the pointed cliff, and stopped there, taking in the fantastic view, looking at the black water below, far below, the surface mirroring the distant stars, the shore, the forest and the mountains.

She half turned, stretching her arms above her head, welcoming him as he appeared from the forest, giving him the best possible smile of burning passion.

– I'm much… bigger than the last time you saw me, am I not?

He nodded. She winked, a teasing wink, before she jumped from the cliff and dived towards the black surface. He reached the point in time to see the final part of her dive and the gracious landing. A white splash rose high up towards him, enticing him, like everything did at this moment. He saw everything from the opposite side of the lake, saw her form as she hit the water, her beyond tempting curves and enticing call of the wild. His surroundings seemed to fade. He focused his entire attention on the female down there, and dived after her.

A pull, a slight pain he quickly forgot. The water pushed at him from all sides as the force of the dive pushed him into the black lake's depth. He slowed down, and began orienting himself, to search for her in the pitch-black environment. He spotted first her arms as she swam deeper into the darkness. Her brown skin seemed white and cold, even as its glow kept luring and enticing him. He followed her, followed as he began to feel the pressure in his ears.

*They stepped ashore dripping wet, right in the middle of the wild forest. Water steamed from their bodies. The cold of the depths had increased their heat, not in any way weakened it. She wriggled between the tight trees right there, a few steps ahead, in a leisurely pace. When she let a natural hole in the ground capture her body the smile she sent over her shoulder, the entire stretched-out body, every thought, every minor act left little doubt about her desires, her demands.*

*She turned fully around and studied him frankly and undiluted, and with awe as he charged her.*

*– You brought the wind, My Lord, she said huskily. – And you're the incarnation of the Storm.*

*He hardly managed to speak, to respond vocally.*

*– No, that's not right. We are! Together!*

*The two storms collided and the trees shook.*

They embraced down there in the deep. The water boiled around them. They kissed hungrily, beyond passion. Lips pushed against lips. They shared air, while they slowly, inevitably began rising in the water. She embraced him with her arms and legs and Hunger. And then pushed his prodding limb into her. Both were compelled to bend their heads back. It was yet another involuntary act, totally immersed in the moment.

Neither mouth nor nostrils were filled with water. In a way they were like newborn again, instinctively aware of how to keep the water out.

They broke the surface in silence, in a whirl of frothing water. The hot stream flowed from him and into her, from her, into the small pond in which they dipped their bodies. Two pair of fireeyes flashed and glowed. The third pair joined as their hands did. And then sound returned. They both gasped as they greedily sucked air into their mouth, smiling and laughing in ecstasy.

The water, the forest, it was all the same.

He lifted her up and pushed her against the tree. She writhed impatiently and enticingly in his arms. He lost his footing, and they fell to the ground, to the wet, dry forest bed, and it felt soft and pleasant beyond words. She laughed thrillingly and almost managed to free herself from his grip. He caught the female's foot, as she was about to jump, and pulled her beneath him. A simple burst of power and he had turned the twisting body around on its belly. Her violent, but obviously half-hearted protests were weakened every second, as their moves became increasingly synchronized. When he pushed into her from behind they stopped completely. He *bit* into her neck, and she screamed in delight. She felt exactly the same as he did. Not the ridiculous pain.

The dizzying taste of blood.

She wailed and complained, impatiently, moaning in need. He pushed deep within her, harder every time. They both growled. Her arms reached like snakes or branches across the forest bed. He grabbed them and held on, hard. A wind rotated around them, surrounded them. Dry twigs began breaking. Rocks flew through the air and collided. Leaves and dirt rained down from above, but not where they moved and gasped and mated. He pulled her up on her knees, but kept biting into her neck. Her body began swaying. She rotated her hips and tightened them around his rock-hard thing. Both knelt. Their hands touched over her breasts. He was no longer able to bite into her skin. His louder growl rose undiluted between the trees, spread on the pond that was the forest. She turned her head and reached back with her lips towards his, needed to make several attempts before succeeding, but finally she managed to push her lips against his.

And taste the blood.

Her pleasure-cry chased birds and animals away. Their blood and life mixed. Her arms fell down. She didn't have the strength needed to keep them up anymore. He squeezed her shoulders hard. She moaned and growled in wild abandon. Both had long since passed the state of reason, the very state of cognitive thought. His and her roar of Hunger mixed, no longer possible to separate from each other.

They rested somewhat, stretched out on a bed of moss and grass. The fire and the night burned with a lower flame. They rested body against body, enjoying the close contact, the peace and silence, only slowly growing aware of their surroundings.

– Love you, she mumbled. – Lovely, lovely fierce Ted.

He wanted to speak, to reply, but she held on to his lips and whispered soft kisses in his ears. They both mumbled and their whisper rose towards the crowns at the forest's heights.

They sat up, quite stunned, but not stunned to the point they probably would have been at an earlier point in their lives.

Both looked at the pattern of broken twigs and rocks surrounding them in a united, exalted surprise.

– We did this, she stated. – Without even thinking about it. We are that powerful.

Her eyes flared. She climbed on top of him with sensual, catlike movements.

– Mmmm, she purred. Her large breasts rubbing against his chest. Her hips moving against his. He reacted instantly on her efforts. – I can remember us doing it twice in the water. How many times after we reached shore?

– I can't recall.

His hands slid across the female's round muscular thighs, her smooth skin.
– Neither do I. It isn't important, anyway. We don't care about such details, right?
She kissed him, and her tongue played with his.
– It's different, now, she giggled. – I'm still horny, but it's not all encompassing anymore. We can let the beast rest and enjoy… the flavor a bit more.
Her hips began rising and falling. A pleased smile spread from half open eyes and lit the lazy expression.
– It feels so good to have your cock inside me, she breathed. – I want it there all the time.
– This stud loves to feel the mare's tight cunt squeeze tight around him.
He was very deliberately being ironic. It didn't ruin the mood.
It couldn't be ruined. Out here there was no pretense, no hiding.
They rolled around and he was on top again.
– It's so strange. She moaned slowly, content. – We're not birds…
– But we made a nest anyway, he stated.
Her eyes turned misty. She heard a female bird call out to her mate. A final distraction. He buried his head between her breasts. The long raven hair covered all of her upper body. She breathed through it. Fangs sought his shoulder and she bit the soft skin. It cracked like a ripe fruit. She slurped the blood. He stayed on top. She felt the hardness of the wet heat once again, and cried out in joy. He cried back.
He remained inside her for a long, long time. It felt so good, good, good. When they finally rose it wasn't in regret, but in expectation. There would always be another time.
– I will never join with another man without thinking about you, she said proudly. – You will never fuck another woman without thinking about me. It was rough, primitive, filled with abandon. May it ever be thus.
She gave him another sultry kiss, and that, too, felt like forever.
– It's purely physical, she wondered. – And still it isn't. A piecemeal gathering of the whole, without contradictions, of course. The technological/religious society makes artificial divisions between the physical and the spiritual. But we know better. There are no contradictions.
– You're just a slip of a girl…
She looked at him, waiting patiently.
– But you have always been the smartest and with a clarity of mind and purpose far beyond mine.
– You say the nicest things, she purred.
– I feel like an idiot, he said sourly. – Considering I postponed this heavenly and hellish multiple fuck for five years.
She rewarded him with a thrilling laughter.
They felt joy. The sting of sadness remained. And it all felt right.
Awareness of their surrounding returned with a vengeance. It flowed into them like air into their lungs. They climbed out of their nest. He, too, felt the first

sting of pride when he saw all the dried semen on her thighs. It looked like many men had fucked her. She followed the line of his stare and her smile widened.

– You should be empty, she said, – but you're not. You never will be.

At dawn they stepped yawning out of the forest. They held hands and stopped to enjoy each other's closeness and touch. He did feel empty, and her fire also burned low. They passed the smoking ruin that had been the Cornwall Mansion at a distance. None of the firemen striving to put out the still monstrous fire noticed them. Neither did the journalists and curious flocking to the place.

Practically the entire valley was present and staring this morning.

The nagging worry returned briefly to Ted. He had seen what the two of them could accomplish on their own, and he wondered what they would be able to do together.

People stared at the fire and invisible fire with fascination mixed with fear, with terror, stared at an event rocking their world to the core. Eugene was there, the Barker's and Scott Thompson. Eugene shook his head, in terror and denial.

Ted and Elizabeth walked up the shingle road to the Kendall main building, not really caring if they were seen or not. They were only pinpricks seen from the Cornwall place anyway.

– We are a sight for sore eyes, aren't we? She giggled.

They were covered in blood, moss and dirt, mud-like properties. The raven hair was a single tangled mass. Linsey watched them from the window, clearly apprehensive. Elizabeth waved enthusiastically to him. He was clearly relieved.

The main door was open. They walked inside and went directly to the large bathtub.

– This is new, right?

– Yeah, she grinned, – Eugene had it installed in a bout of megalomania…

Ted turned on the water and they stepped into the frothing heat. Liz poured on with soap and the bubbles enveloped them. They began rubbing and washing each other.

– Shit! She cried out. – It burns in the eyes. And this is supposed to be natural soap.

She rubbed him behind the ears in a good-natured kind of way. The long hair, much longer than hers offered special challenges, but she dealt with it full of go-ahead spirit. She rubbed him tenderly on his back with a hand and her cheek.

– No new scars, she said speculatively. – And the distinct scars after the ugly whip are practically gone. You have a fabulous ability to heal yourself, sir.

She released her girlish giggle again. He had to remind himself that, in spite of her obvious maturity she hadn't quite passed that age.

But in her eyes were stars and fires, and also a solemnity beyond appearances.

He raised his left arm and grabbed his elbow with the other hand.

– There were many marks after needles here. I don't know exactly when they vanished. One morning when I looked they were gone.

She touched her neck.

– It's still tender, she complained.

He took a look. The skin on her neck was clearly inflamed and a different shade then the rest. But there was no sign of crust or the wound itself.

– I broke my shoulder in there. It healed in minutes. By the time I began running it was as if it had never been.

They took a look at his shoulder. While they watched even the inflamed color faded, and the piece of skin was impossible to discern from the rest.

– Eric demonstrated on me, she said, with both anger and joy in her voice. – He cut me, and the wound closed as we watched. He called me Goddess.

– It's so easy to believe, isn't it?

He washed her, somewhat cautious, until she threw him a caustic look.

It made him angry, angry with himself, and he overcompensated, made her cry out in pain.

– That's *better!* She nodded. – You know I'm not a piece of china, easily broken.

– You're absolutely correct, he concurred. – I know that! During a London night not two full moons ago, I swore to myself I would never more hold back, that I would enthusiastically explore every avenue.

She shook then, in anxiety and anticipation. His eyes had suddenly turned dark, dark as pools of the blackest night.

They washed each other, rough and affectionate, very rough, very affectionate. Their hands were soft as petals and rough as rocks.

Hands touched, so very astute, tenderly and sensitive. They soaped each other in again. The dirt clearly needed more than one turn, and just now they needed to be clean, needed it badly. Moisture stuck to their faces as they embraced, as they sat there tight, as they touched in every way they could. They just sat there and enjoyed each other's closeness. Sometimes, like now they needed it so badly that it scared them.

The water purified them, a ritual washing off the slag. They left the ashes behind.

Yet again.

## 2

She blinked, as they entered the big bedroom, with the double bed, the one no one else used anymore.

– I am… sleepy, she said. – I feel… drained.

– No wonder. With everything you've done, without… without…

– Without feeding, she nodded.

They dropped down on the bed. Heavy, dark curtains drew themselves and covered the window, hiding the day for sore eyes. The two embraced with tiny, instinctive movements, and lay there entwined. Sleep came practically instantaneous, uncompromising. They slept and rested and healed.

When they woke up it was dark. They were surprised to find that their limbs were stiff and sore. Silence reigned in the house. They dressed as fast as they were able with their stiff limbs, and walked to the living room. Linsey waited for them there. He sat on the couch with Michelle in his lap. She jumped off it and ran to them. Ted managed, only with great difficulty to bend down and sweep her up in arms that felt very stiff. The little girl stared excitedly and inquiringly at him with the large and eerie pale eyes burning with intelligence and maturity far beyond her years.

– I was about to wake you, Linsey said curtly. – A delegation including the acting sheriff is on its way. He called five minutes ago.

Liz looked out the window, down the shingle road. Trudy walked in front, characteristically a bit ahead of Eugene. There were no signs of ash or dirt on her. Eugene was dirty everywhere. He had taken part in the rescue operation.

Some considerable amount of steps behind, the delegation, with numerous official and unofficial representatives from the county walked in a very anxious and determined pace.

– Bell is the acting sheriff, Liz cried excitedly. – The chorus line has finally reached the big league. What a blast!

– That's the guy who always agrees with the latest speaker? Ted wondered.

– You can take that to the bank, Linsey snorted ironically.

– The sheep can reveal itself to be a wolf, though, Ted grinned.

She looked cheerfully at him. They understood each other so well.

She remembered how clear-cut the spunky eleven year-old girl had seen the world, her clarity of vision, and desperately wanted that back.

– I've made a call to some lawyers, Linsey said. – I thought we might need them.

– You were not wrong, his sister nodded.

– Strangely enough Carl Palmer in London called me, and offered his help.

– And he did it early today, right, before any news had broken?

– Yeah, he did. How did you…

– That makes sense, Ted grinned. – That makes perfect sense.

– He comes on the first available flight, Linsey noted, clearly upset.

– Good thinking about the lawyers, Ted said. – We need all the help we can get. It will take time before this goes away.

Liz glanced curiously at him. She didn't think it would ever «go away».

And more. She knew that Ted didn't think it would either.

The house, the entire valley was seething in a variety of emotions, both working with and against one another. There was no lynch mob approaching just now. There was too much paralyzing fear and too little hatred and rage present for that to happen. They were drawn here because this was the only remaining power center left in the valley, the remains of what had been pulverized the night before. Men and women like Bell, and the entourage on his heels could sense shifts in power the way people with arthritis could feel a change in the weather. They had learned early what had also been hammered into Ted and Liz: A power vacuum had to be filled quickly, or others would rush in to fill it.

The four of them all walked to the door. Michelle enjoyed herself on her father's arm. Bell didn't manage to ring the bell before the door opened. And before he could open his mouth to speak Elizabeth had caught his eyes.

– Good evening, she said, quite solemn compared to her usual happy front. – What can we help you guys with?

– We come here to pay our respects, Miss Kendall. He coughed. – We're very sorry about what happened.

– Thank you, she said, with just the right taint of sadness and catching in her voice.

– We don't know what caused the fire, Bell nodded, – but it was a hell of epic proportions there. It will take weeks just to identify some of the bodies.

– We know what happened, Linsey said curtly. – We were there all four of us. It has shaken my sister deeply, but she's still willing to answer questions.

Bell nodded almost imperceptible. The priest's wife and Neal Grey glanced accusingly at him.

– Of course, my dear. The priest's wife took Elizabeth's arm. – You must be devastated.

Elizabeth nodded, sniffing hard.

Then, for some reason everybody's eyes locked on to the little girl in their midst.

– And who is this? The woman said heartily.

– Oh, that's right, Ted said. – I don't believe you've met. This is Michelle. My daughter. Mine and Claudia's… Michelle, say hello to Ellen.

– 'ello, Ellen, Michelle cried, very happy, not really used to be included in the conversation.

– H-hello, Ellen Brady managed, somewhat challenged.

The others present looked astounded at the little girl, the heir to the enormous Cornwall fortune.

– We haven't seen much of her before, have we?

That was an understatement, of course. Neal attempted to keep the suspicion from manifesting in his voice. He tried hard, but it was no use.

– Claudia didn't let her out much, Ted replied curtly. – I know you've heard the rumors, but I guess the servants were ordered to keep their mouth shut. A blood test should prove the truth of the matter… if there is any doubt, that is?

No one took him up on it.

– Please, come inside, Liz offered pleasantly, playing the grieving «widow». – It has been quite a day, so we haven't much to offer you, though.

– We understand, Miss Kendall, Bell coughed some more. – You shouldn't strain yourself.

Mumbling, more or less honest declarations came from them all.

They followed her into the living room. She placed herself in front of the fireplace. For some reason they imagined there was still fire there.

– We went there, the three of us. Liz drew breath. – I was the only one being invited to the party, but Ted and Linsey insisted on following me…

– Why is that, honey, Mrs. Brady wondered, suddenly very understanding.

– People have threatened Paul's life for weeks, and several of those very people were present in the Mansion last night.

She sniffed a bit. The others waited patiently.

– I didn't agree with Paul in everything, but I loved him.

*And hated him.*

She straightened, and continued bravely.

– I asked Ted and Linsey to take Michelle out of there almost immediately. It all degenerated very quickly into a shouting argument, and worse. «Take her», I told the boys. «Keep her safe». They did. I stayed at Paul's side.

Elizabeth Kendall's voice lowered to a virtual whisper.

– I watched as old grievances and hostility culminated into what can't be described as anything but open enmity and… and w-warfare. People had brought g-guns. People just stood and shouted to each other, and then it h-happened. Suddenly the new sheriff, obviously on the other side's payroll drew his guns and s-shot Hunter in the head. Everything just turned totally chaotic after that. It was almost impossible to know who was fighting whom. The pig of a sheriff fired and fired. Everybody fought everybody. I saw the sheriff be hit, be stopped, finally. Suddenly there was smoke and the curtains burned. Everything that could burn… burned. Someone had blocked the doors. I saw Kent Farley strive to open them, in vain. He was hit. I didn't see him fall. People fought with knives. One of the servants beat up on Claudia, before throwing her m-mangled body through the window. I remember that Paul threw me out through that opening, saving me. He never made it outside.

She hid her face in her shaking hands, and did her best to produce the tears, but failed. She wondered about this. Here she was mixing truth and lies excellently, and made a lifetime performance, but there were no tears.

Eugene entered the room. Trudy practically pushed him forward. He had taken a shower and looked somewhat clean and fresh.

– Ted pulled me away. She sniffed. – He carried me back here. I fell asleep, and didn't wake up until a few minutes before you came. We saw the fire-trucks on our way home, but we just had to get away from it all. The stench of fire and ashes stuck in my nose, and won't l-let g-go, and I can't *escape* it.

Trudy walked to her. The seventeen-year-old girl broke down in her mother's arms, not quite seventeen yet.

– You're a tough little cookie. Trudy comforted her. – But everybody has a limit, and you've reached yours.

– It's so sad, Liz sniffed.

– Speak for yourself, Trudy responded curtly. – I'm not sorry that the assholes are dead. Now, there will still be a valley, one we can all actually live in.

No one commented her statement.

That was it. All the remaining spunk had left the delegation. The few among them that had anything to say… didn't.

Trudy supported the girl out of the room. In the doorway she turned half around.

– My daughter will be at your disposal anytime you might wish her to, sheriff, she said. – If you want a legal statement…

– Thank you, Bell coughed, cursing his coughing.

– After a few days rest we'll bring her to your office. As I said whenever will suit you.
– I'll be in touch, Bell said, with his hat in his hands.
The delegation left the Kendall ranch. The house that was never quiet turned quiet.
Trudy returned to the living room. She closed the door behind her.
– Poor girl, she said, pondering a bit. – She was truly exhausted, falling asleep again the moment her head hit the pillow.
Trudy looked at Ted, clearly curious.
– How do you feel, Edward? She asked in a motherly, smothering tone.
– I feel fantastic! He stated.
– Then you haven't single-handedly pulverized an empire either, she nodded.
– That is correct, he stated.

## 3

Michelle was registered in the county's archives as Claudia's daughter. No father was listed. Claudia's supposed marriage with Claus Schiffner wasn't listed anywhere. Ted and Michelle gave blood as Liz went to the sheriff's office playing grieving widow, accompanied by a lawyer. Both acts were mere formalities. Ted received the confirmation from the laboratory and Liz wasn't really bothered by the officers of the law.
– There's absolutely no doubt, Mr. Warren, the doctor said. – In fact, during my years of practice I've never seen a better likeness, physical or genetic. It's… remarkable.
The judicial meeting didn't last long. The judge turned a few pages in the documents on his desk, taking a single look at the adult man and the girl sitting there side by side before ending the case.
It also helped that Linsey was in the courtroom, doing his best, his very best to help them charm the man behind the desk.
There had been no one, public officials or distant Cornwalls that had contested Ted's claim.
– Congratulations, Liz said to him afterwards, in front of the journalists, kissing him on the cheek, sickeningly proper.
She wore a dress decorated with flower motives and a broad hat, and she turned a parasol between her fingers. She didn't resemble herself and resembled herself perfectly.
Trudy and Linsey embraced him. Michelle stood in their midst and looked cheerfully up at them. They looked like quite the happy family.
Eugene stood further down on the steps leading to the court building. They ignored him.
– Five members of the Janus Clan together, Ted said and stared hard at Trudy.
– Yes, isn't it *wonderful?*
She responded to him with an innocence far superior to what her daughter could muster.

Carl Palmer came to them, and came to their aid pushing through the gathered crowd of journalists and curious people. He had had some experience in that.

– This might have threatened to become a storm initially, he said, – but it turned out to be hardly more than a light breeze. If this keeps up I can return to London in no time.

– Why don't you stay for a while, anyway? Trudy squeezed his hand coquettishly. – Relaxing a bit, enjoying life?

– Well, perhaps I will, he nodded, a bit flustered. – The office will run itself for a while. There are more than enough people there to cover anything that might happen. And I have told them and myself for years that I will have a vacation soon… It's worth pondering.

And his reward was a blinding smile from the woman holding his hand.

The ranch sounded unnaturally silent, now, after all the noise in and outside the courtroom. Liz removed her hat and threw it on the couch. She and Ted were alone together in the living room.

– Trudy is coming into her own, she said pointedly. – The chrysalis is cracking wide open.

– Just like ours are. In a flash he covered the distance between them.

– Do you like my dress? She inquired teasingly, winking.

– I love it, he replied. – I would have loved it even if you had worn rags.

– I'll *bet!*

Her laughter was rich and full.

They could have had sex, now, they knew that, uncomplicated and fulfilling. They had done it any time during the day and night recently.

But other desires drove them right now, something they had postponed, for some reason.

There was dinner. They ate with a scorching appetite, no longer hiding their Hunger, but ignoring Eugene's disapproving look, ignoring him.

They played with Michelle a bit in the yard, between the house and the barn, strangely apprehensive. She was bright and quick on her legs, just as they had expected.

– Do you think she…? They led a low-keyed conversation. Liz stood there tiptoeing. – You know…

– I don't know. He shook his head. – How are we supposed to know?

– Trudy dug a lot just before and during my first period. She obviously waited for it for days, and then, when it happened she went nuts and practically assaulted me with questions and curiosity. She knew or at least suspected strongly that something would happen.

– Adolescence brings many changes to a person. Ted nodded. – It's not strange to think that its beginning would be even more dramatic… for us. Was she convinced?

– Not really, at least not until I disrupted a sweet moment between her and Eugene later that night, and told them about a bunch of weirdoes levitating outside the window of my room. After that her behavior clearly changed towards me. She turned possessive and capricious.

Ted nodded. She had always behaved strangely towards him.
Trudy appeared in the entrance door. She studied them, like she always did, but now something new had entered her eyes.
– Come to me, Michelle, she cried. – Daddy and Aunt Liz are a bit busy right now.
Michelle looked at them. They looked at each other, nodded, and sent Michelle to the woman in the doorway.
Curiosity burned within them, as they made their way to the basement. They walked the outer route, through the basement door. The smell of mold grew stronger the closer they got to the dark tunnel and room. There had been nothing of that when Elizabeth had paid her first visit years earlier.
They brought no lights. There was no need for that. They saw better in the dark than ever before.
They experienced it like entering a cabin, one deep in the woods.
– There's a sense of ancient times, he said slowly, – of antiquity and mystery… and danger.
– Danger, she whispered.
Two pairs of fireeyes met above the dusty cardboard boxes. Burning stares focused on the box that no dust would fall on. All had been unpacked except this one.
– I couldn't open it, she freely admitted. – I told myself that I would wait for you, but I couldn't and tried my best, and failed. You have no idea how irritating that is.
And she failed in her attempt to keep her voice light. She challenged him without saying a word.
– You try…
He returned the stare. She didn't give an inch. He placed his hands on the box, traced his fingers along the obvious cracks. It felt like cardboard. It was cardboard. He pulled, first with his hands, his physical strength. Nothing moved. He was unable to open the box and even to lift it from the ground. It was all completely ridiculous. He grew angry, a flash of emotions quickly growing strong. He felt the power grow, like it always did when his black rage manifested itself. With all the power of his mind he attacked the outrageously solid box. His eyes flared and boiled. The surroundings turned indistinct. The room shook. The ceiling bulged. She stared startled at him, at her soul mate. The ground under the box began quaking. It dawned on her that he was striving, truly striving. Sweaty pearls of frustration and savagery jumped from his skin. Weak-kneed she sensed her only moderately weakened desire and Hunger awaken. When he attacked the box with all the strength he possessed, with his claws of night and fire.
She blinked, and in that blink was the image of horror from a thousand nightmares. She gasped, and he did, too.
He stopped, let go of the box and straightened. She saw something very similar to fear in his eyes.

– Did you see it? She whispered, ashamed of the all too present fear in her voice.

– Yes, he replied, his eyes and brief wording revealing exactly the same fear overwhelming her. – A face in the air, the face from my most troubled dreams… of… of the dragon.

– The dragon, she whispered.

He grabbed her hands. She grabbed his.

– Let us try again.

– Let us. She nodded in a frenzy. And then, a bit of doubt. – Aren't you tired?

– Not the slightest.

He kissed her passionately. She knew he was telling the truth. He didn't need to convince her.

Like one person they grabbed the box… and tore it apart. It was a piece of cake, as if it had been only an ordinary cardboard box.

Joy flashed like lightning through them. It burned and tickled.

– Whoever has placed this stuff here meant for us to open the final box…

– … together, she completed.

They looked into the box with hungry eyes.

## 4

The words cut into them, like a cold draft from a grave.

The words and writing seemed extraordinary strange, with an added depth, like layer upon layer, read by their see-in-the-dark eyes.

«To Ted and Liz. Half of what you find here is written by me. Half is written by others. And… it's also safe to say that I may not even have written everything written by me. The future may not be the future, but just as much the past. Experience the riddle within the enigma. Read the Tapestry. See it shift and twist before your sensitive eyes».

That was one single sheet of cryptic text at the top of the heap. The rest was one single stable of books and notes and paper, and strange types of paper.

– It's the Warren family history. Liz nodded startled, after having opened the book at the top of the heap. – But it is *so* much.

On the first page was a drawing of a man with fireeyes. Under the drawing was a name, words and a number:

**Adam Warren**
Born: Unknown.

Dead? 1780

Just one number, not two.

– The first Warren was named Adam, she giggled. – How ironic.

– He had amnesia, Ted noted, – and didn't remember anything about his former life. He chose both his first and last name. He was truly the first Warren, at least in name.

He had appeared on the battlefield in the war between England and France, in what would become the English colonies and later the United States of America, with a rather serious head injury. He had married, fathered a son, and after twenty-five years he had vanished without a trace.

There was writing on the front of the second book.

DIARY OF A TRAVELING MAN - NICHOLAS WARREN 1912 - 1952

They began reading that, without really putting down the first. His writing seemed so personal to them, as if they actually heard his voice.

«I start my new life today, and fervently hope it will lessen the pain of my old».

– He traveled with Titanic, Liz said wide eyed. She swallowed hard. – He and his wife and son. And his wife… died.

They breathlessly read on, at the unfolding drama, forgetting any time and place, except what the story unveiled. Days and nights might pass outside, without them noticing. They had waited so long for this, for an explanation, a deeper connection concerning their lives.

– It's so… much, Ted said. – So overwhelming. An entire tapestry of reality on its own merit.

– He both likes and dislikes… what he is, she noted.

Others were born. Others like him. But he remained unique, even compared to them.

They browsed a bit, couldn't really take it all in at a glance.

– Nancy's «master» in New Orleans had green eyes, Ted said in a subdued, shaking voice.

– Look at this, Liz exclaimed, – at their birth and death. Very few of them were old when they died. And they didn't just die, die young, but were killed, either in random, seemingly meaningless «accidents», or they were murdered.

The implications dawned on them, inevitably.

– There are people out there that just don't *like* us, Liz emphasized. – And it goes on and on, through the generations.

– Nick will be eighty-six now, if he is still alive.

– Yes, and Trudy told me he looked *young* when he brought all this here, when he was sixty-five.

– Perhaps we can grow very old, Ted said.

– Perhaps we are like the people of legend walking the Earth in ancient times? She sighed cheerfully and frosty simultaneously. – Like the gods and vampires and immortals… creatures without beginning, without end…

Later she would carefully consider those words, and wonder if she had truly realized what they entailed.

– John died young-looking, after surviving countless accidents, shootouts and enemies.

They practically dived into the material, more than a little obsessive. They memorized it all, perhaps fearing they would never more cast their eyes on all this again.

When the headache finally arrived, with a vengeance, they were surprised it hadn't come earlier.

They sat back, supporting their back against the walls, the soft walls, the walls turning soft, turning into mist and shadow… and as they progressed, turning into fangs and claws of the Earth.

– There's more there, she nodded.

– We haven't fed for a while. Are you hungry?

– Not the slightest, she decided.

So they hit the books again, hit the books of books.

Liz held the family book open.

– The last entry is the birth of Patrick in 1948…

He looked up. There was a question mark at the end there, something in her voice, a kind of *doubt*.

And he couldn't understand why.

And neither, apparently could she.

– It isn't really the final entry, she said.

– No, of course it isn't, he said non-committal.

– I remember Linsey writing down the films he had seen, she continued. – Sometimes he watched them twice, and the second time could sometimes be months after the first, so that particular entry would be made after a film he had seen the previous week, for instance, but still appear before it.

Where are you going with this? He asked her with a naughty look.

And it wasn't truly a silent question.

She reopened the book on its last page.

**Patrick Warren**
Born: 1948
Dead:

Just a baby picture.

She turned one page back, and there it was, really.

**Iris Warren**
Born: 1946
Dead: 1974

– I know her, Ted cried. – I saw her be killed in the storm ravaging Perth.

– But…? Liz grinned frostily.

– But how could he know that? *Did* he know or did he return here unnoticed and…

The page on the left…

They took their time. Ted moved over to her, and they both looked.

And then, it stared them in the face, impossible to ignore, what had played for an eternity in their subconscious.

**Mark Stewart**
Born: 1937
Dead: 1979

Liz quickly turned the page further back.

**Ethel Edith Warren**
Born: 1935
Dead:

The photo was of her as a girl with fireeyes, but the drawing… the drawing was of her as an adult, of a woman bathed in shadow and a face that looked as familiar to the two of them as would a mirror, framed by blonde hair with a major red hue dancing in the shadows.

– Nick drew this, Liz said. – I wonder if he showed it to her, if he showed it to anyone… until now.

The opposite side was also strange in its own way.

**Trudy Warren**
Born: 1933
Dead:

The photo was of Trudy as they knew her, a fairly ordinary face, a young girl with a sweet and not that pretty a face.

The drawing was of a creature quite different, with large, deep dark eyes and a more than different face. It was Trudy, but a completely different Trudy.

On the left side was Joel. He had been born in 1931 and had died in 1952. Or… so it seemed.

Liz, impatiently, turned another page.

**Jack Warren**
Born: 1928
Dead: 1984

Liz threw the book away and grabbed the next at the top. More and younger family history. They didn't have to look far to have their hopes and horrors confirmed. The first few pages had it all, and it just kept coming.

**Michael Warren**
Born: 1952
Dead: 1992

And on the next page.

**Edward Warren**
Born: May 1st 1955
Dead: December 22nd 2008

Linsey was on the right. Both on his drawing and picture he had fireeyes, and a white streak in his hair, clearly older.

There was no death date on him.

Liz was on the next page.

**Elizabeth Warren**
Born: May 1st 1959
Dead: December 22nd 2008

– Now, that is truly amazing… isn't it…

Liz whispered.

And ran out of there the fastest she could.

He had just reached the stable when she rode a horse out of there, rode it hard, as if Death itself chased her.

It was far into the mountains, when he finally caught up with her. She had stopped by a pond. The horse drank greedily. She sat there, staring down at the water's surface.

– It's good news, isn't it? She snarled, as she turned towards him. – Getting to know you're gonna live to be forty-nine is *good* fucking news.

Tears flooded her face, impossible to ignore.

He approached her carefully, but he needn't have worried.

She was quite calm, deadly calm.

He took her hands. He squeezed them, squeezed them hard. She bit her lower lip.

– We're going to do it, he said. – We're going to face the world, on our terms. No one or nothing shall be our master, not even Death itself.

And she squeezed, too, and she saw the pain, the joy, in his eyes, his glowing eyes.

– Amen, she said.

They returned to the house, to the dark and dank room, and it was as if they had never left. She had a dark streak of dirt on her cheek, from when she had dried her tears, dipped her hand in mud and dried her tears. He rubbed it off.

– The dates, she said. – Our birth dates. They are different from what we have been told, what we've been led to believe our entire lives.

– If they are correct, we've been lied to - again. Ted's lips tightened. – We've have been told we were born on the eight. Even our birthdays have been «celebrated» then.

– Yeah, his mate said weakly.

– But why? He said, suddenly enraged. – Why… the bother?

– A part of a general diversion, I gather, she said lightly. – There has been more than enough of that, hasn't it?

One more detail, fairly unimportant, but still helping to confirm the big picture.

She leaned at the wall in a wild movement, and when she grabbed his hand stars lit her eyes. She seemed so innocent then, so brittle, reminding him of Linda at their… what they had been told was their twelfth birthday… before… before…

– Thirty-two years are a long way off, he said, just as lightly. – I'm afraid we have a lot of other dangers to worry about until then.

– You're worried on my behalf, she grinned coquettishly. – That's so sweet of you. I don't know if I want to kiss you or rip you to shreds…

## 5

They carried the stuff to his room, which was closest. There was a lot of it, also all the recipes and stuff he had never seen.

– Ethel's diary, Liz commented. – A lot of stuff I'll bet she hasn't even actually written yet. The notes of one David Warren, born in the year 2061… Where did he get all of this? *How* did he get it?

– It might be forgeries, partly of fully, Ted pointed out. – We can't rule that out. Made by him or others. We can't rule anything out.

They went back and forth in time, in books and diaries, unable to focus on anything.

– He says he met Jonas Bergli in New York in 1931. If that's true, they've known each other for forty-five years, and Bergli was in Denver at least the last ten years of your time there.

She threw the diary away, in a fit of rage and despair.

– This is bullshit, all of it. It doesn't tell us anything of value, anything we truly need to know.

She picked up the Born and Dead book, the Book of the Dead, again, shifting through it. They had been loath to reread it, but she reluctantly did, forced herself to overcome the sense of dread rising in her.

– Damn it! She cried. – Look at this.

She handed the book to him. He didn't notice it at first, but he couldn't really avoid seeing it eventually.

The writing of the «future deaths and births» was gone, erased, as if it had never been there in the first place. The pictures and drawings were still there, but no letters, no names, and no dates. They looked through it all twice, before convincing themselves of what the eyes saw.

– Is he toying with us, is that it? Fuck!

She swore bitterly.

– Perhaps he's showing us what he *can* show us, Ted insisted. – What was or is available to him, nothing more, nothing less.

There was a bit of silence between them.

– Perhaps, he said.

– Perhaps this is nothing but the albeit weird family album it pretends to be. He's telling us stories about kin and loss and longing. That might count for something… right?

She sighed. There was just no way of knowing.

– He has an agenda, Ted finally said. – He has, as well.

– Who hasn't? She said exasperated.

They left the room, weary and not exactly in high spirits, and they wondered if that was also Nick's aim. She turned off the lights as an afterthought with her mind after the door had closed behind them. They walked upstairs and had dinner, a late dinner they made themselves. There was no one else present. They ate in silence. The food tasted bland, almost to the point that it didn't taste like food at all. They looked in on Michelle. She was sound asleep. Liz closed the door quietly, with a little smile on her lips.

– I can't hear her breathe, she whispered.

There might have been reason for worry, if they hadn't sensed her heartbeat and the blood flowing through her veins. She was alive, and fully so, vibrant and young.

Liz closed the door, and they walked away.

– Too bad she will be totally fucked up in about a ten years' time… if she's lucky.

They returned to the room, to their room, not bothering to switch on the lights. Well fed they walked right to the bed, barely avoiding all the books thrown on the floor.

– Man, she groaned, somewhat content, – I'm so tired that I could sleep for days.

One of the books lay open. Her eyes fell on her own demonic face.

– The text, she said slowly. – It's back.

He picked up the book before she had finished speaking.

– I don't think it ever «left», he said. – It just hid… in normal light. It's meant for us, not the casual historian.

She turned on the lamp. The letters and numbers vanished. She turned off the light again. The letters and numbers appeared anew.

– Well, that's always something, I guess…

They sought closer to the other as they went to bed, full clothed, as they felt sleep come, as exhaustion finally overwhelmed them.

And their dreams of night and fire were more jumbled than ever. They woke up in the morning, blinking once, blinking twice.

– It feels so good having you close to me. She kissed him on the cheek, on the lips. – I love waking up by your side. Yesterday already feels distant. This is a new day. What about a ride before breakfast?

– I think we might want to have breakfast first for once, he replied.

– Okay for me, she shrugged, as she jumped out of bed. – But I feel fine!

But she wasn't, really. She sensed it in her limbs, a kind of lethargy almost unknown to her, at least lately. They had overextended themselves the last few days. They had limits.

Trudy and Carl sat by the breakfast table, more snuggling than eating. Clothes and hair were still in disorder. Linsey and Michelle ignored them, and seemed to be caught in their own, private universe, not eating that much either, playing with the forks and knives and spoons.

Liz and Ted sat down and began devouring the food.

– Tonight is our birthday, she said cheerfully. – Tonight we were born.

– Then we have thrice the reason to celebrate tonight, Carl said.

Today was April 30th according to the Common Era calendar, western christian timeframe. Tonight was Beltane, Witchnight.

– So he told you, Trudy nodded. – I'm not surprised.

– Why don't we all have a ride after breakfast? Carl cried enthusiastically, not really noticing the caustic look the others sent each other. – I absolutely love the terrain around here, and want to experience as much as possible before I leave.

– Ride, Michelle cried, not quite right, brightening the room with her smile.

The meal ended, slowly, almost reluctantly, on the edge of their lips and their vision, and they made their way out of the kitchen, out of the house, towards the barn.

– It's all in the eyes, Liz said. – Do you guys know that? It's all in the eyes, you know.

And in her voice was the same wonder, tinged with sadness.

They entered the barn through the large opening in front, and stopped, stopped cold.

Eugene Kendall hung from the ceiling bar with a noose around his neck, his rigid body spinning fast back and forth, and he had evidently done that for quite a while. His face had turned bluish and swollen. To those watching, it seemed like he would never stop spinning.

Michelle looked up, not really understanding anything of what was happening, and the others didn't really either.

Trudy looked enraged up at him, her face turning white as milk.

– Is this it? She spat, clenching her teeth. – Is this your way of punishing me? Well, I'm happy to tell you that it doesn't *work.*

Everybody looked at each other, exchanging flickering glances.

They weren't exactly sure what they felt, but what burned most of all in their guts was *relief.*

## 6

It turned dark. The day passed quiet as a dream. Paramedics came and fetched Eugene's body, and then he was gone. But his spirit lingered. They all sensed it, his disapproving frown of contempt.

Liz stood by the window, pushing her forehead at the cold glass.

– What are you doing? Trudy wondered.

– I stare into the darkness in hope of seeing the fire.

– Stare long and hard enough, and you will see it.

The mother, both tenderly and harshly advised her distraught daughter.

Liz tried, kept staring hard enough to make her eyes hurt, but the image of the stiff, swinging body kept distracting her, kept the ball expanding in her throat, and she felt like she was suffocating. A tight-woven fist struck the window in silence, kept striking it repeatedly without making a sound.

– I feel such anger, mommy, such contempt, and I don't want to, not in this case. He isn't *worth* it!

– He said farewell to the world, to life, long ago, mommy said softly. – You must never do that.

Trudy walked closer to her, but didn't walk to her.

– You are still young. Most tend to forget that with your otherwise mature ways. But you've tasted Power, now, and you will never be the same.

The walls and windows of the house faded around them, giving way to the wide-open air of the Hill. They were all there, all the Warrens present in these parts of the world. And Carl, too. Trudy handed a torch to Ted. He threw it on the heap of wood and dry paper and grass. The larger flame rose almost instantly at the night sky. The world turned red and yellow and shadow. Heat singed their exposed body hairs and they sighed in joy.

– Death has touched us, Trudy said. – It always will.

She stood there, finally revealed how she truly looked like, how she truly was. To Carl's credit he didn't react with too much astonishment when she changed. She didn't look at him, practically ignored him. Her entire focus was on the others, on her kin.

– You're one of the «mermaids» of the family, Liz grinned. – Nick wrote about them.

– You look great. Ted shrugged.

– Gleat! Michelle cried.

There was laughter, loud and brittle and strong.

The fire danced in their midst. It reached up, illuminating the dark sky, turning into mist and shadow.

– You're being born, Trudy the mermaid said. – Taking the first, painful steps in the big bad world.

Ted studied her, studied the half naked body with just a little bit of arousal.

She had scales on her shoulders, elbows, hips and knees, clearly a kind of genetic protection measure. Even a bullet might bounce off the hard skin. Her ability to change form was another obvious defense ability. She looked magnificent.

– Once, when you're ready, Trudy Warren said. – You'll seek out the Valley of Kings, and you'll find all the answers to all the questions you've ever asked.

– One more cryptic remark like that, and I will kill you, Liz emphasized.

There was more hearty laughter, though that of Trudy and Liz was clearly more than a bit strained…

– Sing, Trudy told Michelle.

– 'ing? Michelle wondered.

– Sing with me. Hum my words, little one. Know what you already know.

And she began, and Michelle joined her, catching up fast, very natural and right.

Fly
The bird can fly
Fly in fire, fly in shadow
It doesn't need to fear anything
Except perhaps death
The walking death
I see a valley
A circle of fire and shadow
And I dance in its shade
On the edge of its abyss

And the others' spine came alive with cold, with icy and hot splinters of the mind's eye. And when Trudy repeated the verse they all sang with her,

And the choir rose in the night. It descended into the Abyss, fell into the ravine of their souls, and they felt rage, remorse, joy and sadness, and everything rinsed them, until that, too faded away, and nothing but the Night and Fire remained.

# Chapter Two: The city in the desert

Fourth part (excerpt and summary) of:
«Observations on evolution and development of Life in The Universe».
The further observations of Gabrielle Asteroth, born 1984-02-29

– It's fucking Grand Canyon, Liz whispered.

They both felt the chill then, as if it was something tangible, as they stared down, into the rust-colored abyss.

Both saw them.

The indistinct mirages of the children of Earth, of the wolf dancing in the woods

They saw it, images of the ancient city in the forest.

They heard it, in the roar of the engine they rode, in the wind whistling in their ears. The two of them sat by the open window and listened to the dust rising from the land, to the words and voice of the unknown, unborn woman playing out in their mind. They heard the voice of the Storyteller.

The neck hairs of the young man and woman stand up as they read about themselves in the Storyteller's annals, as they turn the pages of the Book of Shadows, the written words of night and fire, with contributions from witches past, present and future, of fluid words beyond time.

A young woman, dark haired and tall walked through the strange forest. It seemed *made* in a way, a forest not a forest. She trembled while glancing around, as she heard the growls of the wolves, while turning her head, clearly apprehensive.

The ancient, mythic land is revealing itself before my eyes. I write it down as I see it, as I experience it, I, the Storyteller, the Weaver of Worlds. I give names to what is hidden, what is unknown.

The young girl sensed the rustle of the treetops, the screeching of the ravens in the air and on the branches. The large, black birds were strange, so different from any other bird she had ever seen. She imagined she walked through the forest for ages. It was so big, so very big. Night seemed to come and go, as she stayed on her path, the path she had so recently found.

There were the small straight and roaring rivers, flowing outwards from the center, on the forest bed. It showed her the way, pointing to her destination, and she recognized it all. It was as familiar as the back of her hand.

She reached a clearing in the growth. The moment she stepped out from the forest the desert heat embraced her, invaded her, dried her mouth. There were quite a few strange huts at the clearing's center, at the beige and pale reddish land. And… at the center's center was a large, tall hut, one not of wood, but of stone, woven, not built, but made, growing from the very ground below. Not made by nature, but by Man. The tingling feeling rose within the girl, overwhelming her as it had never done before.

A group of people, suddenly appearing from nowhere, men and women cloaked in Shadow waited for her in front of the strange large hut. She stopped, unable to stop shivering. She kept walking, on rubbery legs.

An older woman, with long grayish hair stepped forward to greet her, reaching out a hand for her to reach for. The girl took the final, decisive step forward, and let the woman take her hand.

– Welcome, Maya of the Scorpion Tribe. Welcome to Atlantis.

The girl curtseyed involuntarily, scolding herself, but unable to shake the sense of inferiority the encounter brought her.

– Remove your clothes, the woman snapped.

Maya obeyed instantly, dropping the fine dress her mother had made for her in the dust.

– Sit!

She sat down on her ass, crossing the legs in front of her, a position of meditation she had been taught from an early age.

They surrounded her, encircled her, bathing her in shadows, relieving the pressure created by the ravaging daystar above. They spoke to her. She knew that, even though she couldn't understand the words.

*– Sit!*

She heard the voice from far away. Suddenly, just like that, they were gone. She sat there alone, in front of the center hut.

– We will return for you, the woman said. – Do not move until we return. Do you understand, novice?

Her voice was cruel and filled with acid. Maya nodded, and swallowed hard. Swallowing was already hard, as moisture rapidly vaporized in her mouth,

She sat there, totally unprotected. The mighty daystar burned her skin, boiled her veins and stole her sanity. She glanced up occasionally, waiting for it to move on the white sky, but it didn't. Her eyes caught the dress, there in the dust, just outside her range. She closed her eyes again, attempting to concentrate, to clear her mind of thoughts, of all the horrible thoughts randomly striking her consciousness, imagining that the ground was covered by white cold, the white cold she had never experienced, but yet remembered. That was one of the things that had brought her to the attention of the Seers, and ultimately had taken her away from her tribe, and brought her here. She remembered ancient times, long before her birth.

Eyes blinked, slowly, as dizziness gripped her, as her swollen tongue made it hard to breathe, as her head felt twice as big as normal. She looked up, desperately waiting for the daystar to move, until she finally had to realize the horrible truth: that it wouldn't. It hadn't for a long time, and it wouldn't. She moaned in terror.

The heat… invaded her. It boiled her insides and turned it all to mush, and she couldn't move. She tried, but everything was frozen, useless. The black birds flapped their wings and squeaked in her ears. Her eyes didn't blink anymore. They stayed open, stayed closed, leaving only a pained impression of the hell outside her burned body. There were shadows around her then, but they brought her no relief. They encircled her. She stared straight ahead, staring blindly at the hooded figures surrounding her. Everything faded away. She fell, fell on her side, her head hitting the hard, dusty ground. Everything faded away, and only black and red remained.

She rested on soft blankets in a cool hut. Through the opening in the wall she saw that it was still day outside, but its heat no longer reached her.

The woman held her head and brought a cup to her lips. She drank it empty, and the water filled her and strengthened her.

– Rest, the woman whispered. – Replenish yourself.

And she did. Night finally came, and nightmares struck her mind. New ones, adding to those she had suffered since childhood. She writhed in terror on the soft blankets.

Even the next morning movement was difficult. The bread and soup they fed her strengthened her and reached every piece of her body. And she felt it, felt it happening.

The woman gave her her dress. It was as clean and as beautiful as the day her mother had given it to her. Maya rose from the blankets and slipped the piece of cloth over her head. She stopped in the doorway, fearful of the smoldering heat.

They stood outside, looking at her. She stepped forward and crossed the invisible threshold.

One of the men stepped forward.

– This is Jahavalo, Maya, the woman said. – He will be your teacher, your Guide in the Mysteries.

Maya looked shyly at him, hardly daring to raise her head. His cold intense eyes pierced her like daggers.

– Greetings, Maya, Jahavalo said, his voice invading her like a desert storm.

– Greetings, Jaha…

– You may call me Master, he said gently, bowing.

– Greetings, Master, she bowed.

– Walk with me.

He said.

And she did.

He walked first, and she walked in his tracks, his tracks fading in the dust and the wind.

They walked forever. She was used to walking, to crossing the vast Waste back and forth. She knew the desert, but she had never been here before, on this mighty, desolate place, and she gasped in exhaustion and fear. When he stopped, when she stumbled the last few steps towards the Master, when she looked up… She found herself in hollow ground, in a kind of… bowl, with steep walls around it. The heat from the daystar baked the ground, making it hot and arid, far beyond that of the desert around it. There was no sand on this place, no sand at all, only hard ground boiling the air, boiling the two humans foolish enough to venture here.

This was the Hollow Ground, the place she had heard the elders whisper about in fear and reverence.

Master held a flask to her lips and she drank greedily, the water healing and reinvigorating her.

– Move the dust, he commanded her.

She looked at him in incomprehension. There was dust here, like a mist floating through the air. She saw it when squinting her eyes. But… how could she…

He struck her with his stick, a stick appearing in his hand from nowhere. It hit her butt, and it hurt terribly. She yelped and shrunk under his steady, unwavering stare.

– Move the dust, he commanded her.

She waved her hands in front of her, waved them frantically.

But the dust didn't move.

He hit her again. She cried out in pain, and water, incredibly enough flowed from her eyes.

He didn't speak this time, moved his stick in the air, raised it and lowered it, just stared at her, stared right through her, as if she wasn't there.

She bit her lower lip. It wasn't intentional, but she bit it so hard that she cracked the skin, and she tasted the red iron fluid in her mouth. She didn't move, not her hands or anything else, just stared at the dust, the floating, shiny dust, and she moved it. It danced by her command. And at that precise time she also sensed something move in her head, a flow, a release. Suddenly it was as if she became the bowl, the Hollow, was the dust blowing in its quiet wind. She stared at the Master, her attention fully focused on him, a huge, triumphant grin transforming her face.

– Yes, that's it, he said hoarsely. – You feel the Power, the Power of the Dust.

He touched her jaw with the stick, rewarding her.

The night came. The night finally came. He lit a fire with his hands, lit the dust, and it burned in the very air, floating above them, sucking dust from the ground. She could hardly take her eyes away from it. It was cold here at night. She froze in her thin dress. He sat there in his black robe, seemingly totally relaxed and comfortable. But she sensed his churning insides, now, and shivered some more.

Nights and days passed like dust, as they sat there, as he taught her, as he filled her with his wisdom.

– Why are you… all of you…

She held her tongue.

– Speak, he bade her.

– Why are you… why are we isolating ourselves from the outside?

– This place is dedicated to Seekers, even to special seekers, those eager to study what is Beyond, what is outside the world. As you know, even those living out there in the Waste, those of the five tribes you once were a part of have chosen to isolate themselves from others. We all came to this place long ago, to escape persecution and death. The other tribes of the Earth can't reach us here, can't touch us with their dull knives.

– The forest is different around here, she hummed. – Everything is different. I know what a forest is. I know the land, but this is something Other from the rest. This is… Us, isn't it? It's all us.

He nodded in acknowledgement.

– You're a bright one, he said. – I knew that the moment I first laid my eyes on you.

There was something in his voice, something she didn't quite get.

– This was a barren land when we came here. We had to form it with our will, with our very souls. Some of us shaped the stone. Others made the land bloom. We transformed the land, transformed ourselves.

Jahavalo shivered a bit. She looked startled at him. She wasn't wrong… was she?

– The Storm visits us here, he said. – It comes for us wherever we go, even here. It comes as sand. It comes as water, or flesh, and we have to be prepared for it, prepared for its destructive Power.

He rose, towering above her, signing for her to rise.

She did so.

– On your knees, he snapped.

She obeyed, apprehensive and out of breath. He walked around her, and knelt behind her. She could sense him. He lifted the lower part of her dress, pushed it up her back, exposing her. She opened her mouth, about to move her lips.

– Don't speak, he said hoarsely. – Don't speak a word.

He touched her, touched her spot. She gasped instantly, realizing startled what was happening. This wasn't new to her. She had mated a few times during the previous moons, since her very first time. But this was… different.

– Be quiet, he admonished her. – Quiet as dust.

Her heat rose, inevitably. He wanted her. No doubt about that. Her breathing increased in tune with his. He moved her, like dust. She moaned aloud.

– You're a treasure, he snorted. – Such a treasure.

And then he pushed himself inside her, pushed hard, like the warrior after a hunt. He was hard and thick and deep. She moved as he moved, moved under his command. He flooded her belly, and he spread everywhere inside her. Her weak arms collapsed from under her. Her head hit the ground. He pulled out of her with a content snort. She heard the rustling of his clothes as he rose. Her head hurt after hitting the hard ground. She remained in that position, frozen, paralyzed.

– Go and fetch water, he said icily.

She rose on unsteady feet, avoiding his scolding stare, wondering if she had done anything wrong.

It was dark out there, beyond the Hollow, but she knew where to go. She smelled the water. All children of the Waste were able to do that, at an early age.

She still felt lazy and content from the mating, the pleasure and pain lingering inside. Water from her eyes flooded her face, and she couldn't quite tell why. The shiny dust danced around her. She blinked, and it grew, and she imagined she could glimpse her own angry face.

The jar splashed into the pond between the palms. She almost dropped it, and wondered what was wrong with her.

You clumsy girl, he scolded her, and she sniffed.

He was there, with her. He was everywhere around her.
She filled the jar with water, put it on her head, balancing it there, and hurried back.
He sat there, beneath his fire. She put the jar in front of him, and stood there waiting. He filled his cup and drank. Then he signed for her to kneel in front of him. She looked attentive at him. He filled her cup with water and spices, and gave it to her. She drank. The bitter taste made her gag. The fluid, with its content slid down her throat, fell into her depths. She blinked, suddenly, just like that, dazed, sleepy.
– Pay attention! You will not fall asleep for minutes. There will be more than enough time.
Eyes focused on him. She was nothing but those eyes.
He held something in his hand.
– This is my gift to you, he said. – Wear it always. Never remove it, even for a second.
It was a necklace, or it resembled one, but was more elaborate, thicker and heavier. He put it around her neck, and he locked it in place. It felt tight and cold.
She found the lock on the side of her neck, but it was so strong that she couldn't open or break it, not with both her hands.
The strength in her hands faded. Her arms fell down.
Time passed.
– Open your eyes.
She did, and a completely different world revealed itself. He was there. She heard his voice, but she didn't see him.
– Tell me what you see, he hissed. – Tell me in detail.
– I see the Wave, she said sleepily. – That of sand, that of water. I see Atlantis drown in the sea. I see a girl sit in a hut writing down my words.
– Tell me about the girl.
– She's a Seer. She sees ancient times and the far future with equal strength. I like her clothes. They're so soft and pleasant to wear. The Dust is like putty in her hand.
– You're such a treasure, he marveled. – I rather thought you would be, the first time I laid my eyes on you.
His words echoed in her head, and she couldn't understand why.
He walked and she walked in his tracks.
They returned to the huts, through the forest, and it glowed around her, and she looked at him with eyes glowing in gratitude.
– There's so much, she mumbled. – Thank you, Master. Thank you.
– And this is just the beginning, he told her. – Together we will find everything worth seeking.
The circle awaited them. The older woman stepped forward. The novice looked at her, but also looked behind her at the others, especially noticing a man, hideously disfigured, with a strange forehead growth.

– Jahavalo speaks highly of you, Maya of the Scorpion Tribe. He says you're ready, prepared for the Secrets.

– Yes, Mistress, Maya said. – I'm eager. The need burns within me. I want to *know!*

– Enter then, the Cave of Darkness, of your own free will, and pray you will find your way back out.

They stepped aside, revealing the dark portal to the largest hut. A sudden draft sucked her in. It was a big mouth, one with large and pointed fangs. She glanced anxiously at Jahavalo. He nodded encouragingly. One more turn of the head, one final glance, before she said farewell to what she had known. She crossed the threshold. Everything changed around her.

She walked down steps of stone, hard under her feet. Hollow ground. Thin walls. She heard the sea and the all outside, the whispers existence itself made. This place had been forged long ago, forged by people like those outside, like her, the Dust People. The cave was huge, and the smallest move she made echoed and was amplified across the space. She realized she had heard this before, upon crossing the Waste, when the ground itself had spoken to her.

*I sit here, writing, Gabrielle, the Weaver of Worlds writes, and I can hear it, too, and the Dust is all around me, embracing me like a womb.*

I'm afraid. He's coming. I'm sore afraid.

It was easy going down, as if she was actually floating most of the time, as if the currents embraced her desert-skinny frame, and levitated her to the center of the darkness. She sat there, curled up like a pre-born, while the currents tore her apart.

She screamed, screamed her lungs out, in the silence of the womb. There was water there, on the floor. She sipped some, and it was the spice giving her life. Life was pulled out of her, and pulled back in. The outside revealed itself to her, as she was being born. The contractions began, as she was giving birth, giving birth to herself.

Suddenly she was outside, among her future peers, looking straight through them, learning all their weaknesses and traits. It happened in a flash. In a flash it was gone. She spread out like the wind, outside the clearing of huts, outside the circle of forest, to her kin, the five tribes living in the Waste.

She saw all the Waste. She was outside it, in the frothing sea surrounding it all. The World was so small, and the world, the true world outside was so big. Contractions became tremors, became quakes. She rose up through the tunnel towards the light, walking the last few steps through the doorway, feeling the weight of her legs as her feet touched the woven stone.

They welcomed her, the ten and two did, welcomed her as an equal. They could do no less, faced with the radiance of her being.

The air burned at the center of the circle. It was night. Maya looked at her peers with her new eyes, and they looked completely different from what they had looked only the day before.

There was the ceremony, simple and potent. The older woman Cawolfa, handed her the black robe, and she robed, and she spoke:

– I, given the name of Maya by my parents, take the name of Lillith, the Raven. I give name to my Shadow, my eternal Self.

– This is who you are! The others choired.

– This is who I am! She hummed.

They all came forward to greet her, to include her.

– Welcome, Lillith.

He took her hands and held on to them.

– Thank you, Jahavalo, she said huskily.

And looking at him, that strange feeling came over her again. She freed herself of him, and she knew she didn't imagine the flare of irritation coming from him.

But she didn't understand it.

She reached out a hand. A single raven settled on her arm.

They all had their animal close by, or she could read it when looking at them.

Calisto was a snake.

Carlo was the big tooth, the kind that made the ground shake.

Jahavalo was a dog, the kind that had been wolves, but had been taken in by humans and changed through the generations.

Zotre was the hyena.

Morningstar was the buffalo, with its big horns.

They all had a totem, a personal self they could draw strength from and sort of emulate.

Lillith sensed them all, and in some cases felt them all, as they embraced, body and mind.

– From now on we will all be your teachers and aides, Cawolfa said kindly. – Like you will be ours.

Jahavalo walked to the oblong tube pointing to the sky. There was a fuse sticking out of it. He lit it with a dramatic wave of his hand. Its base exploded and it rose into the air, its rainbow content spreading silently across the sky.

They came, came from all the five corners of the Earth, to witness the proscribed event. She sensed them, as they left the Waste and walked through the forest, the forest she knew, now, like the back of her hand.

– Look at them, Jahavalo said in her ear. – They all come, all the children, to look at the cloudless sky, to glance at the Chosen, to glow in our presence.

Again his word made her tremble. He reminded her of something, something she couldn't recall.

The five tribes broke out of the forest, prompted by the call in the night, the adults and the yawning, wide-eyed children.

They gathered in a half moon around the front of the large hut.

– Welcome, my children! Wolf cried, waving her wand in the air, creating wisps of Dust. – She you knew as Maya is now Lillith the Raven, and Maya no more. Come and meet her. Come and make her your servant.

– Come and bow for her Might, Jahavalo cried.

They filed past her. They all did. The females curtseyed, the males bowed. Lillith touched them, touched their brow, and she saw the Dust dance above their head.

The line seemed endless, as if they all filed past her twice or even thrice. There was such reverence in their eyes, and even her mother and father and former siblings looked at her with new, wary eyes.

Lone Dove curtseyed deeply, almost touching the ground, almost paralyzed with fright. Lillith wanted to speak to her, but Jahavalo stopped her with a light touch on her shoulder.

It ended, with song and dance, with reckless abandon, where the ten and three, and the rest mingled and joined. Lillith noticed that groups of four or five, gathering in a completely random pattern sought out each member of the Circle. She noticed the larger number presenting themselves before Jahavalo, pulled to him like moth to the flame.

– They seek to please you, placate you Lillith, he told her, bade her. – Accept them, and set them free.

She did. She watched how the others removed their covers, and she did as well, watched eager cohorts approaching the fire in the night.

And there was much sweat, much sound, and a lot of heavy breathing, on the dry ground, and inside the parched forest.

Lillith walked with Jahavalo on a day when dark clouds had gathered in the sky.

– My sister didn't recognize me, Lillith said. – Am I that changed?

– Yes, you've grown beyond them, Jahavalo nodded, – grown beyond their feeble perception of existence.

They had all shown her great respect. She still recalled what a strangely pleasing experience that had been, almost, in its own way as much as the Pleasures afterwards.

– You're a great addition to our ranks, the man at her side said. – And they sense that, sense how our power has grown, and they know our ability to protect them has increased significantly.

Again she sensed that strange ambiguity in him, and she wondered, wondered what it was about.

He stopped and nodded, and she fixed her large, almond eyes on him.

– Yes, he hissed. – You *understand.* I just knew you would, knew it the moment I first saw your outside, your infinite inside. Come, come with me, and know Power.

He led her to the bottom, first point, of the five-pointed star, to a place where the very air seethed and burned.

– They came this way, he said. – They came here eons ago, sealing the path behind them, blocking their enemies' walk. Touch it, touch the wall.

There was nothing here, nothing her eyes could see, but she still sensed it, sensed what was ahead of her, even before she reached out a hand and *touched* it.

There was nothing there, nothing to touch. Her hand vanished into nothing, as if it ceased to exist, and there was pain, and she pulled the hand back as soon as she was able.

She stared at him in absolute astonishment.

– Our ancestors came to this land, and somehow bonded with it, made it their own.

– This is what the Spear Dance is for, she exclaimed.

– Yes, he said, a gleam in his eyes. – Our enemies are delayed, but they will come, and now we are sufficient numbers to deal with them. When the barrier breaks down, and one day it will, we will be ready.

– Yes, she whispered. – Yes!

– Our mothers and fathers made sacrifices in blood, Jahavalo said. – Death and Life consecrated this place, and made it ours.

– But there is… a price? The waves of sand and water?

– Yes, he nodded. – The power runs through the Earth here, and they took that power, and directed it, balanced everything, and the unbalance returns to us once every Season. And we of the ten and three are the only force keeping it at bay. Feel it, feel the power beneath your feet.

She sensed it, sensed the rumble, the pull, and she was sore afraid.

– Something fell from the sky here long ago, he said, his voice distant, as if he was actually there, seeing it before his very eyes, – bringing death and destruction unheard of. Demons ruled the Earth then, and not men. But they were all vanquished, gone in a blink of an eye, and men were free to take their rightful place as Masters of the Earth.

He grabbed her and positioned her.

– Behold, he said, waving his hand in the air.

He removed the air before her eyes, making her see.

And she saw it, saw them, through a hole, a mist in the air. There were people there, scores of them, not that far away from the two of them. But… they stood still, frozen like statues.

– They are not moving… are they?

– Oh, they are. He grinned in triumph. – I come here once a Season, I have done so since childhood, and I see how they have advanced, perhaps raised a foot a bit more, just a little bit more, how the spear they have thrown has reached a bit further ahead.

She looked at him, striving to understand, to wrap her mind around what he had told her, his astonishing gift of understanding.

– They are engaged in a bubble of time. We are in the world. They are not! This is the power we, the high members of the five tribes have at our command.

His words made her dizzy, tasting like sweet honey at the tip of her tongue.

She slipped out of her dress, and they did it, there, at the edge of the Abyss.

It was not many days after that she began throwing up in the morning. She walked to Wolf to tell her the happy news, but Wolf already knew.

There were no words, no silly, solemn statements, but a lot of smiles and nods and greetings and hugs. The twelve embraced her in a thousand small and big ways, and she felt much loved.

The little one grew within her day by day, until it was visible as the characteristic bulge on her belly. The desert-skinny girl gave way to something resembling a well-fed mother-to-be.

It was night. The girl looked at her face in the pond, in the light of the fire. It was the eyes, the eyes that more than anything made her face.
– They're truly something, aren't they? The older woman said. – It's like they are the entire face, like pools of dark blood rising from our depths.
Something made her move, made her leave the gathering of huts and go to the place in the south. She looked at the warriors and their weapons floating in the air. There was daylight in there, in the sphere. There always was.
– It was necessary to do this, Wolf growled, her growl turning to despair. – But now I begin to think we would have been better off if we had made our stand and not resorted to Magick. We're suffocating here all of us, dying in our Shadow, instead of only in body.
Lillith turned, but didn't see Wolf anywhere.
She turned back towards the unmoving flesh and blood, wondering if they saw her, how long she would have to stand here, to become more than a fleeting phantom to them.
To them day and night would constantly flicker and never truly settle, while years would pass outside their prison. But so far hardly more than a moment had passed from their point of view. Perhaps they had still to actually register how the group they persecuted and hounded and killed quite simply faded away before their eyes.
– I have never been comfortable in Magick, Wolf told her. – But you, you are born in it, bathing in it from your very first breath and so will your brood.
Lillith walked in the dry forest, pondering Wolf and Jahavalo's words. She heard their voices in the wind, heard them fading in and out of the Dust dancing around her.
Wolf and Jahavalo were her two mirrors, she realized startled, the foundation on which she would build her life. They might wage war within her.
– The Dust is… different from the air, she said excitedly to Carlo a cloudy day.
Carlo, a laidback, solemn man, her teacher for the day nodded approvingly.
– It's like I can glimpse… things in it, see into… another world.
– Another world is being born in the Dust, he nodded. – It has been for a long time, growing a bit more for every new generation. One of Shadow, a reflection of us and this world.
He hesitated. She looked enticingly at him. He relented, bathed in her dazzling smile.
– I was told by my elders, my teachers that long ago the world had only been what we could touch with our hands, our flesh. But long ago that changed. Something happened, something making us all more than we were.
– And we could reach out and touch the very air, she cried, – even touch what isn't yet here. We're *growing,* growing into what we have always been.
Moments, only moments later she realized startled that he looked at her with apprehension in his eyes.
The eyes were the face, were the soul, were the male or female.
She stepped close to him, and kissed him, used her tongue to caress his skin.
His manhood rose hard and pulsing. She felt it against her bigger lips.

– Males are so easily aroused, she grinned. – So easy to touch.
He grabbed her arm and held on, held on hard. It hurt. She couldn't get free. Males were so much stronger than females physically. He let go of her and she stumbled backwards, whimpering, lashing out at him with venomous words.
– Jahavalo wanted me, and he used me. He found me desirable, so desirable that he didn't care about what I thought at all.
Carlo frowned, clearly confused, confusing her as well.
– Are you saying that he took you without your… consent?
Lillith frowned, too, understanding eluding her. She replied without replying, her silence speaking louder than any words.
– That's… unprecedented, Carlo said astonished.
A tear, an astonishing tear appeared in the female's corner of the left eye.
– I thought it was supposed to be like that. Initiations are supposed to be… hard, right?
– Yes, Carlo nodded. – But…
– But not like that, right?
The female's voice was now hard and edgy.
He replied without replying.
– He didn't care about me, about my awakening, about me learning, but used me, used me callously for the sake of his own pleasure, his own desire. He even gave me a collar, like he would his dogs.
Dust danced in the air surrounding them, swarming like angry flies.
The apprehension in Carlo's eyes was no longer because of her, but because of what had risen, what had been exposed.
Lillith grabbed the necklace and tore it off in one powerful pull.
– Eviana and Cevi wear collars as well. He taught them, too, right? And they bore the spawn of their «union» with him?
Carlo's silence spoke volumes.
– But you knew about this? You must have!
– We suspected, Carlo said, in a very strained voice. – But we didn't *know,* not for sure. He was always so eager in his desire to teach the newcomers, so… passionate.
She rushed back towards the center, and he followed her, fear painted in his face, now.
Above them the clouds gathered and thickened.
– The Wave, Carlo cried. – The Wave of sand and water.
Lillith sensed it, as tangible as she sensed her own inside storm.
Morningstar met them at the gate. He clearly looked worried. Her features softened for a moment. His strange forehead growth didn't scare her anymore.
– The Wave is coming fast this time, he told them. – Faster than I've ever seen.
The ground shook, shook so hard that they almost lost their footing.
The ten and three met in front of the large hut.
Lillith's eyes locked onto Jahavalo and never let go. Not even when they opened further, opened so much that they didn't see what was right in front of her, but instead the time to come.

She fell to her knees, as she saw herself walk up long stairs, forged in stone.

– I see, she cried. – I see strange shapes float in the sky, and I see the wave of sand and water. It comes for us.

Blood flowed from her mouth. She had bit herself.

– Why did you do it? She asked Jahavalo. – Why did you make us crawl beneath you like insects on the ground?

And he knew, everybody knew what she meant, knew the reason for the snarl in her voice. Eviana and Cevi looked ashamed, even as they sought closer to his shadow. Lillith looked like a giant where she knelt on the hard ground.

– You were nothing, he said, with the chill in his voice. – I raised you from the mud and pulled you up in the Dust.

– But you didn't let us go afterwards, Lillith pointed out. – You kept us, as pets.

– Harsh times are coming, he countered. – People with vision and cunning and *will* should lead, should decide what is good and not for the People.

– Jahavalo is right, Zotre said. – He has the answers.

Lillith noticed that Zotre had no necklace.

– It is wrong! Wolf stepped forward.

Lillith rose. Something happened, something very definite, irreversible. There was a sense of finality. It was a good thing, but also indefinitely bad. The three women and one man sought to Jahavalo. Three others gathered around Wolf and Lillith. The other three stood there, between the rock and a hard place, clearly at a loss and totally clueless what to do, where to go. The two groups faced each other, a wall rising between them.

– We'll leave, Lillith stated, anger burning within her, making her powerful, making her strong. – We'll leave this dead place, right now. It will destroy us if we stay.

– L-leave? Eviana whined.

– Leave, Morningstar confirmed. – This place was right for us at one, crucial point in our existence, but it isn't any longer.

– I think you are correct, Jahavalo said. – We should leave.

They stared at him.

– But we should wait until after the Wave, until we've tamed it one more time.

– That makes sense. Carlo nodded. – We'll have more time, then. We don't have to flee like rabbits, but can plan ahead, prepare.

Everybody nodded slowly. It did make sense.

The two groups, the three groups mingled and became one once more. They went to work with fevered and anxious thoughts.

The drums began beating at dawn. The flutes and the whistle in the forest began speaking at noon. The whisper of the sand began howling at dusk. The thirteen sat inside a circle of fire, in a circle of Dust. The five tribes gathered around them, beating the butt end of their spears at the ground, and the ground shook.

– Feel the smallest things, Morningstar began.

– What we can't see, only sense, Wolf said.

– The world is those things, Calisto said.
– What we want it to be, Morningstar said.
– Is not what it is, Wolf said.
– The world is Power, Jahavalo said.
– And that is not wrong, Lillith nodded.
– The blood and howls in the night, Carlo growled.
– The world is Magick, Lillith cried.

And there was movement, as they sensed the Dust, as they invented it with their being, as it was inversed into them. As they raised their hands and arms, and the world changed color around them, as the sound of the beating of the sticks on the ground changed into a deeper, murkier quality.

As the veil fell before their eyes, and the Wave and the Storm revealed itself to them in all its horror and beauty.

And then they experienced Power, its majesty and seduction. It filled them to the brink of their being. They saw it, saw the Wave, the sand and the water, every grain of sand, every drop of water.

The thirteen, supported by their five tribes, reached out with one mighty hand and grabbed, for one moment, one tiny piece of eternity the Storm by its balls, stopping it in its tracks, halting, delaying its rampage.

The Power faded within them, returning to the Infinity it had once come from.

They sat there, drained, content, relieved, receiving the gratitude and devotion of their people.

They rose, on unsteady, spry feet. The ceremony drained them, but strengthened them, too. It was such an enormous sense of accomplishment, of Life. It lingered within them, never to quite go away.

The celebration began, hesitatingly, passionately. Something nipped at Lillith's mind, but she shook her head, discarded it as unimportant and threw herself into the Dance.

She faced the other twelve in turn, as she also faced all her brethren from the five tribes.

I know you, she said, she laughed her trilling laughter. And I know you. And you. And you. We first met long ago, in a place far from here.

Knowledge and understanding burned within her, now, in the aftermath of the Infinite Touch. The masks fell, and people were revealed as who and what they truly were.

They roamed the spaces between the huts, the huts, and forest and the dunes outside. Lillith ran with six others, naked and hearty to the southern point, where Power seethed and pulsed. A man kissed her, a woman kissed her. Lillith returned the caresses, but she kept staring at the patterns, the ever-shifting patterns in the air. There was a hole here, a hole in the very reality itself.

A sharp, sudden pain nipped the insides of her nostrils. She touched her upper lip. There was blood on it. She stood there, as if listening for a moment or two, then she screamed.

– Exalted one…?

One of the men touched her cautiously. He pulled his hand back, burning it on her red-hot skin.

She stared at what was right in front of her. Her eyes opened so hard that it hurt. She screamed again. Stumbling at first, she rushed back towards the huts, gaining her footing, losing it. The others supported her.

– Gather everybody, she mumbled. – Everybody! *Force them,* if you have to.

They shook under her startling, extraordinary uncivil behavior.

– The grains are rolling, she cried, – slipping between our fingers, and the ground is crumbling beneath our feet.

They left her, sore afraid.

She stumbled alone back to the huts, somehow able to stay on her feet. The ground shook under her, and she had no way of knowing what was the fever assaulting her, and what was real. She sat down in front of the large hut, and they all came to her, came to the burning shadow in their mist. The twelve stopped before her, looking absolutely startled at the dark, dark eyes.

– We didn't vanquish the Wave, she said. – It's still coming.

– What are you talking about? Jahavalo shook his head. – We did what we have done every year since before all of us were born. This time we even had your added Power to aid us.

– I saw it, she stated pointedly. – It's coming. What worked before will work no longer. The instability our ancestors created here is catching up with us. It's coming through the ground, too, this time, and the foundation this land rests on is already crumbling. Can't you feel the ground shake?

They looked bewildered at each other, like children.

– I can, she stated. – And soon, not many days from now, you will, too.

– But we can't leave, Jahavalo cried. – This is our home. It's…

He believed her. That, more than anything was what convinced the others.

– We need more power, he said. – More people in the circle…

– You don't *get it,* she snarled, the Raven squeaked. – Not all the power or power adepts in the world can keep this from happening. We attempted to tame the world, but the world won't be tamed. Your *guile* stands exposed, «master». The world itself exposed you. You never intended for us to leave, but now we don't have any choice, and I, for one can't wait.

They all listened, and they all turned to her, though some did so reluctantly.

But the moment the decision had been made, they all began moving, began making haste. Survival overshadowed everything else.

The night was spent gathering weapons and a few, rudimentary belongings. They made more rucksacks to carry things, and all the food and water they could possibly bring. Lillith saw the land, the vast island in the sea, saw the journey only a few had ever taken, to the much bigger land beyond, the land their ancestors had fled in fear and persecution.

– What about the warriors in the time bubble? Morningstar asked her.

They turned to her, for wisdom, for assurances and for leadership.

– Whatever people they are, their tribe is long gone. She shrugged. – Let them stay. When the bubble finally dissolves by itself, the solid ground will vanish beneath them and turn into sea. Let them swim to the far shores.

She saw it, saw this entire land fall beneath the large wave, the soon to be smooth ocean surface.

– It will take us many days to reach the distant shores, Wolf said. – Will it be enough?

– I don't know, Lillith whispered.

Then her voice hardened, strengthened:

– I just know that we will all succumb if we stay here, and that all of our story will be undone.

At sunset the next day they set out east, leaving behind the only home they had known. They all looked back, safe in the certainty that they would never return, certain of nothing else. Lillith knew that Jahavalo stared at her. She returned the stare, giving him a teasing smile in return.

The Long Walk began, the one that would never end.

– I see us wander, Wolf said. – I see us walk to the end of time and beyond. This is a good thing. We suffocated here.

– Now, we'll rejoin the world, Morningstar said.

– Risking waking up with a spear in our gut, Jahavalo cried passionately.

– Now we can *deal* with that, Morningstar countered. – As we should have done in the first place.

Lillith stayed silent. It was as if she couldn't close her eyes, those inside her head. She saw starvation and death, endless suffering and boundless freedom, worlds unheard of.

They rested and slept in the pitiful shadows under the covers at day and walked at night, their walk without end.

The ground began shaking on the tenth day, and from then on it grew steadily worse. One morning, by consent they kept walking. Lillith kept turning her head, until she stopped by an act of will, and rushed forward, throwing away her load, and most of the others did the same.

There was a loud crack. She saw it, bore witness to the large island splitting in two. The mainland was just a few hundred steps ahead, so close, so far away. A woman turned her head and looked back, and froze to a statue that very moment. Lillith knew what she saw, knew she saw the giant water wall rise towards the heavens and shadow the sun, and chase them with deadly speed and accuracy. Its roar grew overwhelming in a matter of a few heartbeats. There was a narrow bridge of land connecting the island and the mainland. They crossed it in something resembling more an animal stampede than an orderly evacuation. Keep running, Lillith cried, knowing fully how useless it was, fully aware that she couldn't hear herself scream in the roar of the water wall chasing the tiny group of human beings.

The deluge hit them and flushed their bones and flesh far away to distant lands and times.

## 2

It was on the verge of fall when they made their way west. They took the bike, waved goodbye to those remaining, and left the valley, never to return.

The two of them stayed at the Kendall Ranch the entire summer, strangely relaxed, fully aware that their current relative bliss wouldn't last, but they did see fit to enjoy it, to enjoy their brief respite from the Storm, never allowing themselves to forget, forget anything. And they had no desire to do that, anyway. They kept their eyes sharp as a hawk.

They swam nude in the lake, deep below its surface. Its murky depths revealed itself to their sensitive eyes. They swam down to the bottom. It took them minutes, but they were not any worse off. They didn't share air this time, but grabbed a large rock to make themselves stand on the ground. It brought a strange feeling, to deliberately keep themselves from rising. They kept their eyes on each other, smiling in spite of the pressure of the hostile surroundings. She let go of a huge bubble of air, and he did, too. They crouched, letting go of the rock and kicked off at the ground, shooting like arrows towards the surface.

Forever passed as they swam upwards, but there wasn't really any panic. They began to feel the first faint signs of asphyxiation, but they weren't truly worried.

They broke the surface simultaneously, gasping for air, howling in laughter.

– That was so COOL! Liz cried.

They let themselves float in the water, relaxing, enjoying to the max the feeling of the moment, the warm, warm sun against their face, the cool fluid embalming their skin.

The two bodies floated towards each other, met and softly clinched, and joined, a powerful, explosive need without guilt. They walked up on the shore a long time after that, walking close, sitting close, allowing the sun to dry them, to burn them.

– I remember when I was a cute little girl…

– You're still a cute little girl, he grinned.

She scowled at him.

– When I was little, she continued. – Bathing to cool off during the summer did little good. After the walk home we were just as sweaty as we were before the bath. It isn't like that anymore. The hottest summer sun is simply pleasant. It doesn't burn anymore.

It did turn their skin to a darker hue, though, easily, much faster than it would and did ordinary people.

– I've noticed. He nodded. – We change and adapt to our surroundings in a manner far more pronounced than others do.

They deliberately forgot about the world outside that summer, embracing a joy inevitably laced with bitterness. Laughter echoed through the Southern Colorado forests and mountains. People heard it, but they didn't see the culprits, and they were believed to be ghosts. The two Warrens rested nude and tight on a bare rock in the mountains, as close as they could come to the Sun.

– We needed this, Liz said dreamily. – Needed this brief respite, this walk in the wild.

Bathed in the colder afternoon sun she stood in the forest glen with the Peacemaker in her hand. She squeezed the trigger, and thunder rolled across the field.

– Don't squeeze, he admonished her.

The shot went haywire, far away from the marked target on the tree twenty steps ahead.

– I know. She nodded in frustration. – It's a flow, not a pull.

But she did learn. The gun that initially felt awkward in her grip, eventually felt like it truly belonged in her malleable hands, as if it was an extension of her being. She began hitting the tree, and a certain sense of peace settled in her. She knew it was just a matter of time before she would be able to hit her mark in her sleep, and that both worried and exhilarated her.

They fought, trained, honed their reflexes and skills, even though it wasn't much of a fight, since he always won. He was clearly both stronger and faster than her.

He held her down. She hit the ground with her free hand as a sign of admitting defeat. Irritation was visible as she allowed him to help her up.

– As you know, I've had a rather unpleasant and intense training course, he said. – Don't worry about it. You'll catch up.

Her expression turned somber, filled with regret.

– I know. She touched his cheek. – I haven't had years of practice crammed into a few months, forced-fed into my body and mind.

And there it was again, the pain, strangely enough even more in her than in him.

– I can feel the wrongness, feel it everywhere.

She fired the gun. The bullet hit the branch she had been aiming at, and broke it in pieces.

The list. The list of death paraded before their inner eye. They would never forget, never allowing themselves to forget.

The thunder of the powerful engine below them shook their mind. The two-wheeler raged on the New Mexico highway on its way west. She was driving. He was learning, too, but she seemed to be thriving on the bike in a way he couldn't, and he let her. They didn't wear helmets, and the wind constantly caressed their hair, their long tresses dancing like shadows in the slipstream of the bike.

They looked down on Grand Canyon, looked in awe at its majesty and power.

He struggled with words. She looked at him, rubbing his neck, patiently, even tenderly.

– This is… indescribable.

– There is no greater word, she replied, she cried across the divide.

The red earth resonated under their wheels as they were making their way west, diluting the gray under their feet. They stopped by a red mountain right across the Arizona border. A few Native Americans had set up a way station there, with a souvenir store and a makeshift toilet at the back. The place came off as both inspiring and infinitely sad. There were despair here, lingering and prevailing. They deliberately stayed longer than they needed to, to confront similar notions within themselves.

They stopped later, at dusk, at an old, worn motel. Paying up front they received a key from the man behind the counter, a key to a room a bit farther down the road.

A room with stairs to the bed. No paint on most of the walls. But a room telling a long story. It told the two of them, in fleeting images and whispers.

– Why do we see all this? She wondered. – Why now?

– I don't know. He shook his head. – There's nothing here, nothing having any direct connection with us. Perhaps it's just random, a result of our powers growing in the leaps and bounds they always do?

She didn't comment aloud on that, but she pondered it, kept analyzing it, like she did everything.

He stepped over to the window, looking at the cars passing by.

– There's a kind of almost… religious fervor to Trudy, don't you think?

– Yes! She stated. – I definitely think that. Something happened to them, to her and Nick and the others, in 1952 and/or afterwards, something profound changing their lives, for better or worse.

– A life-changing experience, he said, his voice cracking.

She walked to him, turning him around, making him look at her.

– You're thinking about Tilla again, aren't you?

He nodded, didn't trust his voice.

– Good! She stated.

He looked startled at her.

– I *want* you to think about her, she said passionately. – I want you to grieve, want you to think of the happiness you shared with her, to never forget her. I want all of you, not just a compartmentalized part you reserve for me.

She kissed him hard, drawing blood.

– I don't love you. She shrugged. – Not more than you love me. That word is such a limited description, at best, for what I feel about you, such a very narrow way of describing life.

He still didn't say anything.

– Love is just crumbs on one table, in a room with many tables, and in a Universe with many rooms. It's heavily overrated. The Human Being has far more on its plate. Love is not the supreme power of the Universe. Life itself is!

There was noise outside, a number of trucks passing by, noise slowly fading.

– We're free, now. He finally spoke. – Free from others' agenda. We can do what we want. The very Universe, Life itself is waiting for us to grab it.

– Yes, she whispered. – *Yes!*

At dusk the next day they cruised into the city of Las Vegas, Nevada.

# Chapter Three: The fake flowers

*FROM THE ANNALS OF ETHEL EDITH WARREN - BORN 1935*

*Cold sweat breaks all over me.*

*I can see the Tapestry unfolding, like strands of night and fire. I can see the waves collapse. I'm observing action and reaction, cause and effect constantly folding back on itself.*

*Warriors unending, eternal are falling, not through Space, but through Time. What happened once may not happen twice, or thrice. The Tapestry is ever changing, ever shifting, as reality itself is turned inside out. Yes, the fireeyes, created by Life, created by Fire will ever be the song of the Universe.*

*I can see slave laborers toil under the whip on the Konya Heights in ancient Turkey, on the Salisbury Plains on the British Isles, see them die horrible deaths on the Arena in Old Rome, experience it all as they suffer and die in droves in the asteroid mines.*

*I can see flashes of Shadow in the coldest of ashes.*

*There is a tablet in gray hovering in the air. It's not one of stone, but more formed out of mist. On it, in the many-dimensional space there are figures moving, some alike, some not.*

*The Tapestry is constantly moving and changing.*

2

Las Vegas was long and broad straight streets and avenues. Everything was big here, both grand and pompous.

They drove south, down Las Vegas Boulevard, popularly called The Strip. The air boiled and quivered around them. The wind brought by their high speed was hardly noticeable. Liz eased on the hand control when Tropicana Hotel and Casino appeared in their vision, but it was still a hard turn left. She made it with astonishing ease, smiling as she sensed his appreciation. They stopped outside the hotel entrance, not very gently, on screaming tires. People stared hard at them. They ignored it, ignored the flashes of fear and angry bursts they sensed in the onlookers.

She turned off the engine, and they climbed off the bike.

– This place is ours, she declared. – We own it.

He looked at her, looked through the dust covering her face, and felt the hard ball inside loosen a little, felt the icy river begin to melt by the first stirrings of spring.

– We do own it, he confirmed. – Look at us as we stride unfazed into this wretched house.

She giggled and shook imperceptibly, as he took her hand, as he covered it in his bigger, stronger. He brought their one, small suitcase, and they walked inside.

The heat of the desert waned as they entered the cooled, controlled environment. They looked at themselves from outside themselves, from various points in the reception area. It was easy, and they saw how they glowed, how they stood out from everybody, truly walking through the place as if they owned it.

They walked to the reception desk. Liz spoke to the porter and charmed him into oblivion.

– So, did I do a good job? She asked Ted in the elevator.

– Undoubtedly, he replied dryly. – I'm willing to bet he recalls nothing from your conversation but your dazzling smile.

– And it isn't even a Power, she cried excitedly.

– Not if you don't count the power of your dazzling personality, he said lightly.

She turned dark and misty in her eyes.

– You say the nicest things… she cooed.

And pulled closer to him.

And it was like an explosion behind both pair of eyes. And the next thing they noticed were bodies pushing against each other as water from the shower poured down and surrounded them.

They rubbed each other with towels afterwards, in slow, lazy movements.

– I feel so free, she whispered, – so wild and unafraid.

She walked to the mirror, posing before it, posing for him. She was always posing for him.

– This place was used in the Godfather movie, she said. – A good choice. It's a dangerous place, filled with mystery and brutality.

– And it's evidently making you jittery, he commented. – I must question whether you have overdone the eye movement we do since we arrived here…

She turned towards him, smiling sweetly.

– You're so astute, My Lord, she said. – I feel so safe with you.

Was there a hint of sarcasm and accusation in her voice? He couldn't tell.

She shrugged.

– The last time I passed through here, I and my two companions were rather unlucky in our choice of victim. In desperate need of some hard cash, we robbed the wrong man. Not only is he this proud city's Chief of Police, but he also has connections… organized crime connections.

– That might be fun, he said neutrally.

– It was dark, she said, – and I had short hair like a boy, so I don't know if he would recognize me, but we better be prepared for some mischief.

– We always are, he stated.

She looked at him, sensing no anger in him, nothing directed at her. There was a brief, brief silence. She sighed happily, and rushed into his arms, like a little girl. He swallowed hard. She was a little girl, in some ways, still innocent, in spite of it all, still not that much fucked up by the world.

Night dawned on Las Vegas. Neon lights supplanted natural light. The two Warrens dressed, clothed themselves in fabric, and headed down to the casino.

The excitement below rose towards them as they took the elevator down, bathing them in its seething energies. They sensed it, even felt it physically, a tangible force they could draw strength from.

– We both look older than our years tonight, she remarked as she admired herself in the mirror.

He grinned as he kept his eyes on her. Her face might cause her to be confused with a child, but there was no way the fully developed body could lead to such a misunderstanding. He looked like an overgrown boy in comparison. If not for the eyes. Those deep, deep eyes of dark, dark fire.

The gaming room was large, seemingly stretching on forever. Row on row of slot machines and roulette and Black Jack tables, and other games they didn't recognize. Their skin began tingling, in both expectation and because of the generous gifts the other players unknowingly bestowed upon them.

They walked to a roulette table, surrounded by fluttering wings, as they stretched out their senses, as they prepared, as they began *touching* the spinning wheel ahead.

– I feel it, she whispered. – The previous time I tried this I couldn't make it work, but now I can. I know I can.

The white ball jumped up in the air. It did that on occasion. No one reacted to the sight of its brief air dance, except the two approaching. A thrill shot through Liz as the ball landed on 36, exactly where she had wanted it to land.

– New color, Ted said.

They hardly heard each other's voices. Hardly heard others speak. Everything was muted by the sound, the buzz inside, the roar of their inner voices ascending.

This was a ten-dollar table. That meant that ten dollars was the minimum bet, even on the numbers. They bought a roll of blue chips for 1000 dollars. He used everything to cover about sixty percent of the numbers, as was the right thing to do, mathematically, like most of the other players also did, but he chose two numbers on the opposite side of the wheel as his mark, and put his highest stacks, hundred dollars there.

He focused on the number 20, and on the ball, the dancing white ball turning red, touching it with his fluttering wings, tuning in on the spinning wheel. Minutes passed by, during the seconds the ball danced. He became the dance, became the ball, the wheel, and made the ball land on 20. It wasn't hard, wasn't hard at all, and no one was the wiser. No one suspected foul play, because there was nothing to see, nothing to point a finger at. The ball had quite simply landed on a number, as it always did. They had just won 3600 dollars.

Liz clapped her hands excitedly, giving him a sultry kiss, playing the vamp, as the croupier pushed a lot of chips, including several marked $100 in their direction. She was up next and repeated his method, except placing the highest values on different numbers. They won again.

And thus the evening passed, in a blur of motion and a haze of boiling blood. They took turns betting, cautiously, not overdoing it, loosing deliberately most of the time, not giving in to the rush inside, not giving anyone the slightest reason for suspicion. Slowly, but surely their winnings increased, not that much faster than other winners in the casino.

When they began slipping, when their control and focus slid, they had already decided to quit for the evening. They walked to the cashier, receiving their money. The large bruiser of a cashier stared hard at them as he counted the bills. They were ready for trouble, but nothing happened. This was just small change anyway. The high rollers visiting the casino could leave with millions in winnings. The two of them had increased their fortune significantly, but then again, that wasn't unusual in Vegas. Even if most people left broke, there were a few lucky ones that didn't, and an even smaller number leaving with a lot more money than they had arrived with.

They sat on the bed in their quiet, quiet room, sipping champagne, their eyes glowing, warming the other.

– That was *amazing,* she cried. – It felt so good. And we weren't even cutting loose. It was so *easy!* Exactly like taking candy from a baby.

– And such candy, he marveled.

He took some Russian caviar from the plate and put in her mouth. She swallowed it with a shudder, with half closed eyes.

– Overrated, she grinned softly. – Highly overrated…

She jumped out of the bed, dancing to the muted music.

– I can picture it easily, she giggled. – The conversation between the manager and his thugs: «But boss, there's no way they could have cheated. The croupier was one of our most trusted guys. I could lean on him a little, but quite frankly, I don't think we'll find any *irregularities.* They won fair and square. It happens, you know».

She did the imitation to perfection. Her voice even turned an octave or so lower, almost like that of a man. It was eerie, even to him.

– And it's so funny… what we did down there… *This* is just a parlor trick, the surface, the visible iceberg of something far deeper, far *more.*

An apple rose from the bowl and into her hand. She took a large bite.

– What you and Tilla and Mark did in London… *that* is Magick.

It was as if the room darkened a little, just a little, and everything turned clearer, the texture of their vision that much more lucid.

– You focused, she marveled, her eyes glowing distinctively stronger. – You focused everything inside, your rage on one single target, and the result was gloriously terrible to behold.

This was the *Witch* speaking, the force of nature manifesting itself beneath the shell of the bimbo, the carefree young woman.

She found the black candles in the suitcase, and he wasn't at all surprised that she had brought them.

– I see Wolf, Jahavalo and Lillith and the others in my visions, she said. – I did that long before I read about them.

– I do, too, he said hoarsely. – I did, too.
– And beyond them all…
– … I see the Dragon, he completed in a whisper.
She put out all the electrical lights in the room, drawing the curtains tight. She did so with hardly any conscious thought at all. It had become second nature to her, like it had to him. The candles floated up in the air around the two of them sitting on the bed, forming a circle. She lit them with a lighter. The tiny flames stretched and reached onto the room. She undressed, and he did, too.
– No focus this time, she said. – Just let the thoughts drift. Let them wander, wander through eternity and back, wherever they may take us.
She held out a hand, and his pouch floated from the suitcase and to her. He concentrated slightly and the tap water began to flow on the restroom, filling a glass. The glass danced through the air to them. Not a single drop was spilled. They approached this carefully, thinking it through while they were doing it. Their movements were coordinated, a mirror of the other. It was as if they had always been doing it.
They grabbed each their small tube and filled a few, precious grains on them, and then dousing them with water.
– These are seeds, she said. – Where do they grow?
– I don't know.
He shook his head.
– I suppose we will learn to do this without them one day, she pondered. – Without… crutches.
– We do that in dreams, involuntarily all the time, he said. – But it's blurry then, a series of chaotic images and impressions not being of much help to us.
The seeds began swelling in the water, cracking, turning into one, homogenous mass swelling uncontrollably, expanding out of the tubes. They filled their palms with it, and began smearing it across the other's chest.
– Gods and demons of infernal realms, she cried. – We CALL upon you all. We want to ride your wings to distant places and times.
Hands sought down, sought to cock and cunt, and they applied the ointment with just a slight hesitation, with a determination steely and stubborn beyond words.
Words and chants unknown began making sense, as their voices mixed with that of the shadow world, the shimmering surroundings turning ever clearer.
She gasped, a startled smile crossing her face.
– I'm… swelling, she said. – It feels so good, so very good.
His cock stood out hard and thick.
Then there was a wrenching sound somewhere, and they felt it as if their skin was turned inside out.
– It hurts, she said, clenching her teeth.
The pressure in his manhood increased to an unbearable level, but there was no relief.
– Pain, she whispered. – I didn't think there would be pain.

The searing pain increased to the point of becoming unbearable, and they cried out, as their powerful shadows left their bodies and set out on their Journey.

What wasn't matter rose from their still bodies. The room seemed to both contract and expand. It changed, becoming something Other, something vastly different from how they had perceived it.

They stood there, levitating in the air, hovering above their tiny bodies far below. But they were yet still in the room.

– My, oh, my, the Shadow that was Liz exclaimed.

They were still not free of their bodies, and quickly realized that they wouldn't be, shouldn't be. A silver cord connected them to the physical reality they were about to temporarily leave behind. They stared at each other, stared at themselves. It was a frightening, yet amazing sight.

– This is so much, she whispered, she thundered. – I never dreamed…

– And yet you did, he stated.

Lips moved, but they weren't really speaking, but communicating in a way making speech seem like a barrier, a thing they had left behind long, long ago.

And they had.

This was already long ago, as the room dissolved around them, as Everything opened up before them.

They saw through mist, through shadow, saw the past, the present and the future, and other times besides, and couldn't quite tell which was which.

The door not the door opened for them, and they walked through it. Suddenly they were outside, outside the Tropicana, in the intersection between The Boulevard and Tropicana Avenue. But it wasn't the same place they had arrived at earlier. They looked around, and there were far more tall buildings. But they were dark and burning, with large holes in their walls. People rushed back and forth in panic, and sirens were heard everywhere. Explosions shook the ground. A huge chunk of the Tropicana Hotel fell off the south wall and hit the street.

This is… she thought (and he heard her). This is amazing. This is incredible!

As one their eyes were drawn to the large clock somewhere ahead. It said:

**01.45 06-06-1988**

And they knew.

– We are here, he said.

A ghostly sound picked up by the people around them, and they pointed at them, at the ghosts in their midst.

Two ghosts that began walking north, the same way they had arrived earlier, backtracking, revisiting the path they had taken, fading from the view of those who looked at them as fast as they had appeared. They saw themselves on the bike, a fleeting image soon vanquished.

And they heard what their ears couldn't hear.

The journey is different every time.

A voiceless voice said.

The path is never the same.

The wind not wind whispered.

Learn all there is to learn.

The thunder rolled.

Because it's all changing.

There was a fog, like clouds splitting before flying birds. They saw the woman with the wolf's head stand on what appeared to be a battlefield, standing between heaps of mangled bodies.

– Jahavalo came to this place, this people, she said. – And he destroyed it, destroyed them.

Ted turned, and he saw Stonehenge, saw it not as he, Ted Warren knew it, had seen it the previous year, but how it had been in its heyday, in its prime. And there was pain, like a sword in the gut, and as he looked down there was blood on his hands. He stared at her, and she, too was covered in blood. They stood beside Wolf in a field of death.

Everything faded away, fading into mist, becoming the mist.

Dry, dry sand under their feet, their bare feet. Children's feet. They looked startled at each other, at the young, brown faces. Above them loomed the pyramids and palaces of Egypt, not as the ruins they looked like in the twentieth century, but in their days of splendor and power. They knelt on the stone floor with a lot of other children, knelt before the woman of high stature on the throne. Her face was covered by golden make up, and tightened ritualistically around her eyes, but they recognized her, and they trembled in fear. She smacked her lips in displeasure and they froze in terror.

She rose and hurried out of the room. There was no obvious signal, only the slight buzz tiny Ted and tiny Liz recognized in their head. They rose, too, and followed the foaming regent, leaving the other children kneeling on the ground.

They entered a smaller room, one with windows, windows without glass, opening up to the searing desert.

The Queen removed her hat, revealing her long black and silken hair. She turned abruptly towards them, and they fell on their knees, sore afraid.

Black, her eyes were black.

– That's better, she snapped. – That's much better. Now, rise, and take your place in your mother's court.

They jumped on their feet and rushed to her. She nodded, somewhat pleased. They sensed it, and they rejoiced in their hearts.

– This is the Golden Land, she stated proudly, patronizingly. – And we are its masters. And you, you two are the next in line, the two next children of the gods. And you can't even show your Queen proper respect.

– I'm sorry, mother, the girl said. – We…

– Silence! The Queen stopped her with a fierce move of the hand. – I order flagellated lowly palace servants not kneeling properly. So what then, my children, shall I do with you?

– P-please, m-mother, the boy sniveled.

She grabbed him, grabbed them both. Pain shot through them, as she squeezed them with her invisible hands, her godly power. They wanted to scream, but they couldn't release a single sound.

Hands let go, and they fell to floor, sobbing in terror and relief, and sensing the hard ball inside hardening further.

– You will learn, she said softly. – Learn the ways of Power, its pitfalls and joy.

It was as if she… changed then, as she and the room faded away, as if her attention shifted a little, from the two children, to the spirits floating in the void, as the strange and so familiar light was lit in her eyes.

He sensed it immediately, the stench of burning flesh in his nostrils. They sailed down the river in a blink of an eye, and were cast ashore on this place, this place of Death and suffering. Mist dissolved and many a tall fire pierced the sky, and it was a sight horrible beyond belief.

The many screams resounded in their ears and souls. Ted, or he who would one night become Ted blinked with sore eyes. The heavy smoke hurt them, just as much as his wounds hurt his hide. A long line of pyres lit up the yard outside the large castle. He blinked and saw the witches being burned, rows and rows of them. One man walked along rows of witches, lighting their pyres with an oozing torch. Liz, she who would one day be Liz was the last in line, bound to a stake on the largest pyre.

A large congregation was gathered here, to enjoy the festivities. A regal figure sat on a throne-like chair, the resident, presiding bishop. The girl struggled against the ropes, wild panic in her eyes, but she was bound tight, and struggled in vain. The boy knew that, somehow, as he worked his own bonds, as skin and blood flowed freely from his body and fell to the ground.

The man with the torch stopped before the last witch. The honorable bishop rose and by lifting a hand silenced the mocking cries from the large crowd. Burnings were great entertainment. For every new day of cleansing the crowd had grown, until now, on the final day, the entire yard was filled with shouting, shallow people.

– This is harsh but necessary punishment, the bishop cried. – Neither the good people of this town nor I are to blame for this. The witches and their warlocks have brought this upon themselves, by serving Satan, by giving themselves to the infernal realms.

The boy gagged in a burst of laughter.

– Your pretty, pretty speeches have always impressed me, he shouted at the bishop. – It has always inspired the godhood in me.

– You mock, warlock. The man on the throne raised a finger. – But beware, your destiny will be far more horrible than all your witches combined.

– They are not my witches you insane…

He was struck in the ribs by two of the guards. But the blows were not very hard, because his voice had changed in mid-sentence, turned deeper and ghostly. He used the opportunity to work on his bonds, work in a frenzied state of beyond desperation, beyond panic. Strange and alien thoughts flooded his mind. The tears flowing down his cheeks began burning his skin.

– LIGHT THE PYRE, the bishop shouted dramatically.

– LIGHT THE PYRE, the crowd echoed.

The man with the torch stuck it in the dry heap of wood and hay, and it caught fire immediately.

– NO! The boy cried, falling on his knees, as the guards let go of him and everybody laughed cruelly.

The flames licked the girl's feet and everybody turned… turned… *to enjoy the show*. The boy jumped up. He grabbed a man's sword and killed him with it, jumping away from there in one mighty jump, heading for the pyre and the girl.

– STOP HIM! The bishop shrieked.

The boy killed the first two attempting to block his way in one single blow, and went head to head with the blur of men between him and the girl. The girl's screams grew louder, and it cut into him as hard as the blade he wielded. He brushed a man aside, cut off yet another man's head, but they were so many. He doubled, redoubled his efforts, but he never seemed to come any closer.

Two pair of fireeyes met, as he made his heart-wrenching, horrible decision.

*– Forever!*

He cried, lifting the sword, his threatening, savage appearance halting the advance of the soldiers.

– Forever! She replied, in a coarse, but strangely strong voice.

He turned, and jumped towards the bishop. The flames surrounded the girl now, and her screams were cut off abruptly. He landed right in front of the bishop, and penetrated his heart in one, mighty thrust. The guards rushed in from all sides, stabbing him with their swords. He twisted the blade. The bishop screamed. Ted Warren stared into the eyes of Eugene Kendall.

– You're not the mind behind this, all this, the boy gasped. – I know him, and you're not him. You're just another tool, another *servant*.

And impossibly enough, as both he and the bishop breathed their last, as they slowly fell to the ground, he turned and stared at the crowd, catching the eyes of the tall man with the gray braid.

– WE'RE COMING FOR YOU, his voice like Thunder shouted. – Your days are numbered! We're *coming* for you, JAHAVALO!

And the Earth and the ether shook and quivered. The bishop hit the ground, dead and done. The boy died. The girl died. There was a wrenching pain, and it felt like dying, like being born, and what was not flesh rose from their bodies, and behind the veil Jahavalo appeared, too, waiting for them. They brushed his advances off as if they were nothing, and attacked him with claws of night and fire. And on the other side of the veil, in the castle yard the man with the gray braid crouched and screamed. He backed off in absolute panic, there on the verge of the Shadow Realm, the world beyond, pulling away from their boundless Wrath.

– Who ARE you? He screamed in despair and desperation and incredulity.

They rose and joined their bigger shadows. He caught just a glimpse of them, as they briefly appeared, before once more fading away.

– We are the Adversary, they choired. – We know you. We are your Enemy. One day, soon, there will be a reckoning. We are COMING FOR YOU, JAHAVALO

There was frantic knocking on the door. Ted and Liz' eyes flung open there on the bed.

– Hey, what's going ON in there? An angry voice shouted from the hallway.

They sat there on the bed, gasping for air, feeling as if their bodies had been turned inside out. Each breath was an ordeal, and there never seemed to be enough air. Cold Sweat kept pouring from their skin like acid. They fell back. She hit the wall, and he fell off the bed and down on the floor. Her lips moved a few times before they were finally able to form words.

– Go fuck yourself, she shouted at the door with venom in her voice.

She could practically visualize how the fat man outside backed off in horror.

Ted shook his head in repeated attempts to clear it. But at the same time he felt clearer than ever.

– Too bad he didn't come in. We need to feed. We would have sucked him dry. We need to feed slowly.

Confused thoughts and imagery and conflicting emotions and desires continued to race through their minds.

– That was incredible, she cried. – That was terrible. It keeps playing before my eyes. I can hardly believe it. I do, with all my heart. I *know,* know beyond any doubt.

He fought himself up on his knees, had to try several times before he even managed that much. She crawled to him across the bed, and they embraced, shaking like leaves. Only slowly, slowly they reached a somewhat tranquil state.

– Yes, now we know, he nodded. – Now, there's no turning back.

– There never was, she said.

Forever, his eyes said.

Forever, her eyes replied.

– You're covered by dust, he said.

– You, too, she said. – Covered by Dust.

She touched it, brushed it off his brow. It stuck to her fingers for a while, but then it seemed to… dissolve before their eyes, and once again realization lit their eyes.

They showered again, washed each other in slow, lazy strokes. The towels were still wet, so they used the sheets to dry themselves, not bothering with doing a very thorough job of it. It was night outside. They were already out there, walking the streets, before actually leaving the room, before they took the elevator down and walked through the reception area, and hit the wall of heat outside. Their skin and hair dried in seconds, in the smoldering heat of the desert night. They touched people's skin briefly as they passed them on the busy sidewalk and felt the bursts of energy as soft lightning to their system. It did the job. It healed and invigorated them until the stiffness and pain in their limbs were practically gone. Filled with Hunger as they were, they didn't have to consciously drain anybody for a while to make it work. It expanded their senses further. Their surroundings invaded them, as they invaded their surroundings.

– We've been here only a few hours, she said, her voice thick with gratification, – and we've already made this city our home.

And people hardly noticed. A brief pain on the spot of contact, a momentary weakness, that was all.

– It *lingers,* she noted, smiling. – Lingers, even as it's fading. Just now I caught a flash of us walking through the streets of San Francisco. It feels eerie. It's many years from now, and we're not alone, but surrounded by… by *others*. There are fireeyes and other strangers. I can feel the exalted mood like a tangible force. «We never went to California», you ponder. «We never set our feet there».

Ted had seen many pictures and movies from San Francisco, and when he concentrated he could see what she saw, sense what she sensed, and hear the music.

«There are good times, too», the young woman with black eyes cried in front of a strange-looking castle on a lake, in a place that was definitely not San Francisco. «And this is a good time, one long in waiting».

They visited several other casinos, played a little, won some and lost some, didn't bother to strain themselves.

There was a row of plastic flowers in one reception area.

– Look at this, Liz cried. – What a glorious collection of fake flowers.

– Aren't they adorable? A woman with blue hair whined.

– They are disgusting, Liz snarled.

Ted noted amazed and pleased that there was no true malice in her voice, only a healthy contempt for the artificial life they found here.

And she still danced, still sang, as she walked through the valley of death.

– It's amazing, she marveled. – Everything here is fake. All both urban and rural areas are to some extent, but Las Vegas takes it to an unprecedented, all time high. Even the organic tissue actually being organic tissue is wrong, wrong beyond words.

They eventually moved upwards, from the strip to Downtown, not bothering to catch a taxi, but using the 24/7 Boulevard bus service. There were a lot of people on the bus, and the two of them bathed in the air's ambient energies. They didn't even have to touch anyone skin to skin in this pool of refreshing water. It felt like dying. It felt like too much life, and it burned them, as it freed their perception, as it burned their mind.

– One touch, she whispered. – One touch is all it takes… to beckon eternity.

And the Hunger beckoned in her eyes.

They never allowed themselves to forget the Hunger, its joy and pitfalls.

It was always there, burning in their gut.

They stepped off the bus in seedy Downtown, fresh as flowers, heading down Fremont Street towards the casinos.

– Look! She cried. – A Magick shop. And it's even open.

She looked at a dark part of the street, a place crowded in shadow, where the neon lights just didn't reach.

It was a special place. Ted nodded to himself, feeling yet another thrill of the moment. They walked inside.

They both noticed it. It was like entering another world. There was music, dark and mysterious. It echoed within them from the very first moment. The two of them spotted no electrical lights. Candles cast their muted light across the room. Incense rubbed pleasantly the inside of their nostrils, evoking images and impressions of distant places and times. They looked around, exalted, seeing nothing here that wouldn't have totally curled a christian's toe.

There were two people behind the counter, a man and a woman, dressed in black. The store was about half full, all the potential present customers clearly not the average citizen. Liz and Ted shamelessly studied the others present. Most looked away, but not all. She grabbed a boy. He grabbed a girl.

Making them face them.

– What is your name? They choired softly.

– B-brad, the boy replied.

– Justine, the girl whispered.

– I rather thought so, Ted grinned.

She blushed. She wasn't some helpless innocent, he easily saw that, but she blushed to the point that it was clearly visible through the heavy make up.

Liz kissed Brad, straight and right to the point, no hesitation, no pretense. She was taller than he was, and she held him in a tight grip. Ted began undressing Justine. He did so slowly, unhurriedly. She didn't offer even the slightest sign of objection. On the contrary. She revealed ever more of her excitement for every new fabric he pulled off her.

There was a sound, unmistakable, from the door, the sound of it being locked, from it clearly locking itself. The people gathered in the room froze.

Justine stood there naked. Brad, too, a few seconds later. They shook in need. There were fourteen other people in the room, including the two behind the counter. They all stared at the two ravens in their midst. There was fear. There was endless excitement, a curiosity that couldn't be denied. The male behind the counter attempted to speak, but his voice failed him.

Ted and Liz began to undress, casually, enticingly. He kept his attention on Justine as he did so, his cock rising the moment he pulled down his underwear. He kept his attention on them all. They all felt the stare. It was a tangible, physical thing, paralyzing everybody. Brad closed his eyes briefly as Liz touched him, drawing breath abruptly. She walked to the other males, touching them, as her companion did with the females.

– I just bet you have a large, cozy bed somewhere, she said to the woman behind the counter. – Take us there. Take us there, now.

– Yes, my Goddess. The girl whispered and curtseyed. – At once, my Goddess.

– You are so sweet, Liz grinned. – Such a sweet child. You will serve us well.

She hurried in front, and everybody hurried after her, some glancing uncertain at each other, but still hurrying. They entered a large bedroom, also lit by candles. The bed *was* large, more than big enough for the lot of them. It was placed in a corner, nicely and unassumingly. The two Warrens raised their hands in a dramatic gesture. Most of the others didn't notice what was happening at first, but they knew something happened. And then they froze and stared in earnest.

The carpet began… Something *happened* to the carpet. It was torn along a line at the center of the floor. Then there were several lines joining the one, forming a pentagram, and then a circle was drawn at its points, forming a pentacle. Four of those present backed off, to avoid being caught inside. The large pentacle made up major parts of the room.

– Fate delivered this moment to you, Ted told them. – It's up to you to seize it.

The bed rose into the air, easily, as if grabbed by a mighty hand. There were loud, startled, terrified and amazed gasps.

– You can be afraid, be the little mouse afraid of the cat, or you can grab life by the tail, and never look back.

The bed settled on the floor, on the pentacle, surrounded by its wide circle.

– Behold the circle of the witch, Liz said. – One of danger, mystery and imagination.

Her voice turned ghostly and dark. A couple held on to each other, sore afraid.

– Go! Ted snarled at them. – Crawl into your hole and stay there, for the rest of your miserable life.

They hurried out. Ted and Liz turned to the rest, and touched them, touched them without hands, without skin, harshly, tenderly, invasive, in all ways and none. The two of them crossed into the circle and entered the bed.

– Come here, Liz called lazily, with a dwelling, teasing smile.

And they came, with fear and longing and need warring in their hearts. Justine rushed in front of Ted, eagerly presenting herself to him, her eyes glazed over and sharp simultaneously. Brad came to Liz. The two Warrens looked at their charges, hungry as wolves. The others came, some slowly, some faster.

– Form a circle around us, Liz bade them. – Hold hands and don't let go.

The circle formed, and they held hands. Ted and Liz sensed it, even felt it the moment the circle completed itself. A happy, exuberant smile transformed Liz' face into the sun, into the moon, into fire and mystery. She directed her attention completely at Brad and she put a palm on his chest. He shivered in apprehension and anticipation and thousands of other, less identifiable emotions.

– Your touch b-burns, he whimpered.

There was movement, as the other two also began their dance, their coupling of fire, but he didn't hear any words, didn't really see any movement, except the implication of one. Burning hands touched breasts, he knew that, but he didn't see it. But he felt it, a powerful jolt in his gut. He saw the eyes in front of him, though, saw them lit up like a dark sun.

– Isn't it supposed to? She replied softly. – Isn't all skin in truth fire, waiting to be lit? Yours is. I can feel it, you know, feel it come to life.

He looked down on his cock, the most obvious proof of his growing desire. She grabbed it then, took it in her strong hand. He gasped and cried out, making the entire circle cry out with him. His entire frame shook, and he took that one, crucial step forward, into her embrace, touching her with the entire front of his body.

– Yes, she said pleased. – Now, your touch burn, now, your entire skin is inflamed with need.

They fell on their knees, as the two invisible forms by their side fell as well, all four touching and embracing. Justine writhed in Ted's arms, shuddered as he touched her, crying out in wild abandon. Brad forgot everything, except the enticing form before him. Ted and Liz felt it, felt the Power rise, felt it rise in them, and they welcomed it.

– Now, break the circle, Ted bade them all. – Come to us, all of you. Come to the flame and burn in its heat.

And the circle of bodies broke up and became a sea, a sea of flesh, writhing and howling, there, on the surface of the black satin.

Moans and gasps and growls and grunts filled the room, filled sensitive ears. Liz rocked on a male. Sweat filled her eyes, filled Ted's eyes, as he pulled and pushed on a female in front of him, as the two Warrens stared at each other with absolute clarity. This is it, she thought, he thought. This is how it should be. They swam in a sea of bodies, and ecstasy dominated their entire perception, and there was no recrimination, no regret. Power filled them.

Power without guilt. A natural state of being they had longed for so long, but never quite achieved, until this wretched night.

A male filled her, filled her up, and she cried out in ecstasy, in a pleasure undreamed of. Ted felt the females' curves against his hips as he filled them up, as he flooded them, as he washed them in his sea. Pain exploded in his frontal lobe. He gasped. She gasped. The air changed around them, suddenly filled with… with Dust. Everybody collapsed on the large bed, entangled in the sea of bodies, of burning flesh. Happy, content moans rose from the bed, dancing in the room of shadows and fire and mist. Bodies caressed one another in a long, joyous aftermath stretching into the rust and blood of the dawn.

## 2

They reluctantly untangled from the heap of bodies, the bittersweet touch of skin. Both were wide-awake. Every bit of fatigue they had ever felt was like gone with the wind, as if it had never been. Sleep was far away and they suspected it had never been further away. They studied each other, bathing in each other's glowing eyes.

Water embraced them. They weren't really taking a shower. They were diving deep below the sea, into a place where there was no light, only seething, unending fire. Even when there was no more water it was there, sliding off their skin. They stepped out of the bathroom, already dry.

Justine knelt on the floor. There was no more fear, only a smile, euphoria revealed in her eyes and all over her body, in every small move she made.

The others, stretching pleasantly on the bed, got up and knelt as well, echoing the happy servitude in Justine.

Liz and Ted glanced at each other, and that glance spoke volumes.

– This is yet another junction, I suppose, she queried.

– I would assume it is, he nodded. – Yet another in a long line.
– Too much of that and your knees get sore, he said to them, couldn't bring himself to say more.
They looked uncertain at him at first, until it dawned on them, until they realized that he was truly, sort of joking. Everybody rose on somewhat unsteady, but strong feet. They stepped down from the bed and on to the floor and stared at the two, and the two calmly returned the stare.
– We have very few answers to the questions we see in your eyes, Liz said. – We're looking for them ourselves.
– But we have learned a few important facts, he said.
– We don't want servitude, she said. – Not in any shape or form.
– You were slightly wrong about us, he said. – That's okay. We were slightly wrong ourselves.
Justine stepped close to him, pushing herself at him, kissing him on the lips. And as the ice broke, the others rushed forward as well, and they all stood there, embracing, bonding further.
– Fate delivered this moment to us, Justine said.
– It's up to us to seize it, Brad said.
– It's funny, another man somberly grinned. – I was about to leave the store several minutes earlier, but I changed my mind.
Slowly, painfully the mood of solemnity and awe changed, into something resembling how it should have been in the first place. Ted and Liz felt relief, tinged with apprehension.
– We live dangerous lives, Ted said. – I'm not sure we did you any favor.
– You did, Brad stated, taking his hands. – No matter what happens next, I'll never forget this night.
Stephen, the owner, a man in his early forties looked at the two with a tint of sadness in his eyes.
– You're both very young, he noted, – but you've had your share of grief, and then some. I can't imagine what you must have gone through to become what you have become.
That's right, Ted thought. You can't!
– We've always been like this, Liz stated proudly.
They all looked at each other, finally becoming aware of each other, laughing, giggling, bonding. The two Warrens actually felt it, like a tangible wave washing over them.
A girl looked down at herself.
– I'm *sticky* all over. She shook her head, grinning even wider. – Is there only one shower here?
– I'm afraid so, Stephen confirmed. – I guess we have to use it together in groups of four or so to get cleaned up fairly quickly.
And eyes once again turned misty and excited.
– You have fun, kids, Liz grinned. – We gotta go. There's a poker game waiting for us.
– A… poker game? Brad gaped.

– Precisely. We have an appointment at eleven, I believe, at Binion Horseshoe Casino, and we don't want to be late.

– You're all invited to dinner at Tropicana tonight, Ted said lightly. – Please come. It will be a blast…

And with those words they left behind the boys and girls of the heated night, the boys and girls more stunned than ever.

Their clothes lay exactly where they had left them, on the floor in the outer room, and they dressed. People passing by outside stared, but they ignored that.

There was a necklace with a pentacle pendant under the glass cover of the desk. She walked behind the counter and opened it, picked up the necklace and put it around her neck.

– Such is the witch. She nodded, to herself, to him. – Wearing Satan's mark on her chest.

– You did everything tonight just for that? He said sourly. – Why couldn't you just *buy* the damn thing?

A thrilling laughter rewarded his witty remark.

They stepped outside, into the desert heat, with an afterthought locking the door behind them, continuing the walk down Fremont Street, interrupted so joyfully last night.

– Many of them will die, he said. – Die early, because of us.

– They will live, because of us, she said.

The early morning sunshine already baked Fremont Street in its heat. Totally unfiltered it hit the humans hurrying between buildings.

Las Vegas was quiet, or quieter, in the morning. There were fewer people, both in the streets and inside the casinos, and they were not that loud.

They had the twenty-four hour breakfast on the second floor at Four Queens. It was an uncommonly tasty meal and they actually enjoyed it. But then again, they enjoyed almost everything these days.

– Weird, she giggled. – We're actually having breakfast, during breakfast time…

The feeding proceeded in silence, in a raging fever of more or less random thoughts and insight.

– I wonder about the seeds, he said. – Where they are coming from, what their origin is.

– They will have to be very powerful to affect us the way they do, she pondered, leaning back a little. – One would suspect they have been grown and groomed for that very purpose. Much more so than then those used to heal and cleanse wounds.

There was more silence. They sat there, just enjoying each other's company. For a while that was enough.

– We fucked up, he said, – by allowing them to worship us, by not giving a damn about them, about nothing but our own gratification.

– Yes, she nodded. – But perhaps that turned out to be a healthy turn of events, both to them and us, teaching us all more about mechanisms of oppression. We can all learn more about that, about that, too.

She ran ahead a bit, and began dancing in the street before him. He knew she enjoyed that, loved that, and not just to display herself to him and others, but because of the freedom each and every move gave her. It echoed within him, and he envied her her youth and relative innocence. She was far younger than him than the four years in physical age.

– Dance with me, she called.

– What?

He had major difficulties responding to her, both verbally and at all, as he didn't trust either his voice or his flesh.

– Dance with me. Let us dance hard and fast and soft. Let us create the world.

He did. It wasn't hard. He had learned dancing, learned the steps and its intuitive moves. It was easy. He just let himself go, and allowed his body to take over, just like sex. It wasn't hard at all.

They danced on, and it felt like hours to them, two ghost dancers creating the universe. The surroundings faded into nothing, into unimportance. Threads of fire and shadow sizzled in the slipstream of their bodies and mind.

– What are we going to do with you? She asked in his ear. – You're so tight-woven that I feel you might break anytime.

– And yet I feel as if you're the vulnerable one, he said. – You haven't seen what I've seen, endured what I have endured, and I fear you will.

– But I want to, she said.

He stared at her, startled.

– Well, not exactly, perhaps. She bowed her head. – But I want to be like you, to catch up with you, with your pain. I want to be a razorblade cutting through everything, with you, and you're ahead of me, and I can never quite measure up without that.

She raised her head again, staring intensely, even more intensely than she usually did, into his twin pair of eyes.

He just shook his head, unable to voice his worry, his contempt.

– You're just a spoiled brat, he snarled.

She wanted to strike him, hammer her fists against his chest, but he caught them and held them, held them hard.

– Never say that, she whispered. – Please, never say that, My Lord.

He held on, and squeezed, unable to help himself.

– Perhaps you're afraid of me growing up, she whimpered, she whispered harshly. – Perhaps you won't *like* the sight very much.

She kissed him, kissed him hard on the lips, drawing blood. He let go of her and embraced her, as she buried her claws in his back and held on. They stood there in the merciless sunlight, unfazed by the smoldering heat.

The air-conditioned casino felt so chilly afterwards, like the coldest of tombs.

There were lights in there, thousands of glittering lights, cast between the red, red walls.

– This place hasn't changed much, she remarked. – It needs an interior architect more than ever.

Many heard her. They couldn't avoid doing that, with her loud voice.

It was nine o'clock in the morning. There weren't queues this early. The best game they could find was a $100/$200 limit hold'em table, which was okay. They felt a little insecure and this was a level they could deal with. Them included there were eight players around the table, not quite full. They studied the other players, as they knew they were being studied in return.

This was different than with the roulette. The two of them couldn't just sit down and pick up the money. Their enhanced empathy allowed them to read people's emotions, but they still had to interpret what they sensed, and there were people, like several of the seasoned pros around this table that had made it an art form to hide their emotions. Some of them had developed it to such a degree that it wasn't just their faces anymore, but their insides as well.

It was a challenge, and the two Warrens grabbed it by the balls, more eager than ever to succeed.

– Not much action this early in the morning, is there? Liz grinned. – Vegas does seem to sleep, after all…

After a while they became a little bit impatient, so they began «trash talking», to disturb whatever serenity there was around the table. It had no discernible effect on two of the players, but the rest were clearly affected by it, and began slipping, open up inside, with bursts of irritation and well suppressed rage, but rage nonetheless, and they instantly became easier to read. The two sensed it, flares rising from their depths.

It took them about two hours to clean the table. Not totally. That was never done. There would always be players left. But they, too, were quite demoralized.

– Not much action around here these days, is there? Liz said aloud, putting just the right amount of scorn into her voice.

They quit the table and collected the ten thousand dollars win, a fairly good one on this level. The remaining players were beaten anyway, and hardly dared playing against them.

When they went to collect their money, a voice was heard from the depths of the room.

– What an Amazon, one of the losing players exclaimed in disgust, loud enough for anyone in the room to hear.

Liz grabbed Ted's arm lightly.

– I hope you don't feel like you have to defend your girl's honor or something…

She grinned, calming the sudden, inevitable rage inside them both.

As they casually put their thick rolls of bills into their pockets a man approached them, approached them carefully. They stopped, eying him openly. It didn't particularly faze him, and their interest was piqued.

– Ted Warren? Liz Warren?

– That's absolutely correct, Mister, Liz said impressed. – What is it to you, if I may ask?

He handed each of them a card. They both put it away without looking at it.

– My name is Roger Preston. I'm currently in the employ of Richard Hagman. He and some other gentlemen are engaged in a private game upstairs, and they would like the two of you to join them.

Ted looked at his watch, deliberately, without bothering to hide it. The time was eleven o'clock precisely. He grinned.

– That's so generous of Mr. Hagman, Liz said. – By all means, lead on.

They followed him upstairs. It was quite the walk. This was a rather large place, even though it couldn't compare to Tropicana and the other mega-casinos. The surroundings changed from the red walls and carpets, the blood theme below, to a more restrained standard. But, strangely enough, to the two Warrens it took an even more intimidating meaning. Ted noticed how Liz shivered imperceptibly just before Roger Preston opened the door to the fairly small, darkened room, where only the green felt was lit. He knew no one else noticed, but he easily did.

The door opened to them. The room opened up to them. The table became the entire room, became its shadows and breath.

Four men sat around the table, in its peripheral shadows. Two seats were empty. Another thrill shot through Ted. This was shorthand poker, six players around the table instead of the usual ten, a more ruthless form, because it demanded action of a player far more often.

– May I present Ted and Liz Warren, gentlemen, Preston said, as he stopped by the table and everyone looked up.

There were presentations and handshaking. Ted and Liz hadn't cared much for handshaking earlier in their lives, as it was way too traditional for their taste, but now they had changed their minds, because they knew what it could do for them, for them alone. One brief contact spoke a thousand words.

Richard Hagman, Phillip Caine, Anthony La Grande and Zarkon Zimbalist.

Hagman was the man with the big money, a very typical industrialist and mogul, with a deeper twist not easily discerned, not even by a Warren handshake.

– We play No Limit hold'em here, he bragged patronizingly. – $1000/$2000 forced blinds.

– That suits our wallets quite well, Richard, Ted grinned grimly.

– Then I wish you welcome to our little game, Hagman nodded mercifully, a grim satisfaction present in his eyes and voice.

Ted «recognized» Phillip Caine immediately, even though they had never met. Except for him being one more generation removed from his Mexican ancestry, he quite resembled his father. Ted sensed resentment, one bordering on hatred, and it wasn't difficult to know why.

– We have already met. Liz smiled sweetly upon taking Phillip's hand. – You do remember me, don't you, Phillip?

– I remember you, he said hoarsely.

– Phillip is one of the best up and coming players in town these days, Hagman said pleasantly. – Already surpassing his father, the way I see it.

Caine was young, about Ted's age, but he seemed older, calmer and more collected.

But it was a sham, a mask. Liz sensed his seething insides, what even his years of training in masking his emotions and expressions could not hide, not from her.

They sat down and the game began, one played just as much in the shadows of the mind, as on the bright green felt. Ted had two aces on his hand. On the table was one more ace, two fives, one four and an eight. Ted bet first. Hagman pondered for a while, and then raised quite the substantial amount. There was a wall there, suddenly between Ted and his chips. He forced himself to call, even though he didn't want to. He wanted to see Hagman's cards.

Hagman showed two fives and took the pot.

Ted mucked his cards without revealing them.

The game began. Slowly, surely Ted and Liz gained confidence, in their birthright and in themselves, as it pertained to the Poker table. Ted had an ace and a five matched by the two cards on the table. But there was also three hearts there, making Hagman a possible flush. Ted called his steep bet at the end. Hagman had been bluffing and Ted took the pot.

– Pretty good play there, son, Hagman nodded. – I bet pretty hard to get you out.

The two Warrens identified more and more emotions in their opponents. They were wrong on occasion, but increasingly less so.

Liz flirted with Phillip and beat him almost every time they had a showdown. It was like reading an open book. To her it was.

– That is so cruel of me, she teased him, as she took the pot, another pot from his shaky grasp.

Eventually he was steaming so much that he actually left the table, left it with himself in shambles, not those around the table, an act, an event that was spoken about in Vegas for years.

Hagman was clearly very pleased with something after that, so pleased that he almost got impossible to read. This in spite of him having lost a substantial amount of money. His weird enjoyment overshadowed the variation in his emotion they needed to identify in order to make him a fairly easy mark. So they had to focus hard on their actual poker skills in order to keep up with him.

– As I was saying, just before you two arrived, a long prepared plan of mine is finally becoming to fruition…

– And what plan is that, sir? Liz flirted openly.

And it had no effect whatsoever on him, and that shocked her.

– It's an expedition, my dear, he revealed willingly, – into the depths of the South American jungle. I've looked long and hard for a place down there that's supposed to hold untold riches.

– You want us to join you… on a treasure hunt?

– Precisely. The «treasure hunt» part of it isn't that important, though. I certainly don't need the money, and neither do you, I suspect. No, we all need something more, something driving us from early childhood.

He looked almost demonic, there, in his seat, and they listened.
– So, I have, for some time, now, been gathering a team of adventurous young people like yourselves. Zarkon and Anthony here, and Phillip, and others. We would all love for you to join us.
– I've heard you love to surround yourself with young, pretty people, Liz remarked casually, pointedly.
There was a glitch then, in his carefree mask. Liz sensed the passion within, sensed how it exploded.
– You don't have to decide immediately, he said generously. – In fact my plane isn't taking off from New Orleans until November 21st. It's a big, private jet. There's room for everybody invited.
– And you have invited a *score*. Ted nodded.
– I most certainly have. I've always found it great to have a lot of interesting people to keep me company.
They had read about him. He didn't just usually surround himself with an entire collection of selected people, but was obsessed by it. Most rich people did something similar, surrounding themselves with hundreds of «friends», but he had taken it to a different level entirely.
The poker game faded eventually, fairly quickly, by lack of interest, no longer being the focal point of the gathering. The three once again shook hands with the two and the two willingly obliged.
– He isn't telling us the whole truth, Liz commented.
They walked through the heat again, towards the bus stop.
– Who is? Ted shook his head. – We're living in a world of smoke and mirrors, and we just have to accept that fact.
They had to wait a while for the bus. She kept pacing, clearly agitated or bothered with something. He waited patiently.
– When we… before we entered the room… the door… leered at me.
Her voice shook.
– It made me… reluctant to enter the room. It fucking *scared me!*
She paced some more.
– Our powers are the same. So why do you think I got the shivers and not you? That should mean something, right?
– You had a premonition, he said. – Of something relating to you, and not necessarily to me. It's evidently related to Hagman or someone else in the room. We'll just ignore his «invitation». It's no big deal.
– No, it isn't.
She shrugged, calming down, but not looking at him.
– If we had acted on every bad feeling we've had, we would never have left the cradle.
She said.
And turned towards him.
It was once more night in Las Vegas. A fairly diverse group of people gathered around the large table set by Liz and Ted Warren. Everybody they had invited came. That surprised them and pleased them to no end.

The sound of glasses meeting and parting, a lot of times, a lot of excited talk, resounded in the room, inevitably observed from the other tables in the large dining room, with envious and malicious eyes.

Justine had removed a lot of make-up, and looked distinctly different. She held up a bare arm, smiling with parted lips.

– Look at me. I've got goose bumps all over.

There was laughter, the thunder rising above the crowd, spreading across the room and to the street. Other people kept staring at them, condemning them, but they didn't care.

Liz looked up and he stood there, staring at her.

– Oh, hello, Phillip, she cried, very loud.

– Hello, he mumbled, looking very uncomfortable just then.

– Sit with us, she offered. – Join us in our feast.

They made room for him, and he sat down, joined them in the broken circle.

And they were one more. And it was no big deal. He blended in, and soon he fit in as well. He was one of them. Liz kissed him softly on the cheek, with dark stars in her eyes.

Dinner arrived, a large steak with a dark, crispy hide. Expectation rose a few more notches. Everything seemed enhanced tonight, enlarged, bigger than life, even as they startled realized that nothing truly was.

– A toast… Justine stood up, raising her glass. – One to unsung heroes, to those condemned by society, who continue to make their mark on the world. There is tradition in our circle to toast for the dead of our kind. My choice tonight is Ulrike Meinhof. May her fight continue in her next life!

– Meinhof? Ted exclaimed. – She is dead…?

The others nodded, looking curiously at the two Warrens.

– Boy, have we been out of touch lately, Liz whistled.

– It isn't exactly broadcast through main television, a boy said. – It isn't strange that you missed it. Most people have. We got the news through our own, special grapevine.

– The guards in the Stammheim prison killed her, Stephen said. – The German authorities masked it as a suicide and have continued to claim that, even after all the evidence to the contrary surfacing afterwards. They can, as usual get away with murder, without repercussions.

– Oh, there will be repercussions, Ted swore.

And he sounded so sure, so absolutely confident, and everybody present that evening froze and shook.

– Strange, isn't it? Brad pondered. – To feel sorrow for the death of a person we don't know, and have never met.

– But we do know her, Liz stated softly.

And goose bumps erupted on everybody's skin.

– To Ulrike Meinhof! Justine cried, as they all rose. – The sister we have always known and we one night will know again.

– TO ULRIKE MEINHOF! They choired.

And a thousand glasses met and parted.

It was later that same evening. The group had regrouped to a fake fireplace in a corner. Liz shook her head and smiled, and the others couldn't tell why. But then again, they never could.

– This is weird, a Phillip that had gotten way too much to drink exclaimed. – I feel like I have known you guys my entire life.

– Haven't you? Stephen asked.

And now everybody knew why Ted and Liz were smiling.

The evening, the night lingered and ended only very reluctantly.

Ted and Liz stumbled in each other's arms towards their hotel room without being quite able to tell how they had ended up there. They remembered the others like ghosts in their mind, and they were, sort of. The time, the time was now.

– We seek them out, don't we, Liz mumbled at his shoulder, – like sniffing wolves? And they come to us as well. They will always come to us.

There was a powerful, cold draft, a suction pulling at them throughout their walk down the hallway. At one moment, when Ted opened the door, it was almost pulled out of his grip. He closed the door behind them and made sure he locked it.

– I'm so tired, Liz said. – I feel so good, so very good.

They undressed slowly, not really in a hurry. The chilled air in the room ruffled pleasantly their body hairs, their resting feathers. They lay down on the bed, entwined, breathing the same air, and quickly, almost without noticing, they finally fell into a deep, dreamless sleep.

# Chapter Four: The whispering desert

FROM THE ANNALS OF DAVID WARREN - BORN 2061

*Our story runs deep...*

*Thousands of years into the past something happened. A door, no, a portal opened, and gave way to something dangerous, something inevitable, infinitely precious.*

*We are the Wild made flesh, untamable, a primal scream in what may pretend to be an orderly existence.*

*Humanity has sought too long and too far outside themselves, and misplaced their way. But we have come now. We have always been here, with them, always been them, even through the rise of civilization, and we will be with them through its fall. We were there, at the beginning of the Universe, and we will be there at its end. And Beyond. We are what survives.*

*I've heard it be argued, and I believe it to be true, that Life is the Universe made flesh. But if there is something to it we are the Universe's return... its return to Fire. After all the embers have been put out, all the ashes spread with the wind...*

*We are still There. We will always be here. Kill a thousand of us, kill billions, it doesn't matter. Is it possible to kill Life, to extinguish Fire?*

*The resurrection dreams are always with me. I can hear the flapping of wings, sense the heat burn in the wettest of oceans. In the sea of eternity the Phoenix is waiting, biding Its time, waiting for the moment to burn, to rise from the ashes of its own fire.*

*What has already happened is waiting to happen again.*

2

It was broad daylight when Liz took the bus alone, to downtown Las Vegas. She studied the people outside the bus with keen, almost obsessed interest.

They were different from before. She was different. Her view of them had changed. Her eyes saw so much than before, saw the dark shapes dance around their earthly bodies, their vulnerable flesh. Clouds raced across the sky. Everything stood still while the Witch studied the world. And she realized startled that this was the world, the way it truly was, beneath and beyond appearances and illusions.

They looked so much more interesting, now, revealing so much more about themselves.

She was distracted to the point of her missing her bus stop. Suddenly, sweat poured from her skin. A moment of panic was enough to make it happen. She jumped off the bus at the next stop, impatience stuck in her throat until she stood totally unprotected in the Las Vegas streets, in the desert heat. Everybody brought a bottle of water with them here, and she was no exception. She opened it and drank deep, saving half of it just to be on the safe side. The bus had just brought her a block or so from her intended stop, but a block was an infinite distance here. The residents were fond of saying «oh, just a block or two» when being asked for directions, but what they saw as a short stretch was when using a car.

Phillip Caine waited for her in the shade outside Totrec Bar & sports book.

– You look… sweaty, sweetheart.

– Leaving the bus at the wrong stop can do that to you here.

He nodded.

– A short walk feels like miles, and the water in my bottle is *boiling*. Can you believe it?

– I can believe it, honey, he drawled. – I'm quite used to it.

She let him grab her and give her a kiss on the lips. He projected cockiness and confidence, but she saw straight through him, his façade of arrogance.

They walked into the bar. She breathed the stench of sweat and smoke and alcohol. This place was nothing like the fairly bright and classy casinos she had frequented. There was danger here, generalized, but clear and present.

He noticed her slight concern. That didn't surprise her. He was a profiler, after all. He read people.

– Perhaps this is a mistake? He casually hinted at.

– Certainly not, she said serious minded. – I told you I wanted you to show me the seedy parts of Vegas, did I not?

And he had done that much. She didn't need to take a closer look at the people frequenting this place to know that. It was basically the worst kind of strip joint, with a varnish of respectability. It, like the sight of the strippers, the sweaty nude dancers on the stage both attracted and repulsed her. Nausea swept over her, and she couldn't make it go away.

He noticed her interest. Of course he did, the astute bastard. She turned back to him, meeting his eyes, burning holes in him.

– Some of the dancers do it for the money, she said huskily, – while others clearly enjoy it, even excel in it. I can understand why. There is freedom in such a wild dance, even here, in a place like this.

He swallowed hard.

A waitress approached them.

– May I serve you anything? She said, wriggling her butt.

– Glenmorangie, straight up, please, Liz grinned darkly.

– The same for me, thanks, Phillip said quickly.

They smiled a bit to each other then.

What am I doing here? Liz thought. What the fuck am I doing here?

They were served drinks. The waitress kept wriggling her butt as if she was paid to do so (and she was). Liz wanted to ask her if she felt good with herself, but held her tongue, biting her lower lip.

– Make that a bottle! She ordered, she snapped.

The waitress' eyes turned big and scared.

– Are you serious? Philip wondered with concern and amazement in his eyes.
– Serious? She returned his scolding with a vengeance.
She lifted the small glass and cried out:
– Cheers, good fellow!
He lifted his own small glass. Glasses met and parted. She brought hers to her lips and holding it upside down, emptied the strong liquor into her mouth. He clearly hesitated, before doing the same. It burned, burned all the way down to her stomach and exploded there. A large, content grin spread on her face.
The bottle was put on the table, this time by a large, intimidating bruiser. Liz giggled, as she smiled seductively to him. She forgot about him and saw nothing but Phillip Caine's pretty eyes.
She poured another drink for them both. When she lifted her glass, seeing the challenge in her eyes, he did the same. She didn't say anything this time, but only brought the glass to her lips and drank.
It was some time later. The music machine was slightly wrong tuned or the right speaker was blown. At least there were jarring sounds coming from it, jarring her ears.
The bottle was half full. Caine was red-faced. He clearly had trouble forming syllables, and looked very uncomfortable.
It affected her, too, inevitably, the way she had poured it on, but he was stone drunk, and had major difficulties lifting the glass. The grin felt strange, with the numb lips and all. She rocked on the chair, rocked to the music.
– Are you brother and sister? He asked casually, hoarsely. – You and Ted, I mean.
He attempted to grab her hand in his stupor, but she easily avoided his clumsy attempt.
She emptied her glass again before replying, meeting his eyes, his swimming eyes.
– We are cousins and yes, in case you're wondering we fuck each other. We fuck each other senselessly, make each other burn in delightful ecstasy.
She sensed his hurt pride through the haze, and grinned in triumph.
– How could you *beat* me? He hissed. This time he caught her arm and squeezed, squeezed hard. – You're just a girl and I'm one of the best players in the world.
A twist of his arm and she had freed herself. He yelped, but hardly felt anything through the numbness of intoxication.
– Perhaps you should be a bit less confident in yourself and your abilities, and lay off with the sexism, she snorted icily. – Then you might accomplish something.
She rose. He attempted to look at her, but his eyes practically crossed each other. She laughed throatily.
– Nature calls. She bent down and gave him a feather-light kiss, letting him take a good look at her breasts, the seductive tone back in her voice. – I'll be right back, honey.

Crossing her feet more than actually walking, she stumbled across the floor towards the restroom, acutely aware of all the lusty, possessive stares following her. Fortunately the restroom was the first open door she arrived at. She fell into it more than entering it. The giggle sounded both loud and muted, and she couldn't decide which was which. She almost peed on herself. Sweet relief crossed her face as she pulled down her pants and sat down on the bowl, and the hot stream left her overfilled bladder and hissed as it hit the water below.

Mirror seemed cloudy, but she knew it wasn't the mirror when she turned and the room looked similar. This was wrong. She had been drunk before, and it had never had this effect on her. This was wrong. This was wrong.

A man grabbed her as she returned to the hallway. It was the big bruiser. She attempted to resist him, but he paralyzed her easily with a brutal strike at her ribs. He kept her on her feet, as he dragged her down the hallway, and into a room. A bedroom. Another bedroom. A woman waited right inside the door. It was the wriggling butt waitress. Liz felt the first pangs of fear, but so weak, oh, so weak.

– You must have put too little in the bottle, he swore. – It should have worked a long time ago.

– Don't give me that, the woman said sourly. – You saw her. She drank the poor guy under the table. It certainly worked wonders on him. It's obvious that she has the constitution of a horse. We evidently need to give her something extra.

Liz shook her head. She swam through a quicksand of thought. Panic gripped her. She wanted to do something, anything, but nothing worked. Not even her tongue. When she attempted to speak only gibberish came out. The woman approached her, with a syringe in her right hand.

– Don't be afraid, little girl. A comforting pat on the cheek. – There is no use being afraid. Powerful people have singled you out, and from this moment on you will no longer have any say over your own life.

– Your old friend, the Chief sends his love, the bruiser grinned widely. – He really wanted you, you know. He must have, since he has put up wanted posters of you everywhere, everywhere not public.

– And you have value beyond even that, sweet thing, the waitress said sweetly, viciously.

Fear, tangible and true gripped Liz, now. She struggled in the big man's grip, but he held her in a vice. He squeezed her wrists, making her cry out in pain. Hoping the pain would clear her mind she doubled her efforts, but the excruciating pain cursing through her paralyzed her further. She turned limp in the man's arms. The woman rolled up her sleeve, ready to set the needle, to push its horrible content into Liz' veins.

– Now, sweet thing. Now, everything will soon be all right.

Her mind cleared. A bolt of lightning struck her from below. She kicked at and hit, with deadly precision, the big man's feet, making him lose his balance. She saw it, saw it all in a single, horrible moment, experienced how they took her away, felt how they drugged her further… disconnecting her, chaining her and taking her to a truck filled with nude chained girls, bringing her to the Chief, to Morgan Lombard that was far more than what he had appeared to her, to a woman she couldn't quite picture in her mind, to a place called the Stable, a place in the desert where people, both men and women where destroyed, trained as playthings, reduced to servants, to slaves. And during it all she felt her own, sick surrender, her eventual eagerness to please her masters. She struck backwards with her elbow, hitting the bruiser in his ribs as he fell to the floor, breaking the ribs, crushing his ribcage in one brutal, vicious blow. Bright red lung blood flowed from his mouth. She didn't actually see that with her eyes, but she still saw it, in vivid, vivid color, and it felt so good. The woman attempted to stab her with the needle, but missed. Liz grabbed the woman's wrist, and with a terrible focusing of her power, she crushed the flesh and bone in her hand. The man on the floor died. He perished with every desperate breath he attempted to take. His death nourished her, strengthened her, and empowered her. She tore out the woman's throat with her nails, her long and sharp, sharp claws.

She stood there, breathing, the bright, insane taint slowly fading in her eyes. There were nails, metal nails here in the room, metal chairs. The metal chairs rose into the air and during a matter of seconds they were torn apart. The two bodies rose into the air. Liz pushed the male body at the lower part of the wall, pushed the nails she had made into his wrists and ankles and chest with loud, terrible sounds, and the dead man was nailed to the wall. The woman's body moved. Her bloody arm and hand moved like a brush across the wall, writing one telling sentence:

**I'M COMING FOR YOU, MORGAN!**

Then the woman's dead carcass was also nailed to the wall, under the writing, at her partner's side.

– A camera, Liz mumbled. – A kingdom for a camera. What composition, what art!

She took one step forward and almost fell, her knees almost giving in, her feet suddenly weak as rubber. She took another, firm step, her feet suddenly strong as steel. There was a choke, then a snarl, than a deadly, eerie calm in the dark fireeyes.

The music outside in the bar played on. She noticed it as a distant, unimportant afterthought.

She didn't need a mirror, knowing fully well how she looked, covered in blood. Their blood. Not her own. Think! Don't act before you have thought this through. She wanted to ignore the insistent voice in her head, wanted to go out there, revealing herself to the world. Speed. Speed was a necessity, but not at the sacrifice of rational thought. She was rational, was never more rational than in these decisive moments. *Undressing*. Her hands moved by themselves, removing her clothes, packing the bloody fabrics in a sheet, in several sheets, after picking the wallet, the clean wallet from a pocket. *Showering*. A quick shower. Blood, all the blood disappeared down the drain. Leaving no fingerprints. All touch was by the mind. She didn't bother drying herself much. A ball of hair gathered in her palm and she put it with the bloody sheet. She was very much aware that she wouldn't be able to comb the room for all of it, for all the pieces of her presence. *Time.* Time crawled and raced. She grabbed another sheet and wrapped it around her, covering her otherwise nude body, feeling the hallway outside, sensing no people, and left the room with the sack of bloody clothes in her hand. Not much time had passed. Good. Very good! She was good at this.

She hurried outside, to the backyard, and there it was, the truck was. There was no need, really for her to open the door and discover the girls inside, to see it with her eyes, but she did anyway, and there they were, drugged and nude and helpless. She walked back out, closed the door, and walked to the driver's seat. *Drive.* She couldn't move the wheel and operate the handles with her power. It wasn't precise enough for that, especially not now, when she was a bundle of nerves and rage. She wrapped her hands in the sheet and started the truck, and drove away, slowly. The truck was difficult to handle, but she managed. She hit a lamppost. Damn! She drove on. There was a street close to Fremont Street. She stopped there, unable to tell how she had reached the place. Thoughts, there were so many thoughts. She went through it all in her mind, all her options, all her fears.

It was a quiet street, with no stores and no people, a place she had instinctively sought. She left the truck in a hurried, but not too fast a pace, bringing the bundle of clothes, of bloody, bloody clothes, glancing around without glancing around. After passing one public pay phone she chose the second and dialed a few numbers. First to a few newspapers and then to the police, to three different stations, a few short sentences before hanging up. There were a few minutes longer walk to Fremont Street and the small, dark and chilled Magick Shop. She walked through the shop without stopping or looking much around. Stephen was alone there. She went to the bedroom at the back. He quietly asked the few customers to leave and asked them to return after the lunch break and they did.

She sat on the bed drinking a glass of water, clearly shaking.

– I need to borrow some clothes, she said. – And I need to get rid of this. All this. There must not be a single shred left.

He nodded, somewhat calm, though mildly shocked over witnessing the state she was in, as his eyes moved to the bundle of clothes and remains on the floor.

– We have a burner in the basement, he grinned and joked. – In fact, it was one of the main reasons we chose this location. It has proven very useful.

She had to use Stephen's clothes. The rest in the apartment were too small for her. Even Stephen's were, but she managed somehow. He fired up the oven below. She watched as her former clothes disintegrated in the cellar's fiery heat. There was still daylight when she once again walked through Las Vegas' white-hot streets. She took the bus back south. The close proximity of the other passengers strengthened her physically, but it didn't truly comfort her, not now.

The hotel room was quiet. She changed clothes and put Stephen's in a plastic bag. The body standing in front of the mirror, the hand brushing her hair was steady. It was, once again the eyes that told the story. Liz Warren saw it all in there somewhere. The confident young woman nodded pleased to herself.

She found Ted in one of the private rooms, robbing a bunch of rich amateur players. He saw straight through her guise, and instantly put down his cards and excused himself.

They faced each other, there, in the doorway.

– I think I've had my first, crystal clear premonition, she said aloud and shrieking, not by far loud enough for anybody else to hear.

He rubbed her back, and she rested her head on his shoulder, and it felt so good.

3

They drove their bike. She drove their bike through the white-hot streets. They passed the place where she had parked the truck. It was filled with cops and journalists, and flashes and cries in the twilight. The last few of the girls, covered in blankets, were being helped into the ambulances. The two Warrens drove south, towards the Californian border. The desert swallowed them almost instantly, making the city a distant memory.

– It's no use, she said. – I remember seeing road signs and such, glimpses of the fuckers' memories, but it's all blurry now. We won't find them, won't find them like this.

They had stepped off the bike. The sun had set, and twilight fallen over the desert.

– They've probably closed shop, anyway, Ted said. – At least here, now. The bastards!

– They almost had me, she whispered. – It was so close, so very close.

– We will get them! He told her, touching her cheek. – We will get them all!

– I know that! She replied sourly, playing the wronged party. – Sooner or later they will cross our path again, and we will be *ready*.

With the rage came awareness. She cocked her head and seemed to… listen.

The border was here, there, only a few steps away. She walked to it, touched it, touched the air with her hand.

– It's so strange, she mumbled. – It's almost as if there is a barrier here. It's no problem breaking it, no real resistance, but it's still unmistakably *here*.

– And exactly at lines drawn on a map. He shook his head in wonder. – Astounding! Whoever put it up must be obsessed with borders. Or something.

He left the road, and ran for a while holding up his hand. She did the same on the opposite side. They saw the «sparks» fly from it, from its touch with invisible non-material fabric in the air.

They returned to the road.

– It *is* astounding, she grinned, she shuddered. – I'm willing to bet that the barrier is following the lines on the maps slavishly.

Twilight deepened. They levitated the bike off the road, far off, and hid it behind a dune, and headed deeper into the desert, staying on the Nevada side. He began dancing, dancing the twilight, humming and gesturing. She stared astonished at him.

– I can hear them, he hummed, – the souls of the dead whispering in the sand.
And then she could, as well. The grains of sand touched and spoke, and told secrets and lies, and truths. They gathered branches from dead bushes, and they lit a fire, and the fire spoke to them as well. The air itself spoke.
– I can sense the water. She sat there with her eyes closed, easily seeing the fire. – I can sense it move deep below the surface. And… and…
She gasped.
– It tingles! She cried. – I feel it, feel the world.
And dry tears of joy flowed down her cheeks.
He heard a Salamander on his right side, like he knew she heard one on her left. They reached out to each other across the gulf of fire, and they embraced, their shadows mingling, becoming one.
– We need to practice, she shouted through the buzz of sand. – Practice a lot!
The sand rose in the air, coming alive around them, and so did they. They looked at themselves from the outside, from above, and they saw wings. There were wings of sand, seemingly attached to their shoulders, and they flapped fast and furious and powerful.
– I FEEL IT!
Their ghostly voice choired.
Through the dry, dry sand of the desert they both felt the world, and for a moment, just a tiny moment, their woes felt scant.

## 4

The newspapers waited for them upon their return to the city. The headlines screamed at them from the stands.

*RITUALISTIC SACRIFICES IN DOWNTOWN*

Below was the very graphic photograph, evidently taken by a journalist before the police had arrived at the scene. She looked at it with the familiar distant smile around her mouth.
– That makes me all warm and fuzzy inside, she said dreamily. – I'm thinking about starting a scrapbook…
A little further down the front page, there was a minor notice.

CHIEF LOMBARD ON VACATION

And finally there was a face, one to connect to the dark night and feverish action and almost obscure memory a year ago.
– I never really looked at his face, she said. – That was a mistake. I will remember it from now on. It will never fade from my foremost consciousness again.
– That's good! He nodded his approval.
The news about the kidnapped women wasn't the main headline on any of the front pages.
It was there, but buried beneath the garbage that was the daily journalism. One piece of news stealing its thunder was this important announcement:

FLUFFY WINS THE STRIP EXHIBITION COMPETITION

Fluffy was a dog, a white puddle. The proud mutt stood on a stool, dead and still, very polite and obedient.

The two walked the streets. They drank a lot of water, and even had to buy two more bottles. The desert kept speaking to them, beneath, beyond all the concrete and construction.

– A city is a desert, she nodded, nodded to herself, – a desert of the mind, devoid of life, one made of stone, imitated stone.

– There are lots of ghosts in a stone desert, he commented. – And they all have to scream to be heard, with the predictable result that no one is, of course.

– The spirits are screaming in anguish, she cried, wailed like a banshee, – suffering beyond fucking belief, the dead and alive alike.

A man with half a face, half a face gone, half half-faded, transparent blinked in and out before her, wailing before vanishing, leaving her in peace.

The whispers continued, on a level they could never quite close off.

They often saw patrolling police cars. They only dimly spotted the men inside, but they sensed them.

– There! She cried out. – The driver. That bastard recognized me. But he's just an observer. He has probably been told to stay away.

Ted saw it, how the car moved a little to the right. The driver might dwell within the hallways of power, but he was new at this, at the cloak and dagger game.

The car drove on, and they headed in the opposite direction.

– This will be the way it will always be from now on, won't it?

Her voice shook just a little, in the familiar range of rage, expectation and fear.

– You can take that to the bank or something, he replied, as casually as he could, knowing fully well that he didn't fool her for a second.

They finally decided, on a whim to walk inside, to pay a visit to yet another casino and entertainment facility. There was a lot of activity inside, and unusually so. An old guy in a tux sang tired old songs. The considerable crowd applauded «enthusiastically» between each tune.

– Inspiring, isn't he? A young man said to his companion.

– Like a turtle on the deathbed, Ted said very kindly.

The man and his companion paled.

The two Warrens walked to another hall. There was a fashion show at the other side of the building. Lightly clad females «danced» up there at the «catwalk», showing off one more useless piece of cloth after another.

– What a great assembly of proud women, a woman dressed in fur cried.

Liz stared at her, drawing a circle on her forehead.

– Are you quite well? She asked the woman in fur admiring the fashion models. – Your statement just now didn't exactly suggest that…

The woman turned to make a snide remark, but stopped in her tracks. She attempted to speak, to return the dagger stare.

Liz kept staring at her, until she looked away, and a shudder passed through her, and she sought closer to the people on the other side of her.

– You see, those are not women, Liz giggled darkly, walking close to her, breathing down her neck. – Those are skeletons without flesh, clothed in skin, and so, I guess, are you. And you aren't even wearing your own skin. What's *wrong* with you?

The two stood there, remained there. Quite a lot of those present had heard the exchange of words and wanted to convey their displeasure in the strongest possible way, but they couldn't quite cut it. Liz and Ted stood there, until it was clear that no one would call the guards to have them forcibly removed. Then they left.

The air outside felt good, felt practically life-giving, even in the worst afternoon heat.

There were no clouds in the sky, the wide, wide sky, but they saw clouds still. Dust-devils rolled through the desert as if there was no city here at all. When hands reached for each other it happened exactly at the same time. Skin touched and it felt cool to the touch. Lips met and it was all burning, burning as if heaven and hell were both present on that pinprick of skin. They breathed as they looked at each other, unable to look away, and they didn't want to.

They stiffened, looking at each other in understanding.

– I can hear drums, she said.

– That's funny, he said. – I can, too.

– But no one else apparently, she noted, looking around at the people passing back and forth. – That is significant, right?

– The drums are not here. He reached out, as if sniffing the air. – But far away.

– They're calling to us, she said, speaking in a brittle voice. – Calling us home.

They found themselves back at the Tropicana, having walked far, in a rush of forgetfulness. The vestibule looked no different.

– I need a drink, she decided.

She pulled him with her to the bar.

– I know what you're thinking, she said. – Do I want to make myself vulnerable again?

– I wasn't going to ask that…

– Just let them come at me again, she swore. – Let them try my patience, my infinite rage.

She paid for her glasses and her bottle, and they headed for the deeper recesses of the place. They couldn't help but notice the stares, even more worried than they usually were. The two walked in Shadow, they knew that. They seemed to disappear in the spot between lamps, and dim the light close to the lamps.

She opened the bottle, and put one glass in front of him, as he knew she would, and filled her own glass.

– Have one, she told him.

– No! He shook his head.

Her hand grabbed the glass and lifted it to her mouth. She emptied it in one move.

– Have one. She besieged him.

And finally, after a curtly nod from him, she poured his glass.

He had one. She poured both their glasses, and then he had more. And she poured both their glasses again, and they drank. It began to affect him. He noticed it in small things at first, how his coordination went to hell, how his vision turned blurry, how he couldn't quite recall how many times the glass had touched his lips.

They sat there drinking, slower now.

– I'm the experienced drinker, she peered, – but you have more body fat. That would make it practically an even match, don't you think?

– Match? He returned.

– You Beast, she whispered. – You callous beast.

They danced, danced tight. There was no audible music they could hear. The music came from within. He began humming, and she recognized the melody, and she shuddered.

The bottle was empty, and they started to sober up again. The liquor left a bitter taste in their mouth, as it always did.

– Thirty-two years, she whispered, and he heard her. – That's a very long time. Have you any idea how much can happen during all that time?

– I have given it some thought, he admitted.

– So much can happen, she continued unfazed, – so many variables have to be counted in. I would say nothing is fixed, is given, unless one believes in inevitability, something I certainly don't do.

– Perhaps one would be wise to believe in destiny, but not fate, he sniffed. – Destiny can always be changed. Fate can't.

– But perhaps one that is able to see and follow most of the pieces on the board can move them and plan ahead, she said. – The question is who are the players and who are the pieces.

– Perhaps we're all a little bit of both, he nodded.

She hesitated. Every time she did that astonished him.

– We begin to glimpse the bigger truth… don't we?

He replied without thinking, and the words flowed like wind across a field of tall grass, or through a forest. The trees swayed like the grass.

– «Once, in the distant past or future mankind created, perhaps by accident, perhaps by design, a world beyond the physical, one of mind, one of soul».

And her eyes widened to an abyss.

They attended a party in Justine and Brad's apartment. The crowd was basically the same type they had found in Stephen's store. It was not the newest and most luxurious of apartments, but quite spacey. The two Warrens looked around, as they always did, listened, watched and learned. It was yet another strange experience.

– This is truly strange, Liz said. – Look at Justine and Brad and the others trying to pretend nothing has changed, that they still have something in common with the rest of the people here.

– I see it, Ted agreed.

– But they haven't. They've moved on. None of them can ever go back to who and what they were.

There were two crowds in the large living room, separated along a blurry, but still distinct line.

He nodded, not saying anything.

– Is this what we are then, muses inspiring others to find themselves?

– Yes, he replied.

That, too, he thought.

You are the third force.

He turned, turned around hard, to see the person that had spoken to him. There was nobody there.

Liz grabbed him, turned him back.

– You saw something, heard something, didn't you? What was it? I heard something, too, but nothing I could make out.

He told her.

– This is something closer to home for you, she said excitedly. – Like the vision in front of the door was for me.

– I think perhaps the message was for us both, he said.

– But…? She prompted him.

– I think perhaps the messenger is somewhat closer to home for me.

– This is *so* exciting, she cried, making people turn their heads. – Our lives are and will be *extraordinary!*

He smiled. Her youthful exuberance always made him smile, made him… happy.

– *Yes!* He said aloud, as he turned towards everybody in the room. – Our lives should be extraordinary. We should make them so. That is the least Destiny expects from us.

He commanded their attention. She knew he did. Not by any Power, but by his passion alone. And it and his words made many of the people gathered here sore afraid.

Justine walked to him, smiling, taking his hand.

– This is Ted and Liz I was telling you about, she said. – They are young. They are ancient. They've got so much to teach us, teach us all.

They didn't really look at the two Warrens, those who didn't know them, at least not with more than half-hearted interest, mostly in acquiescence with their hosts, acting polite and interested. The two Warrens sensed them, sensed their dull lack of interest.

Ted snapped his fingers in a dramatic gesture and all the electrical lights in the room were turned off. Only the few candles threw fire and shadow at the two suddenly so imposing figures.

And now they all looked. Now, they were all paying attention.

Is this it? He thought. Is this what it takes to make them *listen?*

– It is said that Magick doesn't exist, he began. – Even in this assembly many harbor that ridiculous claim. Or they claim that it's all a cute fluffy bunny without fangs, without claws. That, in my opinion is yet another attempt to place humanity outside nature's reach, to make us something we're not. The world isn't a nice place, and it will never be, should never be. And Magick isn't either.

It enhances the world, reveals it in all its wonder and cruelty. It doesn't hide it, doesn't conceal reality, but opens it up for all to see and know. Some people don't want that. Instead they want to hide in their ivory tower, and never truly even *taste* the real world. And do you know what's the worst part of it is? They want everyone else to hide as well.

Clearly flustered and anxious a couple made their way towards the exit. The door slammed shut in front of them. Candles flared and almost blew out, before resettling in a kind of calm mode. The couple froze like statues and thus they remained.

– You will listen, Liz said softly. – You may leave afterwards.

Five candles rose from the floor and formed a circle around the two raven-haired cousins. Some of the people stepped back. Others stared and stood their ground, fascinated beyond belief.

– This is Magick, Ted cried. – But only the tip of the iceberg of something far greater… and dangerous.

The two turned toward the other and grabbed hands. Something happened. There was a flash not a flash and lines formed between the candles, forming a pentagram of gossamer filament of both silver and gold, and the two stood at its center, one facing the base of the star, another facing its point.

– Yes, this is white magick, black magick and everything. Liz hummed. – It's all the same. If I were you I would rid myself of the bullshit of duality you've been force-fed since birth immediately. It pulls you down, keeps you from growing, from becoming the person you most of all want to be.

– Step into the circle now, one by one… and *feel* the Magick.

Five points of a circle formed between the candles, completing the pentacle.

Justine was the first. There was a sparkle as she crossed the gossamer circle line, and a mist of shadow and fire seemed to be surrounding her.

– It tingles, she gasped. – It… OH, GODDESS!

It seemed to… ride her, to blanket her frame and penetrate her shell.

– Hear the song, Liz and Ted choired. – Hear the song we all hear, hear horror and joy combined into something far more.

Justine stepped aside, unblocking the portal inside, taking her place in one of the points

Brad was next. The same happened to him. He reacted slightly different, like they all did.

– I see, he attempted to describe, convey his indescribable experience. – I see… I…

It was a large circle. There was a lot of room, more than enough room for them all, for everyone gathered in the room. They all stepped inside, they all stood there, staring at the blurry center. The room outside didn't seem to exist anymore. In its stead had come a vast, indefinite, ever-changing mist. Ted and Liz Warren stepped into their line of vision, bringing clarity and confusion in equal measure.

– Yes, you've done it, Ted said softly. – You've taken one simple step forward, and by doing so you've taken that one, crucial step into the world.

Then all the candles were put out simultaneously, in one, brutal sweep of something that was not wind, was not matter, and the room turned pitch black.
– Now, Ted said. – Now, you have been listening.
And somewhere in the dark there was a silent scream.

5

Morning came, with its gray light and dull saturation.
They sat on the edge of the bed in one of the bedrooms, encouraged and happy, but also more than a little down. The morning light brought understanding and realization beyond words. In its deep silence they couldn't hide from themselves.
– Yesterday brought the world, she whimpered. – Now, there are only us left.
– It's enough, he said empathically. – Even in daylight. We're the world and everything in it.
– Yes, she cried, grabbing his hand. – It is. It is!
They dressed, casually, like they always did, not eager to conceal themselves for the world, to clothe themselves in fabrics.
– Look at us, she grinned. – We have a financially secure future and we're sulking.
He stood by the window, not really looking out, not looking out at all.
– It isn't enough. Having money isn't enough. It can never be.
They stared at each other, in complete agreement.
– This place, this entire city feels dead, dead as rock. Let's leave!
And the stronger fire in her eyes, more than anything else, convinced him.
A door opened. They turned and saw the smile die on the lips of she who entered their space.
– You're… leaving? Justine choked.
– Yes, Liz replied, – there's nothing for us here. Whatever we're looking for isn't in this dead place.
Breakfast was lighthearted and fun. Many gathered around the long table. They usually did, as Ted and Liz understood it. The table was there for a reason.
But coexisting with the exuberant mood was a hushed whisper just as loud as the many bursts of laughter. A somber mood lurked beneath the bright morning light.
The apartment was almost empty of people. Justine came to them as they were about to leave.
– I've… *changed,* she choked. – Too much has happened. I can never go back.
– We understand, Liz said. – Come, then.
And she reached out a hand.
They spent a few more days and nights in Las Vegas. Nothing much happened. It was merely the wait, until they got their ass in gear. They waited and they did not wait in vain.
The two of them made a lot of long walks, pushing themselves, even running, exercising outside, during the worst daytime heat. The others stared at them as if they were insane at first, but then their attitude changed, inevitably, as they

watched how the two excelled in the exhaustion. And then they joined in. Ted and Liz were a bit fearful on their behalf at first, but these people were used to the desert. Some of them had lived here their entire life. They could take it, could endure a little, perhaps even a lot of heat.

One day they brought band-aid and stuff, deliberately revealing it, bringing down the point quite well to the apprehensive crowd. The running began. Each ran with one large bottle filled with water in each hand. They ran flat out (the crowd did) to an abandoned construction site. There were quite a few of them these days.

– Nobody here with a heart condition or anything, I trust?

– Now, he asks that! Stephen gasped, bending over, with his hands on his knees, desperately attempting to catch his breath.

There was laughter, right through the ragged breath, and it strengthened them, strengthened their life.

One of the bottles of water was already empty, and they had started on the second.

– Come. Liz waved to a big, muscular bruiser. – Attack me.

He did, after a prolonged hesitation, after her quiet, sinister insistence.

A few seconds later he crouched on the ground, pretty banged up, but not seriously injured.

It continued like that for a while. The two checked their charges for injuries, but there weren't any.

They sat in the shade for a few minutes, resting.

– Why can't we spar against each other? One asked. – That would be fairer, don't you think?

– Because you aren't skilled enough for that yet, to not injure each other, the male raven said.

– And because this is fun, of course, the crueler female raven added.

On the fourth or fifth (or tenth) day she told them more they didn't know.

– You begin to feel better, I trust? You begin to feel you can do *anything*.

She wasn't asking them. She was telling them. They began to feel wonderfully relaxed and refreshed. Every step felt like a cold shower. The effect of the merciless sun seemed muted, not anymore so sharp a blade.

Early one morning they rolled their two new bikes to the front of the hotel entrance.

– It seems like years since we first came here, she said, wonder and anguish in her voice.

– It is and it isn't, he replied.

There was a distant roar, quickly approaching.

Justine and Brad joined them, on their own bikes, as they had suspected they would. Almost all the rest did as well. Justine looked proudly at them, practically presenting, offering the rest to them, to the gods.

Twenty gathered around them, and it felt right, so right, almost right…

Some of them had long since quit their jobs and sold their assets. The rest had done so or completed their job yesterday. Liz and Ted stared at them, welcoming them on their quest.

– You're making a dangerous decision, Ted told them. – Congratulations. From this moment on your training begin in earnest. The long-term goal is survival… and boundless freedom.

He sounded so sure, so very confident, so very vulnerable. They couldn't decide whether or not he was this ancient, unstoppable force or an insecure, fucked up young boy… and then… they realized he was both.

– You've made the right choice, Liz cried. – My condolences…

Hotel guests stared, and the personnel surely considered calling the police, but they stood there, frozen in inaction.

Everybody checked their bike, the strong straps and the nomad's tools.

And then, just as they were about to leave, yet another biker arrived. He wore a helmet and wasn't instantly recognizable. Liz recognized Phillip Caine before anybody else did.

He stopped before Liz, removed his helmet and threw it away. It gave away a horrible noise as it rolled across the sidewalk. She smiled to him, her special smile, transforming her face.

They set out on their Journey.

Twenty and one ravens followed the first two, the first bikes, leaving Las Vegas, heading east and south, and it felt right, so very, very right.

Silence reigned in the streets after their passing.

# Chapter Five: Vengeance is mine - Part 1

## DISTANT BUTTERFLY WINGS

### Farewell to the arms - Spain 1936-37

«Vengeance harms us more than what originally hurt us».
John Lubbock

The hills and valleys of Spain resounded in blasts and fury. The air stank of smoke and explosives. Jonas Bergli ran with the others, towards a place resembling safety.

He remembered sitting on a bus, then the explosion, then himself running. His forehead was wet. After he touched his head and brought the hand back down he saw it was covered in blood.

A man asked him a question, in Spanish, thank god, not Catalan.

– I'm fine, he replied in the same language. – A little lightheaded, but fine.

There was a long line of people walking on the stony path. Some stumbled forward and some managed walking, somewhat, but they all had a dazed look in their eyes. The afternoon sun burned them, through the light clouds, the lingering smoke. They walked through a mist, ever changing, ever revealing different parts of the landscape surrounding them.

The thunder, close and distant, hurt their ears.

There was a nurse with the bus, and as soon as they had sufficiently removed themselves from the war zone, they all sat down by the road. She surveyed them all, and by a miracle none of them, none still walking at least, were seriously injured. Jonas released an involuntary cry when she put a wet cloth to his head.

– You're probably okay, she told him in halting English. – If you get a serious headache tonight you need to relax, though.

– I thought you were English, he said, a bit put off.

– No. She shook her head. – I'm Norwegian.

– So am I, he smiled. – At least I was.

– That does surprise me, she said. – You must have been gone a long time.

– Yes, he said distantly. – A long time.

– Jeg er Ruth, she said and gave him her hand, as she repeated it in English. – I'm Ruth

– Jonas, he replied, and added. – Thanks for speaking English. It's been twenty years since I left. My guess is that I would hardly understand you anymore.

– That's okay, she shrugged. – I enjoy speaking English.

She tied a bandage around his head. His head said thud, thud, thud, but he felt fine. The walk continued. He carried her suitcase for a while, until she insisted on carrying it herself. She was strong, in more than one sense of the word.

– Many will come here. She sniffed. – They will come here from Norway and all over the world, volunteers in the fight. I just thought I would be among the first.

They walked in silence for a while. He looked at her openly, studying her, without pretense of modesty. She reddened.

– You're not like other men, Jonas Bergli, she stated. – You haven't asked me what a woman is doing here.

– No. He shook his head. – I may wonder about many things in life, but that isn't one of them.

– I wonder why not, she said, purposely returning his stare. – Where have you learned your strange behavior?

– Among the Shadowwalkers, he replied, replied without thinking twice.

Her eyes widened. There were also murmurs among the other travelers, buzzing in his ears like bees.

– We hadn't heard about them in Norway, she said. – We hear nothing in Norway. But since I came here, I've heard them being mentioned many times, mentioned with awe. The way I hear it they must be something between giants and gods.

– They are people, Jonas stressed. – No more, no less.

They walked for hours. Many people reached their home or simply sat down by the roadside, but the two of them and a small number of travelers continued on their way.

– Where are you headed? She wondered.

– An anarchist stronghold somewhere ahead. He indicated a direction with his head. – It might be hours away, might be days, for all I know.

– I'm going there, too, she grinned, still glancing shyly at him. – I know the way.

The group sat down by a crossroads as the twilight set in. All those left carried their own food and water. It was a very international group, with many nationalities represented, many which had left nationality behind. They sat there and spoke and dreamed and lived.

The thunder still resounded in their ears, but it was, for the time being, solely distant. They allowed themselves to relax somewhat.

The talking continued well into the evening and night. No fires were lit. There were no loud voices. Any sound in the night brought added awareness and tension.

There were heated discussions and it felt so good, so very, very good to speak openly about these things in a crowd of absolute strangers. Strangers came to this land from all over the world, and they met and spoke during night and day both.

They spoke openly, about the shadows of the world.

And sleep, when it finally came, was filled with potent dreams.

The morning brought more thunder, more screams of pain and rage. The gray morning light brought sobriety and cold, cold fear. Bodies decorated the land, on and off the road, most in pieces bathed in blood. It both discouraged and encouraged them.

They spoke excitedly among themselves, airing thoughts and theorems that had been buried, buried deep their entire lives. The thing hiding within no longer belonged merely to the night, but to the brightest of days.

– This might be it, you know, a girl cried, – the beginning of the end to oppression and tyranny in the world. People are willingly, even eagerly taking up arms against the forces that will destroy the good things happening here.

– It's the arms, the violence that has brought an end to the good thing we had here, another countered.

The girl turned angrily towards the man, snarling at him.

– So, that's what you think? Perhaps we should ask the *Falangista* to pause a bit in their killing and torture, while we're handing them flowers?

The discussion kept up on their walk, their long walk.

– The day we have democratic elections everywhere, the socialists will win…

– It's true, another insisted. – Then we wouldn't have this destructive arms embargo benefiting only the enemy. All nations could cooperate toward a truly benevolent goal.

– And everything will be great in the world, another cried sarcastically.

Jonas said quietly, casually:

– The labor party won the election in Norway, didn't they, like they have done so many places recently?

– Yes, they did, Ruth nodded fiercely.

– It won't help any, Jonas said with conviction.

– I know that. That was one of many reasons why I left. They have already joined the society they once wanted to replace.

– This place might not be the one we're looking for either, Jonas said, – but it's still ripe with revolution, with *change*.

People looked at him and then they looked at each other, and they whispered among themselves. He heard them, heard them whispering about *shadows,* and he found it pleasing.

There was a turn on the road, a walk around a cliff, and the village opened up to them. It was a small place, at least originally so, with few houses, but now expanded with many a new shed and even more tents. It resounded with activity and energy. People were in *motion,* even when standing still. It was palatable, a tangible force in the air and in their hearts.

The travelers arrived at an open spot, a town center, drawn there from the moment they entered the town's borders. There was a stage there, clearly makeshift and rough-cut, but in spite of that or rather because of that, a true and exciting place. There was a play, played between tall torches and sweaty people. It was twilight again. The travelers had walked far, but suddenly they didn't feel the slightest fatigue. A woman captivated the attention of all the people gathered. Jonas' heart made a jump or ten in his chest. Heat rushed through his blood.

The play (with contribution from a number of other sources and clearly done with a modern outlook and interpretation) was Shakespeare's *Macbeth.*

Out, out, brief candle!
Life's but a walking shadow, a poor player
That struts and frets his hour upon the stage
And then is heard no more; it is a tale
Told by an idiot, full of sound and fury,
Signifying nothing.

There was a lot of applause, subdued, but enthusiastic and passionate.

It might not be the performance itself that made people so excited, but the elation in which she performed it, contrary to the perceived grim words.

Nancy Warren glowed in the dusk, pulling all the eyes in the gathering, male and female, to *her*. All fires, all shadows, all deep forests in existence were drawn…

To her.

He saw that easily, in every face, in the body language of every male and female, adult and child in the gathering.

The performance ended. She curtseyed deeply as she received the accolades from an excited audience, but there was nothing submissive about it, about the traditionally submissive movement. It was, on the contrary, filled with defiance and joy.

She walked straight to Jonas. The eyes of Ruth and the others standing there with him widened to an uncanny degree. She embraced him and kissed him on the lips. Her lips burned. There was a catching in his throat as joy coursed through him.

– You found me, she said huskily. – I always knew you would.

She turned to the others, shocking them with her deep, penetrating stare.

– Hello, Ruth, she greeted the woman. – I've been waiting for you.

Ruth shook.

– How do you know my name? Ruth cried.

– I know more than your name, Ruth. I know you. I know you to the core of your being.

Jonas realized startled that she wasn't hiding anymore. She appeared to the world as she was… infinite.

They walked inside, to the extended Cantina, extended with makeshift walls and a bar that seemed to extend forever.

Jonas spotted the two men immediately. He wasn't sure he recognized Virgil and James, but he saw that they were no longer hiding either. They drank, drank hard, and it didn't really affect them, even though James still looked at the world with vulnerability in his eyes, while Virgil did not. There was nothing left there, but a shell of a human being. Jonas couldn't make himself look at him, and he noticed that Nancy and James couldn't either.

There was sawdust on the floor, already wet this early in the evening. This was a pretty wild place. Most of those present celebrated with abandon, as if it was their last night.

Virgil only drank, and all of it disappeared into the vast black hole inside of him.
– We need to talk, Nancy said to Jonas. – Let's go a somewhere quiet.
A man grabbed her and gave her a passionate kiss on the lips. She returned the kiss, laughing throatily and passionately. Jonas, strangely enough, felt very little jealousy. She got rid of the big man with a few hushed words and a smile. Jonas knew she signed, somehow, to Virgil and James, for them to come with her. He didn't see her doing it, but he knew she did. She walked up the stairs, and he followed her. And somewhere behind him the two other Warrens quietly and unseen followed them both.
The room was quiet. In spite of the bright lights there the white walls didn't quite penetrate the darkness. The four stood at its center, facing each other.
– He's here, she said. – Lance Powell is here, running guns for the reactionary army.
Jonas looked at her, frowning.
– I've followed him. Virgil stepped forward, his voice dead and still. – Followed him across the Earth. I almost caught up with him in Marseille, in one of his *brothels,* but he got away again.
Jonas kept frowning, even as he realized whom they were speaking about.
– Powell? As he recited the name and read understanding and certainty in Nancy's eyes, he knew, knew beyond words. – But that… doesn't make sense. It doesn't make sense at all.
The Abyss opened up beneath him. He felt it happening, felt himself being shredded to pieces when the implications dawned on him.
– But…
He couldn't bring himself to say anymore. The truth was written in everybody's faces.
– You're wrong there, my love. She curled her left hand into a fist. – It doesn't make conventional sense, but my master is just as much a monster as Adolph Foster, the other green-eyed enemy plaguing us the previous century. He doesn't care about his daughter's fate or anything but the need to *hurt* us.
– Nick shouted his name, Jonas said, nodding. – I remember.
– The devil sent April to us, Virgil swore, – knowing fully well… knowing what would… what would happen.
– The three of us met in Paris. Nancy looked at Jonas, almost apologetic.
– So you all came here because of him?
– That wasn't the only reason, she said weakly, – but it was the initial, motivating factor, yes.
– We need to *end* this, James stated, and for a moment there he didn't quite look like himself, but like someone else, a stranger.
And strangely enough, it was the look in his very normal eyes that made the strongest impression on Jonas, that made a beyond cold trickle race down his spine.
– Can you imagine what kind of man he is, that can do this, James continued, – what kind of resolve he has, to send his own daughter to such a horrible fate, to

spend his entire life on the task of *destroying* us? Can you imagine what's motivating him, what dark secret he carries, to do that?

Jonas couldn't, but he feared the three before him could. Three of the people he cared most about in the world, and they were being consumed by hatred and fear.

He and Nancy stood on the balcony later. The full moon was up. The sound of the festivities below rose pleasantly in the air, hitting their ears. Fire and moonlight spilled across her face. She smiled to him, and in that moment it was all worth it.

– Look at the moon, she said breathlessly. – See how its light fills the landscape in ways the sun can never do.

And suddenly, he was out of breath as well.

She turned to him, with fear in her eyes, and the moment was lost.

– A hungry mouth is hunting me, she whispered. – It's large and black and has long sharp fangs.

– You… know this? He said cautiously.

– I sense it. And on occasion I feel I can actually see it as well, a thing waiting in the darkness, waiting to *devour* me.

He saw how she pulled herself together, how she concentrated, focused.

– There's a smell. She frowned. – One of flowers. And I can see them, black, red and white petals falling to the ground from high above.

He looked at her with concern in his eyes.

She forced a smile.

– But don't let me entertain you with tales of gloom, my Jonas. You have news of home, yes?

– Not that much, he replied. – I didn't leave that long after Virgil and James.

– So, how is the little one, the little girl?

It was said so casually, so light that it hit him like a rock.

– Ethel is fine, he replied hoarsely, just as casually. – I got a recent letter from Nick. People can even touch her, now, with only a slight discomfort. Nick and Rachel and Carla take care of her. She's already *running* around, and she's playing with the other children.

The scene of the little baby on the floor surrounded by the two unmoving, stiff bodies haunted him, and Nancy immediately picked up on it.

– I… felt it, she whispered. – Half a world away I *felt* it.

She grabbed his hands and held on. He attempted to pull himself free, for one, two three seconds, before he gave up.

– Jonas, she reached out and *touched* the world.

He saw it, experienced it, through her eyes, through her enhanced perception, and it jarred in his, overwhelmed his completely. The baby sucked all energy, all life out of her mother and the maid, and in one violent outburst of Power she sensed the world.

Nancy had been fairly cautious, fairly guarded in his company. She wasn't anymore. He saw her, experienced her, as she was, now. Her thoughts, emotions, her being leaked and he knew her, more so, than he had ever done. He trembled and so did she.

– Nick killed his mother at birth, too, she said. – But I didn't. I didn't know how it was like, how it... felt. But now I do. Now, I *know!*

The night grew darker. And the cold of far away winter invaded them both.

## 2

They walked through the streets of Barcelona, visiting La Sagrada Familia, the insane works of Antonio Gaudi. Buildings not buildings, but a homage to something far beyond ordinary thought. Sculptures not sculptures, but twisted, beautiful figures repeatedly sending daggers of ice down your spine.

Gaudi had been very religious, but in spite of that his work fit well with what was happening around his work right now.

There were sounds of distant thunder, distant battle, but people still filled the streets, still celebrated as if their last day had come.

Nancy danced among them, as she did at Jonas' side. And it was clearly unnerving for most people, even among the freethinkers present here, because she beneath the shell, the varnish of skin, hardly looked like a human being at all, but like a wild beast in the wilderness. And that was no exaggeration, no silly description told through the eyes of a mundane person, but the obvious truth.

The torches burned high, the smoke oozed thick, as she stepped up on the stage.

– What happens here have value far beyond this city, this land, she cried.

Her words were greeted with applause and loud cries.

She spoke Catalan. He couldn't really tell, but he more than suspected that she spoke without a discernible accent. She spoke like a native.

It was a storm standing up there with its fist raised, one clothed in flesh, but nonetheless the Storm personified.

– The world is looking at us, she cried. – Current human society looks at us in fear and loathing. Do you know why? Because we can't be ignored anymore. We can't be intimidated into silence anymore. We can no longer be swept under the rug or thrown into a dark dungeon without repercussions.

She invaded him, invaded his very being, and like a tall wave she swept him with her, swept him far at sea.

– The world has criticized us for many things, she said. – Included in this is the fact that we're burning churches and killing the church' men and women. But that's inevitable, of course... since the church and its people are such an integrated part of the tyranny that has for so long held sway over us all. There's a horrible hole in the world where christians have walked.

A strange glance was cast on her two close relatives. Virgil and James pushed a stricken, terrified priest forward. Rage seemed to be present in the very air around them and the woman on the stage. It was a seething, visible thing.

– Come, she snarled, – let's take a look at your church, padre.

She jumped down from the stage and charged into the stone building. She didn't run, but she still appeared to move fast, fast as lightning. Shadow and fire and the entire excited gathering followed her inside.

The catholic congregation had huddled on benches inside, timid and tiny creatures calling on nothing but contempt within Jonas.

These creatures were the current masters of the world.

Something primeval rose within him, something beyond life, beyond death.

Virgil pushed the priest towards his subjects. The man stumbled a few steps before he managed to straighten himself.

– Be calm, he admonished the people on his benches. – God will protect us. Let us pray, pray for deliverance.

At the last word he directed his eyes towards the ceiling, towards the heavens, and there was no small amount of venom in those small eyes.

– Yes, pray, Virgil chuckled, – and see how far it gets you.

He walked right into their midst.

– Let them pray, and see if their God comes to their rescue.

And Jonas wasn't sure what scared him the most, his friend's insane laughter or the horrible, eerie glare of the christians.

A few of them began to sway and they all folded their hands, sounds rising from their throats, from their very being. They fell on their knees, heads bowed, hands folded. The prayer was in Latin, but Jonas understood it. It wasn't that hard, really.

«Mighty God, hallow is thy name. Protect us in our moment of need and smite our enemies».

And the primeval trickle down his spine was ice-cold and paralyzing. He watched Nancy right then, as he often did, her restless frame, her nostrils seemingly, actually sniffing the air. She looked uncharacteristically… skittish, the expression of apprehension and rage magnified to a beyond uncanny degree. She spoke. He couldn't hear her because of the loud chant filling the church… but he still knew her words with absolute certainty:

Something is here.

She took one step forward, casting a pointed stare around her. There was hatred there, and contempt and an unbridled rage.

I know you, she said.

– I KNOW YOU, she repeated, she cried at the ceiling.

And now Jonas heard her, her mighty voice thundering in his ears.

– I KNOW WHO YOU ARE!

He rushed to her. She turned to him, stared at him with pity, with abandon, with love.

– He can't touch me, can't touch us, she whispered in his ear. – He can touch almost everybody else, even you, but he can't touch us.

She turned away from him, and then, then Jonas Bergli saw something he would never, never, never forget. He saw what everybody else in the church witnessed.

He saw what wasn't fire, wasn't shadow rise from Nancy Warren's frame, saw it engulf her. He imagined the dark, fiery figure she had become grow to touch the ceiling, towering over them all. And then he, and everyone else in the church directed their attention at the point in the air she focused on, and they saw something there, a presence, a form in the air, an ethereal figure, a face glaring incredulous at the woman of Fire and Shadow facing him.

– Who are you? It hissed. – What in the seven hells are you?

– I'm your doom, she snarled, not really speaking but forming words out of the air itself. – I'm coming for you. You will never have your kingdom on Earth.

And fear touched the face, and it faded away. Nancy remained, in all her horror and glory. What looked to them all as a giant shape faded, and only Nancy remained.

The stricken congregation had stopped praying. They looked in horror at the demon in their midst. She stared at everybody, at everybody present.

– Get out! All of you get out, *now!*

She shouted, a voice not a voice at all, but something out of the darkest nightmare.

They obeyed without thinking, they all did. Jonas' legs burned after just a few steps, as if he had just run a marathon. He saw, like they all did, even with closed eyes, the witch standing there, in the midst of a rubble of broken benches and wood, saw her reach out and touch the air, saw her shake violently, saw a ball, a large ball of fire erupt from her abdomen, ripping apart her clothes. It struck the wall, the brick wall, and ignited it like it would paper. The wood caught fire. Everything erupted in fire, a seething inferno felt more than seen, experienced more than felt. Everybody rushed outside, coughing and gasping. She was last, surrounded in flames, walking calmly towards them as the proud building disintegrated behind her.

## 3

It was a quiet night in the hills. Nancy walked towards him between the campfires. She put a finger on his lips, as he was about to speak, and led him away.

To the cliff, where they could see the valley below, with its mist and bright spots.

– You wonder about what happened in the church, she told him.

He didn't reply. There was no need for that.

– I'm not sure myself, not anymore, but I can show you what I saw, what I experienced.

She touched his brow with her fingers, and instantly, in a span of seconds he experienced it all through her senses. He saw, once again the congregation praying, but now he did so through her eyes, truly through her eyes. There was a flow, a release. Something began rising from the kneeling people, a kind of cloud being sucked up into the air, vanishing somewhere under the ceiling. He shivered as he shared her rage, and the realization of what was actually

happening. The face appeared and the cloud was sucked into it in an even stream.
– That thing… he gasped, – whatever it is, is gaining power from their prayer… their worship?
– Yes, he is, she nodded. – From every person, every group praying to, worshipping his various incarnations all over the planet.
– He? He said frosty.
The face and the giant shadow faced off in the church, shaking the building, shaking the ground. He sensed the frustration in them both, as they were unable to truly affect each other. She reached out, stealing some of his even flow, and then she could hurt him, and he whimpered in pain, and he left, and her frustration, her rage flowed completely out of control. She exploded in rage and her surroundings with her.
– Behold the power, Jonas Bergli, she said softly, – behold a lifetime of bottled-up hatred and rage.
He looked at his beloved, at the compelling, sweet face, but all he could see was the twisted, demonic features.
– I told you that you had stumbled upon a vast drama, she said, she whimpered, she joked. – I clearly underestimated its extent, though.
He grabbed her and pulled her closer, held her hard in a desperate effort to keep her close. She sighed in relief and joy and sick gratitude. She was like a child sometimes, so needy, so much in need of comfort, of support.
They walked between the campfires, holding hands like all would-be lovers. Between the fires they saw Ruth go to Virgil with a sack of wine, giving it to him with a blushing face. He stared at her with cold, envious eyes. Jonas experienced that, that, too, through Nancy's expanded, expanding senses, and he wondered for the thousandth time what she was becoming.
– Another one falling in love with Virgil's tragedy, Nancy sighed. – Poor girl.
A group of men and women performed between other fires. They stood on the shoulders of those beneath them, forming a construct stretching deep into the night sky.
– It's a *Castell.* A tourist cried. – A human tower.
– Yes, Jonas Bergli, Nancy Warren nodded, as usual picking up on his conflicting moods, on all of them, – this is humanity, all of it, all its thousand fires and ashes.
A whirling in the air, a vortex at a center somewhere brought them all together. There was a place, a large spot in the middle of nowhere, surrounded by five campfires, and an undeniable force pulled them all there.
To her.
She undressed, very casually and very matter of fact, but in spite of that it was the most sensual movements they had all ever witnessed. Without thinking, burning with a passion impossible to deny, they joined her there on the rocky ground.
The fires flared. Jonas didn't notice, except in the deepest recesses of his mind. There were bodies, bodies everywhere. They were all swimming in an ocean of

fiery embraces. Jonas gasped, echoing that of the thousand echoes surrounding him. Skin against skin writhed on the hard ground, noticing only the soft, hot and moist flesh, the waves of pleasure traversing the molten sea.

Jonas crawled to the center. She called him, beckoned him there. He crawled on top of her, gasping for breath, desperately attempting to breathe in the ignited air. There was a breath of cold wind, but he hardly noticed. She welcomed him, igniting his cold lips. There was sand, its scent very powerful in his nostrils. In a glimpse lasting an eternity he saw an old woman walking the infinite sands of Egypt. She spoke, she, too spoke to him, spoke his name. He kissed Nancy, the demon, he tasted her blood. He pushed against her glowing body, pushed again and again and again, until he fell on her, and she kissed his brow and rubbed his back.

– Good, she whispered, – very good.

And for once, in that brief moment, everything was right with the world.

## 4

It was winter, and when the thaw arrived next spring the winter remained.

The four was only a small number in a long row of people loaded with arms. The woman was visibly pregnant, but she still moved with an ease and grace envied by the most hardened warrior. And she killed with a ferocity none in her company could match.

Virgil killed with a cold rage and an efficiency that strangely enough scared his fellow soldiers far more. He seemed more like a machine than a human being, totally deprived of what made a person breathe, touch and live.

But he kept going still, driven by something unnamable, something beyond hatred.

Jonas fired his gun. The gunpowder stuck in his nostrils and eyes, and he could hardly see through the mist. He saw nothing except the geyser of red somewhere ahead.

A cannon was fired not that far away, its thunder not that muted through the cotton in his ears. Many cannons, many guns were fired, on both sides, all parts of the battlefield, turning his ears to mush. The explosions sounded like one, continuous thunder.

A bullet hit him. He couldn’t tell where. But it couldn’t be that bad, because he continued to fight, to function, to kill. He saw Virgil be hit, and there was no reaction, no reaction whatsoever in his friend’s ashen, impassive face.

The battle ended, the battle continued. They rested, not resting in a camp of tents and moans and suffering. Ruth cleaned his wound and bandaged it. It hurt. That pleased him somewhat. He saw Nancy stand guard with her rifle on the shoulder. Her beige jacket was bloody. He suspected it was her blood, even though he couldn’t be sure. But he knew there wasn’t any wound, not anymore on her flawless skin. He saw it before his eyes, his feverish eyes, saw her skin heal in a matter of seconds.

The others looked at her in awe, as a mix of the Madonna and Diana, the Goddess of the Hunt, but she ignored them, treating them with the contempt they deserved. But not him. Never him. She was at his side at all times. He didn't always see her, but he sensed her, sensed her smothering passion.

She spoke to him in his feverish dreams, as he lay there, writhing on the volcanic rock.

– Others may speculate, but you know who I am, Jonas, you know my name. *Say* it, say my name.

And he cried it out, cried it for all the world to hear, mumbled it in his fever, and she responded, and in that moment he also knew, beyond doubt, beyond reason who he was.

Morning broke in mist and rain. The full brunt of General Franco's forces descended on the warriors loyal to what had briefly been the government of Spain.

She ran in front of him across the bridge, still agile and easily able to outrun him and everyone else present.

They had been cut off from the main army. Like many other splinter groups they sought refuge anywhere they could find it. A grenade landed in the midst of the fleeing force behind them, blowing a large hole in the bridge. They reached the other side in relative safety. Looking back they felt a kind of sick relief. It was clear that the enemy forces couldn't pursue them over that bridge.

Later that day, during the twilight, they were finally able to get some rest. Even Nancy was tired. Not physically perhaps, but he saw the dark bags under her eyes.

They walked back and forth through the makeshift camp. She looked *wild* this woman. Even though her voice was tired, nothing of her savagery was gone or even diminished.

On the contrary. It was clearly growing.

When she spoke the fatigue was hardly there at all. The rage was thick in her voice and eyes.

– Look at them, she said, in a strange, soft tone.

They stood on a higher ground, looking down at the camp.

– They fight well. I can't fault them for that. But they, we, didn't lose this war last night or last week, but long ago.

He didn't say anything. She saw his reply in his eyes. She always did.

– The reactionary forces have already won, she said, – by making «us» abandon our ideals. The freedom found everywhere in this land only a few months ago is now practically extinct, also in «our» camps. This…

She struck out a hand, indicating what was beneath her, the battered, miserable soldiers and volunteers.

– … is yet another illusion of rebellion.

He opened his mouth to speak, and suddenly she was there, close to him. There was nothing between them.

– I could do a lot here, she whispered. – I can… by *letting go,* giving the enemy a true taste of what they wish for the world. But I'm only one, and one is never enough. What does it take, I wonder? What does it take to *transform* the world?

Her words lingered within him in the ever more desperate days and weeks to come. He could recite them flawlessly in his head without straining.

They fought on the road to Aragon, one of the last strongholds of the anarchist forces. The enemy, superior in manpower and logistics closed in on them in ever-stronger waves. Explosions shook the ground around them. Bullets rained like hail on them. One hit Jonas. And while he stumbled back, yet another hit him, and he fell.

She was at his side in an instant, but she didn't touch him, and he knew why. In her agitated state she was deadly to anybody she touched.

– Help me up, he gasped. – I can stand. I can run and fight.

Virgil and James were there immediately, helping him stand, helping him run. The four of them and a few others rushed up a slope, towards a good defense spot.

Jonas fell, fell again the moment they reached the cover. Nancy was on her way to him, when she stopped and cried out.

– Damn, she gasped. – The water just broke.

They looked at her in disbelief.

– Bad timing, she mumbled. – Such damn bad timing.

Jonas crawled to the front of the hideout, their miniature fortress. He spotted the approaching soldiers down there. They were coming, as certain as day followed night.

– You go, he said. – Get out of here, all of you.

They looked astonished at him. He saw her, her watery eyes with his back turned.

– It isn't an army following us, just a search and clean-up crew. From this position I can delay them for hours, long enough for you to get away. I can't walk, and you will have more than enough to do, carrying her. And you must, must get her away from here.

They all stared at him with water in their eyes. He found that strangely appropriate.

He watched them as they made a stretcher for her, made it from clothes and anything in their possession. They left a fairly large amount of their weapons in his care, enough for him to fire a lot of rounds, more than enough. He felt strangely lightheaded and strong. He felt it deep inside, the rage, quelling the gathering despair completely. Something had always been there, inside, something he had never truly acknowledged, not until now.

They left, had left a long time ago.

Every second contained weeks and months. His sharp eyes were able to follow small drops of rain as they fell, follow them on their long way falling down.

He fired, killing two of the enemy soldiers the moment they stuck their heads up down below. They clearly got more cautious after that. He was able to rest for a few seconds. It was enough, and unnecessary. The fire flowed in him. It filled him with power. He saw them move down there, in their attempt to circle closer to him. They were good, and didn't often expose themselves. But the moment they did, he killed them, as easy as he would be snapping his fingers. He saw Nancy's face as they carried her off. It was hours and hours ago, but he still recalled it, every feature burned into his memory.

They circled around him, he knew that, knew they were closing in on him, inevitably. He loaded as much of the weapons on his shoulders as he could possibly carry without being seriously hampered, and pulled back to a better position. A soldier appeared over the ridge. Jonas shot him in the face. He was still amazed, after all these months how good he was with weapons, all kind of weapons. It was like they were a part of him, a part of his flesh and mind and soul, an arm, a leg reaching far beyond ordinary reach.

Feet thundered behind him. He ran. The sun appeared behind the clouds, its light turning to gray. He found the easily defendable position he had been frantically looking for. When the first wave began its attack he was ready and fired in their midst. They dropped like flies, but they kept coming, like he had known they would. He grabbed the other machinegun, using both simultaneously.

He saw her lips move, as they carried her away: «We'll always meet again». He saw her tears flash like the rubies they were. It was as if it was all happening right now. And it was.

His hands whitened around the machinegun, as he pulled the trigger. And then everything faded to white in his eyes, and to thunder in his ears.

## 5

He opened his eyes and saw Ruth stand above him, dressed in her nurse uniform.

I'm dreaming, he thought at first, or I'm back in the Other World, back in the mist.

But there was too much blood, too much screaming and suffering, not at all the relative serenity he remembered from the place Beyond.

Ruth straightened his pillow. Pain was dull and distant, but clearly there, telling him he was alive.

– How did I get here?

– You… walked here. She looked at him, clearly with anxiety in her eyes. – You were more dead than alive. No one understands how you were able to move, much less walk, but you did. No one understands how you were able to survive… but you did.

He strived to say more, but his constricted throat kept him from speaking.

– They thought you were dead. Nancy looked almost dead herself, until… until the baby was born. They left almost immediately after that, all three… four of them, convinced you were gone.

– How long?

His hoarse voice sounded like a crow talking.

– You have been in that bed for a month, Jonas, Ruth cried. – More dead than alive. Many times I was convinced you were dead, but when the morning came, you were always breathing.
– Where did they go?
– Lance Powell had left, left the country, Ruth said apprehensive, beyond apprehension. – So they followed him, followed him to hell.
Jonas slept again, but now his sleep was filled with nightmarish images, and his sleep no longer gave him rest.
Styx, the river of knowledge, death and life flowed through him, and he felt its pull.
But he no longer needed it, needed the rest. From that morning, that day, his condition improved quickly, uncannily. He walked on crutches after three days, and the others steered away from him as they passed, fearing they would burn themselves on the fire. And for the first time he understood more of what Nancy and her brethren felt.
He shaved, removing his beard, removing it completely. He had gotten to know it as a friend the last year. Now they parted company. Jonas Bergli stared at his face in the mirror, his pale, ashen face, wondering who he was.
Ruth watched him gather his few possessions in a rucksack, saw him strap it on his back and shoulders.
– Will I see you again? She wondered, her voice cracking. – Any of you?
He walked away, saying the words he had always known he would say.
– Paths that cross will always cross again.

«I had dropped more or less by chance into the only community of any size in Western Europe where political consciousness and disbelief in capitalism were more normal than their opposites. Up here in Aragon one was among tens of thousands of people, mainly though not entirely of working-class origin, all living at the same level and mingling on terms of equality. In theory it was perfect equality, and even in practice it was not far from it. There is a sense in which it would be true to say that one was experiencing a foretaste of Socialism, by which I mean that the prevailing mental atmosphere was that of Socialism. Many of the normal motives of civilized life--snobbishness, money-grubbing, fear of the boss, etc.--had simply ceased to exist. The ordinary class-division of society had disappeared to an extent that is almost unthinkable in the money-tainted air of England; there was no one there except the peasants and ourselves, and no one owned anyone else as his master».

George Orwell describing a scene in Aragon during this time period in his book *Homage to Catalonia.*

# Part Two:
# The City of the Dead

# Chapter Six: The Path of Lizards

*There is no introduction, no fancy words, only the stroke of a brush painting in blood, building of castles in the sand.*

*To you who are reading this: No, I don't know who you are. Somebody will read this, or has read it, I know that. In the casket before you, you will find everything that has happened in your past, present and future. Study the content well. You may try to change what will happen. You may succeed. You may not.*

*It's a strange thing to sit here, in this distant time and place, and know that this will be read, not only in the future, but in the past as well. And that it will Change the Universe, change it irrevocably. Something happened once, turning a leaf, turning a stone, and many stones were turned, and many leaves were cast in the air. And no one may say where they will fall and rise. They will fall and they will rise. I know that. You know that, too. In a Universe with no constants what so ever, these are two. There is birth. There is death and rebirth. We are the Song of the Universe...*

*This is our Life. We are re-enacting, reinventing its horrors, joys and dance every second of our nights and days and...*

*And Shadow.*

2

They had stopped by the Hoover Dam, not far from Las Vegas. They heard the hum, its distant roar from far away.

– This is contained fury, Ted said, holding a fist before his face. – And that is what we shall unlock from within.

The two of them stood at the center of the circle the twenty-one formed. A tall fire singed their hair and skin, and it didn't seem to bother them, bother them at all. There was no wind, but there was a draft in the air, making the top flames of the fire dance and stretch.

She jumped up on the rock, an impossible jump, a lioness' jump bridging an impossible distance. The lioness walked among them, baring her fangs, touching them with her ice-cold bloody claws. The Witch captivated them with her sorcery.

The two stood at the center of a pentacle, all lines of the five-point star and its circle glowing in a very different St. Elmo's fire. They cut their skin, the soft-sided fleshy side of the hand, and the ruby flow rained down on the barren rock. It hissed and boiled as it turned to red mist and they all breathed its vapors.

– In the beginning we were damned, the sorceress chanted, – and through damnation we found freedom, power and purpose. Rejoice, my siblings, this is us all naked. This is who we are.

And effortlessly it all took off.

A girl mumbled while wildly riding a boy.

– We seek close, seek inside. Flesh mixes, mind melds, and we all dance the Invisible Labyrinth.

They all saw this before they undressed, before they sought close, sought inside, before flesh mixed and mind melded.

It was days later, days before. They couldn't tell and didn't care.

Phillip sat on a rock alone. Liz walked to him.

– Great show, he said. – My compliments.

– This is nothing, she grinned. – You wait until New Orleans. Then you'll see how it's supposed to be done.

Phillip sat on a rock, brooding. Liz walked to him, studying him, looking straight through him.

– Something has changed in you, she pondered. – What is it?

– So you don't know? She sensed triumph in him, and a horrible sadness and rage.

She looked at him, just looked at him, with those big eyes of hers.

His shoulders sagged and he relented.

– I, we… the family received a notification, a message from the police. My father has been killed in New Orleans, shot down in the middle of the street. Apparently there was a delay, a mix-up, and we didn't get the message until long after it had happened, and he's long since buried, in an unmarked grave.

A few seconds passed, and then she put her hand on his shoulder, comforting him somewhat.

– I'm sorry.

He looked at her, stared at her at length, before nodding.

– Whoever has done it will pay, pay a hundred times. I will find them, even if I have to search all the four corners of the Earth.

And the fifth, she thought. And all the empty places in-between and beyond.

They drank lots of water to wet their dry mouths and throats, to compensate for the sponge sucking all moisture from their tongue.

The visions began, assaulting them like blades, releasing the sweet blood in their veins.

Dark and amazed laughter descended the dark heavens. They shook and shook their heads for a long time, until everything started making sense, until joy and awareness burned within them all.

– I go, a boy called. – I go behind the corner, and meet the Shadow.

I go
I go behind the corner
And meet the Shadow
I burn in its face
Its tongue licks my ass
Swallowing my Self whole
And I am it
I find myself
In places I've never looked

Phillip shivered in Liz' arms, crouching in her deep, deep lap. She comforted him as best she could, as existence cut itself open before her, as she tasted the air like blood, and the blood gave up its secrets.

Ted stood on his arms, stood upside down, looking at the world from a right, right angle.

Or at least he imagined he did.

The stars were at his brow and the ground at his feet, his toes drawing beautiful lines in the mud.

Everything faded in time, including the razor sharp mind he could dimly recall.

There was a scream of rage and despair echoing through eternity. Tears like fire dropped from Phillip Caine's black, black eyes.

I LOOK, a boy said, everybody said. I FIND myself in every single spot I look.

Bodies and soaring minds are falling, a voice calls, not through space, but through time.

– I see a girl, Liz said, very remote. – She stands on a flooded beach, speaking to the waves.

And the waves bring them her words.

And the waves gave up their secrets.

– FAAAR out, the girl sighed. – Far ouuuuuuuuuuut. And so good, so very sweet. I love sweet. I love it so much.

Faces danced in the fires and everybody shivered faced with their mirror image.

The creatures in the fire danced and stared at their shadows in the mirror.

– I KNOW, Brad shouted. – I SEE, SEE SO MUCH!

The wind drifted slowly, so very slowly across the darkened land and everything was visible, slowly stopping in its travels, until everything once more stood still.

It was peaceful afterwards, if that word had any meaning. A boy and a girl rested drowsy side-by-side, comparing notes.

– I brought some reading.

It was an old, stained and worn copy of Science 189, from 1975.

– Listen to this: A guy named Wallace Broecker says there will be an enormous global warming the next decades, a warming directly brought on by mankind's burning of fossil fuels releasing CO2 and other greenhouse gases into the atmosphere.

- Did we sleep? The girl wondered.

- Do we sleep? The boy wondered.

Questions and answers kept killing them softly throughout the night, in the eternal existence they found themselves. The stars darkened in the sky, and everything turned bright.

Everybody wore dark glasses the day after, but eyes flashed and burned behind the shades. They reached the ends of New Mexico sometimes during the afternoon. The sun was in the west, the dust in the east. They looked hard at it, and the thousand grains glowed in the dusk.

– Through Texas? He pondered.

– Through Texas, she confirmed.

And a thousand stallions roared in the night.

3

The dust in their vision turned to blood. This didn't surprise them. They rode through the valley of a giant Hollow, and the hard ground stung their feet, and the ground was painted red.

Liz's bike turned sideways on the road, and screeched across the gray path. The others stopped, quite stricken. The bike stopped in a cloud of sand and dust just outside the road.

She sat there, unbelievably enough still on the bike.

He dismounted his bike and walked to her. Everybody turned off their engine, going to her.

She rushed into his arms, pushed herself at him. He looked astonished at her.

– You're shaking, he whispered.

And she stood there for minutes, shivering like a small bird before the Storm.

– I don't know what it is, she said sullenly. – I just know that it is. It is waiting for us out there, no matter where we go.

He patted her back, rubbed her hair.

– Can I ride back with you? She said in a tiny, childish voice. – Please?

Her pouting always irritated him. He couldn't help himself.

– No. He vehemently shook his head.

He let go of her, and pushed her away in contempt.

She stood there shaking, twisting her lips, while she slowly, angrily pulled herself together.

– Fine, she snarled. – Be that way. Just be that way, and see how it benefits you.

She lifted a hand. The bike rose in the air in a dustbin of sand. She put it back on the road with a less than minimal effort.

A truck passing by visibly strayed off course. Ted saw the driver's stunned and apprehensive expression, and it somehow pleased him, pleased him, too.

It clearly pleased Liz. He didn't have to look at her to see that.

She mounted the bike and set off in a roar of rage.

The others looked at him. He shrugged without shrugging, and they relaxed somewhat. He mounted his own bike and drove off in a somewhat controlled manner, and they followed him.

4

– Texas is something of a disappointment, Liz cried loudly. – Nothing much ever happens here.

She looked challengingly around her in the small diner. There were no takers.

Texas slipped away beneath their wheels. Nothing much happened. There were a few skirmishes outside Houston, but it never amounted to much. No one in his right and *unright* mind picked a fight with a bunch of bikers without a damn good reason, and no one they met found one. Not even Liz' constantly venomous tongue managed that.

She spoke to the group, to the wandering tribe late at night, while the campfire burned their skin.

– Some years ago Hells Angels leveled a sheriff's office and most of that small town after they had been treated disrespectfully, she burned. – Very few have dared to hassle bikers after that. So, there's a definite advantage to wear that skin.

She drilled them in combat, both armed and unarmed. They gasped as she demonstrated her skills, convinced the weapons were an extension of her body, her self, her very being. And it felt even more incredible because they knew more about her, now, her age, her general background.

– I feel it, you know, she said dreamily, suddenly softly, – feel the steel in my hands, feel it as if I've felt it for thousands of years.

Phillip missed a target, and he blushed, as he felt her wrath, her desperation, her desperate need for them all to learn, and he redoubled his efforts.

Weapons weren't unknown to him, far from it. He had practiced with them, with and without his father's guidance and consent since he was a kid, but this was different, this was real.

They all learned, even those who had never touched a gun or a knife before.

– Yes, you're all learning, Ted said. – Now, all you have left to learn is to kill or be killed.

And his words were more sinister in a way, because he hadn't spoken much these last few days.

The flatlands of Texas gave way to the swamps of Louisiana, slowly, almost unnoticeable.

They drilled themselves some more. Justine hit a target, and she gasped in joy. They could all see the blood gushing from the inanimate statue, as if there was actually a flesh and blood creature standing there, see the figure fall and die, and excitement and terror warred within them.

The swamp was alive. They sensed that, without even trying. In a moist place, between tall, thick trees, not that far from the main road they found a ramshackle cabin. It was abandoned, tables, furniture and floor and all covered in dust. When they entered it and walked around it became clear there hadn't been people there for a long time. The moisture lingered in the air, but the dust was still dry, easily stirred from its rest.

– This is so great, Brad cried. – It's spacey, and… well spacey. I could do much with this place.

– New Orleans is just over the hill, Phillip said, a new, sinister, strange Phillip. – It's a perfect spot.

– It is! Ted stated darkly. – It will draw the curious and the friendly… and hostile, draw them all, and that is exactly how we want it.

And they marveled and trembled at the sight of him, at the sound of his voice.

The two fireeyes walking among them… they were like walking moons. There were silver light and the color of fire dancing across their many faces.

The tribe arrived in New Orleans at dusk. The metal horses rode slowly through the antique streets, strangely quiet and muted. They recognized Canal Street and the special balconies in the French Quarter from countless photographs and movies. Ted and Liz and also several of the others from a thousand fevered dreams. The two of them clutched the handles on the bikes a bit tighter. Their companions didn't notice.

People stared at them in strange ways, strange ways even for them.

The eerie mood rose from the ground and emanated from the buildings and people, and hit the new arrivals like hardened air, pricking their skin. Others might not sense more than mundane stirrings upon arriving in New Orleans, but they did.

There was a parking lot by a demolished building where there actually was a lot of parking space. It was probably due to the dust blowing in from the demolition site, covering everything in gray powder. But their bikes, their clothes had been on the road for days, and weren't changed in any visible way.

They dismounted and looked around, tasted the air. It was different, way different from what any of them had experienced before. Liz and Ted bathed in it, enjoying the moment to the fullest.

– Cities have personalities, haven't they? Justine breathed in wonder. – Almost like people. And in this city, this City of the Dead it's filled to the brim. I've always wanted to go here, but could never work up the nerve. This is a dream come true.

Her grateful smile, directed at the two Warrens spoke volumes, almost making them blush, but also worry, inevitably.

They left the bikes without guards, and walked up Canal Street.

– Just let them steal from us, Liz grinned. – And they'll know soon enough they've made the greatest mistake in their life.

People stared at them, but in a strange manner. Used to stares at this stage in their lives, in similar circumstances, they noticed the originality of people's reaction to their presence.

– How weird, Liz said incredulously. – They're afraid, or at least skittish, but not of us.

They noticed the moment they turned a corner and crossed the invisible line to the Vieux Carrè, the French Quarter, even before spotting the balconies and the special architecture.

There is an open space opening up to them after they've walked for a while, and they're a bit lost, after having crisscrossed the narrow streets for a while. A man stands at its center. He holds a ball of fire in his hand or close to it, holds it in his grip, even though it doesn't touch his skin.

They stop, and watch and listen.

– There is a valley somewhere, the man clothed in chalk cried in a dead man's voice. – A Valley of Death, one of kings and gods, where all things are possible.

He put the fire in his hand to his mouth and swallowed it, consumed it, and it seemed to glow within him, to the point where his skin brightened and burned.

– I'm Henry Gallier, he cried. – I'm the Loa of the gods.

Liz steps forward.

– Your words move me, sir, she cries. – They make it tingle down my spine.

The man freezes and glares at her, and his expression turns absolutely blank. He speaks, and they can't understand the words.

– Is that… that is French, isn't it? Brad wonders.

Gallier takes a big jump backwards, and with a final, fear-filled glance he runs away like an animal before the Storm.

A girl stops at an odd angle from Liz and the others, between Liz and Ted. Her head is slightly cocked as she speaks.

– «I burn in your presence, Bird of Fire and Shadow. My flame is nothing compared to yours. I dwindle to ashes in your moonlight».

– So what does it mean? Liz asked lightly.

– I have no idea, the girl said evenly. – I've seen Henry perform here every day for years, but he has never behaved like this. Never! You made quite an impression on him.

The girl is young, younger than Ted, perhaps a bit older than Liz. She looks strangely at them, at them all, and there's something in that look that is strangely familiar.

– You're travelers? She stated.

– We are indeed, Ted said. – And we have traveled far to come to this place, this City of the Dead.

– I'm late for supper, the girl said.

And hurried away.

They watched her leave.

– Welcome to New Orleans, Liz said, a huge grin transforming her face.

– I think someone just did, Phillip emphasized. – Did welcome us.

She turned and looked at him. It was as if she saw him, saw his cold, hard face for the first time. Everybody looked for the girl, but she had vanished between the buildings, and no matter how much Liz wanted to pursue her, she knew she would find nothing in there, nothing but ghosts and shadows laughing at her.

Welcome to New Orleans. She looked at Ted. They stood there, breathing in the air of the foreign, but oh, so familiar place. It was like pulling off an old blanket, revealing everything hidden beneath. A thrill shot through them both, of expectation and apprehension, and as always they couldn't tell which was which. It echoed within them time and time again, much more so than the whispers from the streets and buildings surrounding them, as the twilight turned to darkness and the darkness turned to night.

*Welcome to New Orleans!*

## 5

There was an old manor close to the swamps. The car pulled up in front of the gate, and the gate opened on rusty hinges. The car was a limousine. A man wearing white gloves drove it through an alley of old trees to the front of the manor. The driver wearing white gloves stepped outside and walked to one of the back doors, and opened it. Phillip Caine stepped outside. Ignoring the driver he appeared to brush dust from his coat before stepping towards the entrance. He easily noticed the numerous armed guards. It seemed excessive, even for a place like this. And what was even weirder: They didn't hide, didn't even make the attempt at being discreet, which was, the way his father had told him, darn near sacrilege in these surroundings.

Another servant opened the door (the very large and heavy door) for him, and yet another waited for him inside.

– Good evening, sir, may I take your coat.

Caine left him his coat, looking closer at the man. This was a fairly important man in the household, one running its daily chores, the equivalent of an English butler that some filthy rich Americans were fond of employing.

– Thank you, sir. If you will come with me, sir.

There was a question mark at the end of the sentence. There always was on these occasions, it seemed.

Caine followed him upstairs. The marble, carpet-covered stairway was just as expensive and deliberate as the rest of the building. The walk went up the stairway, and down a long, well-lit hallway, to a room at the center of the building, a place with no windows, a place of shadows, the poker room.

He walked inside, very aware of every detail surrounding him, the hand-carved furniture, the lavish lamps, and the sweat in the men's faces.

– Gentlemen, the head honcho servant declared somewhat hastily, – may I present Phillip Caine.

The question mark was there, as always. Phillip suppressed a wicked laughter.

The seven men around the table looked at the newest arrival. Caine shook hands with them. The seventh (or the first), Clayton Powers met his eyes, an act very telling among players. Philip saw nothing there, nothing at all.

– I knew your father, kid, the older man said lightly. – I hear you're carrying on in his memory, and then some. I want to thank you for coming here, for agreeing to join our little game.

– A pleasure, sir, Caine said, just as lightly, – I want to thank you for inviting me. As you may have heard, I never say no to any poker game, not to a *good* one.

Laughter, paper-dry and dead echoed around the table, but not beyond it. The newest arrival sat down in the eighth seat, putting a thick pile of bills on the table. There were two empty seats. He noticed that, of course, but didn't comment on it.

– Too bad your two young friends couldn't join us, another of the men, Taylor Lowell commented. – They, too, have gained quite a reputation as *players*.

– They are otherwise engaged today, I'm afraid, Caine shrugged. – They told me to apologize on their behalf.

The seven men nodded, grunted, not commenting on it.

Caine almost grinned again. That was poker for you. Nothing was ever as it seemed.

– They make quite an impression on people, I hear, Powers inquired.

– Oh, yes, Caine joked, – I myself can hardly reach back in time before the moment I first encountered them.

The game began. He felt exhilaration, inevitably, adding to the increased stirring he had felt for a while. The cards were at his fingertips. He felt the pattern at their back painting in his brain. There was no cheating. He was quickly convinced of that, as he observed his opponents. These men weren't about that, not here, at least. No matter the numerous atrocities they committed and ordered committed outside this room, this was a game of skill even they appreciated. Even though he couldn't truly appreciate it these days, he made a conscious effort to fall back on old desires, those only dimly recalled from his now seemingly ancient past.

He dealt the cards, not too slow, not too fast, attempting to focus on the table, the players before him. Two cards to each player, five «community cards» in total at the center of the table, cards shared by all, to combine with the cards they had in their hands or in front of them.

And he was distracted.

He focused on Clayton Powers. The others were immaterial, anyway.

– Your father was truly a legend in these parts, one of the men said, – long before he departed for that glittertown in the desert. He truly was the Gambler.

– My father is dead! Phillip cried. – I am the Gambler, now!

The men merely nodded. Such a dramatic, theatrical, even emotional outburst during a succession of title and name was quite familiar to them. The fact that it happened at a poker table was ultimately irrelevant.

– He was murdered, shot down in the street like a dog, and I'm going to find the dog doing it.

This time there was a reaction, a brittle ruffle around the table. Phillip sensed it. He had noticed from an early age, how he always seemed to be more sensitive around the table.

Powers dealt the cards. His fleshy fingers looked like those of a piano player when he treated the deck to his eminent technique. The Gambler looked at his cards, and he made a bet. Lowell and another player called. The first three cards were dropped on the table. The Gambler bet some more. Lowell called. The third player raised. The Gambler re-raised him again. Lowell called. The third player folded. The fourth card was turned on the table. The Gambler bet again, bet a lot. Lowell sat there pondering, foaming a lot around the mouth… before folding. The Gambler collected a big pot.

And what he had, his two pocket cards, no one would ever know. He wasn't certain he knew himself.

Cards were and would always be immaterial. People weren't. You played the players, not the cards.

The deck circled the table, and he circled with it, piercing the eyes above it. Each characteristic, every casual move danced in his mind, and he sat there, and Elizabeth Warren filled his mind like a sponge. She became the dance, became the Alpha and Omega, and the cards turned to mist and shadow.

When he looked up, he was amazed that it was still day outside. He felt it as if he had been sitting here for days.
He looked over the table, at Clayton Powers. Phillip's stack and his were about even. The others didn't count. They were just window dressing.
Half an hour later, he paused a bit, before dealing, rubbing his temples.
– Sorry, gentlemen, it doesn't work for me today.
– It doesn't… work for you? Lowell said pointedly, looking at the very much thicker pile of bills in front of the Gambler.
– I'm afraid not. I'll give you gentlemen an hour to win back your losses, and then I'll be on my way.
There was honesty here, brutal and to the point. He knew they «appreciated» that in this matter, no matter how petty they usually were.
When the hour had passed his pile had grown even thicker, and most of the others' were practically gone. They could add to their stack at any time, but he knew they wouldn't do that, not in his presence. He said his polite goodbye, and walked down the stairway. The butler, or «Major Domo», as they were often called in the United States, the man he still couldn't recall the name of, handed him his coat, and he was out of there, out through the big door, in the vast yard, and he could somewhat breathe again.

## 6

The man and woman dressed totally in black wore sunglasses even in the darkest hour.
New Orleans and Vieux Carrè revealed itself to Ted and Liz' glowing eyes.
– Cities have a mood, she said with badly concealed excitement. – A taste, tangible, like blood, spices flickering in your mind.
– Yes. He nodded. – And this one reminds me of London, reminds me in ways I can't identify. They are alike, and they are different. And they both sort of give me the impression of walking through the wilderness, as if it is actually present here, in the midst of concrete and bricks.
– It is! She cried. – It is right here, with us, wherever we go.
She wagged her tail as they rummaged through the streets. People noticed her, and they noticed him, too.
– I can feel myself responding to it, she pondered, sniffing the air without really realizing she was doing it. – Whatever is here, is also… inside us. I feel so proud, Ted, so very proud.
That startled him. It was one of the few times that he could recall that she had actually used his name. She used a lot of other names, but usually not the abbreviation he had grown into, never his name.
She stopped, right at the corner, leaning against it, provocative and irresistible.
Two pair of eyes moved as one, taking in the sights, registering everything happening around them, striving to make sense of it.
– I don't understand them, she finally said.
He didn't say anything. There was no need.

– I mean, they're not an enigma or anything, far from it, on the contrary. I mean, how can they be so mundane, so thoroughly unable to find their own way? Even here, most people don't get it!

He looked at those passing them, back and forth on the street, looked and kept looking, kept observing. Squinting his eyes, he attempted to focus on, to concentrate at that something inside resonating with the surroundings. And suddenly…

Suddenly it was as if he was several places simultaneously. He blinked. She didn't watch the passing people, but watched him, and as she did, she closed her eyes, and a smile broke on her face.

– The Power, she breathed. – The Power is growing.

There was a man at the opposite corner. They heard him breathe, and in more ways than one, it was as if they were standing right there by his side. His scent danced in their nostrils. His sounds lingered in their ears. A woman danced somewhere on the second floor of a nearby building. They felt her moves in their limbs, sensed the invisible glow in her eyes.

They stood there breathing, attempting to catch themselves, catch the wind passing back and forth in their nostrils.

– Unholy cow, she exhaled, – that wasn't our enhanced five senses at work, at least not solely so. There was more, so much More.

Minutes passed, there, on the corner. They heard waves striking the shore, saw the mist of giant waterfalls rise in the air.

It faded, slowly, inevitably.

She sighed and walked to him.

– There's an alley, not far from the Square.

– I know the one you mean, Ted acknowledged.

– It's so dark and mysterious. I get the willies there.

She grabbed his hands.

– Let's go there, she said, eagerly like a young girl.

There was a draft in the air, an invisible trail, shimmering, almost visible air, surrounding them as they walked, as they forged their way through the known and unknown streets.

The alley looked dark. It always did, to their eyes, even in the middle of the day. They stopped a few steps within its confines, staring at the empty street, straining their eyes, straining… And suddenly the street is empty no more.

There's a shift in the air, a change in perception, and even though they're still physically present in the street, they're also in a place of soft, dark light, a place of mist and shadow.

Ted crouches slightly, as if in pain. Liz looks both at him and at the multivision environment.

This is a crossroads, a voice says. As you are crossroads, gates to Infinity.

The voice is not a voice, but sounds forming in the very air. Whether it is male or female they cannot say.

Ted Warren reached out with his left hand, reached out into the thick soup of invisible mist that had become the air, and he touched it. He felt its solid firmament in his grasp.

– How can you do that? They heard a woman speak, her beyond shocked expression painted in their mind. – You shouldn't be able to *do* that.

People, or rather shadows, swarmed around them, no more solid than specters, whirling so fast that most of them could hardly be glimpsed, far less recognized, but a warm breeze of familiarity still washed over the two, the two standing their ground against the onslaught battering them.

This is the Shadow World. The voice kept articulating itself out of thin air. Humanity has, for good or ill created a world less of physical reality, and more of the mind, but still of neither. This is who we are, what sets us apart, what makes us closer to everything than anything else.

There was thunder, unheard, except for the tremble in the ground, the shimmer in the air.

A man, one of the countless, swarming shadows, slowed down in his faster than seen pace, stopped a bit ahead of them, and he turned, looked eerily at them, and headed towards them. His face, his face, its details changed so fast that they were unable to make out one, single look, but somewhere in the whirling mass that was his face, they still recognized him. They stared at him, at the large hole in his chest, at the waterfall of blood leaking from it, and decorating the malleable ground.

His face, impassive as stone, stared at them with its distant, ebony eyes.

– I'm coming, he said, – and there will be a reckoning.

His voice sounded solid and normal, like it would if he was standing right in front of them.

And he was. He walked towards them, but he didn't come any closer, not closer than right in front of them.

– You dreamed of Death, he said, – and Death is coming.

He dissolved, faded to nothing in front of them, and the chill coursing through them was like nothing they had ever felt.

They walked for hours after that, not really noticing the passing of time. They noticed their surroundings, with even sharper and more accurate senses.

Water was constantly pouring down in the streets from the upper floor balconies, from the watered pottery plants. One could smell the dirt, the soil from the pottery.

They smelled it, almost like an invasive force, penetrating them, all their parts.

It didn't rain. It hadn't rained since their arrival, but the air was still humid beyond belief. Everything was constantly wet. Hair, skin and paper, in the midst of sun, shade and wind. They, too, were sweating profusely and constantly in the damp, jungle-like heat.

– My hair feels like it hasn't been washed for weeks, she complained. – And the clothes… Are people ever dry here?

– I think they will grow gills soon, he replied lightly. – Those that haven't already.

She grinned at him, upbeat and wild, in spite of it all.

The inner chill prevailed, no matter what they did to expunge it.

They passed through Bourbon Street for what had to be the hundredth time or something. Sidewalks were narrow here, like all streets in the Quarter, with very short distance to the insides of the buildings. Everything is tight and close.

Both the sidewalks and the street were packed. The occasional car had major trouble driving through. Ted spotted Henry Gallier down a crossing street, spotted him at an impossible angle. He wasn't alone this time, but kept company with a group of people with shadows dancing around their forms. Ted nodded to himself. He knew them, knew them for what they were.

– Some people see auras, Liz nodded, as astute as ever, – but this is a step beyond that.

And as always she hit the nail straight on the head. He pulled her close and kissed her passionately on the lips. She laughed, a thrilling laughter sending thrills and chills through everybody nearby.

Bourbon Street had once been the whorehouse capital of America, and there were still some of them left, even though they no longer dominated the scenery the way they once had, even though they now were less discreet than they had once been. Ted shook his head over this apparent contradiction.

Well-dressed men stood in the open doorways, calling out to those passing by.

- NAKED WOMEN INSIDE, a man shouted. – NAKED WOMEN INSIDE.

Ted went to him, impulsively, after having hesitated a few steps, clearly irritated.

– The way you shout it, it seems like men have never seen a naked woman before.

– What is your problem, man? The man with naked women inside complained, his welcoming smile quickly fading.

– My… *problem* is the way everything is commercialized, trivialized, making shitheads like you a livelihood.

Comprehension failed totally to dawn in the man's face and features. He spotted Liz and his eyes brightened.

– Hi, baby, he whistled. – I can make you a star in a minute if you let me.

– You, sir, are a slug, she replied in a mock representation of a christian upper-class woman. – Not worthy to be in my exalted presence.

There was laughter, loud laughter, and the man in the door was further humiliated.

The two Warrens walked on. Liz pushed herself close to Ted, in a manner definitely not resembling that of a proper lady. She whispered soft words in his ears.

– You're so sweet. I want to reward you so very, very much…

– It was just a whim, he shrugged.

Her expression softened even more, her eyes looking almost tenderly at him.

They sat on Jackson Square, on a bench, watching the clouds dance. There was a kind of silence here, not present elsewhere in the Quarter. People passed by, but they were not loud. The wind was picking up, picking up from one moment to the next.

– There is a Storm coming, she said dreamingly. – I can actually see the wisps, the wisps of Shadow in the air.

He shivered in the warm sunshine. She looked at him.

– Death is coming, he said.

She rose and reached out a hand to him, very deliberately. He took it, and she pulled him up, pulled him on his feet.

Her voice, when she spoke, was both distant and close, with the challenge in her voice that both infuriated and attracted him.

– You didn't have your powers before the… bad things happened to you, not really, not as anything but ghosts and half remembered dreams. But mine has… bloomed, now, and, they tell me what is in store. We aren't ignorant anymore. We know what's coming, and we can prepare for it.

She was very close, her lips and entire being.

– Come, he said, and pulled her with him, gently and rough.

She sensed the eagerness, the these days so rare boyish charm in him, and didn't resist.

They walked to Decatur. She looked inquiringly at him, but he wasn't very forthcoming. There was humor in him, bubbling beneath the surface, and it puzzled her. He stopped by the horse carrier, the very available horse carrier and he bowed to her. She looked incredulous at him.

– Care for a ride, Madame? He said, mimicking to perfection the formal language.

They were mimics, she realized on a side note. They had always been good at it. It had always come naturally to them, without practicing.

– Are you serious? Then she was smiling, an exalted smile. – You are serious, aren't you…

She held out a hand, and he took it. He clearly went too far when he helped her up on the open seat, but she didn't care. She giggled and a warm, warm feeling rose inside her.

– The Grand Tour, Monsieur? The man holding the horses' reins queried.

– The Grand Tour, Ted confirmed cheerfully.

The man rattled the reins, and the horses snuffled and started walking.

Liz sat there, so very astute, drawing her breath.

– There's something in a girl's makeup, making her melt when taken on a romantic horse carrier tour in the evening, she sighed, her voice a clear undercurrent of contempt.

He brought a hand out from behind his back.

– Flowers? She exclaimed happily. – For me?

– For my Dark Maiden, he said ironically.

– My dark knight, in dirty armor, she said softly, kissing him hungrily on the lips.

The world moved slowly around the two youths, revolving around their senses as surroundings and people shifted. They sat still, but the world still moved. It was peaceful and extremely dynamic at the same time. The ride went down Decatur, along the power lines, towards Canal Street. They sat there and listened, to the noise, to the quiet darkness. Someone was playing an accordion, one of those tiny ones typical for the area, playing it slowly, dwelling on every tone. There was a party in an apartment they passed. A boy and a girl stood on a balcony and kissed passionately, their faces concealed, hidden in shadow. Somewhere in the building, on a large bed five people were fucking each other. It was intense and passionate and wild, a savagery totally beyond reason, a reason beyond passion, and the two in the carriage sensed it, felt it glow in their bellies. The girl leaned close and the boy took her in his arms, and they kissed forever in the darkness.

## 7

The sound of the coq-fighting and loud cries resounded, overloaded their sensitive eardrums. They followed the trail of Francis Caine's final hours. It wasn't really hard, wasn't hard at all.

– Yes, we recognized him, a bartender said nervously after just a little prodding. – At least we old-timers did. Francis Caine wasn't exactly an unknown quantity in these parts.

– But something was different that night, wasn't it? Ted said casually. – What was it?

– *What?* Phillip grabbed the man by the collar.

The man behind the desk sent The Gambler a strange look. The look he sent the young man manhandling him wasn't unsympathetic.

– The fact that Caine was here at all felt… wrong. He had long since outgrown us, moved on to better things. He was… misplaced.

He hesitated some more, before nodding to himself. They waited. Phillip let go of him.

– Some of us can see it, you know, he said, looking at Ted and Liz with very intense eyes. – When a man is marked, when Death has touched him, and he doesn't have long left to live. It isn't about external things at all, but rests within the person itself. When a human being has let go of the will to live he or she are far more vulnerable to those outside forces that might exploit such a state of mind, and Francis Caine was ready to receive Death's sweet and bitter touch.

– Voodoo bullshit, Phillip Caine snarled.

He discovered that Ted and Liz stood there and nodded to themselves and got even more agitated, even though he was unable to express it. He felt like a cauldron inside. The pressure was building and he was unable to explode.

The wind was blowing, dust floating in the narrow street. Liz and Ted Warren stood at its beginning, holding hands. This was the «crime site». They had seen the police photographs, but they easily noticed more. Even though it was partly their imagination experiencing the crumbling figure of Francis Caine entering the street and walk through it, they saw him. They saw a shadowy form wait for him with a gun raised, heard the crack of the gun, saw the bullet hit his forehead and blow away the back of his brain, and saw him fall in the dust. And as the dust whirled in the air, they felt him breathe his final breath.

He stood there in the street, right now, staring at them with a look of hatred and bewilderment in his eyes, as if he was still alive.

– What do you see? Phillip called, his voice half coarse, half broken.

– Nothing. Liz shook her head, disentangling her hand from Ted's. – Nothing important.

Phillip carried a briefcase, one with every scrap of information they had been able to dig up about the case. There was a lot there, and still… there was nothing or less than nothing. They sat around a table on a sidewalk restaurant, eating in a distracted fashion, and went through it all, went through it again. Phillip looked at the picture of his dead father, and his expression hardened a bit more.

– There is something here. Liz frowned. – Something I can't quite grasp…

– Something is missing. Ted shrugged. – There is nothing about Mark here, nothing at all.

And they looked at each other with a clarity of thought they often missed.

– It's obvious, now, in hindsight, Liz said. – How come you realized it, and I didn't?

– You didn't spend much time with Mark…

– It makes sense, Phillip said. – It makes perfect sense… doesn't it?

– Yes. Ted nodded. – It does. Mark would want to hide any obvious involvement with a crime from the authorities. The question is what *kind* of sense it makes.

There was an angry subtext to his words and his voice that Liz easily recognized. She grabbed his hand again, squeezing it tightly.

An image came to her of the twenty-three warm and naked bodies just stretching there, in the heated, humid room, touching, relaxed and peacefully.

Touch is important, she thought. We've learned that.

She saw him stiffen, and she did, too. There was movement in the adjacent streets, very fast movement. They noticed it as a disturbance in people's walk, a ripple in the pond. It was quite unsettling. It was a kind of… spatial sense of their extended surroundings far exceeding ordinary telekinesis, as they had learned to define it.

There was a song rising from the back alleys and buildings. Everybody heard it, heard the insane chant cutting to the bone. Phillip's eyes widened. He couldn't keep it from happening, even if he didn't want it to happen. The chant filled every person in the nearby streets with a nameless horror:

*– Iluso is our Master. Iluso is our God. Beware his wrath. We are the People beyond Legend, and we are mighty beyond words.*

– Is that English? Liz wondered through her teeth. – Or some ancient, dead language?

– It's both, Ted said.

She cast a glance at him, nodding, nodding to herself.

– It's Romany, Phillip said.

The two of them looked at him, stunned that he knew.

– Father told me, he told them, – told me the story.

The first two appeared around the corner to the left. Then, shortly afterwards two more appeared around the right corner ahead. They were dressed in white hoods and robes. And…

They held guns in their hands, carrying them completely openly.

– What are those? A girl nearby sniffed. – Ku Klux Klan rejects or something?

Then she spotted the guns, and her eyes grew huge and scared. She remained there, on the spot, frozen and dead.

– I hear it, Liz chanted. – I hear it for the first time, the rush, the buzzing in the ears, the rising Sound of Thunder.

The approaching servants of Iluso heard her, and it sent a perceptible shiver through them, even though it didn't stop their perpetual, inevitable forward motion.

And Phillip did, too, sensing how his body, his mind prepared for what was to come. He saw, sensed more than saw Ted and Liz move, saw them fall from their chairs, saw them draw their guns, a flash, an indistinct shadow more than a move, and he noticed he held his own gun in both his hands, firing it at the attackers.

He was standing with his two companions, running, in a hail of bullets. The insane chant kept filling the streets, and he realized that it wasn't really the attackers that were chanting, at least not them alone. It was as if there was an entire choir hidden somewhere in the streets of New Orleans.

The first red stain appeared on white fabric. The first attacker squealed and died. Phillip Caine watched Ted Warren fire his gun. It was as if it came alive in his hand. And Phillip watched Liz, and the metal glowed and pulsed in her hand as well. Phillip fired and a bullet hit a female hooded figure in the chest. He was hit. He fell, and found himself staring astounded at the red stain on his dark clothes, finding it incredible that the red was visible on the black fabric. His finger kept squeezing the trigger. He kept firing, rolling and moving in the dust. A bullet hit the frozen female bystander. She simply fell, without a sound. Other, fleeing bystanders were hit. Blood and dust filled the streets, complementing the chant hurting Phillip's ears.

Afterwards. Long afterwards, a few seconds, less than a minute at most, he watched, studied the two Warrens walking among the dead and dying, sucking up their energy like sponges sucking water. There were dead people everywhere, a scene beyond unreal and ugly. He saw two ravens flap their wings and felt the impact in the wind, the waves in the air created when they reached his brow. The chant faded, and dread and silence filled the air. It was over so fast. Death had merely touched them, ruffled their feathers.

Liz walked towards him, slowly, nonchalantly, a fury personified, smiling at him with feverish eyes.

– What…

He attempted to speak, to give voice to what had rested inside him.

She nodded to him, encouragingly, the sunset in her eyes blinding him.

Tears filled his eyes, as he attempted to bypass, ignore the searing pain.

– What's the Sound of Thunder? He managed.
– The end of the world, she replied.
She grinned.
– It's your arm. She nodded to herself. – It's a fleabite.
Once again he was unable to speak.
She reached out a hand to him. He reached out, too, and she grabbed his wrist, pulling him up. He gasped, as pain ravaged him. She stood there, seemingly oblivious to his plight.
– Now, you know, she said.
He stared at her through the haze of red, seeing clearer than he ever had, as she restated, sanitized her sentence.
– Now, you know what it's like.

# Chapter Seven: Death and the Maiden

## FLIGHT OF THE RAVEN

*There is a smell of burning, of smoke. That's the very first sensation you notice. The fire was first. We were born in the Fire. And we are its Shadow.*

*You see a foreign place on television, a place you have never visited, feeling a catching in your throat, of longing and pain. You have never been to that place, but you know it still.*

*You experience a foreign smell. You sit in your own kitchen and know this scent doesn't belong here. It is coming from you. It isn't physically there, but has arisen from a prodding of your memory.*

*To many that's how it begins, one of many ways it might begin. And for most present day, narrow-minded people that's how it ends. Life is filled with reincarnation dreams, but we learn to discard them as insignificant from an early age, by parents, and by a society discarding everything deep, everything truly valuable, discarding Life.*

### 2

He found himself in a shadowy, bright colorless landscape beyond description.

The man with the black eyes stared at Ted Warren with an expression of hatred and longing, his eyes twinkling in Shadow.

– Morgan Lombard killed me. But he was just a hand, really, not the actual killer.

The roar in Ted's ears turned silent, absolutely silent. Cold rushed down his spine.

– Jahavalo killed me, the man with the black eyes said. – He has killed me many times, like he has you, but he could never reach you, never touch you.

It was the «man» from the dark, narrow alley, the man with many faces, with a large hole in his chest.

But now there was no hole, and Ted could easily see his face, a face both strangely unfamiliar and familiar.

– He waits for me on the other side, but I won't go there. I will cheat him of his prize.

– Jahavalo? Ted whispered, fits of the coldest cold almost overwhelming him.

– You know him, know him from your earliest night terrors thousands of years back. He haunts all our days. He's both the first and second power. Only a third, truly independent can fight him effectively, can crush him like the bug he is.

And the black hole of a man drew breath, even though he didn't need to breathe.

– You know me. You knew who I was, know who I will be. I will be untouchable then. He won't be able to touch me anymore. I've waited for that, waited for so very long, waited to regain the gift of fire he pulled from my grasp.

Ted wanted to speak, even though he had no tongue, even though he had no mouth, but his voice died unborn. The two men stood there, facing each other, neither averting their eyes.

– *We* are the Third Force. The stranger's tongue turned into a snake and he spat it out, and it curled on the ground and slithered off. – Jahavalo shivers in his comfortable bed, sensing our coming. And that is good, because we need to be all the nightmares we can be to keep him from his final, ultimate ascension. We will stop him, and civilization will drown in blood.

Half his face, half his body shed its skin and flesh, and revealed the glowing skeleton, the one from Ted's thousand nightmares. And just as the entire figure began fading, his one eye began glowing in fire.

At the morning of Samhain, before All Soul's Night, he awoke, drenched in cold sweat, realizing that Liz, his partner, his companion sat beside him on the bed, so much closer than all the other warm bodies also sleeping in the bed beside them.

She comforted him, rubbed his ice-cold skin.

– Death, he gasped. – Death is being born.

The others woke up, too, yawning, sensing his distress, having become fairly attuned to his moods, and they come to him, embracing the shaking body, heating the cold sweat. There was a lot of hugging and kissing.

The others are gone. Only the two of them remain.

– Their presence feels… good? She said hesitatingly.

– Touch is important. He nodded. – We've learned that, haven't we?

She nodded, swallowing hard.

– I see a hospital, a hospital in *London*. He said casually, very casually. She wasn't fooled. – I see a woman. I know. I know her. Death springs from her loins.

There is morning, hours, seconds later, the dawn of October 31st - Halloween. The activity in and around the city begins early, increasing even from the fairly high spike yesterday and the days before that.

She sat in front of the broken mirror, brushing her hair. She sat there for a long time, making it a concentrated effort, before finally turning towards him.

– Damn, this humidity is the pits, she swore. – An hour since I showered and my tresses are still wet. And I'll bet they will be greasy before dusk.

She tilted her head slightly, as if something just occurred to her.

– Do you think I should cut my hair?

Ted sat in an old, dusty chair, mumbling something. They were both still undressed. They always postponed dressing in the morning.

Liz rose from the stool, and began pacing back and forth in the room.

– It will make it easier to manage. She nodded. – There are points to be made for practicality.

– Uh huh, he said distantly.

She turned towards him, grinning.
– I plan on throwing myself into the tar pits, she declared, – and let myself be fucked by the tars.
– A very good idea, he acknowledged, not really acknowledging anything.
Her expression softened. She focused her mind power on the fleshy part of his shoulder and squeezed, squeezed hard, with her mind's claws, drawing blood.
He jumped to his feet, staring astounded at her. She walked to him, her expression softening further, as she crossed the boundaries of his physical reach.
– You were far gone just now, she told him icily and very softly, touching his cheek. – You were unprepared. You must never be that again.
The wound healed. There had been deep gashes. Now, there were hardly more than scratches left, and they were fading fast. She touched the skin, kissing it carefully, licking off the blood.
– Tilla…
He said.
– Tilla?
She whispered, looking up at him, suddenly sore afraid.
– Tilla was here. I sensed her! It was as if I saw her, saw her right in front of me. She spoke to me, but I couldn't hear her words.
Liz shivered, pulling closer to him.
– Was she… was she *angry?*
– No! He considered it, before shaking his head. – She just *was*.
He touches her tenderly, brutally, and she melts into his arms.
The guys, twenty and three of them walked through the French Quarter. The Festival of Samhain, the celebration of Halloween grew towards a climax, as the day proceeded towards night. It was still day, when the official parades and stuff filled the streets. They stayed away from that, having plans of their own.
– There is no way around it, Liz declared with her usual flair. – Vieux Carrè stinks of shit. It isn't just the spices.
Laughter, as usual both brittle and strong.
Drawings of pumpkins, skeletons and witches were on every wall, dolls both unique to New Orleans and not dangled from windows and balconies everywhere.
The tradition of Halloween had come to these lands with the European invaders, but in this area, this cultural melting pot, it had taken on a mix way beyond anything previously experienced.
At the corner of Basin and St. Louis he spotted the cemetery.
Ted stopped there, and the others did, too. The First Cemetery, where someone had finally buried Marie Laveau - the Voodoo Queen, and also other infamous sorcerers had been buried.
– Usually I don't get anything from cemeteries, Liz noted, as they walked inside, between the tall and sophisticated tombstones. – Everything has usually happened to people by the time their bodies arrive here, but here I do feel the tingle, the burning of skin. It can make a girl all hot and sticky, you know.
And more hot air rushed through them all.

She posed before the Voodoo Queen stone in a provocative, very provocative pose, and Brad photographed her. All the women posed, alone or together. And the men, too, later, in other spots. And eventually, strangely enough, everybody together, in various mixes. They all posed together in a few pictures, where the camera floated in the air, also high above any natural vantage point.

– These are the photos I've always wanted to take, Ted said pleased. – What very few others may take.

– A witch might be a unique photographer, Justine teased, and blushed instantly when he approvingly directed his attention at her.

This place was like a city, one within the other larger city surrounded by the white wall. When you walked through it, even considering the obvious wrong scale, the passageways resembled streets, and the crypts houses. It gave them all an eerie, extraordinary sense of being watched. And it lingered and grew the longer they stayed.

Henry Gallier appeared before them, and they all saw him, saw his wicked grin.

– Everybody must take the train, he said, in his eerie voice. – Everybody not taking the train is free game.

And the laughter echoed between the tiny houses of the dead, as his form faded before their eyes.

Several members of the tribe became very distressed by this. Liz and Ted noticed it instantly.

– Is he… a ghost? Has someone k-killed him?

– No, Ted replied, revealing only bits and pieces of his smothering anger. – He's what might be called a «live ghost», just a mean bastard fucking with us.

– I think he was scared of what he saw in us and attempted to get even. Liz shrugged. – Not much of a scary ghost at all, in my opinion.

Laughter, brittle, but true. Incredulity, followed by ascending belief in self among them all.

Phillip looked at her. She had done it again. A few well placed words, and balance and confidence in the group had been restored. She was valuable, so infinitely valuable. He swallowed hard.

He moved his arm in the sling, and it hurt, hurt a lot.

– The world is more, much more than what we were told it is, Ted said to them, adding to her words. – We've all seen that. It might be a little scary at first, but not more so than the mundane horrors we faced during our childhood and adolescence, what every man, woman and child on the planet is facing every fucking day of their lives.

They all felt his suffering and rage, and was somewhat, in a backwards kind of way comforted by it.

He knew that, sensing their emotions and range of emotions as if it was his own. He recalled their reaction to Phillip's wound and upon hearing about the gunfight. Fascination and fear had warred in their eyes.

And they noticed the abrupt change in him, the growing of a sound, a snarl they had learned to recognize and as both they and the girl followed him, they did so with both apprehension and anticipation.

The nascent tribe walked through New Orleans, through the French Quarter, under the hot afternoon sun, to a little house by the river. They couldn't avoid noticing the commotion they created, the looks and pointed fingers. There was nothing overt about it, but it was there, just as obvious as thunder and lightning, rain and sun. They spotted a nameless terror in the eyes following their path, in the way the fingers pointed at them.

– Do you see? Caine asked Liz.

– Of course I do! She replied cockily to him. – And it isn't that strange. This is Voodoo land. They know or at least glimpse the truth about the world here.

Her words sent shivers of terror through him.

*Fury,* she thought, both chilled and very, very excited, as she watched Ted, watched him move, warmed by the heat in his eyes. Raging Fury, pulling everything into its vortex.

Mute witnesses to what followed would afterwards keep relating to each other how Ted Warren, even though he had never been to this street before, had gone straight to Henry Gallier's house, as if he had somehow homed in on it, sniffed its location in the wind.

There was fire. She saw it, dancing in the wind, ghostly flames surrounding him, hotter than any forge.

And then, on cue were the drums. She heard them, even though no on else did, and she swayed to their beat.

Liz, light as feathers on her feet, saw Ted, her mate, her companion put his feet down, and his every step was heavy as thunder, and the very Earth shook under his feet.

He stopped in front of a house, the house at the end of the street. They all did, all falling in line behind him.

A woman, frail, old and nervous, opened the door and appeared on the porch.

– I seek Henry Gallier, Ted Warren stated without foreplay, his voice thick with rage.

– He ain't here, the woman replied, a nervous twist visible in the corner of her mouth.

She frowned, clearly troubled.

– He returned home, distressed beyond belief, and cried that the Loa had taken him over, taken him completely and utterly.

– So, he isn't here, Ted nodded in grim satisfaction. – So, where is he?

– I don't know, the woman replied. – He just… left. I've never seen him like this before, never seen him… distressed, really, until now.

Warren smiled or grinned or stared at her with his cold, hard eyes, grinned wolfishly, cruel. Those watching couldn't quite tell.

– So, he isn't here, huh?

– He isn't here, the woman repeated hoarsely.

– He left? Warren kept at it. – Ran like the dog he is?

– … ran, the woman whispered.

Warren nodded, as he half way turned away to leave.

Everybody jumped and gasped in shock as the man, as Henry Gallier came crashing through the window, and glass was flying everywhere. Liz did, too, even as her heart jumped in joy.

Gallier screamed loud, whined like a child or an old woman as he was pulled through the air, as if by an invisible hand, pulled into Ted Warren's outstretched hand, into his claw-like grip, as the large frame of the dark-haired man seemed to grow even larger, grow even darker.

– Listen. The snarl came from a ravine, a deep abyss shaking those watching to the core, and they could only imagine how Gallier was experiencing it all. – I'm gonna say this once: Leave us alone or *suffer* the consequences.

Gallier began speaking, began spouting words, spitting them like curses, as he in absolute panic and vain attempted to free himself from the strangling grip. It was beyond belief how he managed to speak at all, but he did.

He spoke French again, in harsh, accentuated expression. Liz listened to it, listened to what to her was gibberish, and then she frowned. And then the language changed, becoming something different, vastly different and strange beyond words, and Liz' frown deepened.

Then, amazingly, there were sparks, actual sparks in the air between the two men. Then… then there were flames, ghostly at first, then, suddenly, a full-blown ball of fire embracing them both. People screamed, high-pitched and hysterical.

Gallier's body dissolved in the firestorm. It fell apart, and rained like ashes to the ground, as the flames kept hammering Warren, but never quite reaching him, as his hand never let go of Gallier's neck, until there was nothing more to hold onto.

And just like that, like with a snapping of fingers it was over. Warren fell to his knees gasping, gasping desperately for air, his entire front blackened and burned.

And then, then it was as if the air itself split, cracked open, and they could see into another world, one of mist and shadows, and they all saw the creature there, saw Henry Gallier as he charged the kneeling man, as he was repelled by an invisible force and howled in misery, and with that the mist and shadows faded from their view, and it was just Ted kneeling there in the dust.

The others wanted to go to him, to help him, to aid him in any way they possibly could.

– STAY BACK! Liz cried sharply.

They stopped in mid-step, held in place by her voice and perhaps more.

You'll all die, she thought. He'll pull life from you like a sponge.

She rushed to him, putting out the flames still consuming his hair, brushing its remains off his head. He looked at her, she knew he did, with his blackened eyes. As she watched the burned skin began peeling off by itself, and clean, healthy skin began appearing beneath. From head to toe it reemerged, and after a few more seconds it was almost as if he hadn't been burned at all. She watched in an impossible mix of awe and horror. His eyes reemerged, fixed on her. He was breathing, still labored, but regularly. He rose, towering above her. His eyes watered a bit, before stopping. Tears jumped from her eyes in joy.

He shook off the remains of his clothes, and he stood there naked. She touched his face. It was smooth, new, but still exactly as she remembered it.

She turned towards one of the biggest males in their company, casually, intensively.

– Your pants and jacket, please, she chided.

He removed his pants and jacket in quite a hurry, and handed them to her. She handed them to Ted. He put them on, and they did fit him, or didn't fit him too badly.

– Practical Liz, he nodded, he praised her, his voice still coarse, raw.

– That's me, she acknowledged. – Always prepared for anything.

She pulled him with her into the house, through the open door, and the others in the tribe followed her. The door was open. There was no one else left, not in the entire street. They had fled like rabbits before the storm.

From the predator, she thought proudly.

She went to the bathroom, and she found an electric razor there, as she had hoped for. He sat in a chair. She plugged in the razor, and began shaving off the remains of his hair.

– Your eyebrows grow back immediately, she wondered, – but not the hair on your head. Curious.

She shook her head.

– Dead skin, he said. – Hair is dead skin.

Without that information helping any, of course.

– I guess we will always find out about our powers as we go, she nodded, somewhat content.

His head, too, was smooth as milk when she was done. He shed the rest of the ashen skin there and on his body as they all watched. When she was done with him she started shaving off her own hair, methodically and casually, as if it was merely a trifle, and to her, at that moment, it was. And soon enough her head was bald, too, her hair covering half the room's floor.

She looked at it, looked around her briefly.

– I guess they can use our dead skin against us, if they choose to, or choose to try…

She drawled, before making the decision already made.

There was a lamp on the table, filled with oil. She lifted it up and smashed it at the far wall, and it instantly exploded in a sea of flames. They walked outside, the fire already surrounding the house as they left, as they walked away from there, never to return.

He felt exhausted, spent afterwards, not physically but emotionally. Everything kept boiling and burning within. The volcano had erupted and it remained powerful, undiminished.

The young man sat on a bench at a high point, looking at the passing of the river.

She came to him, as always eager, beyond curious.

– Tell me, she pleaded, she demanded, like a child, like a queen.

– He burned, he said, thoughtfully.

Hesitating a bit before continuing.

– It wasn't me. He did it himself, did it to himself, in his desperate attempt to take me out. But I felt something, felt the fire, felt it *move*.

– I did, too, she whispered excitedly.

And they relived the moment, the flashes of memory, saw Gallier's mouth move like a machine gun, spitting his venomous curses.

– He spoke French at first, and I didn't understand it, but then, suddenly it seemed to make sense, and then he spoke another, ancient, long dead language, and I understood that, too. He said something like This:

Leave me, unholy creature from the deepest Pit
You destroyer of worlds
Leave me be, and return
To the Abyss from where you came
And bother God's people no more

And she began speaking, too, almost immediately, and they choired the words in dark voices.

– He attacked you, she said, – attacked you from beyond the grave, beyond life.

They shivered, and for once the sun and not even the fire within could warm them.

– But he couldn't touch you, she cried triumphantly, – He was a powerful Mage, and an even more powerful spirit, and he couldn't even come near you.

And the fire within flowed yet again, as it always did, and the relative chill of the approaching night didn't touch them, didn't touch them at all.

They walked through the City of the Dead, through its streets and alleys, leading their tribe. The noise of the ongoing celebration didn't escape them, but silence resounded in their sensitive ears. Torches burned brighter when they passed, and people hardly dared look at them with their lowered eyes.

– See how they stare at us in fear and awe, Liz said contemptuously, – the two emotions making the world move.

And something hurt within them all.

They walked through the dark, narrow alley again. There was nothing there this time, except the usual background noises of the city and shadows. Nothing was everything, but nothing out of the ordinary happened, even when Ted attempted to make it happen, with the power, the power of life seething within him, with Henry Gallier's lifeforce slowly fading from his grasp.

He noticed the shape at the end of the street, in silhouette against the background lights. A roar of warning rose in his mind.

It was the girl, the «ghost» they had met on their first evening in New Orleans. She stood there, waiting for them, as they speeded up, as they attempted to catch up with her. As they closed in on the corner, he blinked, and she was gone. He rushed to the corner, and he saw her walk down the street, in a fast, deliberate pace.

She turned another corner, and they rushed to get there, in the hope of catching up with her, but she was the same distance ahead, and they realized what the game was, and fit their pace to hers, and kept following her, at the distance of her choosing, through the intricate labyrinth of the city she created.

Ted realized it was indeed a labyrinth, and as he often did he saw the city from above, as his senses and his powers burned bright and strong. He saw the running girl, saw her path. She turned another corner. He continued straight ahead, down several blocks. There was a house on the left, somewhat isolated from the other houses, with a garden with tall weed. The girl stood in front of the entrance, by the gate on the path leading to the house. She looked up startled, as they approached her from the opposite direction from where she had expected them.

She seemed to melt, to fade away before their eyes. When they reached the position by the gate, she was nowhere to be seen.

They looked at the open gate, the wide open door ahead of them.

– Looks like we're expected, Liz said dryly, very coy.

And they walked into the cool darkness, strangely unworried, strangely worried.

Ted and Liz led on, ready for anything, the short hairs in their neck standing up like newly grown wheat.

There was the dance as they walked, as they moved, there always was. The house had an unusual oblong form. Ahead of them waited a room that covered its entire length. Liz sensed it, beyond the doorway leading to a place even darker than this ebony hallway. She looked at Ted. She observed how he stiffened, how he relaxed, and how his eyes lit up, and she realized startled what waited for them in there.

They entered the room filled with candles and living fire. Mark Stewart sat on a high chair, a throne at the end of the long hall.

## 3

The air in the room was dense, and so was the mood, filled with poignancy. Three people stood alone in there in the circle, surrounded by dozens of others on both sides of an invisible line.

– Ted, Liz, Mark Stewart greeted them. – How nice of you to drop by. Know that you are welcome.

– Mark… Ted nodded curtly, courteously, and nothing more.

The girl, the runner knelt by his side, her head resting in his lap. He ruffled her hair absentmindedly.

– You've met Laurie, I trust? She's such a gem, so fast on her feet that she would put us all to shame. And she walks the shadows, of course, like we all do.

The two studied the one, and he studied them, and none of them made any secret of it, probing each other across an abyss of time and experience.

Jean sat by his side, just as majestic and imposing and terrifying in her way as he was in his. She had changed, grown taller and bigger, almost beyond recognition. Something had happened to her, to Jean Gidman, something major.

Ted realized startled that she reminded him of her half brother.

A church bell nearby tolled eight. It reverberated heavy and poignant and scary in his mind. There was something, something elusive there somewhere, something he instinctively reached for, but couldn't quite grasp.

– A gem indeed, he finally replied, a choir of noise, of grains of desert sand rubbing against each other slowly subsiding in his mind's ears.

– Your twenty and one ravens are welcome, too, of course, Stewart nodded. – We're having quite the party tonight. People are coming from all over the bayou and even beyond.

– That's so gracious of you, Mark, Liz declared graciously, very graciously, a mocking smile gracing her face. – We were planning to hold our own celebration tonight, but yours looks so much more interesting.

Stewart rose from the chair. He walked to Phillip.

– Allow me to take care of that for you, son, he said.

Phillip flinched as the big man grabbed his wounded arm. And then his eyes grew huge and disbelieving as the heat of a thousand suns coursed through his flesh and bones and soul.

He blinked, and looked down at his arm. It moved easy and free, and there was no more pain, not even the slightest remnants of it. He curled his hand into a fist.

– I'm sorry about your father, son, Stewart said.

– Thank you, sir, Phillip said in a daze.

– We still haven't been able to find his killer, but *we will!*

– We will! Phillip repeated.

Liz stepped between the two men. She caught Phillip's eyes. Mesmerized by her stare, he was no longer lost in the moment of Stewart's machinations.

She turned towards Stewart, challenge clear in her pose. He shrugged. They both relaxed somewhat, still tense, still locked eyes meet eyes.

– You should join me, you know, he said, his conviction washing over her like lye.

– Why? She countered, her voice like ragged edges of a recently broken stone.

– You're still excited, are you not? Stewart nodded when she nodded. – You still look at the world with curious eyes.

She still nodded, tilting her head slightly.

– You have no direction, no more focus than the youngest child. I can provide that.

– We're the Third Force, Ted said, his voice from far away ringing in both their ears, as if he stood there, right between them all. – There's nothing you can teach us that we can't and won't learn for ourselves.

– But there is, Stewart grinned, cocky and dangerous. – There is one more thing, one more lesson before the end.

Nothing more was said. The moment ended. Time resumed its flow.

## 4

The guests arrived with the night, filling up the house and also the street outside. Furniture was put in the middle of the street, and the very sight of that pleased Liz and Ted both.

– Sweet Mark has quite a setup here. Liz nodded to him, to herself. – Fear is the key, isn't it?

She looked at him, as if asking.

– It is, he nodded.

– It tingles so well within me, she giggled.

They saw the throne room even when they weren't there. They saw Mark and Jean, and their two Lieutenants Kelly Regehr and Clayton Prescott. Both Regehr and Prescott made them uneasy, for vastly different reasons. Regehr because of her blind devotion and Prescott because he seemed to enjoy himself beyond reason.

Their devotion to the King was different and the same.

People arrived from near and far. There were bells and there were the many candles. Wind chimes shook in the windless air.

Kelly Regehr met everybody in the hall like a perfect hostess.

And she brought them the last stretch to the Promised Land, and their eyes lit up shiny and wet.

The guests sought an audience with Mark and Jean first. Then they partied. The King gave them his nod and his sanction, and they felt vindicated and strong.

Torches were lit and even large bonfires burned in the street. This was Halloween and things not normally allowed were. But this clearly went beyond, far beyond that. There was a sense of abandon that certainly sat well with the two Warrens.

Liz began swaying, began dancing to the pulsing music shaking the houses and foundations for several blocks, and with a final, warning note to herself… she let go.

And it was exactly like a deluge. Ted sensed it, felt it happen. She danced with a man dressed as Baron Samedi, the Voodoun death god, and then, as that image burned into Ted's mind, he once again experienced how the world changed around him. There was hardly any interlude anymore. He was even tempted to believe there was no interlude at all, that this was the world, that he simply had gained the ability to see more of it.

She was the same, even though she had become a deeper shade, as she writhed in the dance. But the others weren't. They weren't the same people, and some of them had eyes glowing in fire, not merely reflecting it. And this place wasn't New Orleans at all, but only one resembling it.

Stewart stopped by his side, unnoticed, like the ghost he was. Warren swore silently to himself, even though he knew Stewart «heard» him.

– She has never known grief, Stewart commented dryly, – not truly, not the kind tearing you up inside.

Warren pulled himself from his dream state, but it was too late. Stewart was gone. All that was left was a voice whispering in the wind.

– But she will!

He observed Laurie Isherwood while she, too, danced, seemingly totally oblivious to her surroundings. The incessant worry, what he always felt when looking at her returned. He was unable to pinpoint or quantify it, but it was always there, like ants crawling beneath his skin.

Someone, somewhere started beating a drum. He couldn't see it, but he could still see hands hit the tight skin in a steady, poignant beat. It started affecting him, boiling his blood, even more than the tall flames did.

He danced with Liz. The two Warrens danced, and they drew silent gasps from the others present. He remembered taking one step forward, remembered Liz' smile, and then they were two. She smiled to him. Her radiant smile, her happy, guttural laughter burned him like ashes.

And it was as if they were really dancing indoors, and also another, totally different place. Everything shifted and burned, casting shadows and mist.

People gathered in the street, gathered inside. Jean Gidman stepped out on the porch. There was something about the large woman that made everybody pause and stop, and look at the imposing figure. Wind and change blew through her. The boards on the porch squeaked beneath her feet.

– Welcome friends, welcome brethren, she cried softly, – to this place of revels and time.

– Hear, hear, people returned her cry.

She had changed, Ted noted, not merely on the outside, but far more so on the inside, where it counted. He hardly recognized her.

– She wasn't always like this, was she? Liz wondered.

He shook his head.

– She certainly wasn't.

– So, what do you think happened to her?

That's what we always seem to wonder about, he thought.

– I can't imagine, he kept shaking his head.

– Mark seems happy enough about it, Liz mused. – She's more… more *in tune* with him, now. Whatever happened, it's more immediate compared to what we went through, which, after all is a fairly prolonged, ongoing process.

– You were always a bright kid. Ted eyed her.

She blushed from head to toe.

Her skin clearly turned a darker hue of brown.

You're still a kid, he thought.

«I can see us», he heard her young voice, «we're adults, we're together, and we're powerful beyond imagination».

He wasn't sure the quote was completely correct, but he recalled it that way.

And it sent shivers down his spine.

The scene shifted and shifted again. They were inside, sitting around a long, broad table, eating and drinking with the rest. Stewart and Jean sat at the head of the table, entertaining and cajoling their guests.

All the people around the table wore masks, and to those not trained and able to see beneath masks, it would be practically impossible to identify many of them.

– Look at us, Stewart mused cheerfully, – saviors born of dreams, the ultimate riders on the storm.

Glasses met and parted. Cheers rose at the ceiling.

Ted raised his glass and directed his silent toast towards his kin. A puzzling look crossed Stewart's face, before he nodded, and nodded again. He returned the toast. They both drank.

Ted spotted a glimpse of the death mask he wore in the window, the open window the wind, the hardly noticeable draft moved back and forth. It was like he could see his own features in it, as if the mask had actually become his face.

And when he looked at Liz, he saw her features there, too, the same strange, fluid movement, not present in any of the other masks. It was their faces, but white, white as the palest marble.

The music ascended a notch, a cue noticeably tickling his frontal lobe.

He rose and turned to her, reaching out a hand. She took it, and rose with him. Her smile grew huge, blushing in joy.

They danced, there, in front of everyone.

– Aren't you glad you learned this? She called huskily to him. – Isn't it great to be able… to let go, to do so without… without fear?

He nodded, unable to reply verbally.

Everybody watched and stared, as the two fluid creatures moved across the floor, and, seemingly, through the very air everybody breathed, ever closer to the approaching midnight, and Mark Stewart's eyes started glowing behind the mask, glowing in the darkest fire.

And in some ways it was as if they were still outside dancing.

The very room darkened, faded around them, until everything and everyone had transformed into spots of fire and shadow. People gathered around the table, the table turned altar. A pig and its head bled freely. Its eyes stared at everybody and blood covered the altar. Stewart and Jean stood at the head of the table, Ted and Liz at its opposite end. Laurie entered the room, calling everybody attention to her. She carried three cages with one coq in each.

She let them out on the table, on the altar, one by one. Wings flapped, and they began picking the crumbs, the bloody crumbs on the slippery surface. Motions were whirls, seemingly endlessly repeating themselves.

– When in Rome, Stewart declared, – dress like a roman.

And in that very moment the closest coq was pulled into his hand. He grabbed it and held on, as the bird was screeching and flapping its wings. The man seemed totally unfazed by its efforts, its useless efforts. He grabbed a bloody knife, and in one single move he cut off the bird's head. The bird kept flapping its wings and moving its feet, until it slowly, slowly was a mere lump of meat in Stewart's hand. There was a glow, seen by everyone, passing from the bird and into the large man. His skin turned darker and his eyes a brighter hue.

– This is merely an appetizer, he nodded, – a light snack.

His attention, never truly wavering, turned visibly to his younger kin, and everybody else present followed his cue. Ted shrugged, deliberately, and Liz did, too. There was a tense mood in the room, even a sense of menace. They pulled to them each their coq, and in one single act, as they grabbed the birds, they decapitated them with their power. And instantly after that, the animals seemed to both implode and explode in the two Warrens' hands. Cries of astonishment and shock and excitement filled the room. Feathers, guts and blood flowed through the air, and landed slowly, slowly at the already stained table, at everybody standing around it. There was that weird glow again, a fire-like twilight seemingly being absorbed by the two creatures standing there. Everybody saw it. There was silence. Absolutely, deafening silence.

And then the nearby bell started on its twelve strikes. Everybody present removed bloodied masks. The stench of blood penetrated the room, but no one seemed put-off by it.

5

Ted felt Stewart's eyes on him, even when he wasn't in the line of sight. As the festivities practically exploded after midnight, and he felt sort of disconnected to it all, he still sensed those both hot and reptilian eyes burn his back.

The two Warrens walked the streets of Samhain New Orleans with their brood, their twenty and one companions.

– I had to get out of there, Liz practically snarled. – There came a point when I couldn't stay there a moment longer.

Ted nodded, finding it difficult to articulate himself.

There was something about this new Stewart and the entire situation, stage making his insides twist in unease.

New, he wondered, or just more visible, now, to their opened and sharper eyes?

A little bit of both, he gathered.

And the sense of frustration and low-burning anger kept churning up inside.

They circled the house in the fairly quiet street, not circling too far away, not too close, visibly uncomfortable and indecisive. New Orleans exploded around them tonight, and mingled, inevitably, with the low-burning explosion inside of them. A fire-breather stood on a corner, juggling torches. Ted thought of Linda instantly. He saw her there on the corner, taking the place of the slim man, doubling her amazing childhood act, and the torches turned from torches to knives and back again.

People moved, in the streets and between them. They were constantly moving. He looked up, at the huge power lines through the city, along the river and riverfront streetcar. People rushed along it, across it, laughing and kissing and living.

He looked at the passing women, at their curves and smiles. Liz noticed, of course. She noticed everything. He sensed how her insides shifted and burned.

– You see a lot of candy here, don't you? That's all right. I do, too. Do indulge yourself. I intend to.

There was honesty in her voice, but also agitation and jealousy, and he couldn't tell it all apart.

They turned another corner, into another fairly quiet area of tonight's noisy town.

He spotted two girls on a couch by a table placed in the middle of the street. It was a broad couch. The two half lay, half sat on it, cushioned by a set of pillows. They didn't move much, but what they moved, and the way they did so, made his throat dry up in an instant. He made a show of turning towards Liz and kissing her, before liberating himself from her grip, and head for the two on the couch.

They looked up as he and the others approached them. There was no fear in their eyes.

– Hi, how is it going? He greeted them, cursing his needy voice.

– It's going quite well, thank you, the melodious voice echoed in his ears.

She was tall. That was easy to see, even in her present position. She had long legs and large breasts. And her friend had a similar build. He felt a thrill surge through him.

– We are wanderers in the night, looking for a brief home, he said.

– There's room for quite a few more in our house, she replied huskily. – You people may go inside. We will sit here a bit longer, enjoying the fine evening before we join you all there.

– I like the evening quite well myself…

He told her.

Caine looked at Liz. She shrugged, very deliberate, and she led the twenty and one inside.

The girl's smile grazed Ted's body. She stretched her own long and curved body in a not to be confused sensual way, meeting his eyes not backing off the slightest, with no pretence of modesty.

– The young one appeared a little… agitated, the soft voice spoke to him. – She's yours, isn't she?

– She belongs to herself, he shrugged, – like we all do, and she can handle herself.

– I'll bet she can…

He sat down on the table, right in front of her.

– I like you. He went right to the point.

She wasn't put off. He saw that easily enough in her eyes, in the way her body moved, and didn't need to sense her deeper emotions to know that.

– Is that a fact? She replied defiantly. – What exactly do you like about me?

He stared into her eyes. She gasped silently, as the first twinges of fear grabbed her.

– I love everything about you, he told her. – I love the way your lips move, the way your hips curve, the way your breasts dance under your blouse when you breathe and among a thousand things: the dangerous gleam in your eyes. It excites me beyond words the way your voice sings in my mind.

Her eyes clouded as a dazed smile transformed her face, and she stretched herself on the couch, exposing herself, clearly showing off for him. Her nipples hardened under the thin fabric of her blouse, and her thighs were suddenly covered in sweat.

– I like you, too, she said huskily. – I like you very much.

He grabbed her and pulled her to him. She didn't resist, but let herself be pulled willingly into his domain. He undressed her in slow, eerily calm movements. She looked at him as if in a trance-like state. A hand found a breast and began playing with it, playing hard. She tensed a bit, just a bit, before becoming even softer, already turned on, becoming putty in his hands. It excited her. Her raw scent as her water began breaking tore at his nostrils. He kissed her neck. Dark Creole Girl moaned long and loud. He pushed his hand between her legs. There was no caution, no sophistication, no holding back. Her moans turned into a wail. He stopped a bit, turning to the other one.

– You, too, he told her.

She looked incredulous at him.

– Come here, he bade her.

Bright Girl rose, in stiff, doll-like moves, as she took the one step, two steps forward, into his embrace. He buried his other hand in her already wet cunt. She fell on him, and then they were both ready and eager in his ruthless grip.

– You're cruel, Bright Girl sniffed. – Cruel!

– Naughty boy, Dark Girl grinned happily. – Strong boy. Lovely boy.

Her voice was hardly a voice at all, but more a series of moans.

– I realized something, he growled. – I realized the truth about what they say about the cold in the heat of the night.

– It's all the sweating, she sighed happily.

He put them both back on the couch, and began undressing, slowly, but yet in uncontrolled, fiery moves. Bright Girl did as well, fast and excited, in painful, desperate need. They saw his cock, his hard and straight cock. He let them.

– You are such sweet candy, he said in a deliberate and patronizing manner, and he hardly had to concentrate on it.

He stood there, kept standing there, not touching them physically, grabbing them with his mind, roaming their sex with his invisible touch. Dark Girl stared at him in shock and wonder, and alarm, but unable to muster the slightest resistance. And it meant nothing to him. Dark Girl's moans turned loud as screams, short bursts of voice, as he played her as he willed. He laughed hard.

– Come to me, he snarled to them both.

And they did. They obeyed instantly. Tears flowed down their cheeks as they knelt before him, as he took their jaws in his hand, and he bent down and finally kissed them, and they wailed in joy, and it meant nothing to him.

– You are Candy and Candice. He baptized them. – From this moment on those are your names, and you will never answer to any others.

They choked as they writhed under his touch, his ruthless touch.

And they were nothing to him.

And their whining voice rose at the heavens.

Phillip stood on the balcony above, looking straight ahead, seeing nothing, hearing nothing but the wails filling his ears.

He saw, with his back turned Liz ride two muscular males on the bed in the bedroom inside, two large body builders, treating them like toys.
– NAUGHTY BOYS, she shouted. – NAUGHTY, NAUGHTY BOYS
As she snarled at him, as she moaned and howled at the moon.
The men lay still. She leaned on the wall of the balcony, looking at him with a dazed smile, still filled with a desire not the slightest diminished. Her eyes burned him, both his skin and his soul. His hard and painful erection turned even harder and more painful.
– They were worthy snacks, she snarled, – but hardly more than that, boys attempting to play an adult game.
He turned towards her, doing his absolute best to hide the longing in his eyes.
Her hard grin turned into a less than hard smile.
He saw the dark fire twinkle and grow in her eyes, and swallowed hard.
– Are you sure?
– What do you mean? He said hoarsely.
– Don't fuck with me. She reacted instantly, grabbing him, grabbing his collar with her invisible claws. – Don't ever fuck with me!
– I won't, he assured her, wanting to fuck her, wanting to kneel before her
Another wail rose from the street below. He shook in the heat of the night.
– Are you sure you want to fuck me? She teased him, she haunted him. – The legend says that once a man has fucked a succubus he can never again find satisfaction with an ordinary woman.
Caine had fucked her before, but never alone, away from the comfort of the tribe, always surrounded by other hot bodies relieving, sharing her passion, her lethal desire.
He pushed at his pants, desperately attempting to break out. She licked her lips, walking to him, grabbing his pants and in one pull tearing them off.
– Come, servant, she bade him. – Do your duty, serve and please your Goddess.
She returned to the room, and the bed, and he followed her, followed her swinging hips, blind deaf and mute. Only the scent overpowering his nostrils, his cognitive functions, his very self mattered. Nothing else did.
– You judge me, she mocked him, as she turned to him, as she welcomed him into her lap. – Judge my actions and my rejection of civilized morality, but I have liberated myself from the illusions growing up in the modern, unwise world imposed on me. I have no more use for them.
She kissed him, and he returned the kiss, passionately, helplessly beyond words.
– My Ḱwaiala, she whispered, – my good and loyal servant.
She touched him, scratched the side of his neck, making the mark of his station. He groaned in pain and need.
– I'm not sated, Kwaiala, she sighed needy. – I'm still hungry, so very, very hungry.
She grabbed his head, and she *kissed* him, and it hurt, as she wantonly drew blood, drew precious life. And there was no consideration beyond rudimentary need, the Hunger he felt roaming him like a storm.

The demon put him down on the bed beside the other men it had recently fed on, and it covered his body in its totality, smoothing it like a kiss.

It moved on him, moved with its claws and fangs, and he saw them in his fever vision, and that single impression would never leave him. He felt her squeeze him as he slipped inside her. She caressed him, and he gasped, gasped loud as a scream.

He felt her drain him. He felt her invade him, destroying any change he ever had of finding peace. The succubus took what she wanted, gave what she desired, and left her victim in shambles. He gasped helplessly as he pushed himself at the she-demon, until he had been completely drained and lay still as a dead body, and dreamed his fevered resurrection dreams.

## 6

The girls caressed him with hands and lips, totally immersed in the place of infinite need he had placed them. His fangs and claws grew. He took from them whatever he wanted, giving them everything they could ever desire, a reason for being. And then… it happened. As he emptied himself in Candy, in Candice the something he had faintly sensed, but never experienced until now, until this moment, rose from the deepest recesses of his being. Ted gasped as he moved on the cushy couch. Liz' mouth remained open as she felt the molten prod empty itself within her womb.

He dreamed. He dreamed awake, about ruins, about a city leveled to the ground, and he saw himself walk its rubble. She saw him walk by her side. There was clarity, as a million, an infinite number of impressions assaulted them simultaneously, as the drum, the New Orleans beat hammered them mercilessly, as it opened them, as they gutted themselves and devoured their entrails. They felt it, felt themselves be gutted by a blade sharper than a billion swords.

Death, he gasped. Death is being born.

In the time approaching the London Samhain midnight six hours past they heard the drums. People, witches celebrated in London Hyde Park. They sang and they beat their drums. Ted Warren stood there, looking at them with his direct, unwavering stare. The boy stopped beating his drum. He cried out and pointed, pointed at the ominous figure standing between the two trees, blending in with the night. Ted stood there, staring at them, smelling them, smelling the trees, hearing the sound of anxious birds not far away.

The entire gathering stared at him, now, sore afraid, and he wondered why.

Iris Carson and Penelope Middleton walked towards him, as if they were one person, hesitatingly at first, then bolder, determined.

– What are you doing here? Iris asked him.

She noticed without trying the intensity, the sense of purpose burning within him. It flooded her.

He looked confused at her, not really confused at all.

– I don't… know.

He shook his head, and the treetops shook in the wind.

Why are you here, Ror Ken? A female voice asked him

He lifted his head, looking around him in what seemed like ancient streets, in a city old as time.

It was gone in an instant, a mirage never really there.

He saw his giant shadowy form reflected in Iris and Penelope's huge eyes.

In a hospital bed not far away a woman breathed and pushed, breathed and pushed in increasingly shorter intervals. He stood there by the bed, watching, but no one saw him.

Liz stood by his side, a curious, beyond curious expression visible in her demonic face.

Who is he? She wondered.

He looked at her. He?

I don't know, he replied.

But he knew. He knew that much, as he sensed the baby within the womb reacting to their presence.

The mother noticed, too, noticed the baby's reaction, and her eyes turned wary and anxious, just like Ted had learned to know her.

The final contractions began. The woman, the mother-to-be screamed, screamed in agony.

We change position… without moving? Liz stated.

To say that he sensed her joy was an understatement of infinite proportions.

Her joy - and beyond curious interest to what was happening before their «eyes».

THIS IS SUCH A THRILL

– THIS IS SUCH A THRILL

Liz shouted it across the rooftops at the New Orleans dawn, standing naked on the balcony, looking at Ted standing naked on the couch.

The woman on the bed shook and a haunted look crossed her face.

– We *are* gods, Liz told Ted, her entire being aflame, – we have to be.

Their bodies were firmly rooted in the City of the Dead, but their minds soared across the sea, the great divide.

They spotted the baby's head between the sweaty thighs. It slid out easily, seemingly without any resistance. The nurse grabbed him and picked him up, lifting him above her head. The boy looked perfectly normal. His eyes was brown, his face quite mundane. But Ted in this form, Traveling great divides, saw what was hidden beneath the exterior, beneath the shell.

– I want to hold him, the woman said anxiously.

The nurses attempted to coax her, to convince her to allow them to clean the child, but she was adamant, and they relented. They had cut the string, and bumped him on the back, completed their task.

They were sore afraid, and wanted to leave.

He doesn't scream, Ted told Liz.

They couldn't take their attention off his eyes. He looked at the world with calm, serene, sinister eyes.

A man entered the room with the classic silly grin painted on his face.

She hasn't told him.

Cathy Randolph gathered the little bundle in her arms, the look of pain and bewilderment never really leaving her face.

Ted and Liz felt the pull, the heavy pull of their bodies, as they faded from the scene, as one final impression revealed itself and stayed with them, stayed with them Forever.

As half of the skin on the baby's face faded away before their sharper eyes, and half of a naked skull revealed itself.

# Chapter Eight: Travelers in Twilight

*A place cloaked in Shadow, the Far Lands, the Other World awaits us all.*

*Shadow Woman stands at the center of a living circle, among living, breathing human beings.*

*They found themselves on a barren rock with a strange constellation of stars and moons above. It was a circle of moons, but it was also a pentacle of moons and stars. The circle found themselves up there, down here, down there, and at the center of the circle they glimpsed the shadowy face*

*Shadow Woman speaks, even though they can see no lips move. There is a face, there, under the hood, but they can only glimpse its features.*

*You come here, seek this place because you seek all places, because you are seekers, Travelers in twilight...*

*Hardship and strife await you on this path, but you walk it still, because you are alive.*

2

Richard Hagman arrived in New Orleans. He did so in style or something very much resembling that with his sideshow of possessions and various people drifting into his circle over the years.

He arrived with yet another army, yet another skewed, half-cooked tribe, to an already war-torn city.

There was something about how the company he kept, at least some of them, how they moved their eyes and held their arms, like a spring feather looking to be released. The airport was filled with reporters and photographers. Richard Hagman, at least when he was on the road with his traveling circus was news. His life had long since been filled with drama and controversy.

An impromptu, perhaps not so impromptu press conference was quickly set up. It was evident, even to the casual observer, how Hagman was used to this and even thrived in this, the spectacle surrounding him.

– I'm pleased to be here, he grinned, – pleased beyond words to visit the fine city of New Orleans. We all are.

Anthony La Grande and Zarkon Zimbalist stood at his side, with a very not there presence. They were not exactly unknown themselves, quite infamous like their boss. Questions were asked to them, too, but this was Hagman's show, and the journalists knew that, and acted accordingly.

– I've been quite an archeology buff for a while. Hagman kept going. – You know that. You've followed my «exploits», as you have dubbed them around the world, from one ancient gravesite to the next. But, anyway, they've been merely a preparation, really… for the real thing to come.

He had their full attention, now, not just their casual interest. The mood changed, imperceptibly.

– You were cruel, as is your want, he stated passionately. – But you were right.
A stunned silence greeted his words.
– Yes, you heard right, he nodded. – I was just a dabbler, a pretender to the throne. And the truth hurts, Ladies and Gentlemen, it always does. So it took me a while to realize the obvious, but when I did new and wondrous doors opened up to me…
The journalists glanced at each other. One of them made a very telling move by the forehead.
– I started, with the help of trusted advisors to do the research, do the math, studying ancient texts and legends, stories upon stories, seeking the impossible, what no people in our jaded day and age have seen or even contemplated. There is a place, Ladies and Gentlemen, where both impossible answers and questions may be found, where the bold and investigative person may succeed beyond his wildest dreams, a place with many names, a true Valley of Kings. We will leave shortly, take off to unknown shores…
– And then the Great Adventure, the treasure at the end of the rainbow awaits.

## 3

Candy awoke, in the midst of pain, of fevered dreams. Candice lay by her side. So did Walter, Ben and dozens of others. There were nude bodies everywhere, all over the room. The stench of semen and cunt water filled her perception. She glanced around the room, the place she had spent years of her life, and it looked alien to her. Very conscious of herself moving, of not stepping on anyone, she rose and left the immediate cluster of bodies.
Nude feet, sensitive, beyond sensitive skin touched the carpet. She moved clumsily, awkward, a stranger to herself. A not very measurable time later she found herself in the bathroom, looking at herself, at Candy in the mirror. There was nothing left of the girl that had used to live here, only a few days earlier. She looked similar, but aside from that there was nothing resembling that girl.
In the brief time since Candy had been born, there had been days of deep sleep, and nights of heat and fire, and nothing besides.
She walked to the toilet bowl, casually, apprehensive. For a minute, a second or two, she stood there, imagining herself staring at the vortex far below. Suddenly nausea struck her, and she fell to her knees and threw up, her entire body covered in cold sweat. Sitting there, for minutes, hours she did nothing but breathe. It was as if she couldn't get enough air. She rose slowly, drying her lips and face of vomit, returning to the sink and the mirror. The sound of the water in the sink was muted, hardly noticeable at all, except for what her eyes told her. She cleaned herself, just a bit, as if preparing herself for a shower.
The tall female form studied her dispassionately with her burning eyes. Candy knew she was there without turning. She had learned to recognize the feeling of her, their presence.
– Feed, the voice bade her. – Nourish yourself.

Fireeyes held an apple to her mouth, and Candy obediently took a bite of it, chewing it, before taking yet another bite, eagerly eating of the other's hand. Then there was an orange, and then another apple, and more. Candy ate it all, and she felt strength return to her famished body. Waves of gratitude assaulted her.

Fireeyes appraised her, turning her around, nodding to herself.

– Yes, she nodded, – you are fit to bear our children.

Our?

Candy felt a cold stab in her gut.

– But I'm on the pill, she protested weakly.

– Please, Kwaiala. Liz just smiled. – You're embarrassing yourself. How can you even entertain the thought that a manmade chemical can be stronger than our seed?

Candy lowered her eyes, deferring to the other's infallible wisdom.

The creature straightened, turning cold and regal.

– Good morning, Candy.

– Good morning, My Lady, Candy curtseyed deeply.

A hand patted her cheek, a bigger, much bigger hand than that of the Lady. Candy glanced at the bigger frame in the doorway and a joyous smile lit up her face, as her juices once more started flowing freely.

Saliva flooded her mouth and flowed from her mouth as the big frame grabbed her and pulled her closer.

Yes, she whispered soundlessly. YES

As she melted into his embrace.

She stood by the window later, half dozing off, actually noticing the still hot semen drying on her thighs, not caring if anybody down on the busy street saw her. That had always bothered her before, bothered her terribly.

Candy showered, showered a while later, with a bundle of other boys and girls. She didn't really know how long time had passed. It could be hours, but could just as well be more days slipping by. There was a lot of laughter and play, faces lit by the joy riding them all.

Candy and Candice, with Walter and Ben, and the guys were out shopping. It was strange wearing clothes again, but it also felt sort of pleasant to have the tight fabric cover her skin, her beyond sensitive skin.

She strived to speak, waving her hands in an attempt to get it out.

– I… see something, she said, – something that was always hidden.

– Tell us about it, Brad grinned, exchanging looks with Justine, laughter with the rest.

Justine turned towards the four new additions.

– They tore the veil of illusion from your eyes, she said softly, – and now you see the world as it is, in all its horror and beauty, sadness and joy.

The warm November breeze hit her slowly, and she felt it, and her happy laughter washed over the others.

Candy heard a name be spoken, one faintly familiar. She turned towards the man speaking it. He wore a police uniform. She studied him with a frown on her brow.

– There you guys are, he said, to the four. – We began to worry about you. I mean, I know it was Halloween and all, but don't you think you're taking it a bit far?

– We're okay. She shrugged, giving him her dazzling smile. – There's nothing wrong with us, if that's what you mean.

The man from another life faded away from her eyes, and she saw him no more.

They walked back home, their arms filled up with groceries. The four sensed, with their newly awakened sensitivity his eyes in their back.

The tribe gathered around the rather too small table or set of tables in the newly transformed living room. There were easy laughter and lots of smiling. The four noticed it easily, how different this life was from the mere existence they had suffered through previously. The twenty and seven ate, and it was a feast. Every time Candy chewed she was practically overwhelmed by the powerful taste of what she had believed was just food.

And it is, she thought feverishly. She sat in Ben's lap and she felt him, not merely at the points of contact, but all of him, his entire being communing with her, with hers.

A ripe orange cracked in her hands, its juice hitting both her and Ben, their glowing skin.

He gasped, as she felt him harden against her thigh.

– It feels so good, he whispered in her ear. – It's almost too much, so very, very much.

I know what you mean, she told him with her eyes, as she kissed him, and everything turned shadow once again.

Ben stood by the window, looking down at the busy street. Semen fell drop-by-drop from his half erect cock, half on his thigh, half on the carpet.

Liz entered his line of vision, and he hardened instantly. She laughed throatily as she slipped close to him, as she started petting him, touching him in ways he had until recently been unable to imagine.

– Eager Kwaiala, she cackled.

The fire in her eyes burned him, filled his entire vision.

Day turned to night once again.

– Please, My Lady, he gasped. – What have you done to me? Please, tell me. Please!

– You were seeking, she granted his request. – In spite of the horrible life you led, you were reaching out, ripe, ready to be transformed, and now you are, and there is no return to the hell you lived.

And she touched him, not only with her skin, but with the very air, shimmering and potent, surrounding her. The fire and shadow embraced him, and he lost himself, until there was nothing but lust and joy and fear and pain left.

It was day again. Liz closed her eyes briefly, and when she opened them again, she and Ted were the only two present in the apartment.

They stood before the mirror, looking at the dark shade on their head already becoming short hair.

– Four police officers. She snapped her fingers. – Four enemies turned. Just like that.

– It's like you told him. Ted said. – They weren't exactly the run of the mill police officers. They were already There, with us. They just needed the final, brutal push.

– We will always draw human beings with our Passion, she said giddily, – those not fearing it. And we'll either liberate or destroy them.

He embraced her from behind, holding her softly, his body glued to hers.

She turned limp in his arms, letting herself be held.

– That feels so good, she said, smiling to him from the mirror.

She slipped out of his grip, her smile widening when she realized he didn't attempt to hold her back. It was just a few steps to the balcony. She walked there and turned back towards him.

– We are setting up shop, aren't we?

– Inevitably, yes, he said hesitatingly.

– I guess it is inevitable. She nodded. – It was said about the ancients, about the old gods that they wouldn't truly become powerful… until they declared their godhood.

He walked to the closest cabinet and opened it. In quite the relaxed manner he grabbed a flask of liquor and two glasses, and brought it to her. He was startled to see suspicion in her luring eyes.

– You haven't drunk lately, he confirmed. – In fact you haven't had a drink since…

– Don't play games with me, My Lord, she hissed sullenly, almost like she had been when he first got to know her.

It was a startling transformation, but he kept his stoic face, his mask, and waited.

The young girl stood there, shivering like a leaf.

– They p-poisoned me, she said weakly, – made me vulnerable. I'll never let that happen, never let myself be weak again. The alcohol masked the taste of poison, and I was unable to detect it. I forced myself to drink the first few days afterwards, but it was useless, just a *pretense* of confidence.

He wanted to take her in his arms and comfort her. He held back. She went and picked up her leather jacket, and returned to him in a rush.

– I've had dreams. She choked. – Dreams where they did capture me. They feel so real. It is as if it truly happened, somewhere, in another reality. Some nights they are so vivid that I fear they are the reality, and this the dream. I was taken, and brought to… a training camp, a place where they enslaved me, and dozens of others. They broke us, and made us their playthings, and no matter how hard I fought I couldn't s-stop them.

There was a special, concealed zipper in the jacket's back. She opened the large pocket and pulled up a small, flat box. She opened it feverishly, practically tore it open with shaking hands. Inside were three needles, filled with a strange liquid.

– The two hoodlums wanted to use this on me. I stopped them a split second before they could do it. It was so close.

She showed him her thumb and index finger, indicating how close it had been.

– In the dream this worked on me, making me pliable and weak. It cancelled my power. I was gone, and they could do whatever they w-wanted with me. I remember the smell of sawdust, of laboratory chemicals, of the metal in the cages they put us in, and sweat from countless nude bodies.

Her voice had become lifeless, totally even.

– The question is, if this truly works: did the couple know what they were doing or was it just a coincidence?

– It makes sense that there would exist… countermeasures against us, Ted said, forcing the words out.

– Is this it, then? She wondered. – Is this… the Hammer of Witches?

He wanted to speak, but couldn't.

– We need to know, she decided. – We need to be sure.

She grabbed one of the needles, and handed the box to him.

– Feel free to do all the necessary testing.

She said.

Before setting the needle in her arm, giving him a look filled with trust.

She hardly managed to empty the needle's content into her vein before she lost all strength, and dropped to the floor like an empty sack, hitting it hard, unable to even cushion the fall.

Panic riddled him, until he had checked her pulse and found it to be perfectly normal. He studied her with ashen eyes, even though he didn't need to. His senses registered everything, easy and unwanted. She was awake, and aware at some level, but it was all muddled, a horrible jumble making cold, acid sweat break all over his body. Her open eyes moved, but they were never in focus, more inorganic material than actual tools of vision, and so, he surmised all her senses «worked». He didn't need to imagine how it was for her. He felt it like wasps stinging his skin, their poison buzzing in his veins.

She had been totally or close to totally disconnected. Nothing worked or worked anyway near properly.

He sat down a chosen distance from the half dead creature, crossing his legs, concentrating. There was an obvious need for that. He felt his control slipping, and warm acid sweat reached his brow, and soon thereafter his eyes.

A kitchen knife appeared above the still body, spinning a bit before stopping, pointing down. He shook the unmoving body, shook it again, hard. There was no discernible reaction. The body rocked a few times, and then it was once more still. The knife fell. He stabbed one arm, cutting it open, making the blood flow, cutting a bit too much with his lack of control. The wound did close, but so slow, like in slow motion. It took an eternity. He touched her without touching her, with his mind, rubbing her cunt, and she was easily aroused, easily suggestible, docile. She smiled, a sick smile making him sick.

They found him, found them there, on the floor, surrounded by darkness.

– Enter! They heard his voice, his command. – Your Lord and Lady need you.

They rushed to her. As they had been taught they surrounded her and put their hands on her skin. There was no transference he was able to sense. They looked anxious at him. He nodded, and they retreated.

– It's all right, he told them with his hollow voice. – It will be all right. You may leave. Everybody but the Kwaiala.

They left. Ben, Walter, Candy and Candice, and Phillip remained.

He sat there for hours, without speaking, and neither did they, until the unmoving figure on the floor, finally moaned and began moving. Her open eyes began focusing, but it still took minutes more before he saw intelligence, anything beyond rudimentary awareness there.

She sat up. He nodded and Walter and Ben rushed to her. They touched her, but nothing happened. Her skin was still dead. She attempted to speak, but she spoke nothing but sounds, gibberish, and stared bewildered at him.

– It's a neural toxin, he said curtly. – Along the lines of what Meinz and bunch used. But I gather they would have been ecstatic about getting their hands on this one. It *is* the Hammer of Witches.

Images came to him, unbidden, about men and women chained in dank cellars, about them being led to the pyre with a sick smile on their lips.

She looked at him, attempting to hold her eyes locked on him, but failing. Her attention constantly slipped away. She cried out in despair and crawled to him, into his arms. Both of them, all seven of them sat there shaking together, for a long time.

A timeless time later she finally opened her eyes, her somewhat calm eyes, and rose, and was able to stand somewhat on steady feet. She fixed her attention on the box on the floor, and attempted to move it, but nothing happened. Something akin to panic gripped her, and managed only by the greatest of efforts to keep calm.

– It works on everybody, of course, she said, – but works best of all on us, on blocking us, keeping us down.

She paced restlessly, using the entire floor of the apartment, while in uneven intervals attempting to use her powers, and finally, when the sun was about to set outside, when despair and misery cast long shadows in her eyes, the apple on the table trembled, and levitated unsteadily into her hand.

Tears broke in her eyes, and continued in an even flow. She was unable to hold back.

– It's a good thing we did this, she finally said. – We are better prepared, and we might develop a form of immunity or at least resistance to it after a while.

The box opened. He held out a hand. One syringe slipped into his palm. They looked at each other, and they didn't have to nod. The swift glance spoke volumes.

He set the needle quickly, without allowing himself to think it through, administering its content into his vein. He fell to the floor, dead to this world.

Liz sat down on the floor, crossing her legs, her lips trembling when she spoke.

– Guard us, she commanded harshly. – Guard us with your lives.

They left her, left them alone, and placed themselves as sentries outside the door and around the house.

She sat there, quiet and gasping, as darkness embraced them both.

There were dreams, there were mind and cognition, deep within, but it was jumbled, muted, and he whimpered through the eternity he failed to make sense of it.

She tickled his cock, and it rose, and he saw the sick smile on his face through her eyes.

You are open, now, an unintelligible voice called to him. Open to the world, to the very depths of the Universe itself.

And he understood nothing.

Tears fell and formed a river and then a sea, and he was a drop mixing with the tide, until there was nothing left, no identity, no sense of being, no… Self.

He lay with his head in her lap afterwards, shaking like a baby.

They sat there, on the floor, desperately holding on to each other, staring at the nothing surrounding them, until the first glimpses of morning, and they finally fell into a deep, deep sleep, and they dreamt vivid, excited dreams of tomorrow.

## 4

Thunder rocked the streets. Everything moved in the crimson dust, and the only possible way to avoid its sharp edges was to be constantly in motion. Impressions mixed with the sense of the glowing gun in her hand hammered and hummed in Elizabeth Warren's mind.

There had been no clear warning this time, hadn't been anything worrying her. They had walked down the street, basically minding their own business. The shooting had begun further down the street. She had sighed, and they had turned around, intending to leave before being caught in the melee, but in seconds the battle had spread to the entire block, surrounding them.

She reloaded while she moved, a process already becoming instinctive. Men and women wearing the characteristic robe of David Gidman's clan appeared everywhere. She killed a young slender girl charging her with a gun spitting fire, killed her with one single bullet in the heart, and triumph rose within. With one sweep of her power she had cleared the street in front of her. She heard bones break, tons of them, as the enemies were thrown at the wall.

– How many of them are there? Candice gasped as they hid behind a corner, with their backs to the wall, her bright hair red with blood.

– Too many to be counted. Liz closed and opened her eyes. – Don't worry, we can always count them later, if we bother.

– You handle your gun great, Candice said, her eyes glowing in open admiration and worship. – Better than any officer I've ever seen.

And then, subdued, respectful and sullen:

– How can that be? How can you be so good?

– Since I'm only a child, you mean, Liz grinned, – with no formal training?

– Forgive me, My Lady, Candice said, bowing her head.

When Candice dared to Look at Liz Warren, to glimpse her fire, Candice was the child.

– I'm born with iron at my side. Liz once again briefly closed and opened her eyes. – In a heat stronger than a thousand forges.

Hers and Stewart's tribe didn't fire at each other, even though it was hard avoiding it, in the heat of battle, especially since they tended to be just as reckless as Gidman's beyond loyal soldiers.

Liz held herself back, deliberately, to not teach her people too many bad habits.

Or so she hoped.

They had to learn, through suffering, pain and death, she knew that.

And learned they did, as people started dying out there. The screams of the wounded and dying echoed mercilessly between the walls of the new and old New Orleans. Silent drums hammered relentlessly at Liz's eardrums. She couldn't tell whether or not it was the sound of her own feet on the ground or some distant thunder rushing at her. The tall, dark demon stood behind a corner using the flickering life forms out there as target practice, and she felt a rush every time blood drew lines in the air behind the indistinct figures.

She pulled back, the reloading an instinctive process she hardly had to even register in her molten mind anymore. The clouds above the battle moved slowly across the sky, at least to her perception. Slowly she stopped, with an effort strangling the boiling blood in her veins, signing for the others to relent, to pull back, as she did herself.

– Let's leave. She shook her head in disgust. – There's nothing for us here.

They looked attentive at her, like puppies. She wanted to shake them, to rattle them to their bones.

– Let them keep it up. Let them destroy each other… for now.

She saw things in the smoke, dancing faces, horrible grins mocking her, as she with a force of will steered her feet away from the cemetery the center of the city had become.

The battle remained behind them, as they kept pulling back. No one attempted to block their way or stop them.

– Where are the cops? Justine exclaimed incredulous.

– Several higher officials were strung up in the night, Candice said frostily. – I've never seen the boss so scared, so it had to be bad. We were told to stay out of it and we did. But the rumors of the unrest and noise your two friends are making are reaching federal authorities, and they will interfere sooner or later, probably with martial law and the works. It's only a matter of time.

– Mark and Gidman know this, too, Liz nodded. – They will move their feud elsewhere, and start all over again.

– They don't care, Phillip said enraged, – not about anything, except the war they're waging against each other.

There he was, by her side, like she expected him to be.

– It is as if it has gained a life of its own. Liz nodded some more, with wondering eyes. – Something perpetual and completely different from what it once started out as, how it once began.

She reached out a hand, and seemed to grab a handful of the whirling dust surrounding her. It danced above her palm, within her curled claws. She stared at it in an attempt to spot something in there, anything giving her the slightest glimmer of understanding, but no particular insight was forthcoming.

Move the Dust, a voice called to her.

– What…

She looked around her, but there was no one there, no one except her flesh and blood followers. Of course.

No one she could see or even sense. She couldn't tell if the voice had been real of imagined or something else entirely. Frustrated she let her hand and arm fall.

She noticed the others' look, their total faith in her. They hadn't noticed anything out of the ordinary. Of course they hadn't.

Distracted she noticed the blood flowing down Candice's arm and down on the ground.

– You're hurt.

– Oh, the girl grinned nervously, – I hadn't noticed.

– Don't worry, it isn't bad, Liz comforted her. – But we'll fix you as soon as we get home.

They moved into the narrow, cozy street, where they had set up camp, their current brief-home. Everybody moved alert and ready for what might come. Liz stretched out her senses. It was just a peaceful and lazy street. She allowed herself to relax, at least a little, and the others, taking their cue from her did, too.

Ted was home, with Candy and most of the others. Candy spoke on the phone. She put it back on the receiver just as Liz and bunch arrived, smiling crookedly to them.

– That was our former Chief, she grinned. – He informed me we were fired, for dereliction of duty. I, on the other hand, informed him we had already quit nights ago.

Ted walked to Candice, quickly but gently grabbing her, removing her blouse. It was torn and soaked in blood. They could all see how the wound leaked, how it seemed to continue to leak in an even flow.

They saw how it stopped leaking the moment he focused on it. He pulled a jacket, his jacket from the couch. There was a zipper there, on the back, like it was in Liz' jacket. He opened it, and pulled out a pouch. There was a box inside that pouch, one of polished wood, and with strange carvings.

– This will hurt a bit, he said gently, making Candice blush, blush hotly and terribly. – The bullet just grazed you, but it hit a vein, and would have bled a lot before stopping.

The box opened, and one of the small bottles with the fine powder at the bottom rose into the air. The corkscrew removed itself, and the bottle levitated to the sink, where the tap turned itself on. Those gathered around Ted and Liz still stared at the display. It still astonished them, and on some level it always would.

Ted sensed the blood, sensed its flow. Liz knew that. Just like she could.

The bottle returned to Ted's hand, its content already fuming and expanding. The porridge-like mass grew too big for the bottle, pushing itself out, and onto Ted's hand. He smeared it on the wound. It stung. They could see it in Candice's expression, but she bravely, stubbornly kept it inside, kept the pain from voicing itself.

– This will make you sleepy, Ted told her. – You will sleep, and when you wake up you'll be good as new.

– Thank you, she whispered.

She began blinking almost instantaneously. He caught her as she stumbled, and carried her to one of the beds. The big woman felt light as a feather in his arms. He put her down just as easily, gently.

– Will I dream? She wondered.

– You will, he assured her. – You will ride the solar winds of distant stars, and find truths hidden in your deepest heart.

And it was all very strange, and that was no longer strange at all.

He bandaged her. The white fabric turned red very fast and very worrisome. He turned after a while and nodded to the others. A sigh of relief flooded his senses.

– Our Shaman, Justine hailed him, – our shadow in darkness.

Laughter, brittle, but yet strong.

And he walked in between the seething bodies and spirits, and bathed in their fire and acceptance.

It was night again. The two of them stood on the balcony, far enough removed from the others in the room inside. The late evening's sounds reached him from afar. Liz held him from behind, nuzzling his neck with her soft lips.

– Why use it on her and not on Phillip? She wondered.

He hesitated, and she understood in a flash.

– Because I saw Death, he replied, staring into the night. – It was close, so very close.

– That's funny, she said, considering it. – I didn't. I wonder why.

She pondered the issue some more.

– You're older, of course, she mused. – And even though I'm female and thereby relatively better developed for my age, I might not have caught up completely yet. Or even though our powers have seemed the same to this point there may be slight variations.

He stared into the night. The light from distant stars reached him, and he felt cold, so very cold.

The two of them rested in bed. The heat from the female form warmed him, and he felt good, so very good.

She was stroking his back, touching his skin with her sensitive hands.

– How strange, she mumbled. – All your new wounds are gone without scars. Even the ugly needle marks are gone. But your old scars, faded as they might be are still there.

Her words created a fizzle of a storm within him.

– They are still there, she stated, a shiver distorting her voice and eyes.

Slowly, only slowly the world outside returned to their senses, immersed as they were in memories and each other's emotions.

They heard steps, steps approaching them, coming at them on hooves of thunder and echoes, and they once more grew alert and ready. Voices reached them from outside. They recognized them and relaxed, as much as they ever were able to.

– IT'S ALL RIGHT, she called to Candy and Ben standing sentry. – LET THEM HAVE THEIR AUDITION!

She giggled. He sighed.

The cheerfulness masked the recent sadness and melancholy. They didn't fool themselves.

Richard Hagman approached them accompanied by Anthony La Grande and Zarkon Zimbalist. He was a bit unsettled in his dignity, no doubt after having been modestly roughed up by the sentries. The three of them had been allowed passage, been granted royal audition, but not with their guns.

– So, have you considered it? Hagman asked them.

– We have considered, Liz said lazily, – but we haven't decided yet.

The two on the bed made no attempt at hiding their nudity, but seemed quite relaxed by it. La Grande and Zimbalist glanced uneasy at the full female form, attempting in vain to hide their interest.

– I'll appreciate an expedited reply, he said stiffly, – since we'll be departing soon.

– You'll have one, she said lightly.

And that was that, really. Richard Hagman, one of the richest and most powerful men in the world, had been brushed off like dust on a jacket, and he knew it.

Liz burst out in laughter long before the echo of the three men's steps had faded from the two's sensitive ears.

– Did you see that? She grinned happily. – How confident we were, how contemptuously we treated them, like servants not fit to lick our feet?

Her excitement flowed through him, but he didn't reply, not with words. He tried to hide his concern from her, and if she picked up on it she made no sign of having done so.

– I remember our mother, you know. The Egyptian Queen, that is. Among all our visions I remember that one the clearest. Why do you think that is?

She was challenging him, taunting him, willfully, deliberately. He chose to ignore it.

– There's a rumbling in the air, isn't it? She cocked her head and listened, a bit more subdued, but yet more excited than ever. – What is that, I wonder? Is it the sound of New Orleans itself echoing in our ears?

They returned to the balcony, nude, not doing the slightest attempt at hiding themselves to all the people passing by below. Ted felt freedom, felt its power surging through his being. The stares, the raised fingers no longer bothered him, but on the contrary liberated him.

– I want to go Traveling again, she said excitedly. – I want to learn all the secrets, want to see the very edge of the Universe.

Her eyes began flashing, and slowly, inevitably his did, too. The accusing glances from below turned fearful, even more timid. He raised the dust in the street, made it surround the pedestrians, and he made sure they heard the hot and cold triumphant laughter when they began walking faster and eventually practically began running off.

– Yes, RUN! He shouted to them. – Run, like the RABBITS you are.

He grabbed the girl's hands, and she gasped in joy, and in two pair of eyes there was an even stronger glow.

It was very telling that glow. It told of everything within them, as it twinkled and pulsed and grew.

– Even here they are afraid, he said. – Even here, in the City of the Dead.

– So, let them, she said. – Let them run like rabbits from the hunter.

She cast her eyes at the street below. An enigmatic smile crossed her serene face. Behind that smile, that face everything moved and bustled like the ocean.

– But perhaps they're not all totally useless, she noted.

A man carrying a rather large drum had more than a few difficulties running with the load on his back. He had to stop frequently to balance it, to not drop it. Liz used her power to touch him, to pinch him in the neck. He looked up startled.

– Yes, you, she cried. – Definitely you. Come here, best speed, into your Goddess' fawn. She's in fervent need of services only you can provide.

She giggled, holding her head high for a moment, before giggling again, willfully exposing herself to the boy below. He hesitated. She nudged him, pushed him in the back, clearly impatient. He rushed forward then, in a fearful mix of desire and cold sweat.

– Drummer, COME TO ME! She laughed aloud.

He came. She saw him, sensed him as he rushed the stairs, and joined the others in the room inside. The circle formed, as she and Ted returned to them. She nodded to the drummer, and he began beating his drum in a heavy, steady beat, adding to the silent drum already beating. The air seemed to shimmer, and the room seemed to be transformed before their eyes.

The rush excited them, spurred them on. The two of them entered the circle, granting themselves access to the unbreakable bond forming. The drumbeat wasn't merely a sound, but something deeper, something reaching below the surface, to what was hidden and resting, and dormant, slowly rising to the shimmer far up there. The two shimmering forms walked to the center of the circle, the slow humming accompanying the drumbeat hitting them like slow moving waves.

Candles floated through the air, lit by floating matches, brief fire, large, black candles surrounding the circle, casting long, giant shadows in the room.

The two sat down on the floor, back to back, slowly and repeatedly closing and opening and closing their eyes, casting their eyes through the shimmering air, the dark wall, the living, pulsing forms so very attentive to their presence.

She raised a hand, and the humming faded and the drum fell silent.

Hesitating a bit before she spoke, she moved the hand, as if she attempted to touch the very air.

– I want to move the ether, she said aloud. – I want to touch reality itself. I want to ride the roaring wave moving through Space and time.

And it seemed to all the people gathered in the fairly small room as if her voice echoed in the very air. She shifted slightly in her chosen position, rubbing her naked ass back and forth on the floor. They all touched her, or felt like they did. She began rubbing her sex, and her hand turned instantly wet. Her mouth stayed open. The potent stench ripped into all their nostrils.

Liz smiled, secure in her mastery over them all. They wanted to turn to each other, but she held them in place, far harder than any iron would do.

Ted's cock rose fast and hard. He didn't touch it. There was no need for that. His stench tore in the nostrils of those gathered as hard as hers did.

Breathing increased to insane levels, as they all were grabbed by the naked lust permeating the room, touching their very souls.

– Yesss, she hissed triumphantly. – Give in to your needs. You're the vessels, the boost we need to travel the Other World.

– GOD… Candy cried.

– … DESS… Ben gasped.

Everybody in the circle sat there mumbling and heaving, ravaged by the relentless forces riding them. There was no respite, no recess from the cruel Storm.

Everybody in the circle fell inward towards the two at the center, and no one ever released the grip of the hands at those by their side. The goddess' mean laughter coursed through them and filled them with joy.

– I see! Ted said, his voice suddenly so very cold and scary. – I see two men locked in battle, never letting go of each other, dying in each other's grip.

– I lie dead on the ground, Liz said, – but I still live. Even as my heart beats its final beat, I cling to life.

– I feel the pain, Ted gasped, – The wounds, the pure viciousness of it all, the pain of dying.

The others gasped, too, writhing in pain on the floor, as he shared it with them, as he shared everything with them.

Being born hurts, Tilla told him.

He blinked. But it wasn't Tilla that had told him that, but Betty, Betty who was as much gone as Tilla from his life, from his reach. He reached for them, reached out to them both, but he couldn't quite get to them. Betty stood with her back to him, but then, as she turned, just as the contact was broken, as she smiled to him, he could sense the smell and visual flashes and bits of her surroundings.

His eyes, his wandering eyes witnessed how she knelt before a man on a throne. Chin was there, kneeling by her side. He saw the man on the throne through Chin's eyes, and shivered in the hot sunlight. It was so strange and so unsettling to sense fear in the dangerous man. And that overwhelming emotion masked his surprise that he, in fact experienced the world through Chin's mind.

That, all that compressed into a tiny, tiny moment.

In one moment was eternity, and he experienced it, and forgot about it the same instant.

It faded, like it always did, into mist and shadow.

It ended so fast this time, so very fast, and a voiceless voice shouted in anger and disappointment.

Some cried in joy, others in fear, sagging on the floor.

Silence descended on the gathering, but the silent cry kept echoing between the walls. Time seemed to actually end as they all lay there, slowly, so slowly picking up the pieces of their lives.

The distant thunder was just as distant, just as close. They were able to touch it with their fingertips, as it ravaged their numb skin.

Liz and Ted stood on the balcony. Everybody else was asleep, dead asleep.

She stared at him, never letting go.

– Why didn't it work? She said sullenly. – It should have worked. Everything was done right, felt right, but nothing happened.

He returned her stare, but his didn't really pack her punch.

– That isn't entirely true, he pointed out, – there were the images, the impressions and visions, and we felt the pain, the actual pain. And hatred, hatred beyond hate. I've never actually experienced it like that before, so… real.

The image, the experience of the two men battling to the death stayed with him. He couldn't get rid of it, no matter how much he tried.

– Trinkets! She retorted. – Crumbs on our large table.

– I don't know how much I wanna feel, he said, shaking his head, visibly shaking, his voice turning high-pitched and childish.

It turned quiet. She focused even harder on him, her expression turning spiteful, mean, the expression always unsettling him. She looked, and she stared, and he felt the daggers in his mind.

– Perhaps your heart wasn't really in it? She said abruptly to him. – Perhaps you didn't want it enough.

– Perhaps you wanted it too much, he mumbled.

He didn't tell her about Betty, and he wondered what she, what Liz kept from him.

She walked to him, and turned limp in his arms. He did embrace her. Her voice turned into a wail.

– It isn't here either. Whatever we're looking for, it isn't here.

## 5

The sudden, beyond loud thunder rocked New Orleans. The final, loud explosion made them all sway on their feet. Everybody looked up. Those with finer tuned senses immediately directed their attention in the correct direction, and Ted and Liz knew, instantly where to go. They recalled unrest and shadows through the night between that moment and this, and that was all.

They began moving, and the others, their followers began moving with them, through streets and avenues and air with increasingly thickening smoke, and then they all knew.

Ruins and destruction beyond destruction surrounded them. It was everywhere, no matter the direction they looked. There was a giant hole in the wall in the house before them, but it still stood, miraculously. Every other house in the previously fairly peaceful neighborhood was flattened beyond recognition.

Pieces still floated in the air. Dust lingered everywhere, and it was hard to breathe. People still ran back and forth in a confused, unfathomable pattern. The others sensed Ted and Liz' jittery easily. They noticed their never resting eyes. Liz touched Ted's shoulder and pointed, pointed at the floating debris. It hit them all simultaneously.

Some of the pieces still floated upwards. They were clearly levitating… or being levitated.

It was an amazing sight, really. As soon as they noticed it, they noticed a lot more of the floating pieces. The wood and glass and everything seemed aware, sentient, as it buzzed around the gathering people like angry wasps.

Ted tilted his head, clearly listening. The others, including Liz heard nothing but the overwhelming noise, but he clearly heard something more.

He walked inside the still standing house. They followed him, apprehensive, mimicking, and not his excited state of being.

They found darkness in there, found shadow, and blinding splinters of light.

A girl sat on the floor, at a spot remarkably clean and free of debris.

– Laurie, Ted called softly.

There was no discernible reaction.

– LAURIE! He shouted.

Everybody shook, the voice cutting through them all like the sharpest of blades.

She looked up, her eyes locking on to his.

– What happened, Laurie? He asked softly.

– Mark told me to r-run, she replied evenly. – He ordered me to leave them and find a safe place to h-hide.

– And you did, Ted nodded, strangely, uncommonly affectionate. – You made this place for yourself.

She looked closer at him, the remote look in her eyes never truly leaving her.

– You did good, he told her.

He gathered her in his arms, and lifted her up. She didn't resist, or didn't in any visible way react. Her head rested on his shoulder. Her eyes stared at nothing.

They moved on, searching further through the rubble. The stench assaulted the two, or rather three in front, ravaging their enhanced senses. Nostrils twitched in

Laurie's unmovable face. Ted and Liz didn't look at each other, but looked anyway.

– There are bodies…

He said.

– But mostly the neighbors, she completed. – They discovered too late what a bad neighborhood it was.

She cackled insanely.

There were blood and flesh and bones everywhere, unrecognizable, left in pieces. They stood in the disaster area that had been the central building, the main focus of the fighting. Jumbled, evasive impressions assaulted Liz and Ted, gone the moment they appeared.

Death was present everywhere. Ted felt him, a potent force in the very ether.

Others appeared slowly, the cops and journalists and officials. The tribe pulled back, into the shadows, practically unseen by those basking in the light. Cops filled the French Quarter that day and night, filled it to the brim. Uniformed people in various incarnations walked around in full armor, and with fingers twitching around the trigger of their weapons.

Flashes of reality haunted them, during their remaining time in New Orleans. The city left them, as they left it, left it behind.

A few days later Liz and a few others visited a so-called classy cafeteria on Canal Street. She looked without looking at the well-dressed men and women dominating the place. Liz and bunch entered the place, all well dressed and groomed for the day, and that fact was suddenly instantly in doubt. She used her eyes and ears, and the others thrilled at seeing her frown, seeing anger rise behind her eyes.

A waiter approached them, and stopped, instinctively by the dominant force at the table. Liz hardly acknowledged his presence.

– Is there anything I can get you? He offered respectfully, adding a soundless «Ma'am» there at the end.

– Coffee, she replied lazily. – For us all.

The coffee arrived, and it didn't seem that they needed to wait for it at all. The fireeyes began glowing, and the others giggled, and Liz feared for them… and for herself.

It was hot and strong. Whatever this place was, they could clearly make good coffee. Liz closed her eyes, her eyelids hurting bad.

Another place further down the street played loud and rough Rock. She sat there rocking to it, and so did a few others in the room. A group, one of four, badly dressed rose from their chairs, and started swinging, started rocking, started dancing. Liz grinned and opened the door. It slid open, seemingly by itself. The music flowed inside, accompanied with a rustle of wind upsetting everybody's hair. The others grinned, too, sensing, seeing her playful mood.

A man with a very sour disposition, flawlessly dressed, rushed forward from the kitchen and headed for the door. It closed by itself before he reached it. He stopped, a study in confusion. There was laughter somewhere, silent, but present. Liz was certain he heard it, somehow. He had that certainty and confusion written all over his face.

– There's a wind blowing, she said. – The Wind of Change.

She didn't speak very loud, but most people in the room heard her, anyway. She knew that, because she was their ears, the worried glances they sent each other, and the slow burning counteracting the sick feeling in their gut.

One of the dancers looked at her. He walked to her, as she knew he would. She could sense his interest. It lit the entire room with shadows. His friends, both male and female came, too.

– You look like you belong here, he said.

She waited patiently.

– At first glance, he completed his reasoning.

– Appearances can be deceiving, she grinned. – First appearances are usual very much so.

On the other hand… she thought, grim in mind.

The supervisor made his way to them, still very much full of himself, guided by his bodyguards, his heavy bouncers. She turned to him, to them, looking very direct at him.

– I must ask you to leave, he said.

– Why? She asked him, both incredulous and contemptuously.

– You're upsetting the other guests.

It was amazing. She hadn't even begun doing her thing, and neither had the other group, and he had sniffed her out, exposed her intentions, like a dog. He was very well trained, very well trained indeed.

She walked to the nearest table.

– Am I upsetting you, Ma'am? She inquired. – This gentleman says I am, and I wonder if you share his sentiment.

There was no reply, except a stiff mask. No matter Liz' rather pleasant demeanor she had just made a scandalous break in etiquette.

Her eyes began glowing. She sensed it, sensed the molten volcano boil within, and the others did, too.

It boils, she thought unprompted. It boils, and all ashes fly away.

The door flew open. There was a loud crack as it hit the wall, and broke in a thousand pieces.

– Come, she called to them all, in an excellent impersonation of a southern lady, the mimic once again effortlessly doing her thing, – let's leave this boorish place.

And to the gentleman supervising the place:

– Ah won't be back, sir, she stated. – Ah won't make the mistake of ever gracing this place with mah presence again.

She walked out of there, her head held high, leading the two groups, two groups already becoming one.

And as soon as they had left… shadows descended on the place.

Everything suddenly seemed so very, very threatening.

A teacup hit the floor and broke in a thousand pieces. How it had fallen from its position at the center of the table no one could say.

– Bokor! A young African-American girl hissed, catching herself immediately when her older, white companion cast her a reproaching glance.

It progressed quickly from there. In a manner of seconds cups and service and all flew across the room, and hit the walls. Windows broke. They broke from one moment to the next. Bottles hit the ceiling. Shards began buzzing around like bees, dangerously close to the people present.

They made their way out, in a more or less dignified manner, sore afraid. The calamity didn't follow them outside, and when they realized this, they stopped, and cast their eyes back.

An unseen force went amok in the place, a place where poorly dressed people constantly had been told to leave the premises.

The destruction just went on and on and on, until there was hardly more than ruins left of what had been a well-respected establishment.

Liz let go slowly, as she made her way down Canal Street, a huge, ecstatic smile brightening her features, her skin and deep shadows.

She turned, first and foremost to her new charges. A brick levitated slowly towards her open palm. It levitated above it, cloaked in dark air. Bathed in the afternoon sun the entire woman was cloaked in shadow, and she looked bigger than she was.

– Are you afraid? She asked the boy.

– Yes, he replied hoarsely.

– You should be, she said lazily. – I can kill you with a thought. I don't even have to try very hard.

They were all stricken, all the new ones. There was no doubt in their eyes as to what she was. A couple behind the boy, their former leader, looked like they were about to kneel. Liz smiled, sensing how she bound them closer to her with each passing second.

– Are you… a girl strived to speak. – Are you a goddess?

– A goddess, Liz nodded, – a Lord of Chaos come to Earth to sow discord and freedom and savage joy.

She walked among them, targeting them, sensing the power, the pitiless wave.

– So, do you deserve mercy? She spat. – Do you deserve to live to bathe in your own shit?

They stopped and froze, and attempted to back off, but she denied them that. The constant, sinister pressure in their back made them stay put.

– We deserve a chance, a girl spat, – to prove ourselves.

Adding respectfully, as her features softened:

– … My Goddess.

The pressure in their back let up.

– Come, then, Liz said to them, as she turned and walked away.

And they did follow her, into the shadows present even in the brightest day.

They hadn't walked far when police officers surrounded them on all sides. Liz held up a hand, to keep her followers from acting rashly. They all stopped, looking attentively at the clearly nervous uniformed people. No weapons were drawn, but that moment wasn't far ahead.

– Is there anything we can help you with, officers? She offered smoothly.

– You are Elizabeth Kendall?

– No, not anymore.

A firm headshake.

– We would like you to come with us, please. You will all come with us.

– What is this? Candy stepped forward, angrily. – Do you have a good reason for taking us in like this?

– It's all right. Liz put a hand on her shoulder. – These people will only speak to us for a while, clear up a few things, that's all.

Candy relented immediately when meeting the other's eyes, and stepped back.

They were grabbed, rather roughly, and led off, pushed and pulled by their honor guard of shitty and angry police officers.

It was less than a minute's walk to the nearest police station. They were thrown into one, big holding cell and forgotten, or so it felt as the hours passed, and the afternoon heat smothered them. Liz didn't sweat. The heat didn't bother her, like it did the others, but everything boiled within her, and all the buzzing wasps she had ever felt inside were loose. The shadow emanated from her, and descended on them all, and she was helpless to stop it. Candy and some of the others recognized the signs and comforted her the best they were able.

– There is a darkness inside me, she whispered, hardly audible. – A beast waiting impatiently and indefinitely patient to be set loose on the world.

Usually, she was okay with this, with it, but not in moments like this, when she was angry, and frustrated beyond frustration.

– It will be over soon, Candy said optimistically. – They're usually content with letting people stew one afternoon. Usually.

But the fine police officers of New Orleans had also been boggled down with frustration lately, and they had clearly decided it was payback time.

Liz began sweating eventually, knowing fully well that it wasn't because of the heat, that it was caused by the dark, dark claws tearing at the walls inside her. They were caged, like animals, and right now Liz felt like an animal shaking the bars. And the bars began shaking, the shake steadily increasing in strength as the hours crawled. Liz couldn't stop it, and eventually she stopped trying, letting the power do its thing, do what it wanted.

There were other prisoners within the cell, but they stayed away, clearly intimidated by both their reputation and what, whatever was happening.

They came for her close to midnight. She nodded to her companions, attempting to lift their spirit, to show them a confidence she didn't feel.

The interrogation room was exactly like she remembered it from the films, a naked place with a table and a few chairs. She sat alone for a few minutes. They let her squirm while watching her behind the one-way mirror, confident in their stupidity that she couldn't see them.

There were two of them. There always were, it seemed. One handed her a cup of coffee. She ignored it. He put it down on the table.

– You look a little… he began.
– I have a slight problem with claustrophobia. She shrugged.
– So you don't like confined spaces, huh? He grinned. He actually grinned.
She didn't comment on that, either verbally or in any other visible way.
– Elizabeth Kendall, one of the men said. – You're Elizabeth Kendall?
It had told and did tell her something that they knew her name. The fact that there was no formal opening to the «interview», and that they used no recording device told her more.
– What if I am? She replied, behaving defensively, like a common criminal.
The man hit the table with his large, very large fist.
She shrugged again, and he seemed to be somewhat content with the «answer».
– I'm Elizabeth Warren, she stated calmly, not really showing any kind of fear at all.
And a flash of worry appeared in the form of the frown on his forehead.
The detective (he didn't present himself and neither did his partner) put two photos on the table before her. They showed Mark Stewart and David Gidman.
– Do you know these two?
– I know of Gidman, she shrugged, deliberately. – I've never met him.
A shadow seemed to pass over her, and she frowned.
– I've met Stewart. Neither of them is my favorite people, if that is what you're asking.
– But Stewart is a relative of yours, right?
– So what? Do you like all your relatives?
They had done their homework, that's for sure.
– Do you like the unwanted distant cousin showing up on every holiday, making a nuisance of himself?
She stared him down, and he blinked.
The other man stepped forward.
– Miss Kendall, the other said formally, but kindly. – These two have turned our city into their own private battleground lately.
– Yeah, I know, she grinned. – It stinks, doesn't it?
– And you haven't exactly been idle yourself. The «bad cop» stepped forward again. – You, and your other distant cousin, Ted Cousin.
She wanted to feel insulted on Ted's behalf, but chose to let it go.
– We were defending ourselves. That is still legal in this country, isn't it?
– You're underage, Missy, and you don't have a permit.
– I would be just as DEAD, she shouted and stunned him.
Dust fell on the floor, and they imagined they heard it, that they could actually hear it.
– Listen, she said in the subsequent silence, – David and Mark have left town, and we're about to. Perhaps that's why you're leaving your hideouts, I don't know… But you shouldn't make too much out of that. We aren't your problem anymore. I would be pleased with that, if I were you.
– It isn't that easy, the good cop began.

– I've given you every courtesy, every consideration, she said with luring eyes. – I've sweated it out in a cell for hours just because you decided it was time for some payback, for some regaining of your manhood, and I've answered your ridiculous questions, but enough is enough.

She rose, the chair tilting behind her, hitting the far wall behind her.

– Please sit back down, Miss, the good cop said, and she sensed the rage beneath his surface.

The strange calm entered her again, or rather flowed from her vast deep.

– Six, she said.

– Huh?

– There are six behind the mirror.

They looked bewildered at each other.

There was no advanced warning. The two of them were pushed, as if by invisible hands at the wall, pushed hard, pushed upward at the ceiling, and she made sure it hurt. They gasped in fear and pain, blinding pain, as their bones were twisted and grinded at the wall.

The mirror broke, and revealed the six behind it. In one sweep of power they were all struck down, and it pleased her, pleased her immensely.

– Little boys, she said scornfully, – biting off so much more than you can chew.

She squeezed them squeezed them all, and they screamed. The two on the wall was dropped on the floor with the others. She walked among them, kicking them and hurting them, in any way she could think of. They crouched there in tears and horror.

– Behold the Goddess of Pain and Sacrifice, she said softly. – Behold her kind wrath. Pray that you will never feel her full rage.

A man reached for his gun. She broke his arm, broke it with a stray thought. He screamed, and the sound resonated so sweet in her ears. She smiled, a horrible, twisted smile that made them pee their pants. The stench rose in the room, tearing at her nostrils. She laughed, her scorn making them shrink even further down the road of shame and degradation.

– I know you, she grinned. – I know your wives and children. I can kill them with a thought if you should ever cross me again.

She kicked another in the ribs. It felt good using her foot, too. She sat down on her heels, tenderly touching their cheeks.

One of them attempted to speak. His lips moved, but no sound rose from him, except the gasps and occasional screams, as she perfected her art.

– Hush, she whispered. – Be silent and listen to your Goddess and listen well.

She stood up, facing them all, a study in wrath. In Wrath.

– You're not safe anywhere, if you decide to cross me, she SHOUTED, and the dark, horrible voice itself made the brick walls shake. – I hope you realize this, for your own good. Please don't take my current good mood, the fact that I choose to show mercy, for weakness. You're afraid, now, and you will be afraid for every single second for the rest of your sorry existence. And I'll be with you every moment of it, enjoying your devotion to your Goddess. And if your devotion and fear should ever turn to rage and thoughts of vengeance and restoration of your lost manhood, I'll be there and remind you of who's in charge.

She left them, letting go, turning half around in the door, as they lay there writhing, free to move, but forever shackled by the unimaginable horror they had just experienced, totally unable to meet her eyes, her burning eyes, the pits of hell she had used to curse them and curse them forever.

There was a lot of buzz, a lot of activity around her, as she returned to the cell area, as messages were sent back and forth, as explicit orders were issued. She met cops. They looked strangely at her, but didn't bother her. She ignored them. The bars began shaking the moment she entered the room. And then, almost instantly, the cell door was pulled off its hinges. It hit the other wall with a shriek, and a loud noise defying any description.

– Time to take our leave, she told her charges. – We have stayed far too long in this shithole.

In spite of the last word, she spoke in a strangely formal way, so different from how they had come to know her, exactly as they had come to know her.

Lethargy left them, slowly, as they made their way to her, as they embraced her with their devotion and love, and she felt loved and appreciated and pleased.

The others in the cell left, too. She wasn't sure of why. Whether they left because they wanted to or if they were terrified of the demon that had briefly touched their lives.

She led her followers through the streets. It felt good. She walked through every street and alley with impunity, and they did, too. They learned about the world, about power, true power.

The impunity reached the special house in the French Quarter, followed by every eye they passed. Ted and the rest stood on the balcony, greeting them with warmth and heat. She spotted him almost immediately, long before she actually saw him with her eyes. His eyes were on her, on her living, dancing Shadow. She smiled, a smile jubilant and joyful hitting him like a hot wave on the beach.

I'm ready, she told him. Let's take on the world.

They embraced, several times before they actually did so physically. And when they touched, skin-to-skin time slipped away, and continued to do so during their last days and hours in New Orleans. They sent an envoy to Richard Hagman, informing him that they accepted his offer. And he, in turn informed them that he was «delighted» they had decided to accept.

It was quiet enough these last days and hours. They had become accustomed to the sounds of guns and bombs. But seekers and the curious and the morbid all continued to seek them out. And they talked to journalists. The fact that they had become a part of Hagman's entourage of travelers didn't pass the journalists by either.

The newshounds, like any other were also welcomed to the house in the French Quarter, but they were sent on their way even more confused.

– Perhaps we should have set up shop, Liz said. – We may never have a better chance.

– We are not ready, Ted said. – And we will.

– You're so wise, she said admiringly.

In moments like this, when she looked at him like a lovesick puppy, he wondered about her.

– They call us «the Ugly Ducklings», she said.

– Yes?

He looked at her, frowning.

– That's sooo *cool!*

She grinned.

To avoid some of the ruckus on departure day, they took cabs to the airport. They quite simply left the house as it was, and brought their few belongings. The taxi driver in Ted and Liz's car kept yapping nervously.

– The entire area from the central parts to the international airport was a swamp in the late fifties, he told them. – New Orleans is below sea level. The spillways keep the city or at least major parts of it from being flooded.

– Wow, Liz said, – that is interesting. Leave it to knowledgeable taxi drivers to tell us the truly fascinating stuff about the city.

Her face was lit, like that of the eager kid she was. The driver blushed like a tomato.

In another taxi Candy asked Justine with a voice filled with longing:

– What's… what's a Kwaiala?

– I don't… know, Justine replied frustrated.

Hagman welcomed them, not far from his private jet, with the pack of newshounds being very present. The newshounds would dig and keep digging into their past, like they had done before, and there was a lot of… *juicy* stuff to find. Liz and Ted glanced at each other. They were about to grow famous… or infamous.

Ted stood at the top of the stairs, one step away from entering the plane.

He was back in New Orleans, in its streets and cauldron. It was like he was actually there, sensing its smells, sounds and emotions.

And he heard the voice from the alley. The roar of voices coalesced into one, single sentence.

This is the path of your life, Ror Ken.

The saying of the name hit him like an ice-cold spike down his spine.

I am Ror Ken, he thought.

There is still time to unwind that path, unwind Destiny, to choose not to choose.

He shook his head, and replied, defiantly, shouting at the heavens, at existence itself:

The trick is to be busy being born, not busy dying… *come what may.*

It echoed in eternity, more powerful, not less, every time it was repeated.

He took that one, decisive step into the plane, closing off yet another part of his life.

And they were on their way.

# Chapter Nine: Vengeance is mine - Part 2

## DISTANT BUTTERFLY WINGS

### The Open City - Rotterdam 1940

Fear was present, even more than usual in people's eyes these days. It was tangible, thoroughly rooted in every face he saw.

He turned left and walked into the shadow of the tall building, and there he spotted her.

She walked towards him with the characteristic sack on her back and a man and a small boy at her side.

– Jonas? She cried out. – JONAS!

She ran to him, ran into his arms and embraced him.

They stood there, facing each other. He stared at her blushing face.

– I knew I would see you again, she said giddily. – I just didn't think it would happen so soon.

He understood that statement, at least he thought he did, and it felt both weird and bad and wonderful.

She pulled back a little and turned.

– Oh, before I forget my manners, she spoke in French. – Jonas, this is my husband, François Stewart. François, this is Jonas Bergli, my old and good friend that I told you about, that I believed to be dead.

Jonas had known. James and Virgil had told him about Stewart.

– A pleasure, the Frenchman said curtly and reached out a hand.

– A pleasure, Jonas echoed.

– And this… Nancy glowed, – is Mark.

Jonas took the small boy's little, outstretched hand, feeling very numb and very anxious.

They stood in the shadow of the 45 meters tall White House building in Rotterdam, but Jonas sensed a far larger Shadow blocking the sun around them, and he shivered in the hot May air.

The street was filled with people racing back and forth, true tangible fear painted on their faces. He met Nancy's eyes, and realized that she wasn't unaffected either.

The German war machine was heading this way and everyone wanted to run for their lives, but there was nowhere to go, at least to those who knew what was happening.

The Dutch government had declared Rotterdam an Open City, one without military importance, and subsequently hoped to save it from being bombed, but uncertainty was running high. No one knew what would happen, what to expect.

– We shouldn't be here, Jonas said in English.

– François works here, Nancy stated, still speaking French, strangely ambiguous.

She pulled closer to her husband, the loyal wife.

Jonas felt the lump in his throat grow.

She believed I was dead, he thought.

Nancy whispered something in her husband's ear, and he nodded.

– We're about to have dinner soon, Stewart said in French. – We live nearby. You are invited to join us.

– Thank you very much, Jonas heard himself say (in French). – That's very kind of you.

French it is, he thought, grinning a bit inside, the sting of pain constantly waxing and waning somewhere in there.

It shouldn't matter. You shouldn't be married, and even if you are it shouldn't matter. Society's rules of conduct shouldn't matter. Not to us.

The word matter seemed to echo inside of him. And it didn't go away, even though he made an effort into making it.

It was just a few blocks.

– François is employed by the French government, Nancy said proudly. – We live here at their expense.

He didn't need to listen to her voice to hear the fine-tuned irony there. His throat ached. He knew her so well.

It was a fashionable building at the east side, clearly above the average standard. A guard opened the door for them, saluting Stewart. They entered a great hall, one housing a number of apartments. Servants greeted them and took their clothes. It was… quiet here, nothing close to the noisy ruckus assaulting them from outside. The stylish apartment itself surrounded Jonas like a vice.

The servants prepared dinner. They put plates and stuff on the table, and then finally the food.

The four of them sat there, mostly in silence. In spite of the civil talk, there was silence.

– Jonas is a sailor, Nancy said brightly. – He has sailed the seven seas all his life.

– I can imagine, Stewart commented dryly.

Jonas wanted to ask him if he could imagine anything, but held his tongue.

They had dinner. Jonas couldn't remember what it was afterwards, how it had tasted. Nancy ate with her usual passionate appetite, though with a certain restraint unfamiliar to him. But it was Nancy. He saw that behind her eyes, in every minor or major movement.

The noise from the street outside didn't really enter the building, even though he registered it the same way he ate the food, in a detached manner.

– That was a lovely meal, Nancy told the waiter. – Thank you, Bertrand.

Stewart didn't say anything.

And just like that dinner was done, gone in a dream or a wisp of smoke. Stewart rose first.

– I need to have some work done before the day is done, he said formally to Jonas. – Will you excuse me?

– Of course, Jonas replied.

Stewart turned towards his wife.

– I need some help with the letters, he said.
– Of course, my husband, she said, giving him a blinding smile.
They excited the room. Jonas sat there in the chair for a while, listening, listening to the building. It was quiet, dead. He shivered.
He moved around. It was a large place, almost like a mansion. The sounds from the street outside sounded distant, even though it wasn't really that far away. The windows were open, now, but he still didn't really hear much. He felt numb.
On the shelf before him he saw their wedding photo. Nancy looked different, indistinct, as if she had somehow erased herself.
A good wife did that.
Another was of her, in her «circumstance», her large belly. The next depicted her and Mark. He sat in her lap staring at the world with large, curious eyes.
Jonas walked to the window. People kept scurrying back and forth down there, like confused birds, not sure where to fly, or an orchestra not knowing what to play. One major conductor and cronies said jump, and everybody jumped and played his tune. Nothing made sense in the world today. Not that it ever did. He shook his head.
He saw soldiers on the march, saw them dissolve in blood and broken flesh. The sensations came easy to him. They came unbidden, twisted to nightmarish proportions, and he was in no way certain it was truly a dream.
– It happens everywhere these days, she said.
He turned, and saw her enter the room through the small arc leading to the study. Her skin looked pale, radiating a light not of this world.
– It's hard not to notice, isn't it?
He nodded.
– But people like us want to notice, anyway, don't we Jonas? We don't run from the world, like the rabbits currently populating it does.
This time the tall dark man didn't nod.
– *He* is here, she said.
His eyes widened.
– That's why I am here, she said.
She walked close to him, but stopped a step away.
– He's with the Allies, she said, with venom in her voice, – not with the Germans, somewhere with the High Command. He remains elusive, difficult to pin down, but we're getting closer. We tracked him here, my kin and I, and we know we will find him, find him soon.
She had changed. He realized that startled. She had never or rarely exhibited malice before, at least not in his presence, but she did, now. He realized that she was *letting go*.
He saw Stewart down on the street. A car stopped in front of him. A man, the driver opened a door for him, and he sat down in the back seat.
– The distraction is gone, she said. – It is of no consequence, but it means we won't be disturbed, not even by a trifle such as he.
The strange woman in front of him, the way she spoke…
– I'm sorry, she cried. – I'm sorry, my love.

But there was no regret in her fiery, lupine eyes. She nodded, nodded to herself, reaching out to touch his cheek. He grabbed her hand. She cried out in pain. He looked astonished and shocked at her, and he knew. His eyes narrowed to slits as he removed the glove on her hand. The hand was swollen, cracked by recent marks. Jonas recalled the peculiar sounds from the study, those he hadn't been able to identify at first, before this very moment, the sounds of a riding whip hitting flesh and bone.

– That's okay, I want him to treat me badly, she said with her hollow voice. – So I can treat him badly in return.

Jonas recalled the first sight of François Stewart. He looked anything but good, while she, in return looked marvelous. She was practically glowing radiantly there that one step away, glowing like did her eyes, in dark fire.

You're right, she told him with that beautiful fire in her eyes. It doesn't matter.

She went to Jonas, taking that final, crucial step forward, immersing herself in his presence, kissing him hard on the lips, drawing blood.

– I want to live, Jonas Bergli. – Live!

And in that next moment was everything, everything forgotten.

## 2

They rested in bed, close, so very close. She moved away from him with a kiss, a tender touch of her now totally unblemished hand. He felt a little lightheaded, a little weak, but he didn't care.

She giggled, darkly and cheerful and moody and in messy passion.

– Virgil and James are close, aren't they?

– Yes, he confirmed. – Yes, I would say so.

– They have always been close. She nodded, frowning, – Long before April died, even before Sue died, since James' early childhood, I've been told.

– And now joined, in hatred and loss, Jonas insisted.

She flashed her fangs and didn't seem to hear. For a moment there, she didn't seem to notice him at all. He grabbed her and shook her, shook her hard.

– You understand, don't you Jonas? She said in something very similar to a little girl's voice. – Tell me you understand.

– I understand, he replied dully.

She smiled.

– Poor Jonas, she said softly, with both pity and malice in her voice.

They walked through the city at night. There were no lights anywhere, except behind heavy curtains. He got a sense of them walking through a medieval city, which was to a point true, since the city center was in large part made up of buildings hundreds of years old. She moved like a shadow, seemingly totally unfazed by the darkness surrounding them.

He blinked and the city seemed even more like a medieval village to him.

– You remember, don't you? She said softly.

That would have been a strange question to him, if he hadn't found it strangely valid.

– Yes, he replied.

Glimpses of fire, bits of screams and shouts. It unnerved him to no end.

But when he glanced around him and listened he saw only a dark city, heard only the quiet streets.

But when he looked at her he saw far more, saw the fire and mist and shadows of the night.

– I see you, you know, she said.

– What? He looked at her half turned face, at the light eclipsed by the shadow.

She turned fully and stopped, and he did, too.

– I see you in my most vivid dreams. You have a beast's face, but it is you. We are in a strange place, one as old as time itself. There is a full moon, and lots of tall fires. We fuck, together with many males and females close to us, and afterwards I am spent and filled with pleasure, and I rest in your vast lap. I rub against your pelt, and it feels so sensuous, so right on my beyond sensitive skin.

She seemed different but the same. Goosebumps broke all over his body.

– Perhaps it's only a dream…

She pulled back a little, clearly embarrassed, but glowing, glowing.

– But it feels genuine, feels so *real*.

They came to a building, standing a bit on its own. At least it seemed that way to him, though he couldn't say why that was. She smiled to him, and knocked on the door, knocked in a special manner, a signal. He heard a click, and the door opened. They slipped quickly inside.

There was no electrical light inside, only candles casting ghostly lights and shadows across the room and the faces revealing themselves. He recognized Virgil and James, and also Carla, but not all the other unfamiliar, strangely familiar faces gathered around the main table.

Steam rose between the tables, obscuring further the figures. At least Jonas thought it was steam. It seemed to be, seemed to thicken, to transform as he watched… into mist and shadows.

The two joined the circle, stepped into the two last available spots around the round table. Nancy and everyone else nodded as well, and Jonas also found himself nodding

– There are those who know that the world is not how it is supposed to be, she said.

– THERE ARE THOSE WHO KNOW!

Jonas cried it with the others, and it added to his confusion.

– We know, she stated solemnly. – We count among those few who still remember the world as it was when humanity was young, and not the tired, bowed creature of today.

Twenty-five, including him they were twenty-five. Jonas suddenly knew, and he couldn't recall counting them.

– A corruption has long since spread across the world, but it isn't merely the ugly mark most people perceive in these obviously troubled times, but far worse, a fact made abundantly clear by the fact that our old enemy is working for the Allies, for those perceived as the current white hats.

He shook his head, both troubled and in awe because of her eloquence, and the glowing darkness surrounding her.

– We know that the world is not black and white and that the lines are blurred, and that the true line in the sand, if such a beast exists at all is far from where the majority of current humanity believes it is…

He studied the gathering afterwards, as they mingled and interacted. They weren't Belgian. In fact they weren't any particular nationality or race. He saw Africans there, and Afro-Americans, and Orientals and an assorted mix stunning him. There didn't seem to be any reason or rhyme to it, it just *was*.

– Where did you find everybody? He asked Nancy.

– We didn't find them, she replied. – We found them and they found us.

– Enigmatic as ever…

There was meeting and parting of glasses, as people cheered, and spoke like old friends, old friends that hadn't seen each other in years.

– I see something, Jonas, she said with twinkling eyes. – I see glimpses of what has always been *hidden*. I have tried, tried my entire adult life to see through the veil to the Other World, but I never truly succeeded.

Her words… they sent shivers through his entire frame, not only down his spine.

Carla looked at them, and they caught her smiling at them, before she turned away, her attention fading like a mirage.

He walked to her, chased her, suddenly anxious, and caught up with her at the door. She turned her attention to him once more, and he knew her, knew her song, the one he had heard long before ever meeting her.

– It's been a while, hasn't it? She grinned.

He noticed the increasing number of gray hairs, but she didn't look old.

She looked old.

– Yes, a while, he nodded.

– It has been so long, she said. – But now the waiting is almost done.

He heard the sounds of hooves hitting the ground, heard riders in the early morning.

Sometimes there are riders.

She was gone, during the moment he had been distracted. He suspected she had vanished into the ladies' room, but he was in no way certain.

He opened the door and there she was. She stopped a moment and smiled to him, before walking inside the cubicle.

The door closed in front of him with a soft thud, and he shook his head and returned to the party, to what was evidently a celebration. He hadn't been certain it was until he saw Nancy and the others raise their glasses and drink.

A woman spoke to Virgil and James. They seemed hesitant, apprehensive, exactly like old friends that hadn't seen each other in years and wondered if old friendships were still valid, if it was possible to rekindle the past and reignite the good moments they had shared.

– It's exactly like I saw it in my dream, she stated incredulous. – Exactly the same.

Virgil nodded, almost happy, even though no amount of fleeting moments could truly transform the tired lines in his face. He had gray hairs, too. He was one of the youngest present, but he had grown old long ago.

But he Burned, and the burning kept him alive, no matter how much he wanted to die.

It was the way the woman… presented herself to him, to them, offering herself to them that more than anything struck Jonas, and as had often been the case lately he felt both clarity and ridicule.

Nine years had passed since he had met the Warrens, met the Shadowwalkers, and he no longer recalled more than bits and pieces before that crucial point in his life.

– «I walk the path of yesterday», Carla said to him, – «and on its turns and curves I see tomorrow. I walk the path of tomorrow, and in its dim distance I glimpse the past».

Everybody in the room nodded. Jonas did, as well.

– To Tomorrow. James suddenly cried out and raised his glass. – If tomorrow comes.

– TOMORROW, everybody cried, drinking their glass empty.

The red wine burned in Jonas' throat.

– We are the Shadowwalkers, Nancy said. – We are one group of walkers among many and we know who we are, at least in the shadows.

She filled all the glasses. They drank some more. The wine burned on Jonas' lips, suddenly so much stronger than it had in his throat.

He studied her, and he studied Carla, Virgil and James. She was different. They were all slightly different, compared to New York and even Spain.

Nine years, only nine years, but it felt like a lifetime, far more so than his years before that moment in New York when he had met them… for the first time.

The wine filled him, the spices filled him, exploded in his veins, not just in his stomach. He met Nancy's eyes, and they twinkled and her mouth twisted into a smile beyond joyous, beyond desire. Her lips burned against his, even when they didn't touch.

The room at the upper floor surrounded him, them, and he had no idea how they had arrived at this place. She glowed, glowed in the dark and slipped close to him, and nothing else mattered.

And the dark filled him, filled her, and he smelled dust, smelled dry desert sand, and he had no idea where it all came from, and he tumbled down, spiraled into that dark, until it was all he knew, all he would ever know.

## 3

He woke up with her in his arms. She smiled to him. The light broke through the heavy curtains and blinded him. One single flash and they walked outside through the streets. They noticed the increased, frantic activity almost immediately, no matter how they kept looking at each other, kept looking at the other with a warm, warm tingle of a smile.

– We should get out of the city the fastest we can, she stated, and he easily noted the slight shiver in her voice. – The fastest we possibly are able.

With a renewed sense of urgency they hurried through the busy streets.

– Can you hear the planes? A woman said to her companion.

Jonas didn't hear the reply, but he cocked his ear.

– There are no planes, he said to Nancy.

She nodded her agreement, but her eyes had started to flicker, to move back and forth and up at an increasingly faster pace, not resting, not even for a tiny, single moment.

They ran towards the public apartment buildings. The door inside was open, clearly a worrying sign, if he had ever seen one.

Nancy rushed right to the children's ward. The empty room stared at them.

She rushed back into the living room.

– Where is he? She snarled to the maid. – Where is Mark?

The maid backed off a little startled and frightened.

– The Master took him, she replied. – He told us he would go first with the boy, and that we were supposed to follow him later.

– He would say that, the strange, alien woman said, gritting her teeth, and her rage flared again. – When did he leave, you stupid cunt. *When?*

– Only a couple of minutes ago, the woman responded with shaking lips.

And they were outside again, running. There was a long queue of cars down the main street. A raven flapped its wings and rose from the nearest rooftop and he shivered in his bones.

– He won't get far, she shouted, with a voice filled with triumph.

She knew, she didn't just guess or offered a desperate hope to herself. He realized that, once again startled beyond words. The raven circled a street ahead, and Jonas Bergli and his beloved chased it through streets filled with strife and chaos and fear.

They heard the planes before they saw them, before they appeared above the buildings far away. Nancy muttered something under her breath, but he didn't get what. It was neither English nor French or any other language Jonas could understand. She was clearly anxious, driven, even more so than usual.

People ran up and down the street, ran back and forth in all directions, unable to make up their mind as to what was safe, slowly realizing that nowhere really was. Nancy didn't care. Her run was deliberate, directed, filled with purpose.

The cars used the entire street, both lanes and the sidewalks in their zeal to flee the open city. It was hopeless. Everything came to a predictable halt not far ahead.

The wild animal in the guise of a woman slipped between the carcasses of hot metal effortlessly. Its deadly claws didn't even touch her, as she made her way to her destination. Jonas fell behind, no matter how hard he strived to keep up.

He heard music and it distracted him. It seemed to come from everywhere around him. He covered his ears, but it did no good. The scent of… of sand, desert sand played in his nostrils, and he stared bewildered at the world. He closed his eyes briefly and in that blink a million images and sensations flooded his mind.

She gestured, and the door of a car, one particular car blew open. The engine roared, and its parts suddenly burst through the hood. Already panicked people froze and stared, stared at the world through hazy, fevered eyes. Some, quite a few of them remained there, on the spot, paralyzed, unable to move as much as a finger.

François Stewart jumped out of the car with the boy in his arms, a knife pushed at the boy's throat.

– I WILL do it, he shouted, – if you attempt as much as a tiny little *trick.*

Nancy stopped. Jonas stopped. She about ten steps, virtually exactly ten steps away, he a little behind her. He saw everything with a clarity he couldn't recall ever experiencing.

– Please, my husband, she spoke softly, – there's no need for this...

– DAMN RIGHT IT ISN'T, Stewart shouted insanely. – You swore to obey and cherish me and obey and cherish me you shall, for the rest of your life.

– I will, she affirmed. – I am.

– Oh, no. He shook his head in a very twisted version of a smile. – You smile pretty and are very good at pretending, but behind your smile you hiss, and work your satanic ways, and I want it to *stop!*

– It will! She pleaded with him. – I will be pleasing and attentive and everything a good wife is. I will be yours, unconditionally.

She fell on her knees, bowing her head. Jason realized startled that she played the good girl from the brothel in New Orleans again, and he wondered what it cost her, what depths that lurked within her given that she was able to do that.

Spittle flowed down Stewart's jaw, his eyes bulging ever more in their sockets.

– And what about him? Nodding towards Jonas.

– He will leave, she said meekly, – and never bother us again.

Jonas wanted to scream at the other man, but the knife still pressed against the boy's jugular, and Jonas held himself in check by an act of iron will. Seconds passed. Nobody moved. Stewart's eyes seemed to clear and the insanity leaving them. He looked confused at the boy and at the kneeling woman.

The first bomb hit the ground, hit the sidewalk just a block away. Jonas looked up. The air was filled with planes and he hadn't even noticed. He shuddered. Stewart lost his grip on the boy or let go of the small body, Jonas couldn't tell what. And in that moment the stranger on the ground howled in rage and seemed to leap, to flow on her feet, throwing herself at the man an impossible distance away. She went right for his throat, and Bergli saw how she tore it to shreds and blood gushed from the breathing dead man's neck.

Mark was pushed away from the two, by what Bergli knew was an invisible hand. The boy ran into his arms. There was another blast, and then there were *many*. He threw himself down, covering the small body with his big frame, acknowledging the futility, the theatrics of that small attempt at defying fate.

Thunder shook him, as if the entire street seemed to explode around the two of them.

A noise of a level he had never imagined could exist assaulted his ears, all his senses.

Until it all seemed to *stop*. He still heard explosions, he was certain of that, but they seemed muted, distant. He felt the warm body below him, a heart alive and beating. He rose, revealing the boy, the tiny face dissolved in tears, and he stumbled the few steps towards the open hole in the ground.

Stewart was nowhere to be found or seen. Bergli could, if he had chosen to have imagined that the tiny pieces of flesh had been a human being once, but that could never be proven, at least not by him.

His left ear bled, wetting his shoulder and neck. He saw Nancy or at least something resembling her, at the center of the hole, of the hollow. It wasn't hard getting there, to her. He simply stumbled over the edge and kept walking, the few steps to the remains there.

– Mark? She said.

Incredibly enough she was able to speak.

– He's okay. He choked. – He's just a bit roughed up, that's all.

Somewhere he heard the boy's tiny wails.

Jonas knelt by her side. She was completely shredded, to the point that it was so little left whole of her body that it was a miracle she yet lived.

– I see her, she mumbled. – She fell in the sand. She is dying. I see a hooded figure walk down the Thunder Road. In its left hand it holds a wand…

She faltered.

– … with a tiny skull on top. In its right it holds a sword.

She shook, an expression of horror burning in her face. Her body, what was left of it, incredibly enough turned rigid.

– Mickey…

She cried.

Her eyes turned to glass. Her beyond mangled body lay still.

He sat there, on his knees, unable to feel anything, to even register anything of what happened around him. The cries and wails didn't touch him, failed to register in his consciousness. Planes kept passing above him, and explosions kept shaking the ground or so he imagined. He didn't move.

A movement in the air startled him, making him look up, making him react. He watched as the image of something very alike Nancy formed before his burning eyes. The apparition had her eyes on his, looking at him with infinite fondness. He shook and jumped to his feet, stumbling backwards a few steps before finally regaining his balance.

The second apparition faded in before his eyes, and it was an old Egyptian woman. Astounded he saw affection in her eyes as well. One heartbeat, two, and they joined, becoming one, fearsome entity. He stared at the fangs and claws and the beyond demonic face. She stared passionately at him with her lupine eyes.

– Hello, Anubis. She spoke somewhat, creating sound, even though she was only a spirit. – I see that you remember me, remember yourself. That is good. That is so very good.

She faded before his eyes, but the image of her had been burned into his eyes forever. No matter where he turned from now on, he would see her frightening visage.

He fell on his knees again there in the ruins, and thus he remained, for hours, days, and years, until dusk finally settled, and he was forced to move on.

# Third Part:
# The Call of the Wild

# Chapter Ten: The Wasteful Man

The private jet scoured the heavens on its way south. Two people stood at the center of the plane, staring at the clouds outside. They saw them, even if they didn't look through the window. In every cloud they saw a face, a shade, a shape in the mist.

– I have always been weary of flying, she said in a low voice. – Even when I went to London to see you, I was uncomfortable. I've never understood why.

– It is unnatural, he said. – A plane is advanced technology, and I think, I believe strongly, we're adverse to that.

– But so is a motorbike, she said, – and I love riding one.

New Orleans stayed with them, somehow, and always would, he suspected. He heard a fiddle. A man stood on a balcony and played. Ted Warren felt it like he was there, and not here. He and Liz were the only real people on the plane. The people in New Orleans surrounding them, passing them in the streets, were real, not the ghosts here.

Two pair of eyes spotted the two crossing swords on the wall, spotted them simultaneously. They walked there and grabbed them, grabbed the shaft, and pulled the swords from the wall, and the present turned real, turned tangible again.

Richard Hagman studied them. Ted knew that without looking, and he didn't care. The dark man and equally dark woman faced each other with swords in their hands.

They made the first few, tentative strokes. Swinging blades cut the air, making holes in reality. The two of them circled each other, fencing, not really attempting to hurt the other. It was more like a ballet, a choreographed battle, as if the other knew exactly what the other would do at any time. They stopped after a while, looking astounded at each other.

– It's so weird, Liz said. – It is as if the sword is an extension of my very being.

– How many times have you… have you practiced?

Justine frowned at them.

– This is our first, Ted said, also frowning.

– Then I have to say you handle them with an uncanny, practiced ease, Richard Hagman commented.

– We're born with iron at our side. Liz stated proudly. – In a heat stronger than a thousand forges.

And then it was as if she saw herself in a place not a place, a fiery creature of Fire and Shadow. The place slowly condensed into a clearer image. She saw a circle. Mountains surrounded the circle. Desert surrounded the circle. She stepped into it from its outside, crossed the threshold, and her perception of the world, of herself and everything changed. Ted was there, facing her, as she was facing him, burning in Shadow like she was.

It faded, in a matter of moments, of microseconds, faster than even a dream. She was back on the plane, and realized startled that she had never left it.

She met Ted's eyes.

– I was in a *cold* place, she said. – It was nothing. It wasn't just that there was nothing there, but that it *was* Nothing. Then it was filled, filled with *Life,* with *Fire*. And then I was in a completely different place, and a moment later I was elsewhere again. It wasn't just one vision, but two, three, four, five…

Hagman rose from his chair

– You're such interesting young people, he declared. – I certainly made the right decision bringing you along.

He was undoubtedly an enigmatic, powerful figure. Liz felt herself grow queasy and hot while looking at him.

The main cabin was crowded, filled with Hagman's people and those following Liz and Ted, and the number of journalists doing nothing but following Hagman's exploits, but not more than it was fairly easy to move around. It resembled a field more than a cabin, and the aircraft itself more a ship than most passenger planes.

Everybody looked at Liz, but she had grown used to that by now.

She put her sword back on the wall, and so did Ted.

Anthony La Grande stepped forward.

– You didn't hurt each other, he said, more than frowning. – The control to keep that from happening is only found in very experienced fighters.

– It is like I said. She flashed a smile, exposing her fangs to him. – We don't need to learn anything, only rediscover what we have forgotten, something true for all human beings by the way.

She could remember actual sword fighting, seeing flashes of another her in the mirror image of the shining metal.

A female with fireeyes was taught the use of the sword. She was transformed from a slip of a girl to a fiery warrior. Battle-scars painted her body and she wore them proudly. She was on a battlefield, and the fast-moving, shiny sword turned red with enemies' blood. The seventeen year-old-girl gasped in excitement.

She leaned against Ted, her hot skin burning his cheek. Fire danced in her eyes like never before.

– The exercise, she spoke in his ear, – it… released something inside of me, something… primal.

– I felt it, too. He nodded. – Each new stroke brought… enlightenment.

And bloodlust and terror and fear.

– The next more powerful, so much more powerful than the one before, she whispered.

They were alone, in another room, as if the others had quite simply faded from their view, as if they had wished them out of existence.

Candy brought them two glasses of water on a tray. They grabbed it and drank greedily, so thirsty, so filled with… with Hunger.

She sensed that, and she melted willingly, excitedly into their embrace, her dark hair becoming one with theirs.

They returned refreshed, slow burning with sensuality, affecting everybody in the room. Liz sensed that, easily, in each and every one of those present how they reacted to their immediate presence.

Hagman and company stood gathered around the large table at the center of the room. The map room, he called it, and he had spoken about it on earlier occasions, but never revealed it before. Liz felt the inevitable sting of excitement inside.

There was a giant map on the table, a modern one, of the northern half of South America.

– The Amazon forest, he declared dramatically, – the largest jungle in the world, and still largely unexplored by the white race, by the modern world.

She liked his addition there. He wouldn't say things like «Columbus or Leif Eriksson discovered America», like most people would. Everybody knew that there had been natives there before, but even the language and day-to-day conversation ignored that. But he didn't.

A camera was recording it all, in typical, megalomaniacal Hagman style.

– I grew up with the stories of the ancient cities. Hagman spoke to the camera, to posterity, clearly enjoying himself, clearly full of himself. – With the tales of Atlantis, El Dorado, Cibola, Xanadu and their like, whose may all have one origin, and be the same city.

Flashes of the city, the forest in the desert appeared before Ted and Liz's eyes. They didn't have to close them to see it again, to see it unfold.

It wasn't that much, Liz wanted to say. Time and excessive storytelling created the legend of the splendorous city.

But she kept silent.

– But there was one, major problem with them or it, Hagman said. – It didn't exist anymore, and I knew that, even at the beginning of my zeal. Whether it had sunk below the sea or just been abandoned or destroyed in a storm, time itself had made it inaccessible to me. So I had to look elsewhere, and I did. I found, in my travels more recent cities and temples and stuff. But, as I found it I began picking up clues to another place, unbound by space and time, or so the legend says, a valley of kings rivaling that of ancient Egypt. I've tracked and backtracked information for years, and the proof I've gathered gives one, undeniable conclusion: The place still exists.

His voice had turned hoarse there, at the end. They stared at him, as he stared at them with his penetrating eyes. He put another map on the table. This was older, clearly worn by time, and without the modern sophistication of the one beneath.

Ted saw Betty again. She smiled to him.

The map depicted a jungle. That much was clear. It resembled the century-old maps in books Liz and Ted had seen in school. But it was of a land covered in jungle, and at its center was a large open area filled with buildings. Ted and Liz looked at each other with the strange feeling rising from their depths again.

– Look at this map, Hagman told the people leaning forward around the table.

And they all looked.
- Your city… it seems to be in Brazil somewhere, Phillip mused, - but aren't most ancient cities in the west, mostly in Columbia, Peru and Bolivia, and didn't those early German and Spanish «explorers» turn the jungle there upside down and inside out looking for several lost cities, and killed thousands of people in the bargain?
- They looked in the wrong place, the modern explorer replied, - and yes, as you pointed out, they weren't exactly the most imaginative people, mostly mercenaries and ruthless, biased megalomaniacs, doomed to fail.
Then he pulled the old map away, and they saw once again the new, fairly sophisticated map of South America.
– Look at the resemblance, the tycoon said, his voice thick with emotion. – How *similar* they are.
– They are, Candice said, – sort of.
– Yes, yes, Hagman nodded. – There are no absolute certainties when studying old maps. Trust me, I've learned that hard lesson often enough. Many of them are just plain fakes, and the majority of those remaining are, at best unreliable. But rest assured that I have done the research, done the math and all, and I tell you that this…
He pointed at the point on the modern map equivalent to the spot on the other, worn map in his hand.
– … is the most probable place to find the present Valley of Kings.
He looked at them, looked at them all, as if daring them to contradict him, but there was no need.
His words excited them, excited them all, and continued to do so, as they made their way south, as they slipped beneath the clouds and finally landed on the airport outside Caracas, Venezuela.

## 2

They walked through the old colonial district, in the shadows of the new, modern office buildings. The air was hot and humid, more so than any of the travelers except Hagman himself, and a few of his more experienced aides had ever experienced.
He had been most places, all over the planet, and he kept entertaining them with stories of his exploits.
Ted and Liz, and those following them eventually went out on their own, exploring the city, the light of adventure lit in their eyes.
– It's so strange, so different, Justine cried excitedly, adding a bit more subdued, – so familiar.
There were even a few shopping malls to make them feel more at home, and they looked dismayed at the flashy sights, as they hurried past them.
They sought the more unsavory places in the city, and found them, after a lot of legwork and stubbornness. While most visitors sought what was the most

familiar to them in any given place, this group did the opposite, and the feeling of being in a foreign country was boosted further.

It dawned slowly on most of them that they were far away from home. Ted was the only one among them that had been abroad more than briefly, and all this was just as unfamiliar to him. They heard the language, noticed the mostly brownish faces surrounding them, and realized they were further away from home than they had ever been, and also knew this was only the beginning.

That fact filled them with the now familiar tingle of excitement and fear.

Phillip spoke Spanish, and without that they would have been lost fairly quickly. Caracas was a city of mixed cultures rivaling New Orleans, though, and they really had to strive to get around. It became a challenge to them, to manage without a guide or interpreter, and they pressed on in youthful enthusiasm. Ted shuddered momentarily and no one noticed, not even Liz. She was busy laughing with the girls.

They tried on local clothes. She noticed nonplussed his looks and smiled amused.

– «When in Rome, dress like a roman», she grinned.

With the top and skirt and her still short hair a certain way, she almost looked like a local or an original native, an American Indian. At least she would, to people not knowing better. It was the «chameleon effect» again. Experience had told Ted that both of them could blend in, in almost any society, and pass for almost any group of people, especially if they chose to. The others looked astonished at her.

Or perhaps he was being too optimistic. What was probably truer is that they looked black to Caucasians, white to Negroid and so on. They could blend in, but also stood out like a sore nail.

– Richard sure has a lot of stories to tell. Candy shook her head in wonder. – I never knew, never imagined that the world was so strange, so vast, and so… interesting.

The others, including Ted and Liz laughed with her.

– I was a robot, an automaton, doing nothing except serving my corrupt masters, she said, turning to the two of them, – until you two came along. Thank you. Thank you.

– We all have had that feeling occasionally, Kwaiala, Liz said graciously. – That misery telling us we are worthless and unable to do anything to change our situation. The lucky and brave and stubborn encounters other people willing and able to offer another perspective, to be teachers and visionaries in a world dominated by tyrants and their sycophants.

But she was distracted. They all were, and couldn't help it. They heard the song, heard it from rooftops and alleys. It spoke to them from the deepest recesses of their fear and shook their confidence to ribbons.

– *Iluso is our Master. Iluso is our God. Beware his wrath.*

They walked down a busy street, when they heard it again, and they froze.

Ted and Liz attempted to focus, to locate the singers, but they proved illusive, difficult to track down. Liz rushed off, around a corner, on full alert, but there was no one there, no one even remotely suspicious at least. People stared at her, as they always did, as if she was a wild animal, but she could sense no animosity in them beyond that, beyond their mundane ignorance and intolerance and sense of inferiority.

The song seemed to rise from the city, the very ground itself, haunting them.

– He means to rattle us, Liz mumbled, – to get on our nerves. Ignore him.

But she couldn't. Phillip saw that easily, but he kept silent.

Hagman held a banquet, an over-the-top feast for his fellow travelers and for local backers of his venture. As usual he spared no expenses. That was more than evident to all taking part in his *baile,* his party, his celebration of adventure and excess.

– Friends and fellow travelers, he boasted, – allow me to give thanks to you for attending my modest gathering…

Phillip counted about two hundred heads in the room before giving up.

– I want to give special thanks to those people that have chosen to accompany me on my quest to unknown shores. I want us to have a toast, my friends, to the unknown, the unexplored, and to US, seeking the secrets of the world…

Liz drank with a stubborn, determined expression in her face. She drank a lot. Ted pretended to be unconcerned, but he followed her with his eyes and his glance, like he always did. She cheered, and Candy and the others looked at her with apprehensive stares.

They forget, Phillip thought, forget how young she is.

– We should… caution her, Candy told him with worry painted all over her face. – Two full-grown men couldn't have kept up with her. She drinks herself to death.

– It will be okay, he assured her. – She knows what she's doing.

He observed Liz as she stumbled around, taking hard liquor from the trays offered the guests, and he observed Ted observing her. The look of concealed anxiety in Warren's face wasn't exactly reassuring.

It was all so jumbled, so like a jigsaw puzzle observed through dirty glass or something. Phillip had trouble seeing properly. No matter how hard he strained his eyes he never seemed to see the girl clearly, and he wanted to, wanted to desperately, and he could almost imagine that some kind of dirty glass indeed obscured his vision… somehow.

There was some commotion at the door. It grew so loud that everybody in the room turned their heads there. A woman, followed by several women and men brusquely discarded the guards and made their way towards Hagman at the other side of the room.

– It's his wife, a woman whispered to her companion. – They love and hate each other.

There were both nervous and excited giggling among the gathering, as Mr. and Mrs. Hagman came face to face.

– Hello, my dear, Hagman cleared his throat, – I didn't expect to see you here.

– I'll bet you didn't, she replied sheepishly.

There was laughter, nervous and brittle and hearty.

– She's an archeologist, too, the woman kept telling her companion. – They have been competing, been racing to reach new archeological sites first since before they were married.

The woman went on to tell the man by her side the entire life story of Mrs. And Mr. Hagman. Caine didn't really listen. He sought out Liz, but couldn't find her.

He found her, hidden away, on a couch in a dark room on the second floor, drinking large gulps of liquor.

She writhed on her back, her eyes swimming, hardly conscious. He took that one, crucial step into the room, and she instantly turned her head and caught him with her low-burning eyes.

– It silences the voices, she mumbled, – at least for a little while.

He walked closer. She sat up, hissing at him, halting him in his tracks.

– Don't touch me. Don't even come close to touching me. My body is fighting the poison and it can do very nasty things to people touching me in such a state, if given the change.

She sat there, looking at him, staring him down. She had pulled up her legs. He easily saw her cunt, wet and swollen. She smirked at him with her very nasty grin.

– Adepts have always used alcohol in an attempt to control their powers, she said. – Awareness fades, for a little while. No more enhanced senses, no visions or specters of the future. Some have become so desperate that they have become drunks and eventually ruined their powers altogether.

She rose, a little unsteady, laughing.

– Don't worry, it won't work on me. I heal long before any serious damage can be done.

He looked at her, attempting not to stare. He had never before seen her as… frail.

– Come with me, she giggled. – Your Goddess needs you.

She cackled insanely.

And he followed her, and not before long he found himself walking with her through Caracas' streets. He observed how she deliberately, casually touched people she passed on the sidewalk, just a little each time, and how her eyes cleared and began burning again.

He wanted to say something, anything. She raised a hand stopping him from speaking.

– Can you hear it?

– What?

– Of course you can't, she nodded to herself.

He heard the drums first, seemingly rising from the ground itself. Then he heard it, heard the choir, and it seemed to come from inside his head, and goose bumps broke out all over his body, and when he glanced at Liz he was astonished to notice the goose bumps on her skin as well.

– This is new, she said. – I've never felt anything like it before. It's a kind of… buzz in my frontal lobe. The chant is in my head as well as in my ears, if you know what I mean.

He didn't and she knew that. He kept silent.

She moved again. She never really *began* moving, the way he saw it. It was just one, fluid motion. He had suddenly major problems keeping up with her, and very soon he strived to catch his breath. It was infuriating. He knew he was in excellent shape, but he didn't stand a change of keeping up with her.

Everything filed past him in a blur. He lost her around some corners, caught a glimpse of her on other occasions, and he glimpsed her eyes, and he realized she made sure he was still there, that she would have been able to move even faster if she wanted to, and it didn't sit well with him, didn't sit well with him at all, and he felt disgusted with himself, and that, in turn made him feel even worse.

He found her standing above an old beggar, just as he feared he had lost her. She was wild the girl crouching before the man in rags before her. The juxtaposing anxiety and joy within Phillip Caine grew even stronger as he watched her.

– Where is he? She asked.

The chant kept rising from the man's throat. There was nothing there, if you looked at his eyes, really, as if he had become the chant, and that was now everything he was.

The chill down Phillip's spine didn't let go, no matter how hard he tried.

– Where is he? Liz raged, shaking the skinny form in her claws' grip. – Where is your Master?

– Iluso is our Master. The old man's voice cracked for a moment. – Iluso is our God. Beware his wrath.

He laughed, and Phillip saw that his laughter rattled the girl, saw it easily. She touched him skin to skin then, and it was like touching wet paper, and she shivered visibly.

– Iluso is fish and bird, Earth and sky, the man cackled. – Iluso is everywhere. He's a shark, swimming the waters, catching all the little fish in his net.

There was intelligence, awareness just for a moment there, in the watery eyes, and then nothing, except the emptiness Phillip had first seen.

Liz let go of the man and straightened, looking at Phillip as if she only then noticed his presence.

– Come! She told him, and left, and he followed her like a good dog.

– He will catch you, the loud, suddenly crystal-clear dark voice cried.

They turned, and Phillip Caine witnessed something that would haunt him for the rest of his days.

The figure seemed to collapse there, where it sat, collapse into nothing. Flesh just faded, like ice in the sun. One second the two of them saw a heap of clothes, and then there wasn't even that, was no sign of anyone, no proof that there had ever been anyone on that spot.

She crouched there, between the alley and the street, staring at him with insane eyes, and he saw the beast luring within the sensual female form. He saw that it was sore afraid, and he shivered hard.

## 3

The rain season began. Streets and sewers were flooded and sewage rose with the secrets buried in humanity's depths.

Ted Warren sensed it, and as he often did he both marveled and worried about his enhanced and uncanny senses. It rose within him like the flood surrounding him. He sat hot and cold in the midst of warm and pleasant bodies, shivering like a leaf.

Liz' eyes grew wide and wary. She moved, moved towards him and he grew aware of his surroundings, even though that other world, that of his senses retained its power.

– What do you see? She asked, demand and pleading equally present in her voice.

– I see the sea, he replied, hearing himself speak through a tunnel, from a vantage point far away.

She moved closer to him, touching him, kissing his lips, holding her lips, herself there, as if she desired to push herself inside him.

– I see it rise, breaking all surfaces, all confines. It's a tide, but also more than that. It's a flood no one can deny or escape.

– Good, she whispered. – Very good.

He saw her clearly, like he always did. The others, even though he was able to glimpse them, were all concealed in the dancing mist.

– I see ice melting and breaking up. It's happening all over the world, happening right now. It's not apparent yet, but it will be, will be soon.

– So, it is a physical effect then?

– Yes, and… no. I see people on the move. I see them rise. We're rising… ascending, becoming a force in the world. The house in London… I see us there. We're many and powerful. We're in the desert. I can hear it whisper to us, the souls of the dead, empowering us. I see fire and ice and it's all the *same*.

He heard it, heard the whisper rise to a deafening roar.

And he woke up fully, seeing his surroundings in a normal light again, or in a fairly normal light, gasping, striving to pull large gulps of air into his straining lungs.

Candy brought him a chalice of hot, spiced tea. He drank it all in matter of seconds. They came to him, touching him, replenishing him. He rose, and his perspective seemed to change far more than the mere distance his head moved from the floor should have caused. The sights, smell, sounds and taste of the room assaulted him. The party still kept going in other parts of the house. The sensations from all over the house, and even on the streets, flooded him. This was a bedroom (a large bedroom) in a distant wing of the colonial building owned by Hagman's wife or former wife, Alanis Monroe. He spotted several unfamiliar faces among those of his tribe. They had been pulled in when the party had taken flight, and followed him here with the others.

He glanced around for Liz, but saw her nowhere. She had left. He looked down at his cock without shame or shyness. It still dripped of warm juices. The pleasant tingling of power still spread through his body and empowered him.

Someone told him that his ears were moving. He knew they did, zeroing in on sounds sharp and soft. They picked up ice being dropped in a glass somewhere. He didn't hear a wall of sound or anything undistinguishable, but could, at least in part distinguish between the various sources.

He dressed. They all did. A woman asked him with badly concealed desire if he wanted an *assisted* bath. He shook his head. Fully dressed he glanced briefly at himself as he passed the hall mirror. Dressed, not dressed, it didn't seem to matter one way or another for him anymore. He noticed that with a modicum of satisfaction.

The rain continued to pour outside. The flood kept rising in the streets. Inside, outside, it didn't matter. It was all the same.

Laurie caught up with him, a bit breathless, eager like a much younger girl.

– How is it like? She asked. – The Journey?

– You know that, he replied softly. – You have experienced it yourself several times.

– Just glimpses, she cried. – Half baked, unfulfilled promises. Not like you.

He stopped and turned towards her and looked at her. She reddened, but desperately kept meeting his eyes, his eyes growing distant, and once again he was not really present anymore, but out there, in the infinity that was reality.

– It's vast, he said. – Every time I return I feel like I've been gone for many lifetimes. Each moment is an eternity, and there's no end to it. The reality most people experience as real is really an illusion, not in the sense that it doesn't exist, but in its importance.

He wanted to say more, wanted, somehow to still the Hunger inside her, but words failed him.

– Thank you, she whispered, kissing him shyly, but to him her prevailing burning desire was quite evident.

She had excelled throughout the night, in the swirling mist of bodies and fumes, but she was still hungry, still needy. He had never really met anyone as needy as her, and it made him strangely anxious.

He held out an arm to her. She giggled and stuck her own arm inside his. They returned together to the house… and to the party's ground floor. She clung to him like glue, letting him know she was available, that she wanted him, wanted him very much. He couldn't help but respond to her.

*Do you want me?* He heard her voice in his head. She laughed pleased, while looking at him with her opaque eyes. *You want me!*

He did… and he didn't, and he made his best to mask his conflicting emotions from her. It was close to impossible. She was a telepath, like Betty, in addition to her telekinetic talent, but even though clearly less experienced, she was far more powerful. He knew she was straining in crowds; that the «noise» made the telepathy less reliable, but it didn't seem to disturb her that much. She had come a long way from that insecure, moody girl he had met in New Orleans.

She had gained weight, and color and confidence, and she had grown considerably more assertive.

They moved among the gathering, a crowd of both local and international wealth. She looked at them with contempt and a snarl behind the innocent smile.
– Look at them, she said, shaking her head, the voice of the eighteen year old girl turning childish and spiteful. – This is supposed to be members of the world's elite.
He wanted to voice objections to her judgmental statement, but in truth he couldn't. Her words were a mere echo of the strong words he and Liz had made during their conversation on the subject.
– We are the new gods, aren't we? Aren't we, Ted?
– Yes, he heard himself say.
– And when we make our presence known the world will tremble.
She nodded content.
Yes, he thought.
People noticed them. How could they not? The contempt and patronizing glee they radiated were deeper than the ocean. He glimpsed Hagman, glimpsed Richard in a circle of well dressed gentlemen. He had been struggling quite a bit lately, and it had begun to show. Things moved slower down here, compared to what he was used to, and the travelers had trouble getting even the simplest of supplies on their way further south. Ted considered it for a moment, than he forgot about it.
The rise… began, began again, outside, inside, a pressure in his frontal lobe. He heard the first chords or the melody from the room's speakers, and suddenly everything felt good, felt right. There was no need for him to drag Laurie with him to the dance floor. She sensed his eagerness, his dark passion and joined him enthusiastically. They began moving, began dancing even before they reached the polished floor, as he, on a whim turned the sound up, way up. The music and lyrics of All Tomorrow's Parties by Velvet Underground filled the hall, filled the old building. He sensed fear in people's hearts when the couple began excelling out there, in the swirling mist, and it excited him.
Laurie was incredibly fast and light on her feet. He knew that already, but it still astonished him. She giggled as he strived to keep up with her. But then, with only a slight effort he did, he managed, and her eyes turned misty and huge. The scent from her wet, inner thighs cut into his nostrils like the sharpest of blades. The song was slow, no matter how fast their feet moved, and it was even slower in his mind, as their surroundings turned indistinct, fading in a way to his senses, to all his senses, turning sharper than ever.
He saw, with a crystal clarity the interest and rejection in people's eyes afterwards, and he didn't give a damn. Laurie led on, now, and he followed her, pulled by the fevered thoughts she projected into his equally buzzing mind.
She pushed herself at him the moment they were out of sight, teased him with her full and enticing lips, and rubbed herself at him with every piece of her tight body.
Stick it in, she implored him. Please!
She pushed her front against one of the many Roman pillars in the empty hall. He did. He pulled up her skirt, grabbed her tight butt, and pushed himself deep

inside of her, without recalling pulling down his pants. She cried out in ecstasy. He could swear they heard her loud moans all over the house. He sensed them, experienced it from their perspective, and he became even more aroused and pushed even harder.

He gasped, and he knew they heard that, too. Her face rose in his vision, even though she had his back to him. She was in his mind, projecting herself into him, and he couldn't resist her lure. He felt her push, felt her break his defenses and push deep within his self.

One! We are one. We are one, Ted, beloved Ted. Gods making love. Love love love love love love

And then everything just descended into unintelligible rambling. He forgot everything, everything but the Goddess praising him with her every move and thought.

Daylight. Flooding his mind. Birds rose in the wind created by the warm winds from the sea. Animals still climbed higher up inland, to escape the floods, but human life, at least higher up in the hierarchy continued as usual.

He, Phillip, Laurie and Liz played poker on the vast estate of Luis Fernando Ochoa, one of the richest and most powerful men in South America. Ochoa had sent one of his many henchmen with an invitation, and they, waiting for something to happen, in a stroke of pure boredom had accepted.

They were picked up in a chopper on a parking lot, «unless they wanted to drive for miles on bad roads». Ted studied Laurie. She watched absolutely fascinated the shifting landscape below, as they left central Caracas and practically found themselves in the jungle. He could sense the jungle, the savagery between the trees, and he wondered if she could, too.

The chopper landed on the lawn. The silence as the engine died was deafening. They were met by a woman dressed in a smart business suit the moment they stepped outside.

– Mr. and Ms. Warren, Mr. Caine and Ms. Isherwood, I'm Consuela Martinez, a representative of Senor Ochoa. He regrets he wasn't able to meet you in person due to sudden, unforeseen circumstances. He was called away and isn't home right now, but he told me to assure you that he will be back shortly, and ordered me to take care of your needs. The other players are waiting inside.

Warren looked at her with unwavering eyes, as he took her hand. She was blushing instantly. He held her eyes, and she had to pull herself together with an effort. She shook hands with the others, too, but she was clearly distracted, preoccupied, flustered and confused. He looked at Liz to share the moment with her, like he always did, but she, too, was strangely preoccupied lately. She had been like this for days, now, and he wondered why.

Laurie walked by his side, holding his hand.

Poor Consuela is quite taken with you. When you gave her the eye her breasts were instantly swelling and right now her panties are soaked in her juices. She tries not to look at you, or even think of you, in vain, of course. You are present in her every thought. You have invaded her very being.

He didn't comment on that. In fact he gave no indication at all that he had heard her «speak». There had been no need for her to tell him, though. He had noticed easily enough.

You should use her, she shrugged. She's just a snack for a God of your stature, anyway.

And he knew he would.

The house wasn't made in colonial style but in Roman, or Greek, or something very close to it.

– Another megalomaniac with tons of money, Liz remarked.

But in spite of the obvious sting in her voice it didn't sound like her at all.

They met the other players, mostly locals, but a few more or less known to them from their time in Las Vegas and New Orleans.

There were between fifty and sixty people in the room, and not all had arrived yet.

– Ochoa is arranging the South American Championship, one of the players said helpful, when he noticed Warren's expression.

The others hardly acknowledged the four youths' presence, and only with obvious disdain. That excited Warren a bit, enough for him to rise from instant boredom.

Ochoa arrived, «only» half an hour late, accompanied by four new participants.

– Ah, I see you are all here, even our young friends from the United States. Your reputation precedes you.

He bowed, and Warren and Caine returned the bow, and the girls curtsied.

If there was any hint of sarcasm in Ochoa's voice Warren certainly couldn't detect it. Evidently he meant what he said. He was happy to see them, at least as a part of his show.

– Allow me to apologize for my tardiness, Ochoa continued. – Rest assured that I'll make it up to you all. This event will be one to remember.

The event was a poker tournament with $10 000 «buy-in» like the annual World Series tournament in Las Vegas. It started out with the sixty players around six tables, and would continue until everybody except the winner was out.

Ted saw all the tables, in a whirl of motion and emotion and glimpses of reality, and the house itself, how it, in its own, false way was breathing like the jungle outside. He sensed the jungle at his fingertips, so very close.

Laurie was not a poker player. That was easy to see, at least to him that knew what she was. But it helped that she was able to read the minds of most of the people around the table. To most of those present she appeared as an unconventional, but solid player. He almost let out a bark of laughter.

Liz was struggling, and that… distracted him. He almost fucked up royally once, when he got too caught up in her play, and forgot to focus on what was happening around his table and on his opponents.

The jungle was breathing, and he realized he was already there.

And that didn't distract him, but strengthened him.

Ochoa had brought in dealers for the event. Ted kept an eye on them for a while, to see if there was any foul play involved, but that was clearly not the case, so except for the ants crawling through his veins he was able to relax, and enjoy the game.

– Too bad Richard couldn't participate, Ochoa said to him with his cold eyes. – I know how he and his closest confidantes love the game.

– He did want to come, Ted shrugged. – But he's quite busy these days setting up the expedition and all.

Ochoa is a drug baron, Laurie told him quite unnecessary, and Richard can't stand him, which is surely one reason why Richard is having so much trouble.

– But you aren't? Ochoa asked Ted. – You don't share his interest in ancient civilizations?

– Oh, we are *interested,* Ted replied, – or we wouldn't be here. It is safe to say we don't share his passion for it, though.

– You are in it for the ride, Ochoa nodded. – For the thrill it gives you. I understand.

Ted didn't say anything.

Ochoa was hard to read, like Hagman. All single-minded individuals were, strangely enough. And you didn't get to be insanely wealthy without being single-minded.

But like Hagman, the drug baron wore his intentions on the outside like a sore thumb, and that was why he could never be a truly good player. Warren didn't need to get a hand on his emotions in order to beat him, and right now that felt kind of reassuring.

Ted excelled in the electric mood around the tables, and just by acknowledging that fact, he excelled even more. He knew he was good at this, the masks, the half smiles and all.

– I re-raise, he said sheepishly.

The others folded around the table to the other guy that had raised first. The man glared at Ted, sat there for seconds, eternities… and folded, throwing his two hole cards into the muck of yesterday's memory.

There was a break. Warren went for a walk. He didn't see Liz anywhere. But he sensed her, as he always did, even though the signal or whatever it was that made them able to sense each other was faint. He found her on one of the balconies. She was like him, enjoying sights from above.

She stood there, with her back to him, but she noticed him. He knew that because of the way she curled her back.

– I've lost my power, she said to the air.

She turned to face him, deliberately, her eyes cold and dark.

– I've tried everything. I can't even levitate a feather.

– It happened to me, too, he said, after a momentary hesitation. – And it has happened to you before as well. It returned then, and it will again. It's probably connected to our power, somehow, to the way it works.

She rushed to him, into his arms, timid and fearful. He forced himself to hold her, to comfort her, and the fact that she needed comforting made it worse to him.

– The empathy is still there, she said in a low voice. – But even that is weak. It's like I can't hear properly anymore, and I *hate* it.

He nodded. That was how he remembered it.

– I feel so vulnerable, she hissed in his ear, and the sound of her hiss comforted him a bit.

They returned to the tables. The number of players had dropped significantly by now, about half of what they had started out with. It had taken about six hours. It would take the rest of the day and also tomorrow before the end game began.

The players immersed themselves in the game, being at the table, and nowhere else. He sensed Phillip's calm, how he viewed the cards and chips like chess pieces, like mathematical equations, the players like buttons to push. It worked, for him. It didn't for Warren, and never would. To him the table was a living, breathing being, endlessly moving and changing. He felt Liz' raw nerves and distress at the other table, and it distracted him, but it didn't deter him.

A player sitting opposite him, Victor Gomez stared hard at him. Warren smiled, and he knew that made the other man furious. He was fairly good at pushing buttons himself, when he wanted to.

– I raise, he declared.

He had seven and three off-suit. The cards didn't really matter in this game. There was no luck involved, not in the long run. The better a player became the more convinced he or she became of that fact. You played the player, not the cards. He didn't really have to remind himself of that fact anymore.

Gomez mucked. Warren had raised on a sort of planned «whim», to test the other player and Gomez had failed miserably.

He began focusing on Gomez wherever the situation warranted it, and that was quite often, as the Columbian tycoon started some serious fuming. The man was out half an hour later, and the larger part of his chips had drifted off to Warren's ever larger heap.

Day turned to night, and the night to day, and he couldn't really recall sleeping, only resting, with his mind filled with theorems and of other worlds and places and millions of people parading before his inner eye. He sat by the table and the time he spent away from it felt like an intermezzo and nothing more.

Liz was out. He hadn't really noticed it when it happened, but he could still reply it in detail in his mind. She hadn't really done anything wrong or played stupid, but it just didn't work for her. Her despair in his mind was a tangible thing, never straying much from his attention.

Laurie was out, too. She rose, abruptly, looking furiously at her malefactor, before storming out in a cloud of fury.

There were only three players left, Ted and two others. Phillip stared at him, totally uncharacteristically across the table. Ted saw the entire circle of the table, saw its center from all sides, not visibly, but with a sense he couldn't name.

He looked at the jack of diamonds, six of clubs, and deuce of hearts on the table, so beyond compatible with his pocket sixes.

Phillip bet fifteen thousand, a little above half of the pot, a nice solid bet.

– I raise, Ted said. – To forty.

Phillip re-raised him, almost without considering it, to hundred.

– You've got aces, Ted told him casually. – I'm going all-in.

There was a heavy sigh in the room. About half an hour had passed since the previous player; the man that had finished fourth had lost his chips. The game had gone back and forth for a while, without much action until now. Phillip stared at him without really staring at him, but for the Gambler this was staring and everybody knew it.

He called. Ted turned his two sixes. The remaining two cars were meaningless, not affecting the final result in any way. Caine bowed and left the table in a dark cloud of silence. The subsequent heads up game with the final opponent was over in a matter of minutes. Ted didn't really remember any of the play. The applause rose to the ceiling and filled the room and eventually the entire estate.

It was an hour later. Luis Fernando Ochoa led a fairly brief ceremony celebrating the winner. Ted put the money in his pocket, and both he and Ochoa mingled with everybody present. Consuela with a lot of other girls gathered around him, around the winner. He pulled them close and kissed them all, one by one. Liz ran to him and kissed him sultry on the lips, the victor's reward. There was a large swimming pool in the garden. Most of the girls undressed and jumped naked and giggling into it, including Liz. Laurie looked patronizing at her from the patio. Quite a few of the men joined in. Ochoa looked pleased at it all. Both the competition and the subsequent party had clearly surpassed his expectations.

The night breathed around Ted. The torches in the garden danced in his mind, as well as in his vision. He looked at Consuela in the pool. She froze there, and turned, and looked right at him, and she headed out of the water, and straight to him, posing before him eager and ready. And there was a bedroom and a bed, and the sleeping, spent girl, and then there was the garden, the patio again, and no time seemed to have passed.

– You're enjoying yourself, Senor Warren? Ochoa approached him with a glass in his hand.

– I am indeed. Warren bowed. – Both the game and the party have been quite enjoyable. Thank you, Senor.

– Think nothing of it. The drug baron said generously. – I have to say your reputation isn't exaggerated at all, and I quite enjoy your visit. The pleasure, as you Americans put it… is all mine.

You Americans, Ted thought.

– You may keep Consuela, if you wish, by the way. Not that I won't… miss her, but you may want to consider her a part of your prize. She's clearly yours, anyway. Anyone with half a mind and eye can see that.

Mine, Ted thought.

– She's free to join us on our quest, if that's her desire, Warren shrugged.

Ochoa grinned, and the white, very white teeth reminded Ted of that of a shark. It didn't scare him, but it made him more than a little uncomfortable.

– I like the way you treat women, Ted. May I call you Ted? You use them and discard them at will. It's the way they should be treated, of course, like the whores they are.

Ted frowned, and later he wasn't sure why he had frowned. He thought he heard screams, and the next moment he was certain of it, and a few more moments later everybody heard it.

Servants came running from the opposite side of the estate, very distressed.

– It's Senor Phillip, Senor. Men in white robes took him, took him into the jungle.

And then Ted felt the very pronounced tingle down his spine.

– Merde! Ochoa swore. – Those madmen are indulging themselves way too much these days. Something has to be done about them.

They ran, all of them to the other side of the house. There was nothing to see, except distressed servants marking the spot where the aggressors had vanished into the jungle.

– We will send a hunting party, Ochoa declared, – and teach those muchachos a thing or two about the jungle.

Guns, large guns were brought out from hiding.

– We three will take the point. Ted nodded at Liz and Laurie by his side. – We will sniff out the bastards. You will probably not be able to keep up with us, though.

Ochoa considered it for a moment before nodding, and then Ted knew that he had, that he, too had researched them thoroughly.

– Are you ready? Ted asked the two girls, deliberately rough and pointedly.

They nodded, serious minded, clearly marked by the moment, by the drama. Their fear and excitement mingled with his own. He once again tried to imagine David Gidman's face before his inner eye, but couldn't do it. He had never really seen it much in anywhere near a lucid state of mind.

Liz hadn't dressed. She stank of juices, and looked lazily and content at the men, and they couldn't help being affected by it. The gun belt around her waist only made them even more helplessly drawn to her. Ted undressed, quickly and unhesitating. They pulled back, as if being burned. Laurie hesitated a bit, before she, too began removing her clothes.

– We will be wolves sniffing them out, she stated viciously. – They will find no safe haven anywhere for our cruel punishment.

The three of them started running, disappearing into the dense jungle before the others in the hunting party managed to even get moving.

The jungle swallowed the three of them. Ted felt like it did, even though the sense of coming home was totally overwhelming. The tight vegetation didn't stop them, hardly even impeded upon their movement. Feet moved swift and confident across the treacherous ground. Breathing was easy, in spite of the extremely high humidity. They were unused to sweating, and now it flowed from their skin, but that didn't slow them down either.

Laurie ran ahead, took the point, and they had a bit of trouble keeping up with her, and they had to compensate a bit before being able to match her speed.

They saw her in flashes, between the trees and bushes, but it sufficed. He marveled at her moves, glancing cautiously to his side, but he didn't need to worry. Liz was totally focused at the task ahead, and was almost primal in her approach. He sensed the hunter, the predator rise from its slumber within, also from his own depths, and it was a powerful, beyond pleasant sensation.

Liz grinned at him, a flash of fangs and pleasure, and he returned his own.

«This is what we are born to do», she told him. «This is who we are».

And she was right. There were no distractions out here, nothing keeping them… from themselves.

I sense him, Laurie sent to him. They're carrying him. He's stuck up like cordwood. The signal is faint, distant. There are so many different… noises here, damn it.

The animals distracted her. She couldn't close herself off, focus herself. In the many directions she could go she didn't know where to turn. She stopped.

They stopped, too.

– We need to move, Liz said impatiently. – They have a considerable head start already. We need to pick up the trail.

He knew what she meant: their scent.

But there were a million scents here, all of them so damn distracting.

She shook lose some lianas with some difficulty. They were strong. She made a loop. He looked wide eyed at her.

– I'll be the dog, she said.

And he knew she was like a dog sometimes, in her zeal to serve him.

She put the noose around her neck and handed him the other end. He grabbed it and held on. She turned to Laurie.

– You need to… disconnect my higher brain functions. Can you do that?

– Sure! Laurie shrugged and considered it, brightened, and grinned wickedly. – It's easy. You just let me in, and I snap my fingers.

Liz shook a bit, before getting that familiar and insanely determined look in her eyes.

She cast him a final glance, begging with a fear-filled look before submitting to Laurie's cruel touch.

Laurie put a hand on her forehead. It had happened so fast, not giving Ted time to think, and now it happened even faster. The light of fiery intelligence in the fireeyes died and only the fierceness remained. She snarled, and was about to attack Laurie. He pulled the rope, pulled hard. She fell, and rolled on the ground, before standing on all fours, looking up at him with those doglike eyes. Laurie laughed hard.

– How easy she's tamed.

The beast turned and snarled again, whimpering while turning back towards him.

– Phillip, he told her sternly. – Phillip.

She barked, and began sniffing the ground. He let out some rope, but he made sure not to let go of too much. The beast circled back and forth several times, through an ever bigger part of the jungle, before she began narrowing in on a smaller area. She panted and pulled in the restraint. He began running, and she set off with her tongue hanging from the jaw of the steaming snout.

– Good dog, Laurie grinned. – *Good* dog.

He saw its butt point at him, wriggling as it made its way through the jungle. It moved almost perfectly natural on all fours, in spite of the fact that it didn't have the right kind of legs, but it compensated for that in an uncanny way. He sensed its eagerness, its single-minded, predatory mindset and had to pull himself together to not lose himself in it.

A part of him wanted to, and would always want to, he knew that.

He often caught Phillip's scent, but lost it just as often, and he knew they would never have been able to track the man and people they were tracking so fast without the drastic method Liz had devised.

Clever girl, such a clever girl, Laurie sent. Such a *cute* pet.

The range of emotion and thoughts he received from her was incredible, such a detailed texture of information.

*Yes,* she sent excitedly to him. Speech is a barrier.

She touched something deep within him and his frontal lobe buzzed. He saw Phillip Caine, or rather he saw through his clouded vision. The men and women walked upwards, raced upwards on steep ground. Laurie gasped in shock.

– They're going to sacrifice him, sacrifice him to their God, to Gidman.

She was clearly genuinely shocked. The trembling girl couldn't hide anything from him. She didn't even try.

– Gidman isn't here, she stated. – Not anywhere close. He was, in New Orleans. I sensed him.

The men and women dressed in white hoods and robes reached the top of the hill, a flat, circle-round area. Liz pulled in the rope, and he sensed her panicked realization and picked up speed. He would guess that she saw what he saw, the place from the air, the ancient marks of the large pentacle. They saw themselves in the dense jungle below.

Your power, Laurie sent in awe. It's amazing, beyond amazing. I wondered why they took Phillip, such an insignificant gnat, but now I know. They didn't dare grab any of us, anyone equal to their God.

Dusk settled, seemingly from one moment to the next. He saw Caine being chained to the ground, to rings rusty with age and blood. The woman looked pleased at the sacrificial lamb. A large pyre was lit. He heard her, the priestess chant, with the knife in her hand, and sensed how her voice sensed the very ether around the worshippers.

Her power sent shivers through the world.

He nodded impatiently to Laurie. She put her hand on Liz' head, and the shadow of intelligence was once more reigniting the dark girl's eyes.

Liz rose, shaking a bit, gritting her teeth. He returned her gun belt to her, and she took it in a swift and decisive move, holding on to it for dear life, before putting it around her waist.

They ran. They jumped up the hill. Laurie was left behind, no matter how fast she ran. They jumped, as high as Ted had done over the hedge in London and even higher. It was hard doing it continuously upwards, though, and Liz didn't have the advantage of the power boost anymore. Ted also threatened to slide back every time he landed, but he used his power to push himself in the back. Liz couldn't do that, and she was quickly sagging behind.

She turned to Laurie.

– Throw me up there, she told the other.

Laurie looked nonplussed at her.

– But I can't really control it that much. I risk hurting you.

– *Do it!* The dark girl hissed.

And then there was fear in Laurie's eyes.

Liz felt the push, the brutal lift, and she tasted blood in her mouth. The two shadows crossed the edge of the plateau simultaneously. They landed, and threw themselves away from each other, attacking from two sides, firing at the white clad figures ahead. The targets fell like dominoes. They returned the fire. Ted felt only the wild bloodlust, the taste of blood in his mouth, in her mouth. The priestess was gone. He noticed it in a flash. Phillip lay chained on the ground. He was alive, his heart beating hard and strong. Liz' gun clicked on an empty chamber. She threw herself at the nearest target, tearing into him, snarling like a wild beast, and her snarl now was at least as savage as it had been when she had run on all fours. She used her claws and fist and feet and tore him apart. The others fired at her, but their bullets hit his body. She held it up, what was left of it as shield, and used his gun. Ted had also picked up an extra gun, two extra guns, and he fired both. The enemies fled and the two fireeyes used them as target practice, and the enemies fell and died, torn apart by hot lead and fangs and claws of the Earth.

It was over, as fast as it had begun. Silence once more slowly reigned on the high plateau. Elizabeth Warren breathed, a happy grin on her face, her entire body soaked in blood. Ted turned and saw Laurie stand behind them, at the edge of the flat ground, just at the outer line of the pentacle, staring blindly at the bloody and torn apart bodies everywhere, her skin white as milk. He would always remember her like that, even after a thousand years.

They freed Phillip. He had a flesh wound on his hip. A stray bullet had grazed him. They encountered some difficulty when they set out to release him. There was no key anywhere, and they ended up having to break the locks and bend open the rusty metal bracelets.

– Why do I always get hit? He complained aloud, his voice hoarse and angry, his eyes a crazy shade of darkness.

– You were just unlucky and got hit by a stray bullet, Liz said, embracing him and kissing him softly on the cheek. – It happens, you know.

Ted knew that explanation didn't satisfy the Gambler, didn't calm the open wound inside.

They left the circle, the place of sacrifice and death and savage joy, where bodies leaked heat and mist, the mist the three saviors saw so clearly. Down below there was movement in the moist jungle, Ochoa and his hunting party finally arriving.

And again, Ted knew, Phillip Caine saw things clearly.

4

– Give Senor Hagman my regards.

That was the last word Ochoa gave Warren before sending them on their way.

Liz had taken a bath. They all had, in Ochoa's exclusive, very exclusive indoors bath. Laurie had been able to clean herself, barely, never taking her eyes off Liz glowing figure and pleased grin, half consciously, half not emulating the other girl's every move, almost like a mirror image.

She had rushed to her side eventually and begun washing her, her eyes cast down like the lowest of servants. Liz had only grinned, cruelly, and let her keep it up.

More wicked is the female, Ted thought.

If Laurie noticed that, if she picked it from his mind, she gave no indication of having done so.

They returned to the city, the chopper a silent bird, landing on the enforced roof of the old colonial building where their friends and fellow travelers and Hagman's party stayed.

Another party was building, yet another in the endless line they had attended since arriving in Caracas. It was the day before New Year's Eve 1976, and the festivities began early.

Richard Hagman and Alanis Monroe posed together in front of cameras, microphones and journalists. They both looked very pleased or smug, almost content, depending on how you looked at it.

The room fell silent. Expectation ruled the gathering.

– I'm pleased to announce two equally important and great news, he began. – We're now finally ready to continue the great Journey and… it will be a joint venture.

– Which have surely increased our change of success four times, Monroe added. – Two great minds and two camps of skilled and daring people making way into the vast and *exciting* unknown.

He frowned. They all saw that.

– She fixed it, of course, a woman said to her companion, – or they would have been stuck here *forever*.

Ted knew better or figured he knew better, even though he wasn't sure, but he remained silent.

He and Liz stood on the roof, looking at the city, while Caracas was fading around them, like New Orleans and other places had also done, places they would never see again.

– You won so easily, she breathed, stars in her eyes, – treating Phillip and the rest like the amateurs they are.

– It isn't easy, Ted said, frowning. – One needs to focus constantly, to not be too cocky, to not screw up.

– You could never do that when you were a kid, Liz said and nodded, – but you've grown up, now. I'm so proud of you.

She threw herself into his arms, and kissed him, her lips lingering pleasantly on his.

– We both have, he insisted, – and have turned away from childish things…

– … to *blood* and the horrors of the world, she said, kissing his hand. – And there is no turning back anymore.

And they shivered in each other's arms. And what they saw wasn't Caracas at all, but the deep and violent jungle ahead.

# Chapter Eleven: Falling Down

She was back in Las Vegas, and looked around her with confused, befuddled eyes, and she didn't understand it, didn't understand anything of what was happening.

Liz was grabbed by the big bruiser and led down the hallway. She attempted to resist him, but he paralyzed her easily with a brutal strike in her ribs. He kept her on her feet, holding her in his strong arms, pulling her into a room, where the wriggling butt waitress waited for them.

They spoke, but the girl couldn't make out what they were saying, which was strange since she recalled clearly that she had been able to the… the first time.

Liz shook her head. She swam through a quicksand of thought. Panic gripped her. She wanted to do something, anything, but nothing worked. Not even her tongue. When she attempted to speak only gibberish came out. The woman approached her, with a syringe in her right hand.

The woman patted her on the cheek, and said something, something unintelligible and horrible. The man laughed, and his words drowned in the cruel laughter.

Fear, tangible and true gripped Liz, now. She struggled in the big man's grip, but he held her in a vice. He squeezed her wrists, making her cry out in pain. Hoping the pain would clear her mind she doubled her efforts, but the excruciating pain cursing through her paralyzed her further. She grew limp in the man's arms. The woman rolled up her sleeve, and quickly and expertly set the needle, pushing its horrible content into Liz' veins.

– There, sweet thing. Now, everything is all right.

Everything just… disconnected. She noticed everything happening, felt their touch, but she could make no voluntary action, and turned completely limp in their grip. He touched her below, and she instantly felt the first stirrings of need.

– Hot bitch, he noted. – That's good. That makes you a very valuable bitch.

Valuable… She knew, knew what he was talking about.

They undressed her, quickly, efficiently. She felt how the fabric of her clothes slipped off her, but even if she wanted to scream there was no tangible reaction from her. Her breasts were exposed, the wetness below and every piece of her skin, and she could do nothing to prevent it, nothing at all, and she choked. It felt so bad. Her nudity felt bad, and she choked hard.

They chained her, put cold bracelets around her wrists and ankles, working quickly and efficiently, clearly experienced in all of this. He put her over his right shoulder. The woman rushed to the door, opened it and looked outside. She nodded. They hurried out, through the backdoor of the building, into the backyard. There was a van there. The woman opened the door. The bruiser carried Liz into the darkness. The poison didn't impact on her vision. She saw everything undiluted, and she couldn't look away. In a fairly cramped space was a floor covered with chained naked girls. She choked again, catching the woman's undivided attention. A hand squeezed her jaw.

– This is it, little girl. Whatever your life was, it ends here. From this moment you won't have any say in anything. Everything you say and do will be decided by others.

Liz wanted to shout her denial, her rage and despair, but only gibberish crossed her numb lips. She was casually, brutally thrown among the other girls.

The woman walked among them, kicking them around, measuring their reactions. Liz didn't move a finger, but others did. The girls the woman deemed to be too lucid, too sentient and astute, she gave an injection, and the light once more died in their eyes.

The bruiser held Liz' head like a trophy. She sensed his triumphant glee, even before she heard the thick triumph in his voice.

– Look at her. Even in here, even in her drugged state the eyes are distinct, visible.

That told Liz something, something horrible. They knew what she was, what her eyes represented.

– It doesn't matter, the woman stated cruelly. – She will kneel before us, like the rest.

The two left and closed the door. The room turned dark, completely dark. Liz saw nothing, and panic once more rose in her. She should be able to see something.

But there was nothing, no sensation aside from the horrible dull need consuming her.

The engine started and the truck began moving. Liz felt the pressure of naked skin against hers. She expected, desperately expected the flow of power to begin…

But nothing happened. She choked again.

She wondered what they had done to her. She wanted desperately to know, but there was no answer forthcoming.

She drifted off eventually, not dreaming, not sensing anything. She came to after a long time of nothingness, not knowing, not even being able to take the smallest guess about how long time had passed. Tears filled her eyes, but she couldn't dry them.

Her left arm hurt, being squeezed between her body and the floor. She wanted to move, but she was unable to move anything.

There was a flash of light. The door had been opened again. Another sedated girl in chains was thrown on the floor. Liz caught a glimpse of the bruiser's face and the syringe in his hand. It disappeared from her vision. She felt the sting again and the needle came back up empty. The man slapped her.

– You'll bankrupt us with your insane need for juice, girl, he hissed.

He touched her below again, and she gasped, instantly moaning in need.

– If you weren't so insanely eager, that is…

He squeezed her sore breasts, and it hurt. A sound escaped her shivering lips, her open, gasping mouth. He laughed cruelly, and the moan was supplanted by a tiny whimper.

She wanted to be angry, at least feel angry, but was unable of even that feat. The image of his grin stayed in her mind, long after he had left her alone. She couldn't get rid of it no matter how hard she closed her eyes.

And she despised herself.

Time passed. She knew it did, even though she had no sense of it passing. The juice wore off again eventually. She began moving, writhing on the floor, with some of the other girls, involuntary, not really in control of anything.

The light flooded her eyes again, blinding her. She cried out in pain. All the girls did. She glimpsed the woman lift a whip, and saw the bruiser with one, too. They both lashed out with them, at the naked girls on the floor.

– UP, The woman snarled, – up, you lazy bitches.

They stumbled out of the van on unsteady legs, desperate to stay on their feet, to avoid the brutal lash of the whip. But some fell anyway, and screamed in panic and pain when the whip hit their unprotected skin, and they jumped back up, choking in confusion and fear.

– March!

And they did, tripping more than walking, the short chain between their ankles almost making them loose their footing every time they took a step. They stumbled into a hall, one fairly large. There were small cages in two lines there, one line by each long wall. A group of chained and nude males stumbled in from the opposite direction. Liz saw their cocks dangle between their legs, and it was all she seemed to see.

Two others, very similar to the bruiser and the waitress in both body and inclination herded the males.

– ON YOUR KNEES! The four shouted, also letting the whips speak for them.

The chained males and females fell on their knees. Liz hurt her knees when they hit the floor. She whimpered. Everything hurt, a dull pain, and she couldn't make anything work. She tried, tried hard, but nothing happened, no matter how much she attempted to focus what was left of her hatred on their captors.

Even the cognitive part of her mind didn't work properly. It felt like her brain had turned to mud. Fear and confusion seemed to be the only emotions she was capable of having. When orders were barked and the lash hit her skin she obeyed without any real resistance.

They stood there, on their knees, their eyes lowered, suddenly sensing a draft on their sweaty skin. She heard the sound of steps. Two large figures, a man and a woman entered her line of vision. She recognized Morgan Lombard and the woman was obviously his sister. He looked so much more dangerous than the last time she had encountered him, and the woman looked even more so.

They stopped before the four, and the four bowed their heads in subservience.

– They seem like an excellent batch. Good work.

The four didn't reply. She turned to the prisoners.

– Hi, I am Martine. I own you. Your ass and everything else you may possess is mine, now, and forever. You may wonder why and I am going to tell you because it suits my purpose.

Her voice was like her demeanor, cruel and cold. She emanated authority and danger. It was no doubt who was in charge here: She was.

– You are cursed. You were from the moment of your ill-fated conception, long before you grew to adulthood and displayed your godless blight on mankind.

She produced something from her purse. It was a curious thing, resembling a battery and a lamp, a little more sophisticated. Girls and boys lifted their heads. Martine brought the device close to a male's head. It began glowing in a bluish flame. She pulled it away and the flame faded. The boy began shaking.

– Yes, she spat, – I know what a Satan's child you are.

She walked along the line of boys, holding the device to their head. It began glowing for everyone she passed, fading in the in-between. It continued to do so when she stepped across the floor to the girls. Some of them tried dully, and without much energy to pull away. They were quickly whipped back into place.

When the woman reached Liz the device lit up in a brilliant light. Martine smiled.

– Of course, she shrugged. – I would expect no less from a ring bearer. Show me, bitch!

Liz obeyed and held up her chained wrists. Martine grabbed the hand with the ring. She pulled the ring off with a contemptuous smile.

– But you will be just as broken as the others, of course. You will be just one more cursed sibling here at the Stable, one of several places in the world your kind is made to serve the true humanity.

She let go of the hand and it fell back down. She chuckled proudly, and grabbed around the other's jaw, and pushed it up.

– Pretty eyes, she acknowledged. – But soon, very soon that will be all they will ever be, all they will ever signify.

She walked to the end of the line, and stopped there.

– Yes, we know what you are, and how to spot you, she nodded, – and we will seek you all out, and give you what you so richly deserve.

One of the girls attempted to speak, releasing unintelligible sounds. The bruiser lifted his whip, ready to strike. Martine stopped him by raising a hand and with a cruel smile.

– I don't understand, the girl finally managed to spell out. – I don't understand what's happening.

– What is there to understand, dear? Martine inquired puzzled.

– That… device must be… faulty, the girl burst out. – Whatever it's supposed to be showing, I'm not like the others here.

Martine clearly pondered her words, her panicked statement.

– The device isn't infallible. It has proven faulty on occasions.

– Yes, faulty, the girl nodded eagerly. – Please let me go. *Please!*

Martine pulled a syringe from her purse. Its content was clearly different from what they had injected into Liz. The girl crouching before Martine glanced fearfully around, as if wanting to pull back, but then she relented, surrendering, submitting to her fate. A slight nod from Martine sufficed. The girl lifted her arms. Martine grabbed one and expertly injected the needle into the easily broken skin. The content flooded the girl's veins.

Nothing happened at first, nothing pronounced. The female stood there, on her knees, shivering in fear.

Then, at her fingertips there was dark flare, a spark more like shadow then anything electrical Liz had seen. The girl screamed in pain, and folded and fell on the floor. The body shook in cramps, and she kept screaming in violent anguish.

It subsided slowly, so very slowly. The girl lay there, looking up at the tall woman standing above her.

– What did you DO to me? She cried.

– I? Martine grinned cruelly. – I didn't do anything to you, except exposing your true nature. It's all a matter of chemistry, you see. I made your powers appear, forcing them out of hiding, so to speak.

– My… p-powers?

The bewilderment and shock was painted in the girl's tearstained features.

Liz wanted to say it, to cry it from the rooftops, but to her shame she kept silent.

– Your mutant powers, Martine told the girl sweetly.

The girl knew, had known before she had been told. The concept was so well ingrained in the culture from various novels, films and comics that practically everybody knew it one way or another.

– But why… why the pain?

– It's the chains, silly. They disrupt the energies in your body, wrecking havoc and pain when you try to use them. You wouldn't even be able to access them at all, if not for the trigger I injected into your system.

She noticed the glances Liz and a few others sent her, and chuckled. The chilly laughter burned them and froze them.

– Yes, you are absolutely correct. I've been taught how to deal with your kind practically since birth. I know your weaknesses and everything making you tick, and believe me, it will be a pleasure to apply all that knowledge on you, as I have on so many others before you. You will pray for death, and then, a while past that point you will live your life in eternal bliss, eternal servitude.

She nodded, and the other four began moving. The prisoners were dragged off, and thrown into the cages. The doors were slammed shut and locked, and they sat there, in the confined space, on their knees, looking at the world through narrowly spaced bars.

It was hot and uncomfortable and horrible, and when they eventually dozed off Liz didn't know how long time had passed, only that it could just as well have been days. Her throat was dry, so dry that she could hardly swallow. She heard someone cry out his or her misery, and couldn't tell if the voice was male or female or her own parched squeak.

She began dreaming, dreaming within the dream, no longer able to distinguish the nightmare from reality. Liz hung from chains, and they whipped her ruthlessly front and back, and she screamed her lungs out, and she had no voice left except a hoarse, impotent whisper. She stood on her knees in the cage, her eyes and cheeks flooded with tears.

Martine entered the room, followed by males and females with empty eyes, dressed in bland uniforms and shaved heads. They all looked the same, no matter the skin color or facial shape or features, the same lack of expression, the same dead eyes.

A girl walked back and forth before the cages, and all those within them got a dazed expression in their eyes. Liz felt it, how what was left of her cognitive thought left her.

– Ruby here is such a precious thing, Martine said. – She will put you all in the right mood when I tell her to. She will crack you open, and then she will fill you with happy thoughts.

The girl at Liz' side pushed her face between the bars, and Liz noticed that she had done the same. They all stared at Ruby's eyes, totally mesmerized. Liz recognized Ruby, recognized Laurie, and somewhere inside her dull panic attempted in vain to rear its head, its wooly mind.

It was all a dream, she droned on inside. This is the real world. This is real, real, real.

– She's ready, My Lady, Ruby reported, – ready for the imprint.

– Very well. You may proceed.

Liz felt the probe then, felt it invade her, felt it change her, taking away everything she was and could be.

Martine held up a bottle with a teat, pushed the teat into Liz' panting open mouth and eager lips closed around the rubber and instantly began sucking.

– That's my girl, Martine praised her. – I baptize you Rita, and from now on you will never know any other name.

Rita had sucked the bottle empty. She looked at the tall, regal woman standing above her with a happy and docile smile.

– Hello, Rita, the Lady greeted her.

– Hello, My Lady, Rita replied happily, filled with respect and reverence.

A blink and they were elsewhere. They had their heads shaved. Liz remembered being pulled out of the cage, and not more than that. They marched in tandem, one, two, one, two, further on, on their ill fated path.

They rested on tables. Ruby frowned when she stopped at Liz' side.

– She's resisting, My Lady. – No matter what I do, she recuperates when I give her pause.

– Yes, yes, Martine said, standing there in her white uniform. – That was to be expected. She's a ring bearer, after all, but we will fix her, you and I, fix her together, fix her good.

Liz couldn't move. Martine nodded and the bruiser put a collar around her neck. A needle was set in her neck, and it felt like ice, *ice*. The collar released harmonic signals. She felt them, felt how they disrupted her, kept her from forming coherent thoughts. The bruiser carried her to a chair, and strapped her to it, strapped her so hard that she couldn't move a finger. Martine approached her with an electric drill in her hands.

– Don't worry, little one, the big woman said soothingly, – you won't feel a thing, and when I am done here, you will be considerably more compliant. Science, you see is the answer. It's God's gift, his hallowed weapon against Satan's army. We need to keep an eye on you, even more so than with your unholy brethren, but we are used to that, used to managing your kind. We know you better than you know yourselves.

With steady hands she drilled a hole in Liz' skull, removing, with precision surgery the frontal lobe. The hole closed fairly quickly, but the most crucial damage wasn't repaired.

– It will regrow, of course, Martine said. – But by that time you will be so well trained, and with so many safeguards in place that you will have permanently turned into a very obedient and profitable both sweet and deadly thing in our service.

She frowned, looking at the unmoving face beneath her, before continuing.

– Yes, this is an enterprise. We do turn a profit, and with that we are even better equipped to deal with you all once and for all.

Liz was dressed, given the same bland uniform as the others. She looked at the opaque, empty eyes in the mirror, in the mirror that wasn't really there.

The new arrivals marched in tandem. There was no deviation from the norm. They knelt before Martine, before Morgan. They rose on their behest.

Ruby was there, at Martine's side, with another boy with shaven head.

– They're all calm, My Lady, Ruby reported. – Rita is, too. There is no storm in her Deep.

– I concur, My Lady, the boy said, – I sense no signs of rebellion what so ever. Your new servants are ready for the next step in their training.

Liz looked at herself in the mirror. Her hair didn't grow back.

– Pretty Eyes, Martine called.

Rita straightened further. That was the Lady's affectionate name for her. She rushed before her.

– Lift the chair, Pretty Eyes. The Lady commanded.

Rita obeyed. The chair floated into the air.

– Excellent. A gloved hand patted her cheek.

Martine turned to Morgan with a sick grin of triumph.

– We've done it. We've broken one of the People.

– We have indeed, he nodded pleased. – With further training she will be immensely useful to us.

He stepped close to Rita, Rita standing there, looking at herself in the mirror.

– We will breed her extensively, of course, and use her to catch all the others, and she and they will make us the masters of this world.

Liz looked at him. Fear riddled her, sick, revolting fear. She studied the scene dispassionately.

– They will make us Masters of this world, Morgan said.

– We've done it, Martine stated. – We've broken one of the People.
*Everything had become a jigsaw puzzle with no more reality than a calm surface.*
*Liz tried to hold on, wanted to see more, the moment everything turned clear to her, learn everything there was to learn, but moving images before her froze to a painting, and the painting split into a thousand pieces, and*
– I'm going to find you, she said aloud, and somehow, somewhere she imagined that Martine Rubleaux noticed. – I'm going to…
She woke up.

## 2

– … find you all.
She sat up, on the plane, among all the warm and full blooded bodies, her eyes wide and afraid, sweat pouring from her brow. There was a crack, and there was lightning. At least that was what she imagined.
Ted sat by her side. He had awoken with her, shaken as she was shaken.
She focused on her clothes, instinctively wanting to pull them to her, to dress, but nothing happened, still nothing. Ted looked at her. He understood. She looked at him with infinite fondness and boundless irritation.
There was a loud crack. Everybody heard it. The serene moonlight scene of the plane floating above silver clouds was disrupted when one of the engines exploded violently. Liz saw the wing, saw it split in two, and its outer part disengage from the rest.
The plane tilted. There were screams of shock and panic. Ted grabbed Laurie and pulled her on her feet. Liz was pulled away from them. Suddenly everything was loud, numbingly loud. Laurie looked at Ted with boundless affection. They held hands, held on to each other, hard. Liz hit the wall of the plane, at the opposite side of the room. She yelped. Both of them turned towards her. She felt the pull, and a subsequent joy deeper than Space, as she was pulled back into Ted's embrace. She grabbed both hands reaching out to her, both Laurie and Ted's, and there was a kind of shift in the energy between them, when hers was added to theirs.
Your power may be dormant, Ted told her. But it's still there.
She felt Laurie roaming her thoughts, as she acted as a conduit between their minds, silencing the violent ruckus surrounding them.
We must fly the plane, Liz thought. Make a soft landing. At least that.
And there was laughter somewhere, as the irony of her words hit them. Even Laurie smiled. Liz felt a stirring of affection even for her.
The plane went into a spin. The first body hit the wall, hit it hard. It made a splash, dissolving into blood and bone and disintegrated flesh.
The power rose between the three of them. They felt it, like a sledgehammer in their gut. Everybody else was moving, but they were not, standing still in the air, touching nothing, unable to help any of the flying bodies, focusing all their attention on the metal body, the pile of metal falling to Earth like a rock.

The engine of the left wing still burned, pushing the bird ever further off a sane descent. They focused on the right wing, pushing at it, attempting to take the place of the missing engine, hopelessly in vain.

Grab the plane, Ted shouted to the girls. Grab it all, slowly. We are the plane. We are flying through the air, through the night. We fly wherever we go, and we don't feel the pull of the Earth.

We are the plane, they repeated like a mantra. We are the wings, the body and the bird.

He glimpsed the ground, rising to meet them. He felt panic, felt boundless frustration and rage, venting it against Fate, against Death itself. And impossibly, the plane seemed to level its descent, seemed to float a second or two on impossible currents above the ground.

Before crashing into the jungle, hitting the dense growth like the heavy rock it was.

## 3

There were smoke and moans everywhere. There were cries of misery and pain, and those that didn't utter a single sound, and lay dead and still.

Ted moved and groaned in pain. He opened his eyes and looked directly at a shrapnel of metal, and realized that it went straight through his gut.

He saw Justine by his side, saw her arm balance for a moment or two, before falling, hitting his exposed skin. There was some kind of charge, and the girl's arm seemed to be adhered to him. She looked startled at him, while he looked at her with dispassionate interest. There was pain at first, before a cold, infinite pleasure surged through him. She moaned, and then, a moment later she screamed. He stared at her, studied her incredulous in the brief time it took her to die, for him to suck all life from her. She died in unspeakable horror, as she fed him, fed him strength, fed him every shred of life she possessed.

She shriveled and crumbled to dust there by his side. He gasped, one brief moment, before his body attuned itself to its new reality. The shrapnel was pulled from his body and his grave wound healed in an instant. He reached out a hand and grabbed another, a man by his side, recalling the warm body's name in an instant, forgetting it like insignificant a breath later. This time the process was practically instantaneous. The warm, powerful body shriveled and crumbled to dust so fast that the face didn't even change expression.

He rose in the air, healing every single wound of every person all over the vast crash site, hearing every single shred of their thoughts, and it was like birth. They stared at him, all of them, in horror and awe, knowing fully what had happened, and they fell on their knees. He hovered above them, like a hungry bird. Flashes came to him, ever more, ever more powerful, changing him dramatically, transforming him time and time again, for every new, passing heartbeat removing him further from what and who he had been.

His eyes glowed, to the point of almost totally obscuring his face. He saw it through their eyes, in their minds, as easily as he before took one step forward.

Liz knelt like the others, filled with feverous thoughts. He appeared before her, reaching out a hand.

You need only to touch me, but decide fast.

She looked up, smiling in ecstasy.

There is nothing to think about, My Lord. There never was.

She took his outstretched hand. The fire rose from her eyes and reached for the sky, and then she was hovering at his side.

*Come,* they called, – *come to us.*

It wasn't really a thought, wasn't really a voice, but something profoundly deeper.

They came, rushing forward like a wave, to the beach far, far away, kneeling on its overwhelmingly warm and pleasant sand, and never even remembering being wet.

The two reached out with their power, almost without trying, without conscious thought. An ape was killed by a big cat in the next valley. It sustained them. The jaguar froze momentarily, before continuing on its meal. Countless creatures died naturally in the vicinity of their reach and it sustained them. Death sustained them. They looked excitedly at each other. Their Power had reached a level that was sustaining itself indefinitely, ever growing, and reaching outwards in an ever wider circle.

Laurie stepped forward, and in an instant he knew she had attempted to control him with her mind. He couldn't tell if she had done so deliberately or consciously or not, if it was a function of her power she was unaware of. Even now he couldn't tell. She shrunk under his rejection, his contempt, and then she rejoiced when he, after what appeared to be a thousand years accepted her as his loyal subject. Liz smiled cruelly, and her laughter rocked them all, shaking the ground beneath their feet.

Candice rubbed her growing belly with a happy glow in her face, and so did Candy. They all glowed in exalted joy, as they bowed their heads, their very being before the almighty creatures above.

The two above hesitated momentarily, and then they raised their hands slightly, not much. First nothing or nothing substantially happened, but then they heard a rumble in the Earth, and the ground truly shook beneath their feet.

Something happened, something totally unbelievable and unspeakable. A… structure rose from the ground, one the others instantly recognized as a pyramid, one fairly similar to all the other ruins in the area, except this was brand new, polished and shiny, in a matter of moments. Ted and Liz felt it, how the seething energies inside them almost took control, as they took yet another quantum leap in their growth. Where there had once been jungle there was now a tall pyramid, and added to that, in less than a minute was a garden, an entire city in a circle inside the wild growth.

Where there had been noise, there was now silence yet again.

– Behold our Kingdom, Liz cried, with a loud voice.

And everybody did, through the gods' eyes. The two exchanged glances, an old habit not yet left behind. One blink of an eye, and they flowed towards the peak of the pyramid, landing there on the balcony they had made, taking each other's hands, kissing each other passionately. Fabric grew around them, turning into clothes, lavish clothes, weaved in intricate, beautiful patterns.

– Amazing, she glowed, and repeated it, as if once hadn't quite done it. – Amazing.

– So this is Power, he nodded. – This is the infinite well we hold in our hands.

– This is Power, she stated. – This is our birthright, our entitled stature.

He looked behind him, briefly, at the dots making their way to them.

– Don't worry about them, she chuckled. – They will catch up. They always do, as they are scurrying like ants in our presence.

They walked inside, into the luxurious apartment. They made it as they walked. All the fabric, all materials had become fluid to their remote touch. They calmed as the room calmed, settled as the room settled into what made a pleased grin appear on the female's doll-like mask. At least to normal eyes the violent energies inside them no longer made sparks fly from their eyes. But they still saw each other, anytime they desired as walking volcanoes waiting to blow, and they smiled. She made herself a headgear, a «crown», very similar to that of their once-time Mother, the Egyptian Queen, put it on her head, making even more of her black hair flow down her back. She turned, rotated her body, performing for him.

– Am I pleasing to your eyes, sire? She asked softly, knowing the answer before she heard it.

– You are pleasing beyond anything I can ever conceive of, he replied, and she chuckled pleased.

And they walked the broad stairs, to the large throne room below. Any move they made was like a flow, between moments, and they noticed everything happening, every single insect in their Kingdom.

– Richard wanted to study ancient civilizations, Ted remarked, – but there were only ruins left. Well, now he can study it firsthand.

She laughed, and her laughter excited him so.

They sat on the throne as the four, those who would become the Four approached. Candy, Candice, Ben and Laurie didn't kneel. There was no need, no pretence anymore.

– You are still Kwaiala, the Queen Goddess told them. – That hasn't changed.

She didn't need to say anything more. It was laced in her voice, in the texture of her thoughts flooding them. The Gods dreamed, both awake and not, and they remade the world in their image.

The Queen Goddess rose and the air moved around her, moved as she moved. She walked to Candy, touching her cheek. Candy trembled slightly, before standing still, waiting for the inevitable.

– Do not fear, Kwaiala, Liz spoke softly, – with Power comes Control, and I have no desire to end your life. Why should I, when every dying breath on the globe is mine to enjoy?

Fabric grew on sweaty skin, as the Goddess dressed her faithful, a little less flamboyant than was their gods. The others outside were dressed, too, a little less then The Four.

– And you are blessed among women, are you not, carrying our brood?

– Yes, My Goddess, Candy whispered.

Ted stood there, in a flash before them. One moment he was on the throne, the next he was right in front of them. Ben straightened. The three females softened and their juices started flowing in earnest. He knew before it happened, and would have, even without the powerful stench of their sex.

He peeled Laurie's mind away, curious, and she moaned and breathed hard, and couldn't see anything but the dark creature towering above her like the tallest building, and just like that she was his Forever. No matter how far she walked, and how much time passed, she belonged to him, body and soul.

Forever.

With little more than a thought he opened her, brought her to her full potential of her Power, so high, so beneath his. She smiled and there was boundless love in her eyes.

There was a bit of exposed skin on their left shoulder. A mark appeared there. It burned into their skin, and they gasped. They saw it and instantly understood its significance and they cried out in joy.

– This will identify you as our envoys, no matter where you go.

And outside, a different mark burned into the others' shoulder, and they, too understood, and welcomed it with all their hearts.

The Lord and the Lady exchanged glances, even though they no longer needed to look at each other. The Four was gone, just like that, with less, far less than a snapping of fingers.

– We know so much, Ted said.

– So much already, Liz nodded pleased.

And their knowledge kept expanding, as their power and reach expanded. They stood on the balcony and watched their domain, their garden, their world, watched its progress, as the days and nights passed. Their mind, spirit and Shadow chased through the jungle in an ever wider circle. A wild tribe lived not far away. In an instant they knew everything about them. They moved their bodies through the air, and in a blink of an eye they appeared above the village. The villagers noticed them, and pointed, struck with terror. One thought and the Gods were among them, standing in their midst. The Goddess smiled and it was the most wonderful and terrifying sight they had ever seen. A warrior threw his spear. An instant later it pointed at his head. He froze. The Goddess towered above him.

– You will sire many children, she told him in his language.

The spear fell to the ground.

God felt an intrusion, slight but there into his vast mind. He focused on a woman, a priestess, turning her own power back on her. She gasped and fell to the ground. He raised her up and brought her before him, appraising her, opening her, making her his. She shivered confronted with his vast might, mumbling something, falling to her knees before him, her happy thoughts flooding the village. They all fell on their knees, sore afraid, even as the overwhelming joy rose inside of them.

– The gods left you long ago, Ted said in English, and they understood that, too. – Now, they have returned, and your life is at an end. Your Life begins now.

And then the gods were gone from their sight, but flooding their Self, hardly leaving room for anything else.

The tribe reached the city in the jungle a few hours later, having left virtually all their possessions behind, the only thing on their mind to reach the hallowed city as fast as humanly possible. And even though they were used to running flat out for days, they were exhausted and spent upon their arrival, the overwhelming need to serve their gods overpowering everything else.

They were led to the base of the mountain, at the edge of the city, to the pond with the waterfall, and they bathed there, cleansing themselves from what remained of their past. The gods dressed them and gave them tasks to perform, holy tasks to perform in the gods' exalted honor.

The overlords stood on their balcony, overseeing their work. They enjoyed using their physical eyes, even though that wasn't necessary anymore. They observed how two vastly different set of people joined, how they taught each other and learned and grew into something new and different from both their origin.

Candy came to him one night. She had a big belly, and she was bursting at the seams. It was time. He felt the life within her glow in power and need to break out. She stood at the center of the yard below the pyramid, surrounded by her tribe. Candice sat in a chair not far away from her. She was due a few hours from now.

Laurie and Chini, the former tribal priestess, both with big bellies themselves aided Candy, dried her with wet towels, and helped her through her woes. The united tribe chanted ancient songs, until recently unfamiliar to both half moons. They used the ancient language of the gods, words Ted and Liz had pulled from their Memory, the Memory now ascending and dominating.

The Goddess was with child, too. They saw that easily, but more than that they sensed it, the way she glowed and hummed to them. She had been the last of the females in the tribe to conceive.

It was such a good omen, and they rejoiced.

Candy breathed, and it was a song in itself. The birth was hard, like all births, but it was over very fast. The girl, the new life screamed her lungs out, and brought tears to the entire gathering, to everybody present, except the gods in their midst. Candy bled her birth blood, but that was it. A slightly brighter glow in the Goddess' eyes and her servant was completely healed and vigorous again. Candy accepted the baby girl from Laurie, and walked to God and knelt before him, presenting his daughter, the new goddess to him. The girl floated from Candy's outstretched arms and into the air, turned slowly in the air, where God studied her from all sides.

And he let her slip back into her mother's arm.

The festivities began, and moved to an even higher height when Candice' gave birth to a son later that night. The night passed so quickly for the gods, like all time did, even though, if they wished they could make it stop altogether.

– It marches on, Liz told him on the balcony ten nights later, – ever more powerful. We can do more and with more power to back it up with each passing night. We are not almighty yet, my love, but we will be.

– We will be, he echoed her proud statement.

Their influence spread and kept spreading, and even though they deliberately took their time it happened so easily.

– What was me ten seconds ago is already ten eternities behind.

They choired it, with perfect timing, a chant filling the jungle, reaching its outskirts.

Time was indeed meaningless, and space joined it, increasingly so.

They opened a portal to the misty Shadowland, totally effortless, and they marveled, even in their elevated state of godhood. Caracas waited there, right there before them. They slid through the portal. A thousand people died, turned to dust that very moment, and their circle of power widened a tenfold, and they fed on all the creatures dying naturally within it. All Death's excess energies were theirs to possess.

We are what feed on ashes. People of Caracas, hear our Song.

Another pyramid rose towards the sky. The entire inner city was transformed to yet another circle, circle of Power.

Come to us, you with fire burning, and serve us.

And they came, in the dozens. And the gods opened them, showed them their might, exposing them for what they truly were, and they knew, for the first time in their lives who they were.

They were dressed, and given the mark, the mark of the gods, and they became their envoys, their holy representatives. Everybody, all over the vast urban area fell on their knees, and rejoiced. A few might have resisted the overwhelming call for a moment or two, but then they, too belonged to Those Feeding on Ashes. The city of Caracas was no more. In what was basically a blink of an eye, it had been vanquished, and replaced with something new, something ancient and beyond all modern references.

We were never this powerful. Not even close.

Not in all the lives they had lived, not during all their incarnations.

We have grown, and we keep growing beyond… beyond…

Before she could even complete the thought they had surpassed themselves again, had left the ashes of what they had been a second ago far behind.

They opened another portal and stepped through it, leaving a tiny part of themselves behind to rule this land. It took no effort. Mexico City was next on their list, and then everything blurred, happening so fast that they didn't bother noting it. They did the same in every city they settled in, drawing to them the demigods, the pre-gods. Sometimes they left tiny pieces of themselves to rule, and sometimes the new gods were given the reign, without any discernable pattern or rule.

In California they didn't choose San Francisco but a smaller settlement a bit east of the large city. A man with a ponytail distracted them for the tiniest of moments before they reduced him to ashes, and took all his power, all his amassed control over the world's worshippers, and it wasn't hard, wasn't hard at all. They knew they should have marked this moment as significant, but that was the old them, those they had left behind eons ago, on a distant beach of the world.

Ethel looked up, with her fireeyes, in her penthouse in New York City, and amazingly she was able to speak, before they took her, before they made her theirs.

I knew you would come. I dreamed about you.

A moment later she was a blank slate, one they filled with their desire, to their specifications, and she was theirs to command, just a vessel for their purpose.

There were others, too, more mere distractions on their predestined path of conquest. No one could oppose them, and certainly not the insignificant representatives of the established power of the world. If they managed to react at all they had nowhere to send their soldiers, and the soldiers had nowhere to point their guns.

And then, they, too belonged to the gods.

The circle was Earth. There was one pyramid, one pyramid of Power in every possible center of the world, and the world was transformed. There was celebration. The Goddess was about to give birth. Tall fires rose towards the heavens. The very air shook.

It began thus, and then she, the creature hovering in the air Above began shaking as well.

– Don't be afraid, she said to her worshippers. – It's all right. Demon spawn becomes their mother. It's all right.

Her water broke. It flooded the ground below her feet, and turned the green grass to ashes. Flames began licking her middle body. Then, abruptly the fire embraced her entire figure and gasps of horror and joy both rose towards the heavens and joined the fire there. And it wasn't really fire, at least not like they had learned to understand it, but the very Fire of Creation revealing itself in one Human Being, one god walking among them.

It consumed she who had been Elizabeth Warren, been the Goddess. Her skin and bones flowed like Mercury, changing as they watched, as one form faded and another emerged, and supplanted it.

She looked very much like Liz, but not quite. There was something both uncannily different and similar about her.

Greetings, Father were her first words to him. Greetings, My Lord. I am new and improved, and now able to serve you even better than before.

She flowed towards him, kneeling in the air before him.

Call me Patty, My Lord. I was your consort. Now I am even more so.

And he took her hand, and the radiant being melted into his embrace.

Days and nights melted, melded, into one, uninterrupted flow. Weeks and months passed, in what seemed like only a moment to the two on the balcony.

Earth's human society transformed under their guidance, their unopposed rule. The old cities vanished. New took their place. Patty entered the throne room one auspicious night, followed by her maid Jackie, she who had once been Ethel Warren. God stood at the balcony, as he often did. There was only one pyramid. They were all one. He could change view at will, whether it was the Amazonian Jungle, the transformed New York City or something resembling Old London, or Moscow, Beijing or Harare or any of the thousand cities they had chosen. Everything was at his fingertips, little more than toys for him to play with. Jackie fell on her knees, trembling in awe. Patty slipped into his arms, warm and eager.

– We consume, he said. – That's what we do.

– Yes, yes, she nodded eagerly. – And we spread, and now that we have spread to every fiber of the Earth, the Universe itself awaits our touch.

He looked out there, and he could push himself beyond the planet's atmosphere, but only so far before reaching his limits.

– It will take time, My Liege, she said softly. – Our people need to get out there and brave the way for us. It will take millennia, but that's only a blink of our eternal existence. In the meantime there's a lot of work and play for us to conduct. Through testing and breeding we will prepare our children for everything that may challenge us out there.

Yes, he had been able to cast his mind to the Moon, because mankind had visited there, briefly, but no farther.

He looked at Jackie. The big and tall woman had a big belly, and would be ready to give birth soon. She and the man with the ponytail had been the strongest opponents in an endless, short line they had faced, and it had been like swatting flies.

– She is a marvel, isn't she? Patty grinned cruelly. – She would have been able to give us a lot of trouble before our ascension. Now, she's merely more dust at our feet, a tool, a means to an end, albeit an excellent such, a child of the gods, eager to do their bidding.

He felt her power, her ability to gauge the past, present and future. She might have seen them coming for years, but been helpless to do anything about it.

The celebration started early that night. Young boys and girls danced below, at the plaza, all over the world, to honor the gods. He sensed Jackie, as her power slowly became his. There was a quality, a quantity over it that had previously eluded him, eluding him no longer.

It was more than an ability to gauge the past, present and future. She had the power to twist it all, to create her own reality, sideways, backwards and forward. But fear had ruled her, anxiety and insecurity had held her back.

But now she had been liberated in his service. God actually felt twinges down his spine, and the world trembled.

Ethel and everything she had been was no more. She was Jackie now, and she and everything she was, belonged to him, body and soul.

The night arrived, burning with a thousand fires. Five billion people gathered around the pyramids. There had been those, those few that had resisted him, resisted his will for a few seconds at most, but now they were all his children. From this pinprick of the Universe they would spread, and so would he. They chanted and sang God's praise.

Jackie stood at the center of the yard, all the yards, below the pyramid. She swayed, she twirled and she turned, slowly, until she stopped. Her water broke, and the very ground beneath her feet turned to mist and shadow, into a thousand dreams made real. He studied her with his predatory eyes. She rose in the air, and he was surprised, even though he had known what would happen.

The female Demon Spawn became their mothers. There was no fire when she burned, but more mists and shadows, as her flesh and bones melted to nothing, and the child within her grew to adulthood in the course of a few heartbeats. If she hadn't been Jackie before, she was Jackie, now, completely and utterly.

– I'm a mirror, Jackie cried softly. – I'm your mirror. Stare at thyself, My Lord, and behold your Glory.

And she was, at least to him, a thousand mirrors glaring at him from every angle. In the course of one moment, she glowed, like a star, momentarily, sufficient, and he gasped, and existence itself shook, as he saw, beyond deceit, beyond doubt… what he had become, and everything faded to nothing in his wake.

# Chapter Twelve: The Moist Burning Place

Ted blinked.

Pain fired through him as he moved, as he attempted to move, but his body was pinned to the ground. He struck his wound, shouting in pain, finally after one, two three, four never existing heartbeats managing to turn towards Justine by his side. Her arm tumbled and fell, and he caught it with his mind, and pushed it back up, pushed it away, and it fell down on her belly and rested harmlessly there.

He sat there shaking, unable to tell how many times he had actually tried and failed, as he sat there trembling in sick relief, remembering everything. For a moment, a brief moment he recalled his godhood, recalled everything about it, and then, except for a few, tiny glimpses he forgot all about it.

But the one, important fact remained and would stay with him forever.

He turned and Phillip crouched there, on his other side, still warm, still breathing and pulsing with life.

The others emerged from the bushes, shaken, hammered and with bruises and marks, but alive, Liz, Laurie, Ben, Candy and Candice, and so many others. He felt them, like he felt all those dead and dying.

– Don't go near him, Liz spoke up, strangely calm, filled with contradictory emotions.

She pulled Phillip away, and Ben dragged Justine away. The rest gathered around him, but they didn't walk close, heeding Liz' warning and what their own, precious experience told them, screamed at them.

Ted felt himself slipping, felt his survival instinct scurrying to take over, to overcome what his conscious mind fought to stave off. It was all he could do to focus on not doing anything.

– Lift him up, Liz told Laurie. – Push his body upwards.

She took the other girl's hand. Laurie sent her a desperate look before turning to Ted, squinting her eyes slightly, making his body levitate. Ted gasped, biting his lips, and they heard his silent scream.

– I can't watch, someone cried.

Ted felt how the Abyss within him reached for Laurie, across the bridge over the ravine she created with her power. There was nothing there, nothing for his ravenous appetites to grab hold of, but he knew that there could be, if he wanted there to be, if he wanted it hard enough.

She pulled him off the twisted metal pole, and blood gushed from his large wound. His power flared, and she lost her grip, and he fell to the ground. They all stood there, and watched in horror and fascination as his gaping wound closed itself and even stopped bleeding in a matter of seconds.

The excess blood on the ground hissed and boiled, as it attempted to replicate itself, as it calmed and died.

He rose, on shaky legs. Liz rushed into his arms, trembling hard. Laurie stood there, frowning.

– You've closed off your mind to me, she said incredulous. – Why on Earth would you do that? *Why?*

He sensed how upset she was. He wanted to explain it to her, the warning he had passed on to himself, one of the few undeniable facts he recalled from his dream, his vision, his experience. He wanted to tell her, but he was too numb, too shaken to do that small thing. Regret haunted him more and more for each new passing second, as he turned and walked away, but he didn't tell her.

Mangled bodies and parts of the plane decorated a large area. He walked there, slowly, carefully, briefly touching, feeding on trees and animals he pulled to him, before finally daring to touch his human companions, rebuilding his strength.

They found their tools, their medicine pouch and began the hard and hopeless task of healing the wounded. The seeds, growing to the porridge helped tremendously, but it couldn't save those torn up inside, couldn't revive those already in Death's lap.

And he couldn't, now, when he was limited.

He remembered bits and pieces, even the feeling of all the other powers he had possessed, but he couldn't access them. There was frustration, despair. But also more. There was a sense of… renewal. He had changed, improved. The dry tears in his eyes also burned. Death strengthened him. He swallowed hard. He pressed on.

Liz sensed it, even in her weakened state. She looked at him from afar with her penetrating, inquiring eyes.

Alanis walked to Richard, casting him a bitter glance.

– You couldn't even find a proper plane, could you?

It was so out of the blue, so unfair that everybody stopped in their tracks. And it hurt him, they could all easily see that, without enhanced senses.

Ted sensed the tension between them, and it hurt him, and surprised him. He turned to Laurie. She was there, close, at his side.

They stood a bit by themselves, out of hearing range from most of the others.

– What's with them?

– They're not done with each other, she enlightened him.

He sighed. That was so very helpful.

– Tell me, he prompted her.

Her eyes darkened and a shadow passed over her face.

– They're filled with conflicting emotions, she frowned. – It's puzzling. I've never sensed anything exactly like that before. They don't like each other. They like each other.

She was quite conflicted herself, possibly in turmoil, but nothing like the Storm he had always felt growing within himself.

The very sight and sense of the dead clearly bothered her. She had experienced quite a lot of death in her life, possibly as much as he had, but hadn't taken to it… the way he had.

– We should bury them, someone said, shaking him out of his musing.

– Let them be, Liz said, neither sad nor angry. – They don't belong to us anymore. Our duty is to survive, not to guard the dead. The animals will come for them when we don't look. The Earth will reclaim its flesh and bone.

And the young girl's words, no matter how shocking felt right to them all.

They pulled the wounded away, to a ruin nearby, setting up a camp, gathering useful stuff and gear from the wreckage.

– How are we faring? Hagman, always the leader, always taking charge, asked his people.

– Not so bad, La Grande said. – A lot could and can actually be salvaged. We have lots of food and ways to preserve it. Most of the portable refrigerators and batteries are intact.

– And a lot of machetes, Justine grinned.

They all looked at the heap of shining metal on the ground.

– We are faring good, then, Hagman nodded pleased, looking at Alanis with a mixed look of triumph and longing.

She ignored him with contemptuous ease.

Twilight settled in, night dawned. The stench of the smoke, rubber and metal in the air faded in their nostrils, as the scent of the jungle slowly asserted itself.

– The jungle is breathing, isn't it? Justine said, glancing around her, shaking a little by every new loud sound coming from the darkness. – I've heard the soldiers in Vietnam speak of it, but I never really believed it.

They built fires in a circle, to help protecting them from the four-legged creatures they imagined in the dark. There were more than enough furniture and dry stuff from the plane for them to do that. Ted sensed the beasts. He felt them as they started digesting the lifeless bodies lying around. Laurie sought closer to him. Everybody did, but she clung to him. He realized that even though he could get quite a sense of the creatures lurking around them, his sensitivity was nothing compared to hers. She was able to sense everything.

Liz' eyes glowed. Whether it was because of the fire or if they glowed of their own volition he couldn't say. He knew his eyes glowed, saw his own dark figure in the eyes of the predators lurking around the camp, kept away by the tall fires and going apeshit because of his presence on their turf. The reaction he had experienced in the animals in London couldn't possibly compare to this. This was the jungle. This was the wilderness untamed.

A set of images danced before him, more incomplete than ever. Pieces didn't fit, and there was a large missing chunk in the middle. It was a Jigsaw puzzle, like he had heard Phillip speak of many times, but far more complex than anything Caine could imagine. Understanding eluded him to the point of frustration, even though he didn't deny its presence, like Caine did.

The growls, the sounds of the fangs and claws cutting meat kept them awake. They clutched their weapons, clutched each other and kept their attention somewhere between the bright fire and the infinite darkness out there. They fell into a sort of uneasy slumber right before dawn, and dreamt of fangs and claws and growls and the jungle embracing them on every side, from every angle, and their dreams and their waken state were the same, filled with the scent of iron and sweat, the thoughts of blood and death and sacrifice, and it was all the same.

## 2

The day brought light, but no illumination.

– So, where are we? Hagman finally asked La Grande.

– We're in the Amazon, Alanis shrugged deliberately, – somewhere far south, south east or south west of Caracas.

Hagman kept looking at La Grande.

– That pretty much covers it, La Grande shrugged hard. – Anybody and anything that could possibly tell us in more detail is gone.

The cockpit and the pilots had been nowhere to be found.

– There's a village of natives west of here, Warren told them with his back turned. – They've never seen white men before and cannot tell us where we are, but they will help us survive.

No one spoke up, or contradicted him, but accepted his statement as fact.

He knelt by the wounded. One more had died during their sleep. The others, he knew at a glance would survive. The medicine had healed their wounds. Candice looked at him with even more gratitude in her eyes. He grabbed the dead body and hauled it over his shoulder and carried it off into the jungle. When he returned he did so empty handed.

– Everything is so much simpler here, he told them. – It's dying or living, kill or be killed.

They fed, and every single piece of meat tasted so good, so very good.

He sat on a hill, not far away. Time passed so quickly, and he feared he was back in the dream.

She came to him after a while, walking alone through the deadly stretch of dense jungle where beasts prowled and hunted. He turned and snarled at her.

– You shouldn't have come. It isn't safe.

– I can take care of myself, she said calmly. – I'm not frail.

He calmed himself with an effort. She was right. What was wrong with him?

– We told them that Death would find them, he said, his voice thick with emotion.

– Yes, we did, she responded, – and we were right.

She sat down before him, looking at him with her unblinking stare.

– You Dreamed, she stated, her eyes huge and opaque.

She nodded, when observing his reaction to her words.

– I saw it, when you writhed on the metal, she told him. – I can always tell, tell when you're upset.

– That's a good one, he said, agitation tangible in his voice. – I was beside myself with pain and you see dreams.

It wasn't funny.

– Tell me, she prompted him softly.

He had to breathe several times, charge himself to go on.

– Justine's arm… touched me, he said, hardly hearing his own voice, hardly seeing anything except the overpowering memory. – In my Hunger I sucked power from her, took everything from her, far beyond what I needed to survive. She died and the Hunger suddenly became everything. Nothing else mattered. I turned to Phillip and sucked him dry, too. It happened in an instant. I rose, a reborn God. You all knelt before me. I offered you the Power and you accepted it eagerly, and we created, in just a few months our Kingdom on Earth. It was so easy, like twitching a finger, and we ruled, ruled without mercy and compassion.

He told her everything, every little detail he could recall, from the dim mist of forgotten memory.

They sat there, exchanging glances, both with the sore catch in their throats.

– I had the Dream about Vegas again, she finally said. – I was captured and made a servant of a bunch of mutant-hating scum. They knew us inside and out, knew our weaknesses and all, and how to make us compliant and submissive, taking away all our weapons and strength, and I was happy, happy as a flower.

And she told him, told him everything, every little indignity and detail she could remember, and that was practically all of it.

They sat there afterwards, both shaking, mute and blind and deaf, embracing each other vigorously.

– You dreamt of conquest and Power, she said, aggression and need both so very prevalent in her voice and body language. – I dreamt of being a lowly slave. What does that say about us?

And he had no answer for her. He desperately wished he had, but he hadn't.

They sat there for hours, in silence, taking in the sounds of the close and distant jungle. She crawled onto his lap, visibly trembling, making his own shaking even worse.

– Perhaps they were not dreams at all, she said, with her face close to his, – but visions of what could have been?

He smiled, an ironic twist of his mouth, acknowledging the fact that she was the one that had to say it.

– Perhaps it really happened, and we both pulled ourselves back from the brink to change it. I wonder, truly wonder what that says about us.

– It's comforting in a way, she whispered, her eyes twinkling like the dark fire they were. – It proves we are powerful, powerful enough to deal with just about anything.

She didn't let up, but kept talking, kept prodding them both.

– The people in my dream were certainly real. Laurie was there. I wonder what changed and kept her from being captured.

– I would say it is a safe bet that it was you nailing those two bastards to the wall, he said, grinning without humor. – Perhaps they planned on going to New Orleans after they had delivered you to «the Stable».

– The mere mention of the name gives me the creeps, she trembled.

– It should, he stated solemnly. – But not as much as the reason Martine Rubleaux will have for trembling, though, if she really exists.

– You're right. Liz curled her hand into a fist. – We know *Time,* in a way very few beings in existence can ever do. She won't know what's coming for her until we're right there, at her jugular, putting an end to her and her not so motley crew of *racists.*

She pushed herself at him, and kissed him, kissed him hard, and kissed him again.

– I love you, she said. – I love you. I love you. I *love* you!

She kept repeating it, as she writhed out of her rags, as she entangled herself in his arms, as they lay down on the moist ground, repeating it with her mouth, first aloud, then silently, her body and eyes and everything she was, until only passion and hunger and everything similar remained, and the jungle swallowed them whole.

## 3

They chased through the jungle, the lot of them. Everybody followed the two in front through the dense vegetation.

– We will run out of bullets soon, Liz had told them in what seemed like endless days ago. – If we want to survive, we must all learn to hunt without those soon to be useless guns.

It was strange seeing the young girl standing there lecturing them, or it would have been, if they hadn't known her, known her so well, as well as they would ever know her. She had an uncanny ability to convey a harsh message in a somewhat pleasant manner, one that the male, the other darkling by her side lacked.

Laurie followed closest to the two, fairly easy, but she didn't really attempt to catch up, but followed their moves and example with a sort of tense, teeth gritting eagerness painted on her face. Liz sensed her in her mind, barraging her with impressions, with dull blades attempting to cut her up. She had granted her deep access once, and now it proved difficult to keep her out. But Laurie didn't dare venture deeper, and Liz grinned in triumph, exposing her fangs in a snarl keeping the other girl even easier away from what was exposed ever further with every passing second. The hunt was on and the beast gained ascendance.

She sensed it, and welcomed it, and Laurie stayed out of her mind.

They hunted with spears, crude blades made from wreckage and metal tied to sticks… and the sharp, shiny machetes. The game, the little furry thing running on all fours was somewhere ahead, not really quite aware of them yet. Liz knew what they were thinking, these would-be hunters. They had failed so many times, so many days that they had begun to feel the despair, the loss of spirit, but she drove them on, because there wasn't really any other option. Days and nights passed like rain and bullets, and remaining food just as fast.

It was choreographed in a way, a ballet of sorts, the way they moved, still clumsily and awkward, like a unit, surrounding the game. Laurie was the focal point, by necessity. She kept them all in contact. They heard themselves and the others in her mind.

That was one less secret, and Ted could see the wonder in everybody's eyes, sense it in the buzz that was their minds, the flow that was their blood.

The jungle… it… opened him, cut him open, wide open. He heard noises everywhere, and not just with his ears. It was as if he had reached a completely new level…

Of Power.

It flared even further when they attacked the fairly large, furry animal he couldn't recall the name of, even when he held back, as spears and ill-conceived weapons flew through the air, as they missed and hit, as it squeaked and screamed and died, as it attempted to limp to safety as they caught up with it and stabbed it and chopped it to death in a final orgy of force, of hunt that seemed to last hours, but only was a matter of seconds.

Steam and life rose in the moist air, as it faded and died. He walked to the warm, cooling body and touched it and blood flooded his hands. His hands touched his face, marking it in red. They understood and came to him, and he marked them all. Laurie didn't flinch when he painted her face, but glowed with the rest of them, accepted her devours, as they all did with pride in cloudy and crystal clear windows of the soul.

They carried it back to the camp, to the ancient ruins in triumph. Warren sensed the life in those ruins in ways he had never sensed before.

He sat on the hill. Liz came to him later, beside herself with curiosity.

– I can practically see the ghosts. He shook his head. – I don't even have to try.

– Looks like your brush with godhood left you a pretty nifty present, she grinned.

– Yeah, I guess that's one way to put it, he acknowledged.

He waited a bit. She waited a bit.

– I can feel the jungle breathe, he said. – In ways I couldn't imagine. I couldn't stop Laurie from reading my mind, being in my mind before. Now, I can. Easily! My mind is closed if I choose to, open if I want to. I am *open*. It feels as if a thousand veils have been pulled from my eyes.

She kissed him on the cheek, like a sister, and left him to his thoughts. She knew him so well.

He studied the camp, as time passed. Richard and Alanis were quarrelling again. They both were eager to organize things, to make decisions, and to set themselves up as boss. He was quite okay with that, really. It took attention off him and freed him to focus on important things.

Laurie came to him, eventually, finally. He studied her openly, not holding back anything. She reddened.

– I am curios, she admitted. – Why… share the Hunt? Why not use our powers and be done with it?

– Because we would have left them behind, he said curtly, – and believe me, that would have been the worst possible scenario.

– Something *happened* to you, she stated aggressively, like a little girl without her toy. – What was it?

He ignored her. For a while he didn't even acknowledge her presence. She stood her ground, stubbornly, with her newfound confidence.

– You and I and Liz could set out through the jungle alone, he enlightened her, – and probably survive. But there is no denying it: there *is* strength in numbers, and all our companions are already hardened survivors. There is no telling what threats we may encounter. I *know*. So, in other words, also from a purely selfish viewpoint sharing makes *sense*.

She got it. He saw she did, both the obvious and subtle meaning contained in his words. She blinked and a shiver passed before her eyes.

– You have a plan, she said. – I know that, an *agenda* going far beyond this tiny jungle.

And she giggled, giggled hysterically when she saw that she rattled him.

She walked back down while she kept giggling, kept smirking.

He rose and the jungle seemed to rise with him, in his mind, in the cosmos of his senses. He moved and time moved with him.

The batteries, even the recharging units began to fail, their decay amplified by the frequent use and humidity and constant attack of the surroundings.

– This is one of the most hostile environments in the world, La Grande sighed. – I'm afraid every piece of our remaining advanced technology will fail soon.

Ted looked into the jungle. He didn't really consider it hostile, but most of the others did, and he sensed that.

– The jungle is honest, Liz pointed out. – There's no deceit here. It's dangerous, even lethal, yes, but no more than civilization.

And she blushed under his hot and grateful stare. He wanted her and she could sense that, and it filled her with a warm and fuzzy happiness.

They all turned to her, to them, and they both felt it, felt the others' need, for answers, for comfort, and it haunted them.

The reduced group of travelers left the ruins at the first light of morning, never to return. They sensed that, with their new, keen senses. Ted Warren sensed it easily.

They carried nothing but their weapons and a few belongings, a both heavy and light load on their back and mind.

There was no turning back.

They moved, moved through the difficult to move through jungle, as the day quickly turned hot.

– The jungle is so *dense,* Laurie whined. – It never looks like this on film.

Liz nodded, grinning. She walked first, and she could hardly see more than a few steps ahead. Only occasionally they were able to glimpse farther off. She used the machete, cutting like hell at the branches ahead of her, like most of the others, but it didn't do much good.

– They cut the trees, Justine commented, *very* helpful. – They have to, at any given scene, to make it visible to the audience.

– It looks so different, Ben said. – So different, now.

– I guess it is one thing to rush through it in the heat of hunt, she nodded, – and another to merely walk through it with nothing to occupy your mind.

If she could have compared herself with herself just a few short weeks ago, Laurie sent to Ted. She would have been stunned to see the difference. They're learning, learning to walk… as am I.

She walked closer to him.

You were right. You have opened my eyes to so many things.

And beneath her thoughts he sensed the wonder and joy and fear and anxiety war within her like ants constantly pissing in her veins.

Suddenly, for no reason at all he recalled his last night in London, when he had been hunted by Bob's goons, when he had hunted them… when Tilla had died. He had learned, learned by each new encounter to become more dangerous, even more lethal, to become more focused than he had ever been before. It was a lot like that now, except that he was less focused. He was open, and learning, along the entire spectrum of the rainbow. He sucked it up like a sponge. Every new step was an experience. He moved and the world moved with him.

Laurie stared at him. He sensed her, like he sensed them all. She stared at him with feverish eyes, with something beyond fever.

She can sense me, he realized. Sense my Storm.

He sensed life all around him, sensed decay, and he sensed the other cluster of human beings still fairly far ahead.

– It's like a map, he told Liz the moment she stepped close, barely able to conceal his excitement, his joy. – Like when we can see in the dark. It isn't sound waves, not really, but something far beyond that.

He crouched, as if in pain.

– I sense life and death on equal footing… and… in the far distance I sense the corruption, sense…

– Civilization, they choired.

– It's everywhere, he nodded, – or virtually everywhere, and will always be… as long as it *exists*.

He was amazed he could actually vocalize these thoughts, these vast dreams. They were actually so beyond words, beyond his experience that he knew he would never be able to do them justice, and he felt a touch of the sickening contradictory emotions that kept haunting Laurie.

The fire rose in the night, so much bigger than how it actually looked like, stretching into the night, into the infinity of reality they were all a part of. Liz rubbed his shoulders, comforting him as much as she was able. Laurie stayed away, at the other side of the fire. He could only see her face as jigsaw pieces, twisted and corrupted from her sweet, innocent expression. She looked old, drawn, as if he saw her across a vast abyss of time as well as space.

He saw Liz, but it wasn't her, not the Liz that stood right in front of him.

– We are waxing and waning like the moon, she said. – From light to darkness to Shadow and back again, and for each new turn we grow a little stronger, a bit more aware and powerful.

And her face, her face in Shadow was a study in ecstasy and rage and sorrow mingled together, like the strands of night and fire surrounding them.

The next day they moved on, and it wasn't really like the usual ritual of leaving one's home each morning at all, but truly like a new day, filled with promise and dangers.

They walked for hours and kept walking, their hair and skin and what little remained of their clothes soaked in sweat. Everything felt so light. Liz hummed a melody cheerful and bright.

– The humidity is quite simply phenomenal. She shook her head in amazement. – I'm willing to swear we must all be walking underwater.

Ted kept drying his brow, but it was no use. He wasn't used to sweating, at least not during moderate walking. Even when they took breaks and sat still the sweat just kept pouring from wide open pores.

And it didn't really bother him, not like it did most of the others. He realized startled that he knew the melody Liz was humming. It was the same he had always heard Betty sing and hum. He took up the humming, and he suddenly remembered himself humming in his sleep, and he had visions of a group, another group cross a torn, remote landscape.

And that group became many, crossing many different landscapes, mountains, forests and plains.

In that torn, remote landscape a man with a strange growth on his forehead walked first. He led the others through horrible hardship, and they prevailed, and he heard the song chanted from the Abyss: Lord of the Flies, LORD OF THE FLIES, LORD OF THE FLIES.

And he and Laurie and Liz trembled in the humid heat.

Later a woman led them, crossing forests, mountains and plains, and seas. She had black eyes. Ted recognized her instantly.

The three trembled in the humid heat, and their companions, sensing their excitement and distress trembled with them.

He realized something, abruptly, startled: There were no fireeyes among them. That came later, much later. First there were only a few, and then many, and then few again, and then many. Two people, a man and a woman with fireeyes led on, on a flight, an escape across forests, mountains, plains and seas.

They were always on the run or on the move, always one way or another. That was their way, their endless way.

The stranded travelers entered a new valley. They reached a slope, and they walked downwards.

– Thank God, Alanis cried. – Finally a little variation. I was starting to think we would never find anything breaking this *endless* boredom.

– You never could stand the jungle, Hagman commented sourly.

The others laughed, laughed hard, and the two of them looked embarrassed at each other.

They had almost reached the low parts of the valley when Ted stopped and held up a hand, and they all stopped at his behest, knowing and trusting his senses. All of them had, in the time after the crash, to a certain point learned to measure their surroundings, to read variations, movement in the jungle. Now, there was nothing, nothing but silence.

It wasn't silence exactly, since there was some background noise, but much quieter than it used to be, at least to their better developed senses.

Ted began walking again, and they did, too. He led them out on an open area by the river. He raised his hands and stretched his arms to his sides. A few seconds passed, before he sat down on his ass on the shore, on the shore of small pellet stones.

– Lower your weapons, he said casually, – and whatever you do don't raise them again.

Hagman opened his mouth to protest, but stopped himself a moment later.

A group of warriors, of both sexes with spears and bows appeared from between the trees. Ted sat closest to their spot of appearing. He rose. He carried no weapons. Signaling his fellow travelers to stay behind he took two steps forward and stopped. The advancing group of warriors halted, too. They exchanged a few words. A puzzled look appeared on Warren's face.

– I can understand them, Laurie said. – At least what they're thinking, given time, at least. It feels really strange. I didn't use to think that telepathy is beyond language, but now I believe I do.

She has grown, Ted though, and so have I.

But in his case it wasn't telepathy, but something else. He couldn't read their mind, in any way, but he knew their language, or he would, given time.

Images flashed behind his eyelids again, memories of yet another far away time.

One single pellet rose from the ground, from the shore of pellets. One man pointed. Another pellet and then yet another and another rose from the ground, and began dancing in the air. The man threw his spear. It stopped in midair, right in front of the dancing pellets. Ted felt an irritation in his frontal lobe and instantly recognized it for what it was. He buried his eyes, his glowing eyes in the woman behind the man, the tribe's resident priestess or witch. A large number of pellets rose simultaneously, protecting him from a barrage of spear and arrows. The woman stumbled back, shouting for the others to stop. They did. One single pellets was seemingly fired from its spot in the air, fired above the warriors and hit a tree nearby, penetrating it with a loud sound, reemerging on the other side, and stopping there, hovering there, before returning to the others levitating above and before the stranger. Ted lifted a finger. Laurie stepped forward, revealing the mole on her leg. Liz stepped forward as well, revealing the faded mole on her leg, and Ted, turning slightly revealed his. The woman stepped forward, revealing her own mole, hesitatingly, hitting her chest, saying something.

– She's Chini, Laurie stated. – She's Glow.

– She's Glowing in the Dark, Ted said, stunning himself, not showing it.

He had learned the value of appearances early in life.

The pellets returned slowly to the ground, except one, floating slowly, unthreateningly into her hand. She took it, a dazed look in her eyes.

– I am Fireeyes, he said, in her language, stunning himself.

– Are you The Fireeyes? She asked. – The One we've been waiting for, for nights without number?
Laurie translated for him in his mind, sensing his difficulties.
– I am, he replied. – We were meant to come here, meant to meet you, I know that.
She bowed slightly. They all did. But they didn't kneel. And that pleased him.
– I'm still not what I one night will become, he said. – Neither is she.
He indicated Liz without directly pointing to her.
– I… understand. Glow nodded. – The legend says the Fireeyes will only pass through here on their way to
He understood the word as «Glory», but knew that it wasn't exactly that.
– We will share with you, she stated, filled with apprehension and joy, – share everything we are.
Laurie translated for the others. Alanis gazed at the scene from a distance in total amazement, in something akin to shock.
– She seems so… familiar, Liz said.
– She is, Ted nodded.
– I can almost make out what she's saying, too. I guess I will need a little more time,
– A little more time, Ted nodded.
Glow signed for them to follow her, formally, eagerly, inviting them all into her domain. The village rested on a small piece of land a little longer down the river. It seemed to everybody's eyes like a peaceful, quiet and static place, but to Ted it was dynamic and aggressive, vibrant ground and air filled with activity and laughter. Children ran about, staring openly and unafraid at the newcomers. There was no pretence or reserve. Everybody wore their intentions on the outside.
Chini frowned. She noticed the difference, too, of course. Any shaman or similar would.
– You're different from us? Her frown deepened.
– Yes, Ted nodded, – very different. Most of the world has become a bleak and horrible place, and we're inevitably marked by that fact.
She strived to grasp his words, though not as much as the other members of the tribe nearby.
– I know, she said. – The prophecies foretold it, and I have had visions of the world far away.
But she didn't really understand it. How could she?
– I've sensed its approach.
She shuddered visibly, making the other warriors glance curiously at her.
– You do well to fear it, he said. – It doesn't fight, not really, but it still wins, and destroys everything it touches. It isn't one person or even a group of persons, but a dead thing moving without being seen.
And he was amazed by his own reasoning, how astute it was, and how clearly he saw things.
– And now you're here, she nodded. – You come to us openly. You don't hide.

– Yes, he confirmed to her, – but others won't. They will take everything you are and spit on it, and force you to spit on it, and eventually make you detest yourself.

– They are that… mighty?

– No. He shook his head. – Not they, but what they represent. They're deceivers, sent to do the bidding of the dead thing they serve. Make no mistake about it: they will use force, use coercion in every possible way, but that isn't the most powerful tool at their disposal.

He shocked her, shocked her to her core, rocking the very foundation of her being, and even though he knew she could handle it he, and the other travelers had taken the first of the many steps that would eventually destroy her and the tribe.

Every single contact a primitive society had had with civilization had eventually destroyed that society, and he had no illusions that this would be different.

– Come, she insisted, taking his hands, walking backwards as she kept her eyes on him, giving him the sweetest and most sensual and natural of smiles, – come to our heart. We will make a feast to celebrate the arrival of our distant kin and their tribe.

He saw the entire village, envisioning it in his mind without trying, from every possible angle, like a many-dimensional image including smell, sounds and… and touch. The witch, ancient and nascent recognized it as displacement, Farsight stronger than ever before.

– Your Sight, Chini gasped. – So powerful and beautiful.

To her it was the same. She didn't mince words. There was no pretence in her, and no aspiration towards hypocrisy, not even that. No envy or distortion of self. She was a deadly creature and not quite innocent. In her flowed power without guilt.

He found himself envying her.

The drums began beating, a slow, penetrating rhythm opening up the listeners to the world around them. The spicy food excited him, long before it passed between his lips. The females' swinging hips made him delirious with lust, long before they swung close to his. They sat around the fire, the large fire between all the small fires, seeing all things in the plasma and rising glows turning to swirling mist. He saw himself and Liz cross the United States on motorbike, saw the muddled land behind them, the misty imagery ahead. They were alone. He realized startled that undeniable fact. The past was a slow moving canvas, easy to spot and more painful for every new face or smile or hateful expression appearing. Linda, Mike, Tilla, Bob, Glory, Stewart, Gidman, Michelle, Trudy, Iris and the rest, all the rest. His attention shifted from the past to the future. Just like that, and it was done. David Gidman and Mark Stewart filled the road, but Stewart was bigger, practically reducing One-Eye to insignificance. Ted didn't quite understand that, but there was no denying it.

He swam in the sea of naked bodies, soaking up energy like the sponge he was. They were on all sides of him, and it was all so pleasant and natural. Fires burned tall, dancing in his equally burning eyes, and they seemed to speak to him, communicating something beyond sight, beyond words and anything familiar. The tribe welcomed the travelers with an intensity beyond passion, beyond fire. Two females clung to him, filled to the brim with equal parts curiosity and fear and reverence. They knew what he was. To them he wasn't anything unnatural, but an integral part of nature, like any predator. It was prudent to show a healthy respect for such a creature.

They shivered when he focused on them, when he gave them his complete attention. He could let go here, without fear of sucking dry those close to him. This was how it was supposed to be, without fear or shame or second guessing. He could let go, and he did, becoming one with the swirling mass, becoming Life, Death and the End of Time, emptying himself in those two, leaving them spent and happy, moving on to others.

The mist parted, and he saw far ahead. He recognized the city of New York, glimpsed Ethel there and others, both known and not to him. He saw a woman standing on Times Square, greeting him with a wolfish grin, and he knew her, knew her every corner and twinkle. Then it was London again, a long road of streets and impressions, Iris the Witch smiling affectionately to him, the house by Nothing Hill Gate, its lights lit again, like in decades past, Liz in a lavish dress, playing the perfect hostess, a succession of old, dusty castles and transparent figures in the air, and a growing sense of menace, Jonas Bergli in a dirty hut on a beach, and Linda, and Mike, Mike and Linda in a whirl of fire and noise and thunder.

It faded, all of it, even as it remained, forever.

Ted and Liz met at the center, suddenly very conscious of that fact. They spoke, and could no longer be sure the words were spoken aloud.

– I dream, he said. – I dream awake.

– So do I. She greeted him with a sultry kiss. – I have visions of the past, present and future, and we are together.

He grabbed her, and kissed her, kissed her neck, and she cried out in delight.

– The language is old? She wondered, she stated. – I can't believe we know it, and far less speak it.

– It's a part of us, he said, – of our memories, our Total Recall.

They touched each other, kissed and caressed each other, and it was a joy-filled, explosive moment, as if it was the first time.

She drew breath, as she flustered attempted to speak. They grinned at each other, very self consciously.

– Their… dialect is slightly different from ours. I guess time has made it so.

– Yes, time, Ted said.

She wanted to say more, and he wanted to, too, but the rapid heat suddenly overwhelmed them, and the world was touch, and nothing more, everything more. Fear grabbed them, briefly, whether or not they would regain consciousness in a field of dead, cold bodies, but then that faded, as well, and Hunger ruled them, overtook them completely.

Twilight turned to night, and night to the brightest day, and the world Changed into something alien and familiar and totally different, and the many fires turned into one in the small settlement by the river, that tiny spot of the world.

## Chapter Thirteen: The slow jungle drums

– Allow me to show you, Chini said, – to reveal to you what little you may not know.

The two of them stood with her on a rise overlooking the waterfall. Steam rose from below and created the swirling mist they knew so well.

A large bird, an eagle, beyond big appeared in the mist and landed on the dead branch sticking out above the edge of the waterfall. Elation surged through them, strange and terrifying.

– Behold the eagle, Chini said. – You are the eagle.

It didn't really look like an eagle to them, but like an amalgam of birds and animals constantly shifting and changing.

– You are all birds flapping their wings, sharpening your talons on cold, unfeeling rock. You are the cat, shaking your tail, whipping up a storm, an elephant shaking the ground with every step. You are the children of ancient powers and mightier than all of them. You are what is reigniting ashes, and with death and destruction you will destroy the destroyers.

Cold hammered down their spine.

It didn't bother them that she knew what an elephant was or even surprised them much, but her words bothered them.

She turned towards them with her steady stare.

– You show fear. She nodded. – Perhaps that is a good thing. Perhaps it is good that a future God shows human emotion.

She turned away from them and walked away. They remained on the rise, staring into the mist, staring at her, as she made her way back down on light and heavy feet.

– She's sweet, isn't she, Liz grinned, exposing her fangs, – sweet and vicious to no end?

– She is indeed, he nodded.

– And she's wrong, of course, Liz said somberly. – Meshed in legends and superstition.

– Of course, he agreed.

And just like that he remembered vividly the two of them standing at the top of the pyramid, holding life and death and everything in their hands.

They walked back to the village, taking their time, but even in their reluctance the sense of coming home was so very, very obvious. It felt real to them, all of it. For some reason he thought about Betty (again), and he couldn't avoid thinking about her. For some reason.

All of them sat there, feeding together, sat on the ground, in the circle, laughing and living, even more so as the shadows grew long and deep.

This tribe didn't look like any of the other native tribes they had seen or encountered. Those they had seen or encountered had been pretty much domesticated, of course, but these looked clearly diverse visually as well. There were far greater differences than similarities. They were different.

Days passed. Nights passed. The slow moving rhythm of the jungle began settling in the bones of the unfortunate travelers. There were hunts, wild and disorganized, another time of learning for those not born to the jungle, to the wild. Most of them were clearly less experienced than the youngest resident hunter, and it showed, and it would always show, and they felt at least a bit of shame, for some reason, even though the tribe, not seeing the world in absolutes didn't think like that. To them learning was a life-long process, and they didn't denigrate them their inexperience.

– You are not born here, Chini told them. – We would not fare well in your world either.

They frowned. That was undoubtedly true.

Though her words made them feel both better and worse.

Time itself passed, to the point that they longer counted it, not even as the appearance of the many new straw huts by the river, and the females' growing bellies. Candy and Candice couldn't hunt anymore. Justine, Laurie and Chini, and several others had begun to show growth as well. The meeting of the two tribes was about to bring a score of new life into the world.

Those coming from the outside gave up wearing clothes. It was neither practical nor desirable. They walked around practically nude and it embarrassed them less and less each day. It created some *amusing* results at first, but that, too faded with time.

Even memory faded, to a certain extent. The travelers' recall of the world they had come from turned dim and almost insignificant. It was hardly more than a gleam in their eyes anymore.

Night and day turned into one, and each season stretched on forever.

Liz and Chini sat in the treetops a bright night staring at the sky, at the full moon, and the endless stretch of forest across the valley. The young girl felt peace, to the point that she almost no longer had to acknowledge the irritating itch in her dark corners.

– Look at Mother Moon. Chini pointed at the sky.

Liz did.

– She seems to be whole, and she is, but even so, she consists of two halves, two halves joined, becoming One.

– That's too metaphysical for me. Liz joked, knowing fully well that the woman wouldn't fully understand her.

She looked, and even stared, at the shining disk, straining her eyes, not really seeing anything, but wanting to, wanting it desperately. Sighing, she turned to Chini.

– Am I barren? She wondered, she asked the medicine woman. – Is that it?

Chini wasn't put off, since honesty and the direct approach was far more common here, than in civilization, wasn't put off like most of the people Liz had grown up with would have been, but instead of replying she returned the stare calmly.

– I mean, I've been fucking relentlessly, without any kind of contraception, both with Ted and others for years, and even more after we arrived here, without *results*. It isn't like I'm in a hurry, or anything, but the thought has crossed my mind for a while.

– I think you just answered your own question, Goddess of Vengeance, Chini said kindly, – as I guess is your want. You are not ready, but you will be, somewhere, down the river.

And the girl saw the river with her inner, third eye, sensed its quiet flow and overwhelming, majestic power, reaching, passing many villages, many townships, until it reached the roaring waterfall far ahead.

They sat there in silence for a while. Liz took in the silence of the jungle, in a way she would venture that Chini never could, since she did it all the time, and wouldn't know what its absence meant.

– It's so peaceful here, the girl mumbled.

– This is a brief respite from the path you have chosen, Chini nodded.

She moved a bit, from one branch to another, from one viewpoint to another, so effortlessly, even with the added weight affecting her balance. Liz sighed, green with envy. She knew the woman had had five children, two that were still alive, but she didn't look that much older, even though she was, even though they began early here.

– A metal bird fell not far away, not many cycles ago. Chini hesitated, uncharacteristically so. – That was… you?

– That was us, Liz confirmed.

– And you will rise like a bird of flesh, of shadow and fire.

– You are not the only one saying that, or similar things, Liz said, – but what does it *mean?* Is it meant figuratively or literally?

Liz struggled with the last sentence. It came out as garbage and was, really, at least in this language, which contained no words that could properly translate or describe it.

To Chini and her people there was no difference between the corporal and the spiritual. It was all the same. Liz shook her head, deflecting both Chini's puzzled look, and her own clumsy query.

– I know. Liz stated, grinning glumly, – it means what it means.

Dreams are reality, she thought. Doorways.

– Both I and Ted dream about the Dragon, she said, she hesitated.

She knew Chini knew what a dragon symbolized, or rather, discounting symbolism: what it was.

– You are the Dragon, the priestess stated. – But you will also have to face the dragon, possibly more than one, more than once. They may block your path…

– … the path to

Glory, Liz didn't quite voice with the woman.

Wrath! She realized stunned. It means Wrath.

Suddenly she was cold, cold to the bone and she held around herself, attempting to warm herself and naturally failing miserably.

– You're troubled, the priestess said. – He is, too. But you shouldn't be. Does the wave washing the shore care about the grains of sand? Does a Storm care about the land it ravages?
– B-but we're human beings? Liz protested, protested weakly.
– Yes, Chini nodded, – the greatest force of nature that has ever existed, and you are its spear, its spear of destiny illuminating our way.
– It was strange hearing a jungle girl talk like that, Liz said to Ted later, – almost like listening to a multinational executive or something.
– What is completely wrong in one situation can be totally right in another, Ted said. – Civilization is wrong nearly every time, while nature is beyond right and wrong, which is basically a fairly modern, dualistic bullshit invention.
And she wanted to praise him for being wise again, and blew him a long, sultry kiss. She knew all that, but wanted to praise him anyway, for reminding her.
She sat in the treetops with the jungle queen, while change and time blew through her.
Feeling it, frowning, suddenly plagued with double vision.
– I think there's something wrong with my eyes…
Chini studied her, calmly, like a predator.
– I guess it was inevitable that something would be wrong with me eventually. I haven't been able to feed for months. My ability to self-repair is doomed to go bust.
I'm vulnerable, she thought. I'm so fucking vulnerable.
She looked at the moon again, her eyes suddenly glued to it. It seemed to… to change before her eyes.
As the world changed, as she struggled to speak, to voice the unspeakable, breaking all her dams.
– I SEE it, she cried. – And it isn't just two half moons either, but many, so many forming a whole full moon, and it's on *fire*.
And her eyes were burning. She blinked, seeing herself from outside herself.
– The waterfall, she mumbled, – I can hear it…
But it wasn't the waterfall or at least not solely the waterfall, but a roar rising within, a seething ocean, reminiscent of a thousand suns. She had felt it before, but never had it been so pleasant, so filled with pleasure and joy, so beyond powerful.
Something cracked in her nostrils, and when she touched her upper lip her hand drowned in blood.
The rumble rose from the Earth. She heard it, and then she realized that it wasn't symbolic, but fact. Large rocks rose from the ground below, towards the treetops, to her, paying their respect, to *her*.
They danced, swaying in the air. In her honor. Excited cries reached her from below, but it felt so distant, immaterial.
Chini, startled actually lost her footing, and fell from her branch. Her hand reached for it, but missed, and she was in free fall. With just a thought, a distraction Liz froze her in the air.
– I've got you, she said softly. – Don't be afraid. I've got you.

She held the other woman there for a moment, studying her with a cold, impassive and even inhuman expression.

– I don't feel of this world. I feel of this world.

Chin shivered.

Liz put her back on the nest of branches.

– The child inside of me was afraid, Chini whispered.

– I know, Liz snarled, – I felt the sniveling brat. She was complaining endlessly.

A shadow passed over her eyes, and the fire returned. She smiled, and began climbing down the tree. And as soon as she began she suddenly was in a hurry to get down on the ground. The rocks, all the rocks sort of followed her down, lowered themselves with her.

The tribe, the united tribe met her, welcomed her. She put the rocks back in their designated places, moving her arms up and down, in dramatic gestures, before rushing into Ted's arms.

– It's back, she grinned.

– I can see that, he said dryly, his eyes twinkling.

– And it has *grown,* she cried excitedly. – I *feel* the jungle, just like you described it. I cannot properly put it into words. And it isn't necessary, anyway.

A wind not a wind swept the village, embracing them all, and shiver and delight warred within them and there was no winner.

The wind faded, slowly. A few smaller rocks still hovered above. Liz did a few tricks with them, her face glowing in glee, before she let them fall and settle in the ground.

She turned towards Laurie. Laurie couldn't touch her mind anymore. It had locked her out, now, when it was more open than ever.

Chini climbed down from the tree and set foot on the ground. Liz knew that, knew exactly where she was, also with her back turned.

– You're both *chrysalis,* she stated solemnly, – beings in a constant state of flux, of stasis and growth, contraction and expansion, and you don't have your equal anywhere.

– First you said we fed off ashes, Liz commented teasingly, – And that we were The Dragon and you said a lot more besides, and now this. Tell us, what is it?

– Yes, Chini said.

And turned and walked away.

Liz kissed Ted on the cheek, and sent him the sweetest of smiles.

– Excuse me, my love. I need to leave for a while. I'll be back shortly.

His stare burned her, but she ignored it.

She rushed after Chini, taking her time, biding her time, until they were both far away from the confines of the village. The jungle surrounded her and she embraced it, rocked it in her lap. Chini had stopped, waiting for her at the waterfall.

– So, priestess, Liz said casually, – are you one of the dragons we must overcome to reach our destiny?

Chini fell on her knees, shaking badly, bowing her head, baring her neck.

– I would have known instantly if you were concealing anything from me, Liz nodded, grinning her cruel smile. – You saw me being born, and couldn't deal with it. I can understand that, and I sympathize. If you had been present when Ted was born you would have been terrified. I'm telling you this, sparing you from future heartache. He is like me, exactly like me.

One second passed, two, one minute, or no time at all.

Time? Liz thought.

– We will never speak of this again, she told the woman beneath her. – We will never mention it to anybody or even remember it in our Memory.

She walked to the edge of the cliff, bathing in the froth and steam from the fall.

– You may go now, she shrugged.

And Chini jumped on her feet and hurried off, terror surrounding her like a viper.

The raven hair flowed around the creature, there on the cliff. Liz looked down herself, and smiled, as she slowly reached into the air, both with her arms and her mind. There was a sting below, and dark blood flowed between her thighs and hissed like fire when it hit the wet ground.

Elizabeth Warren stood on the precipice, bathing in the rain and steam and the light from the stars and the moon, remembering everything there was to remember.

## 2

Tranquility touched the travelers and their adoptive tribe. The once outsiders, used to the faster pace of a modern life found themselves with little to do… until they realized they always did something, whether it was pure contemplation or swimming in the river or hunted or explored or made some more or less useful tool.

The tribe used everything. Nothing was wasted. They didn't have any word for that either. The skin and bones and everything of an animal, not just a small, selected piece of the flesh. The travelers saw how it was done, and they learned, learned stunningly fast, because in a place like this it was easy to learn.

It was a hot, beautiful day in the village. A group of old and new villagers sat in a circle, speaking, exchanging words and emotions, enjoying themselves, playing in the shadow of the trees covering the ground.

– I feel the warm sunshine. Candy swayed, rocking back and forth on the ground. – It's so pleasant, such an assault on the senses.

She and Candice sat there breathing, breathing in and out, in and out. The early signs of the upcoming birth had shown themselves for them both, and the new life inside of them was almost ready to pop into this world.

– Two hours a day on average, Hagman noted, from his position by the hut, as hunters returned with game. – That's approximately how long a given tribe member needs for pure survival, to uphold life. It fits perfectly with recent radical anthropology theories. That's far less, compared to the average of eight hours in civilization.

He still had his watch around his wrist. It was water proof, able to take strong hits and all and all a technological marvel.
– Busybody, Alanis blew him a kiss, heat and mist in her eyes.
She stood there, performing for him, dancing while standing still.
– You are so changed, he whispered.
– So are you, dumb ass…
She smiled, and pulled back, into the nearest hut, and the slowly awakening sleepwalker followed her in a daze slowly, inevitably dissipating.
The others sat there, enjoying themselves while the moans and gasps reached them from the hut.
– I guess they will be quarreling again tomorrow, Candy noted with grim humor.
– I guess they will. Ben shrugged.
The bad, even ambiguous emotions between the two fucking in the hut felt strange, even alien to the rest of them, now.
They sat there in the shadow, in the pleasant shadow, as the day passed, and awoke with the coming of twilight, of night, as the dark turned truly alive around them, and it hardly bothered any of the travelers anymore.
It was so relaxed, everything, in spite of the low burn intensity that was always with them, always there, whether they moved or sat still, whether they chased through the jungle or swayed around the fire.
Candy's water broke, splashed around her feet. She smiled, and the others smiled, as hectic and relaxed activity surrounded her. Chini, with quite the visible big belly herself joined the group, comforting the mother-to-be with a smile and a light caress. Candy breathed, and her breathing seemed to spread like ripples in water throughout the village. Candice's water broke shortly thereafter, wetting the ground around her feet. Chini called out for more help and they arrived shortly. The two women stood there, face to face and smiled to each other, supported by one person on each side. Ted and Liz sat in the circle surrounding them, smothering them in excited emotion. Everything felt so peaceful… so right.
The mothers to be stood there, breathing, while both tribe members and travelers gently touched and caressed them, everybody present feeling the sensation of the touch, of the caress. Everybody participated, trading places with uneven intervals, taking turns at comforting the two women at the center. It was a beautiful, fluid and constant movement, and they all sensed its flow, its power, and perhaps for the first time in their lives the travelers truly felt part of something, something profound and incredibly precious.
A dance, Liz thought, Liz choked, a dance of life.
Her lips moved. She hummed, chanted and the villagers, stricken and joyful took up the chant, and it was obviously familiar to them, as the back of a hand. They, like Liz, like Ted merely needed to reach out a hand and touch it.
The gasps emanating from Candy and Candice shivered in the moist air. When Ted and Liz looked at them they didn't see, didn't sense only two people but four. They had sensed the babies for quite some time, but the last few hours that

sense had grown exponentially. In a more vocal society they would have expressed that, expressed their incredulity, their potent, growing joy, but here that felt unnecessary, felt totally redundant.

Candy began breathing faster, splitting her thighs even more, as much as she possibly was able. She screamed sharply, once, twice. They saw the small head and the tiny body, and then the new life landed softly on the sheet Justine and Laurie held under her hips. Chini whacked the small form on the back, and then the world turned very vocal again, as the beautiful scream of life filled their ears and world.

Chini cut the cord. Candy fell on her knees and began to consume it and the placenta. It felt so right, so natural, here, to not waste anything, even to the travelers, who had grown up in a devastating consumer society.

Not long afterwards another scream filled the moist air, all the acute senses. Candice consumed the leftovers in the same frenzy her friend had done. Candy and Candice rested with the tiny bundles in their arms. The tribe, the united tribe gathered around them, welcoming the new life to the world, to their home.

– No fireeyes, Liz noted. – Michelle doesn't have them either.

– Not yet, Ted said. – And neither did we that early.

He put one index finger on each of the children's palms. Both pair of eyes, uncannily focused on him, making him almost overwhelmed by emotion.

– Mothers and children are well, Chini declared.

The celebration began only a few minutes later. The new members of the tribe were celebrated with abandon, with a joy transcending all boundaries. Tall fires once again rose in the village by the river. Liz and Ted swayed close together, close in body, close in mind, swayed in a whirl of bodies, of minds.

– This is so… pleasant, she frowned, she grinned lazily. – This is… *life*… how it should be. I can't believe we've missed out on it for so long, and hardly even known what we've missed. The Hollow in me is filled, filled to the brim.

He didn't say anything, didn't voice his comment, except by movement, by touch. There were dozens of others around them, but during those few, brief moments it was as if they were alone, and they enjoyed both states of mind to the max. There were no contradictions. All contradictions were thrown on the garbage heap where they belonged.

– It is so great seeing the guys walk around with half stiff cocks and the gals clearly aroused occasionally, and that it doesn't necessarily creates arousal in others, and when it happens it happens so naturally, so right.

She wasn't crying, but it was close, as she was overwhelmed by emotion.

The dance became swaying. The swaying became touch. And the touch transformed into passion, into fire.

– No shame, she whispered, swaying in the world of breathing and heaving and sighing and moaning. – No shame.

And memory faded, as everything faded and nothing remained but fire, but dancing shadow behind closed eyelids, before wide open eyes, and the river transformed into flowing lava boiling the sea of human beings mating there, on the river bank.

## 3

Justine, Laurie and Chini gave birth to daughters, and several of the villagers gave birth as well. It happened so soon after the previous births that it didn't seem to be any time at all. They knew, intellectually that several moons had passed, but it didn't feel that way. Time didn't exist here and life was marked by the various memorable events in the tribe's existence.

Liz and Ted stood by the fall, squinting their eyes only slightly, making the water change in their view, becoming tongues of heat bathing them in its pleasant reign.

– I sensed something. She frowned. – I stood here when my period began and I sensed a *lot,* but also something that puzzled me. There was actually something hovering in the *air* above me, something *solid,* invisible, something my eyes couldn't distinguish from the air… that my Power could.

The thought resonated within Ted somehow, but he couldn't place it, place the memory. He felt it was important, even crucial, but he couldn't make himself understand.

– The world is so big, so very big.

He shook his head in wonder.

– We are… happy here, she said incredulous, rubbing her lips close to his ear, savoring his scent. – This is where we are born to live.

The mighty fall resonated within them, surrounding them, as if they levitated out there above it. It wasn't merely the water, but the jungle and everything.

– Of all the places we could have come we came here, to this tribe. It almost makes one believe in fate… doesn't it?

He looked straight ahead, at nothing, as was sometimes his want, looked at the million droplets of water dancing in the air, looking back at himself and the girl from those millions of eyes.

– They have stopped moving, though, stopped being nomads, and they were, at some point, and I wonder about that.

She nodded, also, like him constantly analyzing, computing and processing everything around them, everything in their sphere. And they marveled at the sight of Chini, of Glow, about the fact that they hadn't noticed her approach.

Her voice was ambiguous, both filled with awe and fear, with wonder and despair, and they understood.

– We stopped for you. It was true what you said when you first came to our village: it was preordained. You needed to know, beyond doubt an alternative to the corrupted world you were born into and grew up in.

She left again, left them to ponder and contemplate, as was her want. They weren't certain she had truly been there, at least not the Chini they had come to know.

They remained there, at what seemed like a very long time, lying on the ground, skin to skin, resting both mind and body, at peace with the world.

She looked at Mother Moon, not even finding it necessary to squint her eyes to see beyond the obvious.

– What did you see? He asked casually, failing royally, as usual to keep himself from exposing himself to her.

– I see a tall woman with oily, black hair.

She didn't ask him what he saw. He knew she wanted to.

– What are you thinking?

– Pretty much the same as you, I guess. She stretched her body close to his. – I'm thinking that I am indeed very happy right now, and I'm hoping we can stay that way when we return to the dead world, when we go back to live it up.

Return… He looked anxiously at her.

– You didn't think we would remain here, did you? She asked casually. – Here, at this abandoned outpost of the world?

It was she who had to point out that obvious fact, of course. He looked at her with very ambiguous feelings in his gut.

– «Know thyself and thou shall know all the mysteries of the gods and of the Universe».

He recognized the saying without thinking about it. It was the inscription in the forecourt of the temple of Apollo at Delphi.

They stayed there, by the cliff, by the waterfall the rest of the night, staying away from the tribe, staring into the Abyss.

– You're cold, she said, kissing him on his shoulder.

It was a warm, dry night. The moisture from the waterfall couldn't touch them. The hot jungle couldn't warm them. They only found, as was often the case heat and comfort in each other, and as often was the case, that was enough.

The sun, the glowing sun rose above the jungle, the tall mountain ahead. They saw it and recognized its power. It felt real, so very real. The sun blocked their path and left them as nothing more than ashes on the hard, uncaring ground.

They burned and writhed in their restless sleep. It brought them no rest, but an ever stronger sense of menace, and when morning finally came, and they woke in the middle of the day, and the sun bathed them in its light they crouched there, clutching each other, chilled to the bone.

## 4

Laurie gave milk. She sat with the other mothers in the shadows. The small bundles in their arms sucked greedily the treasure concealed in the swollen breasts. It was yet another peaceful scene. She waved happily to Ted and Liz as they were passing by.

The hunt was on. Liz and Ted headed out with the other hunters for the day. One blink, two and they were inside the dark, moist place between the trees, the spear resting comfortably in their hand. The world changed, as perspective changed. It was, as always both a jarring and exciting experience.

They had learned to turn off or at least mute their senses to a degree, but in here, in the moist shadows that was impossible, especially now, when they were more open than ever. The hunt had been bad for some time, now, and the tribe grew hungry. Liz and Ted took the point, and the world split in a thousand pieces, dozens of paths revealing themselves to the two of them. They sifted through massive amounts of information, isolating what they most of all desired in that moment in time.

Liz recalled briefly her time as Laurie's «hound», and felt fear, fear Ted easily caught, but then it was gone, left like ashes, and only the task remained. They ignored the smaller animals scurrying in the underbrush of the jungle, and sought bigger prey. Fangs and claws began flashing before their eyes. They heard the growl and it entered them, and it rose from their throats, a low, guttural snarl making their fellow hunters shake in their tracks.

And beyond the fangs and claws were something they couldn't acknowledge to themselves, even in their most lucid moments.

Silence reigned in the noisy jungle, as the human beings made their way between the tight trees, as minutes turned to hours, to long hours. Their mind, their attention focused on something ahead, something huge and heavy. The other hunters, having learned their signs these seasons caught on and excitement and blood-thirst ruled them all at the expense of everything else.

A tapir, Ted thought in a flash, a thought fading the moment it appeared.

The three-hundred kilo large animal appeared before them, as if out of nowhere, as they rushed through the red haze filling their mind. It towered above them like a giant, bigger than life, and they felt fear and awe and Hunger beyond words, beyond expression. One of the hunters hurled his spear and through two pair of fireeyes it changed, becoming a burning streak in the night. Sound and fury erupted in the jungle, breaking the spell. Liz and Ted threw themselves at the giant, stabbing it with all their physical might. It howled in rage and pain. This was a peaceful animal, not a predator, but it turned into a bundle of muscles and power when being threatened. Ted was being thrown into the air, halfway into unconsciousness by the time he stopped against a tree. He saw, through a thick daze Liz snarl and attack the animal, attack its underbelly and cut at it, as if it was butter. The creature howled (or so it seemed), or rather, far more logical screamed like a pig. Ted winced as he attempted to move, coughing blood, feeling how his ribs knitted themselves, staring absolutely fascinated at the sight of the savage female form ahead. The other hunters joined her. She stuck her burning spear upwards, deep into the prey's body. He felt it pierce its heart, felt like the female the hard muscle give, as she cried out in joy and triumph.

The giant creature swayed and fell. More red mist rose and surrounded them all. Liz Warren stood above the fallen, shrunken form, covered in blood and guts.

The carcass was brought back to the village in triumph, dragged back on a sled like a labor of love. There would be a feast, and Liz knew there would be a lot of fucking. She would have known without knowing in her conscious thoughts. Her entire bloodstained body, inside and out readied itself for the Dance of Life. She looked at Ted through haze and mist, and felt a powerful, visceral heat fill her, fill her slowly, pleasantly, so natural and right. Their brothers and sisters at the village welcomed them, greeted them with passion and shared their joy of the moment.

They sat there, in the wide circle, between the tall fires and fed, fed life and fire. The hunters of the day had washed, had cleaned themselves in the river, but it seemed like the blood still danced and flowed on their bodies. The travelers felt the pieces of food in their mouth, felt it slide down the throat and being digested in their stomach. The villagers did, too, of course, but to those that had come from far away the sensation was a fairly new experience. They enjoyed every piece of meat passing through them, and it felt so good, so very good.

Some in the circle began caressing each other early, impatient, hungry, but Liz held back. Ted saw that she had something on her mind, and nodded encouragingly to her. Chini also noticed and turned towards them.

– The hunt was strange today, Liz said.

Several of the others nodded their agreement, clearly puzzled. What was on her mind, what they, too had experienced today was different, even to them.

She frowned.

– It almost felt like… like a spirit quest.

Ted recalled it in his Memory.

– It was a Path, Liz said, – and at its end the prey changed, transformed…

She, Ted and Chini choired it.

– … into the Dragon.

They all felt the chill then, inevitably, such a profound feeling of dread that it threatened to leave them shaken forever.

– It was a shared vision of the future, Chini said, – concerning the both of you, a trial you must overcome, and a warning that, whatever it is, you will face it alone.

Alone…

Liz and Ted looked at each other, reaching for each other, hugging each other hard.

– No way! Liz cried. – No fucking way!

They all felt the mood, the good, the bad and the ugly. It didn't hurt them. Life, in all its many forms was well known to them. The manifold of fear, excitement, fire and ashes ruled them side by side. Feeding was done and Hunger took its place, like night followed day, and day followed night.

– You are the priestess. Ted spoke to Chini, in a whirl of fire and ashes. – You're used to interpret spirit guests, right?

– Yes, Chini replied

He didn't close his eyes, but still saw what was far, far away. His Farsight, both its space and time impressed itself upon him. In the midst of dancing fire he Saw. It was almost an independent thing, a part of his dancing Shadow. He saw the children, parts of many tribes, many colors, and the new world in their wake, a pipe dream without power, without the brutal, expedient force of life made manifest.

Then, the pressure beneath his forehead truly made itself known, rising with a vengeance. He was sound asleep, resting peacefully among many warm and pleasant bodies, but in more ways than one, than many… he didn't sleep at all.

He relived the hunt, experienced it all in its vivid reality, and this time there was no doubt it was a vision. The colors were different, the scope so much bigger. He saw the jungle, but also the world around it. The hunt lasted longer this time, much longer. Hours turned to days, many days, as the tired but determined hunters crossed valleys and mountains and plains, deserts and seas, as the jungle stayed with them, like a living, breathing thing,

Linda was with them. Betty was there. And others he didn't recognize. The thing they were chasing stamped the ground and each step it took shook the Earth, and Ted knew it was his feet, his wings creating the storm sounding in their ears.

This time it was Liz that attacked it first, that lay bleeding and broken in the corner, and he that made a stab at it with his spear, his spear hitting nothing but air.

And then they were no longer in the jungle, and the vision turned to one he had had before. He walked on a road, and in the far, far mountains he saw what was always there.

They were no longer in the jungle. He stood on an arena, clutching his spear, his spear of destiny, and before him, ahead of him was his opponent, was the Dragon.

## 5

They experienced days, life as fractions of time. They turned that way, and a month, a *moon* passed. It was all just a blur, a blur of time. They turned another, and a season had passed.

And yet, they could recall everything, every single event of their life in the village with immaculate clarity and detail. A tear, a tear of blood in the corner of the eye of Laurie's child. A sigh in the trees surrounding the village. The increased flow of the river. It was all there, constantly passing in and out of consciousness, sometimes like a trickle, sometimes like the river.

Time is not a river, but an overflow, flooding all fields, all lands.

Ted walked effortlessly through the jungle. The ground was both soft and firm beneath his feet. His feet had been made to move on this ground. His senses had been developed through millions of years of evolution to notice the slightest change in his surroundings.

He frowned. The ground turned hard. Buildings rose around him in place of the trees. He walked through the streets of the city of New York, a place he had never been, but recognized easily. The dream, the vision was once more so vivid, so pervasive that it threatened to become real.

In a moment, in a flash it faded away and he breathed a sigh of relief, overwhelmed by despair.

He had long since grown used to the heat and humidity of the jungle. It had become second nature to him, as if he had never spent most of his life in a completely different environment. Everything worked better out here, in the wilderness, and his senses, astute to begin with turned out to be almost more than he could bear.

There was light in one of the huts, in the hut Hagman and mate shared. The dark glow from a torch flickered in Ted's vision. All batteries had failed long ago. He walked into the hut, knowing that Chini tailed him.

Hagman and mate, and almost all his loyal henchmen were there, joined around a primitive table. Ted felt a feeling of disappointment, one he quickly quenched.

– I concur, Alanis nodded, looking at her mate with approval, with shining eyes. – The topography, the tales… everything fits.

Chini said a word, one single sound, in one exhaling breath.

– The City of Light. Hagman almost jumped through the ceiling. – That was what you said, wasn't it?

She looked at Ted, a little lost.

– Yes, Warren nodded. – That was what she said.

Liz and Laurie were there, too, behind him, and that also failed to surprise him.

Chini said more, a whole series of syllables.

Ted knew Hagman understood or understood most of it, but he translated anyway.

– It is also called the Valley of Death, or the Valley of Lost Hopes. Take your pick.

– I knew it, Hagman cried, not really listening. – I knew it was here somewhere.

No one pointed out to him that «here», in this context, was most of Northern or Northeastern South America.

– We have told you before, Liz frowned. – There never has been a city of light. It's all just legends and exaggerations. The fabled Atlantis was merely a few huts, a village in a forest in the desert.

He looked incredulous at her, exchanging glances with Alanis, and they both looked bewildered at the girl, as if they couldn't really fathom what she was saying.

Both Liz and Laurie stepped forward.

– Allow us to show you

Richard and Alanis nodded hesitatingly, not really agreeing.

Laurie put one hand on Liz's brow and one on both Richard and Alanis' head.

There was a flash, one of shadow, and the two relived the memories, the words she had read, the vision resting in Liz' mind. They experienced the tale, the origin of Lillith, of the village in the forest, in the desert, and its ultimate destruction, and were absolutely stunned when the tale was done, when Laurie removed her hand.

– You found this in a book written by a woman who isn't born yet? Hagman said.

– Yes, Liz said, – and it triggered the visions, creating the close to complete picture.

– Remarkable, he shook his head, – absolutely remarkable.

– It feels right, doesn't it, she pushed him, pushed them, – feels *true?*

He nodded slowly.

– I've seen or heard stranger stories, far less believable.

They all looked at Alanis. She returned their look with a desperate flair in her eyes.

– But even if your vision was accurate, there might still be a Valley of Kings. You said so yourself.

– There might be or might have been, Liz kept frowning, – but it could mean anything. The Valley of Kings in Egypt, for instance was given that name thousands of years after the so called kings or pharaohs were dead and buried, and there are only a few ruins or abandoned *buildings,* and that's all it ever was anyway.

Alanis shook here head, looking at Richard.

– There must be something to it, she insisted. – There must be!

The couple took each other's hands and nodded, and the determination and sadness and desperation in them reverberated through Ted, Liz, Laurie and Chini. All four of them nodded slowly.

Ted and Chin were alone by the fall later.

– We have to leave, anyway, he said, – and following the pipe dream of Richard and Alanis is just as good an occasion as another.

– You're so young, she said hotly, – but I keep seeing the world in your fire. You want to help your friends, a very admirable goal.

– We have to leave, he insisted. – The tribe is growing too big, too big for the game. The hunt isn't actually *failing*. The tribe needs too much game to sustain itself. When we're gone the balance will reset itself.

– But you are the tribe, she frowned, – all of you.

– And we will always be.

The roar of the fall softened a bit, fading to silence a few, precious moments.

– I see. She nodded somberly. – I see, as I've always seen. You are not made for this tiny spot of the world.

– The world has become so small, he said. – It will find its way here, with its fake claws and fangs. The servants of the Machine will find you. It may take a while before they come, but they will.

– I know.

For the first time he saw despair in her eyes.

She held something in her hands, something in a piece of skin, He realized startled that it had been there all the time tonight.

- This is yours, she said, - at least for now.

She handed it to him, and he exposed it to his scrutiny. It was a statue, old and withered, polished and shiny of two women, standing back to back, their bodies and heads joined.

- She's Janus, Chini said, - the one that are many, the many that are one, two halves of the whole. The tribe has carried this representation with us since time before memory.

He touched it, and impressions flooded his consciousness, and he strived to make sense of it all.

– Your daughter will find you, Glow said. – All your daughters will find you, and you will have many. They will come to you, blood drawn by blood, the strongest pull there is.

Her words touched him. His blood moved in his veins.

– And you? He grabbed her hand.

– I don't know. She frowned. – Perhaps.

– I saw you, he said, – during the *hunt*. You were there.

And she lit up like a torch.

And sleep claimed him, claimed them all late that night, as all of them renewed their kinship one final time, as they sat in the wide circle around the fire, and exchanged thoughts and passions. His was a jumble of dreams of past, present and future, and what would never be.

When the decision had been made everything happened surprisingly fast.

They bid their farewell at midday three days later. There was no farewell.

– Two tribes met and became One, Chini said. – Once upon a time, as time flows they will become One again.

Hands, bodies met and parted, in joy and sadness, and the travelers moved on, and they were once again alone in the jungle, as the jungle became their home more than ever before, and what they left behind faded into pinpricks in the vast growth surrounding them.

## Chapter Fourteen: The invisible trail

The Long Walk continued, one they saw no end to.

They passed through a no man's land between the territories of two tribes to the north, fully alert and prepared to defend themselves, but in the end it proved unnecessary. The jungle remained peaceful. They slipped through without incident.

The choir of the jungle rose within them, even more than before, into something tangible. It stayed with them, no matter what they did, an ongoing, eternal presence in their lives. To live in the jungle, in one place was one thing. To constantly move around in its basin was something completely different. Their brothers and sisters in that other half moon tribe had been born into it and took it for granted, something the travelers would never do.

They were heading north, setting the course at dusk, just before the sun would fade away in the horizon in the west. The sky was the sole tangible reference point they had. Everything else looked exactly the same. One night or a few nights in one place didn't breed familiarity. They had never been more lost than they were right now.

There was a world outside this endless stretch of green and moisture and pervasive life, they knew that, but it was presumably far away on all sides.

Casual observers would have difficulty distinguish them from any other native group moving through the jungle. One would notice the guns, of course, but that, in itself wasn't sufficient to make them stand out. None of them really looked white or even remotely civilized anymore, especially since skin and hair were covered by camouflage dirt and colors. They looked like the very image of a nomadic tribe.

The mothers carried the babies in tiny sacks on their backs. Their maneuverability was hardly hampered in any way. Movement was fluid, like that of all of the travelers. The members of the tribe moved like one, and they were one with their surroundings, with all its twists and turns.

They were Wild, both in outward appearance and skin deep.

Ted Warren sensed it, sensed the beautiful savagery in them all, and it pleased him beyond anything.

Laurie and Liz alternated at taking point, each using their unique abilities to sniff out potential dangers. They returned to him now and then, reporting their impressions close up, an act fairly unnecessary, since he could sense what they sensed from far away.

They displayed themselves to him, and their poignant smells reeked in his nostrils. Their sex and those of all the females smelled all the time, even not long after they had been bathing. The males' cocks hardened often, and their smells were equally evident to the females. Scents mingled and created a constant and heavy presence of fervor in the air. Ted felt the continuous fever of expectation linger in everybody's mind.

Occasionally they found a river and knelt by its shore to drink and to wash and cool their sweaty and heated bodies. Laurie stood in the stream and fondled her large breasts, and milk flowed from the nipples. Ted felt himself turning hard in an instant. All the females displayed themselves, pleased by the certainty of being looked at with hungry eyes. Everybody knew the march would be cut short today.

Liz stretched pleasantly in Ted's arms a few hours later. Having been taken many times her passion burned on a low flame, but was still there, a constant and lasting presence, one she recognized in everybody.

– We're beasts, she mumbled in his armpit. – Beasts!

All the females carried child, now, except her. She didn't mind, really, and could do without the extra weight impeding her movements. The others had to stop hunting about four to five moons into the pregnancy. She excelled in it, returning bloody and with a huge, triumphant grin on her face and the game thrown casually across her shoulder.

They welcomed her, in a quiet frenzy of thoughts, scents, touches and emotions.

– I didn't have to use my powers this time, she said. – I wasn't even tempted. I love my powers, but I don't want to get dependant on them. There might come a time when such prudence might prove essential.

Her thoughts went to the needles they carried with them, a reminder of what the world was, and she knew, based on the flicker she saw in Ted's eyes and sensed in his depths that his thoughts centered on similar subjects.

This evening turned quieter, less frantic. They used the opportunity to reflect and ponder, both on their own lives and existence in general. The human beings gathered in the circle around the fire, and consumed the fresh kill, and felt time and space itself pass through them.

– It's there, Laurie said, excited like a kid, – here, there and everywhere. It is right in front of everybody, both tangible and not. One might simply reach for it, and grab it, and now we don't even have to do that. It… it is like something I have missed my entire life and now is here.

She hit her chest repeatedly. They looked at her with affection in their eyes.

Perhaps she had changed the most during the months since the crash. The vindictive brat was almost gone, only glimpsed in passing. It didn't define her anymore.

Powers or not, they all felt it. Out there, in the wilderness, there was no way they could hide from themselves and the world.

They were in touch with their deepest instincts, and they didn't have to define or interpret it at all. It didn't need any words or considerations. It… it…

– It *is,* Alanis stated amazed.

Hands grabbed hands, and the circle completed itself. Hands touched. Hands touched skin, in affection, not necessarily lust. Dissolved smiles pulled close. Lips touched, tasted close scents. They embraced, two and two, all and all, standing close, in a cluster in the large world surrounding them.

– It is as if I am blind, Laurie giggled amazed. – All my other senses are ablaze with power.

– You can see better than you ever have, Liz said kindly.

– Yes! Laurie grabbed her hand and kissed it. – I do. I do!

It was raining. It didn't bother them, bothered them even less than it had the last year. The rain wasn't anything other, separate from them. The very air they inhaled was already a part of them all. Even as they exhaled that part remained, beyond valuable, beyond precious. They moved, moved in accordance to each other, and the trees and animals and the jungle, in the vast existence of the Universe, laughing both within and without.

Spirits rose in the air, spread into the surrounding jungle. They spread, spread out like a flower, its scent touching all fields, all forests and mountains. Ted and Liz shook as cold fever briefly touched them. They attempted, halfheartedly to conceal the sense of dread from the others, in vain.

But even that, even the brutal facts of life failed to impress them this night.

It *is,* the draft between the trees whispered, neither good nor bad.

Richard broke the silence, the unspoken agreement, removing them from the true world, and it felt like dying. They couldn't keep themselves from glaring at him.

– It has many names, he lectured. – I guess as many as there are human societies… Cibola, Xanadu, Atlantis…

– They're all myths, Liz lectured him, striving to hold back her anger, to hold on to the sense of wonder. – As stated, there might have existed places with names like that or similar, but their importance and grandeur were greatly exaggerated, and later their legends mixed with mankind's yearnings for what some people see as perfection, but is really a state of grace that will, fortunately not never exist. There's no Nirvana, or Heaven awaiting us at the end of the road, nor should there ever be. There's only continued existence, an infinite «wheel» without beginning or end.

A ruin, yet another overgrown ruin passed them by one night or two. Nothing or very little separated this one from what they had seen before or from what followed. They moved in its revolting shadow, long after they had left it behind.

– Words fall like sand, Liz hummed, – and in the grand scheme they matter not.

Her smile and her song surrounded them, touched them. They reached out to her as well, and touched her. She felt it, like a hammer of soft water caressing her skin and mind and eternal Self.

She frowned, as the first sign expressed itself. They felt it. She moved away from them a bit, into a sandbank by the river. The sharp pain came, and blood flooded her thighs and the ground she stood on. Less than half of it reached the river, but even so its water turned red in a matter of moments, turned red from side to side of the soft-flowing currents, as if dozens of people had just died and been turned to shreds. Plants by her feet withered and died. Even the trees nearby reacted almost instantaneously and whined in pain.

But they all knew, like they had seen so many times, now, that tomorrow, or the day after tomorrow there would be a growth on this place totally exceeding any sort of sensible effect.

The trail, not always so invisible stretched endlessly behind and in front of them.

Alanis reached full term on a day of rain and fury in the heavens. Rain poured and serial lightning crossed the sky. Neither the continuous shower nor the electrical fury bothered them. The rain was hot and a bubble of silence seemed to isolate them from the world, even as they embraced it with all their hearts.

The child's scream overpowered that of nature around them, and they celebrated.

Days and nights without number passed. The invisible trail led them north, ever north. They had long since stopped measuring time and experienced it pretty much like their brethren in that other tribe far to the south had taught them, like a series of interconnecting events, births, hunts, places and anything impressing itself on them in the unending similarity, the endless variety of the jungle.

– Why north? Liz' always inquisitive mind wanted to know.

– Why not? Ted shrugged, deliberately, very deliberately.

– What if we had chosen south instead, or west or east? It would be just as logical or probable or…

– All trails lead to Rome, he noted.

She stared open-mouthed at him.

The girl, now close to the end of her teenage years had grown both taller and bigger. She towered above everybody in the tribe, except Ted, a feral creature no longer scaring any of them, but inspiring them all.

Ted savored the sight of her, as she sat there with the statue, Chini's gift in her hand.

- The ancient Mother, she said.

He nodded. Laurie stared mesmerized at it. Richard and Alanis studied it. It didn't evoke the same powerful sense of recognition in them, but there was interest, for obvious reasons.

- She had it in her possession all the time, Richard said, - and didn't show us.

- It was her parting gift, Ted said curtly.

Even Richard got the point.

- This is thousands of years old, isn't it? Liz asked the couple.

- I would bet a lot on that, Alanis said, clearly beyond dizzy, light headed. – Even though we would need equipment for verification, I would say it predates most of the known cities and early civilizations. There's very little comparison to anything I've seen before. It's older and more sophisticated…

- … and you have no idea how shocking that is, Richard completed her reasoning.

And at that moment they were unquestionable of one mind.

When they moved on the couple was filled with a renewed sense of purpose.

- Perhaps we shouldn't have showed it to them? Liz said to Ted.

- Truth never hurts, Ted said.

But he didn't sound very confident.

The tribe followed the trail north. Much of the rest faded in their mind.

They stopped a bit by yet another pyramid, and for some totally obscure reason they decided to explore it. It was nothing much. They penetrated deep, as deep as they were able into its ruins, its forgotten halls and hallways. Ted and Liz walked first without light, and the others followed with torches. Most places the walls had tumbled down and left only narrow passageways, but there were also large, open spaces. They stopped by one such spot, in what probably had been the great hall of the building. Everybody stared at the decorated altar and walls, and they froze.

This is recent, Laurie sent to all the tribe members, the sting of fear tangible in her sending.

Let's get out of here, Ted ordered.

And they left, on full alert, far more silent than they had arrived.

It was easy to pick up signs of that other tribe, now, when they knew they were there. Liz and Laurie followed the tracks east, a short while before returning.

Nothing, their demeanor told the others, nothing close.

They headed further north, moving a bit faster than usual, jumpy for days, before slowly calming down again, returning to a somewhat relaxed mode.

– That was a place of worship, Liz shook. – A place of sacrifice, of…

She didn't have to paint a picture. They had all smelled the stink of blood.

Slowly, only slowly the experience faded in their short term recall.

They walked, headed north, ever north, staying on high alert every time they approached a ruin, or anything resembling a ruin, staying away from all of them.

Many days, large chunks of time just disappeared to them, fading into the nothingness of memory, they knew that, but they always managed to once more rise from such a state of savagery, and wasn't sure if that was a good or bad thing. Changes were visible in the others' face each time they focused on them, or so it seemed. Hair was longer. Facial paint had been changed and so on. Time flooded all fields, all forests and all mountains, and the details of its «passing» remained elusive in their mind. They continued on their invisible trail, the one they saw in their eye, but couldn't and didn't care to define. Ted and Liz imagined it as a glow in their mind, even if they wouldn't necessarily express it as such aloud, using words or any other sort of explicit expression.

They wondered if it was real or imagined, and knew it didn't matter.

The landscape changed, truly changed around them. They sensed it before they actually realized it. More ruins appeared to their left, but they weren't overgrown like all the rest they had passed on their trail. Startled and shocked it dawned on them that they were hearing voices and the sound of engines. They instantly pulled back and sought higher ground, to more easily assess the situation.

They stared at the small cluster of houses and buildings down there through a haze of time and memory. The sight felt incredibly weird and foreign, and left a hard knot in their belly.

– I feel like the caveman encountering civilization for the first time, Candy joked (and not).

Ants crawled through their veins, and they could swear the ants were real. Cold sweat broke through the skin all over their body.

Suddenly, upon glancing at each other they felt naked.

– Looks like a fairly large town or rather township, Richard remarked.

His voice sounded loud and shrieking in their ears. Suddenly they had difficulties looking at each other. They glanced around like thieves.

– We can't go down there without clothes. Phillip shook his head. – They will think we are… savages and slay us outright.

– Yes, we can, Ted said. – And they won't!

They knew what he was saying, but they were torn and didn't seem to know themselves anymore.

Reluctantly they left the jungle and made their way down to the village below. They caused a little bit of a stir at first, but some of the villagers were just one or two generations removed from their savage life, and were clearly used to encounter other tribes.

Then, slowly the stir increased and people began pointing and speaking among themselves, as it dawned on them that this wasn't an ordinary tribe. People in uniform showed up, too, and the travelers stopped, in the middle of the street, surrounded by curious and apprehensive and potentially aggressive locals.

Alanis tried Spanish first, but got mostly more puzzled looks. Then she spoke Portuguese, and clarity of sorts illuminated the locals' faces.

– We're Americans, she said. – Our plane crashed in a jungle pretty far away… more than a year… close to two years ago. We would appreciate any assistance you could offer us.

They were in Brazil, and strangely enough not that far off their original flight path.

Old names returned. Old behavior slowly reasserted itself. There was a hotel of sorts down the street. They were brought there, the town people slowly relaxing, but not loosing their skeptical look.

– I'm afraid we don't have any money, now, Alanis said, – but we can get some fairly quickly.

The hotel had communications. Alanis and Richard, after taking the time to convince the skeptical hotel manager both had their phone calls. They were clearly hesitant, slow to return to the life they had once known.

The savages stood at the center of the reception area. Nice-dressed people glared at them from all sides. Laurie and a few more smiled back, but it wasn't really that convincing under all the shit and body paint.

– Good news, Richard told the group. – We haven't been declared dead, not legally at least. Our fortunes have also been managed fairly well. We are not broke.

He added, as an afterthought.

Liz and Ted wondered if anybody, anyone out there had missed them, had grieved for them.

– Help is on the way. It will take some time. We're still far into the woods, so to speak.

Richard changed. They saw him, minute by minute returning to the person he had been, an eternity, a timeless time ago.

Everybody showered. The «hotel» was almost empty. There was enough room for them all. They used cold water. Most of the colors etched on their skin disappeared. They had trouble breathing in the tiny, closed off rooms.

The local bank, with only one employee, the director set them up with tailors the moment the confirmation of their elevated monetary status reached him. They all practically shook their head in bewilderment.

Something shouted something to them, clearly an insult, as they walked down the street, still dressed or undressed in a few, ragged clothes given them by the local church.

– «White Indians», Alanis said, – loosely translated.

– They have forgotten who they were, Laurie said sadly, – and they don't want to remember.

But this was a poor area, and the Americans' arrival was the gold rush of the year. They were treated with the servility money granted them. The tailors «grossly overcharged them», as Richard put it, before shrugging.

These clothes, new and clean and without holes felt twice as strange. They returned to the hotel afterwards, still carrying the children in straps and bags. Everybody stayed together in two of the adjacent, bigger rooms the rest of the day and evening. When it was time for sleep, they knew, from experience that it would be close to impossible for them to sleep in the beds.

They lay there, on the floor, breathing together in the darkness, wide awake.

Ted finally rose.

– This won't work, he declared, quite unnecessary.

They walked into the jungle, with their weapons and stayed there, in the silence and noise of life around them for the night, and slept like babies.

## 2

The deluge began two days later. Representatives from Richard's and Alanis' companies arrived and with them journalists and news media from all over the world. The small town was turned totally on its head and its population pulled even further into the twentieth century. Every surviving member from the lost expedition was photographed up and down, their images spread across the world.

– The flashes hurt my eyes, Laurie complained.

– Don't worry, honey, Alanis shrugged. – This is only temporary. And will certainly help us in our endeavor.

She added, in an optimistic tone.

The money thrown at them by sponsors already would certainly give her right.

Ted and Liz glanced at each other, knowing a bit of the media and how it worked, having been through its wringer several times.

– It seems like we can't avoid publicity, even if we try, Ted pondered. – We seem to end up on the front pages at uneven intervals.

– Perhaps that is our destiny, Liz joked, only half joking.

Richard and Alanis were really the news of the hour and fortunately received most of the attention, but everybody got their share. The babies voiced their displeasure in very vocal and loud ways all day.

Finally, at night, when everything turned fairly quiet, except for a portable stereo a journalist had brought with him, they could still hear the thin, loud wails produced by the powerful lungs and boundless frustration.

– It's strange, Phillip said. – Their cries never bothered me in the jungle. They didn't seem *loud* at all, if you know what I mean.

– I know exactly what you mean. Liz nodded and caressed his cheek.

More sore and tired laughter rose from the small group standing on the balcony of the fairly large house, looking at the small town from the hills.

Richard and Alanis had rented it, and kicked out the owner.

Everybody had their own beds, now, and slowly they began using them, even though they occasionally slept on the floor.

The jungle called out to them, but its lure slowly faded in their minds, though not in their souls. It haunted their dreams. In their dreams they returned to the horrible pyramid of fear they had fled from. Its horrible images and sensations gave them no peace or understanding.

– What do you think it means? Liz asked.

She and Ted sought to the mountaintop nearby, where they could see both ways, both into the infinite jungle growth and the increasingly rural and urban communities to the north and east.

– I don't know. The frustration was evident in his voice. – I know it means nothing good.

Liz phoned Trudy in Colorado, but it wasn't really necessary. Trudy had already heard the news. She had been worried, even though she didn't sound too vivid about it, as if that of her daughter and nephew surviving a plane crash and months in the jungle was a mere trifle.

– I'm okay, mom, Liz said. – In fact I'm more than ok. Ted is, too. Say hello to Michelle from us.

– You've grown, haven't you, Trudy said. – The hardship and danger have made you more than you were.

It was as if the phone line suddenly turned bad. It began cracking and breaking up. The girl stared at the phone. She waited for minutes for the connection to return, but it didn't and she hung up.

Liz walked the city streets in bright daylight, wearing the expensive clothes Alanis had procured for her. It was a busy day in town. Every day was busy these days. It hardly resembled the town they had arrived in, such a short while ago. She waved to some of the villagers passing her on the opposite side of the street. They returned the wave reluctantly.

The «city hall», a derelict old building rested to the right, at the end of the street, the end of the road. The reality or the association, she couldn't tell which gave her the chills. She walked up quirky old stairs. It still felt weird after the years in the jungle. Everything felt off.

The mayor sat behind his desk, flanked by his three secretaries. The sense of unrest, of worry persisted. He scared her, and that fact scared her more, and she worked hard to mask her emotions. She saw him as a giant in her mind, even though he looked quite ordinary in her eyes. His three secretaries, mistresses looked at him with undiminished love in their eyes. They were his, belonged to him. He had a power, a sort of charisma power that could be devastating to those not aware of it. She imagined he grew to that scary giant she saw in her mind.

In another world, a parallel to this one he was all-powerful and ruled over a vast jungle kingdom. Perhaps civilization had neutered him, perhaps the circumstances were different. The latter was certainly true.

She experienced it all, as she occasionally did, like flashes in her mind, and it felt very, very real.

– *Hola,* Senorita Kendall, he greeted her, with his usual sleazy grin, – to what do we own the pleasure?

It's Warren, you dumb fuck, she thought.

– I bring the papers you requested from Mr. Hagman, Senor, she replied, playing the dutiful secretary.

She put the papers on the desk with a deliberate, patronizing smile.

He squirmed and shrank in his seat. Relief and triumph rode her. He didn't know, wasn't aware of his potentially awesome power, believing just like the others in town that he was just a ladies' man.

The air outside suddenly felt so good, and her laughter yet again turned wild and carefree. He wasn't an obstacle on their Path, but was merely one of hundreds of concerns they had to deal with in their lives. Relief flooded her, even though a tiny amount of doubt and anxiety remained.

She wanted to confide in Ted, discuss with him what had to be done, but she held back. There were really only two choices of dealing with the mayor and people like him: leave him be or kill him. Any other half measure would only risk awakening his full power.

Ted and the others waved to her from the garden outside their house, their «Palace» in the hills. She returned the wave, putting up a brave face.

He's still just a kid at heart, she thought glumly.

In another part of the house Richard and Alanis resided, and held constant meetings with underlings and advisers. She sensed them, too, their negative energy, and it gave her a headache. Since her latest power-boost she had been able to pick up so much more of what happened in her surroundings, and it wasn't always a good thing.

It felt like she had to relearn the use of her powers all over again. It felt like…

… like she didn't have to worry about the mayor, worry about anything.

She joined what had become her brethren in the garden. They received her with embraces and kisses and caresses, and she felt accepted, felt loved.

It was all a pleasant jumble of impressions and interaction. The touch made her sense the others' moods better, and it empowered and encouraged her. The young girl, hardened by life felt the soft spot inside grow and multiply, as if all the grief and hardship faded into unimportance.

– So, has anything exciting happened during the half hour I've been gone?

– Just more of the same, Laurie reported dryly. – Richard and Alanis are scouring the entire area and its people to quantify their search for the Golden City… any golden city. Sometimes they seem very encouraged. Other times it's nothing but mud.

She hesitated.

– Yes? Liz prompted her

– They're having difficulties handling the return to civilization, even more so than the rest of us, so they are overcompensating, embracing their previous obsession.

Everybody looked at each other with eyes resembling wounds.

– It has been difficult, Justine acknowledged. – The emptiness here, compared to the fullness of life in there.

They had become so astute all of them, even Laurie. Liz was proud of them.

The journalists usually swarmed them all the moment they left the estate, but today Richard and Alanis had actually invited the vultures in, and held an impromptu press conference… again. Liz couldn't avoid hearing them, even though she did her best to try. Her enhanced hearing was one thing she couldn't turn off, no matter what.

It was just noise in her ears, anyway.

The darkness of the night came like it did in the jungle, abrupt and comforting, and not all the electrical lights, all the new and shiny lighting in the streets could keep it at bay.

Insomnia kept plaguing Liz. Nothing helped. She remained wide awake, without being able to tell why. In her desperation she attempted sedatives, but it didn't help and it didn't really work on her anyway. Not even large doses of the poison worked more than a few minutes at best (at worst), and she was kind of relieved.

The group coupling, the kind and demanding hands and lips helped on her mental state, but not on her insomnia. In her desperation she attempted abstention for a few nights, smiling apologetically and heading into the jungle alone, to no avail.

After one night, where she did sleep, she awoke screaming and bathed in ice-cold sweat, not remembering anything of her nightmare.

– The jungle *scares* me, she whispered, sobbing with no tears, seeking the comfort in Ted's arms.

It was such an outlandish statement coming from her that it made the others uncomfortable. She noticed that and pulled herself together with an effort.

But she was unable to hide her plight from them anymore. Ted had probably known all the time, and given her space. A warm, wet feeling rose in her when she looked at him.

– It's never *quiet* here, Laurie said abruptly, unexpectedly, after a prolonged silence. – There's noise here, all the time. In the jungle there's nothing like that, no *noise*.

– She's right, of course, Liz complained to Ted later, when they were alone, when they stood on the roof and looked across the city, – but she doesn't really understand. It's far worse than that. The noise is everywhere. The light from the city dulls the light from the stars, like everything about the city dulls *all* natural sensations.

The others had just faded away around them, and they found themselves alone.

They took in the sight of the city, deliberately, opening themselves up to its corruption, forcing it on themselves. Something very similar to pain cut through them.

– Look at it, she spat. – In just a few weeks it has gone from bad to worse, has grown to almost twice its previous size, all because of two people's megalomania.

Circus Hagman had brought a lot of new business and activity to the city. When it left it would leave only ashes behind.

Liz shook her head.

– Something is wrong, I mean really, urgently wrong, but I can't pinpoint it, can't see it or identify it. It's like a dream without focus, with no tangible reality.

He desired her. She could tell, even without his hungry eyes, but she was restless, beside herself, and couldn't do it, couldn't give in to her own desires.

– There is something we can try, she said slowly, hesitatingly, passionately, decisively, – something I saw in one of Alanis' books.

He knew what she was talking about, saw it in her eyes, and an icy chill passed through him.

– You want to perform the *pain* ritual? Alanis said stunned.

– Yes! The girl nodded. – You have seen it, haven't you, seen it being performed. You know in detail how it is done?

– Yes, yes. Alanis mused. – I have, but still... this is amazing, an absolute amazing change...

– It was only for tourists, Richard shrugged. – The shaman had been a drunk for years, and performed for a few dimes. The participating villagers did it for drinks.

Alanis turned abruptly, raising a finger at him, opening her mouth to speak her mind, but relented and turned back to the girl.

– I have always wanted to see it, she said, – to see it *work*.

– It's dangerous, Richard insisted. – Especially if it works.

– There are precautions we can take, Alanis said fast and desperately to the girl. – You guys know what you are doing and thus...

– You don't need to sell it to me, the girl said. – I approached you, remember.

Alanis bowed her head in shame.

But the glow of sick curiosity remained in her eyes.

The drums began beating just before the tropic, abrupt darkness the next day. Time jumped to that point, without any noticeable interim. Liz certainly didn't notice time passing. She didn't sleep, but sat in the middle of the street the entire day. The sun burned her body and mind. She prepared there, in her own world. Ted paced back and forth on the top floor of the house, not really moving, unable to reach that state of calm, of meditation. Objects moved around him, seemingly by themselves all day. He attempted to control the occasional bursts of power, but couldn't even do that.

Laurie sat in a chair, unmoving, rocking back and forth, her arms clutching her feet, her feet pulled up to her hips. The sun raced across the sky. Ted blinked once and it was practically gone, falling red and dying in the western horizon. During the time-span of that single blink a thousand shiny pearls of sweat flowed from his skin.

The drums began beating just before the tropic, abrupt darkness. Shadowy sparks erupted from Liz' frame, and began doing so to a lesser degree around Ted, too. Liz undressed. Justine and Phillip painted her with their fingers, painstakingly following Alanis' instructions.

Tall fires were built and lit at the square marketplace at the center of the town. Flames danced as they reached for the darkness above, seemingly swallowed by it, by the infinite, the vastness nothing or no one would ever see the end of. Nude dancers swayed between the sources of sweltering heat. Swollen cocks and breasts jumped up and down on sweaty bodies.

Ted and Liz and Laurie recognized Alanis' sick fascination, the beyond curious need to know like a mirror to their own, and they couldn't say what was true and what was reflection. They had all once again become strangers to each other and themselves.

Thunder rolled in from the horizon, dry and low. There were no clouds in the sky, no moisture but sweaty bodies between the pulsing fires. Open mouths gasped for air, even as air filled their lungs and bubbled their blood.

– «Pain is the answer», Alanis read from her own text, her own translations. – «Pain opens up everything, every little corner and shade of the soul, granting insight, understanding of the workings of the Universe, of the vast Shadow roaming it».

Liz began by repeating her words in English. It sounded different, but it was the same words, the same context and texture.

But there was something there making the anthropologist frown, making tinges of fear ice her bones.

She didn't have to repeat it more than a few times, before the young girl got it right, before Elizabeth Warren could repeat it without help.

– That is so amazing, she gasped. – Your short-time memory is nothing short of phenomenal.

Liz stood between the three of them, her body a painting of symbols and images. First they had been crude, formed by hands and pencils and brushes, but then they began taking on a different appearance, began dancing and flowing on her skin like mercury, or so it seemed to those watching her.

She walked to the center of the square and sat down on her ass between the five fires.

She began by reciting the words, phrases and spells in English. They couldn't hear her at first, but then they did, over all the noise and chanting. She put down the five sticks on the ground by her side.

Then, it was no longer English and completely different, not the same words or context or texture, but the same still, and they understood her, understood better than before what she was saying.

– «Memory fades, but pain is eternal».

She picked one of the sticks, rolling her fist around it, holding the other hand up.

– «Pain succeeds where everything else fails».

The spectators looked at her in horror as she stabbed herself in the arm, as she pushed the dull point of the stick straight through the flesh until it appeared on the other side. She screamed, and everybody present screamed with her. There were loud cracks as windows and walls fractured in the buildings surrounding the square.

She kept speaking, kept chanting, and the words, and the words' meaning kept changing further, as she began reciting far more text than Alanis had taught her, and kept doing so, as she picked the second stick, strived to make her hand on the penetrated arm work, as she stabbed her other arm, as she kept reciting, even through the screaming. In the brief scream was a howl of a thousand wounded beasts.

– Why isn't she healing? Phillip almost shouted to Ted. – Why isn't her body rejecting the intrusion?

He knew the answer to that, and didn't need Ted to answer, and he didn't.

She kept it from happening. Her desperation and iron will was overriding the functions of her body.

Her leg pulled up by itself. She grabbed it with one hand and penetrated its fleshy part with the stick with the other.

A brick pulled from a wall flew through the air and hit a man. His arm broke with a loud, sick sound, and his scream joined that of the witch. Everybody heard tiny popping sounds as all kinds of objects, big and small started flying around, briefly, before settling.

The witch penetrated her second leg. They waited for the stick and stones to fly, but nothing happened.

A woman screamed short and sharp, as an invisible force pulled in her skin, almost tearing it off her bones. People's hair blew in the wind (there was no wind). People heard hisses in their ears, and imagined that claws and fangs ripped the air close to their skin, occasionally drawing blood, pain and anxiety ruling them tooth and claw.

The witch picked the final stick from the bloody and dusty ground. She took it in both her slippery hands and pushed in into her belly.

The flames from the five fires were pulled towards her, hungry mouths eager to devour the creature daring to call them. The dancers began slowing down, began stumbling, began falling, dropping like flies. Hands hammering the drums turned weak and rubbery and sounds ended in a cascade of discord.

Liz collapsed. She fell to her side and lay still, no longer visibly breathing. People wanted to come to her aid. Ted stopped them with one word.

– Wait, he said.

They stared at her, at the half unconscious creature there on the ground, as the paintings and words and spells slowly faded, as her powerful acid sweat dissolved it all. Everybody, except Ted watched, as the sticks pushed themselves from her body and fired through the air like pin balls, as her wounds closed, and she slowly rose to face Ted, as he walked to her.

– Nothing, she mumbled, her mouth filled with blood. – Nothing beyond the wall of pain.

She had bitten off a large part of her tongue. It fizzled and burned as she spat it out and it hit the ground. Her tongue healed and she licked her lips, and the persistent taste of blood cleared her eyes.

# Chapter Fifteen: Vengeance is mine - Part 3

## DISTANT BUTTERFLY WINGS

### The World at War - France 1944

There was only one sentence, so finite and so final.

«We've found him».

Virgil didn't really stand there when he said that. He wasn't truly in the room and faded quickly away before their eyes afterwards.

They heard him upstairs, packing. Jonas heard him, too, or imagined he heard him. James already sat in the hall, waiting, oiling his guns.

Rachel turned her tearstained face towards Nick.

– I told him, she said with venom and sadness in her voice. – I told him about me. I was desperate for him to change his mind.

It was as if she wanted to drive the point in, with a stake.

She and James had quarreled for days with a desperation and despair Jonas easily recognized.

Nick didn't reply, not with words, anyway. Jonas felt left out, abandoned.

– Should I have postponed it? Would that have helped any? He was already leaving me. He has always been leaving me.

James heard it in the hall. He couldn't avoid hearing it.

The children were playing in the garden, by the mausoleum, wild and carefree.

That comforted them all a bit, just a bit.

Virgil descended the stairs. He looked as dead as Jonas had ever seen him, filled with a pitch black life.

James picked up his rucksack.

Rachel took one step forward, gazing imploringly at him.

– Don't go, she pleaded.

James froze.

– Don't you see? James Warren told his beloved, as if Virgil wasn't there, and he truly wasn't. – I have to go with him, to help him. No one is anything even approaching «safe» as long as a creature like Powell lives. Perhaps when he is dead and gone we can… we can all put this behind us and start to live, to live again.

Rachel wanted to say more, but she was unable to do so. There was nothing more to say.

– Is it possible to hate a man you've never met? Jonas wondered. – I'm not sure. But what I feel towards Lance Powell is very close to how I have always imagined hatred. I know that.

He grabbed his coat from the closet.

– I'm coming with you.

– This isn't your fight, Virgil said, and for one moment there was life, emotion in his voice.

– It isn't? Jonas curled his left hand into a fist. – *It isn't?*

Virgil nodded imperceptibly. There was nothing left to say.

Jonas didn't bring anything more than his coat, and the gun in it. He had entered the Warren household with nothing and left with nothing.

No goodbyes were voiced, only nods and more gazes of desperation, of despair. The three of them left, and the house grew even emptier, resembling even more the mausoleum outside.

Rachel and Nick faced each other. She made him look at her.

– He won't be back, she said, drying saliva from the corner of her mouth. – He has left me, that asshole.

She was changing before his eyes, into the person he remembered from a distant dream.

– There's nothing for me here.

The children are listening, he sent to her, cautioning her.

She ignored him with a spiteful look and spiteful thoughts.

– I wanted revenge at first, when I first sought your company, I did. I wanted to be my mother, not myself. But that changed. I changed. I love him, Nick.

There was no preparation, no packing. He closed his eyes briefly, and when he opened them again she was gone. The entrance door was ajar. In a sudden panic he rushed out on the stairs, but she was nowhere to be seen. He didn't sense her thoughts anywhere, no matter how hard he strained.

It took him a few minutes to look through the house, as a penance, but he didn't find her. Rachel was gone, too.

## 2

The house gave way to the war-thorn London streets. The three of them walked, not speaking, not looking at each other. War-thorn streets gave way to the steady rhythm of the train. Virgil sat there, staring out of the window. They kept their silence and hardly even acknowledged each other's presence, except when they had to, for practical reasons. Virgil sat there, allowing the vast black hole within to fill him, fill him to the brim, unconditionally. He let go, and he felt something stir, something that had been dormant his entire life.

The train surged through the landscape, slowed down to a halt in his mind, but he didn't care.

He wasn't in a hurry.

The three of them didn't speak, not for hours. The silence rose like a wall between them, but they still felt close to each other, as if an extra strong type of glue connected them across the gulf of air. James looked out of the window, glanced at the people walking up and down the isle. Virgil didn't really do that. His eyes worked, but they didn't move. He turned his head on occasion to pay for coffee or food or show his «ticket», his pass card, but his eyes didn't move in his skull, never wavered from their relentless stare.

Jonas studied Virgil for signs of life, but didn't find any. It was amazing that the man opposite him could move at all.

The train passed through war-torn Britain. The London suburbs, where there were ruins everywhere they turned their attention, the countryside that seemed to be filled with wreckage of planes and machines. The Kent landscape looked ugly in their eyes. James forced himself to look. Jonas looked at the people walking up and down the aisle. Virgil didn't look at anything.

– He's a colonel in the allied command? Jonas asked, feeling a strong need to break the silence.

– I'm afraid so, James replied.

– Why? Jonas wondered.

– He joins the winners, Virgil shrugged. – It isn't surprising, is it?

– No, it isn't, James said, breaking in before Jonas could say anything. – It's also good tactics in other ways, especially… especially if…

– If he knows we're coming, Jonas completed for him.

– He's exposing his weakness, Virgil said. – He isn't immortal, just very hard to kill.

– But he seems to have dug himself in, James pondered. – Why is that? He could just slink away, and start over, as he has many times before.

– Perhaps… he's afraid of something… other than us, Jonas said, frowning. – Perhaps there is a good reason for that fear.

– It is something Nick should give careful thought, James nodded.

The two of them shuddered, easily understanding the further implications of what was being discussed.

Virgil didn't shudder, didn't move. Even when he moved he seemed like an automaton, a machine that hadn't been oiled in a long time.

– He's waiting for us, Virgil acknowledged.

Visions, soon to become fevered sensations hammered them all. Virgil gritted his teeth in pain. Something hurt them, hurt them all, something almost physical, lurking for so long beneath the surface, lurking no longer.

None in the trio had been part of the attack force in New Orleans twenty-seven years' earlier, but they had been given ample description of the battle, the savage, beyond deadly fighting. Vivid images assaulted their consciousness, as they kept hearing Nick's voice and sensing his projected thoughts from years ago, at Nancy's funeral which was the one time he had spoken about it in considerable detail.

And now, for the first time the three of them seemed to be in contact. Virgil, and to an extent also James seemed to be seething with a kind of energy, with power, displaying abilities they had never before revealed to Jonas. They didn't hide anymore, not to him, and not to themselves. Perhaps they had had trouble reconciling themselves with whom and what they were before, but no more.

And Jonas imagined he could hear their thoughts.

He imagined he felt muscles and bone move under his skin, making anxiety surge through him.

Strange notions and horrors surged through his veins and bones and the catching in his throat wouldn't let up, no matter how hard he fought to discard it.

The train stopped for a while, a good while. There was debris on the line. The waiting or the perceived uncertainty didn't truly affect the three. The image that endeared them, what they glimpsed at the end of the line was far too powerful for that.

A meal was served, of sorts. Jonas forgot what it contained the moment he devoured it.

This was basically a military train, with only a few civilians onboard, and those civilians consisted mostly of relatives of the servicemen.

– Nick has done a great job of shielding us so far, Jonas said. – The question is how long it will last.

He felt an almost insane need to talk, to commune with his two companions, two men that were almost like brothers to him.

The thirteen years he had known them, suffered and lived with them felt like centuries.

The two of them didn't really have anything more to say. He felt a desperation he couldn't name.

After a while he deliberately began listening to other people in the coach. It was easy, just a matter of changing frequency. He didn't have to close his eyes or anything.

– This will be one of our last trips, right?

A nasal female voice.

– I'm afraid so, a male coughed. – Even the Germans, horribly bad at aiming their rockets as they are, just have to achieve one decisive hit on an already overtaxed system soon.

There were others, in the half full coach, sharing their daily life worries, speaking as if there was no war, as if enemy rockets wouldn't sweep the area and bomb the train and the railroad to rubble at any minute.

Spare parts were virtually impossible to come by, at least not without making the effort of making a lot of them, allocating a production facility to do it, and that wouldn't be done until after the war.

– It's funny, isn't it? Virgil said.

James and Jonas looked astonished at him.

– What is, exactly? Jonas wondered.

– We have here a group of nations, of allies having taken on and probably overtaking one of the worst and most inhuman domains that have ever existed on Earth, but it isn't really that much of a difference between the two warring factions, not when it comes to create a truly just society. The war, when it ends will have changed a lot, but not the fundamental wrongs existing all over the world.

He didn't care if the rest of the train heard him, neither lowering nor raising his voice.

– So, you have indeed been paying attention, James grinned, his pale skin brightening for a moment. – I knew you were.

Virgil's words stuck in Jonas, for some reason. He had heard Nick used similar wording, but coming from Virgil it struck a chord deep within the tall and big man.

And he felt a kinship with the two men that totally transcended blood and time.

There were many things, the way they looked at each other, the way they interacted, all the ways they interacted. He remembered, in astute and acute detail the meeting at Sarah's in New York, in a way he had never quite done before. When he heard her voice, Sarah's voice, he almost choked.

«I can't do this anymore».

Dread and fear threatened to overwhelm him.

The train, or rather its passengers, turned silent. At least he perceived it that way.

The seat had a tall back, with a place even he could rest his neck. He did, but he didn't sleep, like Virgil and some of the others did, the people not reacting to any new, potentially dangerous sound, waiting for the whistling the rocket made in everybody's ears and nobody could really hear with their conscious mind.

James didn't sleep. He looked like he would never sleep again.

The train raced through the indistinct landscape outside, a slow-moving train unable to jump off its rails.

## 3

They were let through the various checkpoints without much hassle. The guards reacted remarkably similar, even though there were some caustic remarks.

– Clandestine services, huh? A soldier spat, before he returned the papers.

Young soldiers, practically children bordered the ship. Smoke or rather mist drifted along its side. Everybody walked inside. The ship departed almost immediately after that, with hardly any delay. There was no civilian section onboard. That sat fine with the three Warrens. They had never seen themselves as part of society's elite.

The cigarette smoke filled Jonas' lungs. He hardly noticed, and didn't cough.

Space was tight. Almost all of it was filled up by crouching bodies, whether they were clutching rifles or priced belongings. Wet, everything was wet. Clothes turned wet quickly. Drops formed by the thick humidity flowed through his fingers like desert sand, like golden sand.

Everything slipped through his fingers.

One of the soldiers coughed. It was like a signal. One of the little girls coughed, too, and then several others, and then almost all the rest, including James.

Jonas and Virgil didn't.

– It's funny, isn't it? Jonas mused, speaking to his two companions.

– What is?

One of the soldiers asked in a suspicious tone.

Jonas turned towards him with a humorous grin.

– It's wrong for us to keep the window open.

Seawater and wet air flowed in through the small window.
– But if we don't we'll keep coughing throughout the voyage.
The soldier mumbled something to the soldier by his side. To Jonas it sounded somewhat like «smartass».
A woman was laughing somewhere. He couldn't identify the spot.
– You've got a funny accent, man, one of the other soldiers said. – American, huh?
– Yes, Jonas replied. – American.
He leaned his head at the wall and closed his eyes. Unwanted memories haunted him the very moment everything should have turned black.
The film on his eyelids took him through all his steps, from childhood, through the events that had made him leave Norway forever, through the fateful day in New York in 1931 and every time he had held a gun in his hands. There was the occasional sound, too, and smells, stenches of blood. He remembered Nancy's smell and he recalled her face in meticulous detail, and then, in a flash the image of the spirit rising from her dead body. He heard it speak to him. The suddenly so very vivid memory made him shake hard in the warm and humid storage room.
He knew the sharp air and scent of the French forests and villages before they reached it, to the point that he wasn't entirely certain they were actually there, until the stench from the engine in the car they drove penetrated his defenses.
In tiny flashes he recalled the glimpses of Nick and Virgil exchanging words when they thought no one saw or heard them.
– I should join you.
Nick's more than usual pained voice
– You don't need to. We will take care of him. You're needed here.
Virgil's voice was also like it always was: cold, distant, a few bubbles on the surface to hide the boiling rage beneath.
Nick nodding to him… and to Jonas watching them from the shadows.
The three brothers in arms were brought to the local chief of allied operations in the middle of night. The soldiers looked around them with beyond nervous glances. The commander received them in a hidden-away office outside the main camp.
The woods were lovely, dark and deep. They all heard its silence speak to them, communicating to them beyond words.
– The man you seek is here, the American commander confirmed, – in a camp only a few miles away.
– So, we don't have to look for him further then, James growled. – That's certainly good news.
– I still find it hard to believe he's a German spy…
– Not German, Virgil lied with a straight face. – Russian. That's why he's so useful, short term and why he must be stopped cold before he can corrupt our brave soldiers further.
Jonas didn't laugh or felt the need to. Everything felt dead inside.

The commander bought that more easily. An expression of relief crossed his face.

– He has amassed quite a few followers, dedicated followers already, he acknowledged.

– He's quite good at that, Jonas said.

– They will defend him to the last man, the commander said.

– That won't save him, James said.

There was a quality in the man's voice that Jonas had never realized was there until this very moment.

The three men facing the commandant appeared strangely similar. They blended in, in each other.

They fed. The rather large meal slipped down their throats like water, filling them with energy, making them feel the characteristic traitorous drowsiness. The dining hall didn't seem real to Jonas. Nothing did, except the two men in front of him, his comrades in arms, his brothers beyond blood and time.

Jonas said to Virgil, in an aggressive tone of voice:

– You know, don't you? You know you will reach him?

– I know I will reach him, Virgil confirmed, his icy fire even calmer.

Jonas' thoughts drifted, into more potent images and sensations. He remembered Nancy and Carla in Rotterdam, how all the gathered strangers had belonged together, how right his first encounter with the Shadowwalkers in New York had been, the smiles concealed beneath expressions of time and loss.

The three faced their soldiers, their fellow warriors in twilight.

– This is a crucial mission, Virgil told them, seemingly a completely different man compared to all the time Jonas had known him, an awakening giant in the form of a man. – We attack and we keep attacking until every single enemy combatant is dead and cold. Is that clear?

– YES, SIR! They choired.

– The enemy will wear the same uniform you do, but they will still be the enemy. Clear?

– CRYSTAL CLEAR, SIR!

– You're elite soldiers, supposedly the best of the best. Tonight you'll get the change to prove it.

– YES, SIR!

The march, the fast run began, in the silent of night.

## 4

The attack began during the early dawn. No warning was given. The soldiers looked eager, like dogs given free reign. Virgil nodded to James and Jonas, confident the tin-men would perform adequately.

– They're just cannon-fodder anyway, he said, making the other two shudder.

The human blanket moved forward, silent and deadly. Scouts were deployed, probing the weakness of the enemy. Sometimes the three of them joined them, sometimes not. They didn't care, not about keeping up the appearances either.

The soldiers had been trained to obey, not to think, but even if some of them should see through their ruse, they didn't care. It was all set in motion and couldn't be stopped, and that was how they wanted it.

No engines were used. A unit of soldiers dragged the heavy cannons. The wheels didn't help as much as they should have on the uneven ground.

There was a slow walk through a forest, a rush through the shadows of an open field, several more similar treks, before they began slowing down.

Something… happened to the three of them, something that had been there for as long as the soldiers had known them, but that grew minute by minute.

Virgil moved forward in ways that very much resembled that of different animals. James did, too, his progression a little slower. Jonas caught himself sniffing the air like a beast, the stench of the forest and what was ahead suddenly so very distinct in his nostrils. He knew then as well, knew beyond knowing that Lance Powell waited for them exactly where they believed he did.

– I can smell him, Jonas mumbled.

The other two looked at him, clearly not surprised.

– How can that be? I'm not a dog. I can't separate distinct scents across miles and miles of open landscape. The two of us have never met.

– You have, James stated slowly. – We have all been asleep, no matter how alive we may have felt earlier in our lives.

A very different man from only days earlier.

But still, even more so Jonas' friend, his fellow traveler in the wilderness.

Awake!

He thought.

A wolf howled somewhere to the right, so close by.

Awareness surged through him, and he wondered, like a wounded beast, if he had truly been awake, been alive until this very moment.

Eventually the three of them moved more in front than the scouts, were more scouts than the scouts.

The open eyes showed Jonas one changing image, his inner eye one completely different, glimpses of strangely clad men and women moving through a remote, desolate landscape towards what appeared to be some kind of fortress or fortified position ahead.

Then he saw the camp, in the wet forest straight ahead. One tent in particular stood out in his mind, one surrounded by many, one man at the center of hundreds.

The three of them spread out, leading one pack of men forward. Again Jonas was struck by how effortless everything proceeded. He heard James' words repeated in his ears.

The trio imagined they glimpsed Carla somewhere ahead, raising a sword above her head.

But Carla had turned old and frail, and remained in London, at Nick's side.

– You can heal wounds, they heard her voice, – even somewhat mend a broken heart, but you can't stop people from aging.

Virgil, using his large blade killed the first soldier, the first sentry, doing so with a ruthlessness that should have staggered Jonas, but didn't, and when Jonas and James also started the killing, the silent killing, that, too, failed to stun him or even surprise him.

Out of breath already he did his best to follow the two Warrens through the thick underbrush, and he made it with flying colors. It was as if he was able to double and even triple his expenditure of power without major effort. Nancy, or rather her ghoul had called him…

A rifle was fired by fingers extending from a dying body, and the camp ahead was up in arms in seconds. Virgil gave the signal and guns and cannons were fired, and explosions in red and black obscured already burning visions.

The soldiers kept charging forward, hardly ever taking cover from the enemy fire. They dug in for a few seconds, before moving on.

People began dying in droves, including those running at the three brothers' side.

The enemy forces had been taken by surprise, at least to a point. The attackers reached inside the camp before an effective defense could be mounted. Blood and the sounds of guns surrounded them all. Soldiers formed a perimeter around Lance Powell, revealing where he was to everybody, not just to those able to smell him like a pungent stench in the air. Jonas caught a glimpse of him, his haggard, haunted features.

– I knew you would come, he shouted, and impossibly, they heard him. – I knew you would come for me.

He fought, fought like a man possessed, but he didn't seem at all like the demigod Jonas had pictured him, but like a man that hadn't slept well for years.

– Fire! He howled. – Kill them, kill them all!

Jonas saw him, as if he was standing just a few steps away and not dozens.

– We meet again, Powell shouted. – We meet again.

He looked absolutely insane.

Jonas knew he wasn't.

A bullet hit Jonas in the leg, of all places, and he fell, on his feet again before the thought registered in his mind. Powell was hit, hit by several bullets. He didn't go down, but kept firing while others dropped left and right around him. Blood flowed from Virgil's wound. He kept charging forward. James was strangely unscathed, as if the bullets… avoided him. There was no more cover between the clashing forces. Some of the soldiers fled from the battle, and some of them even made it out alive. Most fell and died and nourished the hard French soil.

Jonas' leg failed him, and he fell again. Unable to get up he crawled forward while firing. James was hit for the first time. He fell, but got back up in an instant. There were only a few uniformed men still standing. They fell and stayed down. Virgil fired at Powell. He held guns in both hands. Powell did the same. James charged him, threw himself at him, penetrating his gut with a rifle. Powell fired at him point blank. James was pushed backwards, pieces of his head gone. Virgil jumped at Powell. Powell pulled the trigger again, but the firing pin hit an empty chamber. James and Virgil attacked simultaneously. Fire and charged air seemed to flow from Powell's hands. James was thrown away, but Virgil just kept charging, seemingly totally unaffected by the unearthly power Powell poured at him.

Jonas could no longer move. He crouched there, between the dead, his attention locked on the fight.

He knew Virgil felt something, felt something awaken inside, dormant his entire life. Jonas felt it, too, startled, as all four of them were dying, there, on the bombed-out hill. Virgil pulled his knife, a shining blade clothed in shadow. It began glowing the moment before he pushed it into Powell's heart. Both screamed in immeasurable pain, as the fire and shadow seemed to slowly consume them both.

The fire stemming from Powell's hands seemed to… turn, and fall back on him. Both the two figures locked in a death-grip screamed in pain and rage. Virgil gutted the other from belly to neck. His hand, his arm kept moving long after most of the flesh was gone from the bones. There were no more words, only rage and pain and fire, and the approaching Shadow.

Virgil Warren and Lance Powell fell to the ground, broken up inside, sustaining injuries no creature could endure.

James moved, drawing breath once, twice, thrice, before he stopped.

Three pairs of dead eyes stared at the sky above.

Jonas crouched on the wet ground, feeling neither the moisture nor the cold.

Three shadows emerged from the unmoving, burned-out bodies. Jonas saw them, sensed them, felt them, as the bright morning once again turned to night.

He didn't feel his own.

The shadows appeared only briefly, before once more fading, and the bright sun burned his wet face.

He choked and kept choking, as he sat up, as he remained there for a time without number, as a pain far worse than what his flesh and bones could provide descended on his consciousness, and the path stretched on like forever ahead of him.

# Part Four:
# The Valley of Death

# Chapter Sixteen: The Journey of Death

A séance even weirder than what Liz had pulled took place a few days later. Richard and Alanis held one of their joint press-conferences, and this time every single expedition member, recent and current participated.

– We will walk, Richard Hagman declared dramatically. – Once again we will travel through the jungle searching for the great mysteries of the world.

His hands moved through the air, adding to his bold words.

– Fate is a strange thing, Hagman mused, his voice enhanced through the microphones and the speakers echoing through the village and the jungle. – Through our misfortune and especially to that of our dear, departed colleagues and friends, and us ending up here we may have come closer to the City of Light than ever. My friends, according to the locals it is close by, perhaps only a few days or weeks march from this very spot. We are better equipped than ever, both physically and mentally to succeed in our exciting venture.

*He's full of shit, isn't he?* Laurie sent to Ted and Liz. Ted had to contain a potential burst of hysteric laughter.

She could do that, now, easily direct her sending, isolate it to the person or persons she chose. He closed his eyes, marveling at the rich details of her mental speech.

He looked casually at Liz, sensing her pain and despair, fearing it was festering and growing within her. It wasn't hard to see that she had touched something bad, and that it wouldn't let her go. He knew she was aware of his scrutiny, she always was, but she didn't seem to care, not even about that, and that was perhaps the greatest cause of worry there was.

The jungle imposed itself on him. He felt it, but muted, closed off from him, and an unbearable sadness manifested in his troubled mind.

– We will now open for questions, Alanis declared. – May they be wise, brief and to the point.

She was infamous for this, for being patronizing towards journalists.

A single, brave soul raised his hand. Hagman acknowledged him.

– So, how come you feel so certain the City of Light, as you call it is here, of all places? A journalist asked. – I mean, you've searched for it all over the world, haven't you?

Hagman frowned, visibly, and those present more than suspected that the journalist in question wouldn't be invited to join the party.

– I can't be certain, of course, he replied, his confidence and winning personality quickly reasserting itself. – As you so *eloquently* pointed out I've traveled across the world without finding it. What I can say, though, is that I feel closer to it, now, than ever before.

– But what do you feel about going back into the jungle after your *ordeal* there? Another journalist wondered incredulous.

– Our prolonged time in the jungle turned out to be an ultimately positive experience, actually, Alanis replied. – We survived and thrived. It made us better equipped to deal with whatever is coming.

– But all this… tracing centuries' old legends and innuendos… what do really expect to *find?* What *use* will it be?

– I will put it to you, Alanis said sweetly, – as I do with similar ridiculous questions that knowledge has a value in itself, and the pursuit of it will always be valuable and infinitely precious. In *addition* to that I'm happy to tell you that interviews we have conducted with the locals in a widespread area show that the stories about the City of Light aren't necessarily old at all, but *recent.*

That caused a sensation. Alanis and Richard smiled to each other, as a lot of hands were raised.

– How recent? A single voice cried, and was echoed by the multitude gathered on his spot of the world.

– As recent as it gets, really, Hagman said, clearly pleased (and smug). – A large group of unknown compatriots were spotted and reported to the local authorities *last month.* The first reports of the legends of a city of light in this area can be traced centuries back, since the Europeans first arrived here, but during the last decade the reports, the sightings, if you will have clearly taken a far more tangible quality.

He was good at this, as always, at handling newshounds. They both were, both through experience and their inborn charm. Ted studied them, soaking up the experience, because he didn't have anything else to do and to satisfy his curiosity, and also because he found something in them lacking in himself. He could never have done this, handling all those sharks in such a slick manner.

– I would like to ask a question to the young members of your expedition, a TV-journalist said. – How does it feel, after all this time, to return to civilization?

– There are only ghosts here, ghosts everywhere, Ted replied without thinking.

There was laughter, but also understanding glances from his fellow travelers, and it warmed him, even in the chilling wind surrounding him, as the séance ended and the Journey of Death began.

## 2

The noise stayed with them. The time they had spent in civilization overwhelmed the years they had spent in the jungle. They were flown in choppers to another, bigger city, where jeeps, equipment and more lasting supplies waited for them. There were roads, wide forest roads made by logging parties cutting deep into what recently had been pristine wilderness.

Even deep within the jungle the noise persisted in their minds, their consciousness.

The roads were bad in this particular area and had been for quite some time, and most of the entourage preferred or chose to walk instead of enduring the slow progress, the constant humps and bumps of the jeeps.

– Did you know that there are several hundred native languages in South America?

Phillip engaged in a conversation with Liz, or tried to.

– Yes, dear, Liz replied.

– The way I've heard it, from Richard and Alanis and their experts, these parts are on the outskirts and even well outside the old Inca Empire, and are still largely unexplored.

– Yes, dear, Liz sighed. – According to the experts.

A photographer, a journalist, or one of Richard's «court» photographers, she couldn't tell which took their picture. The flash, fairly pronounced in the twilight landscape between day and night flared, and practically flooded her sensitive eyes. The frown on her brow grew deeper.

The man pulled back, for some reason. She couldn't really tell why. She wasn't angry and hadn't emanated anger either. A fly, coming too close buzzed one, final time and fell to the ground.

The photographer stumbled and almost fell. He looked down, studying the ground in the hope of spotting some root, but there was none. Shaking his head he made his way further back in the line to snap more pictures, to Justine, Candy and Candice carrying their babies on the back. Justine smiled to him, posing in a mocking gesture of what a model might do. He looked down again. This time he did spot a root. It scratched his foot, clearly moving. He pulled back. It followed him. Suddenly, more than a little distressed he turned back and speeded up. He imagined he heard spiteful laughter, as the root caught up with him and snared his leg. It pulled hard, and he screamed in pain. Then it pulled him into the air, and his scream changed into a wail of fear.

He hung there, upside down. Liz didn't turn at all. She wanted to whistle a wicked tune, but denied herself the pleasure. The root let go of the poor man and he fell hard on his back. Laughter surrounded him, and he couldn't understand why they were laughing. He pulled himself on his feet and managed, somewhat to walk.

Something still seemed to squeeze his foot. There was nothing there, when he looked, but he still felt like his foot was in a squeeze. Every time he set out to take more pictures it took a turn for the worse. He didn't snap more pictures that day.

– You don't like this very much, do you? Phillip asked Liz, already knowing the answer.

– No, not particularly, why?

– I quite enjoy it, he said, giving her his smile, one designed to melt the coldest of maidens. – It isn't every day the attention of the world is upon you. We learned to appreciate that in Vegas. It may lead to all kinds of endorsements, you know.

– I know. She nodded. – All kinds.

She reached out a hand and squeezed his lightly. It didn't hurt, not physically.

– I think I'll take point for a while.

– Is that necessary? There isn't any danger, now, is there? And if anybody should take us on, we have a full contingent of bloodthirsty sentinels to help us protect ourselves.

Richard had hired a *lot* of professionals for the entire trip.

– No, there isn't.

She squeezed his hand a little harder.

Then she was gone.

3

The noise stayed with her. She removed herself further from the first jeep, to no avail. Perspective changed, to a point, but hardly to the point she glimpsed through her dim memory. It wasn't merely the constant sound of the engines, but more, like something had gone seriously out of whack. When she looked at the jungle at both sides of the road, the scar in the landscape she experienced something very close to vertigo.

She heard the snarls and hisses of the beasts in there, and managed only through a supreme effort to keep herself from panicking.

A tree had fallen across the road, and she almost collided with it. It looked dark and menacing in her eyes. She froze. The moment she discovered it, just a few steps away it was as if the branches, all the branches reached for her, and she stood there, until she sensed Ted behind her.

– I can't move it, she said.

– It's too damn big, he said.

– You do it, she said.

– It's too damn big, he repeated. – Impossible to handle.

And then it was too late, as the travelers caught up with them, and too much tape was rolling.

She wanted to be angry with him, but instead sought closer, into his warm and safe embrace.

– What's *wrong* with me? She whispered. – I can't seem to get anything to work properly. This isn't like during the powerless periods. My powers worked great with that grease-ball of a photographer, but suddenly it doesn't. What did I *do?*

– We'll find out, he said, he insisted. – It's just more uncharted territory, that's all.

A group of hired hands started chopping up the tree, into manageable pieces. It took time. Hagman sent a long look at the three perceived miracle workers, but didn't make anything out of it. He was still in an over-the-top good mood.

Laurie didn't say anything either, on her spot close to Liz, but just caressed her friend's cheek.

– The natives are doing this, a local informed Hagman and spat, – doing it to delay the loggers.

– I guess they've realized that time is money, Ted said, – at least to the intruders.

Liz kissed him, hard, before pulling back, disgusted with herself, and it only grew worse by the understanding and even approval she imagined in his eyes.

They removed the tree, cleared the way. It took the rest of the day, and they camped there, in the shadow of what had been life, but now was just wet wood. Liz sat on the ground, rocking back and forth, her arms embracing her stuck up knees. She focused on the ritual, the ritual of pain, taking herself back to that night.

– The past is no trouble, she mumbled. – Neither is the present. The future is. I can't see past it, past the pain.

A memory flared in her mind. She had just used a stick to penetrate her second leg. Nothing happened. Earlier bricks had pulled loose from walls and windows had broken, but this time nothing happened.

Then a woman had screamed. An invisible force had almost pulled her skin off her bones. A wind, a draft had surged through the gathering.

And then, BANG, it was like someone had slammed a door in her face, and left her inside with a lot of hungry worms and spiders devouring her.

She crawled to Ted and put her head in his lap.

– I can't see past the pain, she mumbled, – the fear, the horror, the lobster gnawing at my leg.

– It's all right, he assured her. – It's all right.

And that made her want to cry. It was close. The others stared awkward at her drawn face.

She could see the shock and pity in their eyes.

– I'm behaving like a frightened little girl, she said aloud.

No one responded verbally, ashamed of themselves and their thoughts, unable to face their own reaction to the dramatic change in her.

They gathered around the fires to sleep. The sounds of the jungle grew even more invasive with the silence. There was nothing faulty with her five mundane senses. They were as sharp as ever. If anything her sensitivity had increased further. She could no longer shut it off, and wished she could. Her confusion and despair played havoc with her focus and ruined any change of control. She knew a pitiful sleep was approaching. The dream drew closer, a spider trapping her in its web, looking forward to a tasty snack.

She dreaded the coming of night.

## 4

Welcome to my web, the spider said to its prey.

Liz Warren woke up in the bright light of morning with a stricken expression on her face. She had slept, but the sleep had brought her little or no rest. The dark bags under her eyes had grown bigger. She looked tired, practically exhausted.

– Come, honey, Laurie said, reaching out a hand, – there's a small stream a little stretch from here.

Translation: too far away for most people, but not for them.

Liz studied her, briefly, before shrugging. Laurie had really improved dramatically during the two years in the jungle. Only the return to civilization made Liz recall, faintly, her previous dislike of her.

They moved fast through the jungle. The run alone made Liz feel better. It felt good this morning, better than yesterday, for some reason to use her body. It was mostly despair, not so much fear keeping her down. She felt lighter, brighter. They washed there, in the small stream. The others might not need this, as a way of starting the day, but she surely did.

– Thank you, she said to her friend.

– Don't mention it, Laurie shrugged. – You needed this.

Liz slipped below the surface, the cold water surrounding her on all sides. They used the fine sand as soap. She rubbed her skin hard, until it turned red. They stood on land, waiting for their skin to dry enough for them to dress. Laurie had brought a new set of clothes for them both.

– I can only faintly recall a time in my life I've felt more helpless, Liz said in a low voice.

– Something happened to bring you low, Laurie said in a very practical manner. – We must just find out what.

They returned to the camp, taking their time, taking care not to soil their clothes. Liz wanted them clean right now, wanted it desperately, and once again fear touched her, and that emotion, in this context felt so completely unreasonable that it almost made her cry again.

– You're so strong, Laurie told her, half whispering, grabbing her arm. – And that other night… I could never do what you did. Never!

The packing and departure were well along when they approached the camp. They joined in, throwing themselves into busy work, loosing themselves in it.

The physical hardship wasn't a challenge to Liz, even though she deliberately chose to not use her mind power, but it still distracted her, distracted her from the dreary thoughts. It was visible in her demeanor and also affected the others.

The company was on its way. The jeeps and vehicles continued their slow progress and the scouts and others running along could easily keep up. Liz, Ted and Laurie ran ahead. It was yet another relief to escape the stench of exhaust in their nostrils. They ran and moved and constantly shifted their attention, attempting to catch all details, to fall back on the threat mode of the jungle, where a deadly danger could jump at you at any moment.

Ted and Laurie occasionally ventured inside the tight vegetation, but Liz stayed behind on the road. They returned to her, and she felt base relief. The three of them, along with native scouts stopped on a rise several hundred steps ahead of the caravan.

– Look at it, Liz said in contempt. – It looks like an entire village is on the move, carrying with them rocks, wet wood and countless useless items.

– True nomads don't bring more than they can carry, Laurie acknowledged.

They could see the road improving a little ahead, with less holes and bumps, and waited there, for the convoy to catch up with them. Everybody jumped into the vehicles, and the speed improved significantly. Liz sat there crouching, at the back of the jeep and slowly turned deaf, blind and mute.

Her face didn't feel like her own. The fingers she used to touch it felt like dry sticks. The eyes staring at nothing reminded her of dysfunctional glass. Her ears attempting to listen to the world resembled integral parts of the poison-spewing engines carrying her.

Everything she ate and drank tasted and smelled like petrol or thick oil.

The others comforted her the best they could, but they sensed her distress, how deep it reached, and couldn't help but being influenced and diminished by it.

She drank the water from the plastic bottle. It was like she couldn't get enough of it. She heard the sound of the jungle every time she swallowed.

– There is something wrong with me, she mumbled. – I know there is. There is something inside me. I cannot grasp what, but it's there.

Justine put something Liz knew was a cold cloth on her brow. It felt hot as fire.

Ted turned his head, sniffing something in the wind, and in that moment she knew it as well, and felt strangely comforted, in a backwards kind of way.

Everybody looked up.

They all smelled it from far away, something alien, something not the jungle, standing out even more than they did, even long before they spotted the black smoke. An hour later, when they saw the enormous wounds in the landscape, the giant machines cutting down trees, scalping the entire hill they felt sick to their stomach.

The jungle was gone. In its stead a nightmare scenario revealed itself. The entire valley, and most of its surrounding hills, had been cleaned. There were no more standing trees, and giant fires burned away the remaining underbrush. The black smoke covered most of the sky.

– They do this deliberately, Richard said, – destroy as much as possible, in order to make room for farmland, for devious agriculture.

They had never seen him quite like this, quite this upset.

– The rain forests are the lungs of the planet and if this continues at its present pace the lungs will be gone in less than a century. This concerns the entire world.

It made them all feel bad. There was something fundamentally disturbing about the sight unfolding before them. It was easy, but painful to imagine seeing it all from above, to feel the wound cut through the skin of the Earth.

All of them felt it, as if the experience threatened to pull their soul from their bodies.

– They're doing it all over the Amazon, Ted said. – And in the east, in Sumatra and other rainforests. This problem, this, too, is… is worldwide. It's… causes are widespread.

They sensed his rage, his despair, and shared it.

– This could easily be one Valley of Death, Candy said. – It surely looks like one. If there is a hell this is close. What's *wrong* with people?

There were no replies, no immediate answer, and it kept bothering them, kept haunting them. The time in the jungle with their tribe felt even more distant in time and space.

– Chini told us we needed to live with her tribe, Ted said slowly, – to know later, faced with the world's countless horrors how the world can be.

They didn't move, but they all turned to him, and it both pleased and detracted him.

– It's true. We've witnessed so much in the past and will face so much in the future that we need one memory, one tiny spot in our mind to draw strength from, to know how everything is supposed to be.

They drove on, on the edge of the induced devastation. Laurie threw up, and sat pale and quiet in the back of the truck for hours. The others imagined they could smell the sour stench of her vomit for at least that long. Eventually there was no more smoke in the air when they turned around, and no more smoke making their nostrils bleed.

The horror stayed with them, like a waken nightmare.

They stopped at a secluded spot at midday. The river running by the road actually looked pretty clean. The roaring sound of the water cleansed the noise from Liz' mind. She fed like a wolf, like the rest of them.

Some time later, she walked into the forest alone, giving Ted and the others a reassuring smile. It closed around her, like a mouth, smothering her the way she faintly recalled. She walked among the trees, passing them, slipping past them one by one, forgetting herself, able to relax and enjoy the serene experience, at least temporarily.

There was something right beyond her awareness, something that had also been there, that had always been both threatening and playful, now almost exclusively menacing. Voices spoke to her, but made no sense. She dived behind the tree to expose the elf or demon hiding there, but there was nothing, nothing but shimmering air suggesting there had been something there a moment ago. Hands curled into fists, the rage aiding her again, like it used to, the exposure of fangs sending seething power through her body.

She returned to the camp just when they started worrying about her.

– I feel better, now, she told them. – Thank you, I love you all.

There were more hugs and caresses. It comforted her.

– It still feels somewhat awkward in the forest, she admitted willingly. – As if a mouth is chewing and spitting out a frail human being, but I once more know what I am. I guess seeing, experiencing what we did earlier today reminded me that compared to the world my problems, whatever they may be, are tiny and insignificant.

Her eyes glowed, once again burning away the ashes.

They drove on. It hadn't been raining here for a while. The jungle was still moist and natural, but the road was practically reduced to a dustbin. Nothing would grow there anymore, nothing at all. Those sitting behind the first car needed to cover their mouth to not choke. The green paint on the cars turned gray in a matter of minutes.

– Death has come here as well, Liz said, – not so obvious, but still evident, the Death of spirit, far worse than the physical.

– The cities are like cancer cells, aren't they? Richard said pained. – Sending out material to reproduce themselves?

Ted stared at him. Something clicked in him, his friend's words echoing in his mind.

Liz sought out Ted a little bit after that, in her typical sleek, non-obtrusive way. Not even the fact that she jumped from one car to the other seemed strange to the others. They had become used to it.

– I guess we now know why Richard is seeking the past so much, she said to him, as the two of them sat in the back of the rear truck.

– It's such a horribly… compelling image. I think it will stay within me forever.

She nodded. A tender hand touched his cheek. She understood.

As if to drive the point home they arrived at a mining town not long afterwards. There was little or no advance warning here. They arrived at something that could have been an ordinary settler village, something that often predated vast forest burnings, like the one they had witnessed earlier. The fact that the inhabitants of the makeshift town fired at them on sight didn't really give them much additional information.

– RETREAT! La Grande barked.

This was his domain. He had been in countless scraps around the world, a professional bodyguard and even gunman.

They stopped the trucks, pushing the breaks hard, and drove backwards until they reached the previous turn, and was out of sight from the aggressors. Liz jumped out of the truck and took a cautious or not so cautious look around the corner.

– They're not giving chase, she reported.

The men stood there with their weapons, scowling at the unseen unwelcome visitors.

– They're mining gold, Alanis said, – and don't, generally speaking take kindly to strangers.

– You didn't know they were here, did you? Hagman asked her, clearly accusing her of something.

– You are as paranoid as ever, dear, she scowled at him.

– Please! Laurie cried at them both. – We don't *need* this right now, okay.

That stopped them cold. The girl hardly ever raised her voice in anger.

– They use mercury in the production process, Alanis said, very matter of fact. – The river is probably poisonous miles downstream.

– I've actually read about that, Ted said.

His adoptive father had made him and his brother and sister read a lot of newspapers.

He could easily imagine it, down there, how broken and half dead workers strived to find glimmers of a perceived treasure in a handful of sand, breathing the poisonous fumes from the mercury.

– It's just one of several sites in the Amazon, she shrugged.

But she didn't fool him and the other sensitives among them, didn't fool anybody present, really. Her rage was more modulated and contained, but it was there.

– We're moving around them, Hagman said, making the decision for all of them. – Be on your guard, people.

They backtracked a little. The main «road» was further down in the valley. They had taken the high road in order to meet people and possibly get information, but that was out of the question now.

Ted's grin felt alien on his lips.

No one said what everyone was thinking. They could take out the camp. With their added resources they could even take it out without much danger to themselves, if for nothing else than to satisfy their own vanity, but another would be up an hour after they had left, and they knew that for a fact and almost hated their ability to reason, too see beyond the moment.

The three of them, Ted, Liz and Laurie, and their comrades in arms, their fellow travelers didn't look at each other, but the knot turning harder inside them hurt more than ever.

Taking the low road they focused on security, the three running in front attempting to empty their minds of distracting thoughts, becoming scouts again. Ted knew Laurie directed her mind power at the hillside, scouring it for hostile thoughts. There was no need for her to say anything or shake her head. He knew she had sensed nothing, no danger.

They reached the intersection, where the main road met the smaller, reaching it from the miner-community above.

Nothing.

– It seems like they are content to chase off possible competitors and are not carrying a burning desire to obliterate them, Hagman said. – How refreshing, to encounter sane people.

The expedition moved on.

They stopped sometimes in the afternoon, too. It felt good to get yet another respite from the loud engines ruining their hearing. The break was over way too soon.

It turned late. The sun grew big and red in the horizon. Nothing seemed to change around them. There was the jungle, and there was the road. Their surroundings didn't change much. There was a certain comfort in that, considering the alternative.

They arrived at a tribal village of sorts. The decline was instantly recognizable to them. They saw what others, untrained eyes might miss. The villagers performed their tribal dance for a bunch of tourists. Ted and Liz and the others didn't need the stench of liquor in their nostrils to tell them what a thousand big and small signs revealed.

– I guess civilization has arrived at this place quite some time ago, Ben remarked, – teaching the savages sophisticated behavior.

There was a church upstream, a large property with nice cut lawns. A man holding a bible spoke to the children. The newly arrived saw many empty bottles.

The rage between them echoed within Liz. They were all of one mind about this, a fact that comforted and worried her and rocked her world.

The fires burned here as well, smaller fires, the same, poisonous smoke, the same taste of bile in the mouth. The stench of liquor had never bothered her before, but now it did. The ashes of its fire burned in people's mouth, and made her want to puke.

A woman sat on the ground with a bottle in her hand. She became agitated when Liz approached, saying something, repeating it time and time again.

– False spirit, Alanis said. – She says «false spirit».

The woman crawling on the ground looked at Liz with something akin to compassion in her eyes, like a mother would her child. She reached out with her free arm, but it fell back down every time she attempted to raise it.

– She says you're possessed, Alanis said.

Her words touched Liz, touched her deeply and scratched her insides like claws.

– That's the medicine woman, isn't? She heard herself ask.

– Yes, Alanis confirmed. – At least she used to be.

– So what does it mean… her diagnosis?

Alanis looked at the younger woman with concern in her eyes.

– It can mean a lot of things, but…

– A kind of mental disease, right? Liz asked abruptly.

Alanis didn't have to say anything. The answer was written on her face.

Liz wanted to go to the woman crawling on the ground, help her, ask her to explain herself, but couldn't make herself do it.

– I *am* better, she stated, making sure everybody heard her, – but I still feel like my thoughts are moving through quicksand.

– May I? Laurie approached her humbly and warily.

– Be my guest.

Liz strived to make her voice gentle and touched her friend on the cheek, focusing on opening up to the expected intrusion.

Laurie put a hand on her forehead, her features frozen in concentration. She stepped back an instant later, yelping in pain and alarm.

– I still can't get in, she said. – It's like a storm in there.

– But I removed the shield, Liz said. – I'm certain I did.

– Yes, Laurie said, – and revealed the limitless might beneath. If I should even begin to compare it with anything it's like sticking a hand into a seething fire. If I attempt to stay even for a moment my hand turns to ashes. It *hurts,* even from a distance. If that is quicksand then I wonder how you are when… when…

The shock made the girl reel and her voice quiver. The awe was engraved on her stricken face.

Liz saw, in her mindscape Laurie fall on her knees before her, a trembling heap of worship and terror, and felt a little better, a little worse. She put the shield back in place, once more hiding herself from the world.

But yet another veil had been pulled from her eyes, and she saw the village even clearer than before. She noticed how she was breathing faster, very aware of her own reactions, unable to control them, to even achieve a modicum of control.

So, she did like she had always done, letting it happen, going with the flow. The smile lurked at the edge of her lips, she knew it did. She allowed Laurie to follow her around like a dog on a leash.

She allowed it, even if she found the very notion of it profoundly disturbing.

The village, its very presence in her reality… hurt.

– The village is… sick? Laurie asked.

– Yes, Liz acknowledged, confirmed the other's disgust. – It's sick all right, like a dog that has to be put down.

She wanted to grab a torch and set fire to it, and burn everything down, but she held herself in check.

The honored reverend stood by the gate to his church, to the large property surrounding the massive building. A few of the villagers had gathered to listen to him. They didn't look like they were really listening.

– We have made great progress, he cried. – In an amazingly short time span we have made our own garden here, in this previously so godforsaken place.

– A garden isn't nature, Liz cried, with her loud and powerful voice. – It's just more destruction.

She spoke a variation of the local language, spoke it far better than he did. The villagers didn't speak that much different from other domesticated tribes in the area.

All of them had the language of the conqueror in common.

The honored reverend shook under her remorseless stare, and crossed himself. Seeing him do that both pleased and angered her. She moved on.

Richard and Alanis quarreled again. They seemed to do that all the time, now. She and her tail walked past them. The village wasn't a pleasant sight. She forced herself to look at it, to study it thoroughly. Once it had been small, like most primitive villages just a tiny spot by the river, practically concealed from above by the trees, by the seemingly endless jungle.

Now, countless trees had been chopped down, giving way to vast farmland, growing every day. Five tribe members chopped down more trees as they watched.

She realized that she was shaking again. Whether or not it was in rage or fear or something else she couldn't tell.

– Look at this, she said incredulous. – At all the destruction. It's amazing how effective a priest and his entourage are at this. It's such a well-oiled machinery, developed through centuries of organized insanity.

Laurie waited for her to continue, to say more, so very attuned to her.

– Religion is a pox on mankind, Liz said.

Richard and Alanis also had a talk with the honored reverend, somewhat longer and considerably more polite. She didn't hear what they were saying, but knew she could if she wanted to, but she didn't bother. The good reverend actually looked more distressed then he had done after Liz' scalding attack. He kept crossing himself. It was a ridiculous sight, or it would have been, if not for the double-edged sense of menace it evoked.

They decided to stay there for the night. It wasn't something they wanted or desired, but they were tired after a long day of travel and deafening engine roar. The missionaries and their henchmen scowled at them, looked at them with distrust, and it was mutual. The christian samaritans had decided it was safer to let the strangers spend the night than attempting to chase the heavily armed travelers from the village, but it was pretty clear that they didn't care much for the company.

The travelers didn't put away their guns for the night, but kept them in their grasp or close by, if they had to let go of them to pee or feed.

Liz, Ted and Laurie kept their powers constantly turned on, ready to act on a moment's notice.

– Is there is a reason for this… fear? Liz wondered. – I actually feel directly threatened. It's quite remarkable. I don't know if I can turn off the power if I want to.

Their frontal lobe buzzed and burned and grew.

– It hurts, Laurie said, – but is also exhilarating in a way.

– There is something here, Ted said, – something unseen, elusive, fading away every time I reach for it.

They grabbed hands, joining forces, feeding off each other, sensing how their strength increased, becoming more than the sum of the parts, but had no more success in determining whatever… bothered them.

The travelers sought and picked an easily defendable spot by the river.

– So, how safe are we? Hagman asked.

Even he, with his famous selective pragmatism clearly felt shitty, without quite knowing why.

– Unless attackers come at us with rockets and heavy armaments we should be okay, La Grande assured him.

The river was noisy, like all rivers, but that didn't really bother them. Natural noises didn't keep them from sleeping anymore.

The noise from the village was something else altogether. It scratched constantly in their ears and minds.

Liz closed her eyes with her head on Ted's chest, but her eyelids didn't feel heavy at all. He had fallen asleep almost instantly after the fucking. Everybody else had, too. The sex had been good. She rested in the heap of bodies spent and sleepy, but the weariness and restlessness had returned almost immediately. Ted's scent filled her nostrils, making her smile happily, but that, too failed to distract her for long. She writhed and moved in his arms. He hardly stirred, sleeping like the dead.

The very thought, usually not bothering her at all, did, now.

– Something is wrong, she said aloud.

No one woke up or even stirred.

– Something is very wrong, she practically shouted.

No one reacted in any way she was able to notice. She crouched there on the ground, alone, sniffing and eventually choking.

The birds cried from the treetops. They sounded far away. Everybody else seemed to pull away from her. Warm bodies didn't touch her anymore. A vast field appeared between her and them. She wanted to cover the distance, but couldn't move. A wail rose from her sore throat.

Even the river had turned quiet. Someone laughed, displaying contempt for her.

She crouched there, frozen, whimpering and moaning herself to sleep.

## 5

Liz was tired, dog tired. She was back on the ranch in Colorado, walking on the shingle road to the house. Her eyelids felt heavy, but she couldn't close them. She wanted to lie down and sleep, but she kept putting one foot in front of the other.

The shingle under her feet hissed and burned. It hurt, and she moaned in pain. The very wind touching her skin hurt. The house grinned at her, as she approached it, its… mouthy entrance.

She wanted to turn and split, run away, but her feet wouldn't let her. They kept putting one foot in front of the other, walked her through the maws, into the house.

Her surroundings felt totally unfamiliar. She recognized it in a way. It sort of looked the same, she would venture, but it didn't feel anything like she remembered it, or believed she remembered it.

She experienced it all like totally unreal.

They sat around the dinner table, all of them, Eugene, Trudy, Linsey and June.

– Sit down, Eugene told his daughter, very strict.

– But you're dead, Liz gasped incredulous.

Everybody laughed.

– That's our Liz, Eugene chuckled, – always striving to bring witty banter to the party.

Food and drink appeared on the table. They all ate and drank. Liz couldn't tell what kind of food it was, but just consumed it in relative silence. There was talk around the table, she knew that, but no matter how much she strived she couldn't remember what the conversation had been about.

She and June did the dishes afterwards. Liz looked at her sister. It looked like June, smelled like her and sounded and felt like her.

Liz stood straight before her father afterwards, awaiting his words.

– You did arrive at the right time to the dinner today, father nodded pleased. – That is great progress. Being punctual is very important.

– Thank you, sir, Liz said, giving her father a grateful smile.

– Go to your room, now, and wait there until I send for you.

– Yes, sir, Liz said. – Right away, sir.

She walked upstairs in a daze. Her bedroom, the one she shared with June felt still and dead. Its walls were clean, no posters or pictures or anything. More than anything it reminded her of a prison cell. She choked and sat down on the bed, shaking in fear.

The jungle around her breathed, as she raced through it, between its trees and animals, a moment, before it was gone.

She turned her head and looked at the hallway. The door was closed, but she was still able to see through it, to the hallway outside.

– LIZ! Her father shouted.

The voice made her rise and walk in a fast pace down the stairs to the living room. He waited for her there, in his favorite chair. She stood straight before him, like a soldier (or a polite teenage girl facing her strict father).

– You've made great progress lately, he said.

– Thank you, sir, she said eagerly. – I try.

– But there is still room for improvement. Your schoolwork, among other things suffered greatly during your… difficult phase.

– I'll do my best, sir.

Her voice sounded like an echo of his. Even though the actual words were different it sounded pretty much the same.

She smiled.

The catching in her throat never truly caught anything.

– You will stay home and do homework tonight, he declared. – Your cousin will come over and help you catch up with everything you have missed.

– Yes, sir, she said.

– Dismissed, he told her, very pleased.

The good girl, the obedient daughter returned to her room. She waited patiently, until there was a knock on the door. The moment the knock woke her from her trance-like condition she jumped on her feet and rushed to the door.

He stood there with a heap of books in his arms. She wished welcome her cousin on her father's side, and he entered. His name kept eluding her. She wrecked her mind, but she couldn't remember his name.

They sat down on the bed, and the studying began. She read through a chapter. He asked her questions. She would answer some of them correctly, but others she wouldn't, and she reread the chapter, and the questions and answers would begin again, and again and again. World War II began September 1st when Germany invaded Poland, following years of German hostilities and acquisitions. Two days later Great Britain, France, New Zealand and Australia declared war on Germany. The day after that the British Royal Air Force bombed the German Navy. The day after that the United States declared neutrality, and the German troops crossed the Vistula River in Poland. Five days after that Canada declared war on Germany, the battle of the Atlantic began…

She sat there, sweating and shaking hours later.

– Good girl, her cousin on her father's side said pleased, and petted her like he would a dog. – Now, repeat it all.

She did, recited everything yet again, only briefly wondering about the reason why.

It was night and she slept, but facts of the day just kept flowing through her head. Tears flooded the pillow, and she was unable to understand why that was.

The next day, at school, she recited everything again, before the entire class, and Howard Grey looked very pleased at her. If he looked smug that thought only entertained her briefly, before fading away, and the facts of the day filled her mind again.

The next day was pretty much the same, and the day after that again. During the weekends she helped on the ranch, not like a cowgirl, but in the stables, cleaning, cleaning, cleaning stalls, scrubbing, scrubbing, scrubbing horses.

There were parties, and she was primed for them, displayed, the good girl, the good future wife.

– You will marry soon, mother told her. – Father will decide who that will be, of course. Our job is to make you look the part, make you ready for your future role.

– Yes, mother, the dutiful daughter responded.

– You will be attentive and sweet when the men approach you. You have become a good dancer, but never lead in the dance. Let your partner decide the steps, like your future husband will do.

– Yes, mother.

– You're such a sweet and lovely girl. You'll make a great wife.

Yes, mother.

Her dress was fairly revealing, but not the slightest tacky. It was such a beautiful dress.

She caught glimpses of her painted face, of the painted doll, as she moved between the males, as she displayed herself, like the other girls of the right age. It was obvious that she was desirable. She could tell by the looks the males sent her, the hungry eyes they stared at her with.

Everything was very proper and correct.

– You don't really need to be that good at school, you know, Linsey told her. – Father just likes to point to your intelligence, demonstrating the quality of your offspring. Any cow on the meat market is evaluated on the totality of her traits.

– Yes, Linsey, she said

She curtseyed for a man, and they danced. He led and she followed. It was such a great dance, and she looked at her husband-to-be with endearing eyes. The dance ended. Everybody in the room applauded and she felt a warm and pleasant feeling inside.

It was the day of the wedding. The bride-to-be was groomed by her sister and mother. The final preparations were made.

– Good girl, Trudy said.

– Good girl, June said.

Eugene led her down the aisle towards the altar. Her husband waited ahead.

She stood before the priest with her beloved by her side.

– Do you swear to honor and obey your husband, Elizabeth Kendall? Howard Grey asked, insane amounts of froth flowing from his mouth.

– I swear, she said.

– For as long as you both shall live?

– I so swear, she whispered.

Grey turned to the husband.

– You may now devour the bride, he grinned, his long and sharp teeth proudly displayed.

It wasn't just his fangs, but his entire row of teeth.

Liz looked strangely disaffected at him. She turned towards her husband, her house master. He grabbed her and pulled her close, lifted the veil… and then he kissed her, and it was the sweetest, most intense emotion Liz had ever experienced in her entire life.

– I love you, she cried. – I Love you, love you, love you…

Everybody in the church applauded, a silent, thunderous sound filling her ears, her dull mind. Her husband took her hand and led her down the aisle. She followed him in a state of bliss, of prolonged, perpetual joy, knowing that this would last forever and ever and ever and ever…

Liz woke up screaming.

# Chapter Seventeen: The iron forge

The stink of garbage prevailed in his nostrils. He imagined it was stuck there, like a piece of rotting meat.

Ted cleaned his gun, the Peacemaker. It wasn't really necessary, as it had been oiled regularly and been kept well protected in its container in the sack on his back, but he did it anyway, before loading one and one bullet and firing the first round, before hitting the soup boxes lined up far away on the provisional shooting range at the garbage site and reducing them all to scrap iron.

Pieces of garbage rose in the air, flapping their wings like dead birds in the wind.

They had reached another city, another in a long row. He had long since lost count over how many there had been.

Beyond himself he could study himself, watch himself shoot, see the effortless flow of it all.

– There was a time when you couldn't shoot? Laurie said incredulous, and when he nodded: – I am amazed by that fact.

She smiled sweetly to him.

– It didn't feel right then, he said. – But I crossed a threshold, and everything changed.

– It *is* true, Liz said. – We are born with iron at our side, its blades and blazing weapons. The forge keeps giving birth to us, in an ever hotter glow.

– That's poetry, Ted said, a catching in his throat, as he attempted to keep a light and casual tone, and failed miserably.

She drew her gun from the holster on her hips in an even and quick-as-lightning flow. What was left of the boxes danced on the ground.

– Look at us. We haven't practiced in over two years, and it appears like we never stopped.

He noticed, like she noticed herself a slight shaking of her hands, brief and gone.

– I'm just as good as you, now, she said, – if not better.

He didn't accept the challenge and turned away, and the fire in her eyes visibly intensified.

She reloaded quickly, using a loading device, putting all six bullets in simultaneously. Another firing sequence commenced. She fired at a row of boxes on a wall even farther off. One of the bullets missed and ricocheted off the wall and subsequently a piece of metal and whined past her head. She didn't react in any noticeable way.

Her revolver was new, a Smith & Wesson Magnum 44 chosen among Richard's new stock, so big in her hands, held so steady.

She wasn't exactly pale, but the large bags under her eyes remained. There was something unsettling about her that everybody noticed and that he couldn't help react to, something rubbing him off in all the wrong ways.

He reloaded the gun and put it back in the holster, and she did, too. They left the garbage site, and walked back to town.

They and the rest of the travelers didn't really stand out much in this place. It was yet another border town, not to another country, but to the wilderness, the jungle. Almost everybody, even most of the present women wore guns openly, at their hip, or carried a rifle in their hands.

There was no gold-digging here, but gold-diggers ventured to town to sell their gold. The sound of guns being fired raised no eyebrows anywhere in this place. Nor did cries for help or howls of pain

The three of them felt it, just as much as they heard and saw it, and smelled and tasted the blood not properly cleansed from wet floors. Eyes flickered constantly, keeping a lookout for suspicious movement on rooftops or dark doorways.

– They watch us, don't they? Laurie said, her voice clearly revealing her anxiety and revulsion. – No one moves through this city without major backup, and we're just three. They saw the two of you shoot, and they feared us long before that, suspecting what we are, but they still study us, looking for a weakness, a chink in our armor.

She sought closer to him. Liz deliberately kept her distance.

They returned to Richard and Alanis, the people employed by the two, and the tribe. The couple made their usual inquiries among a given population, showing their maps and drawings to everybody they met.

Justine and the others sat on the sidewalk outside what, if one wanted to be kind could be called a cantina.

Hagman and off and on spouse had what could be called a conversation with what quite safely could be said to be a man with poor means.

– You KNOW about it! Richard cried. – You've HEARD about it.

– Relax, Alanis cautioned him. – You don't want to terrify the poor man.

He stared at her with angry, even enraged eyes.

– You don't want to go there, senor, the man said. – It's a bad place, where bad men live, and horrible things happen.

Richard tried for minutes to make the man say more, cajoling him, bribing him, threatening him. Eventually the man pulled back, backed off, clutching his gun, keeping an eye on Richard and the rest of them, until he was almost out of sight. Then he turned abruptly, and ran off, the fastest he was able.

– Look what you did. He glared at Alanis. – I had him, had him eating off my hand, and then you interfered, and *ruined* it all.

– You asshole, she spat. – You imbecile asshole!

– Cheers! Justine cried demonstratively, raising her glass, staring at the two, sending daggers of disgust at them.

Those sitting around the tables cheered and drank.

They sent Richard and Alanis resentful stares, and even though it softened a bit when they glanced at the approaching trio, it didn't disappear completely.

«Is there anything for us here, anymore»? Justine thinks, Laurie sent to Ted and Liz. «Anything at all»?

I confess that I have wondered about that myself, Ted conceded willingly.
Is that irony or do you mean it? Liz wondered.
Her «voice» was totally even, flat, not betraying a hint of emotion.
He reached out with a hand.
– Don't touch me, she snarled.
She struck his outstretched hand and walked away, and left him there to rot. His arm fell.
He sat down in the nearest chair. There was no lack of chairs around, even though some of them were quite ruined. He sat there for quite some time. It was as if the others weren't there. A dark mist formed in his line of vision, and no matter where he looked or how much he strived to get rid of it, it didn't vanish, didn't let go.
Someone should go after her… Laurie sent to him.
He nodded, or at least gave his consent in some way or another. Laurie hurried after Liz.
The contact remained open. He saw through Laurie's eyes, while still experiencing everything around him.
Candy and Candice comforted him. Everything felt slow. The dread lingered on the outside and inside. They still carried the children on their back. Some of the others kept them in their lap, including Laurie's child. The two women sat down on each knee. Candy stroked his hair. They knew his body language, and could, in effect, to a certain degree read his mind, something that wasn't very difficult right now.
Liz turned several corners. He saw her, the way she moved, her body language. So much was off, diminished. It made him cringe. Candy kissed him on the lips, tenderly, being sweet to him. Liz walked into a bar, a dark and dank joint fairly far off their usual haunts in the city. A lot of hard-eyed men and women stared at her without staring at her when she entered. Laurie hesitated a moment or two before following her inside.
The room was filled with smoke. Ted's eyes flooded with tears because Laurie's were. Liz, with her enhanced senses didn't seem to be affected by it at all. She walked to the bar, followed by cruel eyes, ignoring them as well.
– Whiskey, Liz grinned.
The barkeeper hesitated, but then he evidently got the permission from whoever was in charge, and proceeded to serve the newly arrived woman.
She grabbed the tiny glass and brought it to her lips, or rather to under her nose.
– You know, she said, – I don't even have to taste this shit to know that it's laced with poison.
The stench reeked in her nostrils, in Ted's.
A man moved a bit to her left.
– And I should advice you that I can get this gun on my hips free from the holster before you can blink.
The man froze.
They had seen her in action and knew she wasn't bullshitting them. Images of her training earlier today flowed through their minds. Laurie saw that, easily.

She also saw that it didn't impress them, only impressed them enough to stay their hand.

And then she glimpsed something else, and she wanted to cry out a warning, but never got that far.

Four rifles played up. Liz was penetrated from all sides. She fell in a pool of blood.

Ted shook, and almost squeezed too hard, and nearly broke Candy's arm.

No one said anything. A man stepped forward. He lifted up the still body and carried it to the entrance, effortlessly throwing it outside in the dust.

Laurie was suddenly sweating cold drops of sweat, unable to hide her shakes. She knew exactly where the four men with the rifles hid. The fairly low-intensive stench from the fired guns made her eyes flow more.

– You look like a far more accommodating wench, one of the sitting men said, the leader said. – Why don't you come over here and make yourself presentable.

She smiled sweetly to him, but most of all she wanted to laugh at him, and spit in his face.

There was a sound from the entrance. The men frowned a bit, not immediately connecting it with anything.

Liz Warren appeared in the door, stepped inside, steady on her feet, bloody and covered with dust, her fireeyes glowing in cold flames. Everybody froze, but didn't move, not an inch.

– That was quite interesting and invigorating, she nodded, more to herself than to them. – Care to try again?

Horror and superstition coursed through them. Laurie walked to the leader, a smile playing around her lips, as her power played with his fears. She made him see her with demonic features, not holding back, excelling in letting go.

– So, you want me to be accommodating, huh? She hissed sweetly.

– Don't come any closer, he cried pushing his chair back.

She pushed it back forward again, right into her sphere. Everybody gasped.

– As you wish, she shrugged, – it's only fitting that you, the servant, the slave come to me.

She gestured, and he rose into the air, halfway to the ceiling, and then she *squeezed*. He screamed like a baby.

– Have you learned your place, now?

He hesitated a moment, and she instantly squeezed again.

– Yes, he shouted. – YES!

She dropped him on his knees. He knelt before her, trembling violently.

– *You,* behind the walls, Liz snarled. – Come forth and *kneel* before your gods.

They obeyed. It was easy, even without Laurie's telepathy to imagine how they dropped their weapons and scrambled to obey, stumbling over chairs and tables, not stopping for anything.

Everybody knelt before the two women. The two stood there, looking at them all like they would slugs under their feet, and that was also how every single man and woman in the room felt like.

Liz drew her gun and shot the man at the other side of the room in the arm. He squeaked and fainted.

– You think *this,* she said, holding up the gun, – this little mechanical thing is the most powerful weapon in existence? Well, small men think small, I suppose.

Laurie petted the man before her. He was weeping in stark fear.

– I believe you are correct, she said. – These creatures have no imagination, and they are easily led, at least after their obvious inferiority has been revealed to them.

– You were the power in this city before we arrived, Liz said. – But you've given us a little bit of grief solely because we allowed it, because the gods were lenient, patient. I trust you have, at this point gotten a glimpse of what will happen if our patience should run out?

It was clearly a rhetorical question. No one replied or voiced any reply.

– Heads to the ground, Laurie commanded lazily

They bent forward, and pushed their forehead at the floor.

She put a foot on the man's neck.

– You're such fragile creatures, she said softly. – One slight push and you will be no more.

– You will not move until the sun sets, Liz said. – There will be a lot of discomfort. Your limbs will hurt, but you will not move, and you will be very grateful that this, one time the gods chose to explain themselves.

They left, and didn't turn their heads to look back. Laurie swam through everybody's mind easily and enjoyed herself. It was such a vast kingdom, such a pleasant place to roam.

– I needed this, Liz said, nodding to herself.

– You needed to scratch an itch, Laurie stated, also nodding to herself.

– I did indeed, Liz said, – and now it is thoroughly scratched.

They returned to the others, to Ted that had seen and experienced everything.

– I need to clean myself, Liz said.

She kept walking, up the outside stairs, to the room they used, one covering the entire floor.

Laurie slipped down on Ted's lap and into his arms.

– Are you all right? He wondered, rubbing her cheek a bit.

– Sure, she grinned. – I quite enjoyed myself actually.

She crouched in his lap, showing him, making no secret of how she enjoyed it there. Liz removed her bloody and torn cloths as she walked to the shower. She turned on the water and stepped under its cleansing power. Blood fell from her exposed and undamaged skin. Laurie stayed in contact with them both. They saw through each other's eyes. Laurie kissed Ted's lips and Liz felt it. Liz touched herself, and Ted felt it. Ted turned hard against Laurie's thigh. Liz opened her mouth wide, drawing in as much air as she was able, her gasp echoing between the walls.

It's so pleasant, Laurie told them, so very, very pleasant.

A man moved among the kneeling people in the bar. His muscles contracted, and he shifted position. He held his breath, while looking everywhere in the room for brutal, cruel eyes. A hand moved. He stared at it, as if it was a snake. The others noticed, too, and they followed the drama with intense interest. He lifted his head from the floor, grimacing in pain, as his back acted up after such a long time in frozen position. Both arms began moving, and a relieved, triumphant grin spread on his face.

Then he screamed, as the horrible pain shot through him. It came from the inside, from his very mind. He fell and began shaking, harder and harder as the seconds passed by. The scream turned into a whine. The others shook like leaves. They knew, now, beyond doubt that they would stay in place until a deep darkness had settled in the area.

Liz, Ted and Laurie, in close contact couldn't quite tell who, if any had taken the initiative to the man's punishment. In that moment of action they had been one, singular entity.

The sudden stench of blood woke them from the pleasant haze they had descended into. Laurie kept smiling, both before Ted's eyes and his inner eye, but his frown and vigilance alerted her, too, and the rest of the travelers to something else, something taking indomitable precedence.

Dust rose in the outskirts of the cluster of buildings. It was just a tiny wisp at first, at least in their mind, but growing, growing.

Liz turned off the water, and stepped out of the shower. She grabbed a towel and began rubbing herself hard and relentless.

Laurie looked stunned ahead, at the growing dust-cloud approaching them. Out of habit she turned to Ted to speak to him, not convey the news with her mind, but then she realized he already knew.

Mark Stewart and his hunters had arrived in the nameless town.

## 2

Stewart and Jean, and Kelly Regehr and Clayton Prescott, and all the rest appeared from the dust, the mist and smoke of time.

Ted and the others began moving, positioning themselves, checking their weapons and battle-readiness, doing the checklist in their mind.

The cars stopped a little up the street. The other travelers disembarked their vehicles. Liz returned to the street, to Ted's side.

– It's amazing, isn't it? She said aloud. – Two years. Only two years.

– It feels like an eternity, Laurie whispered.

It looked like something out of the old west, when the two groups approached each other, even as one sat still, waiting. The clothes were different, of course, and the presence and demeanor of the many women, but the attitude and overall scenery were pretty much the same.

They faced each other, as the dust slowly settled.

– Ted… Liz, Mark nodded.

– Mark, Ted said.

Shadows burned and expanded and mingled between them. They moved as the people withdrew into the building, even as they remained where the creatures of flesh and bone had been standing seconds earlier, an imprint on eternity.

– He's here, Stewart said.

– Here? Liz asked.

No one bothered to ask who «he» was.

– We tracked him to this general area, Jean said. – The stories of Iluso the Cyclops have spread all over Central and South America, so it's hard to pinpoint.

She towered above them all, and that was still somewhat unsettling to Ted, who had known her before she had changed.

– Except for a brief occurrence in Caracas two years ago we haven't seen him or heard him being mentioned at all. I guess he was keeping track of us, but lost it when our plane crashed.

Ted shrugged.

– I heard about your plane crashing, Stewart said. – But I knew you weren't dead. I felt you stronger than ever.

His change was, in many ways far more unsettling.

There were still very few physical signs of his transformation, but on the inside everything had been turned inside out. Everything repressed had manifested a thousand-fold. Ted was so pleased to release his own power inside, to reveal it, to revel in it, to let it fly free, keeping the dragon in the mirror at bay. He touched all his traveling companions, deliberately. Liz did, too. He did no longer shy away from reliving the memory of himself as a living God, but savored it, knowing that it kept what had been Mark Stewart one step away.

– Any trouble with the locals in this town? Prescott asked.

– Not anymore, Liz grinned.

– Good, Regehr burned at them, in a startling imitation of her master. – They're always such a bother at first, aren't they?

Ted grabbed bottles of Glenmorangie whiskey from the cabinet, both with his hands and mind, popping the corks with his power. The corks hit the ceiling with a bang. He put a lot of the tiny whiskey glasses on the table and filled them to the brim. There was exactly one drink for each individual present.

He grabbed one glass and raised it.

– Salud! He said.

– Salud! Stewart said.

They all drank, emptied it all in one swallow.

Laurie coughed.

– I presumed you would set up shop in New Orleans, Stewart said, several glasses later. – It would seem like the ideal place.

– It wasn't, Ted said.

– You're still looking, Stewart acknowledged.

They lit the fireplace as it turned dark outside, chasing off a bit of the humidity. Light mist seemed to invade the room, the house, both real and imagined.

Everybody noticed it, how it fluctuated and danced around the three people at the center of the attention.
– It's strange, isn't it? Candy mused. – Two years have passed since we left New Orleans. So much has happened, and still it seems like it was yesterday, like no time has passed at all.
– I can hardly recall anything before that Samhain, Ben said, – anything at all.
– The four of you were born that night, Jean said, a little pointed, – given your names and identities, and everything you will carry with you for the rest of your lives.
Her words felt a little unpleasant, but not as much as they would suspect.
– I know, Ben said quietly, – and it doesn't bother me the slightest. Everybody should be so lucky, be pulled from a dreary and horrible existence. During these two years, though we have endured hardship and tragedy, we have lived stronger and more than most people do during a lifetime.
Candice chuckled and kissed him on the cheek.
– One single second of this is better than the existence we left behind. If I died the next second I would have no regrets. And do you guys know what the most amazing of all is? That I can say something like that with absolute conviction, with the absolute certainty that it's the truth.
Most of the people got drunk, of course. Liz, Ted and Stewart didn't. It did affect them, in a way, diverting their focus only briefly, but they were always out there, in the streets surrounding the house, ready for whatever was coming.
Everybody undressed and began fucking, very casual, very straightforward, an act dissolving bits and pieces of the tense mood. Hours passed in a haze of heat and desire.
Liz walked outside to pee. She just spread her thighs against the wall and got on with it. It was another wonderfully lazy and casual act very appealing to her. The stench of the piss invaded her nostrils and her self. The darkness invaded her, like it always did. She didn't fight it, but let down her guard deliberately, opened herself to what it had to offer.
She noticed Laurie long before she actually appeared by her side, of course. Laurie was drunk, but giggling and in a very good mood. The girl joined her, there at the wall.
– It feels so good, doesn't it, peeing, like a release, giving away what remains after fucking?
Liz mumbled something, a bit lost in her own thoughts, in the pleasant darkness.
– I did fuck a few times, before my powers developed, Laurie kept talking, a dreamy look in her eyes. – There's just *no* comparison. Telepathy enhances the experience beyond words, and add telekinesis, and it becomes something… beyond anything.
There was no malice, or triumph in her voice, no bragging or anything because of the advantage she inadvertently pointed out. She was just talking.

Liz had no more piss left, but she didn't move, just remained on her spot with half-closed eyes, the expanded awareness brought on by the fucking slowly giving way to the drowsiness brought on by the fucking.

– What did Mark mean? Laurie asked casually.

Liz didn't reply, patiently waiting for the rest.

– What did he mean by you «setting up shop»?

And now the voice to the left had gained a little more intensity, insistence.

– It's a modern phrase used to describe an ancient act, Liz said, without looking at the other. – When the gods declare their godhood and live among their worshippers.

– That sounds so *cool,* Laurie said excited.

She finished peeing, too. They both stood there, allowing the piss to turn cold between their thighs.

– You are much better, now, you know…

And then Liz looked at her, lazily, her penetrating stare only moderately in use.

– There is very little left, if anything of whatever malady plagued you. I think it was merely a phase you went through. Honest!

– That is comforting, thank you, Liz said, without malice.

The people in the cantina down the street had finally dared to move, but not very far. They had fallen asleep in their tracks, in the midst of their own shit and piss. The rest of the town had also fallen silent. Richard and Alanis, and their employees and advisors resided in an apartment not far away in the opposite direction. Liz realized that she was able to see everything and everybody so clearly because of the constant rapport she and Ted had with Laurie, through her telepathic abilities. It had become a constant, a habit in their lives.

– So, why not New Orleans? Laurie wondered.

Liz considered the question, pondered its implications.

– I don't know. It didn't feel right, I guess. Perhaps we just aren't ready… yet.

I know we will be!

I know, too, Laurie nodded excitedly.

People passed by on the street, kept passing by and looked directly at them, glancing at them in fear, curiosity and lust, before hurrying on. The two women didn't acknowledge them in any way. It couldn't even be said that they ignored them, because they made no conscious decision of doing so.

Liz read it all in Laurie's expressive face, and felt good about it.

They kissed each other on the lips and chuckled throatily.

– How did you meet Mark and bunch? Liz asked lightly.

– It's amazing, isn't? Laurie said. – That I have never told you that and that you guys have never asked?

She shrugged, and the shrug was also perfectly natural, not feigned.

– My family, my parents and sister and brother was killed in a shootout between Mark and Gidman. I just stood there, on the battlefield afterwards, virtually catatonic. Mark fetched me and brought me to his court. He told me later that he had sensed my latent powers, sensed the… the kinship between us.

Liz saw it, experienced it all. Laurie was an amazing storyteller. Everything seemed to become alive as she spoke. Liz saw the smoky street, the stricken girl, smelled the iron, the gunsmoke and blood, experienced her naked terror, though muted by the years that had passed and everything that had happened during that time.

– When I saw you guys for the first time I knew you, too, were kin, related to me beyond blood. I sensed Mark's fire rise when he told me of your arrival, and he sent me to issue his obscure invitation. Perhaps you would have come even if you hadn't encountered Phillip and Richard in Las Vegas, perhaps not. A case can be made that New Orleans is attracting people like us, but it's still an amazing coincidence. It almost seemed… fated, doesn't it?

– Yes, Liz acknowledged. – Fated…

The street, the world moved around them. A cold draft came from nowhere and touched them.

– Ted told me about a conversation he and Tilla and Linda and other kids from Denver had in London with Mark and Eric Carr, the journalist. Eric spoke about a connection between them all, how they all seemed to be a part of a vast tapestry spread throughout space and time. Mark told them his version of the Warren family history that night, pretty much confirming Eric's hypothesis.

– I find that… exciting, Laurie said awestruck.

– I rather thought you would.

Liz grinned lazily, closing and opening her eyes once.

The sound of the animals, of the not so distant jungle grew momentarily slightly more intense. They noticed, and were lost in it for a while.

Laurie writhed and rolled on the wall, very much in the same manner that Liz did, and they shared the moment, the experience and their kinship.

– Eric?

– Eric, what? Liz wondered.

– The way you say his name, Laurie teased her. – What I sense beneath the buzz in your mind. You have… met him, haven't you?

– Yes, I have, Liz acknowledged willingly. – He makes quite an impression on you, a very intense man for a… a human, a Sapiens. He figured out our secret on his own, and proved it by stabbing my arm, watching it heal.

– My Goddess, Laurie breathed. – That sounds more like the trait of an abusive madman to me.

– He is obsessive, Liz admitted. – And that might indeed lead him… astray, like our traits might do to us, but it was that characteristic that made him look beyond the veil and find unimaginable truths.

– Unimaginable truths, Laurie breathed.

Night came, true night. They sensed it, felt it in their sizzling neural pathways.

They yawned, long pleasant yawns. It felt good to feel sleep come. Hands sought hands, and hand in hand they returned inside, to the heap of warm, resting bodies and minds, and the deep, disturbing dreams of tomorrow.

## 3

The group joined Stewart's band of travelers, scouring the area for signs of Gidman, for Iluso, very much the same way that Richard and Alanis sought the Lost City, leaving the children behind with the estranged couple and their hired guns.

Everybody was visibly armed, taking pride in looking as dangerous as humanly possible. It was overkill, really, with a row of armed-to-the-teeth people surrounding the old man on the ground.

– I haven't seen Iluso, the old man said, speaking English, – but I have heard about him, and heard his song.

He paused a bit, before he made the chant, or a not so bad, more than good enough facsimile of it.

– Iluso is our Master. Iluso is our God. Beware his wrath.

And suddenly their heavy armament and excessive manpower and shitty nerves didn't feel like overkill anymore. Warren deliberately watched Stewart at that moment, watched how he cracked at the seams.

– They raid the villages and towns, the old man said, – spreading confusion and fear, and then they vanish like smoke… or ghosts, and the confusion and fear grows. The army has come to our outpost of civilization, has come, on occasion to chase Iluso and his army of spirits, but when they arrive there's nothing to find.

The travelers left the old man and walked down the street to yet another local cantina. There was no one there. The locals had fled the moment the strangers had been observed outside town.

These strangers always chose the cantina as their temporary residence and people in this area knew that.

– *Iluso* is into human sacrifices these days, Ted told Stewart. – His followers tried offering Phillip to their god, and they wouldn't do that, without his explicit approval, would they?

He recalled the sick feeling that had overwhelmed them by the sheer thought.

– I guess he's making medicine or something before his final confrontation with you. He has cracked.

Stewart didn't look good… no matter how good he looked. There was something there, beneath the surface making Ted jittery to the point that he had problems taking his eyes off his older kin, a constant and building pressure behind the eyelids threatening to burst his skull.

Or so it felt.

– He has chosen the shadows, Jean said, – claimed them. But he won't succeed. We'll confront him no matter where he hides.

She sounded pretty much like Stewart, not at all like the fairly gentle person Ted dimly remembered.

He shrugged, deliberately. She had reason to be angry. She had, too. The old Jean had been a lie, a carefully crafted persona, one hiding from the world, pretty much like Ted himself had done.

Dust rose in the distance. He watched it through the dirty window. It rose and fell as the arriving party reached the town.

They had an excellent view from here, easily able to keep an eye on all access points.

– He won't come here, he heard himself say. – He will come at us from a position of advantage.

He turned towards Stewart, very direct and with unflinching eyes.

– If you truly want to confront him you should avoid such a fortress in the future.

The implication was clear. This was as close to an insult he could come without actually delivering one.

He steeled himself, preparing for Stewart's rage to manifest itself, preparing to combat it with everything he, himself possessed.

But nothing happened. Stewart just ignored the outburst, or seemed to.

The dust cloud dispersed, revealing a military unit, not that many soldiers, but enough to pose a possible threat.

– They are what they seem, as far as I can tell, Laurie told him, told Ted and Liz, deliberately speaking aloud.

– You shouldn't be concerned, senores, the bartender said. – The soldiers just come and go. They brag a little, telling everybody how brave and dangerous they are, and then they leave, leaving everybody to continue with their business.

He sounds like a fan, Laurie sent to Ted and Liz. A fan of the meager business we bring, I guess.

So young and so cynical, Liz thought in their mindscape.

The soldiers didn't venture into the town, but remained in their barracks, a few derelict buildings at the edge of the populated area.

We shouldn't be too full of ourselves, Stewart sent to the three of them. They may be here to check us out. We've caused quite a stir, quite a bit of trouble in a rather large area lately. The central government isn't completely unaware of what's happening in the provinces. They allow roaming groups of locals and gringos as long as the trouble doesn't grow out of control.

The three exchanged glances. Stewart had just sent them a message, one very clear and distinct, in at least two meanings of the word.

The hot afternoon gave way to a sultry evening. The two half moons didn't really mingle much, but retreated to their own part of the house they had chosen to occupy.

– He couldn't communicate that well when you were with him, right? Liz asked Laurie.

She spoke quite loud, not caring to lower her voice at all, not caring if he heard her, like he did, anyway, if he chose to.

– No, Laurie confirmed, – it was mostly emotions then, and piecemeal thoughts when he healed us.

– He is growing, Liz pondered, pacing the floor. – Of course he is.

She looked angry, poised, but Ted noticed a tiny flickering of uncertainty in her eyes, but he couldn't tell if she noticed that he noticed.

He wanted to strike the wall with his hand in frustration and irritation, but held himself in check, and that, in turn made him fume even more.

He did sleep that night, even though he couldn't actually be certain when. The haunting dreams visited him, but then again, they often did, also when he was fully awake. He stood by the window and looked down at the small pond in the valley below. Liz snuck up by his side. They turned and looked back at Laurie lying among the rest. With her sleeping it was finally fairly quiet in his head. Down by the pond a group of masked children danced and played. They found themselves pulled back to Colorado and the Kendall ranch.

The evening and the next morning arrived, the next evening that was morning to them, in a slow blink of an eye. The military convoy was still there. Two guards stood on their post, watching the town through binoculars.

Two half moons, briefly met and then parted.

They faced each other in the twilight morning light.

Ted looked at Liz. She had pulled back a little, on his left side, deferring the decision to him. Irritation surged within his mind and body, no matter how much he attempted to contain it.

– We're leaving, he told Stewart and Jean.

Stewart didn't say anything, but what Ted caught from his boiling insides spoke volumes, and Ted threw all caution to the wind. Laurie tensed a little on his right side, preparing herself.

– Quite frankly, we have no interest in participating in the game of hide and seek your brother and you are playing, Ted snarled. – It gets old very fast, you know.

They packed their remaining gear. It wasn't difficult or didn't take up much of their time. Most of it had already been packed. The groups nodded curtly to each other as one filed past the other.

Stewart reached out a hand for Laurie, as she walked past him. She pulled to the side and sought close to Ted, both pride and rejection in her eyes. Stewart shrugged.

They left, walked into the dusty street, to the jeeps standing at the back of the house. Their movement according to each other was like the flow it had long since become, their attention reaching both outwards and inwards. They smiled to each other, but kept looking out for threats. Their eyes never stopped wandering.

Engines started up in a roar of simultaneous action. The jeeps were on the move, leaving yet another dusty town at the edge of the moist jungle.

The soldiers are scurrying towards their posts, Laurie sent.

The convoy approached the derelict fortress. It was the only road out of town.

They have their fingers on the trigger, Laurie sent. They haven't been told to fire.

The three of them began forming protective shields in the air on the right side of the vehicles, ready to really make an effort of it if it would show itself necessary.

The convoy passed the fortress, ten, twenty, fifty meters.

They raged through the nearest turn. Laurie kept sweeping the surrounding area, but she sensed no human thoughts anywhere. They were home free.

It took them less than the day to return to the other nameless town, where Richard and Alanis were busy (and frantic) preparing the final stages of their expedition.

– Richard is pacing back and forth in his makeshift study, Laurie happily reported, drawing laughter from all the tribal members.

They drove into town, approaching the house with the small garden.

– He's rushing to the window, she said. – A huge smile lights his face.

– He'll never live that down if we confront him with it, Phillip chuckled. – We should let him live on in happy ignorance.

– He has a scratch on his neck, she said somberly. – He and Alanis have been… quarreling again.

That information turned them all quiet and made them shake their heads in distress.

– What *are* they quarreling about? Candy wondered nonplussed.

Everybody glanced at each other, but no one could give a satisfying answer.

Richard and Alanis and some of the aides received them in the courtyard. There were smiles and embraces and kisses and bright laughter. No comments were made about the ugly red line on Richard's neck.

– We're ready, Richard declared happily. – We're finally ready!

– Perhaps our young friends would like to refresh and clean themselves after a long day, Alanis said lightly.

– No refreshing or cleaning necessary, Ted said just as lightly. – In the jungle no one frowns at the stench of your sweat.

There wasn't that much to pack. They would travel light from here on, not bring more than they could carry. It didn't take long, didn't take long at all before they were on the move, leaving the jeeps and most of the expensive equipment behind.

– Shouldn't you have someone pick it up? Justine asked Richard and Alanis.

– Think nothing of it, Richard shrugged. – We've left behind equipment on all five continents. It will be gone five minutes after we've stepped into the jungle.

The wanderers walked out of town, sending only tiny dust clouds into the air, very little to mark their passing. It felt comforting in a way. They didn't turn, didn't look back, they never did.

– Yet another town, Liz said in silent despair and rage, – yet another place where the stench of garbage never leaves our nostrils.

– There's only jungle from here on, Ted said. – No more towns or roads or stinking gasoline or garbage.

But it was like Liz said; it still stuck in their nostrils. Far away, when the stench of oxygen and plants and life abundant dominated their perception it was still there.

## 4

It was days, hours later. They no longer stumbled in roots or cared about branches slapping their face.

– So noisy, one of the new men that had joined them complained.

– Are you kidding me? Candy chuckled. – It's so *quiet*. There's no noise in nature. Only civilization has noise.

– There are a thousand different sounds, Candice said, – and I know each and every one.

Ted, Liz and Laurie were the point, as usual. There were no tracks to follow, but they could sniff out potential dangers. They didn't notice any, except the occasional four-legged predator, but kept their attention on their surroundings all the time. It wasn't hard, very much similar to breathing.

Hagman frequently consulted his maps and compass, but they rarely changed course because of that. The three in front had an inner compass that, at the very least was equal to the mechanical the explorer used.

And not only the three of them, but almost any member of the tribe could match the fairly advanced technology.

Ted pointed to broken branches in their path. Laurie instantly relayed that to the others.

Many people, Ted said. Recent.

The others nodded. Interpreting tracks and seeing signs of humans had been one of the first things they had learned during their life as wild people. That knowledge didn't go away, but stayed with them for all time.

Ted… frowned. Suddenly he was sweating in a completely different manner.

– What's wrong? Liz asked, instantly noticing the change in him.

– I… don't know, he replied.

– It's enough that one of us go apeshit, you know, she said lightly.

He didn't know, didn't know why his heart was suddenly hammering in his chest.

They doubled their efforts, expanded upon the area they covered in their scouting capacity. There was nothing there, nothing explaining the feeling of dread assaulting him.

– I think it was sweat, he said. – I smelled sweat.

Cold camp, Laurie sent to everybody, as they made their way to the place they had selected for the night.

It was a nice spot by the river, one evoking more pleasant memories for them, for the wandering tribe.

They sat there in the darkness, and it didn't really feel dark. Everybody saw well enough after a while. That included those not used to do it.

Ted and Liz saw everything with a kind of clarity they didn't quite manage during the day. Laurie made everybody share it through their eyes and everybody marveled and shivered at the startling sight. Ted waited, waited patiently until he had everybody's attention.

– I recognized the scent, he said. – It was the same I smelled in the ruins where there had been human sacrifices, the same people that have been striking terror into the entire extended part of South America.

They sensed fear in him, and that startled them all further.

– Of course, Liz mumbled. – I should have known that, too.

Stark fear had touched her, overwhelmed her.

– And there's more, Ted said, – something I can't quite grasp, right beyond my reach.

– More, Liz whispered.

It was so frustrating, making the welcomed rage swell within him, but even that couldn't help him this time.

– Surely we're well equipped to defend ourselves? Hagman said, clearly anxious, but mostly unconcerned. – There is no reason to turn back.

But the anxiety doubled when Ted Warren set his eyes like hooks in his flesh, something he hadn't quite experienced before.

– I'm not saying we should turn back, Warren said. – We just need to be all that better prepared.

And Richard Hagman started sweating all that more, and he never truly stopped after that.

I should have known, Liz thought, communicating to Ted and Laurie in their common mindscape. Why didn't I know?

Different angle, Ted thought. We see different parts of the puzzle, of the… of The Invisible Labyrinth.

You're so smart. Liz sent him a hot stare. I love you!

She felt great pleasure when she spotted the slight red blush on his neck. It burned in her enhanced vision like a flare. She moved close to him, and sat in his lap.

– *You* smell so good, she whispered in his ear.

It feels so good to be near you, to feed on the nectar of your scent.

He had to swallow, hard, and cat got his tongue. He was momentarily unable to speak, mind or vocal chords.

It was peaceful there, in the darkness, no matter what both their reason and vivid visions of the future told them.

– The fire is always nice, Ben said, – but right now I don't really miss it. The darkness burns just as much.

Candice kissed him.

– I love sensitive males, she grinned.

Touching in the darkness was very much like seeing. They knew that from before and once more confirmed it to themselves.

Liz hummed that strange, haunting melody again. As always it came to her without any conscious decision on her part. It filled the pervasive shadow and everybody within it. Even Richard and Alanis, not very harmonic these days were caught in it, pulled into its powerful lure.

The campfire was there, with flames like dancing shadows. Liz and Ted felt the shiver, but couldn't tell which one was shivering, or if it was both, or the ground below or the trees and their branches whispering to them.

They posted guards. Liz and Ted and Laurie roamed the jungle, unable to sleep, and when Laurie finally succumbed to Morpheus' lure, the other two still sat there, scanning for changes in the surroundings, visible, tangible signs that someone was moving in on them.

The group kept making good speed during the day, as hours became days. Alanis and Richard consulted their maps and compasses, and the three scouts kept choosing the travelers' path.

Their time in civilization turned distant again, even though they didn't really feel like they were leaving it behind this time.

A lot more pictures were taken, the to-be-processed film protected by the waterproof and generally tight containers. They would survive the harsh conditions.

Ted excelled at taking the pictures, but there was something that insisted on distracting him, something that wouldn't let go.

The three of them stopped on a rise, the moment they spotted signs of something that might be a trail, might be made by humans. They looked from their hiding place at a large waterfall across the basin. Ted astounded the two girls when he used the binoculars to study the terrain by the fall.

– I can't see anyone, he said.

He used his vocal chords to speak, for some reason.

– I can't sense anyone, Laurie said.

Liz touched Ted on the cheek, tenderly, harshly.

– It feels like we're heading into trouble, right?

He nodded, not speaking, in any way. What she sensed in him, both through Laurie and her own senses was a churning buzz of sensations, different and startling compared to previous experience.

– Then, why are we spooked?

– I don't *know!*

He replied with an intensity unusual even for him. She shivered under its power.

– This isn't our scene, Laurie shrugged. – Perhaps it isn't fear, but mere frustration over Richard and Alanis' juvenile display and yearning, their search for mirages and ruins. Perhaps we all want to leave that shit behind. Perhaps we should.

They looked at her, disagreeing with her, agreeing with her.

– Alanis and Richard have wasted years of their life, haven't they? Laurie said, not unkindly, a noticeable catching in her throat. – Wasted them on each other and their obsession.

– I think they might have, Liz nodded sadly, looking very young. – I'm not certain.

Ted didn't say anything. He was clearly distracted, and that word was in no way sufficient to describe his churning insides. Liz sensed the ants crawling slowly through his veins.

The jungle spoke to them, as always, but there was little beyond that. They sensed a disturbance, faint, somewhere ahead.

Richard, Alanis, and the tribe approached from the valley behind them. They were clear and distinct in Laurie's mind. The three followed them as they moved forward, also searching physically for people hiding on the surrounding hills. There were none, but their eyes had no problem spotting a broken branch here, a footprint there.

They waited for all the travelers to catch up on the hill across the waterfall.

Richard and Alanis looked expectant at them, waiting for them to speak up, to say something.

– There is something… somewhere, Ted said.

– Somewhere? Alanis prodded him.

– Yes, we found signs of people all over the area, all pointing in the same direction, Liz said. – Most people would miss them, but we are used to tracking in the jungle.

– Good news, then, Hagman brightened.

– Is it? Ted said. – We found prints of shoes, and there are other strange things. All this activity, through centuries should have left distinct trails, but everything is clearly recent.

– That suggests the city is abandoned, Alanis said, just as eager as her occasional husband. – Perhaps other explorers have reached it before us? That isn't so bad. I don't mind sharing.

Ted and Liz glanced at each other and shrugged.

Let's get it over with, she thought curtly.

– So, where is it? Richard wondered, eager like a boy.

– Over there, Liz said, hinting at the waterfall.

Everybody stared at the tall, steep mountain range, the large wall on both sides of the steaming water. It went on for quite a while, left and right.

Hagman despaired for a few seconds, before brightening yet again.

– Several of the people we spoke with said there is a hole, a trail through the mountain. It shouldn't be too hard to find, not with our excellent trackers.

He was clearly spiteful when he looked at them, and they didn't understand him at all.

They cast their attention across the basin.

– It's a wet dream for a sniper, Liz said. – We'll go first. Positions everyone.

The others spread out and pointed their weapons at every possible hiding place.

We're a fearsome force, aren't we? Laurie beamed. The three of us, our fellow travelers and all of us combined?

We are indeed, Ted thought. No matter whom that might stand against us, a violent encounter with us will cause them quite a bit of trouble.

They made their way down the slope, almost on all fours, moving as if they were a part of the terrain, the very ground they walked on. The professional hired hands stared at them with disdain and jealousy, their friends with an admiration that was no longer tinged with awe.

Our charges… they finally see us as human beings, don't they?

Liz mused a bit

I believe so, yes, Ted nodded.

That's something, I guess.

A brief distraction, before all their focus was on their task.

No more talk, not even of the mind, not more than brief exchanges of info and views. The tall and wide wall, a natural divide of stone and might rose in front of them. They probed it, constantly probed their surroundings, looking for hostiles, rushing east for a while, spotting nothing of what they were looking for, rushing back and forth, unable to spot the crack in the giant's armor they were looking for.

We could probably get over here fairly easily, Laurie remarked, but not our charges.

All the tracks they found, rarer the longer west or east they ventured led back to the center, the point they had started out from.

Is it too late, now, Teddy, too late to turn back if we should so decide?

Long ago, I think. We would have to backtrack far for that.

New Orleans, Las Vegas, further?

There were no reply, and she knew he had no answer for her.

She realized startled the he had the slight crouch, the tendency to a humpback he had displayed when he first had arrived at the Kendall Ranch in his early teens ten years ago, the result of the phantom pains from his brother's constant torture. He was sweating, not like she and Laurie, but ice-cold dry-like droplets, forming crystalline spheres on his skin. She noticed how he shook, shook once, before catching himself.

All three of them looked as one at the waterfall. They noticed instantly, as they reached a certain point in the terrain, the almost invisible trail leading to the dark area between the falling water and the wall behind it.

Has to be, Laurie sent excitedly.

They approached, as cautiously as ever. There was no sense of menace, of immediate danger, nothing they smelled or heard or caught with their sensitive minds or forewarning. Ted and Liz signed to Laurie to halt in her tracks, as they continued forward to what was revealed as an entrance to a cave, or as they suspected, a tunnel. She stopped, clearly insulted, but nodded in acknowledgment. They walked inside, into what would eventually be total darkness to others, but not to them.

There were loud sounds in there, echoes for every step they took, equal to the roar of the water from the outside. Even the sound of their breath echoed in the darkness. There was only one passage, no side caves branching out in other directions, no places people could hide, and it wasn't that long a stretch. The light had hardly faded behind them when it started glowing not far ahead.

They walked back. Laurie waited for them at the entrance. She signaled the people across the basin and they sat out to join the advanced group. It took a few minutes, but Hagman and sometime wife were clearly impatient.

Alanis looked around her, as the cave entrance loomed before them, unusually excited.

– The waterfall, the tunnel, she said in wonder. – It all fits. I'm very optimistic.

She looked at Richard with love in her eyes.

– Half with us, Liz said. – The rest of you wait here, for Laurie's signal. No shouting.

The diverse group of travelers followed the three even stranger people into the twilight world of roaring water and echoes. One of the men coughed and it sounded like gunshots, and anybody that had been tempted to speak was discouraged from doing anything like that.

The other side opened up to bright light and more of the lush forest, and no humans. They kept up their precautionary acts, but there was evidently no need. Liz and Ted walked outside first, and then everybody else. There was a distinct trail through this forest. They walked it, with the three circling and scouting ahead, the frown growing deeper on Ted's brow.

Liz looked at Laurie.

Nothing?

Nothing, Laurie confirmed, shaking her head.

Everybody smelled the scent of cooked food in the air. It was very distinct, almost pervasive.

They reached an edge, and the terrain began tilting. Everybody spotted the large building far away, down in the valley. Ted froze. They looked through their binoculars at what was clearly a modern building, a pyramid with a giant, blackened hole in one of its sides.

Suddenly the ants ran through Ted's veins.

– We must turn back, he said. – We must turn back, *now*.

– What… Why?

Hagman looked like he was sleeping.

– You idiot, Ted swore. – You damn idiot!

Understanding and horror crossed Liz's face.

– Goddess! She gasped, clearly stricken, too.

She recalled later, in a fever vision that she had actually snapped some pictures.

Ted grabbed Hagman and turned him around and pushed him forward. One of his henchmen looked like he was considering something, but having seen Warren's power demonstrated beyond doubt he relented quickly. Ted, Liz, Laurie and also most of the tribe pushed at the others, pulling them with them. They ran, not at full speed, but fast, somewhat controlled, Ted's uncanny and unusual panic catching them all.

A modern building. Laurie's thoughts echoed in them all. Only a modern building. Here, in the middle of nowhere.

The run back to the cave and the hasty walk through it felt like it was going on forever. When they had walked ten steps, it felt pretty much like they hadn't moved at all, and that they had to do it all over again. Ted Warren's experience of it formed Laurie's, and thereby them all.

They reached the bright light on the other side, but Ted kept going, kept charging ahead, almost forgetting about the rest, making it hard for them to keep up. Everybody ran, breathing so hard that it hurt, as they kept charging forward, fleeing from whatever horror had awaited them, returning to the slowly comforting deep, deep jungle.

# Chapter eighteen: Journada del Muerto

When they were at their lowest ebb… it happened.

Ted, and thereby the rest stopped hours later, or so it felt.

He leaned against a tree, his mind blazing, his guard up in all directions. Liz felt his power, and marveled at it, in the midst of his sick fear.

– Positions everybody, he commanded. – On your *guard!*

Some of them had been kneeling, totally exhausted, puking their guts out. They grabbed their guns and fought themselves on their feet, forming a perimeter around the clearly easily defended camp he had chosen for them. That told them something, comforted them, and revealed that he wasn't that far gone. The fact that something had spooked him, spooked him beyond anything they had imagined him being capable of being spooked more than kept them on their toes.

– What was that? Hagman shouted. – What the hell was that?

Warren was at him in a flash, grabbing his collar, shaking him, pushing him at a tree, letting him go, dropping him like he would a flea.

Hagman tried to get back up, but failed and remained on his ass, getting his pants wet.

– I'll tell you what it is, Warren said.

Pausing a bit, not really hesitating, only waiting, to drive the point in.

– *That* was the Abraxas Omega building, the place where they kept me and dozens of others prisoner, where they tortured and brainwashed us until we were nothing but mindless husks. That is the City of Light you have been chasing, the *bad place* you've been repeatedly warned about. This is your Cibola, Xanadu, El Dorado, your Atlantis…

Hagman turned pale, turned pale beyond pale.

Alanis turned gray and dead, fading before their eyes.

Ted paced back and forth, clearly beyond distressed, his brain just as much filled with ants as his veins.

– I recognized it, recognized David Gidman's scent, but my conscious mind couldn't identify it. The human sacrifices, the blood-stained altars we've seen, that's him, are Iluso and his insane worshippers. He's down there, in the pyramid, having returned to his old haunts, reaching out to the entire continent with his horror.

– Goddess! Candy cried softly.

She reached out to Ted with a shaking hand, and he let her.

– Those of you that want to return here, with me and Stewart, when we take on Iluso and eradicate him from existence are welcome to do so, but we are leaving.

They all did, a few minutes later, walked back along the same invisible trail they had followed here. No one was looking behind them and all of them constantly scratched the itch on their back, the sign, the fear that the horror so prevalent in their minds was chasing them.

## 2

They looked back, forward and to the sides, more on guard than ever before. There weren't only the three scouts guarding the perimeter anymore, but people in front, at the rear and on the flanks.

Liz was in front with her platoon, Ted at the rear with his, Laurie on the right and others shifting on being on the left, all constantly moving, clutching their weapons, their trigger finger shivering.

When the night finally arrived, after a day that seemed to last forever, or at least like a polar six-month day no one needed any reminder that a cold camp was needed.

It wasn't difficult locating an easily defensible position. They hardly had to think about it. It was like second nature to them all.

They sat there shivering. The children were screaming, sensing the adults' distress. Adults and children sat there, rocking back and forth, the adults desperately attempting to calm themselves, to fight off the panic boiling beneath the surface.

– Why in God's name did we bring the children?

Richard practically whined, in a tone of voice they had never heard him use before. He looked awful.

– It wasn't that long ago you considered it a great idea, «a way of better interacting with the indigenous population».

Alanis' voice was laced with poison. She looked at him with venom in her eyes.

Warren rocked back and forth, his arms locked around his legs. He ignored the two, or at least made a valiant attempt at doing so.

Liz and Laurie and the others did their best to comfort him, and he let them, let them try. Nightmarish images flared before his eyes, equally horrible sensations coursing through his mind. It was as if his hands clutched around cold bars in a wet cell.

The children didn't cry anymore. They whimpered a bit now and then, in their pitiful slumber, pretty much like the adults not on guard duty. The jungle turned quiet, somewhat.

Nothing, Laurie told Ted and Liz, standing at a high point scanning the area behind, in front and to the sides.

You said you sensed something in the valley? Liz prodded.

Something, Laurie acknowledged. I think… think it was Gidman, but I can't be certain. It was so… so powerful. I pulled back in horror.

You touched… his mind?

I believe I did. There were no thoughts. He… kept them from me.

He kept them… from you? But he shouldn't be able to do that. His power is… is physical.

Liz stopped, before she had completed the sentence. A chill passed from her to the other two.

– He's telepathic, she cried out, the moment she thought it, snarling, shaking violently.

– That would explain it, Ted said, equally shaken. – Explain his charisma and the extreme control he has over his followers, the loyalty he commands. They truly see him as a god.

Nightmarish images and sensations revisited Liz. She whimpered.

– It was him, wasn't it? Ted grabbed her. – Him doing it to you, making you afraid and…

– … *weak,* Liz said. – I don't *know!*

There was someone there, someone I still can't see.

– It happened during your ceremony, Laurie said. – I did feel something. You opened yourself up, and he or someone else used the opportunity to slip inside, to make you doubt yourself and everything you are. Whoever it was, was unable to take control, but could sow seeds of uncertainty in your mind. How insidious. I couldn't do that. Sheer power isn't enough. For someone to do something like that he or she must have enormous skill and control born of long experience.

– And being wicked beyond belief.

Phillip suddenly stood there, behind them, and they hadn't sensed him, hadn't noticed him in any way, and that shocked them, shocked them, too.

Liz felt vomit push itself up her throat. She pushed it back down with an effort.

Laurie grabbed her hands.

– But whoever did it was unable to keep doing it to you. You rejected the foreign influence and regained yourself. Please remember that, remember it always.

The tear didn't form in Liz' eye, but it was close. She kissed the other girl in gratitude and joy.

And in passing, she touched Phillip's cheek, appreciating his rage.

Anger and determination surged through them all. They stayed awake, with too much energy to even stand still. The three focused outward so much that it hurt, digging deep within themselves, but sensed nothing, no overt threat, but the sense of menace remained.

This time both Ted and Liz fell asleep before Laurie. She sat down close to them, with her legs crossed, guarding them. Shadows grew out of the night. She faced them, braved their presence. Liz and Ted's thoughts, dreams and visions burned in her thoughts. She bit her lips until it hurt. The giant black faces smiled to her.

I see…. Is it sadness I see?

She slept, too, not that long afterwards. Others in the tribe took her place as sentinel.

Liz dreamed, dreamed vivid and powerful visions. David Gidman's face, one she had never actually seen, except in photographs appeared before her. She shivered under his ruthless attention, and he smiled in contempt. Stewart appeared, so much bigger than Gidman, a giant in her mindscape, and she shook her head in bewilderment and denial.

Liz watched Ted and Laurie, and watched them and herself writhing there on the forest bed, shaking in the onslaught of their fears and prophetic visions, unable to tell which was which.

My foot, Laurie whimpered. My poor foot!

She looked absolutely devastated, as if all sanity and life had left her. Ted reached out a hand to her, but she pulled away. He tried again, harder, desperately reaching out to the distraught girl in order to comfort and soothe her, but she just kept slipping into the darkness, the nothing, where he couldn't follow her. And he didn't understand it. The darkness was his friend, but he couldn't go where she had gone.

Liz was lucid. She waited for Gidman to come, for the horror that had visited her in nightmares to attack again, but there was nothing, no sense of any conscious presence.

They burned through sleep quickly, the force of their dreams waking them up after hardly more than a few hours. Most of the others didn't sleep much either. They were up and going before the first bright light, feeding as they moved.

Warren checked his weapons, checked them for any malfunction. There wasn't any. He also began checking a selection of the others' guns. Both tribe members and the rest glanced at him, but didn't really questioning his motives. These were all people that knew quite well the importance of well-functioning equipment.

They're all good, Liz told him. I checked them all.

You did, huh?

He nodded in acknowledgement, both bemused and not.

Yes. They're all good. No one has tampered with them.

She smiled proudly.

I've checked everybody's mind several times, Laurie thought, done deep scans. If the enemy has any agents among our numbers, I can't detect them.

They both knew, of course, unlike the others, *why* he was so adamant concerning security, understood better than the rest his growing paranoia, knew the story the others only knew pieces of.

It's different this time, Liz assured him. We're all more than capable of defending ourselves, both as individuals and a group.

We're feisty and lethal warriors, Laurie agreed, joked solemnly.

He pulled them both close, taking them into his embrace and kissed them, kissed them hard. They chuckled pleased.

I know, Liz thought, before he could do it. Why, then, do we feel this urgency, this sick sense of impending doom?

The thoughts kept churning in their mind, cutting their insides.

They would want to do a surprise attack, taking us more or less unaware, Ted thought. Perhaps an aerial assault…

… with teargas and anesthetic gas?

Laurie snapped her fingers.

– Everybody, listen up, he said aloud.

He had their instant attention.

– Put on your masks.
They did, a few of them grumbling, but not much. They understood his reasoning well.
– Thank the Goddess Richard has prepared for any eventuality, Justine chuckled, not unkind.
The general laughter wasn't unkind either. The perceived outside threat made them pull together stronger than ever.
I wish we could see him, them, Ted thought. Anything is better than this uncertainty.
Liz looked at him.
No. He shook his head. There are worse fates.
It was impossible to keep the masks on all the time, so they changed on keeping them on, at least for a few hours, until they gave up. It ended up with them keeping them on the hips, ready for use at a moment's notice.
They were prepared, all of them, seeing the threat as real. The three in front, at the rear and on the sides and everywhere else sensed that with a certain satisfaction.
But the enemy remained elusive, out of reach of all senses.
– We need Stewart, Warren said to Liz when they were alone for a moment or two. – You were right.
– I was?
– I sensed your reluctance when we left.
She frowned.
– I don't think I was reluctant.
She shook her head, and shook it again.
– I don't know what I thought. I guess I figured you knew him best. Thinking about it, now, I believe you did the right thing. I think Mark may be of some limited use to us, if push comes to shove, but we can't trust him.
There, it was said, and couldn't be undone.
Eyes sought eyes, bodies sought bodies.
– Please stop second-guessing yourself, My Lord, she said quietly. – Will you do that, for me?
They wanted each other, there and then, but held back, deliberately, denying themselves the distraction, keeping their attention outward.
He didn't reply, not in any way she could easily discern, and once again she felt that sting of sadness, of regret and recrimination.
The jungle stretched out before them, in all directions. And… they felt it, a push in their gut, one beyond the immediate surroundings, a staggering amount of images and sensations both confusing and clear.
They pushed on, making an effort not to exhaust their fellow wanderers. It was difficult, when every piece of their senses screamed at them… to speed up.
Both of them scratched their back, scratched hard, when the first few attempts didn't work, quickly realizing that no physical cause created the itch.
It didn't really feel like an itch either, but like a glowing piece of iron penetrating their skin and burning their insides.

They tried turning around, but it was no use. The glowing poker stabbed their back, no matter where they turned. The threat seemed to come at them from all directions.

Doubt and certainty riled them, until not much more than just that remained.

– He's out there, waiting, Liz mumbled. – I can feel him. He's out there, waiting for his chance, for us to show weakness. Why can't I feel him?

Ted remembered in flashes, brutally detailed sensations of boundless horror what he had almost forgotten, what he would never forget again. A sound, a blink of an eye, the overwhelming stench everywhere made him remember, made him flinch and mutter under his breath.

They stopped for a while, for a brief respite, for more feeding and a few that needed it used the opportunity to sit down on their heels and shit, the shit flowing like water from their sore opening. Not long afterwards they wiped themselves with leaves, and that was it. Everybody was ready to keep moving.

Liz and Laurie shivered under the onslaught of images and emotions they received from Ted, and Laurie couldn't help broadcasting a bit of it to the others as well. Just a bit, but it made them shudder and gasp and heave, and to clutch their guns even harder.

They made a longer stop at midday, too, one sorely needed. Many had overextended themselves and just had to take a break. They sat in a circle at yet another well-defensible position. Sentinels stood with their back to the rest, listening in.

Ted told them, in explicit detail what had happened to him and his friends.

– First they beat and kicked the crap out of us. Then they chained us hand and feet and drove us off like cattle, using whips to encourage slackers to stay on the top of the pace. When we reached the truck, the brainwashing began in earnest. If we were good and learned fast we were «rewarded». If not we were punished. They pumped us full of drugs and used electric prods on us. I remember that Dennis had a heart attack. They just removed him, threw him away like he was nothing and continued the torture unabated. One of those torturing us bragged about his experience from South American counter-revolutions. Gidman was there all the time, overseeing it all, making sure everything went smoothly. Enslavement is his craft, one he has perfected across the world since before he reached adulthood.

He spoke at length, almost forgetting the time and place, in spite of him doing this deliberately to remind himself what was at stake.

When he was done everybody sat there, desperate strength surging through them.

Fear is the key, he thought, seeing the confirmation in their eyes, as hands moved back and forth on weapons, caressing the cold and hot metal and determination surged through them all.

– My Goddess, Ben said, clearly sick to the bone, – how can human beings do such horrors to one another?

He rocked back and forth, even as he held on to his gun.

– You misunderstand human nature, Alanis shrugged. – You imagine that we are basically altruistic, that we, with all things being equal want to help our fellow man, but that's clearly a wrong assumption, isn't it.

It wasn't a question. Nobody commented on it, but fell deep into their private, murky thoughts.

– But you escaped. Candy sought close to Ted. – Almost all of you did. You… triumphed over the slavers' beyond petty elitism and self-interest. Surely that speaks highly of the human spirit, about its ability to conquer adversity and tyranny?

– Yes, it does

Ted squeezed her hand.

They were on their way again, on the run again. The jungle looked the same as it had an hour before, or countless hours before. There was no discernible change, and in the mire of their despair and deep-rooted fear they began to resent that.

The professional gunmen were afraid, too, obviously. This was a new situation to them, too, one gnawing at the cynicism and cruelty they usually implemented to stay on top of things, a different and deadly playground compared to the fairly uncomplicated situations they usually experienced.

– Alanis and Richard look really, really down, Justine whispered to Phillip. – They've even put away their maps and compasses.

They are, Laurie sent to Ted. It's an understatement, really.

Ted could sense it, too, without her help. The couple's despair virtually descended on him, a gray misery bordering on desolation, mixed with regret and anger, so familiar and chilling to him.

– They need something to kill, Phillip replied quietly to Justine.

– Good! She spat, glancing back at the homogeneous jungle.

Ted, Liz and Laurie scouted together, extra vigilant and aware of every variation, any miniscule change in the pattern surrounding them. There was none, nothing significant.

– We've covered a vast distance in such a short time, since we left the valley, Laurie said. – Surely we must be close to… to civilization?

– No. Ted shook his head. – We won't reach it today, and probably not tomorrow either.

They knew they were heading back south, away from the coast. Warren remembered the harbor, where the ship, the «passenger liner» Aphrodite had docked. He took for granted that Gidman, Iluso's soldiers covered the coastline quite extensively.

This was their, his Place of Power, if anything was. This was where he made his medicine.

Flashes, growing to prolonged images and sensations almost overwhelmed him. He rolled his left hand into a fist, digging into the skin of the palm.

– Yes! Liz dug her nails into his arm. – Embrace the rage. Let it flow!

He did, and it pushed him forward, fueled him, helped him cope, like it always did. His power increased, flowed more easily.

– Everything looks the good damn same, Phillip complained, as was his want.

But it didn't, not really, not to the two Warrens. They easily spotted the small variations in the terrain in this particular valley making it different from the last.

Everybody did, if they tried, but Phillip was tired and irritable and exhausted, both physically and mentally. Many of them were, distracted from their true self, what they had been in the jungle so long ago.

They reached a waterfall, with a pond below. It was such an irresistible temptation, and they knew that, but they didn't care.

– We'll take a break, Ted said without raising his voice.

Half of them undressed and jumped into the water. The other half kept studying their surroundings with hawk's eyes. Ted and Liz nodded to each other. It was good. They remained alert.

– This will help, Laurie said optimistically. – A refreshing of body and mind, making us better suited to continue our trials.

It was easy to confirm that, through her power. Those in the water felt better, felt refreshed and more motivated to keep going. So did the other half, when they had switched places with their traveling companions and splashed around in the clean and boiling pond.

Liz, Ted and Laurie dived deep below, to the bottom dug by the waterfall. They stood there, seemingly on two legs. Their powers kept them in place.

Everything is okay above, Laurie reported. Nothing is wrong. They're alert and ready for whatever comes, lean and mean killing machines.

The surface was far above. When they looked up it seemed like an insurmountable distance, and it comforted them.

They exchanged air. It felt so good, such a great and potent act of sharing. Laurie almost boiled over in joy, to the point that she eventually lost control and began floating upwards. The other two glanced at each other, grinned and allowed themselves to be caught in the upward drift, too.

The surface seemed extremely bright after the darkness below. They laughed and drew breath in heavy gasps.

– I'm hungry, Laurie said, – so very hungry.

She pondered her words a bit before nodding.

– I'll go and see if dinner, the cold, cold delicious dinner is ready.

The big and luscious and supple female body flowed across the water surface like a dolphin.

– We're supposed to be three… aren't we? Liz stated slowly.

– I think we are, he agreed.

– Whenever I think of us in the future and the past, I see a third person, Liz said. – A woman with no face.

He didn't need to listen to hear the distress in her voice, or to focus to sense what was shivering deeper down.

They made their way to the shore, its reality once more imposing itself on them, as they did on it. It felt like a natural process, one they both dreaded and welcomed.

Dinner was ready. People sat down in the circle, looking inwards a bit, but still with an eye on the guards, gauging their reactions, looking for signs of elevated stress, of imminent danger.

– This is good, Laurie remarked. – I remember that I once, in a distant past never could imagine that cold food could have such a great taste.

They laughed with her. The laughter was there, along with the caution and brittle nerves.

Everything, Ted thought. We're everything.

Laurie looked at him, studied him with a smile playing on her lips.

I love the way you look at me, she sent to him, her giddiness hardly contained. I remember how you looked at me… once.

He did, too, pulling the unpleasant memory from the distant past.

Everything looks okay, she reported. None of our sentries have noticed anything, any reason for alarm. Justine thought she did, but it was just a jaguar. She snarled at it and it ran away.

Laurie was… happiness, filled with an inner, abundant harmony, a far cry from the brooding, vicious girl they had met in New Orleans. The years in the jungle had done wonders for her.

She rushed into his arms, fussing in his lap.

Thank you! Thankyouthankyouthankyou

The true jungle was with them still, filling them to the brim with life and humanity.

He smiled, and he sensed Liz' smile as well, as she climbed to the top of a tree, and scouted the surrounding terrain. Fireeyes surveyed a vast area in all directions.

Laurie frowned. She zoomed in on Richard and Alanis, seeing through Alanis' eyes.

– They're at it again. The girl shook her head in distress. – I wish they would stop, and be empowered by our experiences, like we have been.

Those hearing her speak didn't need any names. They knew instantly who she was talking about.

Alanis shouted an insult, and Richard returned the favor. It was mostly silent to Ted, even though a syllable or three broke through. Laurie froze in his arms.

– NO! She gasped.

There were loud cracks, twin thunder, heard both through ears and the mind. Ted turned cold to the bone.

Alanis shot Richard in the chest. He looked incredulous at her, as he was pushed backwards and the red spot grew on his jacket. A snarl erupted from his open mouth. He returned the fire. Laurie shook and everybody else shook, too, as they experienced the horror through her. Alanis and Richard fell, even as they kept firing at each other. The last few bullets went haywire, even as they fell on their back and began coughing pink lung blood.

It was pretty much over by the time the others reached them.

– … asshole, Alanis mumbled. – Damn asshole!

That was her final words. Both she and her former mate stared at the sky with dead eyes.

Laurie fell on her knees by her side, staring at Ted with eyes filled with tears.

– It… it happened so fast, she cried. – I couldn't stop it, couldn't do anything.

Everybody gathered around the two bodies, unable to speak.

– I saw them walk away together, Phillip said. – I thought they wanted to… wanted to…

He choked and even though he tried to continue he couldn't.

Everybody just stood there, unmoving. Some of them sat straight down and remained there, distressed beyond words. Ted wanted to say something, anything, but couldn't do it.

– It doesn't make sense, someone said.

Ted was unable to identify the voice. It could have been anyone.

He glanced around, suddenly anxious. Liz wasn't in the tree anymore, and was nowhere to be seen. He found her by the pond, sitting with her butt on her heels, stirring the water with a hand.

– They loved… and hated each other, she said in a low and haunting voice, and her eyes, when she stared at him were like open wounds.

She rose, standing on her shaking feet, staring firmly at him.

– We are waxing and waning like the moon, she said. – From light to darkness to Shadow and back again, and for each new turn we grew a little stronger, a bit more aware and powerful.

And her face, her face in Shadow was an eerie study in ecstasy and rage and sorrow mingled together, like the strands of night and fire surrounding them.

He returned to the unmoving circle, and she followed him.

– What shall we do with them?

He couldn't identify that voice either.

– Let them be, he said.

No one protested.

One of the representatives for Richard's company snapped a few pictures, from different angles.

– For the legal work, he said.

No one made any comment, even though there were a few recriminating glances breaking the dull paralysis.

They pulled away from the slowly cooling flesh, lingering a bit, just a bit, before they found their gear and were on their way.

– The jungle will take care of them, Ben said, – of their bodies.

They had no trouble noticing the fluttering in his voice.

There were tears, not in Ted or Liz' eyes, but in Laurie's and a few of the others.

No one spoke, not for a very long time.

They were on their way again, the fairly prolonged stop feeling like the briefest of moments.

Several times they caught themselves in looking for those who weren't there.

– I see them, Laurie complained. – I see them all the time.

Liz and Ted did, too. Every time they closed their eyes, every time they inevitably blinked they felt the presence of the dead. They made an effort not to close their eyes, but they had to blink. One blink was like closing their eyes.

And that made everybody see them, by default.

– Stop that! Candy shouted. – Stop projecting, you silly goose!

Everybody looked stunned at her, shaken by the naked animosity.

– I'm trying, Laurie choked, – but I can't.

Liz walked to her, deliberately, embracing her, kissing her brow, the contempt in her eyes making Candy and those gathering around her shrink in their tracks.

Can you break the contact with the two of us? Liz thought. Can you do that, honey?

??? Laurie looked at her, wondering, before the connection dawned and her, and she nodded with big eyes.

The two Warrens sensed it, practically felt it, how the mindscape they shared with Laurie dissolved, faded, until they were alone in their mind again.

The pervasive… presence let up a bit. Laurie still picked up stray thoughts from them all, and projected them in moments of weakness, but not with the same invasive power as before. Only Ted and Liz felt the lingering of death, of the angry shadows that wouldn't let go.

– Is it real, or just our guilt asserting itself? Liz whimpered to him in a brief moment of solitude.

– I don't know, he replied, equally anguished.

Alanis hissed at them. They heard Richard's cruel laughter.

And it tired them, made them sweat and gasp. It was like swatting a swarm of flies, fearing they would transform into wasps.

The dark cloud, their heavy heart haunted everybody, all the wanderers. There were more tears.

It burned in Liz and Ted's throat, but there were no tears. Their eyes were as dry as desert sand.

Some of the wanderers eventually hardly more than stumbled forward, all strength gone from their limbs, and the group had to stop again.

– Perhaps we should have cried? She said.

He wanted to say something, anything, but his voice failed him.

They ran, deliberately overextending themselves, resting with their backs to trees.

– They were assholes, Ben exploded, so out of character, – dragging us with them on their insane quest, in the end caring about nothing but their own vanity. Why should we grieve for them?

He choked, his face still bathing in tears. Some looked angry at him. Others just stared straight ahead, at nothing.

Phillip made his way to Liz and Ted with a large frown visible on his face.

– We made… a mistake, he gasped. – We should have attacked the city and thereby fought from a position of strength. To flee like this… was bad tactics.

Liz looked at him with fondness in her eyes, as the relative truth of his words dawned on her. She and Ted nodded to each other, feeling even worse.

– Do you want us to engage in a war, with our children with us? Laurie wondered.

– Not, now, Ted said. – It's too late, now.

– Perhaps I'm wrong, Caine said. – Perhaps it's the foresight of hindsight. I don't know…

– No, you're right, La Grande said. – It's sound tactic.

– But what does it help us, now? One of the men said.

Everybody looked down beyond down, as they were abut to start moving again, as they slowly and painfully began walking.

This is insane, Laurie sent. This is totally

There was no advance warning, nothing they could point to that would have helped them.

They heard a single burst of machinegun fire. A scream filled their ears. They reacted in a whirl of motion, most of them did, with weapons, muscle and mind.

Ted and Liz reacted as one person, as the jungle exploded in gunfire. Images and sensations flowed through their minds, fired through their blood. They sensed two attackers in the underbrush and pushed them backwards, breaking bones and sinew. Everybody fired at the moving jungle and green leaves turned red. Liz saw, in a flash Phillip go down, and felt rage and sorrow swell within her. She jumped through the air at the attackers.

Natives, she thought dumbfounded, only natives. What the…

She grabbed one of them, reaching for his naked skin, but there was no skin. He was covered in leaves and fabric. Her hand let go of him. She stared at her arm, at tiny needles sticking out of it. Pipes, the natives used blowpipes. They…

Liz fell. Almost everyone she knew had done so seconds earlier. Her head hit the ground, hardly even feeling anything.

Poison, she thought dully.

The poison subdued her, paralyzed her. Vision worked somewhat. Eyes closed and slid open, and kept doing so. She glimpsed legs, native men carrying blowpipes, rope and poles, others, non-natives carrying needles, medical needles. They grabbed Ted and injected the content of a needle into his vein. So fast, everything had happened so fast and been executed so effortlessly. The enemy had rolled over them like clockwork. She felt herself being grabbed, felt the sting of the needle, and the last vestiges of voluntary movement went away. Shame, fear and queasiness kept surging through her few remaining conscious thoughts.

Someone kicked her, began kicking all of them. Nothing worked and the bodies on the ground just moved to the force applied to them, totally unresponsive. The standing men grunted content.

A sick sense of relief overwhelmed her when the men started tying them up and included Phillip. There was no blood among the fallen of Liz' tribe. Everybody had been drugged.

She was totally alone in her head, except for occasional flashes from Ted's equally clouded mind.

They were tied up hand and feet and carried from the poles through the jungle, with their face and groin rubbing against the ground. She was drifting in and out of awareness. Once, when she briefly recovered from her stupor, her dead mind, it was suddenly night. Torches had been lit. One of the white men brought one close to her face and grinned cruelly. She breathed fire and it burned her inside and outside, and she moaned in despair.

The humming invaded her. She recognized Iluso's hymn, and whimpered in despair. A female beat up on her with a stick, a brutal smile brightening the woman's face. It was the priestess, she who had led the attempt at sacrificing Phillip. There was something about her. She seemed to slip in and out of the air, close to invisible at times, as if she was the very air surrounding them.

A hand grabbed Liz's hair from behind. The groggy captive recognized Glory Burns from photographs, a face glowing in anger. Glory spat hateful words at her, words not making sense at all.

Ted saw her, too, shaking his head in bewilderment and confusion.

– What are you doing? He cried, almost incredulous.

Glory walked to him and kicked him, kept kicking him.

– You dare ask? She snarled, almost shouted, in a voice turning into a shrill.

Almost losing it, as she went at him.

She pulled back with an effort and looked down at him in triumph and hate.

– You're just a wet spot on the ground, now, she mumbled and chuckled insanely.

He slowly came to, even as pain and hurt stayed in his eyes.

– I'm Glory, the girl said proudly. – I'm pack leader and Iluso's holy priestess. You're my prisoners and you were so easily caught in my fangs and claws. You're nothing without me. I define your worth, now. I will teach you what life is about, teach you eager servitude and blood and pain.

She walked among them with a whip in her hand and she used it on all the prisoners, creating a world of hurt.

Liz saw no fear in Ted's eyes. The rage flowing through his being flooded her. That comforted her a bit, just a bit, as she kept choking, as stark terror threatened to overwhelm her. She saw in flashes the future, saw David Gidman for the first time in her life, saw him grin at her, making her shake like a little girl. The visions came unbidden, totally unbidden, a constant flow ravaging her.

– Poor girl, Glory chuckled, and Liz couldn't tell if it was now or what to come.

– No, the drugs don't cancel your powers, Gidman laughed at her. – I wanted you to have them, wanted you to feel everything happening to you to the fullest.

Ornaments, drawings of a face, more than resembling Gidman's covered the wall confronting them, strange writings reminding them of all kinds of languages, including ancient Egyptian and Mayan.

– The stench never goes away, Laurie said somewhere in the whirl of water and fire.

A different Laurie, one yet again filled with spite and malevolence.

Then there was the jungle again, and the torch burning her face, the constant brutal beating. Liz hung from her hands and feet tied to the horizontal poles, feeling nothing but pain.

Twice, Liz thought dully. Everything will happen twice, will happen many, many times, and I will suffer through it every single time.

It was like a repetitive wave assaulting her. She moaned in her despair and stark, growing terror. Everything she had dreamed about the last few months was coming to pass.

– Don't fear, little girl, Glory soothed her. – Everything will be okay, will be so very, very pleasant.

It was day again. There had been some sleep, some pitiful dormancy, even though she had no sense of their captors resting or even stopping, except briefly. The prisoners were fed water and food with a bitter taste, one containing yet another drug. She noticed it almost immediately, how she turned even more drowsy and sluggish.

The natives moved quickly through the jungle, even with their load. The awful humming rose from their throat yet again, their homage to Iluso, to their god.

Liz saw her hands clutch bars, felt the cold metal against the skin of her palms.

Then there was the jungle again. They were walking, marching to the beat of the whip and stick. Everybody stumbled forward, pulled by the rope around their neck, pushed by the whip and stick painting their back. The rope tightened around the neck, making it difficult to breathe.

They were kept in the pens, in cages like animals, taken out to be displayed and trained.

Bracelets with short chains, just long enough for them to walk were slapped around their wrists and ankles.

– The chains hurt, don't they?

Liz stared uncomprehending, comprehending at Glory.

– They hurt because you can't stop using your powers, and the metal keeps you from properly utilizing them. Isn't that insidious, isn't that clever beyond imagining?

The cold, cruel laughter shook Liz hard, and she couldn't keep the childish, bewildered expression from manifesting in her face.

– You're just a scared little weak girl, Gidman told her triumphantly. – You'll break like a twig.

She scoped for him, but he wasn't there, no matter how hard and distraught her eyes searched for him. There was the crying of the children, descending into thin wails, as they were ignored and mistreated. She imagined she saw them on a sacrificial stone, cut open and bleeding, dead and still, and she believed she heard herself screaming, but there was nothing substantial to hold onto, except the cruel laughter surrounding her, and the constant, searing pain from the ongoing beating and torture they were all subjected to.

Nightmarish images and sensations assaulted Elizabeth Warren. She attempted to grit her teeth at first, to stand it, but it just kept coming, and whimpering she attempted to stop it, stop its flow, but was unable to do so. The sweaty, battered body hung from the pole between two of the natives.

– We will be free, Ted mumbled to her in the night, or at least that was what she told herself. – Believe that. Believe it above all else. One night we'll break free and wreak havoc on the world.

It comforted her somewhat, but didn't stop the nightmarish visions ravaging her.

Nothing did.

– Don't worry. Glory rubbed her cheek. – You'll be such a polite and attentive girl. I know you will.

Liz puked then, not long afterwards. They noticed and quickly made her drink more of the poisoned water. They forced it into her mouth and forced her to swallow it. She attempted to puke again, but couldn't do it, couldn't even do that, and she choked in an even more horrible despair.

– And then you won't despise yourself anymore, but be a happy and humming party girl, and a dedicated priestess at Iluso's court.

Glory's voice and words stayed with her, too. She couldn't get rid of them more than she could the ongoing, encompassing visions.

She shook constantly, at least as long as there was strength in her limbs, but eventually she just hung from the pole like a sack of meat, unable to even feel her arms.

They were walking, she was certain of it, stumbling forward on wobbly legs. Every time a lash hit her skin she felt like it hit every single piece of skin on her body.

She sat on her ass once, in a gray twilight between light and dark somewhere. They fed her, like they would a child. She wanted to puke, but she was unable to do so.

– You are a child, Iluso told her, – a newborn, only recently having joined my service.

His mere presence made her queasy. It filled her with confusing and happy thoughts.

Then he was gone, and she sat there alone, only a chain connecting her to another human being. She sought the closest piece of suffering warm flesh.

– Poor goddess, the voice said softly, – brought so low.

She didn't recognize it, found no similarity or context in its modulation or tone. Her huge eyes glanced around her, seeking Ted, but she didn't spot him anywhere. Distraught, she tried to move, but was brutally kept in place and punished for her insolence.

It was right after they had been fed, not long after the poison had been re-ingested into their system. One of the white males singled her out. She sensed him before she felt his hands groping her. The stench of his breath made her recoil and her reaction made him leer at her in cruel anticipation.

Then there was a sound, one she recognized, of metal penetrating flesh. An astounded expression changed his cruel face into incredulity and fear. Glory stood there, holding him up into the air, spearing him on her machete.

– I haven't cut any major organs, she hissed at him. – You'll last hours before you die, wailing like an old woman.

She carried him out in the open, to the center of the glen.

– This one's life and soul are forfeit, she shouted. – In his sickness he dared try to have his way with one of Iluso's children, one of his future priestesses.

She spoke Romany. Liz understood her.

Glory brought the shaking man to the nearest tree. Two servants brought ropes and tied him to it. He attempted to speak, but his lips shivered so hard that he couldn't utter a word. Liz imagined she had never before observed such fear. The torture, beyond insidious and cruel began.

They stuck sticks into him, right under the skin, right through the arms, pulling off skin, doing it slowly. His screams chased all birds off the branches, all animals with ears away. Liz felt a strange detachment to it all. She remembered a day long ago, when the captured females had been stripped and paraded before their captors, all the captured females except Liz and Laurie. They had been made to watch with the males, as the numerous rapes had progressed endlessly. Liz had watched that, too, with the strange, horrible detachment, and felt dirty, ashamed and weak.

One of the captive males had grown a hard on. He had, in his horror attempted to conceal it, but that was a hopeless venture.

– Ah, one who wants to join in, Glory had cried.

She had walked to him with a smug smile.

– Which one do you want? You may pick and choose any of the available sluts.

He had started crying.

– Choose, or I'll cut your useless manhood into a thousand pieces and force you to eat them.

He stumbled forward in a daze, towards one of the females with her butt stuck up, but after just a few steps his cock began shrinking. Horror and shame struck his features even harder and he fell on his knees, collapsing completely, reduced to a lump of flesh.

– I'm sorry, he choked. – I'm sorry.

– You're useless, aren't you? Glory raised the machete, aiming for his head.

– Stop.

Justine turned and knelt humbly before Glory.

– I'll take care of him, she begged. – Please let me.

– Well, then, that's a twist. Glory grinned cruelly. – You will die for him, too, then, if you should fail?

– Yes, Justine sniffed.

She turned towards Ben, touching his wet cheek, started caressing him gently, but provokingly.

– We're not here, she told him softly. – We're two lovers home in bed, being good to each other.

She touched his cock, rubbed it a bit, enticingly. It began growing again.

– That's my bitch, Glory snarled. – So fucking eager, so much better than that crybaby!

Justine leaned backwards. Ben crawled on top of her, and not long after that he was rocking on her, his sobbing never quite letting up.

The sight of the rapes was superimposed on that of the torture in Liz' vision and mind, the moans and grunts mixed with the man's horrible screams of beyond pain. They cut off his skin and limbs piece by piece, and even when there was hardly anything left of him, he was still breathing.

He died eventually, as Glory had promised, releasing prolonged whimpers, before one final death rattle.

She walked to Liz and Laurie, stopping in front of them, holding up her trophies.

– A gift for the priestesses to be, she said mockingly.

The men held them, while she forced the raw meat into their mouth and forced them to chew and swallow it.

– That's it, she grinned. – Now, you're baptized.

The two girls shook and couldn't stop shaking, face to face with a horror that wouldn't go away.

– You'll come to love it, she told them with absolute conviction, – to savor its sweet taste, to look forward to every new meal.

Liz shrunk in her tracks and was unable to even look at Glory.

– Yes, the black woman said and squeezed her jaw, – you *know* it's true.

They were walking, and this time Liz was positive they actually were. The cold hot iron around her neck, wrists and ankles burned her and hammered her, and convinced her that everything she imagined was happening was actually happening.

The males left her and Laurie pretty much alone, even though they used the opportunity to punish them if they were deemed to slow down the line or stray from the course. They took it out on the other captive females, mistreating them even harder each time they raped them.

Liz imagined she saw her friends' hateful eyes directed at her.

She spotted Ted's frown, she was certain of it.

Glory walked to him, so astute.

– This isn't the same… not as it… was, he mumbled, attempting to think, to break through the haze constantly descending on his mind, on Liz' mind.

– Of course it isn't, Glory said, with a patronizing smile. – Iluso has wised up, no longer allowing himself to be guided by the weakness of others.

They walked on, the perception of their surroundings one big jumble through all their senses.

Liz frowned some time later, as the sound of flowing water grew in her ears. She thought briefly that she was losing her hearing and shook her head in a fit of panic.

The waterfall filled her senses, briefly blocking out everything else. They stumbled down from the rise, across the valley, filled with a profound sense of dread.

The brightness of the foaming water blinded them. Its deafening roar hurt their ears. The shadows of the cave blinded them. They walked forever inside the pervasive darkness, emerging into the pale, gray light at the other side. The valley opened up to them, boxed them in a vice as they were leaving the plateau, stumbling downwards, towards the structure far ahead, suddenly so close. It already dwarfed the sun in their eyes.

## Chapter nineteen: Falling down

Ted Warren heard Liz repeat the words time and time again for what he imagined was hours.

– «We are the Janus Clan», she recited. – «We survive and thrive anywhere, also in a world where death reigns».

They were strangely comforting and encouraging, a valve on a troubled soul.

Then he heard them no longer, as if somebody had cut the sweet and strong voice off from his consciousness with a razorblade, and he imagined he fell into a deep, deep hole.

Skulls on poles grinned at them, as they crossed the boundary of the pyramid, of Iluso's territory, of his inner sanctum, his Place of Power, the spot in the world where he made his medicine, his Magick.

Ornaments, drawings of a face, more than resembling Gidman's covered the wall confronting them, strange writings reminding them of all kinds of languages, including ancient Egyptian and Mayan.

They saw signs of battle everywhere. The holes in the tunnels created a twilight shimmer. There was no electricity anywhere on their path. Torches oozed all over the cellblocks, both on the walls and on poles. Ted recognized the pens. He remembered them. Details flashed before his hazy vision and phantom pains hammered him.

The sick choir rose from the throats of their captors, and confirmed the shivering in his frontal lobe, the certainty that David Gidman was close.

Hatred, pure and visible rose from Ted's depths.

There was a sound of thunder each time a foot hit the ground. Ted heard it and sensed it, as it shook him and rattled him.

The massive form appeared from the wide crack in the wall.

– The sacrifice has already been done, the giant declared. – Blood of hatred and love has quenched the gods.

The choir rose to an even louder level. Most of his congregation fell on their knees, but not before they made sure the prisoners joined them. Ted attempted to fight himself back up, but was dealt cruel and paralyzing strikes to his legs. Sweat poured into his eyes. He didn't notice.

The Cyclops walked among them, looking down at them with a patronizing snarl in his eye. He kicked them now and then, grabbed their hair and pulled them up, assessing them.

Ted burned somewhere deep below. He knew it would break the surface one day, but it didn't happen right now, like he wanted it to. He had never craved the fire more than he did *right now*.

– You better not harm the children, he swore. – If you ever harm a hair on their head, it will take you centuries to die during the torture I will visit upon you.

Gidman stopped and turned. Ted steeled himself, but the rage just kept raging.

– So, this is Ted Warren, the Cyclops mused. – No longer a boy. How much was I a part of your upbringing, your education, I wonder.

– So very little, Warren replied. – Like a draft touching the baby in the crib.

He saw a glimpse of anxiety, even fear in the eye, he knew he did, even though he didn't quite understand that.

– Perhaps that's true, Gidman mused. – But perhaps your tutoring isn't quite complete yet?

He kicked the kneeling and chained man. Warren didn't attempt to avoid the kick, but took it silently. Gidman breathed harder and now Warren was certain of the fact of the flash of fear in the eye.

Gidman turned away, drying spittle from his jaw, pulling himself together with an effort.

– I don't want to harm the children, he cried. – Why should I? They will become a valuable, powerful part of my growing army…

He looked at them all, even with his back turned.

– … like you will be.

His cohorts and worshippers responded to him, but they were rattled, just like he was.

– I will kill you, Warren said, completely relaxed. – I will cut you in pieces and feed them to the jungle.

And then, when he met the Cyclops' eye, he did understand. The warm trickle of excitement and nausea burned his spine.

– You don't understand, One-Eye told him, whispered to him, shouted silently to him. – I'm immortal, do you hear me. Nothing can kill me. Nothing!

– But Mark took care of your eye, at least.

Gidman shrugged, very deliberately.

– I guess there's a curious physiology behind it, evolution… trailing a bit, the healing process not as strong all over my body.

It was like there was only the two of them, as if the rest were mere specters, spectators to what was going on.

Warren felt the telepathic probes, Gidman's invasive thoughts attempting to get inside, but discarded them easily, brushed them aside like curtains.

– You've changed tactics, haven't you? The slave thing isn't quite your scene, after all, is it, not anymore?

And if the young man in chains hadn't known better, he would have said there was a pleased expression in Iluso's face. The giant snorted.

– My former «colleagues» were fools, and so was I, to stand their presence, and in my misspent youth.

He grabbed Liz and Laurie, lifted them up and held them, like they were light as paper.

– You will all join me and my cause, not as brainwashed puppets, but by the strength of my vision.

The girls wriggled in his grip. He pushed a knee into their abdomen, pacifying them without effort. Liz avoided Ted's eyes, no matter how desperately he attempted to catch hers in his.

The giant left.

And Liz was gone. Ted and the other prisoners were grabbed and thrown into the cells. He swore at those holding them, and they were sore afraid, but that didn't make them let go of him. They threw him into a dark dungeon far away from the others, singled him out. It didn't bother him.

– You're afraid of me because *he* is afraid, he shouted at the walls and the darkness.

He paced the cell and shook the bars, shook, shook, shook them. They didn't budge. He kept shaking them.

Exhausted hours, days later he fell on the floor.

– I dream about you. Glory swore to him. – I do nothing but dream about you.

He remembered all the faces again, the faces and even some names he recognized from the headlines of those he and his fellow slaves had served wine, the absolute horrible feeling it created in the deepest recesses of his consciousness.

In his weak moments he feared he was back there, back here. He felt Gidman probe him, but never with any prolonged effort. Visions and Gidman's imposed sensations coursed through him. He couldn't keep them out or away or distinguish between them. They invaded him, remained and lingered, and cut him open piece by piece.

There were sounds and glimpses of people, of shadows now and then. They threw pieces of meat into the cell and he devoured it like an animal.

Or so he imagined.

– Beasts, Liz whispered in a whirl of wind and water. – We're beasts.

He writhed on the cold stone floor, until he stopped moving and writhed no more.

## 2

Two big females, both visibly pregnant led Liz through what looked to her like a nightmare scenario filled with Gidman's presence. He had dumped her in their care, with no audible instructions, and as far as Liz gathered without using his telepathic powers, but they proceeded instantly and without hesitation with their task. She tried to resist them, but they were cruel and skilled, and easily kept her in check.

The chains kept hurting her, kept distorting her perception, working with the administered drugs to keep her from actively using her powers.

One of the females grabbed her jaw, and her entire face was suddenly filled with pain.

She tried to scream, but couldn't even do that.

– I'm Sarah, Iluso's Ghost, visiting great pain on His behalf, one of the females hissed. – I'm great in my Master's service. I make all new recruits and priestesses behave. You will now behave, yes?

She let go. Liz felt like she was falling through a gathering of sharp knives, blades peeling off her skin piece by piece. Her head nodded and her lips moved, but there was no sound. Wide-open eyes saw nothing but the woman's brutal visage.

– Very good. Sarah is confident that you will become an eager and valuable member at Iluso's court. Isn't that true, meat?

– Yes, Liz whimpered.

Hating herself.

– You've never encountered cruel and powerful members of our kind before, have you, now?

No, she thought, too ashamed to respond verbally.

– Thought so. You'll fit in well here, low on the totem-pole in our Master's harem.

The other, biggest female, with hard, visible muscles held her in her powerful grip, obviously with well beyond normal strength, far stronger than Liz, chains or no chains.

Two other females had taken Laurie away. Liz longed for her company right now, desperately so.

They brought Liz into what was clearly more luxurious quarters, even though she still noticed signs of decay.

It was a bathroom, one very much resembling one in her nightmare version of a harem. She began struggling again, but didn't manage more than a few moments before Sarah used her beyond vicious magick on her again, pacifying her further, making her shiver in fright, making her docile and desperate to prove that she wouldn't struggle anymore.

They undressed her, removed her chains and put her in the tub arrangement at the center of the room. She felt them touch her, but felt none of the familiar and pleasant tingle of empowerment and strength flowing through her body and mind. They washed her, using cloths, sponges and soap, clearly very skilled. She should have enjoyed it, she knew she should have, but she kept shivering throughout the exercise.

– Poor thing, Sarah grinned, petting her cheek.

A flash of anger rose within the girl, but not one reaching the surface.

There were no protests when they washed her, when they dried her or when they oiled her on the table, desensitized her all over, when they rubbed her private parts, and the mere fact that she used those words in her mind made her choke in despair.

– Poor girl, Sarah mused. – Your power must have made you believe you were a goddess, but soon you'll know beyond knowing that you're merely God's humble priestess.

– But He will lift you up and you'll crawl at his feet in his heaven, the other female without a name said.

They brushed and painted her face and made her hair meticulously. It felt like hours, days before they were done, until they finally stepped back and grinned ear to ear.

– Yes, Sarah nodded, – I believe you may be ready to face God, now, and you should take comfort in the fact that He won't be too displeased with your poor showing.
– It will take time and effort on your part before you're worthy of his Holy Presence, the woman without a name said.
Glory returned to her when they were done. They made her kneel and then knelt themselves, before She Who Was Next To God. The strong hand grabbed Liz's jaw. There was no pain this time, only a brutal, condescending touch.
– I know you want to puke, Glory said softly. – You want to be able to puke, but you aren't. You love what's happening to you, with you and in your fragile heart secretly yearn for what's coming. You've always longed for a strong male to dominate you.
They didn't refit the chains, but put a collar with a chain around her neck. Glory pulled her on her feet and pushed her forward.
And each time she seemed to be slowing down or they felt for it, they used the whips on her.
– You're used to the whip already, aint ya, used to its tender mercy?
The caustic voice cut as deep as the lashes did.
All her movements were slow, as if she moved under water, and no matter how much she strived she was unable to correct that or anything. Thoughts and reactions remained dull. The choir of cruel laughter echoed and penetrated deep within her.
– Poor girl, Glory chuckled, and Liz couldn't tell if it was now or what had been.
– Look at that wretched doggie, the woman with no name spat, – how lost she looks.
– She believed she knew who she was, Glory said, – but now she understands how wrong that delusion was, and she's rocked to her core.
They reached a small room, or fairly small, a bedroom. There was a bed at its center. Liz stopped halfway, before a rain of lashes pushed her inside.
– You'll *get it* here, bitch, Sarah hissed, – in the first time of many in your endless service to the Master.
They placed her on the knees on the bed.
– You will wait here, until the Master arrives, and then you will serve him, Glory told her. – Know that any attempt at being willful will be severely punished, but I guess you will be so, anyway, in your ignorance.
The three of them left her. They left the room and closed the door behind them, and she was alone.
The quiet machine of the pyramid worked below her somewhere. She imagined she heard it, no matter how quiet it was. It sounded louder than the soft chokes she released and kept releasing.
She looked around her, studied the walls and their seams, through her vision, working not working off and on. After a while a determined look was lit in her eyes and she crawled out of the bed and started to explore the walls and her confines more closely. The door was locked. It was solid enough. She shook it

carefully at first, then throwing caution to the wind she pulled and pushed as hard as she was currently able.

It was useless. She realized that quickly, beyond her dull anger, and returned to the bed, to the position they had left her.

– Just fuck me! She cried. – I don't care!

Then, as if on cue her visions returned, with a vengeance. She sat there, gasping in shock. The bed shook beneath her, and she realized startled that it was her power.

Hope rattled her briefly, until she realized she had no control, no fine-tuning or tuning what so ever. It was useless or beyond useless, totally out of her reach.

She heard loud, horrible screams and recognized Laurie's distorted voice. The shaking turned completely uncontrollable. Laurie's screams didn't let up, but grew louder, until they ended in a rattle of whimpering and loud, helpless moans Liz both felt and imagined she heard.

He fucked her. She knew that, took her as his, leaving nothing but rubble in his wake. Laurie broadcast everything and it was impossible to keep out.

It… affected her, made everything even more sticky and hot and wet below, and she attempted yet again, in vain to vomit, to puke her guts out on the silk sheets.

Time passed, unending seconds, minutes, days and years.

Iluso entered the room. She didn't hear him arrive or open the door, but there he was, nude, his giant cock slamming his thighs, dripping wet. Suddenly there was no air anywhere.

– No, the drugs don't cancel your powers, David Gidman laughed at her. – I wanted you to have them, wanted you to feel everything happening to you to the fullest.

Her visions turned real. Suddenly she was once more shaking like a leaf.

– You're just a scared little weak girl, Gidman told her triumphantly. – You'll break like a twig.

– Don't come any closer, she sniffed. – I will fight. I don't care if you whip the skin off my bones.

It sounded so lame to her. He treated her words with the contempt she deserved.

What he had done to Laurie kept running through her mind, in an endless repetitive loop. She was totally unable to halt its vicious flow and her fear was easy to see.

– You're such a beauty, he said, – such a tasty snack. You'll carry many of my children.

– Heh, she gawked and grinned sickly at him in somewhat happy contempt. – I don't conceive.

– Of course you do, he said, so very confident. – I'll will you to.

A storm of emotion, of disgust and hope, and disgust with herself raged through her, did so yet again.

She felt his invasive probe, felt it bounce off the protection around her mind, and it made her feel better.

– That's some impressive shield you've got there, little girl. I would venture no one in the world would be able to break it. But you see, it doesn't matter, because you'll be my flower. You will open yourself to me and leave me total access to your wonderful and beautiful mind.

She struck out at him, in fear and panic and something somewhat resembling rage, hands like claws reaching for his cock and nuts.

He grabbed her hands easily, like it was nothing to him, and squeezed. She gasped in pain and horror, instantly paralyzed. He squeezed so *hard*. He pulled her up. She hung in his beyond powerful grip, beside herself in mind-numbing pain.

– You're willful and disobedient and will be punished, he shouted.

He let one lower arm go and grabbed the other with both hands, and then, in one swift move he broke it like he would a dry stick. Elizabeth Warren screamed, loud enough to make the walls shake around her.

– This is just the modest start, he growled. – A horrible prolonged punishment awaits those who *dare* defy the will of Iluso. You will know and you will learn how to behave in his elated presence.

He grabbed her other arm and broke that, too. Everybody within the confines of the pyramid and well outside it heard her this time. He let go of her. She fell back on her knees, staring at her useless arms and hands through thick layers of haze.

– Iluso is merciful, David Gidman shouted. – He could have torn you to pieces limb by limb. Instead he will reveal to you tiny bits of the unending pleasures awaiting the now childish bitch in his service.

He pulled her off the bed squeezing the broken arms. Her scream didn't stop, but kept going, and it had become all that she was. He placed her on her knees by the bed and pushed her upper body forward on the bed. Her screams faded. He put a stop to them with the same ease he did everything: with a light strike in her ribs, making it hard for her to breathe, and her scream faded into an endless whimper. She felt his large hands on her, everywhere. He squeezed her breasts, pushed his meaty fingers into her cunt. She felt them, felt him roam her, everywhere. He spread her legs, pushed them apart with the same, indifferent brutality that he did everything. Her ruined arms writhed on the bed like beheaded snakes.

– Yeah, large, juicy boobs, he breathed. – Wide hips. A big, strong body clearly made for unending childbirth.

She wanted to beg him, beg him on her knees, about everything, but was unable to speak.

He grabbed the shivering hips and pushed himself into her from behind, doing so with complete disregard for her. She felt him blow her apart, leaving only tiny, tiny pieces, spreading her for the winds. Every push he made shook her like a dry leaf. He filled her up. She felt herself smother him, as she increasingly moved to his moves, his direction. He overwhelmed her, brushed her feeble protests aside as the nothing they were.

She howled in protest, and then his cruel, triumphant laughter drowned even that. He pumped into her. His seed flushed her insides. It burned everywhere, not just up her sore hole.

He threw her away across the bed with a contemptuous snarl. She crouched there. He sat down on the bed's edge, and signed to her.

– Come here, slut!

It was a command, one pushing deep within the shaking girl. She moved her fingers. Her arms healed, but still hurt. The healing was slow, painful, not at all what she had become accustomed to. She crawled to him.

– Please, she begged him, her face flooded in tears. – I'll be a good girl, a very good girl.

She climbed onto his lap and pushed her lips against his. He slapped her. She looked at him with a dull expression in her eyes. He slapped her again.

– You've never been truly treated badly, have you, never had to live through that?

She shook her head, timid and scared.

– I guess you're just yet another spoiled girl.

He grabbed her and placed her on her belly across his knees. One hand held her hands behind her back. The other began slapping her butt. She tried to pull free, but he easily paralyzed her again with another fist in her ribs. More muffled screams rose from her sore throat. The spanking continued until she feared, beyond fear that it would never stop.

It ended eventually. She hung over his knees like butchered meat, and that was how she felt as well. At one time or another she strived to regain her ability to think and reason, her will to act, but she collapsed in tears and terror.

He grabbed her jaw and made her look at him. She felt it happen, unable to muster a single thought to resist, how the shield protecting her from his indomitable will crumbled to nothing.

– That was better. Isn't that so much better?

She nodded. Her furnace, dulled and reduced in stature rose to meet him. He grabbed hold of it and held on to it easily in his mind's fist. Her very sense of self crumbled in his ruthless grip.

He put her on her back on the bed and lowered himself on top of her. When he kissed her lips she responded instantly. He began touching her. When he pushed a hand at her sex, she pushed against it, and a low moan rose from her throat. A triumphant laughter shook her even harder than before. When he pushed inside her she was wet and warm, more than ready for him. He rocked up and down on top of her, his full weight resting on her, using every big and small opportunity to hurt her, making her cry out in her increased need every single time.

– YES, he shouted. – The little slut is enjoying it. She's mine, now, mine for all time. Mine, mine, *mine*…

He kept repeating it, as he pumped into her one more time, and she cried out in surrender, in total, unconditional surrender.

– That's my good bitch…

Then he turned her over on her belly, grabbed her hair, pulled hard, and started again.
She crouched there on the bed, saliva flowing from her slack mouth, while a gray, dull happiness filled her consciousness and she hardly felt human anymore.

3

They placed Liz and Laurie in cages in front of the other prisoners, in the large hall in the pens. The two were dragged in after the chains fastened to their collar, stumbling in their stupor.
– These are your gods, Glory cried. – Behold how small they have become after their encounter with Mighty Iluso.
Liz hardly heard her. She felt the bars in her hands and the others' deep scorn. She knelt there, in the tiny cage, sweating and suffering in the heat. Her hand sought below, to her wet and warm hole. She didn't want it to, but it did anyway. There was only a slight delay, practically unnoticeable. She started rubbing herself. Laurie did, too. Their unending moans filled the room.
Sporadic thoughts crossed her feverish mind, nothing more.
Glimpses of the world outside the cage reached her eyes, nothing more.
She heard nothing but the sounds of her own, sick moan. The stench of her sex overwhelmed her completely. The shakes had become a constant in her existence.
Laurie projected her own misery, despair and overwhelming need. The others couldn't help but react to it, and when Laurie, in turn picked up on that it was an ever-increasing loop that ravaged and ruined their soul. All of them joined the two girls in their sick hunger. Both the females and males rubbed themselves until they were sore and nearly mad. Hot water and semen flooded the floor outside and inside the cages. When the males couldn't make it work anymore they turned completely crazy, and started scratching themselves and strike the bars, and hammer their heads against the metal.
Eventually Glory took pity on them and they were pulled out of the cages and hung to dry from the chains and bracelets hanging from the ceiling, where they were no longer able to harm themselves.
– You're weak, Iluso's High Priestess spat. – But take comfort in the certainty that I will teach you to be soldiers, to be useful cogs in Iluso's Kingdom.
The unending, ever more horrible loop continued unabated, but now there was no outlet anymore for the rampant emotions. Eventually they just hung there, in the chains, unmoving and unresponsive.
– The Sun shines above, Laurie mumbled a timeless time later.
– THE SUN SHINES ABOVE, she shouted.
She kept repeating it like a drone, unresisting projecting everything on her mind, holding back nothing.
Their skin seemed to sizzle and burn and they moaned in unspeakable anguish.
Liz and Laurie were taken away eventually. Laurie was given an injection, dulling her awareness and the force of her projections. Glory led on back

towards Iluso's quarters. Two of her underlings pulled the captives' chains. The others were returned to their cages, finally given some reprieve, succumbing to a pitiful rest.

Iluso, bright, mighty Iluso waited for them. The enhanced image of him in the two captives' mind grew even more. A happy sigh rose in everybody in the small party long before the giant appeared in their line of vision.

He towered above them, even from across the room.

They fell on their knees. The two captives didn't need any prompting to do it.

He signed for them to approach. They did. He held a kind of prod in his hands. Liz recognized, even in her stupor the special tattoo needle, David Gidman's well used tool.

Laurie was held, held hard and he pressed the tool at her thigh. It burned and drew on her skin. More screams, more high-pitched howls shook the pyramid and its people. Her power kept flaring, in spite of the drug, making Liz sick and queasy, or sicker and queasier.

– You're marked, now, he said pleased. – You're mine forever.

He turned towards Liz. She made no attempt to get away or even struggle when they grabbed her and held her in their iron grip. The pitiful howl rose from her already beyond sore throat as the stench of burned meat once again tore at her nostrils.

She heard a lullaby in her head, slowly putting her to sleep. He was there all the time, roaming her exposed, vulnerable mind.

The green fist and artistic representation of a snake on her thigh faded away, until there was nothing but practically unblemished skin left. She shook her head in distress. He pressed the hot metal at her skin again, and there was more smoke, more horrendous pain and more oblivion. She kept shaking her head.

– Please, she whimpered. – I'm not doing anything. *Please,* Master.

He chuckled. It shocked her that she wasn't more shocked. She bowed her head. The triumphant laughter echoed in her ears. The smile played on her lips. The shiver didn't keep the smile away. She shook her head, or believed she did, but she couldn't convince herself of it.

– Keep branding her, he commanded brusquely, – until the brand stays put.

– Yes, Master, Sarah replied eagerly, with a happy smile. – Thy will be done.

The Master left. Glory took Laurie away. They left Liz at the tender mercies of Sarah and No Name. Fear beyond fear kept touching the priestess to be every time she glanced at No Name. There was something about her, something even more fearsome than Sarah.

They kept pushing the hot needle at the same spot on Liz thigh. The burn, the needle marks kept fading away. Liz begged them to stop at first, but eventually she just knelt there, unresisting, uncomprehending, while they kept obeying Iluso's explicit order.

She couldn't tell exactly the moment she noticed that the tiny green fist encircled by the snake stayed put, but there it was, in exactly the same spot as that of Laurie and the priestesses. Joy filled her, visible in every move and glance and expression.

The two priestesses to be were being prepared for their initiation, bathed and oiled again. They rested their heads on a pillow with eyes half open, looking at their surroundings with a lazy half smile. Their sex burned. The powerful need penetrated their body and mind. They were filled with confusing and happy thoughts, and couldn't reason, only obey, only listen to His overwhelming majesty, the voice flooding their consciousness.

They were being painted and prepared and everything was so pleasant that they felt they would burst. Sarah hummed the homage to Iluso and when they joined in it felt perfectly natural and right.

– Rise, neophytes, Sarah declared, – and take your place among Iluso's selected few.

They obeyed with pride and longing in their eyes, stood straight while their sisters in the order dressed them, clad them in their scant clothing, making them even more desirable in Iluso's eyes. Sarah knew His desires and preferences, and the girls looked at her with endless gratitude.

The procession began. The chant began. Liz and Laurie joined in effortlessly.

– Iluso is our Master. Iluso is our God. Beware his wrath. We are the People of Legend, and we are mighty beyond words.

Bells played somewhere. The girls heard them. Details about the carvings on the walls flashed slowly before their eyes, in and out of focus. Liz felt like her eyes were constantly half closed and impossible to open fully. The faces and bodies of the half moon, of both sexes waiting around the large bed remained indistinct, slippery. She frowned a bit, fearing she had forgotten something, something important, but it just slipped away.

Then she saw Him, so distinct and larger than life, the giant, the God standing at the head of the half moon, and the last of thoughts ended, and only the beyond powerful need and longing remained. She and the female by her side fell on their knees, loud gasps and spittle flowing from their open mouth.

They knelt there, before the bed, Iluso's altar, the One-Eye flooding their attention.

– We welcome two new to our circle, Glory stated in what seemed so much like a serene moment. – Two new strong and eager servants in Iluso's growing fold.

– WE WELCOME THEM, the gathering choired.

All words after that faded into obscurity, but yet being engraved on their impressionable mind forever.

A light prompting, and they rose, and crawled onto the bed where the glowing being waited for them, accepted them and took them in his mighty embrace.

They were both sweating profusely. The thick, mucus-like fluid covered every piece of their skin. Iluso grabbed Liz, grabbed Laurie, and it was like an electric charge of pleasure. They writhed on their back, twitched and moaned under the command of his hands and mind, his beyond invasive touch.

Everything just went away. God used them many times, they knew that, felt it like a pounding in flesh and bone and soul.

It hurt horribly somewhere, but they could do nothing but smile.

– One-Eye, Liz cried out. – I love you, One-Eye. Love you, Iluso.

There were an endless row of moans. She formed her body to the heavy load moving on her, and his might crushed her to nothing.

The Voice spoke in her mind all night, teaching her, making her learn all important things.

She fell and kept falling, and there was no end to her descent. There was nothing above and nothing below.

Nothing! Nothing! Nothing!

The Voice spoke in her mind and dreams all night.

She shouted in pain and endless joy and her declarations of love and gratitude echoed through the empty void.

4

The many moments of the morning after or the many mornings after were all the same.

Mine! The voice inside her head hissed, and she nodded and hummed His tune.

She woke up on the bed with Laurie at her side.

Sarah's whip bit into their hide.

– Up, neophytes, she commanded sternly.

They obeyed without resistance, eager for her word, the further induction into their new world.

– Recite the Oath.

– We are the priestesses of Iluso, they choired. – We are his holy warriors on Earth and we are lucky and blessed beyond words. Iluso is the God and holy guidance in our lives.

– Again! Sarah spat.

They obeyed.

*– Again!*

Again and again and again, until they hardly knew any other words.

They showered and dried each other and dressed. Then it was the morning meal. They served the table in their simple robes, a symbol of their low stature.

When the others were done they were allowed to feed on the scraps. They did so, filled with gratitude.

Liz ran to the toilet one bright morning, unable to count the days. She threw up all over the bathroom, long before she reached the bowl. Shaky legs failed and she fell on her knees. Sarah stood there, looking down at the shaking figure with a happy smile spread on her face.

– You don't know, do you, don't know what this is?

Liz looked up at her, shaking her head.

– You've been blessed with Iluso's child.

Blessed, Liz thought and smiled.

An enormous sense of joy coursed through her.

She ran and knelt before God not long afterwards, not speaking, not thinking. There was no need. Her expression told him everything he needed to know.

The days and nights passed quickly in the beautiful daze her existence had become. Once her and Laurie's pregnancy was confirmed Iluso chose, in his wisdom to share them with the other males at his court. Sarah and Louis were assigned to them, and stayed with them at all times, teaching them with love and cruelty and infinite patience the gospel of Iluso, engraving it in their very being.

Sarah was so clever, so skilled at picking up on unsatisfactory behavior, plucking every little sign of independence and willful thought from them that Liz marveled at the sight of her. She came to look forward to her teaching, the touch of the whip and her kind words, drowning in it.

– Yes, you should be pleasing to Iluso, Louis said, – if you are, you will live in bliss. If you aren't you'll be cursed and cast out, face the worst possible torment and punishment.

His latter words made panic rise like bile in Liz's throat.

– That frown of yours will fade, the teacher snarled, as she let the lashes fall on the girl's back.

Liz looked for it in the mirror, but couldn't see it, and eventually she stopped looking.

And No Name was there, too, all the time, with the needles she administered into the prisoners' veins, and Liz recognized her, but couldn't say from where, but the mere sight of her made fear chill Liz blood.

Liz was given a hood and a robe, and was like transformed, looking no different from her brothers and sisters in the holy order. Happiness expanded within her and it almost made her burst.

Her belly grew and her hips and breasts swelled. She could see it before it happened. It was already a fact in her mind.

She knelt before Iluso at his altar. He had just taken her many times and was momentarily sated, and she was, too, so filled up with his seed and powerful mind that there was room for nothing more.

– Speak to me, he bid her, – about your future.

– My future is at your side, Master, she responded promptly. – I see nothing more, no matter how far ahead I see.

– That's how your precognition works, I gather, Gidman chuckled, his voice thick with triumph, – showing you what's currently most likely to happen, to become true.

– Yes, Master, she sighed happily.

She just sat there, in the smaller chair by his throne, thinking and doing nothing. Nothing happened and she stared ahead at what wasn't there.

All his priestesses, his consorts were present, praising his very existence.

She stopped briefly by a stranger in his cage, looking with disdain at the dirty man with a dusty beard.

– The Master is strong, she told him with boundless contempt in her voice. – He handles me easily, isn't *weak* like you.

She displayed her big belly, rubbing it, sensually, relaxed, happily.

Her right hand rolled into a fist and she squeezed his throat and he gasped, begged for air, and she granted it.

– I, as the goddess I've become breathe life into your pitiful carcass, she spat. – I give you reason to exist.

He didn't speak. He wanted to, but was unable to voice what itched in his throat, at the deep recesses of his tormented mind.

She smiled, a frown filled with spite.

– Yes, she grinned. – You're nothing but dust blowing at my feet.

He wanted to look at her, but his eyes didn't move from the ground. Shame and sick fear and horrible waking dreams kept him from doing anything. Her grin widened. The taste of blood pleased her tongue.

She left him and forgot about him the moment she turned away.

5

He sat there, and didn't move from his tiny world, no matter how far he looked ahead.

Hands shook the bars constantly. They didn't budge, but he kept shaking them.

There were flashes of faces and impressions, but always seen through the bars. When he smelled stinking sweat it was mixed with the stench of metal, the corrosive metal surrounding him, boxing him in.

He had a beard, for the first time in his life. It had finally started growing in earnest. He was catching up with men far younger than him.

His ears picked up distant sounds, seemingly so close. Sights and smells kept assaulting him. He remained out there, with all of them, enclosed in metal and confined space. His hands kept shaking the bars. Even in his sleep, in his pitiful dormancy he imagined he was shaking the bars. The imprint, sensation of the cold metal stayed on his skin and his mind.

They brought him out occasionally, strung him up and displayed him for all to see. At least he imagined they did. He caught glimpses of Liz now and then, of her diminished self and pale colors. The mere thought of what she had been reduced to made him sick. They put him in front of the mirror, and he saw similar horrible signs in himself, though not so far progressed. And the relief he felt made him choke in self-contempt.

– You wonder, don't you? Glory spat softly. – Ask yourself bewildered how My Lord has picked up skills and knowledge he never displayed before?

She held a woman in her grip, displaying her to his sore eyes.

– This is No Name, she introduced them. – Before Master named her thus, before he decimated her and her organization, Martine Rubleaux had quite a position in the human world.

The spreading gray mass within him spread further.

– Ah, I see you recognize the name. Perhaps you've never even seen this pathetic creature with your eyes before, but you know who and what she was. You're in truth a wonder.

Her sarcasm worked, but he didn't allow it to pacify him. He frowned.

– I wonder more about what happened to you, he shrugged, deliberately, very condescending.

It worked. He sensed how she instantly tilted off balance.
He nodded, grasping something, as he stared into her eyes.
– You really believe I did something to you, don't you, something horrible?
– I'm going to crush you to cinder, she swore. – I'm…
– How could you possible think that unless…
She shook in rage and horror and a sickness beyond hatred.
– You silly cunt, he growled. – It was Mike. Mike posed as me and did it to you. Probably because your «master» asked him to, as a favor.
She saw it, how his mind worked, how it exposed layer by layer. The gun appeared in her hand. She couldn't recall drawing it.
– That's the worst excuse I've ever heard, she said incredulous. – Mike is dead.
– No, he isn't. He faked his death and took his place in the Abraxas Omega as The Mask. He was close to you all the time, and you didn't recognize him.
She backed off, literally. No Name remained, until Glory pulled herself together, and dragged the other women with her.
He sat there, on the floor, unable to tell how long time had passed. There was no night, no day in his cage. One of the effects of the poison made him constantly drowsy, almost unable to form coherent thoughts at its worst. Sometimes he experienced a marked improvement, but then they came and administered the drugs again, and he returned to his stupor.
The sounds kept shaking his eardrums, loud banshee-like shrieks cutting into his mind. Every sensation hurt him, in more ways than one. Despair shook him, He kept shaking the bars. It had become a kind of ritual, a way of coping.
He wondered if Glory had been there at all, if he had ever told her whatever he had told her that had shocked her so.
Hands shook the bars, kept shaking the bars, in an even, insane rhythm. He wasn't conscious of doing it all the time, but he felt the cold metal in his hands. Dust shook lose from the upper part of his cage.
In flashes flowed images, just beyond his reach. Everything had turned into a jumble. In his hands clutching the bars, he felt nothing but the ice-cold metal.
The landscape bathed in moonlight. He saw the hollow moon hovering in the thick sky above. On a day where the sunlight burned the ground and boiled the atmosphere he flapped his wings of shadow and fire.
He couldn't put into context what he saw, what he experienced in the deepest recesses of the Abyss.
In one mighty push he broke the door to his cage.
Everything had turned silent. He stumbled outside, seeing, sensing no one, no one close.
They acted almost instantly, those waiting for him, firing darts and arrows puncturing his skin at a dozen open wounds. Dull pain surged through him briefly, before he went away again. They pulled the ropes stuck to the arrows bleeding him, dragging him through dust and across concrete floor, beating up on him, making certain he suffered when they pulled out the arrows, before they threw him into another cage.

His horrible screams kept echoing between the walls, raising additional wicked, triumphant laughter.

– You should conserve your strength, stupid beast, a male spat. – You'll need it for the trials ahead.

He wasn't positive this had happened either, at least not completely. His new cage looked exactly like his previous, or the one before that, and after a few more days and nights it was. Everything had become a blur to him, time and space nothing more than fleeting sensations he couldn't grasp, no matter how hard he tried.

They fed him cold meat. He ripped it apart with his fangs and claws. The floor on the cage was filled with bones.

– I can smell your fear, he shouted at the emptiness surrounding him.

There was no discernible reply. His words and contempt returned to him like echoes cutting him open like knives. The echoes grew louder and louder and louder.

He imagined he pushed his palms at his ears. It did him no good. He fell to the ground, grinding the bones to dust, crouching there on the hard floor, unmoving like the dead.

And that was also how he felt.

Reality dissolved in his surroundings, and only his nightmares remained.

## Chapter twenty: The Valley of Death

The garden midsection of the pyramid had changed dramatically the last few years from the luxurious nightmare storybook version Ted Warren recalled all too well. It had become overgrown and covered in dirt. The jungle had invaded the place. It looked like the outside, surrounded and covered by something resembling walls and ceiling. The draft, strong as a wind blew from all sides. The hall reminded him of the Roman gladiator arena it had become.

He smelled smoke, saw fire somewhere, couldn't say where. On a throne sat the giant, sat the Cyclops. Crouched on the ground was the girl, his new devotee, initiate. Around her the creatures of the circle danced, chanting their permeating song. The girl swayed her head from side to side, back and forth, back and forth. Her eyes widened, until they were no longer eyes, but merely pain in her face. Her lips moved, moved as the others moved, as she joined the choir, as she melted into its circle, its creed.

– One-Eye, she cried out. – I love you, One-Eye. Love you, Iluso.

Another girl rushed in, knelt before the giant, and the process repeated itself, with only minor variations.

The prisoners were lined up at the center of the arena, let out of their cages for the first tiny moment in immeasurable time. The light hurt their eyes and made tears flow and blind them. Ted's eyes didn't flood and he saw everything immeasurably clear.

– Learn from this, he muttered under his breath, spitting it out, as if in a hurry, as if fearing he would never be able to repeat it. – Take it to heart. But never submit!

– But he just snapped his fingers and made Liz and Laurie his creatures, Justine whined.

– So what? Ted snarled. – You aren't Liz and Laurie.

She looked wide-eyed at him, as if seeing him for the first time.

Or he thought she did, believed she responded to him, briefly, in any way, instead of constantly staring straight ahead with empty eyes, as the sun rose in the sky and bathed the insides of the pyramid in its forge.

The Cyclops rose from his throne and reached out with his arms, his logs. A low murmur of expectation rose from the circle of flesh and fever surrounding the group kneeling at the center of the arena.

He paused, for effect, a showman knowing his audience.

– We have new recruits in our fold, he cried. – To earn their place they will fight, and how well they fight will determine their standing among us.

Glory walked into the circle, slamming the edge of the lash of the whip at the ground, the dusty, sandy floor.

– On your feet, dumb beasts, she shouted.

She whipped them forever until they stood there, somewhat straight, swaying under her cruel attention.

The heavy drum began beating somewhere. Ted Warren heard it. He heard the bittersweet music accompanying it. The insane choir once again rose from the ground and penetrated deep within him. Something touched him yet again, but whatever it touched he couldn't make it work, couldn't act. The rage never reached the surface.

A big, lethal female entered the arena, her entire attention locked on him, and he knew, with a sinking feeling in his gut what would happen.

– You! Glory grinned. – Earn your keep.

She grabbed him and pulled him with her to the center of the arena.

– Are you serious? Caine cried. – He can barely stand.

They were on him instantly, beating the crap out of him, leaving him like a wet spot in the dust and desert sand.

Ted watched it all in a daze, in the swamp of his mind he couldn't pull free from. The blood, like the sweat, like everything registered like mist in his vision. Glory pushed him forward, at his «opponent». It wasn't like moving under water, but through quicksand. Every tiny move felt beyond slow and strenuous. He pulled deep within himself to avert the quick-as-lighting kick on its way towards his face, but would guess he had hardly moved his hand at all. The foot hit him and the dull pain grew slightly worse. She struck him down. He fell. She kept kicking him. He didn't lose consciousness. She was skilled in so many ways, so good at keeping him just at the edge of oblivion. He floated in the air above the Abyss, not falling too far. She dragged him off the arena with huge, shiny eyes and dropped him in front of the other recruits. They looked at him with bowed heads and a deep, horrible despair.

The long, brutal exercise began in earnest. The drums turned loud and hammered their ears. The fighting began, between one from the travelers and one from Iluso's worshippers. Two people walked to the center of the arena and one dragged the opponent off in triumph.

Caine didn't take his eyes off it all, no matter how much he wanted to. He imagined he sat by a poker table, studying his possible opponents like he would there, and he felt an unparalleled understanding burst within.

Ben got trashed, Candice and La Grande, the great hunter and explorer as well. Phillip studied every move, until he finally felt it, the tingling in his temples.

– Learn, he hissed at them, at his beaten and weary friends. – Grow hard and dangerous.

His feet tingled as he, after five battles where all from his side had been thoroughly beaten walked voluntarily towards the center of the arena, and just as he had surmised one of the biggest and most dangerous of opponents joined him there.

He had stuck his head out, and was about to get it chopped off. The thought slipped in and out of his consciousness, of the Burning inside, as it rose within him for the first time.

The brute missed by far with his first swing. Caine kicked him in the left knee, almost breaking it with the first attempt. He sensed the movement in his feet and arms and body and mind, as he pulled away from the other's wild attack. There was something in there, something that had always been there, and that he had never dared acknowledge.

A giant fist hit the side of his face. Blood flooded his mouth. He dried it from his jaw, filled his palm with it, and threw it right back in his opponent's face.

The brute limped, attempting to rub blood from his eyes. He had been unable to move right from the start, after the kick that had harmed his knee. Caine kicked his other knee, the knee he wasn't protecting, and this time it broke, broke with a loud crack. The Gambler had revealed his cards, and hammered the other player with them. There was no contest. The game dragged out, but as each new hand was played, there was little doubt about the outcome.

He hit the other in the belly. There was no discernible reaction. He danced away a bit, attacked again on light feet, hitting the belly once more. The other player gasped, and blood flowed from his mouth and ruined his cards. Caine remembered the lessons, the exercise Ted and Liz had made them suffer through. The knowledge and skill burned within him, as he slowly, inevitably beat the crap out of his opponent.

The beaten man stood on his knees, trying, trying, beyond desperation to rise, to keep fighting. Caine kicked him in the face, and the big man fell in a heap of dust.

Phillip felt ice stab his brain, as he stared at the one-eyed man at the throne.

When he turned his back to him and returned to his friends, his comrades in arms he still saw the one eye glare at him.

– Enthusiasm and cruelty fuel these people, he shrugged deliberately, told his fellow travelers. – They can go on for hours on that fuel, and need to be brutally taken out.

Candy rose, apprehensive and eager.

– Careful, he told her. – You'll face even worse trouble, now.

She nodded proudly to him.

He watched her as she danced, watched her flow, seamlessly from one point to another, as paralyzing fear left her, and directed rage filled her, filled her to the brim. It empowered her. Her opponent was a man, one even bigger than the brute Caine had faced, but this one was clearly more sophisticated, designed to counter her expected tactics.

She attacked him head on, kicked him beyond hard and brutal and effective on the side of the head, breaking his neck, killing him instantly.

Hands raised above her head reached for the heavens, as she returned to Caine and the others.

Caine watched Gidman, noticing easily the added layer of sweat on his brow.

The fights continued, continued into night. Hot torches burned sweaty bodies like the sun had done. It just went on and on.

Thoughts… began slipping from Phillip's conscious mind. He almost noticed it as each reflection, each manifestation of independence slipped away. Weary and burning eyes sought Gidman, sought Iluso on his throne. He seemed totally unfazed, and his cards so very, very strong. Thoughts raced and kept racing through the Gambler's mind, and that fact comforted him somewhat. He fought again, won again, lost again, until he could hardly tell the difference.

Everybody rested on the ground, pretty much totally wasted. The fights ended. No more people were called out or dragged to the center of the arena. The drums faded in the dark.

King Iluso rose, and he seemed to tower above the entire structure of the pyramid. It seemed like a toy in his mighty hand.

– The new recruits have done well, he cried. – They may even belong among us, after their long trials have ended. Time will tell.

– You're good, Caine chuckled insanely. – Oh, you're good.

He found himself in a cage again, sometimes into the night. It was somewhat bigger than the one that had enjoyed his visit earlier. He had been paired up with Candy, an arrangement, he suspected similar to others in other small and hot and humid rooms in the pyramid.

They sat there, opposite each other, in their little corner of the cage, glancing at the other in shame and despair and longing, fighting against any perceived weakness within.

His cock itched, but stayed put between his thighs.

He wanted to scratch it, squeeze it, wanted it bad.

The buzz of the others talking or mumbling all around them hurt his ears, the buzz of voices impossible to understand. He would have preferred the silence of the jungle, but that just wasn't there anymore.

Candy scratched her wounds a bit, before stopping. The distant look in her eyes remained. He looked, deliberately, at her dirty and blood-soaked body, maintaining a direct, steady stare. It took a while, but eventually she noticed it, or allowed herself to notice it. He had her attention.

– You're overestimating him, you know.

She returned his look, almost in horror.

– How can someone possibly be overestimating *David Gidman?* She replied angrily. – He has rolled over the strongest people I've ever met like they were *nothing*. He b-brutalized them b-beyond b-belief, doing far worse things to them than what has been done to us, focusing on them and giving them his total attention. No one can withstand something like that.

He waited. The buzz hurt his ears. He ignored it.

– It isn't quite like that, he said.

She stared at him, like he was insane. He felt calm and collected, at least in addition to the pain shaking his body and mind to pieces.

– Telepathy, mind control… takes time… effort. It isn't like in the comics. Watch him while Liz and Laurie are kneeling at his feet, notice the sweat on his deep brow. He's bluffing with it, overextending himself, focusing on those that are the biggest danger to him, playing poker or chess or both against Ted or Stewart or both, doing his utmost to convince the rest of us he's invincible. The impression he makes on the rest of us has to be impressive. He won't win his game unless we *let* him.

He closed and opened his eyes.

– I've never been very good at chess, but I'm learning.

– Do you truly believe your own words? She asked softly. – At best, if this is a poker game, he's holding all the cards, and in chess all our pieces, those still standing hold bad positions.

– It may look that way, he insisted, – but that doesn't necessarily make it correct.

She noticed the soreness, the desperation in his voice. She had to.

He noticed her smile, her slight nod, the curving of her body as she began to shift in her uncomfortable position.

There was another scream somewhere, or he imagined there was. She didn't seem to notice.

He wanted to say more, attempting hard to articulate himself, but no words came out.

They both sat there with their knees pulled up, resting their heads on the kneecaps, as the seconds stretched into hours and nothing seemed to change, as the light seemed to remain the same, as the sun, wherever it was, was frozen in its position in the sky.

He sat there with closed eyes when his cock began to twitch, and not so long after that rose to a painful erection.

Their eyes met.

– Don't worry, she said softly, very softly. – I want it, too.

It was awkward, but they managed to move close to each other, choking and sobbing.

Phillip and Candy embraced, holding on to each other for dear life.

## 2

The priestesses awoke from their sweaty slumber. Their servants, the bottom of the barrel in the hierarchy of the pyramid approached them with lowered eyes and fell on their knees before the bed.

Liz and Laurie and Glory and the rest rose from the bed, and headed for the baths with the boys and girls in tow. They were bathed and coddled and made presentable. Liz stood before the mirror, as one boy and one girl worked on her. She rubbed her belly absentmindedly. It was slowly turning round and big. She briefly imagined that it had grown very big, from one moment to the next, as if months had passed in a second.

– Brush! She snapped at the boy.

Bowing in fear he handed it to her. She brushed her own hair. It was as if she couldn't feel the movement at all, like she wasn't in her body at all.

But she was. She knew that, knew it well.

Her hair seemed to move of its own volition. No matter what she did, it just kept slipping away from her.

The others glanced at her.

– It won't stay in place, she swore.

It ended up with her returning the brush to the boy, and he and the girl together managed, somewhat to do her hair. They tied it in braids.

Then they dressed her and painted her doll-like face.

Liz looked at herself in the mirror, smiling to he that looked at her through her eyes.

She moved her body, performing for him, longing for his touch.

As if on cue Glory and the others began doing it, too. Liz felt Iluso's delight.

They all walked to him. He waited for them in the dining room, at his high seat at the end of the table. His eye grew big in their eyes. They imagined it levitated close to them, like a mouth about to devour them, and Liz shook with expectation.

– That's my girls, he said, his voice thick and coarse. – Come here.

And they did, one by one rushing into his lap, eager to do his bidding, to serve and please him in all things.

He rubbed Liz callously. She moaned in instant need.

– You like this, don't you?

– I love it, Master, she gasped. – Liz loves being touched by her Master.

Glory stared at him with her dark love.

They danced, performed for him, excited by every casual glance, every minor attention he showed them, moved to the drums he started up with a flicker of his fingers. Sarah smiled to him from her deepest heart.

He fed them the warm meat. They accepted it with boundless hunger and gratitude in their eyes.

They had dinner for breakfast, like they had at almost any meal. They drank wine. The taste of blood filled Liz and Laurie to the brink.

– It's good, isn't it? Sarah spat triumphant at them.

– Very good, High Priestess, the girls choired. – Blood of the gods.

Liz was called to serve Iluso later. She knelt before him, before the throne.

– So, what has my Oracle for me today?

– Your kingdom is growing, Master, the girl replied happily. – The Enemy, the Glowing Man is coming, closer for every passing day.

– Stewart, right? He mused. – When?

– Yes, Stewart. She frowned. – I cannot say, Master. The probabilities shift and turn, but he *will* come.

– Who will win? He asked casually.

– You will lose, Master, she said. – Your chance of success is slim, resting on very few, remote probabilities. I want to see them, I want nothing more, but I can't. Your priestess is sorry, Master, so sorry.

She saw clearer in a way, now, than before. There were no distractions.

They were back at the dinner table, just like that, like they had never left. Good thoughts kept flowing through her, and if she sensed frustration in the giant man, it was just during a few, passing moments.

He took them to bed afterwards, he always did, made them scream in ecstasy, in a state of being leaving nothing but his presence.

The days and nights passed like that, in service and joy. Sometimes, during other fleeting moments the priestesses descended from the temple and walked with disdain among the commoners. It was no sacrifice. That, too felt good, like any act of serving.
They participated in the training of the other recruits. Cages were opened and the sorry lot was brought out in the daylight.
– On your feet, infidels, Sarah shouted, – or there will be hell to pay.
She used the whip totally indiscriminately. Liz and Laurie and the rest, spurred on by her zealous ways did too. Faces registered on and off in her mind, but never really remained there. The sound of the whip hitting skin made her feel so good, so infinitely proud. The prisoners looked like the rags they wore and the glow filling her thoughts grew every time she encountered them.
Elizabeth Kendall went to sleep every night with happy dreams on her mind.

## 3

They drowned him in alcohol. It wasn't the first time and not the last. Aside from that he couldn't tell which time it was. The strong liquor tore at his nostrils stronger than he remembered. He attempted to avoid it, but it came from all sides. They put him in a hole in the ground and began peeing on him. He could hardly distinguish between hot and cold anymore.
– I know the pathways to your mind, now, the cold, distant woman told him. – Liz revealed them to me. It's easy if you know how. It's still boiling in there, but turning colder each time I check up on you.
He didn't see Laurie's face, but he recalled her voice, the version of it that had always worried him, frightened him.
She clutched a piece of his hair in her grip of air and mind, easily levitating him above the hole.
Soon, you'll be ready for my soft touch, the gift of forgetting it is within my power to grant you. Then you'll be nothing but a mellow beast resting at my feet, a tamed thing enjoying the collar and the chain.
He crouched shivering in his cell, believing he was alone, fearing he wasn't.
Another day dawned, yet another turn at the arena. He felt the sweet taste of blood in his mouth and realized he had bit himself. Where, he couldn't say.
He glimpsed the giant at the throne and the concubines and servants there, and instantly forgot about them. His shaking feet carried him towards the big man at the center of the circle. It surprised him that it took him so short a time to reach the bundle of muscles and explosive moves, and the hard fist making him see stars.
The next fist hitting his face made him fall. He attempted to roll away, to avoid the kick in the belly, but failed. Suddenly his left foot struck the belly of his opponent, making the big bulked man stumble backwards.
Ted rose, his legs just as shaky. The man struck him in the face. Ted shook it off. The man struck him again. This time Ted hardly felt it. He struck his opponent, his enemy at the side of the jaw. Another fist charged him. He

deflected it with his arm and struck back, deep into the other's abdomen. There was a loud gasp, and then, not much later a cry of pain.

The enemy redoubled his efforts, striking Ted several times. Ted went down again. The face before him twisted itself in a relieved, triumphant grin. Warren grabbed his foot, twisting it, pushing him away, once more rising on shaky legs, not so shaky anymore. He still felt like he was moving in quicksand, but moved nonetheless. It invigorated him, in a way, he knew it did, even though he couldn't actually feel it.

The eagerness of the other man evaporated slowly, inexorably. He kept fighting in a way, but his exuberance was gone, and his confidence evaporated not long after that, like the castle of sand it had been.

Warren broke his arm, held him, shifted his attention to his other arm and broke that, too.

– Do we move on to your feet, then? He asked quietly. – And to your fingers, your toes and your guts and every fucking bone in your body?

The shivering mass of a man shook his head, pulling back, turned and ran from the arena. Glory shot him in the head the moment he reached its outer boundaries. He fell and remained on the ground in a twisted, unmoving position.

Warren turned towards the throne, towards the man he knew was there.

– Beat me senseless, he shouted. – Pump me full of drugs. But if you have any guts at all, meet me at this spot. Meet me at your convenience, now, tomorrow, or in a hundred years. I don't care!

He returned to his brothers and sisters, to their spot in the sun. He saw fear and awe in Caine's eyes, but much more important: also an unmistakable, gathering fire.

The day ended. He allowed them to take him and bring him back to this cell, didn't use any energy to fight them. They pumped him full of drugs this time, so much that he could hardly think a coherent thought.

The next day the fighting continued. His opponent, a tall, weary female struck him and kicked him, but no matter what she did he kept coming at her. The drugs worked, he knew they did, but they didn't keep him from moving, hitting, fighting.

She didn't run away. Fear kept her in place. He didn't break her bones, but beat her senseless, taking his time, savoring it.

– Kneel, he bade her casually.

She obeyed, quickly, without hesitation, without with as much as a glance at the man on the throne.

– Think and act for yourself, he told her.

And left her, there, in the dust, the dry sand.

They drowned him in alcohol. It did something to him, something horrible, as he crouched there, and hardly could move. They stung him with needles and burned him with sticks penetrating deep within his flesh and even his mind. They stared at him with terror in their eyes. He smelled it on them, on her.

She petted him, like she would a dog.

– You're so strong, she mumbled, – such a valued member of the Master's army, and I know you'll see the light sooner or later. You won't rise above your station, but be his loyal servant onto death.

She tried grabbing hold of his mind, but gave up instantly and stepped back, as if she had burned herself

– Not yet, she mumbled, – but it's only a matter of time. I know it, and you know it.

He was left alone again and wished he wasn't. It burned within him, he knew that or fervently hoped it did, but he couldn't find it within himself. The buzz in his mind was muted, a heap of dying wasps. The cry of despair rose from his mind and possibly his throat, and he heard her cruel and triumphant laughter. He crouched shivering in his cage.

## 4

Glory entered Iluso's sanctum. He was alone in there. She always knew when he was. He towered by the throne. She shrunk in his presence. There was no need for her to kneel.

– The training is going well, she reported, standing straight like a schoolgirl.

He wanted her to speak aloud. She knew that. Of course she did.

– Candy submitted today, and several others followed her.

He saw it happen through her mind.

Laurie saw it happen through both their minds. She listened in, with a hammering heart.

Candy fell on her knees.

– I submit myself to Iluso's mercy, she cried, – to his love and devotion and care, forever and ever.

*Forever and ever,* echoed in Laurie's mind.

– Is she sincere? Glory had asked Laurie with a snarl.

– She desires nothing but to lick the Master's feet, Laurie replied, replied again, as she crouched alone on one of the beds in the outside chambers. – She has seen the magnificence of his ways.

– Your true testing begins now, Glory told Candy. – Pray that you, that you all will be worthy of being Iluso's most holy warriors.

A sign from her, and Candy and the others had been taken away.

Glory caught something resembling a frown in Phillip's face and walked to him.

– What's the matter, dog? You believed the cow cared for you when she had the bright sun of Iluso to compare with?

He opened his mouth to reply. She kicked him in the face, and he crumbled in the dust.

– You will fall, too, of course. Your bravery is just that, a front to mask your shivering inside. You will submit, and then you, too will feel the splendor of service, of dedication to Iluso and his holy cause.

She kicked him again, and again, methodically, without rage and emotion.

– They will all be ready soon, Master, ready to join your growing army of dedicated soldiers. It isn't a matter of if, but of when.

Sarah had Candy and the others under her wings.

– Will you kill for Iluso? She snapped.

– I will, Candy replied.

– Will you give your life for Iluso?

– I will, Candy shouted. – My life for him!

The chant rose from the bottom of the pyramid to its very top:

– ILUSO IS OUR MASTER. ILUSO IS OUR GOD. BEWARE HIS WRATH. WE ARE THE PEOPLE OF LEGEND, AND WE ARE MIGHTY BEYOND WORDS.

Laurie joined in on the choir, so easy, like joining a queue at a supermarket a hot afternoon.

– So, how about the prisoner? Gidman asked Glory casually.

– The prisoner will also succumb, she said with confidence. – He will just take a bit more work, that's all. He has endured much before he arrived here, and has grown powerful in the bargain, but he's only human and will succumb in the end, and then he will be all the more useful to you, Master.

He signed for her to climb into his lap, and she did so eagerly.

– You're afraid of him, aren't you? He said softly.

She bowed her head in shame.

– Yes, Master. He's like a force of nature, like the wind, the thunder and lighting razing the land. I've been dreaming about him… about *them* since I was a little girl. It took a long time before I recognized them as the *monsters* in my childhood night terrors, but now the images are loud and clear.

Laurie shuddered on the bed. She pulled a blanket over her, but it did no good. Before she knew it she was up and walking, heading for the pens, rushing there in a somewhat controlled frenzy. The draft whispered in her ears. The scent from the plant she passed ripped open her nostrils.

Phillip sat in his cage with his head between his knees. She had no chance of seeing his eyes. His mind was still blazing, even though she hardly recognized it.

– There isn't much left of you, now, she spat. – Soon you'll fall like ripe fruit, just like that cunt of yours.

There was no need for her to see his eyes. She returned pleased to the Sanctum.

The underlings knelt by the door as she approached it. She hardly noticed them anymore.

Everybody gathered in the dining hall. They knew, like she did that it was time. Everyone finding their place by the table noticed the shortness of breath, the unadulterated joy rising in their gut. They all moved in accordance with the giant man at the head of the table.

Nausea attacked Laurie like a disease. It roamed her and made her stumble and fall, even though she stayed on her feet.

They greeted him with doe-eyes and passionate affection. Liz was ahead of her in the line, and Laurie watched as she slipped into and off Iluso's lap, leaving a hot imprint on God's lips.

Laurie, like Liz, like all of them just… went away in his presence. She felt him roam her and she cried out in exalted happiness.

He rocked her in his lap like she was a little girl. She drowned in his huge and beautiful brown eye.

– Are you all right, little one?

He frowned, and she couldn't fathom why.

– I'm right as rain, Master, she declared, once again assuring him of her boundless dedication.

– There's nothing you wouldn't do for me, right?

– Nothing, she replied, she breathed.

Like an echo of the others, as if they were an extension of her.

She was kept from projecting, but she couldn't keep out Liz' thoughts, her burning insides of today and tomorrow, leaking constantly now. The frown on David Gidman's brow seemed to grow to insane proportions.

It was night when she awoke with a troublesome bladder in the midst of sweaty bodies. She hurried to the bathroom across the hall, fearing, to the point of insanity that she would release her load before reaching the required destination.

When she sat on the bowl in what felt like a very long time later, it felt so incredibly good to release her burden.

Thoughts rambled on in her head, incapable as she was of stopping them.

– You're afraid of him, aren't you? She heard again.

And then Glory's silent reply, her thoughts that the big man probably hadn't heard, that Laurie hadn't acknowledged before.

And so are you.

It echoed one more time through Laurie's mind:

*And so are you.*

Panic crawled through her veins like superfast ants, leaving chaos and disarray.

– Nothing, she mumbled. – My life for you.

Making haste she returned to the pens, to their distant, murky depths.

The lone form in the cage seemed to be so much more than her eyes could see. The sight of him assaulted her on so many levels.

– You're slipping, she spat. – It's just ruins left of what you were.

She clutched the bars, clutched them so hard that her knuckles turned white. Her eyes when they looked at him, when they stared at him were beyond distant.

– It's such a perfect painting, she said. – With you, its final piece it will be complete.

Her mind burned and she lifted him into the air, pushed him at the opposite wall.

– You're nothing but a wet and exhausted rag I shake, she hissed. – A small spot of smear in the painting.

She squeezed him, making him gasp, pushing him time and time again at the wall, sensing how he went away more and more away inside his dwindling mind each time.

His eyes were half closed. She forced them open. There was nothing there, no fire or awareness to speak of. She grinned in excitement. Letting go of his rag-doll body she dropped him on the floor. It didn't move. She studied it, looking for some movement, any movement. There wasn't any.

– You're my beast, now, she chuckled. – I'll bring you to my Master collared and chained, forever crouching at my feet.

There was no shield anymore, or if there was she easily bypassed it, penetrating deep within the mind of shadow and mist before her.

She shook in anticipation, in fear, in terror, as the sensations and memories and random thoughts began revealing themselves to her.

– This is it, she mumbled. – This is…

There was no transition, at least none she noticed. She faced his glowing core.

Open eyes, closed eyes saw the Black Dome, a place sucking all light from the surroundings, a darkness strong enough to keep the day at bay.

He was on his feet, close to the bars, grabbing her hands. His eyes held hers, held her in stasis, unable to move, his consciousness burning very much like she imagined the sun, and she couldn't for the life of her imagine how she could have believed, mere seconds ago that his fire had been fading.

Impressions assaulted her, overwhelmed her, surged through her like pain. His expression changed, from the empty, weary face to the dynamic, enraged grimace she suddenly remembered so well. The thoughts burning in his mind, at his core turned ascendant. She gasped, in horror, in joy, as she regained her faculties, as she was freed from her bondage. It happened in an instant, from one moment to the next. They both howled in rage, in pain and release.

A focused burst of mind energy flowed from her and spread like ripples in the water from that central point. David Gidman, still in direct contact with her, screamed and fell unconscious to the floor. Elizabeth Warren shook and opened eyes cold and clear.

Somewhere in the jungle, not far away Mark Stewart clutched his head and cried out in pain.

The guards rushed into the room. Two pair of glowing eyes turned towards them. They screamed and fell or were hurled at the wall. Bones and heads broke. Arrows and needles and darts fired at the two standing there clutching hands hit an invisible wall or were redirected on their path by a gust of seething air, swatted aside like feathers. Guards still able turned and fled, the raging howl penetrating the deepest, murkiest part of their mind.

Weak-kneed Laurie was held in place by the invisible force ravaging her. Fear touched her briefly, but then she forgot about it, submitting to the superior power she faced.

He let go, a deliberate, conscious choice. Contact was broken, even as it remained, forever. She gasped and fell to the ground. There was a click, as the lock turned, and the door slid open. He stepped outside.

– Choose, he said, using both his voice and mind.

– I already did, she breathed, her face a study in ecstasy and pain. – I love you.

She dried the blood from her lips and rose on unsteady feet, unwavering eyes locked on him.

– Stewart is leading a combined force of his own people and units from the army, she said. – He's coming.

– I know.

The world… opened up to him. He had borrowed her telepathy, like he had Tilla's years ago. It was amazing. When he closed his eyes, or imagined he closed his eyes, he saw the entire valley, through various people's eyes. The attack-force had reached the tunnel, its valley-side already, facing heavy resistance. The soldiers, in their attack-frenzy rolled over the defenders at the other side, massacring them.

He picked up swords and guns from the fallen guards. She did, too. Those they couldn't carry levitated in the air around them. They rushed to the other rooms, the other cages. Ted opened the doors as an afterthought without really exerting himself. Phillip practically jumped from his cage and grabbed weapons from the air, his thoughts a jumble of rage confirming to Ted's own. They gathered around him, his remaining warriors.

No quarter, he pushed at them with his mind. Demand surrender once and no more, and then kill at will, no matter who's at the receiving end of the bullets or blades or arrows.

They saw what he and Laurie saw, the brutal clash by the tunnel, the howling attack force raging down the hillside towards the pyramid, where its defenders waited for them, equally crazed, singing Iluso's praise.

– You fight, he swore. – You keep fighting if you are hit, for as long as you can pull the trigger, for as long as you *breathe*.

The horror of recent weeks remained in their eyes and stance and depth, but it was easily, like a snap of fingers, overwhelmed by the blood-thirst he shared with them. They remembered the greatness, recalled it faintly, and then in powerful bursts, remembered themselves, what had briefly slumbered inside.

Hundreds of people clashed in that forgotten valley, creating a memory in the survivors lasting as long as time itself.

## 5

David Gidman awoke with a banging headache and lethargy dominating his being.

– Can you feel it?

He awoke with an uncomfortable itch in several spots. Liz had one point of a sword in his groin and another pushed at his eye. The sight and stench of dead bodies surrounded them. She had killed, chopped to pieces everybody present in his court.

– I would be very still, if I was you, she said softly. – One twitch in one or both arms will be sufficient.

And he was.

She was Open. There were no barriers to her mind, but there was nothing there, nothing he could affect. She smiled in chilling triumph.

– Can you feel it slip away, every single bit of control you ever had over me? I snapped my fingers, and that was all it took, to free myself from your meager influence.

The blade rubbed his cock. The flesh shrunk and she chuckled wickedly.

– Everybody sees you in the wrong light, don't they? You don't rule by strength, but by guile. I know. I know you, and soon everyone else will, too!

Explosions shook the ground, shook the pyramid.

– It's been weeks. You had total access to my mind, and were never even close to the most important part. You're just a dumb, ignorant fuck!

She stepped backwards, pulling the swords back with her. He rose cautiously, attempting to make his hurting mind work, preparing to rush her. She smiled.

– We're gonna take you apart piece by piece, until your very soul has shrunk to nothing, under the glory that is I, your Goddess.

There was no forewarning, no indication of what she would do.

She pushed a blade into her gut, through her body, in one mighty push, knowing beyond knowing that she had severed the fetus' head from its body. He screamed, as her pain cut into him undiluted, and he hit the floor yet again, with a loud crack.

Liz Warren fell on her back, hitting the floor hard. She lay there, dying, gasping a little less for each new breath. The dead girl looked at the giant above her. She grinned triumphantly at him.

There was power everywhere, seething in the very air between them, outside and inside.

– I can feel it, she marveled. – I can see it all, as it unfolds, and beyond.

There was a lot of commotion outside. They both heard it.

– You crazy cunt, Gidman mumbled under his breath, shouting it yet again. – YOU CRAZY CUNT!

He was sweating profusely, and there was fear, almost blind fear in his eye as he was backing off, fleeing the room, the sight of blood spreading from the female's groin.

– I could have called you «you crazy cock», she sang to him, – but that wouldn't, for some strange reason carry the same punch…

Her dark laughter chased him through the suddenly so very narrow hallways, with the imposing walls and ceiling and floor. He could hardly breathe.

Her nightmarish visions imposed themselves on him. He couldn't avoid them, couldn't shut her out, no matter how hard he tried.

– I knew you would do that, she called after him, her voice loud and powerful. – I knew you were gonna RUN, like the RABBIT you are.

She felt like she was resting there, on the floor, while the visions continued to assault her, as the future continued to be an open book to her, as she flipped its pages back and forth like an almighty being. The words she read turned more and more real for each new passing moment.

Weak fingers fumbled with the slippery hilt of the sword. She grabbed it, and in one, swift move she had pulled the blade out of her belly. Images moved on the canvas of the ceiling. Sounds echoed between all the walls in this ruin of a building.

She rose. Blood and pieces of flesh flowed from the hole between her thighs. The deep cut in her skin closed. In less than a minute it didn't bleed anymore. But the piece of flesh that had been growing in her belly was gone, left somewhere on the floor behind her.

Her legs felt weak and wobbly at first. It took her ten steps or so until she was able to run hard forward, chasing the shadows and dark corners of her path.

Liz Warren hunted the scent of fresh kills in her nostrils.

## Chapter twenty-one: At the End of the Rainbow

She picked up guns as she moved. It wasn't hard finding them. They were everywhere. She wrested them from both cold and warm hands. Her claws buried themselves deep into the flesh, and she felt the first stirrings of the transference, more and more the longer she held on, the more bodies she touched.

Some fired at her from a corner. She returned the fire and cries of pain sounded pleasantly in her ears.

Ted fought at the other side of the building. He stood out like a blazing trail in her mind. She moved towards him with expectation burning in her gut. Another group fired at her. She returned fire, but was then fired at by another group from the opposite side. She was hit and cried out in pain. The rage increased by yet another notch or two and the pain of healing was reduced to insignificance.

They targeted her legs, clearly. She was hit and fell.

– Cease fire, she heard a familiar voice through the haze her mind had become. – CEASE FIRE!

She pulled herself in hiding, in relative safety.

– This is Jean, the woman cried out to her. – I'm coming over to you, okay?

– Okay! Liz replied, feeling a mix of base relief and an impatience she could hardly contain.

The haze faded a bit, allowing her to think, to do more than react to the dangerous, shifting surroundings.

Jean's people lay down a suppressing fire, and she rushed across the divide of the firing range. Liz' legs healed. It felt great, close to joyous to watch it as it happened.

The giant woman reached her and crouched by her side.

– Sorry about that. My people are quite trigger happy, and when they saw you, they turned even more trigger happy out of pure fright…

– Yeah, I have that effect on people, Liz joked, Liz spat, choking inside.

Jean surveyed the leg wound only briefly before shrugging.

The concern in her eyes remained.

More fire targeted them. They returned it at the new platoon of enemies approaching from the third direction. The two of them pulled back. Liz ignored the sharp pain in her leg as she jumped behind cover.

They were pinned down there for a while. Liz fought to move beyond the pain, the pain slowly joining the rage already present.

She noticed the giantess' concerned, knowing look.

– You spent all this time as his captives, Jean said cautiously. – That must have been… hard?

– It was, Liz acknowledged, as the pain inside also slowly joined her rage, – but he didn't really do anything except fucking us, at least the girls. He pumped me up, that asshole, but I took care of his spawn, took care of him. We're taking care of him good.

– We? Jean said softly, very softly.

– Yes, I see us doing it, see us reducing him to a wet spot on the ground, before ending him.

– Listen…

Jean said.

Liz looked at her.

– I know Dave. I know he wouldn't have been content with just fucking you.

– No, he wasn't.

The girl shook her head, very aware of the catching in her throat she was unable to suppress.

Jean grabbed her shoulders in a soft, comforting grip.

– He raped you and made sure it hurt, every time the opportunity presented itself. He used poison to control you, to weaken your powers, your resolve. You became hardly more than a puppet in his hands.

– He was a great puppeteer, Liz snarled, – but that was all he ever was. And the poison didn't even work properly the last few days. I started feeding off him, and his court. The fool attempted to stem the roaring tide. His downfall was inevitable. He was losing and didn't even suspect it. What a dork!

The older woman didn't say anything. She just watched the girl while she sat there, shivering in rage and shame.

– There's a Book of Shadows somewhere, did you know that? I can see it so clearly, see its writing, like layers I can peel off and observe. In glimpses I can see all the angles, or at least too many to be counted. I know Iluso's ultimate fate, and I know my own.

She could see even now, so clearly, how the battle moved away from them, before it actually did.

– GO! Jean told her followers. – I'll catch up with you.

– You should go with them, Liz said. – I'll be okay. I don't need you or anyone.

– I know how you feel, Jean said. – Believe me, you need someone.

She rose and reached out a hand. Liz hesitated a bit, hesitated a bit more and took it, and then…

They both froze.

The result of the two of them touching skin to skin was instantaneous, without warning or pause or regret. Liz realized with a distant shock how hungry she had been, so much in need. Jean struggled to free herself, but Liz held her in a vice. She could neither move her hand, nor the rest of her body. Suddenly Liz felt powerful beyond words, as the giant woman's life energies practically flooded her, or so it felt.

And with that energy came memories, very distinct memories.

Jean and Mark in a dark room.

*Helpless*. One word lingered between them.

I want to be your partner, fully and undeniably she said, her eyes said, as she sat there ravaged by fever, but how can I? I'm not on your level and I can never be anywhere near where I need to be to not be a liability to you.

Liz couldn't tell if it happened right afterwards, or later, but Stewart drew his gun and shot her. He emptied his gun in her heart. She shook there, on her back, dying, fighting against it, seemingly in vain, when the Change came over her, and she grew, in strength and size, until she was almost as tall and big as her half brother.

Mark smiled in ecstasy and love.

Liz had to struggle, really struggle to let go, but she finally succeeded. She stumbled backwards. Jean Gidman fell to the ground, drained to a point where she was unable to move, but still full of life.

– Goddess… Liz gasped.

She looked at the other in shock and fascination.

– He didn't know, she gasped, – only suspected, but he did it anyway. How could he… What kind of person would *do* such a thing?

She… grew, her body taking on the properties of Jean's power. Absolutely fascinated she observed and felt how her muscles and very limbs stretched and reset. There was pain, but she could handle it. She handled it easily.

Then she saw it, saw the Book of Shadows from her vision clear as day, saw it burst into flames.

There was no reply from Jean, except a shame and humiliation Liz easily recognized.

– I didn't know, she said, not looking at the half unconscious woman at her feet at all, but at something or someone elsewhere. – I didn't have all the facts, and looked at it from a completely wrong angle. Everything is different, now, changed beyond recognition.

Jean tried speaking, tried reaching for the girl, but she was way too weak.

– You'll be safe here, Liz assured her. – The fighting will be far away from this spot.

Liz Warren rushed off, flying on the wings of fire and shadow.

## 2

Phillip felt a bullet grace his hair. He could actually feel the heat emanating from it. A few strands were cut off his head. He hardly noticed, even though a tiny part of his attention was busy with the possible ramifications. The war had finally exploded between David Gidman and the various factions opposing his rule. Life had become a single flow of incoming and outgoing bullets and the hammering thunder accompanying the battle.

He fired at a man exposing himself a bit too long, and hit him right in the head. His brain decorated the wall behind him, and he fell, collapsed like wet paper.

– Where's Ted? Someone asked, Phillip couldn't tell who.

– He went to find Gidman, Phillip said.

– Alone? Is that wise?

– I'm not sure, the Gambler grinned. – But who would be insane enough to stop him? Certainly not I. And there will be a *fight* this time, I know that much. And if Iluso…

He spat the name.

– … if Iluso is taken out, his support will crumble like a house of cards. It's a wise move.

He knew there had been no wisdom aiding Warren's considerations, but something far more primal, and he could relate to that, now, finally relate to it.

They moved, they moved constantly, without a moment's break, their feet, arms, eyes and firing fingers. A man close to Caine was hit. Blood flowed from his penetrated back and into the faces of those behind him, the bullet hitting one of them as well.

The army soldiers that had arrived with Stewart's tribe basically fired at everybody not close to them, or, at least did a very good attempt at it. There were three or even four fronts at any time, a seething shimmer in the air of blood and death.

– Why are they firing at us? One man cried distressed. – They shouldn't be firing at us.

– My guess is that they don't care what *yanqui* they hit.

And Stewart had evidently done little or nothing to change that attitude. Damn him!

Caine glimpsed Candy somewhere with Iluso's people. There was very little distinguishing her from the rest. She chanted the same way, and had the same empty expression in her eyes. He made an effort not to fire at her.

The uniformed soldiers and some of Gidman's fanatics clashed close up. It was a massacre. Many of Iluso's «children» fell as they mindlessly charged the soldiers, but the soldiers panicked completely and made a run for it, and was slaughtered from behind.

Caine spotted the walking fire that was Stewart somewhat to the right, making his way into the pyramid in front of his most loyal followers. The very sight made spots appear in his vision.

– ONE-EYE, a distorted voice shouted, filled with a thick rage making the ground itself shake. – WHERE ARE YOU HIDING, ONE-EYE?

It took a few seconds for Caine to realize that it wasn't Stewart, but Ted, another walking fire and shadow making its way across the battlefield practically undisturbed.

They were inside the pyramid again. Caine hardly noticed. Stewart was somewhere ahead. Then Caine and those in his surroundings were outside again. Even the few, remaining solid walls hardly seemed to be there at all, be much more than ruins, a stage set for the battle, a painting decorated by acid blood, pieces of flesh and intestines.

The fighting had spread to the entire lower valley. Phillip noticed, even as his focus was at the immediate clash surrounding him, his personal space. Even in this landscape of confusion and disarray he practically noticed every single detail, *card* at his disposal. He was laughing, laughing loud and hard.

Justine took a hit. She cried out and fell backwards. He saw how she attempted to move, but was unable to do so. Suddenly pinned down, her companions stopped and sought shelter, firing at the advancing enemy squad, firing without pause, relentlessly at the indistinct figures charging them. Phillip saw, or believed he saw Candy among them. He hesitated a moment, two, while all kinds of thoughts about using a tranquilizer gun rushed through his mind. Candy, leading the attack force, clear as day in his vision fired her gun, fired again and again. He shot her. The bullet hit her in the chest. She stumbled a bit, but kept charging forward. He shot her again. She fell.

He kept firing. Each time he pulled the trigger he felt the pain somewhere, everywhere, as if every bullet he fired hit him. Then he was hit and fell, but he kept firing, firing on every shadow charging him. In one way his senses turned dull and unresponsive. In another, as he moved beyond exhaustion they soared higher then he could have imagined they would ever do. The battle, the war turned into one single mass of screams, pain and release, and sentient thought reduced itself to whatever was required to survive.

## 3

Warren could sense Gidman's thoughts off and on. Gidman kept trying to break the connection, in vain. The panic buzzed right under the big man's surface thoughts.

*I've always been there, haven't I, Dave? You've attempted to keep me out for a long time, and failed miserably. Prepare yourself, Dave. No more running.*

He recalled vividly the rooftop in London, the crashing helicopter, the giant jumping from it, saving himself in the nick of time, fully aware that he could have ended it then.

A fleeting thought he swiftly left behind, as he focused all his attention at what was ahead.

The valley opened up to him, the valley, and everybody in it, a dance, one of life and death, fire and shadow, the shadow of life fading in and out. He cut a path towards his enemy, killing people left and right. They only attempted to stop him for a few minutes, before fleeing to all sides the moment they noticed he was close. He practically ignored them, even as he filled them with bullets, as he fed of them every chance he got, fed as he charged forward, towards the giant Cyclops in his path.

The telepathy he had temporarily gained from Laurie, new to him as it was, was hard to properly utilize, but it still served him somewhat.

There, a flash at the edge of his attention, briefly there, then lost, then found again. He rushed up the stairs to what had been the living quarters of those that had been the High Ones, and there, at what was now the Arena Ted Warren caught up with David Gidman, as he realized he had known deep down he would. Ted Cousin stepped through the Forester junior Mansion yet again, knowing that Mike waited for him there. This was different. He was something more this time, far more, and so was his opponent.

He imagined hundreds of soldiers fighting between them, even though only Gidman's most loyal servants gathered around him. Ted Warren imagined briefly he was somewhere else, in a colder place far away, with different trees, before ignoring also that final distraction.

Iluso's children fired at the demon charging their god, defending Iluso with no thought of their own safety. Warren brushed them aside. He knew bullets and darts hit him, but it didn't faze him in any way, except making him stronger. They targeted his legs. He was hit there and stumbled, but didn't fall.

– HAH!

The shout of contempt rattled the giant, he sensed that. Glory fell to her knees, submitting to his mercy. He ignored her and attacked the giant with his mind powers. Gidman was pushed to the side, but felt slippery in the mind's «grip», like he wasn't really there. Warren frowned but wasn't really surprised that Gidman had at least a partly effective defense against his power. There was a brief hesitation, before he discarded it like he did all useless information. Dropping all his weapons, except the swords in his hands Warren attacked the enemy with everything he had. Gidman, too, carried swords, drew them and met him with equal force.

It was like a crash of two immovable objects, two cars with such solid metal hide that they hardly gave an inch at the moment of impact. Warren attacked with the swords and Gidman blocked. Blades screeched as they met. Flesh bent, but didn't fold, howling far louder than the metal.

Wounds appeared on Gidman's arms in what would seem like from nowhere to those without the necessary knowledge to interpret what was happening. He screamed in rage and slapped Warren so hard that he stumbled backwards.

Afraid, white boy? You need to use tricks?

Kettle, pan, black, Warren hissed at him. You're afraid, the poor shit awakening at night with sweat covering your body. We know all about you, now, Tricky Dave.

They weren't really «talking». There were hardly more than flashes of conversation, as they went at each other harder than they had ever gone at anyone else.

Warren cut the giant on the shoulder, cutting him deep, making lots of blood flow. The wound closed fairly quickly, but it made Gidman loosen his grip on the sword, and it fell from his grip. They circled one another. Warren tried to grab him with his mind again, but it didn't quite work. He imagined he saw a grin somewhere in the grimace resembling a face in front of him, but couldn't be sure. Suddenly there was a pain in his arm, and he lost the sword in his left hand. Damn, it was as if the other man had turned partly invisible. Warren tried harder, fought to control the seething rage, to use his analytical mind.

Both held their remaining sword with both hands. Warren's wound closed just as fast as Gidman's had done. Any cut they got closed just as fast. But there were lots of blood and slowly it covered their bodies, making their palms slippery as hell. Time faded out, like all input that didn't belong. Warren was still unable to use his telekinesis effectively. It wasn't just that the other was invisible, but as if…

He wasn't there.

Gidman had used his mind power to confuse the other, to make him see him in a different position from where he really was.

Warren sensed movement, sensed how the air itself changed and shifted, as his awareness grew yet another notch. He smiled, his grin so big and pronounced, both physically and mentally that Gidman couldn't avoid noticing it.

Fear touched the giant again, and his focus slipped. Warren attacked, not where his eyes told him Gidman was, but where his other senses exposed his position, exposed it through a series of simultaneous sensations he didn't currently care to make sense of. The blade penetrated the giant's upper body by the left shoulder. Gidman screamed in rage and pain, and struck out with his hammer hand, hitting Warren straight in the face, almost severing the head from his body.

Warren landed on the hard ground at the other side of the place. He shook his head, desperately attempting to clear it, confident he would. Gidman grabbed the sword and pulled it out, clearly in pain, crouching there, slowly straightening, as the ghastly wound healed itself. Warren picked up a sword from the ground, and the beyond brutal fight picked up again.

– We'll fill your carcass with blades, he grinned. – Then we'll see how you'll deal with it.

The sword handle slipped in his hand, and he saw it did that in Gidman's hand as well. The stench of hot and acid blood tore at his nostrils. Contradicting, discarding his recent words Warren threw his sword away and waited calmly. One moment, two, and Gidman did, too.

Warren's head still hurt, making it hard to focus, to use his power. He waited, waited, for the berserker rage to come, and it did, virtually instantly, and the transcendent joy did, as well.

– Mike warned you about me, and still you didn't get it, you stupid fuck.

– Mike is just a boy in a man's body, Gidman snarled, – just like you, just like she is a girl in a woman's body.

Suddenly Warren felt it as if a thousand needles penetrated his brain. He stumbled. Gidman moved in on him. Warren launched a series of violent kicks, making him pause.

*Nice try!*

It dawned on him instantly what had happened. Gidman had used a mind-blast on him, made him unable to focus his power. Just thinking about using his telekinesis made his head hurt. Warren snarled, the sting of anxiety drowning in an ever more powerful rage.

He threw himself at the other, kicking and striking him in a series of wild attacks, holding back nothing, visibly staggering the considerably bigger man.

They moved at each other, again and again. Warren noticed to his astonishment and triumph that even though he was clearly smaller than Gidman… it didn't feel that way. He saw himself through Gidman's eyes, saw the demon, the Shadow. Gidman had one, too, but it didn't extend beyond his body.

Warren struck Gidman's face. Gidman struck back, but missed, and Warren struck him in the abdomen, jumping back before the next strike came. Gidman looked completely unaffected. Warren struck out with his power, ignoring the pain, delegating it to a place it didn't matter. It was as if a giant sledgehammer hit the giant, and he was pushed backwards. Warren jumped at him, before he could recover, and kicked him in the head. Gidman kicked out with his foot, and sent Warren high up in the air. More blood flowed from them both. Warren landed on his feet. The fight continued.

A few people gathered around the battleground, but at a fairly safe distance. They didn't do anything, but just stood there and stared at the horrible, beyond savage combat.

Ted struck Gidman in the jaw. Several teeth fell out. Gidman hit him with an uppercut. Ted snarled and hit Gidman in the ribs. Several ribs broke. Gidman coughed blood. Ted jumped for the eye with his claws. Gidman deflected his attack. They circled each other some more. This was no rest. They moved so fast and intense that they hardly gained any respite. There was no talk anymore, no more shouting of insults. Their jaw was so damaged that it didn't manage to repair itself until the next hit, and they could hardly do anything else but mumble curses and spiteful words. They both shook off what would have killed or at least maimed an ordinary human being.

Gidman jumped at Ted, pushing him down on his back, striking out with his right fist. Ted grabbed the fist and squeezed it with his power, and broke it in countless places. Iluso screamed in something beyond pain. Ted struck him with both hands locked to each other. Gidman was extremely heavy and heavyset, but was pushed off his opponent's back and Ted struck out with another kick. Gidman managed to avoid it at the very last moment.

It dawned on everybody that this was an even battle. The horror was palatable in faces and stricken minds.

Ted grabbed the big man by the throat and held on, focusing on draining the other. Gidman tried striking him, squeezing him or shaking him loose, everything in vain. He stumbled. Desperately he struck upwards with his arms. Ted was pushed backwards and coughed pink blood when broken bones penetrated his lungs.

It was healed in a series of moments. Dark laughter erupted from the fluid-filled throat. He struck out against the eye again, but Gidman deflected the attack.

Ted realized incredulous that…

Gidman protected the eye.

He feigned an attack on the eye, and Gidman instantly moved to protect it… and left himself wide open. Ted struck him in the exposed belly, a strike augmented with his telekinesis, breaking the skin, and this time he was clearly affected by it. Gidman gasped. For the very first time the expression of gathering horror Ted had sensed like a faint echo earlier was visible in his face.

Gidman threw his considerable body mass at him, pushing him back, making him gasp, his sledgehammer hands striking at his defenses. Ted threw him off.

Both jumped to their feet and continued hammering at each other, with every erg of power they possessed.

Those watching, fairly close and from far away didn't speak, didn't move. The eyes of all Iluso's blind servants opened wide.

Ted jumped at him, and hammered his head at him, making more blood flow from his nose.

You didn't try to grab me, huh? You didn't want me to drain you. That was two weaknesses. Fear rules you.

Gidman struck him, and even though Ted's defenses were up, and the fist only hit his left arm, the blow was so hard that the arm almost broke and Ted was pushed several steps backwards.

And I will drain you, take everything you are.

The banter was no distraction. It was just there, like the cold, hot rage, aiding him in this fight to the death.

The giant fist graced his head, making him see stars.

Height and reach and strength do matter, doesn't it? Gidman hissed at him.

Ted ignored him, ignored everything but his own dancing body and the man moving through the world in red before him.

Moves were fluid, like the skin of both the combatants seemed to be, healing shortly after an injury. They were breathing hard, beyond hard, at the borderline of their capacity. They didn't have a single piece of clothing left on their body. Skin was covered in lacerations. Blood flowed in several places.

Both broadcast, involuntarily their leaking thoughts, images and sensations of the fight to every mind in the valley. Even the animals crouched and whimpered. Slowly all other fights ceased, they all just stood there, frozen, watching the screen of their inner eye.

Another hit by the giant fist dislocated Ted's jaw. The pain charged through everybody watching. His garbled snarl hurt them worse. This was how it was when telepaths, when the parahumans of ancient Earth made war, when they didn't hold themselves back the slightest, and these two had become like the great ancient ones, unfettered by morality and consideration, the only thing on their mind was to vanquish the enemy.

Ted swung his arm, hitting the other's jaw from below, seemingly making Gidman's head jump backwards, independent of the body. Gidman stumbled. Ted went for him. Gidman protected his eye. Ted ignored that and hit him in the belly, digging in as far as he was able, his claws of fire and shadow ripping open the skin and exposing the insides. Gidman screamed, an almost childish scream, his voice totally unrecognizable.

There was a tingle in Ted's hand, one swiftly spreading to this entire body, and then he felt as if he was burning, and he staggered a bit, even as he realized that he wasn't weakening, but quite the opposite. Energy flowed from Gidman and into him. Gidman leaked through the ghastly wound, and Ted soaked it up.

He struck the Cyclops' eye. It wasn't a clean hit, but it still made more blood flow, making the eye swell to the point of closing it. Gidman, sweating and wheezing attempted to fight back. Ted struck him in the heart and stopped it, for one second, two, three, until it finally began beating again. A vicious left hand struck the eye, so hard that it was smashed to a pulp. Gidman only stumbled around from then on. It dawned on the more than stunned spectators that this wasn't an even fight.

A hard fist struck already weakened ribs, breaking them in several places. They stuck out from the body on all sides up and down. Gurgles rose from Gidman's pulpy throat, as his body was weakening and more and more resembled a flowing mass of dirt and puss. Warren grabbed the bones and twisted them. Gidman froze and his hand fell down along his side.

There was a rifle close to him. Ted picked it up. It rose from the ground and into his hand. He didn't fire it, but pushed it through Gidman lower upper body.

The giant couldn't even scream properly anymore. The once so powerful body shook. Ted slowed down, deliberately, taking his time. He could have ended it there, but he didn't.

Glory picked up a sword from the ground. She looked at Ted with begging eyes. He nodded. She rushed in behind her former God and pushed the sword through his heart. There were muffled screams now and then, as David Gidman died little by little, piece by piece. Ted grabbed both the rifle and the sword, and twisted it around in the other's flesh, cut him open, from one side of the torso, to another.

– You grow weaker. I grow stronger. You're waning and I'm waxing.

He grew visibly bigger, as he held on to the carcass in his grip. Its wounds still attempted to knit themselves, but failed. The dark, dark laughter filled the arena, filled the valley and the world. He let go, deliberately. The mangled body fell unmoving to the ground.

Ted Warren stood there swaying for a moment, two, three, before finally catching his breath. He bowed ironically to Glory.

– Thank you, he said.

– I didn't do it for you, she said. – It was done for purely selfish reasons.

– So young and so cynical

Ted shook his head.

Incredibly enough the man on the ground was still alive. Warren would have been quite stricken by that fact if he didn't feel so good, so incredibly great.

– You deceived and hurt me far more than all the rest, «master». Glory spat. – No matter how bad the world treated me, you beat it soundly. I salute you!

Saliva flowed from her mouth, accompanied by a series of kicks. She eventually stopped, completely exhausted.

Ted reached out a hand. She handed him the sword. Then she fell on her knees before him.

– I see Gidman's twisted words, she said. He heard the echo of her voice. – I see myself. I'm sorry, and I know that no matter how many times I say it I can never make it all right. I wasn't misled. I misled myself. Fuck me! I deserve whatever fate you have in store for me.

He drew back the sword and pushed it through the Cyclops' eye, nailing his head to the ground. The giant body shook in violent cramps.

And just as Ted did that, he turned his head, and he saw Stewart appear from one of the tunnels, and he stepped away from the thing on the ground and turned around to face the new arrival.

Stewart crossed the threshold to the arena. At that moment Ted Warren could sense him fully, sense his power, his gleeful happiness and triumph. Sensations came to the younger man in flashes, how the hardly recognizable man for months had been seeping off Jean's power, her strength and size, patiently strengthening himself.

There was a loud crack. Ted shook. A bullet penetrated Stewart's head from behind, practically blowing it up, blowing away most of his face. The body crumbled and fell, and crouched unmoving on the ground. Ted knew he was dead, dead beyond repair.

Burning eyes zoomed in on movement, on a man standing on the upper hallways with a smoking gun in his hand.

Chin!

The oriental assassin rushed back into the shadows. Ted couldn't sense him with his mind, no matter how hard he strived.

– Find him! Ted snarled to Glory. – I don't care what it takes. Take a group and comb everything here, and bring him before me.

She obeyed without delay the living god in her presence, rushing off, leading her equally beyond dedicated platoon.

He remained there, with Gidman, with the soaked in blood and guts piece of flesh on the ground. Everybody in the valley gathered in the Arena, eyes wide staring at its center.

Glory and her people faded from his view. Elizabeth appeared, just as stark naked and bloody and covered in flesh and guts as he was. He smelled the stench of the fight on her and felt pride.

– Hi, warrior, he greeted her.

– Hi, yourself.

He felt the raging, contradicting emotions in her and strived to keep his face impassive.

– I knew we would take him, she said softly. – He was a walking dead man.

She smiled to him, before turning to the writhing, wounded beast on the ground.

– You took me when I was vulnerable, she said, – at my lowest ebb, when I was easy. What do you think of me, now, Master?

Gidman could indeed still see them, through the minds and eyes of others, their inflated impressions, through fear and paralysis and admiration beyond worship.

Liz knelt on him, draining him, sucking life out of him, and she grew as large and ominous as Ted.

– We could keep him around, she pondered briefly, – draining him at regular intervals…

She tore at everything in there, making more guts and blood fall out. Gidman yelped. David Gidman belched like a small child. She grabbed his right arm and pulled, breaking it in several places, tearing at it, holding on, tearing it off, in one, final pull. She grabbed the throat, holding on, draining energy, feeling beyond fantastic, clawing everything in front of her to pieces. Blood gushed from the arm and the throat, the healing failing to focus, to work. Liz focused… it took no more than a little frown… and broke the left arm, then the left foot, and the right foot. Gidman writhed there, on his back, unable to move much, coughing, coughing, coughing. Liz pulled out the sword from his head.

– BEHOLD, she yelled, – those among you that worshipped this pathetic wreck of a man as a living God.

She rose and stood there for a few seconds, looking down at the helpless, conquered creature, before pulling his body into the air with her mind, her beyond powerful mind, before pushing that blade, too, through the shaking body, through its hammering heart from another angle.

It levitated there. She turned it, squeezed it, eliciting more whimpers from his sore throat.

– You're almost done, now, she told him. – There isn't much left of your body, and certainly not much of your mind. You're hardly more than a whimpering child.

Liz pulled another sword into her hand. In one, swift stroke she severed David Gidman's head from his body, and they could feel his mind and life no more.

– Build three bonfires, she ordered them.

They rushed to obey her royal command.

The two of them walked to Stewart's dead body.

– This is all they've got to show for themselves.

She shook her head in despair and contempt.

– This is the entire «legacy» they leave behind.

Gidman's head was put on one bonfire, his dismembered body on the second. On the third they placed Stewart's rapidly cooling body.

And then they lit the fires.

Jean stood a little away from the others, large, salty tears flowing from her big eyes.

Glory returned with her group. She shook her head, as she approached the two of them.

They looked at her, probed her, not caring how much it hurt. She whimpered.

– No Name wasn't that woman, she said, she quickly, feverishly spat out. – It was just something Sleazy Dave picked from Liz' mind and used against you, to make you lose hope faster.

They had already discerned this, but allowed Glory a moment of indiscretion.

– I've had nightmares about you, she said, – about the two of you, not Mike. I was afraid of you. I still am.

– Good…

They replied to her with both voice and mind.

She shrunk under their stare and unresistingly bared her neck to them.

Liz Warren turned to everybody present, and stared them in the eye.

– You're all one, now, she cried. – No matter what you were before, you're ours, now.

And there was no need for demonstrations, no one even considering contradicting her words. Everybody present, the remaining army soldiers, what had been Stewart's and Gidman's groups bowed their heads and bared their necks, and silently cried allegiance to the new order. The two sensed how everybody fell in line.

Time passed, hours, days, nights, only a few hours. Liz sat on the ground, a bit to herself. Laurie approached her.

– The stench never goes away, Laurie said.

Liz looked puzzled up at her.

– The seed sticks to the skin forever, Laurie told her, her voice and expression a curious mix of sympathy and spite. – No matter how much we rub it and wash it, it stays put.

And then she smiled wickedly and sickly, and left.

Liz found Ted in Iluso's quarters. He paced back and forth there, turning as she approached him, stopped before him, suddenly shaking like a leaf, unable to hold back any longer.

– Can you feel my heart? I sure can't. It's been ripped from my chest.

She looked down, shrinking in her tracks, looking small and vulnerable.

– I wanted to catch up to you, she sniffed, – to match your horrible experiences and suffering. What a fool me.

She rolled her hands into fists, choking aloud.

He looked at her, a mirror not giving away anything of himself, and she made no effort at reading him, no effort at all at penetrating the wall he had erected around himself.

– He fucked me, Teddy, fucked me over, and I hardly even fucking resisted him.

She fell to her knees, not crying, huge, cracking sobs shaking the powerful frame.

– Get up, he said gently.

She didn't react. It was as if she didn't hear him.

– I'm useless, she mumbled. – You should leave me, leave me behind. I'm no good to you.

– Get up! He snarled, he ordered her.

She obeyed instantly, raising her head, her eyes widening, standing before him as a shivering piece of cloth.

His hands, his claws grabbed her, her jaw, her breasts, everything she didn't want him to touch. He touched her, in very cruel and invasive ways, prolonging it indefinitely, not letting up for a moment, and she let him.

And when he spoke it seemed that an eternity had passed.

– You're a nice morsel, he acknowledged. – Quite the pleasing slave… if you choose to be.

Her eyes cleared. She nodded, and a touch of relief flooded his eyes.

He grabbed her hands, holding them, hard, as he spoke:

– Mike did this. He took part in it, and developed it, gave it form. We will find him and we will punish and kill him.

– Yes, she gasped, grasping at the straw he dangled in front of her. – Yes!
She grabbed his hands, her claws breaking their skin.
– I hate him, now, too, she hissed softly. – I hate him even more than you do.
She accompanied him outside, as he addressed those gathered there.
Ted Warren spoke to them and they listened. They had no choice but to listen to the beyond imposing voice.
– THE TIME HAS YET NOT COME, he cried.
He spoke at some length. Liz didn't really listen, but stood by his side, catching only the few, important words.
– You return to the world. We aren't ready for you yet, but we will be. Once, perhaps many years from now, we will send for you, and then… then it begins. Then, Phoenix and its warriors will fight and win.
Torn, secluded pieces of ideas of what might be roamed his mind. The people of the gathering all showed their allegiance, in small and big ways, cheered and shouted and raised their hands and fell on their knees and bared their neck, even as the two that would lead them pulled back, retreated to their sanctuary of silence and solitude.
She walked briefly among her people, while he stayed behind, touching them and giving them comfort, even as she felt none, as they prepared to depart from the pyramid of fear, bringing it with them, inevitably into the world. They saw her smile and outward confidence, but not her shivering insides.
– Will you remain… big? Justine wondered, her eyes burning in fever from the wound.
It would take weeks before all the wounded would be well enough to travel. It was okay. They had time.
She was okay. They were all okay, remarkably so, all those remaining alive.
– No. Liz shook his head. – It will probably linger a day or two, before fading.
– I will take care of both of them, Candice said, holding both her own and Candy's child in her arms, – until you come and claim us all.
– Good, Liz said, striving to sound confident, to sound pleased. – That's good.
She didn't even walk close to Phillip, couldn't stand to see the death in his eyes.
Many wanted to talk to her, but she didn't talk with them, not really, and it wasn't hard spotting even more admiration in their eyes precisely because of that fact, because of her perceived contempt. She said her goodbyes in a cold, distant and patronizing manner, exactly like they would expect from her, and they stared at her in awe.
She returned to the brief sanctum, stumbling more than walking. It was first when she saw him stand at the middle of the floor, she understood somewhat, and was in a backwards way comforted.
Others might not see his beyond distressed expression, but she did, easily.
– Coming back here, being reminded about everything… it gets to you, you know.
His lips shook so hard that he could hardly speak.
– I know. She choked. – Don't think I don't. Please don't!

– The very notion of spending a single second more in this place fills me with dread, he said, – but we will do it. We won't leave until everybody can leave.

Liz strived to comfort him, even as she was comforted. She imagined endless nights and horrors in this cold, desolate place of the human heart.

And they both fell to their knees, embracing there, in the empty ruins, as dry, invisible tears flooded their cheeks.

# Epilogue: leaving Las Vegas

The well-dressed man walked down Fremont Street in Las Vegas. There was something about him, an aura of menace and tragedy, something drawing people's attention. He walked what to him had been so very familiar streets and he didn't recognize them, not really. They looked different, even alien to him. It had been too long and he, himself had changed too much to feel at home here.

He walked inside the Horseshoe Casino, into the cool and pleasant shadows. The murmur picked up the moment he entered the poker section. They recognized him, both from the papers and from previous experience. The stranger, the changed man looked drawn in face, skinny in body, even though he perhaps wasn't. He looked considerably older than his years. Those who had known him didn't really recognize him.

Those present knowing such things saw that he carried a concealed gun under the jacket. They saw how his eyes and fingers constantly twitched in tandem, in imperfect harmony, how the man never rested, even when standing still.

He stopped by a table. It was a high stakes table. There were no seats available. He stood there, with the other spectators, studying the game for a while. Practically everybody else stared at him.

The cards and the movement by the table turned indistinguishable to him. He read both effortlessly, instinctively, as if everybody played with open cards. He was *open*. It seemed so easy, now, what he had pictured being so hard in his youth.

He had never imagined it would be possible to be so open then. Now, it felt like a second skin.

A player quit, broke. He looked almost relieved when he glanced at the stranger and left the room. No one took possession of the vacant seat. People in the queue were called, but didn't step forward to claim their place.

– Weston, the announcer cried.

Weston, whoever he was didn't move or give any indication of who he was.

– Crawford, the announcer cried.

There were no takers.

Six people, all in all were called, but didn't claim their seat. The voice of the announcer seemed to change, to be fading, until it was nothing more than a faint echo.

One of the players at the table eventually looked directly at the stranger.

– Would you care to join us?

Phillip Caine hesitated only briefly before stepping forward and sitting down. He flashed a smile, nodding to the other players, but still looked preoccupied, as if he was far away, not looking at the table or the cards or the players at all, but somewhere else, a place and event that wouldn't let go.

– I never say no to a poker game.

## Author's word:

This is the fourth book in the Janus Clan series. Even though only seconds have passed in the actual story from the third book, there is an almost twenty-year gap between the writing, from I ended Birds Flying in the Dark to the start of this one.

It feels strange and pretty amazing.

From 1986 to 2005 I wrote other books and did other things. As I've related elsewhere I saw no point in continuing on book four when no publisher would touch the first three. But the Janus Clan never left my thoughts. I kept writing the story in my head, like I do all stories, a story that I had first conceived of as a teenager doing a rather futile movie-project.

In other words: this story waited thirty years to be written.

All the original elements are there, fleshed out a bit, slightly altered, clearly matured, but basically the same tale I had envisioned.

It is a journey, one across the United States and parts of South America, one I did in real life in 2002 and 2003, doing both further research and feeling alive beyond excitement and joy in the bargain. I made the journey because of the story. The story became even more what it was because of the journey.

The Janus Clan is travelers, taking themselves across the Earth and the human mind, time and space of humanity.

I walk in their footprints. They walk in mine.

With this book we're almost halfway through their story.

I feel very good about this, indescribably good.

This is my second longest novel (182 000 words). It was what was needed to tell the story in full. There will always be doubt whether or not it should have been even longer, especially the ending, but this is what I ended up with. I spent two years reading and rereading the novel after its completion, as I usually do before publication, taking my time as always.

An established publisher and its «professional editor» would have asked me to trim it, of course, but I always end up with more than I started out with, not less.

It's the tenth book I am publishing in little more than two years and the last so far I've completed that is ready for publication. I will probably not release any new novels in 2013 and the next Janus Clan book is far off, unless I suddenly can afford that before-mentioned skilled and fast-typing personal secretary.

Even so, the last two years still feel like a dream to me, in many ways and definitely like a dream come true, an ongoing celebration I can savor and enjoy beyond words.

And my stories take time doing, inevitably. I know I might have a hard time completing all the books in the series in this lifetime, but I will do my very best.

Other upcoming novels by Amos Keppler from **Midnight Fire Media**:

**The Janus Clan** - (ten chapters about the Wild Man in the modern world, a world balancing on a razor's edge):

**The Defenseless**
**The Slaves**
**Birds Flying in the Dark**
**At the End of the Rainbow**
Lewis of Modern York
The Werewolf of Locus Bradle
The Valley of Kings
Eye in the Sky
The Iron Cage
Phoenix Green Earth

**Lewis of Modern York**

Twin towers are decorating the Manhattan skyline, paragons of oppression and destruction.
Down below, in the Stone Desert's gray emptiness people are desperately striving to survive, to live a semblance of a life.

Lewis Talbot and Carla Wolf are not who they are. They know this. But they don't know why, at least he doesn't. They are growing up. Carla is only eighteen, but she has already traveled the world, in search of what she may never find. Lewis is only fifteen, but strange stirrings and notions have haunted him since the early nights of his life.
And they encounter many interesting people on their Journey, the four Warrens, Patrick, Ethel, Ted and Liz, Jean Gidman and Eric Carr, and others. They all have a reason for being in Modern York, for visiting, for living there. Ted and Liz arrive in town, sick and tired of life, of everything, desperately seeking Life, seeking renewal, a reason to go on living.
Modern York is not so different from old York. War is being prepared there. Peace is being prepared there. The drama of life called the Janus Clan will come to a preliminary conclusion there.
It's an old and true saying: Nobody is exactly who they appear. The question is what is lurking beneath the mask, below the surface, and what may happen when the masks fall.

Preliminary release date October 31, 2017

www.ingramcontent.com/pod-product-compliance
Lightning Source LLC
Chambersburg PA
CBHW060604310726
48982CB00008B/1236/J
*9788291693149*